A New Way of Life
A New Dimension of Art

They came from Europe to America, seeking escape from the want and oppression of the past. But with them they brought a part of the past they treasured—a religion, a tradition, an emotional and intellectual stance nurtured by thousands of years of apartness.

As Jewish immigrants moved from first-generation slum tenements to second-generation apartments to third-generation suburban homes, they gained the prosperity and acceptance they sought —but at the loss of much they did not willingly surrender.

From their drama of gain and loss, from the dilemma of their divided hearts and minds, from their morality and sense of irony and sometimes from their agony, came a uniquely important strain of the American experience and one of the most exciting achievements of American literature.

Jewish-American Stories

ABOUT THE EDITOR
IRVING HOWE was born in 1920 in New York City. Currently Distinguished Professor of English at the Graduate Center of City University of New York and Hunter College, Mr. Howe is one of America's most eminent literary critics and social chroniclers. Among his many highly acclaimed books is the recent bestselling triumph, *World of Our Fathers*.

MENTOR Anthologies of Special Interest

Jewish-American Stories

Edited and
with an Introduction by

Irving Howe

A MENTOR BOOK

NEW AMERICAN LIBRARY

TIMES MIRROR
NEW YORK AND SCARBOROUGH, ONTARIO

ACKNOWLEDGMENTS

Aleichem, Sholom: "On Account of a Hat." From *A Treasury
of Yiddish Stories,* edited by Irving Howe and Eliezer
Greenberg. Copyright 1954 by The Viking Press, Inc. Reprinted by permission of Viking Penguin, Inc.

Allen, Woody: "No Kaddish for Weinstein." From *Without
Feathers* by Woody Allen. Copyright © 1975 by Woody
Allen. Originally appeared in *The New Yorker.* Reprinted
by permission of Random House, Inc.

Babel, Isaac: "The Story of My Dovecot." From *The Collected
Stories of Isaac Babel.* Copyright © 1955 by S. G. Phillips,
Inc. Reprinted by permission of S. G. Phillips, Inc.

Bellow, Saul: "The Old System." From *Mosby's Memoirs and
Other Stories* by Saul Bellow. Copyright © 1967 by Saul
Bellow. All rights reserved. Reprinted by permission of
Viking Penguin, Inc.

Elkin, Stanley: "Criers and Kibitzers, Kibitzers and Criers." From
Criers and Kibitzers, Kibitzers and Criers by Stanley
Elkin. Copyright © 1961 by Stanley Elkin. Reprinted by
permission of Random House, Inc.

Fuchs, Daniel: "Twilight in Southern California." From *Stories*
by Stafford, Cheever, Fuchs, and Maxwell. Copyright ©
1953 by *The New Yorker* Magazine, Inc. Copyright ©
1956, 1966 by Farrar, Straus & Giroux, Inc. Reprinted by
permission of Farrar, Straus & Giroux, Inc.

Gold, Herbert: "The Heart of the Artichoke." From *Hudson Review Anthology.* Copyright © 1961 by Herbert Gold. Reprinted by permission of the author and his agent, James
Brown Associates, Inc.

Goodman, Paul: "The Facts of Life." Copyright 1945 by Paul
Goodman. Reprinted by permission of Sally Goodman.

Kaplan, Johanna: "Sour or Suntanned, It Makes No Difference."
From *Other People's Lives* by Johanna Kaplan. Copyright
© 1968, 1969, 1970, 1971, 1975 by Johanna Kaplan. Reprinted by permission of Alfred A. Knopf, Inc.

Liben, Meyer: "Homage to Benny Leonard." From *Justice Hunger* by Meyer Liben. Copyright © 1956, 1957, 1959, 1961,
1962, 1967 by Meyer Liben. Reprinted by permission of
the estate of Meyer Liben. This story first appeared in
Commentary Magazine, June, 1959.

Mailer, Norman: "The Man Who Studied Yoga." First appeared in *New Short Novels II*, Ballantine Books, New York. Copyright © 1956 by Norman Mailer. Reprinted by permission of the author and the author's agent, Scott Meredith Literary Agency, Inc., 845 Third Avenue, New York, New York 10022.

Malamud, Bernard: "The Magic Barrel." From *The Magic Barrel* by Bernard Malamud. Copyright © 1954–1958 by Bernard Malamud. Reprinted by permission of Farrar, Straus and Giroux, Inc.

Markfield, Wallace: "Under the Marquee." First appeared in *New York Herald Tribune*, February 13, 1966. Copyright © 1966 by Wallace Markfield. Reprinted by permission of Candida Donadio & Associates, Inc.

Olsen, Tillie: "Tell Me A Riddle." From *Tell Me A Riddle* by Tillie Olsen. Copyright © 1960, 1961 by Tillie Olsen. Reprinted by permission of Delacorte Press/Seymour Lawrence.

Ozick, Cynthia: "Envy; Or, Yiddish in America." From *The Pagan Rabbi and Other Stories* by Cynthia Ozick. Copyright © 1969 by Cynthia Ozick. Reprinted by permission of Alfred A. Knopf.

Paley, Grace: "The Loudest Voice." From *The Little Disturbances of Man* by Grace Paley. Copyright © 1959 by Grace Paley. Reprinted by permission of Viking Penguin, Inc.

Perelman, S. J.: "Waiting for Santy." From *The Most of S. J. Perelman*. Copyright © 1930, 1931, 1932, 1933, 1935, 1936, 1953, 1955, 1956, 1957, 1958 by S. J. Perelman. Reprinted by permission of Simon & Schuster, Inc. This story first appeared in the *New Yorker* Magazine.

Rogin, Gilbert: "What Happens Next?" From *What Happens Next?* by Gilbert Rogin. Copyright © 1971 by Gilbert Rogin. Reprinted by permission of Random House, Inc. Originally appeared in *The New Yorker*.

Rosenfeld, Isaac: "King Solomon." From *Alpha and Omega* by Isaac Rosenfeld. Copyright © 1956 by the Estate of Isaac Rosenfeld. Reprinted by permission of Viking Penguin, Inc.

Roth, Henry: "The Surveyor." First appeared in the *New Yorker* Magazine, August 6, 1966. Copyright © 1966 by Henry Roth. Permission granted by the author's literary agent, Roslyn Targ Literary Agency, 250 West 57th Street, New York 10019.

Roth, Philip: "Defender of the Faith." From *Goodbye, Columbus* by Philip Roth. Copyright © 1959 by Philip Roth. Reprinted by permission of Houghton Mifflin Company.

Schwartz, Delmore: "In Dreams Begin Responsibilities." First appeared in *Partisan Review*. Copyright March, 1938. Reprinted by permission of *Partisan Review* and the Estate of Delmore Schwartz.

———: "America! America!" First appeared in *Partisan Review*. Copyright 1940. Reprinted by permission of *Partisan Review* and the Estate of Delmore Schwartz.

Seide, Michael: "Back to Bread." From *The Common Thread* by Michael Seide. Copyright 1944, 1972, published by Harcourt, Brace and Company 1944. Reprinted by Arno Press Inc. 1975. Reprinted by permission of the author.

Singer, Isaac Bashevis: "Gimpel the Fool." Translated by Saul
    Bellow. From *A Treasury of Yiddish Stories*, edited by Irving
    Howe and Eliezer Greenberg. Copyright 1953 by Isaac Bash-
    evis Singer. Reprinted by permission of Viking Penguin, Inc.
Weidman, Jerome: "My Father Sits in the Dark." From *My Father
    Sits in the Dark and Other Stories* by Jerome Weidman.
    Copyright 1934 and renewed 1962 by Jerome Weidman. Re-
    printed by permission of Random House, Inc.

SIGNET, SIGNET CLASSICS, MENTOR, PLUME AND MERIDIAN BOOKS
are published *in the United States* by
The New American Library, Inc.,
1301 Avenue of the Americas, New York, New York 10019,
in Canada by The New American Library of Canada Limited,
81 Mack Avenue, Scarborough, Ontario M1L1M8

First Mentor Printing, May, 1977

2 3 4 5 6 7 8 9

PRINTED IN THE UNITED STATES OF AMERICA

Contents

INTRODUCTION 1

1. ON ACCOUNT OF A HAT, Sholom Aleichem 18
2. THE STORY OF MY DOVECOT, Isaac Babel 26
3. GIMPEL THE FOOL, Bashevis Singer 37
4. THE SURVEYOR, Henry Roth 51
5. KING SOLOMON, Isaac Rosenfeld 67
6. TELL ME A RIDDLE, Tillie Olsen 82
7. MY FATHER SITS IN THE DARK, Jerome Weidman 118
8. WHAT HAPPENS NEXT? *An Uncompleted Investigation*, Gilbert Rogin 122
9. ENVY; OR, YIDDISH IN AMERICA, Cynthia Ozick 129
10. HOMAGE TO BENNY LEONARD, Meyer Liben 178
11. IN DREAMS BEGIN RESPONSIBILITIES, Delmore Schwartz 186
12. AMERICA! AMERICA!, Delmore Schwartz 195
13. NO KADDISH FOR WEINSTEIN, Woody Allen 217
14. THE FACTS OF LIFE, Paul Goodman 222
15. THE MAGIC BARREL, Bernard Malamud 235
16. TWILIGHT IN SOUTHERN CALIFORNIA, Daniel Fuchs 252
17. THE HEART OF THE ARTICHOKE, Herbert Gold 270
18. THE OLD SYSTEM, Saul Bellow 301
19. CRIERS AND KIBITZERS, KIBITZERS AND CRIERS, Stanley Elkin 333
20. UNDER THE MARQUEE, Wallace Markfield 361
21. DEFENDER OF THE FAITH, Philip Roth 373
22. BACK TO BREAD, Michael Seide 402
23. THE MAN WHO STUDIED YOGA, Norman Mailer 413
24. SOUR OR SUNTANNED, IT MAKES NO DIFFERENCE, Johanna Kaplan 443
25. WAITING FOR SANTY, S. J. Perelman 462
26. THE LOUDEST VOICE, Grace Paley 465

Introduction

Irving Howe

Over the decades, by now stretching into centuries, American literature has steadily drawn fresh energies from regions, sub-cultures and ethnic and racial groups which, if taken together, form a pleasing heterogeneity. These communities prepare themselves in unnoticed spaces of our continent and then, through a blend of charm and aggression, break into the national literature. I say "break into" because there is often resistance from the established elites, who look upon the new groups of writers as culturally, and sometimes physically, unwashed, or as a threat to the purity of the English language, or as carriers of subversive ideas.

At least until the 1920s one could hardly speak of a national literature in America as something above or apart from the gatherings of talent that appear in these regions, subcultures and ethnic and racial groups. Throughout the nineteenth century American literature consists largely of works, a few of them masterpieces, that emerge out of the smaller segments of our culture: let's agree to call them regions even though some are not geographically compact. The literature of these regions—New England, the "old Southwest," the Midwest, later the settlements of European immigrants, and then the Jews and the blacks—become part of our national literature once they manage to shake off provincial self-centeredness yet retain the pungency of local speech and the strength of local settings. Then, by a sometimes wonderful leap of the imagination, they can move directly from regional preoccupations to a moral and metaphysical universality. This is what happens to Twain, and later to Faulkner.

Fresh talents gather among the humorists of the "old Southwest," mostly popular entertainers, and out of them emerges the genius of Mark Twain. Ripe talents gather in the villages of New England, and out of them emerges the genius of Hawthorne. A bit later, talents spring up in the bleak spaces of the Midwest, from which we gain the genius of Dreiser.

All of this enables us to improvise a useful formula with which to chart growth and transformation in nineteenth-century American writing, though after a while, of course, the formula breaks down. It fails to account for Poe: perhaps nothing could. It leaves Whitman and Melville dangling as "New York writers," a category of small value in the nineteenth century. Still, no formula need account for everything, and there is enough truth wound up with this one to make it useful.

Even for the twentieth century, when things get a good deal more complicated, the formula has its value. By the twentieth century, it is Southern writing which seems the most significant regional culture to break into national consciousness—and also to become a major part of that international culture of modernism that takes over in America. Yoknapatawpha County and all its brilliant figures thrive upon local myth, indeed, are inconceivable without the obsessive Southern stories; but the local myth rises to art through a sensibility shaken and stimulated by European modernism. Faulkner as mere provincial would not be very interesting. In any case, not the Faulkner we know.

A somewhat similar development occurs among the novelists and story writers whom we call the American Jewish writers: figures like Saul Bellow, Henry Roth, Grace Paley, Daniel Fuchs, Bernard Malamud, Tillie Olsen, Delmore Schwartz, Philip Roth. They don't, to be sure, all come from the same part of the country, yet they do come from a kind of regional culture. Some of them have recently expressed an understandable impatience at being locked into a "school" or "group," yet their work shows major similarities and continuities with regard to subject matter, setting, tone. As long as we remember that we are using the term "regional literature" in a rather loose or metaphorical way, we can speak of the American Jewish writers as constituting a regional literature. Probably it is one of the last this country is going to have. And an important advantage of speaking about them as a regional literature is that it forces us to emphasize that, even as they still bear the marks of old-world and immigrant Jewish culture, they are indisputably *American* writers. They write in English. They live and publish in America. Their work is usually set in this country. And while their novels, stories and poems cannot finally be understood without some awareness of their Jewish origins, still, they are not part of any Jewish literature. They are not part of Hebrew or Yiddish literature.

Their work is regional in that it derives from and deals overwhelmingly with one locale, usually the streets and tenements of the immigrant Jewish neighborhoods or the "better" neighborhoods to which the children of the immigrants have moved; regional in that it offers exotic or curious local customs for the inspection of native readers; and regional in that it comes to us as an outburst of literary consciousness resulting from an encounter between an immigrant group and the host culture of America. So regarded, the writing of American Jews over the past few decades can be seen as fitting into the general pattern of American literary history.

The temptation to compare American Jewish writing with that which has come out of the South is almost irresistible—the two, after all, are the main regional literatures we have had thus far in the twentieth century. In both instances, a subculture finds its voice and its passion at exactly the moment it approaches disintegration. Such a moment of high self-consciousness offers writers the advantages of an inescapable subject: the judgment, affection and hatred they bring to bear upon the remembered world of their youth, and the costs exacted by their struggle to tear themselves away. It offers the emotional strength that comes from traditional styles of conduct—honor for the South, "chosenness" for the Jews—which these writers seek to regain, escape, overcome, while thereby finding their gift of tongue. It offers the vibration of old stories remembered and retold, whether by aging Confederate soldiers or skull-capped grandfathers recalling the terrors of the Czars. It offers the lure of nostalgia, a recapture of moments felt to be greater in their emotional resonance, perhaps more heroic than the present, all now entangled with a will toward violent denial of the past.

"To be the child of immigrants from eastern Europe," wrote Delmore Schwartz, "is in itself a special kind of experience; and an important one to an author. He has heard two languages throughout childhood, the one spoken with ease at home, and the other spoken with ease in the streets and at school, but spoken poorly at home. . . . To an author and especially to a poet [this double experience of language] may give a heightened sensitivity to language, a sense of idiom, and a sense of how much expresses itself through colloquialism. But it also produces in some a fear of mispronunciation; a hesitation in speech; and a sharpened focus upon the character of the parents."

At a crucial point the comparison between Southern and American Jewish writing breaks down, as it should. It breaks down at the point where we abandon the formal parallels in relationship between a receding culture and obsessed writers and examine the content of each culture.

The culture of the South, whatever its corruptions or idiosyncrasies, has been a Christian culture. The culture of the Jews, no matter how comfortably settled into the folds of American society, has remained fundamentally apart—at least until recently. It remains at odds with, perhaps even alien to, the host culture, insofar as being Christian or Jew still affects our lives. And of course it does affect our lives, deeply and in innumerable ways, despite the fading of religious persuasion and the secularization of religious experience. Southern writers view American society from a distance, with the sharpness of insight occasionally granted the outsider; but their condition as outsiders seems a partial and temporary one, by now almost at an end. That does not seem to me quite true with regard to American Jewish writers, even though the Jews as a whole are more integrated into American society today than they have ever been before. Yet, insofar as the American Jewish writers respond to the past— and nothing is more deeply ingrained in the Jewish experience than the idea of the past, the claim of memory—they must still feel a profound, even a mysterious sense of distinctiveness. For better or worse, often both, being Jewish remains something "special." If no longer an experience coloring every moment of life, as no doubt it was for earlier generations of Jews, it still affects crucial portions and moments of life. Nor can the hospitality, tolerance, and generosity of American democracy quite dispel the Jewish sense of distinctiveness. There is too much history, too much pain, behind that sense of distinctiveness. What the American Jewish writers make of it in the context of their experience, how they transform, play with, and try sometimes to suppress it—this forms the major burden of their art.

Let me now try, a bit quixotically, to establish some of the main characteristics of American Jewish writing. I know there are many differences among the American Jewish writers; I know they do not run in packs; yet I am convinced that there are shared memories, shared experiences, shared sensibilities. How could there not be?

Novelists like Henry Roth and Saul Bellow, storytellers like Delmore Schwartz and Bernard Malamud have been blessed, sometimes cursed, with a collective memory that arches over their work, at once liberating and confining the imagination. That frantic casting about for material, that desperate search for action and setting through which a writer can give fictional body to a glimpsed idea—this plight of deracination characterizing so much of American writing these days, even to the point where for some writers it has itself become a usable subject, is largely absent from the work of the American Jewish writers. Absent, at least, from their earlier work, when they are still in the fierce grip of childhood and adolescent memories. Later, as they drain their memories, they may come to share the plight of other American writers.

Not all the stories in this collection deal with the immigrant Jewish milieu, but almost all of them bear its stamp, and almost all would be incomprehensible to a reader who lacked some memory or impression—firsthand or through reading—of the immigrant Jewish milieu. (Could anyone read Dickens without *some* sense of nineteenth-century London?) Nostalgia, return, hatred, nausea, affection, guilt—all these are among the familiar, urgent feelings which memories of immigrant streets, tenements and (most of all) families can stir up in the American Jewish writers. For most of them the great literary problem is not that of summoning, or forcing, recollections of things past; it is that of finding narrative strategies with which to control and order those recollections. They face repeatedly the problem of avoiding the traps of sentimentalism and contempt, sleazy nostalgia and mean-spirited repudiation. Abundance of memory has to be turned into discipline of narration. And here the American Jewish writers are blessed somewhat as Hardy was blessed with Wessex, Faulkner with Yoknapatawpha, even John O'Hara within his portion of Pennsylvania. They possess a "separate world" linked to the world of actuality but recast by imagination, a "separate world" tied backward in time, to the places and manners of a regional subculture. But with this important difference: the immigrant Jewish experience does not seem sufficiently stable or abiding to give the writers who have come out of it that abundance of impressions and stories which Wessex could give Hardy and Yoknapatawpha Faulkner. Everything in the immigrant Jewish experience, and thereby, it now seems, the writing based upon it, is comparatively brief, transient, a flicker of history.

In the stories of Delmore Schwartz, Tillie Olsen, Grace Paley, Jerome Weidman, Michael Seide and Wallace Markfield, we encounter that immigrant world full-face. We see its pinched circumstances, its uncontainable aspirations, its pathos of self-definition, its explosions of street vitality. The death of an aging Jewish woman becomes, in Tillie Olsen's great story "Tell Me a Riddle," a threnody for a vanishing world. The sense of homelessness felt by a second-generation intellectual, raised in that world but no longer part of it, becomes the theme of Schwartz's story "America, America." For Michael Seide, the memories of its life are still glowingly warm, maternal. For Jerome Weidman, in his brilliant story "My Father Sits in the Dark," the immigrant experience yields a sense of terrible loss in the relationship between generations: a loss beyond measuring or speech. And so it goes in most of these stories: familiar myth turned into focused narrative, the stock of culture transformed into particular actions.

One remembers here a shrewd remark of Graham Greene, that an unhappy childhood is a writer's goldmine. While there is no reason to suppose that all American Jewish writers had unhappy childhoods—indeed, my own sense of growing up in the immigrant milieu is that, together with burdens, embarrassments, and awkwardness, there were also bracing security and love—these writers brought to bear upon their work something of what Greene must have had in mind. They brought to bear the overflow of memories of childhood and youth, memories both more fulfilled and deprived than those, perhaps, of other, mainstream Americans.

Some writers in this book, like Gilbert Rogin, Paul Goodman, and Daniel Fuchs, turn to the experience of second-generation Jews, those who by now are presumably at home in America, more prosperous than their immigrant parents and able to speak without Yiddish accents. Yet what comes through, as pathos, comedy, or both, is the continued power of origins, the ineradicable stamp of New York or Chicago slums, even upon grandsons and granddaughters who may never have lived in or seen them. But is that not an essential aspect of the Jewish experience?—the way the past grips and forms us, and will not allow us to escape even when we desperately want to. Or the way we come to feel an anxiety of loss, a depression of abandonment, even when we do escape.

This sense of a common past depends, in the fiction of these writers, primarily on the presence of a given locale, intimately known, scoured in its every nook and cranny, recalled proudly for its details of style and appearance. The sense of place, the sense of Delancey Street in New York or Maxwell Street in Chicago or Napoleon Street in Montreal, the looming grandeur and gewgaws of the Hotel Ansonia on Manhattan's West Side, the grime and noise of Pitkin Avenue in Brownsville or of Blue Hill Avenue in Boston—all these are wonderful inducements, props, stimulants to the American Jewish writers.

There is a fine essay by Eudora Welty called "Place in Fiction," discussing the ways in which the physical setting of a novel or story—the St. Petersburg streets and boarding houses of Dostoevsky, the London grime and fog of Dickens, the Mississippi towns and boats of Mark Twain—helps to validate meanings. Place is where the writer "has his roots, place is where he stands; in his experience out of which he writes it provides the base of reference, in his work the point of view." From seemingly inert locale, place becomes an organizing principle in a work of fiction, setting the tone, bounding the possibilities, declaring the hopes of the life it would represent. Bellow's Chicago, Henry Roth's East Side, Fuchs's Brooklyn: to visualize these settings with sufficient clarity is to grasp themes, ideas. For as Welty nicely observes, "The moment the place in which the novel (or story) happens is accepted as true, through it will begin to glow, in a kind of recognizable glory, the feelings and thought that inhabited the novel (or story) in the author's head and animated the whole of his work."

Our feelings are bound up with and inseparable from place. "I say, 'the Yorkshire moors,' and you will say, '*Wuthering Heights*,' and I have only to murmur, 'If Father were only alive—' for you to come back with, 'We could go to Moscow' . . . The truth is, fiction depends for its life on place. Location is the crossroads of circumstance, the proving ground of 'What happened? Who's here? Who's coming?' and that is the heart's field."

A lovely phrase. For many American Jewish writers, "the heart's field" will forever be those gray packed streets, turbulent and smelly, which they have kept from childhood, holding them in memory long after the actuality has been transformed or erased.

If a story's locale can serve so powerfully to release its

inner meanings, one reason is that the locale has become intimately associated with ways of living—custom, tradition,
sensibility, celebration, ritual, fright, repression. The fiction
of the American Jews is peculiarly rich, sometimes oppres-
sively heavy, with cherished details of old neighborhoods:
modes and styles which the immigrant world made its own,
weaving them out of fragments of the past transported across
the ocean or out of bits and pieces of whatever could be
picked up in the new world. Herbert Gold evoking the aches
of a Jewish storekeeper, Wallace Markfield the pleasure of
Saturday-afternoon movies, Meyer Liben the sporting favor-
ites of the streets—these aren't just the usual "backgrounds"
such as every writer of fiction needs in order to give his
story some verisimilitude. They take on, among American
Jewish writers, an additional tremor of feeling because they
are linked to a belief or delusion that "we" have grown up
under circumstances different from all others. In a good portion of American Jewish fiction, this belief can lead uncomfortably close to sentimentalism and self-indulgence, to say
nothing of the tiresome bric-a-brac of local color. But if
treated honestly, it is a belief that can yield ironic strength.

The centrality of the family in Jewish life, and thereby in
the fiction written about that life, seems to me a major instance of this feeling of having been exposed to a special
destiny. An agency of discipline and coherence, the family
has given the children of the immigrants enormous emotional
resources, but also a mess of psychic troubles. To have
grown up in an immigrant Jewish milieu is to be persuaded
that the family is an institution unbreakable and inviolable,
the one bulwark against the chaos of the world but also the
one barrier to tasting its delights. In American Jewish fiction,
the family becomes an overwhelming, indeed, obsessive presence: it is container of narrative, theater of character, agent
of significance.

How sharply different this seems from the attitude toward
the family that prevails in large stretches of American literature! When you come to think of it, where *is* the family in
Emerson and Thoreau, in Whitman and Melville? Where is it
in Hemingway and Fitzgerald? Occasionally glimpsed, more
often a constraint to be left behind, but rarely a dominating
and enclosing presence. Among the important American
writers, Faulkner is one of the few who shares with the Jewish writers the feeling that the family is at the very center of
existence.

Bellow's "The Old System" reads like a compressed version of those leisurely family chronicles which European novelists wrote at the turn of the century; the characters in this story matter mostly as representative figures in the saga of a family. Both of Delmore Schwartz's stories in this book focus upon family life, in "America, America," with a pained recognition of how much has been lost through the process of "Americanization," and in "In Dreams Begin Responsibilities" with a sardonic consideration of how sad and chafing Jewish family life can be. Only in Michael Seide's stories do we have a recall of the family almost entirely tender, though in Gilbert Rogin's sketch and, with darker tones, in Tillie Olsen's "Tell Me a Riddle" there is a touching warmth, a pleasure in return.

The family, of course, is also that which younger characters rebel against. To break from the family comes to seem a precondition of freedom, an escape from all that was suffocating and parochial in our youth. Herbert Gold's powerful story "The Heart of the Artichoke" captures both the embarrassment of a boy who feels his storekeeper parents lack refinement and the shame he feels with regard to that embarrassment, since he knows that they are people who merit his love and respect. In Malamud's "The Magic Barrel," the distance between the generations comes to seem lacerating: all decorum gone, all dignity and restraint, and nothing left but a muttering of prayers for the dead. And in Schwartz's "America, America," Shenandoah Fish, the intellectual protagonist, reflects: "The lower middle-class of the generation of Shenandoah's parents had engendered perversions of its own nature, children full of contempt for everything important to their parents." Listening to his mother narrate, with shrewd asides, the story of a neighboring Jewish family, Shenandoah "felt for the first time how closely bound he was to these people. His separation was actual enough, but there existed also an unbreakable unity. . . . The life he breathed in was full of these lives and the age in which they had acted and suffered." And all of this—the aching helplessness that marks the split between generations—is realized in the climax of Jerome Weidman's "My Father Sits in the Dark," one of the most memorable stories composed by an American Jewish writer.

Self-consciously or by mere routine, through a worked-out ideology or as a fragment of emotion, many of the American Jewish writers have started with the assumption that there remains—perhaps in secure possession, perhaps no longer in their grasp—a body of inherited traditions, values, and attitudes that we call "Jewishness." That these signify in both their lives and work seems beyond dispute: sometimes as positive beliefs, sometimes as negations hard to shake off. The very term "Jewishness" suggests, of course, a certain vagueness, pointing to the diffusion of a cultural heritage. When one speaks of Judaism or the Jewish religion, it is to invoke a coherent tradition of belief and custom; when one speaks of "Jewishness," it is to invoke a spectrum of styles and symbols, a range of cultural memories, no longer as ordered or weighty as once they were yet still able to affect experience.

This persuasion of distinctiveness remains even among nonbelieving Jews, difficult though it may be for them to specify its exact nature. In story after story there are characters moved by the persuasion of distinctiveness, or at least by recollections of its earlier power. Jewish belief and custom may have become attenuated, and the writers themselves only feebly connected with them; yet the persuasion remains that "we" (whoever that may be, however defined or bound) must live with a sense of our differentness and perhaps draw some sustenance from it. That sense of differentness may, at its best, enable a rich moral perspective upon the ways of the outer world: for which serious man or woman wants entirely to feel at home with the world? And even at its least, it comes to occasional encroachments of memory, bouts of sentiment regarding food, holidays, and customs. But at whatever pitch of value, the awareness of "Jewishness" remains.

Take, for example, Philip Roth's fine story "Defender of the Faith." It starts from a premise shared by all of its characters, the premise that certain ethical values persist in Jewish experience. Sergeant Marx, the central figure in Roth's story, takes seriously the value of rectitude: he feels that a Jew merits what he merits, neither more nor less. The Jewish soldiers who seek to exploit him through appeals to ethnic solidarity are in fact undermining the values of the tradition. Without the assumption that there is something distinctive in "Jewishness," a standard for many to affirm or others to violate, the story would verge on incoherence. It is not, of course, incoherent; it is firmly worked out as a dramatic action. And much the same holds true for the stories by Ozick, Elkin, Malamud, Olsen, and Paley: all rest on the force or the fading of shared values.

Just what is the distinctiveness that Jews experience? No two writers may quite agree. Yet there are felt connections, overlappings of sensibility, kinships of belief. Here, chosen almost at random, is a sampler from a number of writers and critics, all of whom struggle to put into words what they experience as urgency and need:

Ossip Mandelstam: "As a little bit of musk fills an entire house, so the least influence of Judaism overflows all of one's life."

Saul Bellow: "In the stories of the Jewish tradition, the world, and even the universe, have a human meaning. Indeed, the Jewish imagination has sometimes been found guilty of over-humanizing everything, of making too much of a case for us, for mankind. . . . [In Jewish stories] laughter and trembling are so curiously intermingled that it is not easy to determine the relations of the two. At times the laughter seems simply to restore the equilibrium of sanity; at times the figures of the story, or parable, appear to invite or encourage trembling with the secret aim of overcoming it by means of laughter."

Irving Howe: "Insofar as they chose still to regard themselves as Jews, even if nonreligious Jews, [the immigrants] were left with a nagging problem in self-perception, a crisis of identity, as it came to be called, which seems beyond solution or removal, except perhaps through a full return to religious faith or a complete abandonment of Jewish identification. They had achieved 'a normal life' in America, and for those with any taste for self-scrutiny, it was a life permanently beset by the question: who am I and why do I so declare myself? To live with this problem in a state of useful discontent was perhaps what it now meant to be a Jew."

Harold Rosenberg: "If there were a Jewish community in the old sense, with Jewish identity established beyond question by one's membership in that community, to be anything less than a Jew would be an individual aberration. Such, however, is plainly not the case with us, when Jewish identity is so much a matter of acts of the will and intellect. Since it is a matter of seeking one's identity within an open community, the perspective of the [Jewish] semi-outsider has its validity. . . . He is a Jew in that his experience contains the possibility of linking himself with the collective and individual experience of earlier Jews."

Isaac Rosenfeld: "The insight available to most Jewish writers is a natural result of their position in American life and culture. Jews are marginal men. As marginal men, living in cities and coming from the middle classes they are open to more influences than perhaps any other group. I vaguely recall a Yiddish proverb to the effect that bad luck always knows where to find a Jew. . . ."

Philip Rahv: "Bernard Malamud differs [from other Jewish writers] in that he fills his 'Jewishness' with a positive content. I mean that 'Jewishness,' as he understands and above all feels it, is one of the principal sources of value in his work. . . . Another 'Jewish' trait in Malamud is his feeling for human suffering on the one hand and for a life of value, order and dignity on the other. Thus he is one of the very few contemporary writers who seems to have escaped the clutch of historical circumstance that has turned nihilism into so powerful a temptation; nihilistic attitudes, whether of the hedonistic or absurdist variety, can never be squared with Malamud's essentially humanistic inspiration. The feeling for human suffering is of course far from being an exclusively 'Jewish' quality. It figures even more prominently in Dostoevsky. The Russian novelist, however, understands suffering primarily as a means of purification and of eventual salvation, whereas in Malamud suffering is not idealized; suffering is not what you are looking for but what you are likely to get."

Most American Jewish writers have had only an enfeebled relationship—indeed, a torn and deprived relationship—with the Jewish tradition in its fullness. Insofar as their work bears a relationship to the Jewish past, it is mainly through the historical phase of Yiddish, which lasted for several centuries both in eastern Europe and the immigrant quarters of America. But this phase itself represents a major break within, and perhaps from, the Jewish tradition, and moreover, the relationship of the American Jewish writers to the culture of Yiddish, source and root though it may be of their early experience, is often marked by rupture, break, dissociation. (That it is also often masked with sentiments of nostalgia serves finally to enable rupture, break, dissociation.) So that in speaking here of the line of Jewish sensibility which can still be found in the work of these writers, it should be clear that we are speaking about historical fragments, bits and pieces of memory.

Yet even a lapsed tradition, even portions of the past that have been brushed aside, even cultural associations that float about in the atmosphere, all have a way of infiltrating the work of the American Jewish writers. Tradition broken and crippled still displays enormous power over those most ready to shake it off. And tradition seemingly discarded can survive underground for a generation and then, through channels hard to locate, surface in the work of writers who may not even be aware of what is affecting their consciousness. Tradition as discontinuity—this is the central fact in the cultural experience of the American Jewish writers.

In one respect, however, the tradition, not of classical Judaism but of immigrant Jewish culture, still operates strongly in their work. To feel at some distance from society; to experience, almost as if it were cultural legacy, an ironic relationship to power; to assume, almost by way of birthright, a critical stance toward received dogmas; to recognize oneself as not quite at home in the world and thereby to be "assigned" tasks of social and moral criticism—these assumptions, whether taken with high seriousness or deflated toward the mannerism of absurdity, continue to inform the work of many American Jewish writers. Nay-sayers, table-pounders, shoulder-shruggers, eyebrow-raisers, they keep some portion of their parents' and grandparents' irony, skepticism, sometimes rebelliousness. And here the American Jewish writers, who had perhaps felt themselves somewhat estranged or distant from the mainstream of American literature, find that they can feel a genuine kinship with the democratic radicalism and the profound skepticism regarding native myths which course through our literature.

Finally, it has been upon language that the American Jewish writers have most sharply left their mark. To the language of fiction they have brought turnings of voice, feats of irony, and tempos of delivery that helped create a new American style—probably a shortlived style and one that reached its fulfillment in a mere handful of writers, but a new style nonetheless. Style speaks of sensibility, slant, vision; speaks here of a certain high excitability, a rich pumping of blood, a grating mixture of the sardonic and the sentimental, which the Jews brought across the Atlantic together with their baggage. I think it no exaggeration to say that since Faulkner and Hemingway the one major innovation in American prose style has been the yoking of street raciness and high-culture mandarin that we associate with the American Jewish writers.

Not, to be sure, all of them. There really is no single style

shared by all these writers, as any reader of this book can
easily see; and some of them—Delmore Schwartz in the
artifice of his anti-rhetoric, Michael Seide in the mild purity
of his diction, Tillie Olsen in her passionate, high-strung in-
tonation—clearly challenge the generalizations I shall nevertheless make. For what I want to assert is that the dominant
American Jewish style is the one brought to a pitch by Saul
Bellow and imitated and modified by a good many others.

Let us turn back for a moment to some of the earlier
American Jewish writers as they struggle to work out an
appropriate diction. The first collection of stories by Abraham
Cahan, *Yekl* (1896), is written in a baneful dialect so natu-
ralistically faithful, or intent upon being faithful, to the immigrant moment that it now seems about as exotic and inaccessible as the Southern folk argot of Sut Lovingood.
Cahan's major novel, *The Rise of David Levinsky* (1917),
employs, by contrast, a flavorless standard English, the prose
of an earnest but somewhat tone-deaf student worried about
proper usage. More interesting for its narrative line than for
verbal detail, the novel shows Cahan to be not quite in
possession of *any* language, either English or Yiddish, a condition common enough among the immigrants and, in the
case of their occasionally talented sons, to become the shifting ground upon which to build a shifty new style. The problem foreshadowed in Cahan's work is whether the Yiddish-
isms of East Side street talk and an ill-absorbed "correct"
prose painfully acquired in night school can be fused into
some higher stylistic enterprise.

One answer, still the most brilliant, came in Henry Roth's
Call It Sleep, a major novel blending a Joyce roughened to
the tonalities of New York with a Yiddish oddly transposed
into a pure and lyrical English but with its rhythms slightly
askew, as if to reveal immigrant sources. In Roth's novel the
children speak a ghastly, mutilated sort of English while the
main characters talk in Yiddish, which Roth renders as a
high poetic, somewhat offbeat English. Thus, the mother
tells her little boy: "Aren't you just a pair of eyes and ears!
You see, you hear, you remember, but when will you know?
. . . And no kisses? There! Savory, thrifty lips!" The last
phrase may seem a bit too "poetic" in English speech, but if
you translate it into Yiddish—*Na! geshmake, karge lipelakh!*
—it rings exactly right, beautifully idiomatic. Roth is here
continuing the tradition of Jewish bilingualism, in the past a

coexistence of Hebrew as sacred and Yiddish as demotic language; but he does this in an oddly surreptitious way, by making of English, in effect, two languages, or by writing his book in one language and expecting that at some points his readers will be able to hear it in another.

Yet, so far as I can tell, Roth has not been a major stylistic influence upon later American Jewish writers, perhaps because his work seems so self-contained; there is little one can do with it except to admire. A more useful precursor is Daniel Fuchs, a lovely and neglected writer, especially in his second novel, *Homage to Blenholt,* where one begins to hear a new music, a new tempo, as if to echo the beat of life in the slums.

This American Jewish style, which comes to climax and perhaps conclusion in Bellow, I would describe in a few desperate phrases:

A yoking of opposites, gutter vividness with university refinement, street energy with high-culture rhetoric;

a strong infusion of Yiddish, not so much through the occasional use of a phrase or word as through ironic twistings that transform the whole of language;

a rapid, nervous, breathless tempo, like the hurry of a garment salesman traying to con a buyer or a highbrow lecturer trying to dazzle an audience;

a deliberate loosening of syntax, as if to mock those niceties of Correct English which Gore Vidal and other untainted Americans hold dear, so that in consequence there is much greater weight upon transitory patches of color than upon sentences in repose or paragraphs in composure;

a deliberate play with the phrasings of plebeian speech, but often, also, the kind that vibrates with cultural ambition, seeking to zoom into regions of higher thought;

in short, the linguistic tokens of writers who must hurry into articulateness if they are to be heard at all, indeed, who must scrape together a language.

This style reflects a demotic upsurge, the effort to give literary scale to the speech of immigrant streets, or put another way, to create a "third language," richer and less stuffy, out of the fusion of English and Yiddish that had already occurred spontaneously in those streets. These writers did not, of course, create a new language, and in the encounter between English and Yiddish, the first has survived far better than the second; still, it is neither boast nor exaggeration to say that "we" have left our scar, tiny though it may be, upon "their" map.

There remains the question, worth asking if impossible to answer with certainty: What is the likely future of American Jewish writing? Has it already passed its peak of achievement and influence? Can we expect a new generation of writers to appear who will contribute to American literature a distinctive sensibility and style derived from the Jewish experience in this country?

My own view is that American Jewish fiction has probably moved past its high point. Insofar as this body of writing draws heavily from the immigrant experience, it must suffer a depletion of resources, a thinning-out of materials and memories. Other than in books and sentiment, there just isn't enough left of that experience. Even some of the writers, men and women of middle age or beyond, who have themselves lived through the immigrant experience now seem to be finding that their recollections have run dry. Or, that in their stories and novels they have done about as much with those recollections as they can. The sense of an overpowering subject, the sense that this subject imposes itself upon their imaginations—this grows weaker, necessarily, with the passing of the years. There remains, to be sure, the problem of "Jewishnessness," and the rewards and difficulties of definition it may bring us. But this problem, though experienced as an urgent one by at least some people, does not yield a thick enough sediment of felt life to enable a new outburst of writing about American Jews. It is too much a matter of will, or nerves, and not enough of shared experience. Besides, not everything which concerns or interests us can be transmuted into imaginative literature.

I find confirmation of these views in a recent essay by Ruth Wisse, who writes about the problems of the younger Jewish novelists and storytellers: "For those who take Judaism seriously as a cultural alternative, and wish to weave new brilliant cloth from its ancient threads, the sociological reality of the present-day American Jewish community would seem to present an almost insurmountable obstacle. Writers . . . who feel the historic, moral and religious weight of Judaism, and want to represent it in literature, have had to ship their characters out of town by Greyhound or magic carpet, to an unlikely *shtetl*, to Israel, . . . to other times and other climes, in search of pan-Jewish fictional atmospheres."

Others think differently. Younger Jewish writers grow impatient and irritated with the view I have expressed above. They suspect that people like me are trying to monopolize American Jewish writing for the experience of my generation and the one just before it. They would argue that there is a post-immigrant Jewish experience in America which can be located in its own milieu, usually suburbs or middle-class urban neighborhoods; that it has virtues and vices distinctly its own; and that it offers a body of experience which a serious writer can draw upon in creating fictions. Is not their phase of Jewish life in America as authentic and interesting as that of the earlier immigrants? Do they not have a right, also, to make of their involvements and confusions with Jewishness the foundation for stories and novels?

Perhaps these younger writers are in the right. I hope so, though I doubt it, since what seems to me at issue is not so much the intrinsic importance of the post-immigrant Jewish experience as its usability for the making of fictions. Does that experience go deep enough into the lives of the younger, "Americanized" Jews? Does it form the very marrow of their being? Does it provide images of conflict, memories of exaltation and suffering, such as enable the creating of stories?

About all this we need not be dogmatic. Far better to be open and tentative (even if also skeptical). But what can be said with some assurance is that by now, entering the last quarter of the century, there have appeared a significant number of Jewish writers in this country who have made of their memories, largely of the immigrant years, the material for valuable works of fiction. Their stories and novels have already enriched American literature, even, to a modest extent, transforming it as other risings of new Americans have transformed it in the past.

Note to the Reader: The first three stories in this book—those by Sholom Aleichem and Isaac Beshevis Singer written in Yiddish, that by Isaac Babel written in Russian—emerge from east European Jewish experience and have clearly influenced a number of the Jewish-American writers who follow in these pages. I have included these three stories in order to show the continuity from Europe to America of Jewish experience and the writings about it.

On Account of a Hat

Sholom Aleichem

"Did I hear you say absent-minded? Now, in our town, that is, in Kasrilevke, we've really got someone for you—do you hear what I say? His name is Sholem Shachnah, but we call him Sholem Shachnah Rattlebrain, and is he absent-minded, is this a distracted creature, Lord have mercy on us! The stories they tell about him, about this Sholem Shachnah— bushels and baskets of stories—I tell you, whole crates full of stories and anecdotes! It's too bad you're in such a hurry on account of the Passover, because what I could tell you, Mr. Sholom Aleichem—do you hear what I say?—you could go on writing it down forever. But if you can spare a moment I'll tell you a story about what happened to Sholem Shachnah on a Passover eve—a story about a hat, a true story, I should live so, even if it does sound like someone made it up."

These were the words of a Kasrilevke merchant, a dealer in stationery, that is to say, snips of paper. He smoothed out his beard, folded it down over his neck, and went on smoking his thin little cigarettes, one after the other.

I must confess that this true story, which he related to me, does indeed sound like a concocted one, and for a long time I couldn't make up my mind whether or not I should pass it on to you. But I thought it over and decided that if a respectable merchant and dignitary of Kasrilevke, who deals in stationery and is surely no *litterateur*—if he vouches for a story, it must be true. What would he be doing with fiction? Here it is in his own words. I had nothing to do with it.

This Sholem Shachnah I'm telling you about, whom we call Sholem Shachnah Rattlebrain, is a real-estate broker— you hear what I say? He's always with landowners, negotiating transactions. Transactions? Well, at least he hangs around the landowners. So what's the point? I'll tell you. Since he hangs around the landed gentry, naturally some of their manner has rubbed off on him, and he always has a mouth full of farms, homesteads, plots, acreage, soil, threshing machines, renovations, woods, timber, and other such terms having to do with estates.

One day God took pity on Sholem Shachnah, and for the first time in his career as a real-estate broker—are you listening?—he actually worked out a deal. That is to say, the work itself, as you can imagine, was done by others, and when the time came to collect the fee, the big rattler turned out to be not Sholem Shachnah Rattlebrain, bu Drobkin, a Jew from Minsk province, a great big fearsome rattler, a real-estate broker from way back—he and his two brothers, also brokers and also big rattlers. So you can take my word for it, there was quite a to-do. A Jew has contrived and connived and has finally, with God's help, managed to cut himself in—so what do they do but come along and cut him out! Where's Justice? Sholem Shachnah wouldn't stand for it—are you listening to me? He set up such a holler and an outcry— "Look what they've done to me!"—that at last they gave in to shut him up, and good riddance it was too.

When he got his few cents Sholem Shachnah sent the greater part of it home to his wife, so she could pay off some debts, shoo the wolf from the door, fix up new outfits for the children, and make ready for the Passover holidays. And as for himself, he also needed a few things, and besides he had to buy presents for his family, as was the custom.

Meanwhile the time flew by, and before he knew it, it was almost Passover. So Sholem Shachnah—now listen to this— ran to the telegraph office and sent home a wire: *Arriving home Passover without fail.* It's easy to say "arriving" and "without fail" at that. But you just try it! Just try riding out our way on the new train and see how fast you'll arrive. Ah, what a pleasure! Did they do us a favor! I tell you, Mr. Sholom Aleichem, for a taste of Paradise such as this you'd gladly forsake your own grandchildren! You see how it is: until you get to Zlodievka there isn't much you can do about it, so you just lean back and ride. But at Zlodievka the fun begins, because that's where you have to change, to get onto the new train, which they did us such a favor by running out to Kasrilevke. But not so fast. First, there's the little matter of several hours' wait, exactly as announced in the schedule—provided, of course, that you don't pull in after the Kasrilevke train has left. And at what time of night may you look forward to this treat? The very middle, thank you, when you're dead tired and disgusted, without a friend in the world except sleep—and there's not one single place in the whole station where you can lay your head, not one. When the wise men of Kasrilevke quote the passage from the Holy Book, *"Tov shem meshemon tov,"* they know what they're doing. I'll translate it for you: We were better off without the train.

To make a long story short, when our Sholem Shachnah arrived in Zlodievka with his carpetbag he was half dead; he had already spent two nights without sleep. But that was nothing at all to what was facing him—he still had to spend the whole night waiting in the station. What shall he do? Naturally he looked around for a place to sit down. Whoever heard of such a thing? Nowhere. Nothing. No place to sit. The walls of the station were covered with soot, the floor was covered with spit. It was dark, it was terrible. He finally discovered one miserable spot on a bench where he had just room enough to squeeze in, and no more than that, because the bench was occupied by an official of some sort in a uniform full of buttons, who was lying there all stretched out and snoring away to beat the band. Who this Buttons was, whether he was coming or going, he hadn't the vaguest idea, Sholem Shachnah, that is. But he could tell that Buttons was no dime-a-dozen official. This was plain by his cap, a military cap with a red band and a visor. He could have been an officer or a police official. Who knows? But surely he had drawn up to the station with ringing of bells, had staggered in, full to the ears with meat and drink, laid himself out on the bench, as in his father's vineyard, and worked up a glorious snoring.

It's not such a bad life to be a gentile, and an official one at that, with buttons, thinks he, Sholem Shachnah, that is, and he wonders, dare he sit next to this Buttons, or hadn't he better keep his distance? Nowadays you never can tell whom you're sitting next to. If he's no more than a plain inspector, that's still all right. But what if he turns out to be a district inspector? Or a provincial commander? Or even higher than that? And supposing this is even Purishkevitch himself, the famous anti-Semite, may his name perish? Let someone else deal with him and Sholem Shachnah turns cold at the mere thought of falling into such a fellow's hands. But then he says to himself—now listen to this—Buttons, he says,

who the hell is Buttons? And who gives a hang for Purishkevitch? Don't I pay my fare the same as Purishkevitch? So
why should he have all the comforts of life and I none? If
Buttons is entitled to a delicious night's sleep, then doesn't
he, Sholem Shachnah that is, at least have a nap coming?
After all, he's human too, and besides, he's already gone two
nights without a wink. And so he sits down, on a corner of
the bench, and leans his head back, not, God forbid, to sleep,
but just like that, to snooze. But all of a sudden he remembers—he's supposed to be home for Passover, and tomorrow
is Passover eve! What if, God have mercy, he should fall
asleep and miss his train? But that's why he's got a Jewish
head on his shoulders—are you listening to me or not?—so
he figures out the answer to that one too, Sholem Shachnah,
that is, and goes looking for the porter, a certain Yeremei,
he knows him well, to make a deal with him. Whereas he,
Sholem Shachnah, is already on his third sleepless night and
is afraid, God forbid, that he may miss his train, therefore
let him, Yeremei, that is, in God's name, be sure to wake him,
Sholem Shachnah, because tomorrow night is a holiday,
Passover. "Easter," he says to him in Russian and lays a coin
in Yeremei's mitt. "Easter, Yeremei, do you understand,
goyisher kop? Our Easter." The peasant pockets the coin, no
doubt about that, and promises to wake him at the first sign
of the train—he can sleep soundly and put his mind at rest.
So Sholem Shachnah sits down in his corner of the bench,
gingerly, pressed up against the wall, with his carpetbag curled
around him so that no one should steal it. Little by little he
sinks back, makes himself comfortable, and half shuts his eyes
—no more than forty winks, you understand. But before long
he's got one foot propped up on the bench and then the
other; he stretches out and drifts off to sleep. Sleep? I'll say
sleep, like God commanded us: with his head thrown back
and his hat rolling away on the floor, Sholem Shachnah is
snoring like an eight-day wonder. After all, a human being,
up two nights in a row—what would you have him do?

He had a strange dream. He tells this himself, that is,
Sholem Shachnah does. He dreamed that he was riding home
for Passover—are you listening to me?—but not on the train,
in a wagon, driven by a thievish peasant, Ivan Zlodi we call
him. The horses were terribly slow, they barely dragged
along. Sholem Shachnah was impatient, and he poked the
peasant between the shoulders and cried, "May you only drop

dead, Ivan darling! Hurry up, you lout! Passover is coming, our Jewish Easter!" Once he called out to him, twice, three times. The thief paid him no mind. But all of a sudden he whipped his horses to a gallop and they went whirling away, up hill and down, like demons. Sholem Shachnah lost his hat. Another minute of this and he woud have lost God knows what. "Whoa, there, Ivan old boy! Where's the fire? Not so fast!" cried Sholem Shachnah. He covered his head with his hands—he was worried, you see, over his lost hat. How can he drive into town bareheaded? But for all the good it did him, he could have been hollering at a post. Ivan the Thief was racing the horses as if forty devils were after him. All of a sudden—tppprrru!—they came to a dead stop, right in the middle of the field—you hear me?—a dead stop. What's the matter? Nothing. "Get up," said Ivan, "time to get up."

Time? What time? Sholem Shachnah is all confused. He wakes up, rubs his eyes, and is all set to step out of the wagon when he realizes he has lost his hat. Is he dreaming or not? And what's he doing here? Sholem Shachnah finally comes to his senses and recognizes the peasant—this isn't Ivan Zlodi at all but Yeremei the porter. So he concludes that he isn't on the high road after all, but in the station at Zlodievka, on the way home for Passover, and that if he means to get there he'd better run to the window for a ticket, but fast. Now what? No hat. The carpetbag is right where he left it, but his hat? He pokes around under the bench, reaching all over, until he comes up with a hat—not his own, to be sure, but the official's, with the red band and the visor. But Sholem Shachnah has no time for details and he rushes off to buy a ticket. The ticket window is jammed, everybody and his cousins are crowding in. Sholem Shachnah thinks he won't get to the window in time, perish the thought, and he starts pushing forward, carpetbag and all. The people see the red band and the visor and they make way for him. "Where to, Your Excellency?" asks the ticket agent. What's this Excellency, all of a sudden? wonders Sholem Shachnah, and he rather resents it. Some joke, a gentile poking fun at a Jew. All the same he says, Sholem Shachnah, that is, "Kasrilevke." "Which class, Your Excellency?" The ticket agent is looking straight at the red band and the visor. Sholem Shachnah is angrier than ever. I'll give him an Excellency, so he'll know how to make fun of a poor Jew! But then he thinks, Oh, well, we Jews are in Diaspora—do you hear what I say?—

let it pass. And he asks for a ticket third class. "Which class?" The agent blinks at him, very much surprised. This time Sholem Shachnah gets good and sore and he really tells him off. "Third!" says he. All right, thinks the agent, third is third.

In short, Sholem Shachnah buys his ticket, takes up his carpetbag, runs out onto the platform, plunges into the crowd of Jews and gentiles, no comparison intended, and goes looking for the third-class carriage. Again the red band and the visor work like a charm, everyone makes way for the official. Sholem Shachnah is wondering, What goes on here? But he runs along the platform till he meets a conductor carrying a lantern. "Is this third class?" asks Sholem Shachnah, putting one foot on the stairs and shoving his bag into the door of the compartment. "Yes, Your Excellency," says the conductor, but he holds him back. "If you please, sir, it's packed full, as tight as your fist. You couldn't squeeze a needle into that crowd." And he takes Sholem Shachnah's carpetbag—you hear what I'm saying?—and sings out, "Right this way, Your Excellency, I'll find you a seat." "What the Devil!" cries Sholem Shachnah. "Your Excellency and Your Excellency!" But he hasn't much time for the fine points; he's worried about his carpetbag. He's afraid, you see, that with all these Excellencies he'll be swindled out of his belongings. So he runs after the conductor with the lantern, who leads him into a second-class carriage. This is also packed to the rafters, no room even to yawn in there. "This way please, Your Excellency!" And again the conductor grabs the bag and Sholem Shachnah lights out after him. "Where in blazes is he taking me?" Sholem Shachnah is racking his brains over this Excellency business, but meanwhile he keeps his eye on the main thing—the carpetbag. They enter the first-class carriage, the conductor sets down the bag, salutes, and backs away, bowing. Sholem Shachnah bows right back. And there he is, alone at last.

Left alone in the carriage, Sholem Shachnah looks around to get his bearings—you hear what I say? He has no idea why all these honors have suddenly been heaped on him—first class, salutes, Your Excellency. Can it be on account of the real-estate deal he just closed? That's it! But wait a minute. If his own people, Jews, that is, honored him for this, it would be understandable. But gentiles! The conductor! The ticket agent! What's it to them? Maybe he's dreaming. Sholem Shachnah rubs his forehead, and while passing down the corridor glances into the mirror on the wall. It nearly knocks him over! He sees not himself but the official with the red band. That's who it is! "All my bad dreams on Yeremei's head and on his hands and feet, that lug! Twenty times I tell him to wake me and I even give him a tip, and what does he do, that dumb ox, may he catch cholera in his face, but wake the official instead. And me he leaves asleep on the bench! Tough luck, Sholem Shachnah old boy, but this year you'll spend Passover in Zlodievka, not at home."

Now get a load of this. Sholem Shachnah scoops up his carpetbag and rushes off once more, right back to the station where he is sleeping on the bench. He's going to wake himself up before the locomotive, God forbid, lets out a blast and blasts his Passover to pieces. And so it was. No sooner had Sholem Shachnah leaped out of the carriage with his carpetbag than the locomotive did let go with a blast—do you hear me?—one followed by another, and then, good night!

The paper dealer smiled as he lit a fresh cigarette, thin as a straw. "And would you like to hear the rest of the story? The rest isn't so nice. On account of being such a rattlebrain, our dizzy Sholem Shachnah had a miserable Passover, spending both Seders among strangers in the house of a Jew in Zlodievka. But this was nothing—listen to what happened afterward. First of all, he has a wife, Sholem Shachnah, that is, and his wife—how shall I describe her to you? *I* have a wife, *you* have a wife, we all have wives, we've had a taste of Paradise, we know what it means to be married. All I can say about Sholem Shachnah's wife is that she's A Number One. And did she give him a royal welcome! Did she lay into him! Mind you, she didn't complain about his spending the holiday away from home, and she said nothing about the red band and the visor. She let that stand for the time being; she'd take it up with him later. The only thing she complained about was—the telegram! And not so much the telegram— you hear what I say?—as the one short phrase, *without fail*. What possessed him to put that into the wire: *Arriving home Passover without fail*. Was he trying to make the telegraph company rich? And besides, how dare a human being say 'without fail' in the first place? It did him no good to answer and explain. She buried him alive. Oh, well, that's what wives are for. And not that she was altogether wrong—after all, she had been waiting so anxiously. But this was nothing compared with what he caught from the town, Kasrilevke, that is. Even before he returned the whole town—you hear what I say?—knew all about Yeremei and the official and the red band and the visor and the conductor's Your Excellency—the whole show. He himself, Sholem Shachnah, that is, denied everything and swore up and down that the Kasrilevke smart-alecks had invented the entire story for lack of anything better to do. It was all very simple—the reason he came home late, after the holidays, was that he had made a special trip to inspect a wooded estate. Woods? Estate? Not a chance—no one bought *that!* They pointed him out in the streets and held their sides, laughing. And everybody asked him, 'How does it feel, Reb Sholem Shachnah, to wear a cap with a red band and a visor?' 'And tell us,' said others, 'what's it like to travel first class?' As for the children, this was made to order for them—you hear what I say? Wherever he went they trooped after him, shouting, 'Your Excellency! Your excellent Excellency! Your most excellent Excellency!'

"You think it's so easy to put one over on Kasrilevke?"

Translated by Isaac Rosenfeld

The Story of My Dovecot

Isaac Babel

When I was a kid I longed for a dovecot. Never in all my life have I wanted a thing more. But not till I was nine did father promise the wherewithal to buy the wood to make one and three pairs of pigeons to stock it with. It was then 1904, and I was studying for the entrance exam to the preparatory class of the secondary school at Nikolayev in the Province of Kherson, where my people were at that time living. This province of course no longer exists, and our town has been incorporated in the Odessa Region.

I was only nine, and I was scared stiff of the exams. In both subjects, Russian language and arithmetic, I couldn't afford to get less than top marks. At our secondary school the *numerus clausus* was stiff: a mere five percent. So that out of forty boys only two that were Jews could get into the preparatory class. The teachers used to put cunning questions to Jewish boys; no one else was asked such devilish questions. So when father promised to buy the pigeons he demanded top marks with distinction in both subjects. He absolutely tortured me to death. I fell into a state of permanent daydream, into an endless, despairing, childish reverie. I went to the exam deep in this dream, and nevertheless did better than everybody else.

I had a knack for book-learning. Even though they asked cunning questions, the teachers could not rob me of my intelligence and my avid memory. I was good at learning, and got top marks in both subjects. But then everything went wrong. Khariton Efrussi, the corn-dealer who exported wheat to Marseille, slipped someone a 500-rouble bribe. My mark was changed from A to A–, and Efrussi Junior went to the secondary school instead of me. Father took it very badly. From the time I was six he had been cramming me with every scrap of learning he could, and that A– drove him to despair. He wanted to beat Efrussi up, or at least bribe two longshoremen to beat Efrussi up, but mother talked him out of the idea, and I started studying for the second exam the following year, the one for the lowest class. Behind my back my people got the teacher to take me in one year through the preparatory and first-year courses simultaneously, and conscious of the family's despair, I got three whole books by heart. These were Smirnovsky's *Russian Grammar,* Yevtushevsky's *Problems,* and Putsykovich's *Manual of Early Russian History.* Children no longer cram from these books, but I learned them by heart line upon line, and the following year in the Russian exam Karavayev gave me an unrivaled A+.

This Karavayev was a red-faced, irritable fellow, a graduate of Moscow University. He was hardly more than thirty. Crimson glowed in his manly cheeks as it does in the cheeks of peasant children. A wart sat perched on one cheek, and from it there sprouted a tuft of ash-colored cat's whiskers. At the exam, besides Karavayev, there was the Assistant Curator Pyatnitsky, who was reckoned a big noise in the school and throughout the province. When the Assistant Curator asked me about Peter the Great a feeling of complete oblivion came over me, an awareness that the end was near: an abyss seemed to yawn before me, an arid abyss lined with exultation and despair.

About Peter the Great I knew things by heart from Putsykovich's book and Pushkin's verses. Sobbing, I recited these verses, while the faces before me suddenly turned upside down, were shuffled as a pack of cards is shuffled. This cardshuffling went on, and meanwhile, shivering, jerking my back straight, galloping headlong, I was shouting Pushkin's stanzas at the top of my voice. On and on I yelled them, and no one broke into my crazy mouthings. Through a crimson blindness, through the sense of absolute freedom that had filled me, I was aware of nothing but Pyatnitsky's old face with its silver-touched beard bent toward me. He didn't interrupt me, and merely said to Karavayev, who was rejoicing for my sake and Pushkin's:

"What a people," the old man whispered, "those little Jews of yours. There's a devil in them!"

And when at last I could shout no more, he said:

"Very well, run along, my little friend."

I went out from the classroom into the corridor, and there, leaning against a wall that needed a coat of whitewash, I began to awake from my trance. About me Russian boys were playing, the school bell hung not far away above the stairs, the caretaker was snoozing on a chair with a broken seat. I looked at the caretaker, and gradually woke up. Boys were creeping toward me from all sides. They wanted to give me a jab, or perhaps just have a game, but Pyatnitsky suddenly loomed up in the corridor. As he passed me he halted for a moment, the frock coat flowing down his back in a slow heavy wave. I discerned embarrassment in that large, fleshy, upper-class back, and got closer to the old man.

"Children," he said to the boys, "don't touch this lad." And he laid a fat hand tenderly on my shoulder.

"My little friend," he went on, turning me towards him, "tell your father that you are admitted to the first class."

On his chest a great star flashed, and decorations jingled in his lapel. His great black uniformed body started to move away on its stiff legs. Hemmed in by the shadowy walls, moving between them as a barge moves through a deep canal, it disappeared in the doorway of the headmaster's study. The little servingman took in a tray of tea, clinking solemnly, and I ran home to the shop.

In the shop a peasant customer, tortured by doubt, sat scratching himself. When he saw me my father stopped trying to help the peasant make up his mind, and without a moment's hesitation believed everything I had to say. Calling to the assistant to start shutting up shop, he dashed out into Cathedral Street to buy me a school cap with a badge on it. My poor mother had her work cut out getting me away from the crazy fellow. She was pale at the moment, she was experiencing destiny. She kept smoothing me, and pushing me away as though she hated me. She said there was always a notice in the paper about those who had been admitted to the school, and that God would punish us, and that folk would laugh at us if we bought a school cap too soon. My mother was pale; she was experiencing destiny through my eyes. She looked at me with bitter compassion as one might look at a little cripple boy, because she alone knew what a family ours was for misfortunes.

All the men in our family were trusting by nature, and quick to ill-considered actions. We were unlucky in everything we undertook. My grandfather had been a rabbi somewhere in the Belaya Tserkov region. He had been thrown out for blasphemy, and for another forty years he lived noisily and sparsely, teaching foreign languages. In his eightieth year he started going off his head. My Uncle Leo, my father's brother, had studied at the Talmudic Academy in Volozhin. In 1892 he ran away to avoid doing military service, eloping with the daughter of someone serving in the commissariat in the Kiev military district. Uncle Leo took this woman to California, to Los Angeles, and there he abandoned her, and died in a house of ill fame among Negroes and Malays. After his death the American police sent us a heritage from Los Angeles, a large trunk bound with brown iron hoops. In this trunk there were dumbbells, locks of women's hair, uncle's talith, horsewhips with gilt handles, scented tea in boxes trimmed with imitation pearls. Of all the family there remained only crazy Uncle Simon-Wolf, who lived in Odessa, my father, and I. But my father had faith in people, and he used to put them off with the transports of first love. People could not forgive him for this, and used to play him false. So my father believed that his life was guided by an evil fate, an inexplicable being that pursued him, a being in every respect unlike him. And so I alone of all our family was left to my mother. Like all Jews I was short, weakly, and had headaches from studying. My mother saw all this. She had never been dazzled by her husband's pauper pride, by his incomprehensible belief that our family would one day be richer and more powerful than all others on earth. She desired no success for us, was scared of buying a school jacket too soon, and all she would consent to was that I should have my photo taken.

On September 20, 1905, a list of those admitted to the first class was hung up at the school. In the list my name figured too. All our kith and kin kept going to look at this paper, and even Shoyl, my granduncle, went along. I loved that boastful old man, for he sold fish at the market. His fat hands were moist, covered with fish-scales, and smelt of worlds chill and beautiful. Shoyl also differed from ordinary folk in the lying stories he used to tell about the Polish Rising of 1861. Years ago Shoyl had been a tavernkeeper at Skvira. He had seen Nicholas I's soldiers shooting Count Godlevski and other Polish insurgents. But perhaps he hadn't. *Now* I know that Shoyl was just an old ignoramus and a simpleminded liar, but his cock-and-bull stories I have never forgotten: they were good stories. Well now, even silly old Shoyl went along to the school to read the list with my name on it, and that evening he danced and pranced at our pauper ball.

My father got up the ball to celebrate my success, and

asked all his pals—grain-dealers, real-estate brokers, and the traveling salesmen who sold agricultural machinery in our parts. These salesmen would sell a machine to anyone. Peasants and landowners went in fear of them: you couldn't break loose without buying something or other. Of all Jews, salesmen are the widest-awake and the jolliest. At our party they sang Hasidic songs consisting of three words only but which took an awful long time to sing, songs performed with endless comical intonations. The beauty of these intonations may only be recognized by those who have had the good fortune to spend Passover with the Hasidim or who have visited their noisy Volhynian synagogues. Besides the salesmen, old Lieberman who had taught me the Torah and ancient Hebrew honored us with his presence. In our circle he was known as Monsieur Lieberman. He drank more Bessarabian wine than he should have. The ends of the traditional silk tassels poked out from beneath his waistcoat, and in ancient Hebrew he proposed my health. In this toast the old man congratulated my parents and said that I had vanquished all my foes in single combat: I had vanquished the Russian boys with their fat cheeks, and I had vanquished the sons of our own vulgar parvenus. So too in ancient times David King of Judah had overcome Goliath, and just as I had triumphed over Goliath, so too would our people by the strength of their intellect conquer the foes who had encircled us and were thirsting for our blood. Monsieur Lieberman started to weep as he said this, drank more wine as he wept, and shouted *"Vivat!"* The guests formed a circle and danced an old-fashioned quadrille with him in the middle, just as at a wedding in a little Jewish town. Everyone was happy at our ball. Even mother took a sip of vodka, though she neither liked the stuff nor understood how anyone else could—because of this she considered all Russians cracked, and just couldn't imagine how women managed with Russian husbands.

But our happy days came later. For mother they came when of a morning, before I set off for school, she would start making me sandwiches; when we went shopping to buy my school things—pencil box, money box, satchel, new books in cardboard bindings, and exercise books in shiny covers. No one in the world has a keener feeling for new things than children have. Children shudder at the smell of newness as a dog does when it scents a hare, experiencing the madness which later, when we grow up, is called inspiration. And mother acquired this pure and childish sense of the owner-ship of new things. It took us a whole month to get used to the pencil box, to the morning twilight as I drank my tea on the corner of the large, brightly-lit table and packed my books in my satchel. It took us a month to grow accustomed to our happiness, and it was only after the first half-term that I remembered about the pigeons.

I had everything ready for them: one rouble fifty and a dovecot made from a box by Grandfather Shoyl, as we called him. The dovecot was painted brown. It had nests for twelve pairs of pigeons, carved strips on the roof, and a special grating that I had devised to facilitate the capture of strange birds. All was in readiness. On Sunday, October 20, I set out for the bird market, but unexpected obstacles arose in my path.

The events I am relating, that is to say my admission to the first class at the secondary school, occurred in the autumn of 1905. The Emperor Nicholas was then bestowing a con-stitution on the Russian people. Orators in shabby overcoats were clambering onto tall curbstones and haranguing the people. At night shots had been heard in the streets, and so mother didn't want me to go to the bird market. From early morning on October 20 the boys next door were flying a kite right by the police station, and our water carrier, abondoning all his buckets, was walking about the streets with a red face and brilliantined hair. Then we saw baker Kalistov's sons drag a leather vaulting-horse out into the street and start doing gym in the middle of the roadway. No one tried to stop them: Semernikov the policeman even kept inciting them to jump higher. Semernikov was girt with a silk belt his wife had made him, and his boots had been polished that day as they had never been polished before. Out of his customary uniform, the policeman frightened my mother more than anything else. Because of him she didn't want me to go out, but I sneaked out by the back way and ran to the bird market, which in our town was behind the station.

At the bird market Ivan Nikodimych, the pigeon-fancier, sat in his customary place. Apart from pigeons, he had rab-bits for sale too, and a peacock. The peacock, spreading its tail, sat on a perch moving a passionless head from side to side. To its paw was tied a twisted cord, and the other end of the cord was caught beneath one leg of Ivan Nikodimych's wicker chair. The moment I got there I bought from the old man a pair of cherry-colored pigeons with luscious tousled tails, and a pair of crowned pigeons, and put them away in a bag on my chest under my shirt. After these purchases I had only forty copecks left, and for this price the old man was not prepared to let me have a male and female pigeon of the Kryukov breed. What I liked about Kryukov pigeons was their short, knobbly, good-natured beaks. Forty copecks was the proper price, but the fancier insisted on haggling, averting from me a yellow face scorched by the unsociable passions of bird-snarers. At the end of our bargaining, seeing that there were no other customers, Ivan Nikodimych beckoned me closer. All went as I wished, and all went badly.

Toward twelve o'clock, or perhaps a bit later, a man in felt boots passed across the square. He was stepping lightly on swollen feet, and in his worn-out face lively eyes glittered.

"Ivan Nikodimych," he said as he walked past the bird-fancier, "pack up your gear. In town the Jerusalem aristocrats are being granted a constitution. On Fish Street Grandfather Babel has been constitutioned to death."

He said this and walked lightly on between the cages like a barefoot ploughman walking along the edge of a field.

"They shouldn't," murmured Ivan Nikodimych in his wake. "They shouldn't!" he cried more sternly. He started collecting his rabbits and his peacock, and shoved the Kryukov pigeons at me for forty copecks. I hid them in my bosom and watched the people running away from the bird market. The peacock on Ivan Nikodimych's shoulder was last of all to depart. It sat there like the sun in a raw autumnal sky; it sat as July sits on a pink riverbank, a white-hot July in the long cool grass. No one was left in the market, and not far off shots were rattling. Then I ran to the station, cut across a square that had gone topsy-turvy, and flew down an empty lane of trampled yellow earth. At the end of the lane, in a little wheeled armchair, sat the legless Makarenko, who rode about town in his wheel-chair selling cigarettes from a tray. The boys in our street used to buy smokes from him, children loved him, I dashed toward him down the lane.

"Makarenko," I gasped, panting from my run, and I stroked the legless one's shoulder, "have you seen Shoyl?"

The cripple did not reply. A light seemed to be shining through his coarse face built up of red fat, clenched fists, chunks of iron. He was fidgeting on his chair in his excitement, while his wife Kate, presenting a wadded behind, was sorting out some things scattered on the ground.

"How far have you counted?" asked the legless man, and moved his whole bulk away from the woman, as though aware in advance that her answer would be unbearable.

"Fourteen pair of leggings," said Kate, still bending over, "six undersheets. Now I'm a-counting the bonnets."

"Bonnets!" cried Makarenko, with a choking sound like a sob, "it's clear, Catherine, that God has picked on me, that I must answer for all. People are carting off whole rolls of cloth, people have everything they should, and we're stuck with bonnets."

And indeed a woman with a beautiful burning face ran past us down the lane. She was clutching an armful of fezzes in one arm and a piece of cloth in the other, and in a voice of joyful despair she was yelling for her children, who had strayed. A silk dress and a blue blouse fluttered after her as she flew, and she paid no attention to Makarenko who was rolling his chair in pursuit of her. The legless man couldn't catch up. His wheels clattered as he turned the handles for all he was worth.

"Little lady," he cried in a deafening voice, "where did you get that striped stuff?"

But the woman with the fluttering dress was gone. Round the corner to meet her leaped a rickety cart in which a peasant lad stood upright.

"Where've they all run to?" asked the lad, raising a red rein above the nags jerking in their collars.

"Everybody's on Cathedral Street," said Makarenko pleadingly, "everybody's there, sonny. Anything you happen to pick up, bring it along to me. I'll give you a good price."

The lad bent down over the front of the cart and whipped up his piebald nags. Tossing their filthy croups like calves, the horses shot off at a gallop. The yellow lane was once more yellow and empty. Then the legless man turned his quenched eyes upon me.

"God's picked on me, I reckon," he said lifelessly, "I'm a son of man, I reckon."

And he stretched a hand spotted with leprosy toward me.

"What's that you've got in your sack?" he demanded, and took the bag that had been warming his heart.

With his fat hand the cripple fumbled among the tumbler pigeons and dragged to light a cherry-colored she-bird. Jerking back its feet, the bird lay still on his palm.

"Pigeons," said Makarenko, and squeaking his wheels he

rode right up to me. "Damned pigeons," he repeated, and struck me on the cheek.

He dealt me a flying blow with the hand that was clutching the bird. Kate's wadded back seemed to turn upside down, and I fell to the ground in my new overcoat.

"Their spawn must be wiped out," said Kate, straightening up over the bonnets. "I can't a-bear their spawn, nor their stinking menfolk."

She said more things about our spawn, but I heard nothing of it. I lay on the ground, and the guts of the crushed bird trickled down from my temple. They flowed down my cheek, winding this way and that, splashing, blinding me. The tender pigeon-guts slid down over my forehead, and I closed my solitary unstopped-up eye so as not to see the world that spread out before me. This world was tiny, and it was awful. A stone lay just before my eyes, a little stone so chipped as to resemble the face of an old woman with a large jaw. A piece of string lay not far away, and a bunch of feathers that still breathed. My world was tiny, and it was awful. I closed my eyes so as not to see it, and pressed myself tight into the ground that lay beneath me in soothing dumbness. This trampled earth in no way resembled real life, waiting for exams in real life. Somewhere far away Woe rode across it on a great steed, but the noise of the hoofbeats grew weaker and died away, and silence, the bitter silence that sometimes overwhelms children in their sorrow, suddenly deleted the boundary between my body and the earth that was moving nowhither. The earth smelled of raw depths, of the tomb, of flowers. I smelled its smell and started crying, unafraid. I was walking along an unknown street set on either side with white boxes, walking in a getup of bloodstained feathers, alone between the pavements swept clean as on Sunday, weeping bitterly, fully and happily as I never wept again in all my life. Wires that had grown white hummed above my head, a watchdog trotted on in front, in the lane on one side a young peasant in a waistcoat was smashing a window frame in the house of Khariton Efrussi. He was smashing it with a wooden mallet, striking out with his whole body. Sighing, he smiled all around with the amiable grin of drunkenness, sweat, and spiritual power. The whole street was filled with a splitting, a snapping, the song of flying wood. The peasant's whole existence consisted in bending over, sweating, shouting queer words in some unknown, non-Russian language. He shouted the words and sang, shot out his blue eyes; till in the street there appeared a procession bearing the Cross and moving from the Municipal Building. Old men bore aloft the portrait of the neatly-combed Tsar, banners with graveyard saints swayed above their heads, inflamed old women flew on in front. Seeing the procession, the peasant pressed his mallet to his chest and dashed off in pursuit of the banners, while I, waiting till the tail-end of the procession had passed, made my furtive way home. The house was empty. Its white doors were open, the grass by the dovecot had been trampled down. Only Kuzma was still in the yard. Kuzma the yardman was sitting in the shed laying out the dead Shoyl.

"The wind bears you about like an evil wood-chip," said the old man when he saw me. "You've been away ages. And now look what they've done to granddad."

Kuzma wheezed, turned away from me, and started pulling a fish out of a rent in grandfather's trousers. Two pike perch had been stuck into grandfather: one into the rent in his trousers, the other into his mouth. And while grandfather was dead, one of the fish was still alive, and struggling.

"They've done grandfather in, but nobody else," said Kuzma, tossing the fish to the cat. "He cursed them all good and proper, a wonderful damning and blasting it was. You might fetch a couple of pennies to put on his eyes."

But then, at ten years of age, I didn't know what need the dead had of pennies.

"Kuzma," I whispered, "save us."

And I went over to the yardman, hugged his crooked old back with its one shoulder higher than the other, and over this back I saw grandfather. Shoyl lay in the sawdust, his chest squashed in, his beard twisted upwards, battered shoes on his bare feet. His feet, thrown wide apart, were dirty, lilac-colored, dead. Kuzma was fussing over him. He tied the dead man's jaws and kept glancing over the body to see what else he could do. He fussed as though over a newly-purchased garment, and only cooled down when he had given the dead man's beard a good combing.

"He cursed the lot of 'em right and left," he said, smiling, and cast a loving look over the corpse. "If Tartars had crossed his path he'd have sent them packing, but Russians came, and their women with them, Rooski women. Russians just can't bring themselves to forgive, I know what Rooskis are."

The yardman spread some more sawdust beneath the body, threw off his carpenter's apron, and took me by the hand.

"Let's go to father," he mumbled, squeezing my hand

tighter and tighter. "Your father has been searching for you since morning, sure as fate you was dead."

And so with Kuzma I went to the house of the tax-inspector, where my parents, escaping the pogrom, had sought refuge.

Gimpel the Fool

I. Bashevis Singer

1

I am Gimpel the fool. I don't think myself a fool. On the contrary. But that's what folks call me. They gave me the name while I was still in school. I had seven names in all: imbecile, donkey, flax-head, dope, glump, ninny, and fool. The last name stuck. What did my foolishness consist of? I was easy to take in. They said, "Gimpel, you know the rabbi's wife has been brought to childbed?" So I skipped school. Well, it turned out to be a lie. How was I supposed to know? She hadn't had a big belly. But I never looked at her belly. Was that really so foolish? The gang laughed and hee-hawed, stomped and danced and chanted a good-night prayer. And instead of the raisins they give when a woman's lying in, they stuffed my hand full of goat turds. I was no weakling. If I slapped someone he'd see all the way to Cracow. But I'm really not a slugger by nature. I think to myself, Let it pass. So they take advantage of me.

I was coming home from school and heard a dog barking. I'm not afraid of dogs, but of course I never want to start up with them. One of them may be mad, and if he bites there's not a Tartar in the world who can help you. So I made tracks. Then I looked around and saw the whole market place wild with laughter. It was no dog at all but Wolf-Leib the thief. How was I supposed to know it was he? It sounded like a howling bitch.

When the pranksters and leg-pullers found that I was easy to fool, every one of them tried his luck with me. "Gimpel, the Czar is coming to Frampol; Gimpel, the moon fell down in Turbeen; Gimpel, little Hodel Furpiece found a treasure behind the bathhouse." And I like a *golem* believed everyone. In the first place, everything is possible, as it is written in the Wisdom of the Fathers, I've forgotten just how. Second, I had to believe when the whole town came down on me! If I ever dared to say, "Ah, you're kidding!" there was trouble. People got angry. "What do you mean! You want to call everyone a liar?" What was I to do? I believed them, and I hope at least that did some good.

I was an orphan. My grandfather who brought me up was already bent toward the grave. So they turned me over to a baker, and what a time they gave me there! Every woman or girl who came to bake a pan of cookies or dry a batch of noodles had to fool me at least once. "Gimpel, there's a fair in heaven; Gimpel, the rabbi gave birth to a calf in the seventh month; Gimpel, a cow flew over the roof and laid brass eggs." A student from the yeshiva came once to buy a roll, and he said, "You, Gimpel, while you stand here scraping with your baker's shovel the Messiah has come. The dead have arisen." "What do you mean?" I said. "I heard no one blowing the ram's horn!" He said, "Are you deaf?" And all began to cry, "We heard it, we heard!" Then in came Reitze the candle-dipper and called out in her hoarse voice, "Gimpel, your father and mother have stood up from the grave. They're looking for you."

To tell the truth, I knew very well that nothing of the sort had happened, but all the same, as folks were talking, I threw on my wool vest and went out. Maybe something had happened. What did I stand to lose by looking? Well, what a cat music went up! And then I took a vow so that I didn't know the big end from the small.

I went to the rabbi to get some advice. He said, "It is written, better to be a fool all your days than for one hour to be evil. You are not a fool. They are the fools. For he who causes his neighbor to feel shame loses Paradise himself." Nevertheless the rabbi's daughter took me in. As I left the rabbinical court she said, "Have you kissed the wall yet?" I said, "No; what for?" She answered, "It's a law; you've got to do it after every visit." Well, there didn't seem to be any harm in it. And she burst out laughing. It was a fine trick. She put one over on me, all right.

I wanted to go off to another town, but then everyone got busy matchmaking, and they were after me so they nearly tore my coat tails off. They talked at me and talked until I got water on the ear. She was no chaste maiden, but they told me she was virgin pure. She had a limp, and they said it was deliberate, from coyness. She had a bastard, and they told me the child was her little brother. I cried, "You're wasting your time. I'll never marry that whore." But they said indignantly, "What a way to talk! Aren't you ashamed of yourself? We can take you to the rabbi and have you fined for giving her a bad name." I saw then that I wouldn't escape them so easily and I thought, They're set on making me their butt. But when you're married the husband's the master, and if that's all right with her it's agreeable to me too. Besides, you can't pass through life unscathed, nor expect to.

I went to her clay house, which was built on the sand, and the whole gang, hollering and chorusing, came after me. They acted like bearbaiters. When we came to the well they stopped all the same. They were afraid to start anything with Elka. Her mouth would open as if it were on a hinge, and she had a fierce tongue. I entered the house. Lines were strung from wall to wall and clothes were drying. Barefoot she stood by the tub, doing the wash. She was dressed in a worn hand-me-down gown of plush. She had her hair put in braids and pinned across her head. It took my breath away, almost, the reek of it all.

Evidently she knew who I was. She took a look at me and said, "Look who's here! He's come, the drip. Grab a seat."

I told her all; I denied nothing. "Tell me the truth," I said, "are you really a virgin, and is that mischievous Yechiel actually your little brother? Don't be deceitful with me, for I'm an orphan."

"I'm an orphan myself," she answered, "and whoever tries to twist you up, may the end of his nose take a twist. But don't let them think they can take advantage of me. I want a dowry of fifty guilders, and let them take up a collection besides. Otherwise they can kiss my you-know-what." She was very plainspoken. I said, "It's the bride and not the groom who gives a dowry." Then she said, "Don't bargain with me. Either a flat 'yes' or a flat 'no'—go back where you came from."

I thought, No bread will ever be baked from *this* dough. But ours is not a poor town. They consented to everything and proceeded with the wedding. It so happened that there was a dysentery epidemic at the time. The ceremony was held at the cemetery gates, near the little corpse-washing hut. The fellows got drunk. While the marriage contract was being drawn up I heard the most pious high rabbi ask, "Is the bride a widow or a divorced woman?" And the sexton's wife answered for her, "Both a widow and divorced." It was a black moment for me.

But what was I to do, run away from under the marriage canopy?

There was singing and dancing. An old granny danced opposite me, hugging a braided white *chalah*. The master of revels made a "God 'a mercy" in memory of the bride's parents. The schoolboys threw burrs, as on *Tishe b'Av* fast day. There were a lot of gifts after the sermon: a noodle board, a kneading trough, a bucket, brooms, ladles, household articles galore. Then I took a look and saw two strapping young men carrying a crib. "What do we need this for?" I asked. So they said, "Don't rack your brains about it. It's all right, it'll come in handy." I realized I was going to be rooked. Take it another way though, what did I stand to lose? I reflected, I'll see what comes of it. A whole town can't go altogether crazy.

2

At night I came where my wife lay, but she wouldn't let me in. "Say, look here, is this what they married us for?" I said. And she said, "My monthly has come." "But yesterday they took you to the ritual bath, and that's afterward, isn't it supposed to be?" "Today isn't yesterday," said she, "and yesterday's not today. You can beat it if you don't like it." In short, I waited.

Not four months later she was in childbed. The townsfolk hid their laughter with their knuckles. But what could I do? She suffered intolerable pains and clawed at the walls. "Gimpel," she cried, "I'm going. Forgive me!" The house filled with women. They were boiling pans of water. The screams rose to the welkin.

The thing to do was to go to the House of Prayer to repeat Psalms, and that was what I did.

The townsfolk liked that, all right. I stood in a corner saying Psalms and prayers, and they shook their heads at me. "Pray, pray!" they told me. "Prayer never made any woman pregnant." One of the congregation put a straw to my mouth and said, "Hay for the cows." There was something to that too, by God!

She gave birth to a boy. Friday at the synagogue the sexton stood up before the Ark, pounded on the reading table, and announced, "The wealthy Reb Gimpel invites the congregation to a feast in honor of the birth of a son." The whole House of Prayer rang with laughter. My face was flaming. But there was nothing I could do. After all, I *was* the one responsible for the circumcision honors and rituals.

Half the town came running. You couldn't wedge another soul in. Women brought peppered chick-peas, and there was a keg of beer from the tavern. I ate and drank as much as anyone, and they all congratulated me. Then there was a circumcision, and I named the boy after my father, may he rest in peace. When all were gone and I was left with my wife alone, she thrust her head through the bed-curtain and called me to her.

"Gimpel," said she, "why are you silent? Has your ship gone and sunk?"

"What shall I say?" I answered. "A fine thing you've done to me! If my mother had known of it she'd have died a second time."

She said, "Are you crazy, or what?"

"How can you make such a fool," I said, "of one who should be the lord and master?"

"What's the matter with you?" she said. "What have you taken it into your head to imagine?"

I saw that I must speak bluntly and openly. "Do you think this is the way to use an orphan?" I said. "You have borne a bastard."

She answered, "Drive this foolishness out of your head. The child is yours."

"How can he be mine?" I argued. "He was born seventeen weeks after the wedding."

She told me then that he was premature. I said, "Isn't he a little too premature?" She said she had had a grandmother who carried just as short a time and she resembled this grandmother of hers as one drop of water does another. She swore to it with such oaths that you would have believed a peasant at the fair if he had used them. To tell the plain truth, I didn't believe her; but when I talked it over next day with the schoolmaster he told me that the very same thing had happened to Adam and Eve. Two they went up to bed, and four they descended.

"There isn't a woman in the world who is not the granddaughter of Eve," he said.

That was how it was—they argued me dumb. But then, who really knows how such things are?

I began to forget my sorrow. I loved the child madly, and he loved me too. As soon as he saw me he'd wave his little hands and want me to pick him up, and when he was colicky I was the only one who could pacify him. I bought him a little bone teething ring and a little gilded cap. He was forever catching the evil eye from someone, and then I had to run to get one of those abracadabras for him that would get him out of it. I worked like an ox. You know how expenses go up when there's an infant in the house. I don't want to lie about it; I didn't dislike Elka either, for that matter. She swore at me and cursed, and I couldn't get enough of her. What strength she had! One of her looks could rob you of the power of speech. And her orations! Pitch and sulphur, that's what they were full of, and yet somehow also full of charm. I adored her every word. She gave me bloody wounds though.

In the evening I brought her a white loaf as well as a dark one, and also poppyseed rolls I baked myself. I thieved because of her and swiped everything I could lay hands on, macaroons, raisins, almonds, cakes. I hope I may be forgiven for stealing from the Saturday pots the women left to warm in the baker's oven. I would take out scraps of meat, a chunk of pudding, a chicken leg or head, a piece of tripe, whatever I could nip quickly. She ate and became fat and handsome.

I had to sleep away from home all during the week, at the bakery. On Friday nights when I got home she always made an excuse of some sort. Either she had heartburn, or a stitch in the side, or hiccups, or headaches. You know what women's excuses are. I had a bitter time of it. It was rough. To add to it, this little brother of hers, the bastard, was growing bigger. He'd put lumps on me, and when I wanted to hit back she'd open her mouth and curse so powerfully I saw a green haze floating before my eyes. Ten times a day she threatened to divorce me. Another man in my place would have taken French leave and disappeared. But I'm the type that bears it and says nothing. What's one to do? Shoulders are from God, and burdens too.

One night there was a calamity in the bakery; the oven burst, and we almost had a fire. There was nothing to do but go home, so I went home. Let me, I thought, also taste the joy of sleeping in bed in midweek. I didn't want to wake the sleeping mite and tiptoed into the house. Coming in, it seemed to me that I heard not the snoring of one but, as it were, a double snore, one a thin enough snore and the other like the snoring of a slaughtered ox. Oh, I didn't like that! I didn't like it at all. I went up to bed, and things suddenly turned black. Next to Elka lay a man's form. Another in my place would have made an uproar, and enough noise to rouse the whole town, but the thought occurred to me that I might wake the child. A little thing like that—why frighten a little swallow like that, I thought. All right then, I went back to the bakery and stretched out on a sack of flour, and till morning I never shut an eye. I shivered as if I had had malaria. "Enough of being a donkey," I said to myself. "Gimpel isn't going to be a sucker all his life. There's a limit even to the foolishness of a fool like Gimpel."

In the morning I went to the rabbi to get advice, and it made a great commotion in the town. They sent the beadle for Elka right away. She came, carrying the child. And what do you think she did? She denied it, denied everything, bone and stone! "He's out of his head," she said. "I know nothing of dreams or divinations." They yelled at her, warned her, hammered on the table, but she stuck to her guns: it was a false accusation, she said.

The butchers and the horse-traders took her part. One of the lads from the slaughterhouse came by and said to me, "We've got our eye on you, you're a marked man." Meanwhile the child started to bear down and soiled itself. In the rabbinical court there was an Ark of the Covenant, and they couldn't allow that, so they sent Elka away.

I said to the rabbi, "What shall I do?"

"You must divorce her at once," said he.

"And what if she refuses?" I asked.

He said, "You must serve the divorce, that's all you'll have to do."

I said, "Well, all right, Rabbi. Let me think about it."

"There's nothing to think about," said he. "You mustn't remain under the same roof with her."

"And if I want to see the child?" I asked.

"Let her go, the harlot," said he, "and her brood of bastards with her."

The verdict he gave was that I mustn't even cross her threshold—never again, as long as I should live.

During the day it didn't bother me so much. I thought, It was bound to happen, the abscess had to burst. But at night when I stretched out upon the sacks I felt it all very bitterly. A longing took me, for her and for the child. I wanted to be angry, but that's my misfortune exactly, I don't have it in me to be really angry. In the first place—this was how my thoughts went—there's bound to be a slip sometimes. You can't live without errors. Probably that lad who was with her led her on and gave her presents and what not, and women are often long on hair and short on sense, and so he got around her. And then since she denies it so, maybe I was only seeing things? Hallucinations do happen. You see a figure or a mannikin or something, but when you come up closer it's nothing, there's not a thing there. And if that's so, I'm doing her an injustice. And when I got so far in my thoughts I started to weep. I sobbed so that I wet the flour where I lay. In the morning I went to the rabbi and told him that I had made a mistake. The rabbi wrote on with his quill, and he said that if that were so he would have to reconsider the whole case. Until he had finished I wasn't to go near my wife, but I might send her bread and money by messenger.

3

Nine months passed before all the rabbis could come to an agreement. Letters went back and forth. I hadn't realized that there could be so much erudition about a matter like this.

Meantime Elka gave birth to still another child, a girl this time. On the Sabbath I went to the synagogue and invoked a blessing on her. They called me up to the Torah, and I named the child for my mother-in-law, may she rest in peace. The louts and loudmouths of the town who came into the bakery gave me a going over. All Frampol refreshed its spirits because of my trouble and grief. However, I resolved that I would always believe what I was told. What's the good of *not* believing? Today it's your wife you don't believe; tomorrow it's God Himself you won't take stock in.

By an apprentice who was her neighbor I sent her daily a corn or a wheat loaf, or a piece of pastry, rolls or bagels, or, when I got the chance, a slab of pudding, a slice of honeycake, or wedding strudel—whatever came my way. The apprentice was a goodhearted lad, and more than once he added something on his own. He had formerly annoyed me a lot, plucking my nose and digging me in the ribs, but when he started to be a visitor to my house he became kind and friendly. "Hey, you, Gimpel," he said to me, "you have a very decent little wife and two fine kids. You don't deserve them."

"But the things people say about her," I said.

"Well, they have long tongues," he said, "and nothing to do with them but babble. Ignore it as you ignore the cold of last winter."

One day the rabbi sent for me and said, "Are you certain, Gimpel, that you were wrong about your wife?"

I said, "I'm certain."

"Why, but look here! You yourself saw it."

"It must have been a shadow," I said.

"The shadow of what?"

"Just of one of the beams, I think."

"You can go home then. You owe thanks to the Yanover rabbi. He found an obscure reference in Maimonides that favored you."

I seized the rabbi's hand and kissed it.

I wanted to run home immediately. It's no small thing to be separated for so long a time from wife and child. Then I reflected, I'd better go back to work now, and go home in the evening. I said nothing to anyone, although as far as my heart was concerned it was like one of the Holy Days. The women teased and twitted me as they did every day, but my thought was, Go on, with your loose talk. The truth is out, like the oil upon the water. Maimonides says it's right, and therefore it is right!

At night, when I had covered the dough to let it rise, I took my share of bread and a little sack of flour and started homeward. The moon was full and the stars were glistening, something to terrify the soul. I hurried onward, and before me darted a long shadow. It was winter, and a fresh snow had fallen. I had a mind to sing, but it was growing late and I didn't want to wake the householders. Then I felt like whistling, but remembered that you don't whistle at night because it brings the demons out. So I was silent and walked as fast as I could.

Dogs in the Christian yards barked at me when I passed, but I thought, Bark your teeth out! What are you but mere dogs? Whereas I am a man, the husband of a fine wife, the father of promising children.

As I approached the house my heart started to pound as though it were the heart of a criminal. I felt no fear, but my heart went thump! thump! Well, no drawing back. I quietly lifted the latch and went in. Elka was asleep. I looked at the infant's cradle. The shutter was closed, but the moon forced its way through the cracks. I saw the newborn child's face and loved it as soon as I saw it—immediately—each tiny bone.

Then I came nearer to the bed. And what did I see but the apprentice lying there beside Elka. The moon went out all at once. It was utterly black, and I trembled. My teeth chattered. The bread fell from my hands and my wife waked and said, "Who is that, ah?"

I muttered, "It's me."

"Gimpel?" she asked. "How come you're here? I thought it was forbidden."

"The rabbi said," I answered and shook as with a fever.

"Listen to me, Gimpel," she said, "go out to the shed and see if the goat's all right. It seems she's been sick." I have forgotten to say that we had a goat. When I heard she was unwell I went into the yard. The nannygoat was a good little creature. I had a nearly human feeling for her.

With hesitant steps I went up to the shed and opened the door. The goat stood there on her four feet. I felt her everywhere, drew her by the horns, examined her udders, and found nothing wrong. She had probably eaten too much bark. "Good night, little goat," I said. "Keep well." And the little beast answered with a "Maa" as though to thank me for the good will.

I went back. The apprentice had vanished.

"Where," I asked, "is the lad?"

"What lad?" my wife answered.

"What do you mean?" I said. "The apprentice. You were sleeping with him."

"The things I have dreamed this night and the night before," she said, "may they come true and lay you low, body and soul! An evil spirit has taken root in you and dazzles your sight." She screamed out, "You hateful creature! You moon calf! You spook! You uncouth mane! Get out, or I'll scream all Frampol out of bed!"

Before I could move, her brother sprang out from behind the oven and struck me a blow on the back of the head. I thought he had broken my neck. I felt that something about me was deeply wrong, and I said, "Don't make a scandal. All that's needed now is that people should accuse me of raising spooks and *dybbuks*." For that was what she meant. "No one will touch bread of my baking."

In short, I somehow calmed her.

"Well," she said, "that's enough. Lie down, and be shattered by wheels."

Next morning I called the apprentice aside. "Listen here, brother!" I said. And so on and so forth. "What do you say?" He stared at me as though I had dropped from the roof or something.

"I swear," he said, "you'd better go to an herb doctor or some healer. I'm afraid you have a screw loose, but I'll hush it up for you." And that's how the thing stood.

To make a long story short, I lived twenty years with my wife. She bore me six children, four daughters and two sons. All kinds of things happened, but I neither saw nor heard. I believed, and that's all. The rabbi recently said to me, "Belief in itself is beneficial. It is written that a good man lives by his faith."

Suddenly my wife took sick. It began with a trifle, a little growth upon the breast. But she evidently was not destined to live long; she had no years. I spent a fortune on her. I have forgotten to say that by this time I had a bakery of my own and in Frampol was considered to be something of a rich man. Daily the healer came, and every witch doctor in the neighborhood was brought. They decided to use leeches, and after that to try cupping. They even called a doctor from Lublin, but it was too late. Before she died she called me to her bed and said, "Forgive me, Gimpel."

I said, "What is there to forgive? You have been a good and faithful wife."

"Woe, Gimpel!" she said. "It was ugly how I deceived you all these years. I want to go clean to my Maker, and so I have to tell you that the children are not yours."

If I had been clouted on the head with a piece of wood it couldn't have bewildered me more.

"Whose are they?" I asked.

"I don't know," she said, "there were a lot . . . But they're not yours." And as she spoke she tossed her head to the side, her eyes turned glassy, and it was all up with Elka. On her whitened lips there remained a smile.

I imagined that, dead as she was, she was saying, "I deceived Gimpel. That was the meaning of my brief life."

4

One night, when the period of mourning was done, as I lay dreaming on the flour sacks, there came the Spirit of Evil himself and said to me, "Gimpel, why do you sleep?"

I said, "What should I be doing? Eating *kreplach?*"

"The whole world deceives you," he said, "and you ought to deceive the world in your turn."

"How can I deceive all the world?" I asked him.

He answered, "You might accumulate a bucket of urine every day and at night pour it into the dough. Let the sages of Frampol eat filth."

"What about judgment in the world to come?" I said.

"There is no world to come," he said. "They've sold you a bill of goods and talked you into believing you carried a cat in your belly. What nonsense!"

"Well then," I said, "and is there a God?"

He answered, "There is no God either."

"What," I said, "*is* there, then?"

"A thick mire."

He stood before my eyes with a goatish beard and horns, long-toothed, and with a tail. Hearing such words, I wanted to snatch him by the tail, but I tumbled from the flour sacks and nearly broke a rib. Then it happened that I had to answer the call of nature, and, passing, I saw the risen dough, which seemed to say to me, "Do it!" In brief, I let myself be persuaded.

At dawn the apprentice came. We kneaded the bread, scattered caraway seeds on it, and set it to bake. Then the apprentice went away, and I was left sitting in the little trench by the oven, on a pile of rags. Well, Gimpel, I thought, you've revenged yourself on them for all the shame they've put on you. Outside the frost glittered, but it was warm beside the oven. The flames heated my face. I bent my head and fell into a doze.

I saw in a dream, at once, Elka in her shroud. She called to me, "What have you done, Gimpel?"

I said to her, "It's all your fault," and started to cry.

"You fool!" she said. "You fool! Because I was false is everything false too? I never deceived anyone but myself. I'm paying for it all, Gimpel. They spare you nothing here."

I looked at her face. It was black. I was startled and waked, and remained sitting dumb. I sensed that everything hung in the balance. A false step now and I'd lose Eternal Life. But God gave me His help. I seized the long shovel and took out the loaves, carried them into the yard, and started to dig a hole in the frozen earth.

My apprentice came back as I was doing it. "What are you doing, boss?" he said, and grew pale as a corpse.

"I know what I'm doing," I said, and I buried it all before his very eyes.

Then I went home, took my hoard from its hiding place, and divided it among the children. "I saw your mother to-night," I said. "She's turning black, poor thing."

They were so astounded they couldn't speak a word.

"Be well," I said, "and forget that such a one as Gimpel ever existed." I put on my short coat, a pair of boots, took the bag that held my prayer shawl in one hand, my stick in the other, and kissed the *mezzuzah*. When people saw me in the street they were greatly surprised.

"Where are you going?" they said.

I answered, "Into the world." And so I departed from Frampol.

I wandered over the land, and good people did not neglect me. After many years I became old and white; I heard a great deal, many lies and falsehoods, but the longer I lived the more I understood that there were really no lies. Whatever doesn't really happen is dreamed at night. It happens to one if it doesn't happen to another, tomorrow if not today, or a century hence if not next year. What difference can it make? Often I heard tales of which I said, "Now this is a thing that cannot happen." But before a year had elapsed I heard that it actually had come to pass somewhere.

Going from place to place, eating at strange tables, it often happens that I spin yarns—improbable things that could never have happened—about devils, magicians, windmills, and the like. The children run after me, calling, "Grandfather, tell us a story." Sometimes they ask for particular stories, and I try to please them. A fat young boy once said to me, "Grandfather, it's the same story you told us before." The little rogue, he was right.

So it is with dreams too. It is many years since I left Frampol, but as soon as I shut my eyes I am there again. And whom do you think I see? Elka. She is standing by the washtub, as at our first encounter, but her face is shining and her eyes are as radiant as the eyes of a saint, and she speaks outlandish words to me, strange things. When I wake I have forgotten it all. But while the dream lasts I am comforted. She answers all my queries, and what comes out is that all is right. I weep and implore, "Let me be with you." And she consoles me and tells me to be patient. The time is nearer than it is far. Sometimes she strokes and kisses me and weeps upon my face. When I awaken I feel her lips and taste the salt of her tears.

No doubt the world is entirely an imaginary world, but it is only once removed from the true world. At the door of the hovel where I lie, there stands the plank on which the dead are taken away. The gravedigger Jew has his spade ready. The grave waits and the worms are hungry; the shrouds are prepared—I carry them in my beggar's sack. Another *shnorrer* is waiting to inherit my bed of straw. When the time comes I will go joyfully. Whatever may be there, it will be real, without complication, without ridicule, without deception. God be praised: there even Gimpel cannot be deceived.

Translated by Saul Bellow

The Surveyor

Henry Roth

It was with an air of suppressed excitement that the slight, middle-aged man with the unruly gray hair put down the box he was carrying, snapped open a tripod, and drew out of the box a small surveyor's transit. He swiftly mounted the transit on the tripod. He seemed to work as though he were doing something he was not thoroughly practiced at but something he had rehearsed, adjusting the legs of the tripod and the levelling screws with a certain nervous haste. A short few minutes ago, he and the woman who accompanied him had got out of a taxi with their equipment. He had paid the driver and had led the way at once to the spot they were now on. This, too, he had done with an assurance that indicated the location had been decided on beforehand. In a little while, he had the transit levelled to his own satisfaction and was steadying the plumb bob beneath. The woman, who was also middle-aged, but taller and more slender than the man, with a gentle face and a high forehead, was carrying a telescoped levelling rod, which she now extended part way.

They were on the west walk of the short, very wide Avenida del Cid, in Seville, and the man had set up his transit in the middle of the entrance to the Fábrica de Tabacos, a huge, gray edifice, rising only two stories high but sprawling out immensely in length and width. Cigarettes had once been manufactured there; now the building housed the University of Seville. On both sides of the surveyor and his assistant stretched a low stone wall that fronted a deep, wide, waterless moat, overgrown with grass, which ran parallel to the façade of the Fábrica de Tabacos behind them.

"The exact center of the gate. Right?" asked the man, straightening up and adjusting his spectacles. The woman nodded. She seemed more self-possessed than he, not so much because she was under less strain as by temperament. The man drew out of his jacket pocket a small notebook. "No, I don't need that now," he muttered, and thrust the notebook back into his pocket impatiently. "The tape. No, the rod. You've got the work to do."

"I'm ready," she said.

"O.K. You pace off about fifty steps along the wall," he said. "When you've gone that far, just turn around. Keep snug to the wall."

Obediently, the woman walked away from him with steady, measured stride, holding the levelling rod as she went. She stopped, turned, and planted the foot of the rod on the ground.

"O.K. Now hold it up so I can sight it." She held the levelling rod erect; he swung the transit around rapidly, sighted through the telescope, and began making adjustments. "Lean the stick toward me. Good. Hold it there. Right there. O.K. Now come back." Swiftly, he drew out his notebook, leaned over the protractor of the instrument, and jotted down some numbers. The woman, holding the levelling rod upright before her like a staff, came back to join him.

About them, a Sunday-morning quiet prevailed. Most of Seville had probably not arisen, and the Avenida del Cid was almost empty of people. Few automobiles or buses were in sight. At one end of the wide avenue was the *glorieta*, or traffic circle, of Don Juan de Austria, where the waters of a large fountain glinted intricately in the morning sunlight as they played from periphery to center and splashed from basin to basin. A short distance beyond the *glorieta* a large radial crane stood like a red, ungainly cross in the midst of new government buildings under construction. At the other end of the Avenida was the *glorieta* of San Diego, an open space encompassed by the Maria Luisa Park and buildings left over from the Spanish-American Exposition of the nineteen-twenties. Trees lined the Avenida, and a number of streets entered the *glorietas* from different directions. Dominating all this was the central figure of the area, the monumental equestrian statue of El Cid Campeador, semi-legendary hero out of eleventh-century Spain. Horse and rider were poised on a massive granite pedestal that stood in the middle of an oval traffic island on the Avenida. Around the base of the pedestal, there were flower beds surrounded by grass and filled with plants no longer in bloom. High above, El Cid stood in his stirrups and brandished his bannered spear. There was no mistaking what the bronze statue was meant to portray:

Spain's martial valor and audacity, the prowess that had re-won the peninsula from the Moors and later subjugated a new world.

There were one or two people waiting for buses at various *paradas* along the Avenida. All of them by now were watching the activities of the surveyor and his assistant. A man walking by, the lone stroller on their side of the avenue, stopped to stare with unabashed curiosity.

"Buenos días," he said.

"Buenos días," said the surveyor shortly. "Now begins the tough job, Mary. You cross. I'll compute the angle."

A woman with a levelling rod crossing a thoroughfare would have been a strange sight anywhere, and Seville on Sunday morning was hardly an exception. A man left one of the *paradas* and sauntered over. A couple of strollers across the street changed course and directed their steps toward the surveying operations. A cyclist teetered on his wheel a moment without making any forward progress, then dismounted and brought his bicycle up over the curb. The tall, parti-colored staff seemed to be attracting people from a greater and greater distance.

Ignoring all this, the man at the transit worked intently at his computation, swung the instrument in the direction of the woman, who was now standing on the traffic island below the statue of El Cid, and began adjusting the vernier. "A little to the left, Mary," he called. "About two short steps."

"Qué es esto, señor?" inquired a young man in the white shirt and tie of Sunday.

"Un momento. Mary, a little more left!" he shouted to the woman across the street. *"Por favor, señor,* do me the favor of standing to one side." The surveyor immediately crouched before his instrument. His spectacles had apparently fogged. He snatched them off. "A little more," he directed. He looked up from the telescope. "Where are you? Good! Mark it right there." The woman crayoned a cross at the base of the levelling rod. "Come on back," he called. "I can't leave the transit."

"Fotógrafo?" a woman in black asked him.

"No, no," he replied. *"A grimensor."*

"Por qué? Es extranjero," she said. The man shrugged his shoulders.

"Señor." One of the bystanders, a man in a Basque beret, came forward. *"Qué está usted haciendo?"*

"Measurements," the surveyor replied in Spanish. His assistant was approaching. "O.K. I'll take it," he said to her, and stepped forward to relieve her of the levelling rod. "Now," he said grimly, handing her the tape. "Fifty-six and three-fourths metres."

"Yes, I know the number. Don't get rattled, Aaron." She was already backing away from him, unreeling the tape, one end of which he continued to hold.

He laid the levelling rod down, hurried back with his end of the tape to the transit, and knelt at the plumb bob beneath it. "Are you there, Mary?" he called.

The tape was now across the highway, and the woman had reached the traffic island and was aligning the tape with the mark she had previously made. The bystanders' wonder increased, and so did their numbers. Newcomers began to ply those already there with questions. "*Ingleses*? . . . *Me parecen americanos*. . . . *Qué hacen*?"

"A car!" The woman's warning cry came from across the Avenida.

"Lower the tape!" the surveyor yelled from his stooped position. "Lower the tape, Mary. Wave him on!"

The woman, at her end of the tape, smiled pleadingly at the driver of a small Seat that had stopped before the narrow ribbon of metal. "*Por favor! Pase, por favor!*" The driver proceeded reluctantly.

"Where are you?" said the man at the plumb bob.

"Fifty-five and one-half!"

"It has to be fifty-six and three-quarters!"

"That's the flower bed!"

"Oh, hell! Note the number! Mark the edge!" The woman quickly made a cross where the pavement of the traffic oval met the grass border of the flower bed. With one accord, they arose, the woman reeling in the tape, the man walking toward her. "Did you have the tape tight?" he asked her. He was perspiring.

"Yes. I made two marks, one behind the other."

"Wonderful," he said, a little breathlessly. "There! Let's scoot out of here." He had already taken the reel from her, and was winding in the ribbon of tape with a rapidity that made it writhe and slither on the ground. He shoved the reel into his pocket. "Telescope the rod. I'll dismantle."

With the small crowd still watching them, as puzzled as ever, the pair packed their equipment, and in a few minutes they carried it to the curb. "Taxi!" the man called, and waved.

The driver of a cab going by on the other side of the traffic island waved back, circled about the oval, and came their way. The surveyor swung the transit box into the cab as soon as it came to a stop. The driver, who appeared to be accustomed to the strange ways of tourists, got out and helped him mount tripod and levelling rod on the carrier above the cab. "Hotel Inglaterra, *por favor*," said the surveyor, and then, settling in his seat, whistled with relief. "I wasn't any too soon, you know."

"Why?" the woman asked.

"Look back. I think you can still see him."

At one of the corners of the Glorieta de San Diego stood a gray-clad member of Spain's Policía Armada.

"What rashness!" Aaron Stigman reflected aloud as he and his wife approached the Avenida del Cid once more, this time on foot. "Why didn't I pace it off and let it go at that? No, I had to find the very spot. As rash as anything I've ever done. Was it my passion for accuracy, do you think? Or am I turning into an absurd old man?"

"No, I just think it's Seville," she replied.

"Why?" He was carrying a raincoat over his arm, and reached under the coat to adjust something beneath it.

"Too many cathedrals, too many *retablos*, stained-glass windows, saints, crucifixes, Virgins—Virgins! Even a Protestant mind like mine rebels at it." She laughed. "It's just too much."

"Yes, too many martyrs of their faith. None for mine—or what used to be mine. Why shouldn't there be some acknowledgment?"

"Well, of course, Aaron. That's why I approved."

It was now about two hours later, and the Avenida del Cid presented a livelier appearance. Amorous couples, the young man's hand often resting in Spanish fashion on his sweetheart's shoulder, strolled along in and out of the shade of the acacias. Short, robust infantrymen in their coarse khaki uniforms mingled with sober Sevillians returning from Mass. On one corner, before the Fábrica de Tabacos, a street vender had opened his little stand and was arranging his candy and loose cigarettes. Tourists in a yellow-wheeled, horse-drawn cab gazed diffidently about while the coachman leaned sideways to comment on points of interest. Three tall, obviously Scandinavian youths, their bare heads shining like brass in the Sevillian sunlight, turned the dark heads of the Spanish *señoritas* who passed them. All the *paradas* on the Avenida now had their queues of people waiting for the bus. Traffic moved in all directions to and from the *glorietas;* jaunty little Seats droned along, interspersed with buzzing scooters and suddenly out-distanced by snarling motorcycles. From his traffic island in the midst of all this, the monumental El Cid still stood in his stirrups, brandishing his bronze spear.

"I'm sure no one will notice," said Stigman as they waited at the curb.

"I'm sure no one will."

"I could have triangulated it to be absolutely certain, but I guess one measurement was enough. All we had time for." He took his wife's arm. "We can cross now."

"I was only afraid the measurement would end at that catch basin over there."

"Oh, no! What a grisly thought! And yet you know they *have* found bones in the most unlikely places. Anybody watching?" They had reached the traffic island and were standing by the marks his wife had made on the pavement earlier.

"No, I don't see anyone," she said.

"I'll just lay it here. All right?" He had stepped over the grass as far as the flower bed. "O.K.?"

"O.K."

He took a small wreath of fern and boxwood from beneath the raincoat over his arm and placed it on the flower bed. "There! I've done it." He stepped back to the pavement. "A little tribute where it was due. It's scant enough, isn't it?"

"I'm surprised how much I feel about it, Aaron. I didn't think I would."

"Yes?" He stood looking at the flower bed. "What kind of flowers are those?"

"Canna lilies, I think. They've been cut."

"Canna lilies—I don't know them." There was an expression of contemplative sadness on his face. "The gardener or somebody will find a wreath here and wonder why. He'll probably move it to El Cid, but there's nothing I can do about it. There's little one can do against oblivion, anyway." He was silent. "And now?" He finally turned toward his wife. "Where shall we go now?"

"Anywhere. María Luisa Park?"

"All right. Let's find a bench there and sit down."

They skirted the base of the monument—and saw, walking toward them, a gray-clad policeman. He still had a few steps to go before he reached them. *"Buenos días, señores,"* he said, and saluted.

"Buenos días," said Stigman.

"Are you by any chance the same English couple who were seen surveying here this morning?"

"We are Americans, not English," said Stigman, speaking in Spanish. "But we were surveying."

"In that case, I have a few questions to ask you."

"Yes?"

"I am sure you can answer them easily. Can you explain why you were surveying?"

"Yes. I was attempting to locate a spot of some sentimental value to myself," said Stigman. "A place no longer shown on the maps of Seville."

"What place is that, Señor?" The policeman was a stalwart figure. Gray hair showed under his scarlet-ribboned military cap. The skin of his large face was pink, as though freshly shaven. His competence and good judgment were manifest.

"It is a—well, I would rather not say. It is a private matter."

"Señor, surveying in public places among public establishments is no private matter. I could point out further that you laid a measuring tape across a highway, impeding traffic—"

"It was only for a minute."

"A minute is enough for an accident. You attracted a crowd."

"I could not very well help that."

"No, but these are not private matters. Do you have a permit from the proper authority to do this kind of work?"

"I did not know I needed one," said Stigman.

"It is customary to have a permit from the proper authority to avoid difficulties such as those I have just mentioned. However, you are a tourist, and sometimes we overlook what tourists do. But what is this surveying about?"

"Well . . ." Stigman took a deep breath. "I said I tried to locate a place of some sentimental value to myself. I had no other reason for doing so. In fact, I have just laid a wreath over there."

"A wreath?" The policeman turned and looked at the flower bed.

"Yes. Do you want me to remove it?"

"Naturally. I would like to see it." All three of them moved toward the flower bed. Stigman picked up the wreath and showed it to the policeman, whose face gave every indication of extreme perplexity. "Señor, you realize that you have not yet explained yourself."

"I have tried to."

"But what you have told me is no explanation. I have asked you what the surveying was about."

"I have already told you what the surveying was about. What explanation do you want me to make?"

"Aaron . . ." his wife cautioned.

"No, I haven't anything more to say to him." Stigman reverted to English. "I told him all I could. What does he want?"

The policeman showed signs of impatience. "Señor, once more, will you explain what you were doing?"

"I have already told you what I was doing."

"You have told me nothing. Nothing I can understand."

"That is not my fault!"

"Señor!" The policeman raised the hand that held his gloves. "Please accompany me."

"What for?" Stigman braced his legs against the ground.

"There are too many private matters involved here. Too many things that need explanation. This way, *por favor*. The Señora, too."

"Well, for God's sake," Stigman said, looking bleakly at his wife.

They crossed the Avenida to the low wall before the Fábrica de Tabacos, and there the policeman turned to lead the way toward Menendez Pelayo, the main thoroughfare. Two monks who were at that moment striding toward them, vigorous, bearded young men with bare feet in sandals and white cord about brown robes, noted the wreath in Stigman's hand and looked at the trio alertly. It was evident they thought the policeman was escorting two tourists bent on a commemorative act. And so others appeared to think—those they met strolling along the Paseo, and those sitting among the colored tables and chairs of the outdoor cafés. Street photographers arranging their miniature horses and black bulls nodded in deference, and a chestnut vender halted his stirring of the chestnuts to peer at the wreath through the white smoke. Between the traffic and the wall—between the rumbling of vehicles on Menendez Pelayo, reverberating against stucco buildings and store fronts across the street, and the ancient wall of the Alcázar deploying its series of pyramidal caps—the three passed the double pillars of the monument to Columbus and drew near the orange trees of the Jardines de Murillo. In the distance, above the Cathedral, the weathervane Giralda, frail and diaphanous against the blue sky, seemed to acompany them as they walked. Stigman glanced at his wife as if seeking reassurance. With parted lips, she seemed to be drinking in the scene. She seemed to be enjoying it.

There were two men behind the railing in the drab *comisaría*, one man at the desk and one standing. The man at the desk wore a blue sweater and large tinted glasses. His head tapered, and this, together with the large glasses and his heavy torso in its dark sweater, gave him a froglike appearance. There was a touch of the forbidding about him. The man standing wore a business suit and a white shirt. He was uncommonly tall for a Spaniard, and the way he stood, in a stooped, hollow fashion, was even more uncommon. Under thick, iron-gray hair, his features seemed to wince, as if his face were too close to a hot fire. Behind the two men hung a fading portrait of Francisco Franco, in which the Caudillo looked out at the newcomers with benign eyes. Below the portrait, a large map of the district was tacked up. A ring of heavy ancient keys on one wall had scored an arc in the plaster; on the opposite wall, the hands of a new electric clock neared noon. The two men on the other side of the barrier stopped talking.

"*Buenos días*," said Stigman mechanically. His wife repeated the salutation.

"*Buenos días*," the two men before them replied.

The policeman saluted the man at the desk. "Señor Inspector," he began. "On two occasions today, I was at the Glorieta de San Diego when I saw this gentleman and his wife doing what seemed to me very strange things. On the first occasion, they left in a taxi before I had an opportunity to question them."

The two men behind the railing regarded Stigman and his wife noncommittally. The policeman went into a detailed description of what he had observed and the information he had gathered: that the couple had used surveying instruments on the Avenida del Cid for purposes they refused to disclose; that they had carried out this activity in a hurried and surreptitious manner; and that later in the day they had allegedly placed a wreath on one of the flower beds near El Cid, a wreath that he had not even seen them bring. "The Señor is carrying the wreath," he concluded.

Stigman held it up.

"May I see it?" the Inspector asked. Stigman handed over the wreath; the Inspector examined it briefly and then set it down on the desk.

"And the surveying instruments—where are they?"

"They are at our hotel, the Inglaterra."

"You travel with surveying instruments?"

"They are not mine. I rented them. If you wish . . .'" Stigman brought out his wallet, produced a slip of paper, and passed it across the railing. "This is the voucher for my deposit for the use of the instruments."

The Inspector examined the voucher and laid it on the desk. "And your passports?" The documents were produced and surrendered. After a glance at each booklet, the Inspector placed them on his desk.

"You have been conducting surveying operations on a public thoroughfare in Seville, Señor. What is their purpose?"

"Their purpose was to find the place for that wreath."

"And that place was the flower bed beside El Cid. What lies in the flower bed?"

"Nothing that I am sure of, Señor Inspector."

"What did you think was there?"

"That is something I do not care to discuss."

"Come, Señor."

"No, I do not care to discuss it," Stigman said. "If there is a fine attached to what I have done, I am prepared to pay it. If the case is more serious, I demand my right to speak to the American consul."

"We are not at that pass, Señor. I am merely asking for clarification of certain mysterious activities that you have been conducting in public. The police have a right to inquire into their meaning."

Stigman moved his head abruptly to one side and looked up. "Señor Inspector, what would you think of a person who was a guest in your house and insulted you—a guest who insults his host?"

The Inspector made a deprecating gesture. "Obviously, I would feel contempt. What has this to do with you?"

"I am attempting to refrain from insulting the country I am visiting."

"Let us not worry about insults, Señor. All I ask for is a little clarification. Why were you surveying? What lies in the flower bed? What are the facts?"

"I have already told you all the facts that are pertinent," Stigman said. He gripped the railing. "The rest I refuse to tell you. I have done no one any harm."

The Inspector sat back. "What is your occupation?" he asked quietly.

"I am a general-science teacher, retired," said Stigman. "My wife gives music lessons in private."

"I note that you speak Spanish very well."

"We have spent many summers in Mexico."

"And what possible reasons can you have, Señor, for refusing to tell me what was the object of your surveying?"

"I did tell you. It was to place a wreath. Nothing more."

The Inspector looked up at the man beside him as if at one with greater authority. Wincing and unwincing, the tall man's difficult face seemed to belong at times to two different individuals. He had studied Stigman for a while and then Stigman's wife. Most of the time, his eyes rested on her, and when they did his features became lighter. He now addressed a question to the policeman. "Where, once again, was this wreath laid?"

"There, Señor Abogado, at this end of the oval." The policeman leaned over the railing and pointed at the wall map. "The end toward the Glorieta de Don Juan."

"Ah."

The Inspector swivelled about. "There is nothing there of importance," he said, pointing to the wall map. "The Capitanía, the Portuguese Consulate—nothing more. The Palace of Justice is only in its foundation."

"Right here?" The tall man put his finger on the small end of the oval and looked at the policeman.

"*Sí, señor.*"

The lines in the tall man's face cleared. "You need not detain them any longer," he said to the Inspector.

Not the slightest shade of expression came over the seated man's face. He picked up the passports and the voucher and handed them over the railing to Stigman. "I would caution you against continuing to use surveying instruments in public without a permit," he said.

"Then we may go?"

"*Sí, señor. Adiós. Adiós, señora.*" They were free to leave.

The tall man had brought the wreath through the gate of the wooden barrier. He handed it to Stigman. "You know your way back?" he said.

"Oh, yes," said Stigman. "The way we came."

"It would be a privilege if I could accompany you for a while."

"By all means, if you wish," Stigman said.

The three paused for a moment outside, under the red and yellow flag of Spain over the doorway. "I am Miguel Ortega," the tall man said. "I am a state attorney."

"I understood as much," said Stigman.

"We can go to the Inglaterra this way"—he indicated Menendez Pelayo—"or this way, through the Barrio de Santa Cruz. It is more picturesque." His face unkinked as he spoke to Mary Stigman. "Every Sevillano fancies himself a guide."

"We shall need a guide, Señor Ortega, if we go through the Barrio de Santa Cruz," she said.

"And I shall be delighted to conduct you."

"I am sure that no one will mind if I throw this raincoat over my wreath," said Stigman.

The little café to which the lawyer had invited them was, as he said, something more like old Seville than new. The *expreso* machines were there, as they were in all Seville cafés, and the barrels of wine and sherry as well as the ranks of colorful bottles on the shelves in the rear. The usual paper wrappers of sugar cubes littered the floor. But the atmosphere in the place was more neighborly than in any of the cafés Stigman and his wife had been to. To the right of the bar, in the rear of the establishment, was a small provision shop. Aging hams covered with gray mold hung from a pipe near the ceiling, and next to them was an assortment of smoked sausages equally aged. There were basins of chick-peas visible on the small counter, lentils, rice, a large slab of brown quince jelly, and a crock of olives. A youngster with a fresh roll in his hand stood before the counter while the proprietress cut russet slices of *chorizo* for a filler. Three or four men were leaning on the bar in the café, one of them quietly shaking a dice cup. There were only three tables in the place; at one of them a bespectacled old man was busy filling in some sort of form. He had a large glass of white wine and a bundle of lottery tickets in front of him. On the wall behind the bartender hung a slate with the appetizers for the day chalked on it.

"Yes, I do like it," Stigman's wife replied to the lawyer's question. "It has all the appeal of something long lived in."

The lawyer nodded. "Ever since my youth and long before," he said.

The waiter brought the three cognacs they had ordered. "*Salud*," Ortega said, and lifted his glass. Stigman and his wife lifted theirs, and they drank.

Ortega put his glass down. "You know, Señor Stigman, I quite appreciate your feelings," he said. He tilted his head slightly toward the wreath, which Stigman had put on a chair under the table. "In fact, if you wish, I will escort you back to the Avenida del Cid. Would you like to leave it there?"

"Oh, no," replied Stigman shortly. "I have made my gesture, for whatever it was worth."

"You found this place to your satisfaction? I mean, you are reasonably satisfied with the accuracy of your location?" Ortega's face knit and darkened.

"Oh, yes. Shall I say, within a half metre?"

The lawyer shook his head. "You intrigue me enormously."

"Why?"

"That any man would be so—I hesitate to use the word— so naïve. I do not know what word to use."

"I was determined that I was going to make my gesture. I made it."

"Of course." The man's face, wrinkling and unwrinkling, must have been a formidable thing to confront from a witness stand. "Señor Stigman," he went on, "I have old maps on the wall of my study. They are not maps, no. They are old views of Seville. Have you seen such views?"

"I have seen reproductions."

"I have three. In two of mine there is shown a certain landmark of the city, outside the walls. Where El Cid now stands. Approximately."

Stigman sat back listening.

"It is no longer there."

"No, it is no longer there," Stigman conceded.

"And this is the *quemadero,* where criminals were burned to death."

"That is where I laid the wreath."

"So I concluded."

In the pause that followed, only the dry rattle of the dice in the dice cup could be heard, and the scratching of the pen of the man doing his accounts at the table nearby. The café door opened, and three well-dressed patrons walked in—Spaniards with placid faces. They ordered *café con leche* and looked about. A hum of conversation began. A hissing sound came from the *expreso* machine.

"That is where I laid the wreath," Stigman repeated. "Your conclusion is correct. But do you know why I laid the wreath?"

"Yes. Because this was the same *quemadero* where heretics found guilty by the Holy Inquisition were burned—among others, relapsed *conversos*, those Catholics who secretly clung to their old Judaic faith."

"They were men and women who were put to death because they would not renounce their faith," Stigman said. "They were martyrs. I honored them because they deserved to be honored, because of their heroic constancy in the hour of trial. I honored them because no one in Spain honors them."

"I understand," said Ortega. "I am not offended, if that is what you were concerned about. All this is part of the Spanish heritage, along wth her age-old greatness."

"I am happy to hear it," said Stigman. "I am happy you were not offended. It was a small enough tribute I paid—but, even so, it seems to have had some consequences."

Ortega's squint might have been a smile. "Among them, I have had the pleasure of meeting you and your charming wife."

"Thank you. It has been a pleasure for us, too."

Again there was a pause, this time an awkward one.

"Señor Ortega," Stigman said finally, "it seems to me a strange thing that a gentleman in your position, even with such views of Seville as you have on your walls, should have fixed so immediately on the *quemadero*—should have focussed on that spot at once. No one else realized what it was. Not the crowd around us this morning, not the policeman, not the Inspector." He hesitated. "You say this is part of the Spanish heritage. Why is everyone ignorant of it but you?"

"There may have been personal reasons. An idiosyncrasy."

"What, for example? I am eager to know how you could locate a thing like that so quickly. I had a good deal of research to do before I could be sure."

Ortega grimaced. He seemed to be deliberating. He brushed a small flake of cigarette ash from the table. "You have a point," he said.

"But how?"

The Spaniard clouded his eyes briefly with his hand. "Señor Stigman," he said, "what if I informed you that my grandfather told me that his father, when he became very old, would light a candle on Friday nights—would do it as a matter of compulsion? Would light a candle and put it in a pitcher?"

"Ah, so that is why," Stigman said. "That is why you knew where the *quemadero* was."

"In part. I knew where the *quemadero* was because I feel the same way about the people who died there that you do. Because I cannot forget their heroic constancy, as you call it. It was the heroic constancy of Spaniards who were also Jews."

"Spaniards!" Stigman looked at the other man with a startled expression. "It was the heroic constancy of Jews who were also Spaniards!"

Ortega sat motionless. For once, his uncertain face seemed at rest.

"And do you light a candle on Friday nights?" asked Stigman.

The lawyer shook his head, almost as if disdaining the thought. "A candle in consciousness is enough, is it not? And you?"

"Oh, no," Stigman said. "I left the faith of my ancestors many years ago."

Their glasses were empty. Ortega signalled the waiter, who brought three full ones and removed the others.

"I think the word now should be '*l'chaim*,'" said Mary Stigman.

"Do you know it?" asked Stigman, lifting his glass.

Ortega lifted his. "Of course. It is the equivalent of our Spanish '*salud*.'"

From some open window or café door, a male voice hovering in a flamenco quaver reached the Stigmans as they walked through a cramped street of the Barrio. A thin reek of urine emanated from the unsunned cobblestones. Huge doors supporting other doors within them and studded with brass nipples in showy array opened on the flagstones of tranquil patios.

Inside, copper salvers gleamed amid the potted plants; there was a courtyard well in one patio, vases and conch shells in another. Above their heads hung the shallow balconies of the houses, glassed in or laden with greenery, and above these the very roofs grew moss and weeds among their curved tiles.

"This is charming," said Mary Stigman. She was walking close to her husband's side along the narrow pavement.

"Are we going all right?"

"Yes, I think so. The next should be Mateos Gago, and then we should see the Cathedral."

"Quite a remarkable man, Señor Ortega, isn't he?" Stigman observed. " 'Spaniards always pay,' he said when I tried to pay the waiter. '*Los españoles siempre pagan*'—as if it were a tradition." He looked at his wife. "I'll think you're remarkable, too, if you can find a way out of this maze," he said, smiling. "I wish you hadn't been so insistent with him about our ability to find our way without his help."

"I've got the city guide to Seville in my purse."

"So you have. I don't know whether there's something wrong with my sense of reality or my sense of direction," Stigman said. He took his wife's arm. "It must be those two cognacs," he added lamely.

They reached the corner and turned into Mateos Gago. The orange trees that lined the street were in the way for a moment, and then they saw it—the Giralda, *la Fe*, the weathervane. Faith stood on her high pinnacle above the Cathedral, pointing at every wind with her palm branch of triumph. A few more steps and the lofty Moorish minaret that supported her came wholly into view, rearing high its small balconies and sinuous arches, its marble pillars from whose capitals delicate brickwork tracery rose like spreading smoke from a brazier.

"Yes, there it is. You found it," said Stigman. "Now I know where the hotel is." They walked confidently ahead. "Wait a minute!" he said, and arrested his stride.

"What is it?" Involuntarily, his wife looked back.

"Oh, no, no one is following us. Do you know what I did?" Stigman held up his raincoat. "I forgot the wreath."

King Solomon

Isaac Rosenfeld

1. With His Woman

Every year, a certain number of girls. They come to him, lie down beside him, place their hands on his breast, and offer to become his slaves.

This goes on all the time. It is a simple transaction, a lovely thing: "I will be your slave," say the girls, and no more need be said. But Solomon's men, his counselors, can't bear it— what is this power of his? Some maintain it is no power at all, he is merely the King. Oh yes, admit the rest, his being the King has something to do with it—but there have been other kings, so it can't be that. Nor is it anything else. Consider how unprepossessing he is, what a poor impression he makes—why, most of the counselors are taller, handsomer, and leaner than he. To be sure, he has an excellent voice, but his voice comes through best on the telephone, and he has an unlisted number which no one would give out. Certainly not, say the men. Still, the girls keep coming, and they lie down beside him with their hands on his breast.

It is not enough to say the counselors are jealous. After all, there is something strange here, the like of it has not been seen. But who shall explain the King?

Solomon himself makes no comment, he does not speak of his personal affairs. He may drop a hint or two, but these hints are contradictory and vague, and he drops them only for his own amusement; perhaps he, too, doesn't know. Every few years he publishes a collection of his sayings, most of which he has never said, but the sayings have little to do with the case, and their melancholy tone is held to be an affectation. The wisest counselors pay no attention to his words. If anything is to be learned, the wise men say, it had better be sought among his girls.

But the girls also say nothing. The rejected go away in

tears, in anger or regret—in which case one cannot expect them to speak coherently or with regard for truth; or they are determined yet to win his love—and again they will tell lies. As for the women he accepts, they are useless. Almost at once they become so much like Solomon, adopting his mannerisms of gesture and speech and sharing his views of things, that they say only what he would say—and Solomon does not speak his heart. Besides, the counselors think they are stupid. Oh, they are gifted, no doubt of that, and none lacks charm. One dances, another sings, a third makes cheese; some bake, some spin, some are skilled at floral decorations. Still others wear their hair, or cultivate the expression of their eyes, in some mysterious way, impossible to fathom. Or altogether their talent lies in their bare feet, a way of arching the instep or turning up the toes. Yet so far as outsiders can judge, these girls are unqualified to minister to the King, and the counselors waste no time asking questions.

So it has become the custom in the court to study Solomon's women in their work: perhaps the manner in which they serve him will make it clear. The counselors watch over the harem, each chooses a woman to follow about the palace, over the grounds, and through the town. One woman . . . there she goes! . . . sets out early in the morning with a basket, trailed by a counselor. She makes her way to the largest and most crowded kosher market, where she will stand in line for hours, haggling and hefting, crying highway robbery! And what delicacies does she buy? Surely pickles and spices, the rarest and the best . . . Not necessarily, it may even be turnips. So who is the wiser? And as for the obvious conclusion—that Solomon sets store by economy—this has long since been drawn. He even lunches on leftovers.

Another goes to the laundry with his shirts. Solomon wants them done just so, and she gives out instructions on the washing, starching, and ironing, then waits in the steamy atmosphere for hours, till the shirts are done; and carries them back on her head, walking swiftly, deftly, with infinite pride. Why such pride? This is precisely the mystery.

Others clean his shoes, open and sort the mail, tend the garden and the vineyards, keep his musical instruments polished and in tune. A few go to the well for water—a curious assignment, as the palace has had hot and cold running water for years. Perhaps he sends them to the well on purpose, to confuse the counselors. But if this occupation serves only to deceive, why not all the rest? This may well be the case. King Solomon has a staff of regular servants, quite capable of looking after his needs.

Therefore nothing has been learned. The counselors are always confronted by the same questions at nightfall, when their need to know the King is greatest. Much of the time, he sits quietly with a girl or two, pasting stamps in an album, while they massage his scalp. On festive nights, the counselors note the revelry and participate, when invited, in the dancing and carousing. Over and over again they have resolved to stay sober and observant, but always they give way; the moment they enter the King's apartments they are overcome by the radiance which waits—or which they imagine waits—for them there. All is gold, ivory, inlay of silver, velvet, damask, and brocade; incense and odor of spice and musk, with sound of timberles, flutes, and drums; carvings, hangings, carpets ankle-deep. Not that all of this enchants them; many counselors complain that the King has no taste in entertainments, that he relies, for instance, too heavily on tambourines, which he has his dancing girls flutter in their hands till the jingling gives one a headache; that much the same or better amusements can be had in the cabarets about the town which —so much for Solomon's originality—have been the source of many a spectacle of the King's court—and they even have newspaper clippings to prove the point. Nevertheless, they succumb to the King's merrymaking, join it or are swayed by it, and even if it makes them puke with disdain, still they lose the essential detachment. And then at the hour when the King retires to his chamber with his chosen love, all is lost, the counselors are defeated and go disgruntled to their own quarters, to lie awake or dream enviously through the night.

All the same, a pertinacious lot. What stratagems, disguising themselves as eunuchs or hiding in vases or behind the furniture to learn what goes on at night! Here, too, they have been disappointed. Though Solomon burns soft lights beside his couch, no one has witnessed anything—or at least has ever reported what he saw. At the last moment the hidden counselors have shut their eyes or turned away; no one has dared look at the King's nakedness, dared to watch his love. A few, it is said, have so dared, but these have either disappeared (the consensus is, they left of their own accord) or, remaining, have worn a dazed and guilty look ever after, so that people say they went blind. Still, sounds have been heard floating in deep summer air over the garden and the lily pond, mingling with the voices of frogs: sighs, outcries, moans, and exclamations—but the intrusion has been its own punishment, maddening those who have overheard the King and driving them wild with lust or despair. Sooner or later, the counselors have been compelled to stopper their ears. Now when these sounds issue from the King's apartments, the counselors take up instruments and play, softly but in concert, to hide his sounds within their own.

None has seen the King's nakedness; yet all have seen him in shirt sleeves or suspenders, paunchy, loose-jowled, in need of a trim. Often in the heat of the day he appears bareheaded, and all have looked upon his baldness; sometimes he comes forth in his bare feet, and the men have observed bunions and corns. When he appears in this fashion with, say, a cigar in his mouth and circles under his eyes; his armpits showing yellowish and hairy over the arm holes of his undershirt; his wrinkles deep and his skin slack; a wallet protruding from one hip pocket and a kerchief from the other—at such moments, whether he be concerned with issues of government or merely the condition of the plumbing, he does show himself in human nakedness after all, he is much like any man, he even resembles a policeman on his day off or a small-time gambler. And sometimes, unexpectedly, he summons the cabinet to a game of pinochle—then all are aware he has again transcended them.

Some of the counselors have formed liaisons with his rejected mistresses, women he has grown tired of and no longer summons to his couch. Often it seemed to them that they were on the verge of discovery, but persistence undid them. These liaisons have invariably degenerated into marriages, the counselor become a husband, the mistress, a nag. Then the counselor has forgotten his purpose, and the mistress, her knowledge; what the curiosity of the one and the bitterness of the other were to have produced in union, has been dissipated in recriminations: hang up your clothes, don't spend so much money, brush your teeth before coming to bed. Men and women have grown old in this dissembling, but nothing has been learned. From these fruitless experiments has come the statement, erroneously attributed to the King: vanity of vanities, all is vanity.

Of late, King Solomon has turned his attention to the young. He has organized bicycle races for children, entertained them with magicians, taken them on picnics and excursions to the zoo. He loves to sit on a shady bench with a youngster on either knee, a boy and a girl, about four or five in age. They pull at his beard, tug at his ears and finger his spectacles till he can no longer see through the smudges. Sometimes, the children are his own, more often not. It makes no difference, the King has many sons and daughters. He tells stories, not nearly so amusing as they should be, old stories which the children grew tired of in the nursery, or poor inventions, rather pointless on the whole. And he seldom finishes a story but begins to nod in the telling, his words thicken and stumble; eventually he falls asleep. Solomon is a disappointment to the young, seldom will children come twice to his garden. Yet for them he is truly a king: robed and gowned, golden-sandaled, wearing a crown, his hair trimmed, his beard washed lustrous, combed, and waved, and the hairs plucked out of his nostrils. And in this splendor, in which he seldom appears, not even for the reception of ambassadors, he loves to bounce a rubber ball and play catch with the children. He is unskilled at these games, they call him fuckyknuckles. A man turning sixty, an aging king.

But how clear is the expression of his eyes as he plays with the children—if only one knew what it meant! Perhaps he longs to reveal himself but does not know how; or does not know that the people await this revelation; or is unable to see beyond the children, who are bored with him. Perhaps he has nothing to reveal, and all his wisdom lies scattered from his hand: he is merely this, that, and the other, a few buildings raised, roads leveled, a number of words spoken, unthinking, on an idle afternoon. Occasionally, when he recognizes the expectation of the people, he tries to remember an appropriate saying from one of the collections he has published. Most of the time, he is unaware of all this.

The children are fretful in the garden, they wait to be delivered. They have been brought by mothers, nurses, older sisters, who stand outside the gate, looking in through the palings. The mothers and nurses whisper together, their feet and eyes and hands are restless, they look at his shining beard. Later in the afternoon, when the children have been led home, perhaps one of the older girls, one of the sisters, will enter the same garden, approach the spot where the King lies resting, lie down beside him, fold her hands upon his breast, and offer to become his slave.

2. The Queen of Sheba

From all over they have come, and they keep coming, though the King is now an old man. It may be owing to his age that he has grown lenient, admitting women to concubinage whom, the counselors swear, he would have sent packing in the old days. He has reached the years when anything looks good to him. This may not be true, there may be other reasons; but the counselors have a point in saying that the standards have fallen, and they prove it by telling the story of the Queen of Sheba.

A letter came, it was the first application to be received by mail. From a foreign country, the woman signed herself The Queen. She flattered Solomon's wisdom, word of which had reached her from afar; her own ears longed to hear his discourse, her own eyes, to behold his person. An unorthodox application, written in a powerful, forward-rushing, though feminine, hand on strangely scented paper: the King said it reminded him of jungles. He inspected the postmark, clipped off the stamp, and pasted it on a page by itself in his album. His expression was hidden in his beard.

The woman meant it. Boxes began to arrive, plastered with travel stickers. They came on sand-choked, sneezing camels, in long trains, attended by drivers, natives of the Land of Sheba. The next day, more boxes, and again on the third. Gifts of all description, of money and goods, spangles and bangles for the entire court. It made an excellent impression, but Solomon, who distributed the gifts, did not seem pleased. On the last day but one came another shipment, as large as all the others combined. . . . Here the counselors pretend to know the King's mind. First of all, they say, he was annoyed at having to put up so many camels, whole droves of them— his stables were crowded, and there was a shortage of feed for his own animals. Then the camel drivers, rough and barbarous men, were inflamed by the sight of Solomon's women, and the King had to double the guard and pay overtime; this killed him. But their greatest presumption lies in saying that Solomon, when he opened the last and largest load of boxes which contained the Queen's personal effects, thought, "Adonai Elohenu! Is she coming to stay?" No one knows what the King thought.

He may well have been glad that the Queen was coming.

No queen had ever before asked to be his slave—and she was a queen for sure, and of a rich country, think of the gifts she had sent. Solomon put his economists to work and they submitted a report: the financial structure was sound, and the country led in the production of myrrh, pepper, and oil. Now to be sure, the Queen's letter made no direct application; apart from the flattery, it merely said, *coming for a visit,* as an equal might say. But the interpretation was clear. An equal would not come uninvited, only one who meant to offer herself would do so—unless the Queen was rude; but the gifts she had sent took care of that. Yet as a queen, writing from her own palace, she could not have expressed the intention, it would have been treason to her own people. Nevertheless, she had every intention: otherwise, why would she have gone to the trouble? The fact is, there was rejoicing in the palace, Solomon himself led the dancing, and he declared a holiday when the Queen of Sheba arrived.

She came in a howdah, on a camel, preceded by troops of archers and trumpeters. Solomon helped her down and washed and anointed her feet in the courtyard. This didn't come off so well. Sheba used coloring matter on her toenails and the soles of her feet, and the coloring ran; Solomon was out of practice, he tickled her feet a few times and made her laugh. The ceremony was supposed to be a solemn one, the people took it very seriously, and they were offended by her toenails—feet were supposed to be presented dusty; as for the giggling, it was unpardonable, and the priests took offense. A poor set of omens. Besides, Sheba was not quite so young as the autographed picture, which she had sent in advance to Solomon, would have led one to expect. Her skin was nearly black, relieved here and there along her arms and shoulders with spots of a lighter color, a leopard design. Her black hair, which she had apparently made some effort to straighten, had gone frizzled and kinky again in the heat of the desert crossing. Her lips were thick and purplish brown, her palms and the soles of her feet were a light, bright saffron yellow. She wore anklets of delicate chain, gold bracelets all over her arms, and jewels in both obvious and unexpected places, so that the eye was never done seeing them; their light was kept in constant agitation by the massive rhythm of her breathing, which involved her entire body. A sense of tremendous power and authenticity emanated from her breasts. Some thought she was beautiful, others, not. No one knows what the King thought; but he may well have felt what everyone else did who came to witness her arrival—drawn, and at the same time, stunned.

But the King is glad in his heart as he leads Sheba to the table, where he has put on a great spread for her. He is attended by his court and surrounded by his women—and how lordly are his movements as he eats meat and rinses his mouth with wine! At the same time he is uneasy in the Queen's presence, his usual resources may not be enough— after all, this is no maiden lurking in the garden to trip up to him and fold her hands upon his breast. The meal goes well enough: Sheba asks for seconds, and seems impressed with the napkins and silverware. But suddenly, right in the middle of dessert, she turns to him and demands, in front of everyone and that all may hear, that he show her his famous wisdom. This comes as something of a shock. The implication is twofold: that so far he has spoken commonplaces; and secondly, that he is to suffer no illusions, it was really for the sake of his wisdom that she made the difficult trip. The people turn their eyes on the King, who handles the awkward moment with skill; he clears his throat on schedule, and raises his hand in the usual gesture, admonishing silence. But nothing comes.

In the official account of the visit, which Solomon had written to order, he was supposed to have

> . . . *told her all questions: There was not anything . . . which he told her not. And when the Queen of Sheba had seen all Solomon's wisdom, and the house that he had built, and the meat of his table and the sitting of his servants . . .*

etc.,

> *There was no more spirit in her. And she said to the King, It was a true report that I heard in mine own land, of thy acts and thy wisdom. Howbeit, I believed not the words, until I came and mine eyes had seen it; and behold, the half was not told me: Thy wisdom and prosperity exceedeth the fame which I heard. Happy are thy men . . . which stand continually before thee and that hear thy wisdom.*

After which there was supposed to have been further exchange of compliments and gifts.

Now this is not only a bit thick, it gets round the question of Solomon's wisdom. What *did* the King say, when put to it by the Queen? That there were so many feet in a mile? That all circles were round? That the number of stars visible on a clear night from a point well out of town was neither more nor less than a certain number? Did he advise her what to take for colds, give her a recipe for salad dressing, or speak of building temples and ships? Just what does a man say under the circumstances?

Certainly, he hadn't the nerve, the gall, to repeat the abominable invention to her face of the two women who disputed motherhood of a child. She would have seen through it right away. And surely he knew this was not the time to quote his sayings; besides, he always had trouble remembering them. Then what did he say?

His economists had worked up a report on the Land of Sheba. He may have sent for a copy; more likely, he knew the essential facts cold, and spoke what came to mind: industry, agriculture, natural resources. Of the financial structure, the public debt, the condition of business. Of the production of pepper, myrrh, and oil, especially oil. Grant him his wisdom.

Certainly, the Queen was impressed, but one need not suppose that the spirit was knocked out of her or that she said, "It was a true report that I heard in mine own land . . ." etc. Chances are, she paid no attention to his words (except to note the drift) but watched him as he spoke, taking in the cut of his beard, the fit of his clothes, and wondering, betimes, what sort of man he was. She saw his initial uncertainty give way and his confidence grow as he reached the meaty part of his delivery. And all along, she observed how he drew on the admiring glances of his girls, soaked up their adoration, as they lay open-mouthed on couches and rugs at his feet, all criticism suspended, incapacitated by love. Love ringed him round, love sustained him, he was the splendid heart of their hearts. She must have forgotten the heat and sand images of the desert crossing, she, too, lapped from all sides and borne gently afloat . . .

So much one may imagine. But the Queen spent a number of days or weeks, perhaps even a month or two in the King's company, and of what happened during the time of her stay, let alone the subsequent events of the first night, the official chronicles say nothing. A merciful omission, according to the counselors, who report that it went badly from the start. When the King had finished his discourse, they say the Queen felt called upon to answer. But words failed her, or she felt no need of words: she was the Queen. What she did was to lean forward and, in utter disregard of the company, take his head into her hands, gaze at him for a long time with a smile on her thick lips, and at last bestow on him a kiss, which landed somewhere in his beard. Then she jumped onto the table, commanded music, and danced among the cups and bowls, the dishes and the crumpled napkins. The counselors were shocked, the girls smirked painfully, the servants held their breath. Nor was Sheba so slender as the autographed picture may have led one to believe. When she set her feet down, the table shook, and the carafes of wine and sweetened water swayed and threatened to topple. Solomon himself hastily cleared a way for her, pushing the dishes to one side; his hands were trembling. But she proceeded with the dance, the chain anklets tinkled, her fingers snapped, the many jewels she wore flashed wealthily. Her toes left marks on the tablecloth, as though animals had run there. And run she did, back and forth over the length of the table, bending over the counselors to tweak this one's nose and that one's ears. But always she glanced back to see if she had the King's eye.

She had it, darker than usual. To her, this meant that he was admiring her, gravely, as befits King and Queen, and her feet quickened. How stern he was! Already she felt the King's love, harder than any courtier's and so much more severe. She increased the tempo, the musicians scrambling to keep up with her, and whirled. Round and round she sped, drawing nearer the end of the table where the King sat. It was a dance in the style of her country, unknown in these parts, and she did it with the abandon of a tribesgirl, though one must assume she was conscious, in her abandonment, that it was she, the Queen, none other than Sheba, who abandoned herself to King Solomon. That was the whole point of it, the mastery of the thing. Pride did not leave her face, it entered her ecstasy and raised it in degree. Already cries, guttural, impersonal, were barking in her throat; then with a final whoop she spun round and threw herself, arms outstretched and intertwined, like one bound captive, to fall before him on the table where his meal had been.

It was a terrible mistake. The women and the counselors knew the King so much better than she, and their hearts went out in pity. The Queen had offered herself in the only way she knew, majesty, power, and reign implied, throwing herself prone with a condescending crash for the King to rise and assault her. What presumption! He did not move. He sat infinitely removed, almost sorrowing over this great embarrassment. The music had stopped, there was an unbearable silence in the banquet hall. The King rumbled something deep in his beard; perhaps he was merely clearing his throat, preparatory to saying a few words (if only his wisdom did not fail him!). Some of the servants took it to mean more wine, others, more meat, still others, fingerbowls. They ran in all directions. Sheba lowered herself into her seat at the King's side. Her dark face burned. . . . Somehow the time went by, and the evening was over. Solomon led Sheba off to his chamber, as courtesy demanded. Even as she went with him, it was apparent that she still went in hope; even at the last moment. The older women wept.

Day by day, the strain mounted. Sheba was sometimes with the King, they played chess or listened to the radio, they bent their heads over maps, discussed politics, and played croquet. But there were no festivities and she did not dance again. She bore herself with dignity, but she had grown pale, and her smile, when she forgot herself, was cringing and meek. Sometimes, when she was alone, she was seen to run her finger over the table tops and the woodwork, looking for dust. She could not bear the sight of her waiting women, lest the revival of her hope, as they did her toilet, become apparent to them, and would chase them out of the room; only to call them back, and help her prepare for an audience with the King. Finally, she quarreled with some of the girls of the harem. And when this happened, Sheba knew that the day had come and she began to pack.

A pinochle game was in progress when the Queen of Sheba, unannounced and without knocking, came into the room to say she wanted a word with the King. He dismissed his counselors, but one of them swears he managed to hide behind the draperies, where he witnessed the scene.

The King was in his undershirt, smoking a cigar. He apologized for his dishevelment and offered to repair it. The affairs of state, he explained, were so trying lately, he found he worked better in deshabille. Had he been working? asked the Queen with a smile. She thought this was some sort of game, and she fingered the cards with pictures of kings and queens. Solomon, knowing that women do not play pinochle, told her the cabinet had been in extraordinary session, trying fortunes with the picture cards. The times were good, but one must look to the future, and he offered to show her how it was done. No, I don't want to keep you, said the Queen of Sheba, I beg only a few words. Speak, said Solomon.

"Solomon, Solomon," said the Queen, "I am going away. No, don't answer me. You will say something polite and regretful, but my decision can only be a relief to you." She paused, taking on courage. "You must not allow this to be a disappointment to you, you must let me take the whole expense of our emotion upon myself. I did a foolish thing. I am a proud woman, being a Queen, and my pride carried me too far. I thought I would take pride in transcending pride, in offering myself to the King. But still that was pride, since I wanted the King for myself. You did wisely to refuse me. Yes, you are wise, Solomon, let no one question your wisdom. Yours is the wisdom of love, which is the highest. But your love is love only of yourself; yet you share it with others by letting them love you—and this is next to the highest. Either way you look at it, Solomon is wise enough. Understand me—" She took a step forward, a dance step, as though she were again on the table top, but her eyes spoke a different meaning. "I am not pleading with you that you love me or allow me to love you. For you are the King, your taking is your giving. But allow me to say, your power rests on despair. Yours is the power of drawing love, the like of which has not been seen. But you despair of loving with your own heart. I have come to tell the King he must not despair. Surely, Solomon, who has built temples and made the desert flourish, is a powerful king, and he has the power to do what the simplest slave girl or washerwoman of his harem can do—to love with his own heart. And if he does not have this power, it will come to him, he need only accept the love which it is his nature to call forth in everyone, especially in us poor women. This is his glory. Rejoice in it, O King, for you are the King!"

The counselor who hid behind the drapes said he regretted his action, to see how his King stood burdened before the Queen. His own heart filled with loving shame. Solomon looked lost, deprived of his power, as though the years in the palace and the garden had never been. He made an effort to stand dignified in his undershirt, he bore his head as though he were wearing the crown, but it was pitiful to see him.

"The Queen is wise," said he. Then he broke down, and the counselor did not hear his next words. He did hear him say that the Queen was magnificent, that she had the courage of lions and tigers . . . but by now his head was lowered. Suddenly, he clasped the Queen to his breast in an embrace of farewell, and the Queen smiled and stroked his curly beard. They did not immediately take leave of each other, but went on to speak of other matters. Before the Queen of Sheba left the country, King Solomon had leased her oil lands for ninety-nine years.

But on the day of her departure, he stood bare headed in the crowded courtyard to watch her set out, with her trumpeters and archers mounted on supercilious camels, all of them bold and reflecting midday sun. He extended his hand to help her up, and she, with her free hand, chucked him under the chin. Then she leaned out of the howdah to cry, "Long live the King!" King Solomon stood with bowed head to receive the ovation, and it was terrible for the people to see his humility, humble in acknowledgment of his power. Now more than ever they yearned for him.

When Sheba moved off, at the head of the procession, Solomon led the people onto the roof, to watch the camels file across the sand. He stood till evening fell, and the rump of the last plodding animal had twitched out of sight beyond the sand hills. Then he averted his face and wept silently, for it is a terrible thing for the people to see their King's tears.

3. With His Fathers

So the counselors have a point when they say the standards have fallen. Once the Queen of Sheba herself was unable to make it; and now, look. But no wonder, her like will not come again, and besides, Solomon is old. He has been running the country forty years and has begun to speak of retiring; but the people know he will never retire, and so they whisper, it is time for the King to die.

How does this strike him? To look at him—his beard is white, his spotted hands shake, he walks bent, his eyes are rheumy and dim—to look at him one would suppose he dwells on the thought of death. But he is no better known now than he was in his prime. The only certainty is that the King is old.

But what follows from this, how does it reveal him? Or this?—that he had an attack of pleurisy not long ago, and since then his side has been taped. And what does it mean to say that he now has more women than ever cluttering up the palace, one thousand in all, including seven hundred wives? (Is it merely that the standards have fallen?) It was necessary to tear down the harem (while the women, to everyone's displeasure, were quartered in the town) and raise a new building, so large, it has taken up ground formerly allotted to the garden. They are a great source of trouble to him, these women, and the counselors complain—that's where all the money is going, to support the harem. Harem? Why, it's a whole population, the country will be ruined! And the priests complain, every week they send fresh ultimatums, objecting to the fact that so many of Solomon's girls are heathen; they have even accused him of idolatry and threatened him with loss of the Kingdom and the wrath of God. And the people grumble, it's a shame, when they find his women loitering in beauty shops or quarreling right out in the open, as they have begun to do, in the very streets. But Solomon ignores the discontent and goes on collecting women as he once collected stamps.

Why? Or what does this mean?—that he seldom takes the trouble to interview applicants, but establishes a policy for several months, during which time the rule is, no vacancies. Then he will change the rule and take on newcomers by the dozen, most of whom he does not even see, the work being done by the counselors. And how complicated the work has become, compared with the old days, when all that was necessary was for a girl to lie down beside the King with her hands upon his breast. Now there are forms to fill out and letters of recommendation to obtain, several interviews and a medical examination to go through, and even then the girls must wait until their references have been checked. The filing cabinets have mounted to the ceiling. What sense does it make?

And above all in view of the following? The counselors vouch for it, they swear they have seen the proof. That King Solomon now takes to bed, not with a virgin, as his father, David, did in his old age, or even with a dancing girl, but with a hot water bottle to warm him. Think of him lying in bed with a hot water bottle. If this report is true, then doesn't something follow? For this is the extreme, between life and death, where all thoughts meet; an extreme, not a mean; and a wrong guess is impossible, everything is true, as at the topmost point, where all direction is down. It follows that he warms his hands on the water bottle, presses it to his cheek, passes it down along his belly. Now when he thinks of his prime, he of all men must wonder: what was the glory of the King? Who bestowed the power, and what did it consist in? When he had it, he did not consider, and now it is gone. Passing the rubber bottle down to his feet and digging with his toes for warmth, he sees he did everything possible in his life, and left no possibility untouched, of manhood, statesmanship, love. What else can a man do? There is no answer. Except to say, he was in God's grace then? And now no longer? Or is he still in a state of grace, witness the water bottle at his feet? And perhaps he is only being tried, and may look forward to even greater rewards? Such are the advantages of being a believer. If he were one, he would know—at least believe that he knew. But a man who knows only that once love was with him, which now is no more—what does he know, what shall he believe, old, exhausted, shivering alone in bed at night with a hot water bottle, when all's quiet in the palace? And if all's not quiet, that's no longer his concern.

No, if there were any rewards, he'd settle for a good night's sleep. But sleep does not come. He hears strange noises in the apartment, scratching . . . Mice? He must remember to speak to the caretakers. . . . at last he drowses off, to sleep awhile. And if he does not sleep? Or later, when he wakes, and it is still the same night? . . . Does he think of the Queen of Sheba and wonder, whom is she visiting now? Does he remember how she danced upon the table? Or the song he wrote soon after her departure, with her words still fresh in his mind, resolved to pour out his love for her, but from the very first line pouring out, instead, her love for him? *Let him kiss me with the kisses of his mouth, for thy love is better than wine.* It has been years since he heard from her. . . .

Meanwhile, the bottle has grown cold. Shall he ring for another? He shifts the bottle, kneads it between his knees. *And be thou like a young hart upon the mountains of spices.* Look forward, look back, to darkness, at the light, both ways blind. He raises the bottle to his breast; it does not warm him. He gropes for the cord, and while his hand reaches, he thinks, as he has thought so many times, there is a time and a season for everything, a time to be born and a time to die. Is it time now? They will lay him out, washed, anointed, shrouded. They will fold his arms across his chest, with the palms turned in, completing the figure. Now his own hands will lie pressed to his breast, and he will sleep with his fathers.

Tell Me A Riddle

Tillie Olsen

1

For forty-seven years they had been married. How deep back the stubborn, gnarled roots of the quarrel reached, no one could say—but only now, when tending to the needs of others no longer shackled them together, the roots swelled up visible, split the earth between them, and the tearing shook even to the children, long since grown.

Why now, why now? wailed Hannah.

As if when we grew up weren't enough, said Paul.

Poor Ma. Poor Dad. It hurts so for both of them, said Vivi. They never had very much; at least in old age they should be happy.

Knock their heads together, insisted Sammy; tell 'em: you're too old for this kind of thing; no reason not to get along now.

Lennie wrote to Clara: They've lived over so much together; what could possibly tear them apart?

Something tangible enough.

Arthritic hands, and such work as he got, occasional. Poverty all his life, and there was little breath left for the running. He could not, could not turn away from this desire: to have the troubling of responsibility, the fretting with money, over and done with; to be free, to be *care*free where success was not measured by accumulation, and there was use for the vitality still in him.

There was a way. They could sell the house, and with the money join his lodge's Haven, cooperative for the aged. Happy communal life, and was he not already an official; had he not helped organize it, raise funds, served as a trustee?

But she—would not consider it.

"What do we need all this for?" he would ask loudly, for her hearing aid was turned down and the vacuum was shrilling. "Five rooms" (pushing the sofa so she could get into the corner) "furniture" (smoothing down the rug) "floors and surfaces to make work. Tell me, why do we need it?" And he was glad he could ask in a scream.

"Because I'm use't."

"Because you're use't. This is a reason, Mrs. Word Miser? Used to can get unused!"

"Enough unused I have to get used to already . . . Not enough words?" turning off the vacuum a moment to hear herself answer. "Because soon enough we'll need only a little closet, no windows, no furniture, nothing to make work but for worms. Because now I want room . . . Screech and blow like you're doing, you'll need that closet even sooner . . . Ha, again!" for the vacuum bag wailed, puffed half up, hung stubbornly limp. "This time fix it so it stays; quick before the phone rings and you get too important-busy."

But while he struggled with the motor, it seethed in him. Why fix it? Why have to bother? And if it can't be fixed, have to wring the mind with how to pay the repair? At the Haven they come in with their own machines to clean your room or your cottage; you fish, or play cards, or make jokes in the sun, not with knotty fingers fight to mend vacuums.

Over the dishes, coaxingly: "For once in your life, to be free, to have everything done for you, like a queen."

"I never liked queens."

"No dishes, no garbage, no towel to sop, no worry what to buy, what to eat."

"And what else would I do with my empty hands? Better to eat at my own table when I want, and to cook and eat how I want."

"In the cottages they buy what you ask, and cook it how you like. *You* are the one who always used to say: better mankind born without mouths and stomachs than always to worry for money to buy, to shop, to fix, to cook, to wash, to clean."

"How cleverly you hid that you heard. I said it then because eighteen hours a day I ran. And you never scraped a carrot or knew a dish towel sops. Now—for you and me—who cares? A herring out of a jar is enough. But when *I* want, and nobody to bother." And she turned off her ear button, so she would not have to hear.

But as *he* had no peace, juggling and rejuggling the money to figure: how will I pay for this now?; prying out the storm windows (there they take care of this); jolting in the streetcar on errands (there I would not have to ride to take care of this or that); fending the patronizing of relatives just back from Florida (it matters what one is, not what one can afford), he gave *her* no peace.

"Look! In their bulletin. A reading circle. Twice a week it meets."

"Haumm," her answer of not listening.

"A reading circle. Chekhov they read that you like, and Peretz. Cultured people at the Haven that you would enjoy."

"Enjoy!" She tasted the word. "Now, when it pleases you, you find a reading circle for me. And forty years ago when the children were morsels and there was a Circle, did you stay home with them once so I could go? Even once? You trained me well. I do not need others to enjoy. Others!" Her voice trembled. "Because *you* want to be there with others. Already it makes me sick to think of you always around others. Clown, grimacer, floormat, yesman, entertainer, whatever they want of you."

And now it was he who turned on the television loud so he need not hear.

Old scar tissue ruptured and the wounds festered anew. Chekhov indeed. She thought without softness of that young wife, who in deep night hours while she nursed the current baby, and perhaps held another in her lap, would try to stay awake for the only time there was to read. She would feel again the weather of the outside on his cheek when, coming late from a meeting, he would find her so, and stimulated and ardent, sniffing her skin, coax: "I'll put the baby to bed, and you—put the book away, don't read, don't read."

That had been the most beguiling of all the "don't read, put your book away" her life had been. Chekhov indeed!

"Money?" She shrugged him off. "Could we get poorer than once we were? And in America, who starves?"

But as still he pressed:

"Let me alone about money. Was there ever enough? Seven little ones—for every penny I had to ask—and sometimes, remember, there was nothing. But always *I* had to manage. Now *you* manage. Rub your nose in it good."

But from those years she had had to manage, old humiliations and terrors rose up, lived again, and forced her to relive

them. The children's needings; that grocer's face or this merchant's wife she had had to beg credit from when credit was a
disgrace, the scenery of the long blocks walked around when
she could not pay; school coming, and the desperate going
over the old to see what could yet be remade; the soups of
meat bones begged "for-the-dog" one winter . . .

Enough. Now they had no children. Let *him* wrack his head
for how they would live. She would not exchange her solitude
for anything. *Never again to be forced to move the rhythms
of others.*

For in this solitude she had won to a reconciled peace.

Tranquillity from having the empty house no longer an enemy, for it stayed clean—not as in the days when it was her
family, the life in it, that had seemed the enemy: tracking,
smudging, littering, dirtying, engaging her in endless de-
feating battle—and on whom her endless defeat had been
spewed.

The few old books, memorized from rereading; the pictures
to ponder (the magnifying glass superimposed on her heavy
eyeglasses). Or if she wishes, when he is gone, the phonograph, that if she turns up very loud and strains, she can hear:
the ordered sounds, and the struggling.

Out in the garden, growing things to nurture. Birds to be
kept out of the pear tree, and when the pears are heavy and
ripe, the old fury of work, for all must be canned, nothing
wasted.

And her one social duty (for she will not go to luncheons or
meetings) the boxes of old clothes left with her, as with a life-
practiced eye for finding what is still wearable within the worn
(again the magnifying glass superimposed on the heavy glasses) she scans and sorts—this for rag or rummage, that for
mending and cleaning, and this for sending away.

*Being able at last to live within, and not move to the
rhythms of others,* as life had helped her to: denying; remov-
ing; isolating; taking the children one by one; then deafening,
half-blinding—and at last, presenting her solitude.

And in it she had won to a reconciled peace.

Now he was violating it with his constant campaigning:
Sell the house and move to the Haven. (*You* sit, you sit—there
too you could sit like a stone.) He was making of her a battle-
ground where old grievances tore. (Turn on your ear button—

I am talking.) And stubbornly she resisted—so that from wheedling, reasoning, manipulation, it was bitterness he now started with.

And it came to where every happening lashed up a quarrel.

"I will sell the house anyway," he flung at her one night. "I am putting it up for sale. There will be a way to make you sign."

The television blared, as always it did on the evenings he stayed home, and as always it reached her only as noise. She did not know if the tumult was in her or outside. Snap! she turned the sound off. "Shadows," she whispered to him, pointing to the screen, "look, it is only shadows." And in a scream: "Did you say that you will sell the house? Look at me, not at that. I am no shadow. You cannot sell without me."

"Leave on the television. I am watching."

"Like Paulie, like Jenny, a four-year-old. Staring at shadows. *You cannot sell the house.*"

"I will. We are going to the Haven. There you would not have the television when you do not want it. I could sit in the social room and watch. You could lock yourself up to smell your unpleasantness in a room by yourself—for who would want to come near you?"

"No, no selling." A whisper now.

"The television is shadows. Mrs. Enlightened! Mrs. Cultured! A world comes into your house—and it is shadows. People you would never meet in a thousand lifetimes. Wonders. When you were four years old, yes, like Paulie, like Jenny, did you know of Indian dances, alligators, how they use bamboo in Malaya? No, you scratched in your dirt with the chickens and thought Olshana was the world. Yes, Mrs. Unpleasant, I will sell the house, for there better can we be rid of each other than here."

She did not know if the tumult was outside, or in her. Always a ravening inside, a pull to the bed, to lie down, to succumb.

"Have you thought maybe Ma should let a doctor have a look at her?" asked their son Paul after Sunday dinner, regarding his mother crumpled on the couch, instead of, as was her custom, busying herself in Nancy's kitchen.

"Why not the President too?"

"Seriously, Dad. This is the third Sunday she's lain down like that after dinner. Is she that way at home?"

"A regular love affair with the bed. Every time I start to talk to her."

Good protective reaction, observed Nancy to herself. The workings of hos-til-ity.

"Nancy could take her. I just don't like how she looks. Let's have Nancy arrange an appointment."

"You think she'll go?" regarding his wife gloomily. "All right, we have to have doctor bills, we have to have doctor bills." Loudly: "Something hurts you?"

She startled, looked to his lips. He repeated: "Mrs. Take It Easy, something hurts?"

"Nothing . . . Only you."

"A woman of honey. That's why you're lying down?"

"Soon I'll get up to do the dishes, Nancy."

"Leave them, Mother, I like it better this way."

"Mrs. Take It Easy, Paul says you should start ballet. You should go see a doctor and ask: how soon can you start ballet?"

"A doctor?" she begged. "Ballet?"

"We were talking, Ma," explained Paul, "you don't seem any too well. It would be a good idea for you to see a doctor for a checkup."

"I get up now to do the kitchen. Doctors are bills and foolishness, my son. I need no doctors."

"At the Haven," he could not resist pointing out, "a doctor is *not* bills. He lives beside you. You start to sneeze, he is there before you open up a Kleenex. You can be sick there for free, all you want."

"Diarrhea of the mouth, is there a doctor to make you dumb?"

"Ma. Promise me you'll go. Nancy will arrange it."

"It's all of a piece when you think of it," said Nancy, "the way she attacks my kitchen, scrubbing under every cup hook, doing the inside of the oven so I can't enjoy Sunday dinner, knowing that half-blind or not, she's going to find every speck of dirt . . ."

"Don't, Nancy, I've told you—it's the only way she knows to be useful. What did the *doctor* say?"

"A real fatherly lecture. Sixty-nine is young these days. Go out, enjoy life, find interests. Get a new hearing aid, this one is antiquated. Old age is sickness only if one makes it so. Geriatrics, Inc."

"So there was nothing physical."

"Of course there was. How can you live to yourself like she does without there being? Evidence of a kidney disorder, and her blood count is low. He gave her a diet, and she's to come back for follow-up and lab work . . . But he was clear enough: Number One prescription—start living like a human being. When I think of your dad, who could really play the invalid with that arthritis of his, as active as a teenager, and twice as much fun . . ."

"You didn't tell me the doctor says your sickness is in you, how you live." He pushed his advantage. "Life and enjoyments you need better than medicine. And this diet, how can you keep it? To weigh each morsel and scrape away the bits of fat, to make this soup, that pudding. There, at the Haven, they have a dietician, they would do it for you."

She is silent.

"You would feel better there, I know it," he says gently. "There there is life and enjoyments all around."

"What is the matter, Mr. Importantbusy, you have no card game or meeting you can go to?"—turning her face to the pillow.

For a while he cut his meetings and going out, fussed over her diet, tried to wheedle her into leaving the house, brought in visitors:

"I should come to a fashion tea. I should sit and look at pretty babies in clothes I cannot buy. This is pleasure?"

"Always you are better than everyone else. The doctor said you should go out. Mrs. Brem comes to you with goodness and you turn her away."

"Because *you* asked her to, she asked me."

"They won't come back. People you need. the doctor said. Your own cousins I asked; they were willing to come and make peace as if nothing had happened . . ."

"No more crushers of people, pushers, hypocrites, around me. No more in *my* house. You go to them if you like."

"Kind he is to visit. And you, like ice."

"A babbler. All my life around babblers. Enough!"

"She's even worse, Dad? Then let her stew a while," advised Nancy. "You can't let it destroy you; it's a psychological thing, maybe too far gone for any of us to help."

So he let her stew. More and more she lay silent in bed, and sometimes did not even get up to make the meals. No longer was the tongue-lashing inevitable if he left the coffee cup where it did not belong, or forgot to take out the garbage or mislaid the broom. The birds grew bold that summer and for once pocked the pears, undisturbed.

A bellyful of bitterness, and every day the same quarrel in a new way and a different old grievance the quarrel forced her to enter and relive. And the new torment: I am not really sick, the doctor said it, then why do I feel so sick?

One night she asked him: "You have a meeting tonight? Do not go. Stay . . . with me."

He had planned to watch "This Is Your Life," but half sick himself from the heavy heat, and sickening therefore the more after the brooks and woods of the Haven, with satisfaction he grated:

"Hah, Mrs. Live Alone And Like It wants company all of a sudden. It doesn't seem so good the time of solitary when she was a girl exile in Siberia. 'Do not go. Stay with me.' A new song for Mrs. Free As A Bird. Yes, I am going out, and while I am gone chew this aloneness good, and think how you keep us both from where if you want people you do not need to be alone."

"Go, go. All your life you have gone without me."

After him she sobbed curses he had not heard in years, old-country curses from their childhood: Grow, oh shall you grow like an onion, with your head in the ground. Like the hide of a drum shall you be, beaten in life, beaten in death. Oh shall you be like a chandelier, to hang, and to burn . . .

She was not in their bed when he came back. She lay on the cot on the sun porch. All week she did not speak or come near him; nor did he try to make peace or care for her.

He slept badly, so used to her next to him. After all the years, old harmonies and dependencies deep in their bodies; she curled to him, or he coiled to her, each warmed, warming, turning as the other turned, the nights a long embrace.

It was not the empty bed or the storm that woke him, but a faint singing. *She* was singing. Shaking off the drops of rain, the lightning riving her lifted face, he saw her so; the cot covers on the floor.

"This is a private concert?" he asked. "Come in, you are wet."

"I can breathe now," she answered; "my lungs are rich." Though indeed the sound was hardly a breath.

"Come in, come in." Loosing the bamboo shades. "Look how wet you are." Half helping, half carrying her, still faint-breathing her song.

A Russian love song of fifty years ago.

He had found a buyer, but before he told her, he called together those children who were close enough to come. Paul, of course, Sammy from New Jersey, Hannah from Connecticut, Vivi from Ohio.

With a kindling of energy for her beloved visitors, she arrayed the house, cooked and baked. She was not prepared for the solemn after-dinner conclave, they too probing in and tearing. Her frightened eyes watched from mouth to mouth as each spoke.

His stories were eloquent and funny of her refusal to go back to the doctor; of the scorned invitations; of her stubborn silences or the bile "like a Niagara"; of her contrariness: "If I clean it's no good how I cleaned; if I don't clean, I'm still a master who thinks he has a slave."

("Vinegar he poured on me all his life; I am well marinated; how can I be honey now?")

Deftly he marched in the rightness for moving to the Haven; their money from social security free for visiting the children, not sucked into daily needs and into the house; the activities in the Haven for him; but mostly the Haven for *her:* her health, her need of care, distraction, amusement, friends who shared her interests.

"This does offer an outlet for Dad," said Paul; "he's always been an active person. And economic peace of mind isn't to be sneezed at, either, I could use a little of that myself."

But when they asked: "And you, Ma, how do you feel about it?" could only whisper:

"For him it is good. It is not for me. I can no longer live between people."

"You lived all your life *for* people," Vivi cried.

"Not with." Suffering doubly for the unhappiness on her children's faces.

"You have to find some compromise," Sammy insisted. "Maybe sell the house and buy a trailer. After forty-seven years there's surely some way you can find to live in peace."

"There is no help, my children. Different things we need."

"Then live alone!" He could control himself no longer. "I have a buyer for the house. Half the money for you, half for me. Either alone or with me to the Haven. You think I can live any longer as we are doing now?"

"Ma doesn't have to make a decision this minute, however you feel, Dad," Paul said quickly, "and you wouldn't want her to. Let's let it lay a few months, and then talk some more.

"I think I can work it out to take Mother home with me for a while," Hannah said. "You both look terrible, but especially you, Mother. I'm going to ask Phil to have a look at you."

"Sure," cracked Sammy. "What's the use of a doctor husband if you can't get free service out of him once in a while for the family? And absence might make the heart . . . you know."

"There was something after all," Paul told Nancy in a colorless voice. "That was Hannah's Phil calling. Her gall bladder . . . Surgery."

"Her *gall* bladder. If that isn't classic. 'Bitter as gall'—talk of psychosom—"

He stepped closer, put his hand over her mouth and said in the same colorless, plodding voice. "We have to get Dad. They operated at once. The cancer was everywhere, surrounding the liver, everywhere. They did what they could . . . at best she has a year. Dad . . . we have to tell him."

2

Honest in his weakness when they told him, and that she was not to know. "I'm not an actor. She'll know right away by how I am. O that poor woman. I am old too, it will break me into pieces. O that poor woman. She will spit on me: 'So my sickness was how I live.' O Paulie, how she will be, that poor woman. Only she should not suffer . . . I can't stand sickness, Paulie, I can't go with you."

But went. And play-acted.

"A grand opening and you did not even wait for me . . . A good thing Hannah took you with her."

"Fashion teas I needed. They cut out what tore in me; just in my throat something hurts yet . . . Look! so many flowers, like a funeral. Vivi called, did Hannah tell you? And Lennie from San Francisco, and Clara; and Sammy is coming." Her gnome's face pressed happily into the flowers.

It is impossible to predict in these cases, but once over the immediate effects of the operation, she should have several months of comparative well-being.

The money, where will come the money?

Travel with her, Dad. Don't take her home to the old associations. The other children will want to see her.

The money, where will I wring the money?

Whatever happens, she is not to know. No, you can't ask her to sign papers to sell the house; nothing to upset her. Borrow instead, then after . . .

I had wanted to leave you each a few dollars to make life easier, as other fathers do. There will be nothing left now. (Failure! you and your "business is exploitation." Why didn't you make it when it could be made?—Is that what you're thinking Sammy?)

Sure she's unreasonable, Dad—but you have to stay with her; if there's to be any happiness in what's left of her life, it depends on you.

Prop me up children, think of me, too. Shuffled, chained with her, bitter woman. No Haven, and the little money going . . . How happy she looks, poor creature.

The look of excitement. The straining to hear everything (the new hearing aid turned full). Why are you so happy, dying woman?

How the petals are, fold on fold, and the gladioli color. The autumn air.

Stranger grandsons, tall above the little gnome grandmother, the little spry grandfather. Paul in a frenzy of picture-taking before going.

She, wandering the great house. Feeling the books; laugh-

ing at the maple shoemaker's bench of a hundred years ago
used as a table. The ear turned to music.

"Let us go home. See how good I walk now."

"One step from the hospital," he answers, "and she wants
to fly. Wait till Doctor Phil says."

"Look—the birds too are flying home. Very good Phil is
and will not show it, but he is sick of sickness by the time he
comes home."

"Mrs. Telepathy, to read minds," he answers; "read mine
what it says: when the trunks of medicines become a suitcase, then we will go."

The grandboys, they do not know what to say to us . . .
Hannah, she runs around here, there, when is there time for
herself?

Let us go home. Let us go home.

Musing; gentleness—*but for the incidents of the rabbi in
the hospital, and of the candles of benediction.*

Of the rabbi in the hospital:

Now tell me what happened, Mother.

From the sleep I awoke, Hannah's Phil, and he
stands there like a devil in a dream and calls me by
name. I cannot hear. I think he prays. Go away please,
I tell him, I am not a believer. Still he stands, while my
heart knocks with fright.

You scared *him*, Mother. He thought you were delirious.

Who sent him? Why did he come to me?

It is a custom. The men of God come to visit those of
their religion they might help. The hospital makes up the
list for them, and you are on the Jewish list.

Not for rabbis. At once go and make them change.
Tell them to write: Race, human; Religion, none.

And of the candles of benediction:

Look how you have upset yourself, Mrs. Excited
Over Nothing. Pleasant memories you should leave.

Go in, go back to Hannah and the lights. Two weeks
I saw the candles and said nothing. But she asked me.

So what was so terrible? She forgets you never did, she
asks you to light the Friday candles and say the benediction like Phil's mother when she visits. If the candles give

her pleasure, why shouldn't she have the pleasure?

Not for pleasure she does it. For emptiness. Because his family does. Because all around her do.

That is not a good reason too? But you did not hear her. For heritage, she told you. For the boys. From the past they should have tradition.

Superstition! From our ancestors, savages, afraid of the dark, of themselves: mumbo words and magic lights to scare away ghosts.

She told you: how it started does not take away the goodness. For centuries, peace in the house it means.

Swindler! does she look back on the dark centuries? Candles bought instead of bread and stuck into a potato for a candlestick? Religion that stifled and said: in Paradise, woman, you will be the footstool of your husband, and in life—poor chosen Jew—ground under, despised, trembling in cellars. And cremated. And cremated.

This is religion's fault? You think you are still an orator of the 1905 revolution? Where are the pills for quieting? Which are they?

Heritage. How have we come from our savage past, how no longer to be savages—this to teach. To look back and learn what ennobles man—this to teach. To smash all ghettos that divide us—not to go back, not to go back—this to teach. Learned books in the house, will humankind live or die, and she gives to her boys—superstition.

Hannah that is so good to you. Take your pill, Mrs. Excited For Nothing, swallow.

Heritage! But when did I have time to teach? Of Hannah I asked only hands to help.

Swallow.

Otherwise—musing; gentleness.

Not to travel. To go home.

The children want to see you. We have to show them you are as thorny a flower as ever.

Not to travel.

Vivi wants you should see her new baby. She sent the tickets—airplane tickets—a Mrs. Roosevelt she wants to make of you. To Vivi's we have to go.

A new baby. How many warm, seductive babies. She holds him stiffly, *away* from her, so that he wails. And a long shudder begins, and the sweat beads on her forehead.

"Hush, shush," croons the grandfather, lifting him back. "You should forgive your grandmamma, little prince, she has never held a baby before, only seen them in glass cases. Hush, shush."

"You're tired, Ma," says Vivi. "The travel and the noisy dinner. I'll take you to lie down."

(*A long travel from, to, what the feel of a baby evokes.*)

In the airplane, cunningly designed to encase from motion (no wind, no feel of flight), she had sat severely and still, her face turned to the sky through which they cleaved and left no scar.

So this was how it looked, the determining, the crucial sky, and this was how man moved through it, remote above the dwindled earth, the concealed human life. Vulnerable life, that could scar.

There was a steerage ship of memory that shook across a great, circular sea: clustered, ill human beings; and through the thick-stained air, tiny fretting waters in a window round like the airplane's—sun round, moon round. (The round thatched hut roofs of Olshana.) Eye round—like the smaller window that framed distance the solitary year of exile where only her eyes could travel, and no voice spoke. And the polar winds hurled themselves across snow trackless and endless and white—like the clouds which had closed together below and hidden the earth.

Now they put a baby in her lap. Do not ask me, she would have liked to beg. Enough the worn face of Vivi, the remembered grandchildren. I cannot, cannot . . .

Cannot what? Unnatural grandmother, not able to make herself embrace a baby.

She lay there in the bed of the two little girls, her new hearing aid turned full, listening to the sound of the children going to sleep, the baby's fretful crying and hushing, the clatter of dishes being washed and put away. They thought she slept. Still she rode on.

It was not that she had not loved her babies, her children. The love—the passion of tending—had risen with the need like a torrent; and like a torrent drowned and immolated all

else. But when the need was done—o the power that was lost
in the painful damming back and drying up of what still
surged, but had nowhere to go. Only the thin pulsing left that
could not quiet, suffering over lives one felt, but could no
longer hold nor help.

On that torrent she had borne them to their own lives, and
the riverbed was desert long years now. Not there would she
dwell, a memoried wraith. Surely that was not all, surely there
was more. Still the springs, the springs were in her seeking.
Somewhere an older power that beat for life. Somewhere
coherence, transport, meaning. If they would but leave her
in the air now stilled of clamor, in the reconciled solitude, to
journey to her self.

And they put a baby in her lap. Immediacy to embrace,
and the breath of *that* past: warm flesh like this that had claims
and nuzzled away all else and with lovely mouths devoured;
hot-living like an animal—intensely and now; the turning
maze; the long drunkenness; the drowning into needing and
being needed. Severely she looked back—and the shudder
seized her again, and the sweat. Not that way. Not there, not
now could she, not yet . . .

And all that visit, she could not touch the baby.

"Daddy, is it the . . . sickness she's like that?" asked Vivi.
"I was so glad to be having the baby—for her. I told Tim,
it'll give her more happiness than anything, being around a
baby again. And she hasn't played with him once."

He was not listening, "Aahh little seed of life, little
charmer," he crooned, "Hollywood should see you. A heart
of ice you would melt. Kick, kick. The future you'll have for
a ball. In 2050 still kick. Kick for your granddaddy then."

Attentive with the older children; sat through their per-
formances (command performance; we command you to be
the audience); helped Ann sort autumn leaves to find the best
for a school program; listened gravely to Richard tell about
his rock collection, while her lips mutely formed the words
to remember: *igneous, sedimentary, metamorphic;* looked for
missing socks, books and bus tickets; watched the children
whoop after their grandfather who knew how to tickle, chuck,
lift, toss, do tricks, tell secrets, make jokes, match riddle for

riddle. (Tell me a riddle, Grammy. I know no riddles, child.)
Scrubbed sills and woodwork and furniture in every room;
folded the laundry; straightened drawers; emptied the heaped
baskets waiting for ironing (while he or Vivi or Tim nagged:
You're supposed to rest here, you've been sick) but to none
tended or gave food—and could not touch the baby.

After a week she said: "Let us go home. Today call about
the tickets."

"You have important business, Mrs. Inahurry? The President wants to consult with you?" He shouted, for the fear of
the future raced in him. "The clothes are still warm from the
suitcase, your children cannot show enough how glad they
are to see you, and you want home. There is plenty of time
for home. We cannot be with the children at home."

"Blind to around you as always: the little ones sleep four
in a room because we take their bed. We are two more people
in a house with a new baby, and no help."

"Vivi is happy so. The children should have their grandparents a while, she told to me. I should have my mommy
and daddy . . ."

"Babbler and blind. Do you look at her so tired? How she
starts to talk and she cries? I am not strong enough yet to
help. Let us go home."

(To reconciled solitude.)

*For it seemed to her the crowded noisy house was listening
to her, listening for her. She could feel it like a great ear
pressed under her heart. And everything knocked: quick constant raps: let me in, let me in.*

*How was it that soft reaching tendrils also became blows
that knocked?*

C'mon Grandma, I want to show you . . .
Tell me a riddle, Grandma. (*I know no riddles*)
Look Grammy, he's so dumb he can't even find his hands.
(Dody and the baby on a blanket over the fermenting
autumn mound)
I made it—for you. (Flat paper dolls with aprons that
lifted on scalloped skirts that lifted on flowered pants; hair
of yarn and great ringed questioning eyes) (Ann)
Watch me, Grandma. (Richard snaking up the tree, hang-
ing exultant, free, with one hand at the top. Below Dody

hunching over in pretend-cooking.) (Climb too, Dody, climb and look)

Be my nap bed, Grammy. (The "No!" too late.) Morty's abandoned heaviness, while his fingers ladder up and down her hearing-aid cord to his drowsy chant: eentsiebeentsie-spider. (*Children trust*)

It's to start off your own rock collection, Grandma. That's a trilobite fossil, 200 million years old (millions of years on a boy's mouth) and that one's obsidian, black glass.

Knocked and knocked.

Mother, I *told* you the teacher said we had to bring it back all filled out this morning. Didn't you even ask Daddy? Then tell *me* which plan and I'll check it: evacuate or stay in the city or wait for you to come and take me away. (Seeing the look of straining to hear) It's for Disaster, Grandma. (*Children trust.*)

Vivi in the maze of the long, the lovely drunkenness. The old old noises: baby sounds; screaming of a mother flayed to exasperation; children quarreling; children playing; singing; laughter.

And Vivi's tears and memories, spilling so fast, half the words not understood.

She had started remembering out loud deliberately, so her mother would know the past was cherished, still lived in her.

Nursing the baby: My friends marvel, and I tell them, oh it's easy to be such a cow. I remember how beautiful my mother seemed nursing my brother, and the milk just flows . . . Was that Davy? It must have been Davy . . .

Lowering a hem: How did you ever . . . when I think how you made everything we wore . . . Tim, just think, seven kids and Mommy sewed everything . . . do I remember you sang while you sewed? That white dress with the red apples on the skirt you fixed over for me, was it Hannah's or Clara's before it was mine?

Washing sweaters: Ma, I'll never forget, one of those days so nice you washed clothes outside; one of the first spring days it must have been. The bubbles just danced up and down while you scrubbed, and we chased after, and you stopped to show us how to blow our own bubbles with green onion stalks . . . you always . . .

"Strong onion, to still make you cry after so many years," her father said, to turn the tears into laughter.

While Richard bent over his homework: Where is it now, do we still have it, the Book of the Martyrs? It always seemed so, well—exalted, when you'd put it on the round table and we'd all look at it together; there was even a halo from the lamp. The lamp with the beaded fringe you could move up and down; they're in style again, pulley lamps like that, but without the fringe. You know the book I'm talking about, Daddy, the Book of the Martyrs, the first picture was a bust of Spartacus . . . Socrates? I wish there was something like that for the children, Mommy, to give them what you . . . (And the tears splashed again)

(What I intended and did not? Stop it, daughter, stop it, leave that time. And he, the hypocrite, sitting there with tears in his eyes too—it was nothing to you then, nothing.)

. . . The time you came to school and I almost died of shame because of your accent and because I knew you knew I was ashamed; how could I? . . . Sammy's harmonica and you danced to it once, yes you did, you and Davy squealing in your arms . . . That time you bundled us up and walked us down to the railroad station to stay the night 'cause it was heated and we didn't have any coal, that winter of the strike, you didn't think I remembered that, did you, Mommy? . . . How you'd call us out to see the sunsets . . .

Day after day, the spilling memories. Worse now, questions, too. Even the grandchildren: Grandma, in the olden days, when you were little . . .

It was the afternoons that saved.

While they thought she napped, she would leave the mosaic on the wall (of children's drawings, maps, calendars, pictures, Ann's cardboard dolls with their great ringed questioning eyes) and hunch in the girls' closet, on the low shelf where the shoes stood, and the girls' dresses covered.

For that while she would painfully sheathe against the listening house, the tendrils and noises that knocked, and Vivi's spilling memories. Sometimes it helped to braid and unbraid the sashes that dangled, or to trace the pattern on the hoop slips.

Today she had jacks and children under jet trails to forget. Last night, Ann and Dody silhouetted in the window against a sunset of flaming man-made clouds of jet trail, their jacks ball accenting the peaceful noise of dinner being made. Had she told them, yes she had told them of how they played jacks in her village though there was no ball, no jacks. Six stones, round and flat, toss them out, the seventh on the back of the hand, toss, catch and swoop up as many as possible, toss again . . .

Of stones (repeating Richard) there are three kinds: earth's fire jetting; rock of layered centuries; crucibled new out of the old (*igneous, sedimentary, metamorphic*). But there was that other—frozen to black glass, never to transform or hold the fossil memory . . . (let not my seed fall on stone). There was an ancient man who fought to heights a great rock that crashed back down eternally—eternal labor, freedom, labor . . . (stone will perish, but the word remain). And you, David, who with a stone slew, screaming: Lord, take my heart of stone and give me flesh

Who was screaming? Why was she back in the common room of the prison, the sun motes dancing in the shafts of light, and the informer being brought in, a prisoner now, like themselves. And Lisa leaping, yes, Lisa, the gentle and tender, biting at the betrayer's jugular. Screaming and screaming.

No, it is the children screaming. Another of Paul and Sammy's terrible fights?

In Vivi's house. Severely: you are in Vivi's house.

Blows, screams, a call: "Grandma!" For her? O please not for her. Hide, hunch behind the dresses deeper. But a trembling little body hurls itself beside her—surprised, smothered laughter, arms surround her neck, tears rub dry on her cheek, and words too soft to understand whisper into her ear (Is this where you hide too, Grammy? It's my secret place, we have a secret now).

And the sweat beads, and the long shudder seizes.

It seemed the great ear pressed inside now, and the knocking. "We have to go home," she told him, "I grow ill here."

"It is your own fault, Mrs. Bodybusy, you do not rest, you do too much." He raged, but the fear was in his eyes. "It was a serious operation, they told you to take care . . . All right, we will go to where you can rest."

But where? Not home to death, not yet. He had thought to Lennie's, to Clara's; beautiful visits with each of the children. She would have to rest first, be stronger. If they could but go to Florida—it glittered before him, the never-realized promise of Florida. California: of course. (The money, the money dwindling!) Los Angeles first for sun and rest, then to Lennie's in San Francisco.

He told her the next day. "You saw what Nancy wrote: snow and wind back home, a terrible winter. And look at you—all bones and a swollen belly. I called Phil: he said: 'A prescription, Los Angeles sun and rest.'"

She watched the words on his lips: "You have sold the house," she cried, "that is why we do not go home. That is why you talk no more of the Haven, why there is money for travel. After the children you will drag me to the Haven."

"The Haven! Who thinks of the Haven any more? Tell her, Vivi, tell Mrs. Suspicious: a prescription, sun and rest, to make you healthy . . . And how could I sell the house without *you?*"

At the place of farewells and greetings, of winds of coming and winds of going, they say their goodbys.

They look back at her with the eyes of others before them: Richard with her own blue blaze; Ann with the Nordic eyes of Tim; Morty's dreaming brown of a great-grandmother he will never know; Dody with the laughing eyes of him who had been her springtime love (who stands beside her now); Vivi's, all tears.

The baby's eyes are closed in sleep.
Good-by, my children.

3

It is to the back of the great city he brought her, to the dwelling places of the cast-off old. Bounded by two lines of amusement piers to the north and to the south, and between a long straight paving rimmed with black benches facing the sand—sands so wide the ocean is only a far fluting.

In the brief vacation season, some of the boarded stores fronting the sands open, and families, young people and children, may be seen. A little tasseled tram shuttles between the piers, and the lights of roller coasters prink and tweak over those who come to have sensation made in them.

The rest of the year it is abandoned to the old, all else boarded up and still; seemingly empty, except the occasional days and hours when the sun, like a tide, sucks them out of the low rooming houses, casts them onto the benches and sandy rim of the walk—and sweeps them into decaying enclosures back again.

A few newer apartments glint among the low bleached squares. It is in one of these Lennie's Jeannie has arranged their rooms. "Only a few miles north and south people pay hundreds of dollars a month for just this gorgeous air, Granddaddy, just this ocean closeness."

She had been ill on the plane, lay ill for days in the unfamiliar room. Several times the doctor came by—left medicine she would not take. Several times Jeannie drove in the twenty miles from work, still in her Visiting Nurse Uniform, the lightness and brightness of her like a healing.

"Who can believe it is winter?" he said one morning. "Beautiful it is outside like an ad. Come, Mrs. Invalid, come to taste it. You are well enough to sit in here, you are well enough to sit outside. The doctor said it too."

But the benches were encrusted with people, and the sands at the sidewalk's edge. Besides, she had seen the far ruffle of the sea: "there take me," and though she leaned against him, it was she who led.

Plodding and plodding, sitting often to rest, he grumbling. Patting the sand so warm. Once she scooped up a handful, cradling it close to her better eye; peered, and flung it back. And as they came almost to the brink and she could see the glistening wet, she sat down, pulled off her shoes and stockings, left him and began to run. "You'll catch cold," he screamed, but the sand in his shoes weighed him down—he who had always been the agile one—and already the white spray creamed her feet.

He pulled her back, took a handkerchief to wipe off the wet and the sand. "O no," she said, "the sun will dry," seized the square and smoothed it flat, dropped on it a mound of sand, knotted the kerchief corners and tied it to a bag—"to look at with the strong glass" (for the first time in years explaining an action of hers)—and lay down with the little bag against her cheek, looking toward the shore that nurtured life as it first crawled toward consciousness the millions of years ago.

He took her one Sunday in the evil-smelling bus, past flat miles of blister houses, to the home of relatives. O what is this? she cried as the light began to smoke and the houses to dim and recede. Smog, he said, everyone knows but you . . . Outside he kept his arms about her, but she walked with hands pushing the heavy air as if to open it, whispered: who has done this? sat down suddenly to vomit at the curb and for a long while refused to rise.

One's age as seen on the altered face of those known in youth. Is this they he has come to visit? This Max and Rose, smooth and pleasant, introducing them to polite children, disinterested grandchildren, "the whole family, once a month on Sundays. And why not? We have the room, the help, the food."

Talk of cars, of houses, of success: this son that, that daughter this. And *your* children? Hastily skimped over, the intermarriages, the obscure work—"my doctor son-in-law, Phil"—all he has to offer. She silent in a corner. (Car-sick like a baby, he explains.) Years since he has taken her to visit anyone but the children, and old apprehensions prickle: "no incidents," he silently begs, "no incidents." He itched to tell them. "A very sick woman," significantly, indicating her with his eyes, "a very sick woman." Their restricted faces did not react. "Have you thought maybe she'd do better at Palm Springs?" Rose asked. "Or at least a nicer section of the beach, nicer people, a pool." Not to have to say "money" he said instead: "would she have sand to look at through a magnifying glass?" and went on, detail after detail, the old habit betraying of parading the queerness of her for laughter.

After dinner—the others into the living room in men- or women-clusters, or into the den to watch TV—the four of them alone. She sat close to him, and did not speak. Jokes, stories, people they had known, beginning of reminiscence, Russia fifty-sixty years ago. Strange words across the Duncan Phyfe table: *hunger; secret meetings; human rights; spies; betrayals; prison; escape*—interrupted by one of the grandchildren: "Commercial's on; any Coke left? Gee, you're missing a real hair-raiser." And then a granddaughter (Max proudly: "look at her, an American queen") drove them home on her way back to U.C.L.A. No incident—except that there had been no incidents.

The first few mornings she had taken with her the magnifying glass, but he would sit only on the benches, so she rested at the foot, where slatted bench shadows fell, and unless she turned her hearing aid down, other voices invaded.

Now on the days when the sun shone and she felt well

enough, he took her on the tram to where the benches ranged in oblongs, some with tables for checkers or cards. Again the blanket on the sand in the striped shadows, but she no longer brought the magnifying glass. He played cards, and she lay in the sun and looked toward the waters; or they walked—two blocks down to the scaling hotel, two blocks back—past chili-hamburger stands, open-doored bars, Next to New and Perpetual Rummage Sale stores.

Once, out of the aimless walkers, slow and shuffling like themselves, someone ran unevenly toward them, embraced, kissed, wept: "dear friends, old friends." A friend of *hers*, not his: Mrs. Mays who had lived next door to them in Denver when the children were small.

Thirty years are compressed into a dozen sentences; and the present, not even in three. All is told: the children scattered; the husband dead; she lives in a room two blocks up from the sing hall—and points to the domed auditorium jutting before the pier. The leg? phlebitis; the heavy breathing? that, one does not ask. She too comes to the benches each nice day to sit. And tomorrow, tomorrow, are they going to the community sing? Of course he would have heard of it, everybody goes—the big doings they wait for all week. They have never been? She will come to them for dinner tomorrow and they will all go together.

So it is that she sits in the wind of the singing, among the thousand various faces of age.

She had turned off her hearing aid at once they came into the auditorium—as she would have wished to turn off sight.

One by one they streamed by and imprinted on her—and though the savage zest of their singing came voicelessly soft and distant, the faces still roared—the faces densened the air —chorded

children-chants, mother-croons, singing of the chained; love serenades, Beethoven storms, mad Lucia's scream; drunken joy-songs, keens for the dead, work-singing

> *while from floor to balcony to dome a barefooted sore-covered little girl threaded the sound-thronged tumult, danced her ecstasy of grimace to flutes that scratched at a crossroads village wedding*

Yes, faces became sound, and the sound became faces; and faces and sound became weight—pushed, pressed

"Air"—her hand claws his.

"Whenever I enjoy myself . . ." Then he saw the gray sweat on her face. "Here. Up. Help me, Mrs. Mays," and they support her out to where she can gulp the air in sob after sob.

"A doctor, we should get for her a doctor."

"Tch, it's nothing," says Ellen Mays, "I get it all the time . . . You've missed the tram; come to my place. Fix your hearing aid, honey . . . close . . . tea. My view. See, she *wants* to come. Steady now, that's how." Adding mysteriously: "Remember your advice, easy to keep your head above water, empty things float. Float."

The singing a fading march for them, tall woman with a swollen leg, weaving little man, and the swollen thinness they help between.

The stench in the hall: mildew? decay? "We sit and rest then climb. My gorgeous view. We help each other and here we are."

The stench along into the slab of room. A washstand for a sink, a box with oilcloth tacked around for a cupboard, a three-burner gas plate. Artificial flowers, colorless with dust. Everywhere pictures foaming: wedding, baby, party, vacation, graduation, family pictures. From the narrow couch under a slit of window, sure enough the view: lurching rooftops and a scallop of ocean heaving, preening, twitching under the moon.

"While the water heats. Excuse me . . . down the hall." Ellen Mays has gone.

"You'll live?" he asks mechanically, sat down to feel his fright; tried to pull her alongside.

She pushed him away. "For air," she said; stood clinging to the dresser. Then, in a terrible voice:

After a lifetime of room. Of many rooms.

Shhh.

You remember how she lived. Eight children. And now one room   like a coffin. Shrinking the life of her   into one room

She pays rent!

Shrinking the life of her   into one room   like a coffin

Rooms and rooms like this   I lie on the quilt and hear them talk

Please, Mrs. Orator-without-Breath.

Once you went for coffee   I walked   I saw A Balzac   a Chekhov to write it   Rummage Alone On scraps

Better old here than in the old country!

On scraps   Yet they sang like   like   Wondrous! *Humankind one has to believe*   So strong for what? To rot   not grow?

Your poor lungs beg you. They sob between each word.

Singing. Unused   the life in them.   She   in this poor room   with her   pictures   Max   You   The children   Everywhere   unused   the life   And who has meaning?   Century after century   still all in us   not   to grow?

Coffins, rummage, plants: sick woman. Oh lay down. We will get for you the doctor.

"And when will it end. Oh, *the end.*" *That* nightmare thought, and this time she writhed, crumpled against him, seized his hand (for a moment again the weight, the soft distant roaring of humanity) and on the strangled-for breath, begged: "Man . . . we'll destroy ourselves?"

And looking for answer—in the helpless pity and fear for her (for *her*) that distorted his face—she understood the last months, and knew that she was dying.

4

"Let us go home," she said after several days.

"You are in training for a cross-country run? That is why you do not even walk across the room? Here, like a prescription Phil said, till you are stronger from the operation. You want to break doctor's orders?"

She saw the fiction was necessary to him, was silent; then: "At home I will get better. If the doctor here says?"

"And winter? And the visits to Lennie and to Clara? All right," for he saw the tears in her eyes, "I will write Phil, and talk to the doctor."

Days passed. He reported nothing. Jeannie came and took her out for air, past the boarded concessions, the hooded and tented amusement rides, to the end of the pier. They watched the spent waves feed the new, the gulls in the clouded sky; even up where they sat, the windblown sand stung.

She did not ask to go down the crooked steps to the sea.

Back in her bed, while he was gone to the store, she said:

"Jeannie, this doctor, he is not one I can ask questions. Ask him for me, can I go home?"

Jeannie looked at her, said quickly: "Of course, poor Granny, you want your own things around you, don't you? I'll call him tonight . . . Look, I've something to show you," and from her purse unwrapped a large cookie, intricately shaped like a little girl. "Look at the curls—can you hear me well, Granny?—and the darling eyelashes. I just came from a house where they were baking them."

"The dimples, there in the knees," she marveled, holding it to the better light, turning, studying, "like art. Each singly they cut, or a mold?"

"Singly," said Jeannie, "and if it is a child only the mother can make them. O Granny, it's the likeness of a real little girl who died yesterday—Rosita. She was three years old. *Pan del Muerto,* the Bread of the Dead. It was the custom in the part of Mexico they came from."

Still she turned and inspected. "Look, the hollow in the throat, the little cross necklace . . . I think for the mother it is a good thing to be busy with such bread. You know the family?"

Jeannie nodded. "On my rounds. I nursed . . . O Granny, it is like a party; they play songs she liked to dance to. The coffin is lined with pink velvet and she wears a white dress. There are candles . . ."

"In the house?" Surprised, "They keep her in the house?"

"Yes," said Jeannie, "and it is against the health law. I think she is . . . prepared there. The father said it will be sad to bury her in this country; in Oaxaca they have a feast night with candles each year; everyone picnics on the graves of those they loved until dawn."

"Yes Jeannie, the living must comfort themselves." And closed her eyes.

"You want to sleep, Granny?"

"Yes, tired from the pleasure of you. I may keep the Rosita? There stand it, on the dresser, where I can see; something of my own around me."

In the kitchenette, helping her grandfather unpack the groceries, Jeannie said in her light voice:

"I'm resigning my job, Granddaddy."

"Ah, the lucky young man. Which one is he?"

"Too late. You're spoken for." She made a pyramid of cans, unstacked, and built again.

"Something is wrong with the job?"

"With me. I can't be"—she searched for the word—"what they call professional enough. I let myself feel things. And tomorrow I have to report a family . . ." The cans clicked again. "It's not that, either. I just don't know what I want to do, maybe go back to school, maybe go to art school. I thought if you went to San Francisco I'd come along and talk it over with Mommy and Daddy. But I don't see how you can go. She wants to go home. She asked me to ask the doctor."

The doctor told her himself. "Next week you may travel, when you are a little stronger." But next week there was the fever of an infection, and by the time that was over, she could not leave the bed—a rented hospital bed that stood beside the double bed he slept in alone now.

Outwardly the days repeated themselves. Every other afternoon and evening he went out to his new-found cronies, to talk and play cards. Twice a week, Mrs. Mays came. And the rest of the time, Jeannie was there.

By the sickbed stood Jeannie's FM radio. Often into the room the shapes of music came. She would lie curled on her side, her knees drawn up, intense in listening (Jeannie sketched her so, coiled, convoluted like an ear), then thresh her hand out and abruptly snap the radio mute—still to lie in her attitude of listening, concealing tears.

Once Jeannie brought in a young Marine to visit, a friend from high-school days she had found wandering near the empty pier. Because Jeannie asked him to, gravely, without self-consciousness, he sat himself cross-legged on the floor and performed for them a dance of his native Samoa.

Long after they left, a tiny thrumming sound could be heard where, in her bed, she strove to repeat the beckon, flight, surrender of his hands, the fluttering footbeats, and his low plaintive calls.

Hannah and Phil sent flowers. To deepen her pleasure, he placed one in her hair. "Like a girl," he said, and brought the hand mirror so she could see. She looked at the pulsing red flower, the yellow skull face; a desolate, excited laugh shuddered from her, and she pushed the mirror away—but let the flower burn.

The week Lennie and Helen came, the fever returned. With it the excited laugh, and incessant words. She, who in her life had spoken but seldom and then only when necessary (never having learned the easy, social uses of words), now in dying, spoke incessantly.

In a half-whisper: "Like Lisa she is, your Jeannie. Have I told you of Lisa, she who taught me to read? Of the high-born she was, but noble in herself. I was sixteen; they beat me; my father beat me so I would not go to her. It was for-bidden, she was a Tolstoyan. At night, past dogs that howled, terrible dogs, my son, in the snows of winter to the road, I to ride in her carriage like a lady, to books. To her, life was holy, knowledge was holy, and she taught me to read. They hung her. Everything that happens one must try to under-stand why. She killed one who betrayed many. Because of betrayal, betrayed all she lived and believed. In one minute she killed, before my eyes (there is so much blood in a human being, my son), in prison with me. All that happens, one must try to understand.

"The name?" Her lips would work. "The name that was their pole star; the doors of the death houses fixed to open on it; I read of it my year of penal servitude. Thuban!" very excited, "Thuban, in ancient Egypt the pole star. Can you see, look out to see it, Jeannie, if it swings around *our* pole star that seems to *us* not to move.

"Yes, Jeannie, at your age my mother and grandmother had already buried children . . . yes, Jeannie, it is more than oceans between Olshana and you . . . yes, Jeannie, they danced, and for all the bodies they had they might as well be chickens, and indeed, they scratched and flapped their arms and hopped.

"And Andrei Yefimitch, who for twenty years had never known of it and never wanted to know, said as if he wanted to cry: but why my dear friend this malicious laughter?" Telling to herself half-memorized phrases from her few books. "Pain I answer with tears and cries, baseness with indignation, meanness with repulsion . . . for life may be hated or wearied of, but never despised."

Delirious: "Tell me, my neighbor, Mrs. Mays, the pictures never lived, but what of the flowers? Tell them who ask: no rabbis, no ministers, no priests, no speeches, no ceremonies: ah, false—let the living comfort themselves. Tell Sammy's boy, he who flies, tell him to go to Stuttgart and see where Davy has no grave. And what?" A conspirator's laugh. "And what? where millions have no graves—save air."

In delirium or not, wanting the radio on; not seeming to listen, the words still jetting, wanting the music on. Once, silencing it abruptly as of old, she began to cry, unconcealed tears this time. "You have pain, Granny?" Jeannie asked.

"The music," she said, "still it is there and we do not hear; knocks, and our poor human ears too weak. What else, what else we do not hear?"

Once she knocked his hand aside as he gave her a pill, swept the bottles from her bedside table: "no pills, let me feel what I feel," and laughed as on his hands and knees he groped to pick them up.

Nighttimes her hand reached across the bed to hold his.

A constant retching began. Her breath was too faint for sustained speech now, but still the lips moved:

When no longer necessary   to injure others
Pick   pick pick   Blind chicken
As a human being   responsibility for

"David!" imperious, "Basin!" and she would vomit, rinse her mouth, the wasted throat working to swallow, and begin the chant again.

She will be better off in the hospital now, the doctor said.

He sent the telegrams to the children, was packing her suitcase, when her hoarse voice startled. She had roused, was pulling herself to sitting.

"Where now?" she asked. "Where now do you drag me?"

"You do not even have to have a baby to go this time," he soothed, looking for the brush to pack. "Remember, after Davy you told me—worthy to have a baby for the pleasure of the rest in the hospital?"

"Where now? Not home yet?" Her voice mourned. "Where *is* my home?"

He rose to ease her back. "The doctor, the hospital," he started to explain, but deftly, like a snake, she had slithered out of bed and stood swaying, propped behind the night table.

"Coward," she hissed, "runner."

"You stand," he said senselessly.

"To take me there and run. Afraid of a little vomit."

He reached her as she fell. She struggled against him, half slipped from his arms, pulled herself up again.

"Weakling," she taunted, "to leave me there and run. Betrayer. All your life you have run."

He sobbed, telling Jeannie. "A Marilyn Monroe to run for her virtue. Fifty-nine pounds she weighs, the doctor said, and she beats at me like a Dempsey. Betrayer, she cries, and I running like a dog when she calls; day and night, running to her, her vomit, the bedpan . . ."

"She wants you, Granddaddy," said Jeannie. "Isn't that what they call love? I'll see if she sleeps, and if she does, poor worn-out darling, we'll have a party, you and I; I brought us rum babas."

They did not move her. By her bed now stood the tall hooked pillar that held the solutions—blood and dextrose—to feed her veins. Jeannie moved down the hall to take over the sickroom, her face so radiant, her grandfather asked her once: "you are in love?" (Shameful the joy, the pure overwhelming joy from being with her grandmother; the peace, the serenity that breathed.) "My darling escape," she answered incoherently, "my darling Granny"—as if that explained.

Now one by one the children came, those that were able. Hannah, Paul, Sammy. Too late to ask: and what did you learn with your living, Mother, and what do we need to know?

Clara, the eldest, clenched:

Pay me back, Mother, pay me back for all you took from me. Those others you crowded into your heart. The hands I needed to be for you, the heaviness, the responsibility.
Is this she? Noises the dying make, the crablike hands crawling over the covers. The ethereal singing.
She hears that music, that singing from childhood; forgotten sound—not heard since, since . . . And the hardness breaks like a cry: Where did we lose each other, first mother, singing mother?
Annulled: the quarrels, the gibing, the harshness between; the fall into silence and the withdrawal.
I do not know you, Mother. Mother, I never knew you.

Lennie, suffering not alone for her who was dying, but for that in her which never lived (for that which in him might never live). From him too, unspoken words: *good-by mother who taught me to mother myself*.

Not Vivi, who must stay with her children; not Davy, but he is already here, having to die again with *her* this time, for the living take their dead with them when they die.

Light she grew, like a bird, and, like a bird, sound bubbled in her throat while the body fluttered in agony. Night and day, asleep or awake (though indeed there was no difference now) the songs and the phrases leaping.

And he, who had once dreaded a long dying (from fear of himself, from horror of the dwindling money) now desired her quick death profoundly, for *her* sake. He no longer went out, except when Jeannie forced him; no longer laughed, except when, in the bright kitchenette, Jeannie coaxed his laughter (and she, who seemed to hear nothing else, would laugh too, conspiratorial wisps of laughter).

Light, like a bird, the fluttering body, the little claw hands. the beaked shadow on her face; and the throat, bubbling, straining:

He tried not to listen, as he tried not to look on the face in which only the forehead remained familiar, but trapped with her the long nights in that little room, the sounds worked themselves into his consciousness, with their punctuation of death swallows, whimpers, gurglings.

Even in reality (swallow) *life's lack of it*
The bell   Summon   what ennobles
78,000 in one minute (whisper of a scream) *78,000 human beings   we'll destroy ourselves?*

"Aah, Mrs. Miserable," he said, as if she could hear, "all your life working, and now in bed you lie, servants to tend, you do not even need to call to be tended, and still you work. Such hard work it is to die? Such hard work?"

The body threshed, her hand clung in his. A melody, ghost-thin, hovered on her lips, and like a guilty ghost, the vision of her bent in listening to it, silencing the record instantly he was near. Now, heedless of his presence, she floated the melody on and on.

"Hid it from me," he complained, "how many times you listened to remember it so?" And tried to think when she had first played it, or first begun to silence her few records when he came near—but could reconstruct nothing. There was only this room with its tall hooked pillar and its swarm of sounds.

No man one   except through others
Strong with the not yet in the now
Dogma dead war dead one country

"It helps, Mrs. Philosopher, words from books? It helps?" And it seemed to him that for seventy years she had hidden a tape recorder, infinitely microscopic, within her, that it had coiled infinite mile on mile, trapping every song, every melody, every word read, heard and spoken—and that maliciously she was playing back only what said nothing of him, of the children, of their intimate life together.

"Left us indeed, Mrs. Babbler," he reproached, "you who called others babbler and cunningly saved your words. A lifetime you tended and loved, and now not a word of us, for us. Left us indeed? Left me."

And he took out his solitaire deck, shuffled the cards loudly, slapped them down.

Lift high   banner of reason (tatter of an orator's voice)
justice   freedom   light
   Humankind   life worthy   capacities
Seeks (blur of shudder) *belong   human being*

"Words, words," he accused, "and what human beings did *you* seek around you, Mrs. Live Alone, and what mankind think worthy?"

Though even as he spoke, he remembered she had not always been isolated, had not always wanted to be alone (as he knew there had been a voice before this gossamer one; before the hoarse voice that broke from silence to lash, make incidents, shame him—a girl's voice of eloquence that spoke their holiest dreams). But again he could reconstruct, image, nothing of what had been before, or when, or how, it had changed.

Ace, queen, jack. The pillar shadow fell, so, in two tracks; in the mirror depths glistened a moonlike blob, the empty solution bottle. And it worked in him: *of reason and justice and freedom. Dogma dead:* he remembered the quotation, laughed bitterly. "Hah, good you do not know what you say; good Victor Hugo died and did not see it, his twentieth century."

Deuce, ten, five. Dauntlessly she began a song of their youth of belief:

These things shall be, a loftier race
than e'er the world hath known shall rise
with flame of freedom in their souls
and light of knowledge in their eyes

King, four, jack. "In the twentieth century, hah!"

They shall be gentle, brave and strong
to spill no drop of blood, but dare
all . . .
on earth and fire and sea and air

"To spill no drop of blood, hah! So, cadaver, and you too, cadaver Hugo, 'in the twentieth century ignorance will be dead, dogma will be dead, war will be dead, and for all mankind one country—of fulfillment?' Hah!"

And every life (long strangling cough) *shall*
     be a song

The cards fell from his fingers. Without warning, the bereavement and betrayal he had sheltered—compounded through the years—hidden even from himself—revealed itself,
     uncoiled,
     released,
     sprung
and with it the monstrous shapes of what had actually happened in the century.

A ravening hunger or thirst seized him. He groped into the kitchenette, switched on all three lights, piled a tray—"you have finished your night snack, Mrs. Cadaver, now I will have mine." And he was shocked at the tears that splashed on the tray.

"Salt tears. For free. I forgot to shake on salt?"

Whispered: "Lost, how much I lost."

Escaped to the grandchildren whose childhoods were childish, who had never hungered, who lived unravaged by disease in warm houses of many rooms, had all the school for which they cared, could walk on any street, stood a head taller than their grandparents, towered above—beautiful skins, straight backs, clear straightforward eyes. "Yes, you in Olshana," he said to the town of sixty years ago, "they would be nobility to you."

And was this not the dream then, come true in ways undreamed? he asked.

And are there no other children in the world? he answered, as if in her harsh voice.

And the flame of freedom, the light of knowledge?
And the drop, to spill no drop of blood?

And he thought that at six Jeannie would get up and it would be his turn to go to her room and sleep, that he could press the buzzer and she would come now; that in the afternoon Ellen Mays was coming, and this time they would play cards and he could marvel at how rouge can stand half an inch on the cheek; that in the evening the doctor would come, and he could beg him to be merciful, to stop the feeding solutions, to let her die.

To let her die, and with her their youth of belief out of which her bright, betrayed words foamed; stained words, that on her working lips came stainless.

Hours yet before Jeannie's turn. He could press the buzzer and wake her to come now; he could take a pill, and with it sleep; he could pour more brandy into his milk glass, though what he had poured was not yet touched.

Instead he went back, checked her pulse, gently tended with his knotty fingers as Jeannie had taught.

She was whimpering; her hand crawled across the covers for his. Compassionately he enfolded it, and with his free hand gathered up the cards again. Still was there thirst or hunger ravening in him.

That world of their youth—dark, ignorant, terrible with hate and disease—how was it that living in it, in the midst of corruption, filth, treachery, degradation, they had not mistrusted man nor themselves; had believed so beautifully, so . . . falsely?

"Aaah, children," he said out loud, "how we believed, how we belonged." And he yearned to package for each of the children, the grandchildren, for everyone, *that joyous certainty, that sense of mattering, of moving and being moved, of being one and indivisible with the great of the past, with all that freed, ennobled.* Package it, stand on corners, in front of stadiums and on crowded beaches, knock on doors, give it as a fabled gift.

"And why not in cereal boxes, in soap packages?" he mocked himself. "Aah. You have taken my senses, cadaver."

Words foamed, died unsounded. Her body writhed; she

made kissing motions with her mouth. (Her lips moving as she read, poring over the Book of the Martyrs, the magnifying glass superimposed over the heavy eyeglasses.) *Still she believed?* "Eva!" he whispered. "Still you believed? You lived by it? These Things Shall Be?"

"One pound soup meat," she answered distinctly, "one soup bone."

"My ears heard you. Ellen Mays was witness: 'Humankind . . . one has to believe.'" Imploringly: "Eva!"

"Bread, day-old." She was mumbling. "Please, in a wooden box . . . for kindling. The thread, hah, the thread breaks. Cheap thread"—and a gurgling, enormously loud, began in her throat.

"I ask for stone; she gives me bread—day-old." He pulled his hand away, shouted: "Who wanted questions? Everything you have to wake?" Then dully, "Ah, let me help you turn, poor creature."

Words jumbled, cleared. In a voice of crowded terror:

"Paul, Sammy, don't fight.

"Hannah, have I ten hands?"

"How can I give it, Clara, how can I give it if I don't have?"

"You lie," he said sturdily, "there was joy too." Bitterly: "Ah how cheap you speak of us at the last."

As if to rebuke him, as if her voice had no relationship with her flailing body, she sang clearly, beautifully, a school song the children had taught her when they were little; begged:

"Not look   my hair   where they cut . . ."

(The crown of braids shorn.) And instantly he left the mute old woman poring over the Book of the Martyrs; went past the mother treadling at the sewing machine, singing with the children; past the girl in her wrinkled prison dress, hiding her hair with scarred hands, lifting to him her awkward, shamed, imploring eyes of love; and took her in his arms, dear, personal, fleshed, in all the heavy passion he had loved to rouse from her.

"Eva!"

Her little claw hand beat the covers. How much, how much can a man stand? He took up the cards, put them down, circled the beds, walked to the dresser, opened, shut drawers, brushed his hair, moved his hand bit by bit over the mirror to see what of the reflection he could blot out with each move, and felt that at any moment he would die of what was unendurable. Went to press the buzzer to wake Jeannie, looked down, saw on Jeannie's sketch pad the hospital bed, with *her;* the double bed alongside, with him; the tall pillar feeding into her veins, and their hands, his and hers, clasped, feeding each other. And as if he had been instructed he went to his bed, lay down, holding the sketch as if it could shield against the monstrous shapes of loss, of betrayal, of death—and with his free hand took hers back into his.

So Jeannie found them in the morning.

That last day the agony was perpetual. Time after time it lifted her almost off the bed, so they had to fight to hold her down. He could not endure and left the room; wept as if there never would be tears enough.

Jeannie came to comfort him. In her light voice she said: Granddaddy, Granddaddy don't cry. She is not there, she promised me. On the last day, she said she would go back to when she first heard music, a little girl on the road of the village where she was born. She promised me. It is a wedding and they dance, while the flutes so joyous and vibrant tremble in the air. Leave her there, Granddaddy, it is all right. She promised me. Come back, come back and help her poor body to die.

For two of that generation
Seevya and Genya
Infinite, dauntless, incorruptible.

Death deepens the wonder

My Father Sits in the Dark

Jerome Weidman

My father has a peculiar habit. He is fond of sitting in the dark, alone. Sometimes I come home very late. The house is dark. I let myself in quietly because I do not want to disturb my mother. She is a light sleeper. I tiptoe into my room and undress in the dark. I go to the kitchen for a drink of water. My bare feet make no noise. I step into the room and almost trip over my father. He is sitting in a kitchen chair, in his pajamas, smoking his pipe.

"Hello, Pop," I say.

"Hello, son."

"Why don't you go to bed, Pa?"

"I will," he says.

But he remains there. Long after I am asleep I feel sure that he is still sitting there, smoking.

Many times I am reading in my room. I hear my mother get the house ready for the night. I hear my kid brother go to bed. I hear my sister come in. I hear her do things with jars and combs until she, too, is quiet. I know she has gone to sleep. In a little while I hear my mother say good night to my father. I continue to read. Soon I become thirsty. (I drink a lot of water.) I go to the kitchen for a drink. Again I almost stumble across my father. Many times it startles me. I forget about him. And there he is—smoking, sitting, thinking.

"Why don't you go to bed, Pop?"

"I will, son."

But he doesn't. He just sits there and smokes and thinks. It worries me. I can't understand it. What can he be thinking about? Once I asked him.

"What are you thinking about, Pa?"

"Nothing," he said.

Once I left him there and went to bed. I awoke several hours later. I was thirsty. I went to the kitchen. There he was. His pipe was out. But he sat there, staring into a corner of the kitchen. After a moment I became accustomed to the darkness. I took my drink. He still sat and stared. His eyes did not blink. I thought he was not even aware of me. I was afraid.

"Why don't you go to bed, Pop?"

"I will, son," he said. "Don't wait up for me."

"But," I said, "you've been sitting here for hours. What's wrong? What are you thinking about?"

"Nothing, son," he said. "Nothing. It's just restful. That's all."

The way he said it was convincing. He did not seem worried. His voice was even and pleasant. It always is. But I could not understand it. How could it be restful to sit alone in an uncomfortable chair far into the night, in darkness?

What can it be?

I review all the possibilities. It can't be money. I know that. We haven't much, but when he is worried about money he makes no secret of it. It can't be his health. He is not reticent about that either. It can't be the health of anyone in the family. We are a bit short on money, but we are long on health. (Knock wood, my mother would say.) What can it be? I am afraid I do not know. But that does not stop me from worrying.

Maybe he is thinking of his brothers in the old country. Or of his mother and two step-mothers. Or of his father. But they are all dead. And he would not brood about them like that. I say brood, but it is not really true. He does not brood. He does not even seem to be thinking. He looks too peaceful, too, well not contented, just too peaceful, to be brooding. Perhaps it is as he says. Perhaps it is restful. But it does not seem possible. It worries me.

If I only knew what he thinks about. If I only knew that he thinks at all. I might not be able to help him. He might not even need help. It may be as he says. It may be restful. But at least I would not worry about it.

Why does he just sit there, in the dark? Is his mind failing? No, it can't be. He is only fifty-three. And he is just as keen-witted as ever. In fact, he is the same in every respect. He still likes beet soup. He still reads the second section of the *Times* first. He still wears wing collars. He still believes that Debs could have saved the country and that T.R. was a tool of the moneyed interests. He is the same in every way. He does not even look older than he did five years ago. Everybody remarks about that. Well-preserved, they say. But he sits in the dark, alone, smoking, staring straight ahead of him, unblinking, into the small hours of the night.

If it is as he says, if it is restful, I will let it go at that. But suppose it is not. Suppose it is something I cannot fathom. Perhaps he needs help. Why doesn't he speak? Why doesn't he frown or laugh or cry? Why doesn't he do something? Why does he just sit there?

Finally I become angry. Maybe it is just my unsatisfied curiosity. Maybe I *am* a bit worried. Anyway, I become angry.

"Is something wrong, Pop?"

"Nothing, son. Nothing at all."

But this time I am determined not to be put off. I am angry.

"Then why do you sit here all alone, thinking, till late?"

"It's restful, son. I like it."

I am getting nowhere. Tomorrow he will be sitting there again. I will be puzzled. I will be worried. I will not stop now. I am angry.

"Well, what do you *think* about, Pa? Why do you just sit here? What's worrying you? What do you think about?"

"Nothing's worrying me, son. I'm all right. It's just restful. That's all. Go to bed, son."

My anger has left me. But the feeling of worry is still there. I must get an answer. It seems so silly. Why doesn't he tell me? I have a funny feeling that unless I get an answer I will go crazy. I am insistent.

"But what do you *think* about, Pa? What is it?"

"Nothing, son. Just things in general. Nothing special. Just things."

I can get no answer.

It is very late. The street is quiet and the house is dark. I climb the steps softly, skipping the ones that creak. I let myself in with my key and tiptoe into my room. I remove my clothes and remember that I am thirsty. In my bare feet I walk to the kitchen. Before I reach it I know he is there.

I can see the deeper darkness of his hunched shape. He is sitting in the same chair, his elbows on his knees, his cold pipe in his teeth, his unblinking eyes staring straight ahead. He does not seem to know I am there. He did not hear me come in. I stand quietly in the doorway and watch him.

Everything is quiet, but the night is full of little sounds. As I stand there motionless I begin to notice them. The ticking of the alarm clock on the icebox. The low hum of an automobile passing many blocks away. The swish of papers moved along the street by the breeze. A whispering rise and fall of sound, like low breathing. It is strangely pleasant.

The dryness in my throat reminds me. I step briskly into the kitchen.

"Hello, Pop," I say.

"Hello, son," he says. His voice is low and dream-like. He does not change his position or shift his gaze.

I cannot find the faucet. The dim shadow of light that comes through the window from the street lamp only makes the room seem darker. I reach for the short chain in the center of the room. I snap on the light.

He straightens up with a jerk, as though he has been struck. "What's the matter, Pop?" I ask.

"Nothing," he says. "I don't like the light."

"What's the matter with the light?" I say. "What's wrong?"

"Nothing," he says. "I don't like the light."

I snap the light off. I drink my water slowly. I must take it easy, I say to myself. I must get to the bottom of this.

"Why don't you go to bed? Why do you sit here so late in the dark?"

"It's nice," he says. "I can't get used to lights. We didn't have lights when I was a boy in Europe."

My heart skips a beat and I catch my breath happily. I begin to think I understand. I remember the stories of his boyhood in Austria. I see the wide-beamed *kretchma*, with my grandfather behind the bar. It is late, the customers are gone, and he is dozing. I see the bed of glowing coals, the last of the roaring fire. The room is already dark, and growing darker. I see a small boy, crouched on a pile of twigs at one side of the huge fireplace, his starry gaze fixed on the dull remains of the dead flames. The boy is my father.

I remember the pleasure of those few moments while I stood quietly in the doorway watching him.

"You mean there's nothing wrong? You just sit in the dark because you like it, Pop?" I find it hard to keep my voice from rising in a happy shout.

"Sure," he says. "I can't think with the light on."

I set my glass down and turn to go back to my room. "Good night, Pop," I say.

"Good night," he says.

Then I remember. I turn back. "What do you think about, Pop?" I ask.

His voice seems to come from far away. It is quiet and even again. "Nothing," he says softly. "Nothing special."

What Happens Next?

An Uncompleted Investigation

Gilbert Rogin

I tell my father of my intention to write about him, and that I expect him to hold still for an interview.

"You'll have to hurry, Julian," he says.

Uh-oh, he's back with death again.

"You're only sixty-nine," I say.

"Mother and I are going on a cruise the eighteenth instant," he says, delving into his pocket and handing me a carbon of his itinerary done on onionskin.

When I complain it is too faint to make out, he says I never even send them a postcard.

I fear he will die at sea and, wrapped in the flag he loves, be tipped over the rail between one illegible island and another.

We are sitting in the Park by the shuffleboard courts. I detect that my father has been imperceptibly turning, like an hour hand, in order that the sun's rays might smite him flush on the forehead.

I ask, "Do you think we look at all alike?"

"You have the stronger chin," he says. "If you'd only stand up straight. Would you like me to run through my life?"

I ceremoniously open my notebook.

"I was born in Lutzin, in Latvia," he says. "It has another name now. I have four memories of this little town. The first is walking with somebody by a fence behind which gooseberries are growing. I pick several and proceed to eat them, and they are like nectar. My second memory is it is a very cold winter's day. I have done something or other. I am being kept in. Am I being punished? I recall my mother coming, covered in shawls. My third memory is that I am at my grandfather's house. Behind his bench—he is a cobbler—is a high window. I walk through it into a garden, in which tall sunflowers are growing, from which I pick the seeds—"

"If they are tall, how can you reach the seeds?" I ask.

"How can I?" he says. "I forget my fourth memory. I knew it last year, I feel certain. I have five memories of coming to America. My first memory is the train to Libau stopping in a forest and my sister getting off, for a reason which escapes me. I don't see her get on, and when the train starts I am worried that she has been left behind. My second memory occurs in Liverpool, where I see a sign advertising oranges nine for a penny—"

"But surely you can't read English?"

"I am afraid I am mistaken then," he says. "My third memory is having a little playmate on the ship, and my impression that he is going back to Europe at the same time I am going to America. My fourth memory is riding away from Castle Garden in an open cart. It is my sixth birthday. In the streets are innumerable shouting people, and I believe they have all gathered to celebrate my birthday."

"But they are calling you 'greenhorn' and so forth," I say.

"I am inclined to agree," he says.

I am leaning against my father's shoulder, and he has his arm about me.

"Why haven't you told me the fifth memory?" I ask.

"I did," he says, "but you had fallen asleep."

Several days later, I call my father up and ask him if I may continue the interview.

"Was that good stuff I gave you?" he asks.

I assure him it was. I suspect he is in the foyer, in his voluminous pajamas; above his bowed head is an engraving of the Bridge of Sighs. If I don't ask my questions at once, he'll miss the eleven-o'clock news, which is the last news broadcast he listens to—but I falter.

He prompts me: "Do you want me to go on in the same vein?"

"Today I would appreciate it if you would tell me how you regard yourself."

"I am inclined to be roguish," he says.

"No baloney," I say.

"You don't know me in my extra-parental guise," he says. "I'm quick at repartee. I'm known for that. I have a way with language. I've developed a capacity in English superior to most of my circle—a wider vocabulary, an easier flow. On a couple of occasions, fellow-attorneys have asked me, 'Are you a Harvard man?' Are you in fact putting down everything I say?"

"I am, but I'm going to change it."

"But who could possibly be interested?"

"That's not the point."

"My life is inherently ordinary."

"I didn't marry a nobody." This is my mother speaking.

"She listens on the extension," says my father.

She is unlit rooms away, in her bed; upon the headboard are painted roses.

"I won't interrupt further," she says, "but I just want to say that once, in a corridor of the New York County Courthouse, an attorney of no small repute stopped your father and told him, 'You're a formidable opponent.' That's all I've got to say."

"I can hold my own with most of the boys," my father says. "I know I've done a first-rate job in the representation of people. Lately, however, I don't feel like working as hard as heretofore. You feel like easing up. Only yesterday, emerging from the subway en route to the office, I found myself saying to myself, 'Good God, this is the same pattern.' "

"He is unswerving," says my mother. "Oops. Pardon me."

"I am a well-organized human being," my father says. "Curiously, many years ago, Mother and I were at some seashore, walking along the boardwalk. We met a fellow-stroller —perhaps it was that Mother was acquainted with his wife (sh-h-h, permit me to finish)—who read character. Straight off, he told me I was well organized. I was astonished at the accuracy. No doubt, he divined my nature by the way I was dressed, my phiz."

"I thought I told you we set it up beforehand," my mother says. "It was a joke."

"Is that right?" my father says. "I was on the point of saying that life has gone along in a successful pattern. I have never suffered any deprivation. Mother hasn't been denied anything to think of."

"A house in the country," says my mother.

"I have accumulated reserves, which is a great comfort," my father goes on. "Furthermore—"

"Lawns."

"—I think I've been a worthwhile member of society in that—"

"A flower garden."

"—I haven't solely devoted myself to my own affairs—"

"Badminton."

My mother, much younger, stands on one foot like Mercury, her racket raised. A hit? A miss? Presumably, my father is on the other side of the net; at least, I imagine it is he whom I hear chuckling in the dusk.

"—and well-being. I've done something to justify my place as a human being. As I look it over, I find my life has been a rewarding one. I'm satisfied, or, more precisely, I'm not dissatisfied."

"What he's trying to say is that he's not greedy," says my mother.

"I'm an amiable person," says my father.

"He thinks the cup's half full; I think it's half empty."

"You're a gloomy romantic," says my father.

"I'm unrealistic. He keeps me realistic. He doesn't allow me to express myself."

"Ah," says my father.

"You see," says my mother.

"I've missed the news," says my father.

"Don't blame me," I say.

"You may blame me, if you wish," my mother says.

In a while, we hang up. I imagine my father feeling his way along the dark, crooked halls to the bedroom and getting into his bed next to my mother's. They pull the little beaded chains that turn out their lights and, as is their habit, shake hands across the abyss that separates their beds.

I write my father a letter at sea:

Dear Dad:

Here are some more questions:

1. Are you obedient to a moral code?

2. Do you dream? If so, how much? Are your dreams disquieting? Do they have any great themes?

3. When was the last time you shed tears?

4. What do you regret?

5. What are the kindest words a stranger ever addressed to you?

6. Eight years ago last December, I am nearly positive I saw you at the bar of the Woodstock in the company of a

woman wearing a black suit, whose partly revealed bosom you were steadfastly regarding. Please comment.

Love,
Julian

My father's reply, postmarked Fort-de-France, Martinique, reaches me two days after my parents' return:

Dear Son:

In re your queries:

1. I believe in a world of law, but I realize man's infirmities. I dislike ruthlessness, unkindness, and dishonesty. What I do, I do to the utmost of my ability. I am considerate within limits. Never regard me as a paragon.

2. I dream incessantly. The majority of my dreams are peaceable, and they are mostly topical.

3. I don't usually surrender to emotions. The last occasion on which I wept must have been in a movie house.

4. The few times I spanked you, I felt so guilty. It was cruel, and I have never got rid of this great sense of remorse.

5. Once, on a flight from Indianapolis, where I had gone to address a meeting of United Cerebral Palsy, I sat next to a six-year-old boy, with whom I had a conversation. Luncheon was served, and I cut up his chicken for him. When we parted at the airport, this little shaver said to me, "You're a good man, Mr. Stinger." (You notice he didn't get our name quite right. Don't you think that made it all the more affecting? Mother, who has good instincts, doesn't.)

6. I have never been in the Hotel Woodstock.

Love,
Dad

P.S. Thanks for the mystery. Alas, I find I no longer care who kills whom, much less why.

P.P.S. Did I ever tell you that my father, whom you never met, wrote, too? I don't know what, but I think it was poetry. Otherwise, you are dissimilar. You were hovered over during the first part of your life, and have all the stigmata of the artist: essentially self-centered, forbidding, a nonconformist. You were not a friendly child, and smiled rarely, but when you did it lit up your face so. My father was a very decent, gentle, literate human being who was ground down by economic pressures. He was slightly built and never considered strong, but I remember him carrying me in his arms when I fell in the wagon shop on Cherry Street.

My father sits in his undershirt, his head in the sink. My mother stands above him, washing his long, distinguished white hair. I lounge against the tiles, taking notes. Oh, boy, this is it.

My mother, rubbing the steam off the medicine-cabinet mirror, discovers me at work.

"I thought you were done with him weeks ago," she says.

"I've dreamed up some more questions," I say.

"He's at it again," my mother says in my father's ear, over the running water.

"Who's at what?"

"Julian's here, gathering material for his biography."

"It's not going to be true," I say.

"Enunciate," says my father.

"Oh," says my mother.

"First of all, may I ask you what sort of a marriage you two have had?" I shout.

"Beautiful," my father mutters from the depths of the sink.

"But you're entirely different."

"Compromise," my father says.

"For your father I forsook my career on the legitimate stage," my mother says.

"I've developed a great tolerance and understanding," my father says.

"I've found out how to deal with him, too," my mother says, gently pushing my father's face underwater. I hear him gurgling and sputtering.

"What's he saying, Ma?"

"That he's always loved me, that he'll love me till the day he dies," she says, letting go.

It is 11:20 P.M., the news is over, and the lights are extinguished. My mother and father lie in their beds, the covers up to their chins. I am sitting in the dark at my father's feet.

"Dad," I am saying, "remember when you used to push me in my stroller along the river and sing to me about the crocodile? How did it go?"

My father makes no reply.

"He must be in dreamland," my mother says. "Has he told you about the time I was appearing in *Aloma of the South Seas* and he waited for me every night at the stage door, even when it was raining? Once, he gave me a spray of little green orchids."

My father sings faintly.

"Croc, croc, croc, crocodile . . ."

"Oh, we thought you were fast asleep," my mother says.

"Croc, croc, croc, crocodile,
Swimming in the shining Nile . . ."

Envy; or, Yiddish in America

Cynthia Ozick

Edelshtein, an American for forty years, was a ravenous reader of novels by writers "of"—he said this with a snarl—"Jewish extraction." He found them puerile, vicious, pitiable, ignorant, contemptible, above all stupid. In judging them he dug for his deepest vituperation—they were, he said, *"Amerikaner-geboren."* Spawned in America, pogroms a rumor, *mamaloshen* a stranger, history a vacuum. Also many of them were still young, and had black eyes, black hair, and red beards. A few were blue-eyed, like the *cheder-yinglach* of his youth. Schoolboys. He was certain he did not envy them, but he read them like a sickness. They were reviewed and praised, and meanwhile they were considered Jews, and knew nothing. There was even a body of Gentile writers in reaction, beginning to show familiarly whetted teeth: the Jewish Intellectual Establishment was misrepresenting American letters, coloring it with an alien dye, taking it over, and so forth. Like Berlin and Vienna in the twenties. *Judenrein ist Kulturrein* was Edelshtein's opinion. Take away the Jews and where, O so-called Western Civilization, is your literary culture?

For Edelshtein Western Civilization was a sore point. He had never been to Berlin, Vienna, Paris, or even London. He had been to Kiev, though, but only once, as a young boy. His father, a *melamed*, had traveled there on a tutoring job and had taken him along. In Kiev they lived in the cellar of a big house owned by rich Jews, the Kirilovs. They had been born Katz, but bribed an official in order to Russify their name. Every morning he and his father would go up a green staircase to the kitchen for a breakfast of coffee and stale bread and then into the schoolroom to teach *chumash* to Alexei Kirilov, a red-cheeked little boy. The younger Edelshtein would drill him while his father dozed. What had become of Alexei Kirilov? Edelshtein, a widower in New York, sixty-seven years old, a Yiddishist (so-called), a poet, could stare at anything at all—a subway car-card, a garbage can lid, a streetlight—and cause the return of Alexei Kirilov's face, his bright cheeks, his Ukraine-accented Yiddish, his shelves of mechanical toys from Germany—trucks, cranes, wheel-barrows, little colored autos with awnings overhead. Only Edelshtein's father was expected to call him Alexei—everyone else, including the young Edelshtein, said Avremeleh. Avremeleh had a knack of getting things by heart. He had a golden head. Today he was a citizen of the Soviet Union. Or was he finished, dead, in the ravine at Babi Yar? Edelshtein remembered every coveted screw of the German toys. With his father he left Kiev in the spring and returned to Minsk. The mud, frozen into peaks, was melting. The train carriage reeked of urine and dirt seeped through their shoelaces into their socks.

And the language was lost, murdered. The language—a museum. Of what other language can it be said that it died a sudden and definite death, in a given decade, on a given piece of soil? Where are the speakers of ancient Etruscan? Who was the last man to write a poem in Linear B? Attrition, assimilation. Death by mystery not gas. The last Etruscan walks around inside some Sicilian. Western Civilization, that pod of muck, lingers on and on. The Sick Man of Europe with his big globe-head, rotting, but at home in bed. Yiddish, a littleness, a tiny light—oh little holy light!—dead, vanished. Perished. Sent into darkness.

This was Edelshtein's subject. On this subject he lectured for a living. He swallowed scraps. Synagogues, community centers, labor unions underpaid him to suck on the bones of the dead. Smoke. He traveled from borough to borough, suburb to suburb, mourning in English the death of Yiddish. Sometimes he tried to read one or two of his poems. At the first Yiddish word the painted old ladies of the Reform Temples would begin to titter from shame, as at a stand-up television comedian. Orthodox and Conservative men fell instantly asleep. So he reconsidered, and told jokes:

Before the war there was held a great International Esperanto Convention. It met in Geneva. Esperanto scholars, doctors of letters, learned men, came from all over the world to deliver papers on the genesis, syntax, and functionalism of Esperanto. Some spoke of the social value of an international language, others of its beauty. Every nation on earth was represented among the lecturers. All the papers were given in Esperanto. Finally the meeting was concluded, and the tired great men wandered companionably along the corridors, where at last they began to converse casually among themselves in their international language: *"Nu, vos macht a yid?"*

After the war a funeral cortège was moving slowly down a narrow street on the Lower East Side. The cars had left the parking lot behind the chapel in the Bronx and were on their way to the cemetery in Staten Island. Their route took them past the newspaper offices of the last Yiddish daily left in the city. There were two editors, one to run the papers off the press and the other to look out the window. The one looking out the window saw the funeral procession passing by and called to his colleague: "Hey Mottel, print one less!"

But both Edelshtein and his audiences found the jokes worthless. Old jokes. They were not the right kind. They wanted jokes about weddings—spiral staircases, doves flying out of cages, bashful medical students—and he gave them funerals. To speak of Yiddish was to preside over a funeral. He was a rabbi who had survived his whole congregation. Those for whom his tongue was no riddle were specters.

The new Temples scared Edelshtein. He was afraid to use the word *shul* in these palaces—inside, vast mock-bronze Tablets, mobiles of oustretched hands rotating on a motor, gigantic dangling Tetragrammatons in transparent plastic like chandeliers, platforms, altars, daises, pulpits, aisles, pews, polished-oak bins for prayerbooks printed in English with made-up new prayers in them. Everything smelled of wet plaster. Everything was new. The refreshment tables were long and luminous—he saw glazed cakes, snowheaps of egg salad, herring, salmon, tuna, whitefish, gefilte fish, pools of sour cream, silver electric coffee urns, bowls of lemon-slices, pyramids of bread, waferlike teacups from the Black Forest, Indian-brass trays of hard cheeses, golden bottles set up in rows like ninepins, great sculptured butter-birds, Hansel-and-Gretel houses of cream cheese and fruitcake, bars, butlers, fat napery, carpeting deep as honey. He learned their term for their architecture: "soaring." In one place—a flat wall of beige brick in Westchester—he read Scripture riveted on in letters fashioned from 14-karat gold molds: "And thou shalt see My back; but My face shall not be seen." Later that night he

spoke in Mount Vernon, and in the marble lobby afterward
he heard an adolescent girl mimic his inflections. It amazed
him: often he forgot he had an accent. In the train going
back to Manhattan he slid into a miniature jogging doze—it
was a little nest of sweetness there inside the flaps of his overcoat, and he dreamed he was in Kiev, with his father. He
looked through the open schoolroom door at the smoking
cheeks of Alexei Kirilov, eight years old. "Avremeleh," he
called, "Avremeleh, *kum tsu mir, lebst ts' geshtorben?*" He
heard himself yelling in English: Thou shalt see my asshole!
A belch woke him to hot fear. He was afraid he might be,
unknown to himself all his life long, a secret pederast.

He had no children and only a few remote relations (a
druggist cousin in White Plains, a cleaning store in-law hanging on somewhere among the blacks in Brownsville), so he
loitered often in Baumzweig's apartment—dirty mirrors and
rusting crystal, a hazard and invitation to cracks, an abandoned exhausted corridor. Lives had passed through it and
were gone. Watching Baumzweig and his wife—gray-eyed,
sluggish, with a plump Polish nose—it came to him that at
this age, his own and theirs, it was the same having children
or not having them. Baumzweig had two sons, one married
and a professor at San Diego, the other at Stanford, not yet
thirty, in love with his car. The San Diego son had a son.
Sometimes it seemed that it must be in deference to his child-
lessness that Baumzweig and his wife pretended a detachment
from their offspring. The grandson's photo—a fat-lipped blond
child of three or so—was wedged between two wine glasses
on top of the china closet. But then it became plain that they
could not imagine the lives of their children. Nor could the
children imagine their lives. The parents were too helpless to
explain, the sons were too impatient to explain. So they had
given each other up to a common muteness. In that apartment
Josh and Mickey had grown up answering in English the Yiddish of their parents. Mutes. Mutations. What right had these
boys to spit out the Yiddish that had bred them, and only for
the sake of Western Civilization? Edelshtein knew the titles
of their Ph.D. theses: literary boys, one was on Sir Gawain
and the Green Knight, the other was on the novels of Carson
McCullers.

Baumzweig's lethargic wife was intelligent. She told Edelshtein he too had a child, also a son. "Yourself, yourself," she
said. "You remember yourself when you were a little boy,

and *that* little boy is the one you love, *him* you trust, *him* you bless, *him* you bring up in hope to a good manhood." She spoke a rich Yiddish, but high-pitched.

Baumzweig had a good job, a sinecure, a pension in disguise, with an office, a part-time secretary, a typewriter with Hebrew characters, ten-to-three hours. In 1910 a laxative manufacturer—a philanthropist—had founded an organization called the Yiddish-American Alliance for Letters and Social Progress. The original illustrious members were all dead—even the famous poet Yehoash was said to have paid dues for a month or so—but there was a trust providing for the group's continuation, and enough money to pay for a biannual periodical in Yiddish. Baumzweig was the editor of this, but of the Alliance nothing was left, only some crumbling brown snapshots of Jews in derbies. His salary check came from the laxative manufacturer's grandson—a Republican politician, an Episcopalian. The name of the celebrated product was LUKEWARM: it was advertised as delightful to children when dissolved in lukewarm cocoa. The name of the obscure periodical was *Bitterer Yam,* Bitter Sea, but it had so few subscribers that Baumzweig's wife called it Invisible Ink. In it Baumzweig published much of his own poetry and a little of Edelshtein's. Baumzweig wrote mostly of Death, Edelshtein mostly of Love. They were both sentimentalists, but not about each other. They did not like each other, though they were close friends.

Sometimes they read aloud among the dust of empty bowls their newest poems, with an agreement beforehand not to criticize: Paula should be the critic. Carrying coffee back and forth in cloudy glasses, Baumzweig's wife said: "Oh, very nice, very nice. But so sad. Gentlemen, life is not that sad." After this she would always kiss Edelshtein on the forehead, a lazy kiss, often leaving stuck on his eyebrow a crumb of Danish: very slightly she was a slattern.

Edelshtein's friendship with Baumzweig had a ferocious secret: it was moored entirely to their agreed hatred for the man they called *der chazer.* He was named Pig because of his extraordinarily white skin, like a tissue of pale ham, and also because in the last decade he had become unbelievably famous. When they did not call him Pig they called him *shed* —Devil. They also called him Yankee Doodle. His name was Yankel Ostrover, and he was a writer of stories.

They hated him for the amazing thing that had happened

to him—his fame—but this they never referred to. Instead they discussed his style: his Yiddish was impure, his sentences lacked grace and sweep, his paragraph transitions were amateur, vile. Or else they raged against his subject matter which was insanely sexual, pornographic, paranoid, freakish—men who embraced men, women who caressed women, sodomists of every variety, boys copulating with hens, butchers who drank blood for strength behind the knife. All the stories were set in an imaginary Polish village, Zwrdl, and by now there was almost no American literary intellectual alive who had not learned to say Zwrdl when he meant lewd. Ostrover's wife was reputed to be a high-born Polish Gentile woman from the "real" Zwrdl, the daughter in fact of a minor princeling, who did not know a word of Yiddish and read her husband's fiction falteringly, in English translation—but both Edelshtein and Baumzweig had encountered her often enough over the years, at this meeting and that, and regarded her as no more impressive than a pot of stale fish. Her Yiddish had an unpleasant gargling Galician accent, her vocabulary was a thin soup—they joked that it was correct to say she spoke no Yiddish—and she mewed it like a peasant, comparing prices. She was a short square woman, a cube with low-slung udders and a flat backside. It was partly Ostrover's mockery, partly his self-advertising, that had converted her into a little princess. He would make her go into their bedroom to get a whip he claimed she had used on her bay, Romeo, trotting over her father's lands in her girlhood. Baumzweig often said this same whip was applied to the earlobes of Ostrover's translators, unhappy pairs of collaborators he changed from month to month, never satisfied.

Ostrover's glory was exactly in this: that he required translators. Though he wrote only in Yiddish, his fame was American, national, international. They considered him a "modern." Ostrover was free of the prison of Yiddish! Out, out—he had burst out, he was in the world of reality.

And how had he begun? The same as anybody, a columnist for one of the Yiddish dailies, a humorist, a cheap fast article-writer, a squeezer-out of real-life tales. Like anybody else, he saved up a few dollars, put a paper clip over his stories, and hired a Yiddish press to print up a hundred copies. A book. Twenty-five copies he gave to people he counted as relatives, another twenty-five he sent to enemies and rivals, the rest he kept under his bed in the original cartons. Like anybody else, his literary gods were Chekhov and Tolstoy, Peretz and Sholem Aleichem. From this, how did he come to *The New Yorker*, to *Playboy*, to big lecture fees, invitations to Yale and M.I.T. and Vassar, to the Midwest, to Buenos Aires, to a literary agent, to a publisher on Madison Avenue?

"He sleeps with the right translators," Paula said. Edelshtein gave out a whinny. He knew some of Ostrover's translators—a spinster hack in dresses below the knee, occasionally a certain half-mad and drunken lexicographer, college boys with a dictionary.

Thirty years ago, straight out of Poland via Tel Aviv, Ostrover crept into a toying affair with Mireleh, Edelshtein's wife. He had left Palestine during the 1939 Arab riots, not, he said, out of fear, out of integrity rather—it was a country which had turned its face against Yiddish. Yiddish was not honored in Tel Aviv or Jerusalem. In the Negev it was worthless. In the God-given State of Israel they had no use for the language of the bad little interval between Canaan and now. Yiddish was inhabited by the past, the new Jews did not want it. Mireleh liked to hear these anecdotes of how rotten it was in Israel for Yiddish and Yiddishists. In Israel the case was even lamer than in New York, thank God! There was after all a reason to live the life they lived: it was worse somewhere else. Mireleh was a tragedian. She carried herself according to her impression of how a barren woman should sit, squat, stand, eat and sleep, talked constantly of her six miscarriages, and was vindictive about Edelshtein's sperm-count. Ostrover would arrive in the rain, crunch down on the sofa, complain about the transportation from the Bronx to the West Side, and begin to woo Mireleh. He took her out to supper, to his special café, to Second Avenue vaudeville, even home to his apartment near Crotona Park to meet his little princess Pesha. Edelshtein noticed with self-curiosity that he felt no jealousy whatever, but he thought himself obliged to throw a kitchen chair at Ostrover. Ostrover had very fine teeth, his own; the chair knocked off half a lateral incisor, and Edelshtein wept at the flaw. Immediately he led Ostrover to the dentist around the corner.

The two wives, Mireleh and Pesha, seemed to be falling in love: they had dates, they went to museums and movies together, they poked one another and laughed day and night, they shared little privacies, they carried pencil-box rulers in their purses and showed each other certain hilarious measurements, they even became pregnant in the same month. Pesha had her third daughter, Mireleh her seventh miscarriage. Edelshtein was griefstricken but elated. "*My* sperm-count?" he screamed. "*Your* belly! Go fix the machine before you blame the oil!" When the dentist's bill came for Ostrover's jacket crown, Edelshtein sent it to Ostrover. At this injustice Ostrover dismissed Mireleh and forbade Pesha to go anywhere with her ever again.

About Mireleh's affair with Ostrover Edelshtein wrote the following malediction:

> *You, why do you snuff out my sons, my daughters?*
> *Worse than Mother Eve, cursed to break waters*
> *for little ones to float out upon in their tiny barks of skin,*
> *you, merciless one, cannot even bear the fruit of sin.*

It was published to much gossip in *Bitterer Yam* in the spring of that year—one point at issue being whether "snuff out" was the right term in such a watery context. (Baumzweig, a less oblique stylist, had suggested "drown.") The late Zimmerman, Edelshtein's cruelest rival, wrote in a letter to Baumzweig (which Baumzweig read on the telephone to Edelshtein):

> Who is the merciless one, after all, the barren woman who makes the house peaceful with no infantile caterwauling, or the excessively fertile poet who bears the fruit of his sin—namely his untalented verses? He bears it, but who can bear it? In one breath he runs from seas to trees. Like his ancestors the amphibians, puffed up with arrogance. Hersheleh Frog! Why did God give Hersheleh Edelshtein an unfaithful wife? To punish him for writing trash.

Around the same time Ostrover wrote a story: two women loved each other so much they mourned because they could not give birth to one another's children. Both had husbands, one virile and hearty, the other impotent, with a withered organ, a *shlimazal*. They seized the idea of making a tool out of one of the husbands: they agreed to transfer their love for each other into the man, and bear the child of their love through him. So both women turned to the virile husband, and both women conceived. But the woman who had the withered husband could not bear her child: it withered in her womb. "As it is written," Ostrover concluded, "Paradise is only for those who have already been there."

A stupid fable! Three decades later—Mireleh dead of a cancerous uterus, Pesha encrusted with royal lies in *Time* magazine (which photographed the whip)—this piece of insignificant mystification, this *pollution*, included also in Ostrover's *Complete Tales* (Kimmel & Segal, 1968), was the subject of graduate dissertations in comparative literature, as if Ostrover were Thomas Mann, or even Albert Camus. When all that happened was that Pesha and Mireleh had gone to the movies together now and then—and such a long time ago! All the same, Ostrover was released from the dungeon of the dailies, from *Bitterer Yam* and even seedier nullities, he was free, the outside world knew his name. And why Ostrover? Why not somebody else? Was Ostrover more gifted than Komorsky? Did he think up better stories than Horowitz? Why does the world outside pick on an Ostrover instead of an Edelshtein or even a Baumzweig? What occult knack, what craft, what crooked convergence of planets drove translators to grovel before Ostrover's naked swollen sentences with their thin little threadbare pants always pulled down? Who had discovered that Ostrover was a "modern"? His Yiddish, however fevered on itself, bloated, was still Yiddish, it was still *mamaloshen*, it still squeaked up to God with a littleness, a familiarity, an elbow-poke, it was still pieced together out of *shtetl* rags, out of a baby *aleph*, a toddler *beys*—so why Ostrover? Why only Ostrover? Ostrover should be the only one? Everyone else sentenced to darkness, Ostrover alone saved? Ostrover the survivor? As if hidden in the Dutch attic like that child. *His* diary, so to speak, the only documentation of what was. Like Ringelblum of Warsaw. Ostrover was to be the only evidence that there was once a Yiddish tongue, a Yiddish literature? And all the others lost? Lost! Drowned. Snuffed out. Under the earth. As if never.

Edelshtein composed a letter to Ostrover's publishers:

Kimmel & Segal
244 Madison Avenue, New York City

My dear Mr. Kimmel, and very honored Mr. Segal:

I am writing to you in reference to one Y. Ostrover, whose works you are the company that places them before the public's eyes. Be kindly enough to forgive all flaws of English Expression. Undoubtedly, in the course of his business with you, you have received from Y. Ostrover, letters in English, even worse than this. (I HAVE NO TRANSLATOR!) We immigrants, no matter how long already Yankified, stay inside always green and never attain to actual native writing Smoothness. For one million green writers, one Nabokov, one Kosinski. I mention these to show my extreme familiarness with American Literature in all Contemporaneous avatars. In your language I read, let us say, wolfishly. I regard myself as a very Keen critic, esp. concerning so-called Amer.-Jewish writers. If you would give time I could willingly explain to you many clear opinions I have concerning these Jewish-Amer. boys and girls such as (not alphabetical) Roth Philip/ Rosen Norma/ Melammed Bernie/ Friedman B.J./ Paley Grace/ Bellow Saul/ Mailer Norman. Of the latter having just read several recent works including political I would like to remind him what F. Kafka, rest in peace, said to the German-speaking, already very comfortable, Jews of Prague, Czechoslovakia: "Jews of Prague! You know more Yiddish than you think!"

Perhaps, since doubtless you do not read the Jewish Press, you are not informed. Only this month all were taken by surprise! In that filthy propaganda *Sovietish Heymland* which in Russia they run to show that their prisoners the Jews are not prisoners—a poem! By a 20-year-old young Russian Jewish girl! Yiddish will yet live through our young. Though I doubt it as do other pessimists. However, this is not the point! I ask you—what does the following personages mean to you, you who are Sensitive men, Intelligent, and with closely-warmed Feelings! Lyessin, Reisen, Yehoash! H. Leivik himself! Itzik Manger, Chaim Grade, Aaron Zeitlen, Jacob Glatshtein, Eliezer Greenberg! Molodowsky and Korn, ladies, gifted! Dovid Ignatov, Morris Rosenfeld, Moishe Nadir, Moishe Leib Halpern, Reuven Eisland, Mani Leib, Zisha Landau! I ask you! Frug, Peretz, Vintchevski, Bovshover, Edelshtat! Velvl Zbharzher, Avrom Goldfaden! A. Rosenblatt! Y.Y. Schwartz, Yoisef Rollnick! These are all our glorious Yiddish poets. And if I would add to them our beautiful recent Russian brother-poets that were killed by Stalin with his pockmarks, for instance Peretz Markish, would you know any name of theirs? No! THEY HAVE NO TRANSLATORS!

Esteemed Gentlemen, you publish only one Yiddish writer, not even a Poet, only a Story-writer. I humbly submit you give serious wrong Impressions. That we have produced nothing else. I again refer to your associate Y. Ostrover. I do not intend to take away from him any possible talent by this letter, but wish to WITH VIGOROUSNESS assure you that others also exist without notice being bothered over them! I myself am the author and also publisher of four tomes of poetry:

N'shomeh un Guf, Zingen un Freyen, A Velt ohn Vint, A Shtundeh mit Shney. To wit, "Soul and Body," "Singing and Being Happy," "A World with No Wind," "An Hour of Snow," these are my Deep-Feeling titles.

Please inform me if you will be willing to provide me with a translator for these very worthwhile pieces of hidden writings, or, to use a Hebrew Expression, "Buried Light."

Yours very deeply respectful.

He received an answer in the same week.

Dear Mr. Edelstein:

Thank you for your interesting and informative letter. We regret that, unfortunately, we cannot furnish you with a translator. Though your poetry may well be of the quality you claim for it, practically speaking, reputation must precede translation.

Yours sincerely.

A lie! Liars!

Dear Kimmel, dear Segal,

Did YOU, Jews without tongues, ever hear of Ostrover before you found him translated everywhere? In Yiddish he didn't exist for you! For you Yiddish has no existence! A darkness inside a cloud! Who can see it, who can hear it? The world has no ears for the prisoner! You sign yourself "Yours." You're not mine and I'm not Yours!

Sincerely.

He then began to search in earnest for a translator. Expecting little, he wrote to the spinster hack.

Esteemed Edelshtein [she replied]:

To put it as plainly as I can—a plain woman should be as plain in her words—you do not know the world of practicality, of reality. Why should you? You're a poet, an idealist. When a big magazine pays Ostrover $500, how much do I get? Maybe $75. If he takes a rest for a month and doesn't write, what then? Since he's the only one they want to print he's the only one worth translating. Suppose I translated one of your nice little love songs? Would anyone buy it? Foolishness even to ask. And if they bought it, should I slave for the $5? You don't know what I go through with Ostrover anyhow. He sits me down in his dining room, his wife brings in a samovar of tea—did you ever hear anything as pretentious as this—and sits also, watching me. She has jealous eyes. She watches my ankles, which aren't bad. Then we begin. Ostrover reads aloud the first sentence the way he wrote it, in Yiddish. I write it down, in English. Right away it starts. Pesha reads what I put down and says, "That's no good, you don't catch his idiom." Idiom! She knows! Ostrover says, "The last word sticks in my throat. Can't you do better than that? A little more robustness." We look in the dictionary, the thesaurus, we scream out different words, trying, trying. Ostrover doesn't like any of them. Suppose the word is "big." We go through huge, vast, gigantic, enormous, gargantuan, monstrous, etc., etc., etc., and finally Ostrover says—by now it's five hours later, my tonsils hurt, I can hardly stand—"all right, so let it be 'big.' Simplicity above all." Day after day like this! And for $75 is it worth it? Then after this he fires me and gets himself a college boy! Or that imbecile who cracked up over the mathematics dictionary! Until he needs me. However I get a little glory out of it. Everyone says, "There goes Ostrover's translator." In actuality I'm his pig, his stool (I mean that in both senses, I assure you). You write that he has no talent. That's your opinion, maybe you're not wrong, but let me tell you he has a talent for pressure. The way among *them* they write careless novels, hoping they'll be transformed into beautiful movies and sometimes it happens—that's how it is with him. Never mind the quality of his Yiddish, what will it turn into when it becomes English? Transformation is all he cares for— and in English he's a cripple—like, please excuse me, yourself and everyone of your generation. But Ostrover has the sense to be a suitor. He keeps all his translators in a perpetual frenzy of envy for each other, but they're just rubble and offal to him, they aren't the object of his suit. What he woos is *them*. Them! You understand me, Edelshtein? He stands on the backs of hacks to reach. I know you call me hack, and it's all right, by myself I'm what you think me, no imagination, so-so ability (I too once wanted to be a poet, but that's another life)—with Ostrover on my back I'm something else: I'm "Ostrover's translator." You think that's nothing? It's an entrance into *them*. I'm invited everywhere, I go to the same parties Ostrover goes to. Everyone looks at me and thinks I'm a bit freakish, but they say: "It's Ostrover's translator." A marriage. Pesha, that junk-heap, is less married to Ostrover than I am. Like a wife, I have the supposedly passive role.

Supposedly: who knows what goes on in the bedroom? An unmarried person like myself becomes good at guessing at these matters. The same with translation. Who makes the language Ostrover is famous for? You ask: what has persuaded *them* that he's a "so-called modern"?—a sneer. Aha. *Who* has read James Joyce, Ostrover or I? I'm fifty-three years old. I wasn't born back of Hlusk for nothing, I didn't go to Vassar for nothing—do you understand me? I got caught in between, so I got squeezed. Between two organisms. A cultural hermaphrodite, neither one nor the other. I have a forked tongue. When I fight for five hours to make Ostrover say "big" instead of "gargantuan," when I take out all the nice homey commas he sprinkles like a fool, when I drink his wife's stupid tea and then go home with a watery belly—*then* he's being turned into a "modern," you see? I'm the one! No one recognizes this, of course, they think it's something inside the stories themselves, when actually it's the way I dress them up and paint over them. It's all cosmetics, I'm a cosmetician, a painter, the one they pay to do the same job on the corpse in the mortuary, among *them* . . . don't, though, bore me with your criticisms. I tell you his Yiddish doesn't matter. Nobody's Yiddish matters. Whatever's in Yiddish doesn't matter.

The rest of the letter—all women are long-winded, strong-minded—he did not read. He had already seen what she was after: a little bit of money, a little bit of esteem. A miniature megalomaniac: she fancied herself the *real* Ostrover. She believed she had fashioned herself a genius out of a rag. A rag turned into a sack, was that genius? She lived out there in the light, with *them:* naturally she wouldn't waste her time on an Edelshtein. In the bleakness. Dark where he was. An idealist! How had this good word worked itself up in society to become an insult? A darling word nevertheless. Idealist. The difference between him and Ostrover was this: Ostrover wanted to save only himself, Edelshtein wanted to save Yiddish.

Immediately he felt he lied.

With Baumzweig and Paula he went to the 92nd Street Y to hear Ostrover read. "Self-mortification," Paula said of this excursion. It was a snowy night. They had to shove their teeth into the wind, tears of suffering iced down their cheeks, the streets from the subway were Siberia. "Two Christian saints, self-flagellation," she muttered, "with chains of icicles they hit themselves." They paid for the tickets with numb fingers and sat down toward the front. Edelshtein felt paralyzed. His toes stung, prickled, then seemed diseased, gangrenous, furnace-like. The cocoon of his bed at home, the pen he kept on his night table, the first luminous line of his new poem lying there waiting to be born—*Oh that I might like a youth be struck with the blow of belief*—all at once he knew how to go on with it, what it was about and what he meant by it, the hall around him seemed preposterous, unnecessary, why was he here? Crowds, huddling, the whine of folding chairs lifted and dropped, the babble, Paula yawning next to him with squeezed and wrinkled eyelids, Baumzweig blowing his flat nose into a blue plaid handkerchief and exploding a great green flower of snot, why was he in such a place as this? What did such a place have in common with what he knew, what he felt?

Paula craned around her short neck inside a used-up skunk collar to read the frieze, mighty names, golden letters, Moses, Einstein, Maimonides, Heine. Heine. Maybe Heine knew what Edelshtein knew, a convert. But these, ushers in fine jackets, skinny boys carrying books (Ostrover's), wearing them nearly, costumed for blatant bookishness, blatant sexuality, in pants crotch-snug, penciling buttocks on air, mustachioed, some hairy to the collarbone, shins and calves menacing as hammers, and girls, tunics, knees, pants, boots, little hidden sweet tongues, black-eyed. Woolly smell of piles and piles of coats. For Ostrover! The hall was full, the ushers with raised tweed wrists directed all the rest into an unseen gallery nearby: a television screen there, on which the little gray ghost of Ostrover, palpable and otherwise white as a washed pig, would soon flutter. The Y. Why? Edelshtein also lectured at Y's—Elmhurst, Eastchester, Rye, tiny platforms, lecterns too tall for him, catalogues of vexations, his sad recitations to old people. Ladies and Gentlemen, they have cut out my vocal cords, the only language I can freely and fluently address you in, my darling *mamaloshen*, surgery, dead, the operation was a success. Edelshtein's Y's were all old people's homes, convalescent factories, asylums. To himself he sang,

Why	Farvos di Vy?
the Y?	Ich reyd
Lectures	ohn freyd
to specters,	un sheydim tantsen derbei,

aha! specters, if my tongue has no riddle for you, Ladies and Gentlemen, you are specter, wraith, phantom, I have invented you, you are my imagining, there is no one here at all, an empty chamber, a vacant valve, abandoned, desolate. Everyone gone. *Pust vi dem kalten shul mein harts* (another first line left without companion-lines, fellows, followers), the cold study-house, spooks dance there. Ladies and Gentlemen, if you find my tongue a riddle, here is another riddle: How is a Jew like a giraffe? A Jew too has no vocal cords. God blighted Jew and giraffe, one in full, one by half. And no salve. Baumzweig hawked up again. Mucus the sheen of the sea. In God's Creation no thing without beauty however perverse. *Khrakeh khrakeh.* Baumzweig's roar the only noise in the hall. "Shah," Paula said, "*ot kumt der shed.*"

Gleaming, gleaming, Ostrover stood—high, far, the stage broad, brilliant, the lectern punctilious with microphone and water pitcher. A rod of powerful light bored into his eye sockets. He had a moth-mouth as thin and dim as a chalk line, a fence of white hair erect over his ears, a cool voice.

"A new story," he announced, and spittle flashed on his lip. "It isn't obscene, so I consider it a failure."

"Devil," Paula whispered, "washed white pig, Yankee Doodle."

"Shah," Baumzweig said, "*lomir heren.*"

Baumzweig wanted to hear the devil, the pig! Why should anyone want to hear him? Edelshtein, a little bit deaf, hung forward. Before him, his nose nearly in it, the hair of a young girl glistened—some of the stage light had become enmeshed in it. Young, young! Everyone young! Everyone for Ostrover young! A modern.

Cautiously, slyly, Edelshtein let out, as on a rope, little bony shiverings of attentiveness. Two rows in front of him he glimpsed the spinster hack, Chaim Vorovsky the drunken lexicographer whom too much mathematics had crazed, six unknown college boys.

Ostrover's story:

Satan appears to a bad poet. "I desire fame," says the poet, "but I cannot attain it, because I come from Zwrdl, and the only language I can write is Zwrdlish. Unfortunately no one is left in the world who can read Zwrdlish. That is my burden. Give me fame, and I will trade you my soul for it."

"Are you quite sure," says Satan, "that you have estimated the dimensions of your trouble entirely correctly?" "What do you mean?" says the poet. "Perhaps," says Satan, "the trouble lies in your talent. Zwrdl or no Zwrdl, it's very weak." "Not so!" says the poet, "and I'll prove it to you. Teach me French, and in no time I'll be famous." "All right," says Satan, "as soon as I say Glup you'll know French perfectly, better than de Gaulle. But I'll be generous with you. French is such an easy language, I'll take only a quarter of your soul for it."

And he said Glup. And in an instant there was the poet, scribbling away in fluent French. But still no publisher in France wanted him and he remained obscure. Back came Satan: "So the French was no good, *mon vieux? Tant pis!*" "Feh," says the poet, "what do you expect from a people that kept colonies, they should know what's good in the poetry line? Teach me Italian, after all even the Pope dreams in Italian." "Another quarter of your soul," says Satan, ringing it up in his portable cash register. And Glup! There he was again, the poet, writing *terza rima* with such fluency and melancholy that the Pope would have been moved to holy tears of praise if only he had been able to see it in print—unfortunately every publisher in Italy sent the manuscript back with a plain rejection slip, no letter.

"What? Italian no good either?" exclaims Satan. "*Mamma mia*, why don't you believe me, little brother, it's not the language, it's you." It was the same with Swahili and Armenian, Glup!—failure, Glup!—failure, and by now, having rung up a quarter of it at a time, Satan owned the poet's entire soul, and took him back with him to the Place of Fire. "I suppose you'll burn me up," says the poet bitterly. "No, no," says Satan, "we don't go in for that sort of treatment for so silken a creature as a poet. Well? Did you bring everything? I told you to pack carefully! Not to leave behind a scrap!" "I brought my whole file," says the poet, and sure enough, there it was, strapped to his back, a big black metal cabinet. "Now empty it into the Fire," Satan orders. "My poems! Not all my poems? My whole life's output?" cries the poet in anguish. "That's right, do as I say," and the poet obeys, because, after all, he's in hell and Satan owns him. "Good," says Satan, "now come with me, I'll show you to your room."

A perfect room, perfectly appointed, not too cold, not too hot, just the right distance from the great Fire to be comfortable. A jewel of a desk, with a red leather top, a lovely swivel chair cushioned in scarlet, a scarlet Persian rug on the floor, nearby a red refrigerator stocked with cheese and pudding and pickles, a glass of reddish tea already steaming on a little red table. One window without a curtain. "That's your Inspiring View," says Satan, "look out and see." Nothing outside but the Fire cavorting splendidly, flecked with unearthly colors, turning itself and rolling up into unimaginable new forms. "It's beautiful," marvels the poet. "Exactly," says Satan. "It should inspire you to the composition of many new verses." "Yes, yes! May I begin, your Lordship?" "That's why I brought you here," says Satan. "Now sit down and write, since you can't help it anyhow. There is only one stipulation. The moment you finish a stanza you must throw it out of the window, like this." And to illustrate, he tossed out a fresh page.

Instantly a flaming wind picked it up and set it afire, drawing it into the great central conflagration. "Remember that you are in hell," Satan says sternly, "here you write only for oblivion." The poet begins to weep. "No difference, no difference! It was the same up there! O Zwrdl, I curse you that you nurtured me!" "And still he doesn't see the point!" says Satan, exasperated. "Glup glup glup glup glup glup glup! Now write." The poor poet began to scribble, one poem after another, and lo! suddenly he forgot every word of Zwrdlish he ever knew, faster and faster he wrote, he held on to the pen as if it alone kept his legs from flying off on their own, he wrote in Dutch and in English, in German and in Turkish, in Santali and in Sassak, in Lapp and in Kurdish, in Welsh and in Rhaeto-Romanic, in Niasese and in Nicodarese, in Galcha and in Ibanag, in Ho and in Khmer, in Ro and in Volapük, in Jagatai and in Swedish, in Tulu and in Russian, in Irish and in Kalmuck! He wrote in every language but Zwrdlish, and every poem he wrote he had to throw out the window because it was trash anyhow, though he did not realize it. . . .

Edelshtein, spinning off into a furious and alien meditation, was not sure how the story ended. But it was brutal, and Satan was again in the ascendancy: he whipped down aspiration with one of Ostrover's sample aphorisms, dense and swollen as a phallus, but sterile all the same. The terrifying laughter, a

sea-wave all around: it broke toward Edelshtein, meaning to
lash him to bits. Laughter for Ostrover. Little jokes, little
jokes, all they wanted was jokes! "Baumzweig," he said,
pressing himself down across Paula's collar (under it her
plump breasts), "he does it for spite, you see that?"

But Baumzweig was caught in the laughter. The edges of
his mouth were beaten by it. He whirled in it like a bug. "Bastard!" he said.

"Bastard," Edelshtein said reflectively.

"He means *you*," Baumzweig said.

"Me?"

"An allegory. You see how everything fits. . . ."

"If you write letters, you shouldn't mail them," Paula said
reasonably. "It got back to him you're looking for a translator."

"He doesn't need a muse, he needs a butt. Naturally it got
back to him," Baumzweig said. "That witch herself told him."

"Why me?" Edelshtein said. "It could be you."

"I'm not a jealous type," Baumzweig protested. "What he
has you want." He waved over the audience: just then he
looked as insignificant as a little bird.

Paula said, "You both want it."

What they both wanted now began. Homage.

Q. Mr. Ostrover, what would you say is the symbolic weight
    of this story?

A. The symbolic weight is, what you need you deserve. If
    you don't need to be knocked on the head you'll never
    deserve it.

Q. Sir, I'm writing a paper on you for my English class. Can
    you tell me please if you believe in hell?

A. Not since I got rich.

Q. How about God? Do you believe in God?

A. Exactly the way I believe in pneumonia. If you have
    pneumonia, you have it. If you don't, you don't.

Q. Is it true your wife is a Countess? Some people say she's
    really only Jewish.

A. In religion she's a transvestite, and in actuality she's a
    Count.

Q. Is there really such a language as Zwrdlish?

A. You're speaking it right now, it's the language of fools.

Q. What would happen if you weren't translated into
    English?

A. The pygmies and the Eskimos would read me instead.

Nowadays to be Ostrover is to be a worldwide industry.

Q. Then why don't you write about worldwide things like wars?

A. Because I'm afraid of loud noises.

Q. What do you think of the future of Yiddish?

A. What do you think of the future of the Doberman pinscher?

Q. People say other Yiddishists envy you.

A. No, it's I who envy them. I like a quiet life.

Q. Do you keep the Sabbath?

A. Of course, didn't you notice it's gone?—I keep it hidden.

Q. And the dietary laws? Do you observe them?

A. Because of the moral situation of the world I have to. I was heartbroken to learn that the minute an oyster enters my stomach, he becomes an anti-Semite. A bowl of shrimp once started a pogrom against my intestines.

Jokes, jokes! It looked to go on for another hour. The condition of fame, a Question Period: a man can stand up forever and dribble shallow quips and everyone admires him for it. Edelshtein threw up his seat with a squeal and sneaked up the aisle to the double doors and into the lobby. On a bench, half-asleep, he saw the lexicographer. Usually he avoided him—he was a man with a past, all pasts are boring—but when he saw Vorovsky raise his leathery eyelids he went toward him.

"What's new, Chaim?"

"Nothing. Liver pains. And you?"

"Life pains. I saw you inside."

"I walked out, I hate the young."

"You weren't young, no."

"Not like these. I never laughed. Do you realize, at the age of twelve I had already mastered calculus? I practically reinvented it on my own. You haven't read Wittgenstein, Hersheleh, you haven't read Heisenberg, what do you know about the empire of the universe?"

Edelshtein thought to deflect him: "Was it your translation he read in there?"

"Did it sound like mine?"

"I could tell."

"It was and it wasn't. Mine, improved. If you ask that ugly one, she'll say it's hers, improved. Who's really Ostrover's translator? Tell me, Hersheleh, maybe it's you. Nobody knows. It's as they say—by several hands, and all the hands are in Ostrover's pot, burning up. I would like to make a good strong b.m. on your friend Ostrover."

"*My* friend? He's not my friend."

"So why did you pay genuine money to see him? You can see him for free somewhere else, no?"

"The same applies to yourself."

"Youth, I brought youth."

A conversation with a madman: Vorovsky's *meshugas* was to cause other people to suspect him of normality. Edelshtein let himself slide to the bench—he felt his bones accordion downward. He was in the grip of a mournful fatigue. Sitting eye to eye with Vorovsky he confronted the other's hat—a great Russian-style fur monster. A nimbus of droshky-bells surrounded it, shrouds of snow. Vorovsky had a big head, with big kneaded features, except for the nose, which looked like a doll's, pink and formlessly delicate. The only sign of drunkenness was at the bulbs of the nostrils, where the cartilage was swollen, and at the tip, also swollen. Of actual madness there was, in ordinary discourse, no sign, except a tendency toward elusiveness. But it was known that Vorovsky, after compiling his dictionary, a job of seventeen years, one afternoon suddenly began to laugh, and continued laughing for six months, even in his sleep: in order to rest from laughing he had to be given sedatives, though even these could not entirely suppress his laughter. His wife died, and then his father, and he went on laughing. He lost control of his bladder, and then discovered the curative potency, for laughter, of drink. Drink cured him, but he still peed publicly, without realizing it; and even his cure was tentative and unreliable, because if he happened to hear a joke that he liked he might laugh at it for a minute or two, or, on occasion, three hours. Apparently none of Ostrover's jokes had struck home with him—he was sober and desolate-looking. Nevertheless Edelshtein noticed a large dark patch near his fly. He had wet himself, it was impossible to tell how long ago. There was no odor. Edelshtein moved his buttocks back an inch. "Youth?" he inquired.

"My niece. Twenty-three years old, my sister Ida's girl. She reads Yiddish fluently," he said proudly. "She writes."

"In Yiddish?"

"Yiddish," he spat out. "Don't be crazy, Hersheleh, who writes in Yiddish? Twenty-three years old, she should write in Yiddish? What is she, a refugee, an American girl like that?

She's crazy for literature, that's all, she's like the rest in there, to her Ostrover's literature. I brought her, she wanted to be introduced."

"Introduce me," Edelshtein said craftily.

"She wants to be introduced to someone famous, where do you come in?"

"Translated I'd be famous. Listen, Chaim, a talented man like you, so many languages under your belt, why don't you give me a try? A try and a push."

"I'm no good at poetry. You should write stories if you want fame."

"I don't want fame."

"Then what are you talking about?"

"I want—" Edelshtein stopped. What did he want? "To reach," he said.

Vorovsky did not laugh. "I was educated at the University of Berlin. From Vilna to Berlin, that was 1924. Did I reach Berlin? I gave my whole life to collecting a history of the human mind, I mean expressed in mathematics. In mathematics the final and only poetry possible. Did I reach the empire of the universe? Hersheleh, if I could tell you about reaching, I would tell you this: reaching is impossible. Why? Because when you get where you wanted to reach to, that's when you realize that's not what you want to reach to.—Do you know what a bilingual German-English mathematical dictionary is good for?"

Edelshtein covered his knees with his hands. His knuckles glimmered up at him. Row of white skulls.

"Toilet paper," Vorovsky said. "Do you know what poems are good for? The same. And don't call me cynic, what I say isn't cynicism."

"Despair maybe," Edelshtein offered.

"Despair up your ass. I'm a happy man. I know something about laughter." He jumped up—next to the seated Edelshtein he was a giant. Fists gray, thumbnails like bone. The mob was pouring out of the doors of the auditorium. "Something else I'll tell you. Translation is no equation. If you're looking for an equation, better die first. There are no equations, equations don't happen. It's an idea like a two-headed animal, you follow me? The last time I saw an equation it was in a snapshot of myself. I looked in my own eyes, and what did I see there? I saw God in the shape of a murderer. What you should do with your poems is swallow your tongue. There's my niece, behind Ostrover like a tail. Hey Yankel!" he boomed.

The great man did not hear. Hands, arms, heads enclosed him like a fisherman's net. Baumzweig and Paula paddled through eddies, the lobby swirled. Edelshtein saw two little people, elderly, overweight, heavily dressed. He hid himself, he wanted to be lost. Let them go, let them go—

But Paula spotted him. "What happened? We thought you took sick."

"It was too hot in there."

"Come home with us, there's a bed. Instead of your own place alone."

"Thank you no. He signs autographs, look at that."

"Your jealousy will eat you up, Hersheleh."

"I'm not jealous!" Edelshtein shrieked; people turned to see. "Where's Baumzweig?"

"Shaking hands with the pig. An editor has to keep up contacts."

"A poet has to keep down vomit."

Paula considered him. Her chin dipped into her skunk ruff. "How can you vomit, Hersheleh? Pure souls have no stomachs, only ectoplasm. Maybe Ostrover's right, you have too much ambition for your size. What if your dear friend Baumzweig didn't publish you? You wouldn't know your own name. My husband doesn't mention this to you, he's a kind man, but I'm not afraid of the truth. Without him you wouldn't exist."

"With him I don't exist," Edelshtein said. "What is existence?"

"I'm not a Question Period," Paula said.

"That's all right," Edelshtein said, "because I'm an Answer Period. The answer is period. Your husband is finished, period. Also I'm finished, period. We're already dead. Whoever uses Yiddish to keep himself alive is already dead. Either you realize this or you don't realize it. I'm one who realizes."

"I tell him all the time he shouldn't bother with you. You come and you hang around."

"Your house is a gallows, mine is a gas chamber, what's the difference?"

"Don't come any more, nobody needs you."

"My philosophy exactly. We are superfluous on the face of the earth."

"You're a scoundrel."

"Your husband's a weasel, and you're the wife of a weasel."

"Pig and devil yourself."

"Mother of puppydogs." (Paula, such a good woman, the end, he would never see her again!)

He blundered away licking his tears, hitting shoulders with his shoulder, blind with the accident of his grief. A yearning all at once shouted itself in his brain:

EDELSHTEIN: Chaim, teach me to be a drunk!

VOROVSKY: First you need to be crazy.

EDELSHTEIN: Teach me to go crazy!

VOROVSKY: First you need to fail.

EDELSHTEIN: I've failed, I'm schooled in failure, I'm a master of failure!

VOROVSKY: Go back and study some more.

One wall was a mirror. In it he saw an old man crying, dragging a striped scarf like a prayer shawl. He stood and looked at himself. He wished he had been born a Gentile. Pieces of old poems littered his nostrils, he smelled the hour of their creation, his wife in bed beside him, asleep after he had rubbed her to compensate her for bitterness. *The sky is cluttered with stars of David. . . . If everything is something else, then I am something else. . . . Am I a thing and not a bird? Does my way fork though I am one? Will God take back history? Who will let me begin again. . . .*

OSTROVER: Hersheleh, I admit I insulted you, but who will know? It's only a make-believe story, a game.

EDELSHTEIN: Literature isn't a game! Literature isn't little stories!

OSTROVER: So what is it, Torah? You scream out loud like a Jew, Edelshtein. Be quiet, they'll hear you.

EDELSHTEIN: And you, Mr. Elegance, you aren't a Jew?

OSTROVER: Not at all, I'm one of *them*. You too are lured, aren't you, Hersheleh? Shakespeare is better than a shadow, Pushkin is better than a pipsqueak, hah?

EDELSHTEIN: If you become a Gentile you don't automatically become a Shakespeare.

OSTROVER: Oho! A lot you know. I'll let you in on the facts, Hersheleh, because I feel we're really brothers, I feel you straining toward the core of the world. Now listen—did you ever hear of Velvl Shikkerparev? Never. A Yiddish scribbler writing romances for the Yiddish stage in the

East End, I'm speaking of London, England. He finds a translator and overnight he becomes Willie Shakespeare. . . .

EDELSHTEIN: Jokes aside, is this what you advise?

OSTROVER: I would advise my own father no less. Give it up, Hersheleh, stop believing in Yiddish.

EDELSHTEIN: But I don't believe in it!

OSTROVER: You do. I see you do. It's no use talking to you, you won't let go. Tell me, Edelshtein, what language does Moses speak in the world-to-come?

EDELSHTEIN: From babyhood I know this. Hebrew on the Sabbath, on weekdays Yiddish.

OSTROVER: Lost soul, don't make Yiddish into the Sabbath-tongue! If you believe in holiness, you're finished. Holiness is for make-believe.

EDELSHTEIN: I want to be a Gentile like you!

OSTROVER: I'm only a make-believe Gentile. This means that I play at being a Jew to satisfy them. In my village when I was a boy they used to bring in a dancing bear for the carnival, and everyone said, "It's human!"—They said this because they knew it was a bear, though it stood on two legs and waltzed. But it was a bear.

Baumzweig came to him then. "Paula and her temper. Never mind, Hersheleh, come and say hello to the big celebrity, what can you lose?" He went docilely, shook hands with Ostrover, even complimented him on his story. Ostrover was courtly, wiped his lip, let ooze a drop of ink from a slow pen, and continued autographing books. Vorovsky lingered humbly at the rim of Ostrover's circle: his head was fierce, his eyes timid; he was steering a girl by the elbow, but the girl was mooning over an open flyleaf, where Ostrover had written his name. Edelshtein, catching a flash of letters, was startled: it was the Yiddish version she held.

"Excuse me," he said.

"My niece," Vorovsky said.

"I see you read Yiddish," Edelshtein addressed her. "In your generation a miracle."

"Hannah, before you stands H. Edelshtein the poet."

"Edelshtein?"

"Yes."

She recited, *"Little fathers, little uncles, you with your beards and glass and curly hair. . . ."*

Edelshtein shut his lids and again wept.

"If it's the same Edelshtein?"

"The same," he croaked.

"My grandfather used to do that one all the time. It was in a book he had. *A Velt ohn Vint.* But it's not possible."

"Not possible?"

"That you're still alive."

"You're right, you're right," Edelshtein said, struck. "We're all ghosts here."

"My grandfather's dead."

"Forgive him."

"*He* used to read you! And he was an old man, he died years ago, and you're still alive—"

"I'm sorry," Edelshtein said. "Maybe I was young then, I began young."

"Why do you say ghosts? Ostrover's no ghost."

"No, no," he agreed. He was afraid to offend. "Listen, I'll say the rest for you. I'll take a minute only, I promise. Listen, see if you can remember from your grandfather—"

Around him, behind him, in front of him Ostrover, Vorovsky, Baumzweig, perfumed ladies, students, the young, the young, he clawed at his wet face and declaimed, he stood like a wanton stalk in the heart of an empty field:

> *How you spring out of the ground covered with poverty!*
> *In your long coats, fingers rolling wax, tallow eyes.*
> *How can I speak to you, little fathers?*
> *You who nestled me with lyu, lyu, lyu,*
> *lip-lullaby. Jabber of blue-eyed sailors,*
> *how am I fallen into a stranger's womb?*
>
> *Take me back with you, history has left me out.*
> *You belong to the Angel of Death,*
> *I to you.*
> *Braided wraiths, smoke,*
> *let me fall into your graves,*
> *I have no business being your future.*

He gargled, breathed, coughed, choked, tears invaded some false channel in his throat—meanwhile he swallowed up with the seizure of each bawled word this niece, this Hannah, like the rest, boots, rough full hair, a forehead made on a Jewish last, chink eyes—

At the edge of the village a little river.
Herons tip into it pecking at their images
when the waders pass whistling like Gentiles.
The herons hang, hammocks above the sweet summer-water.
Their skulls are full of secrets, their feathers scented.
The village is so little it fits into my nostril.
The roofs shimmer tar,
the sun licks thick as cow.
No one knows what will come.
How crowded with mushrooms the forest's dark floor.

Into his ear Paula said, "Hersheleh, I apologize, come home with us, please, please, I apologize." Edelshtein gave her a push, he intended to finish. "*Littleness,*" he screamed,

I speak to you.
We are such a little huddle.
Our little hovels, our grandfathers' hard hands, how little,
our little, little words,
this lullaby
sung at the lip of your grave,

he screamed.

Baumzweig said, "That's one of your old good ones, the best."

"The one on my table, in progress, is the best," Edelshtein screamed, clamor still high over his head; but he felt soft, rested, calm; he knew how patient.

Ostrover said, "That one you shouldn't throw out the window."

Vorovsky began to laugh.

"This is the dead man's poem, now you know it," Edelshtein said, looking all around, pulling at his shawl, pulling and pulling at it: this too made Vorovsky laugh.

"Hannah, better take home your uncle Chaim," Ostrover said: handsome, all white, a public genius, a feather.

Edelshtein discovered he was cheated, he had not examined the girl sufficiently.

He slept in the sons' room—bunk beds piled on each other. The top one was crowded with Paula's storage boxes. He rolled back and forth on the bottom, dreaming, jerking awake, again dreaming. Now and then, with a vomitous taste, he belched up the hot cocoa Paula had given him for reconciliation. Between the Baumzweigs and himself a private violence: lacking him, whom would they patronize? They were moralists, they needed someone to feel guilty over. Another belch. He abandoned his fine but uninnocent dream—young, he was kissing Alexei's cheeks like ripe peaches, he drew away . . . it was not Alexei, it was a girl, Vorovsky's niece. After the kiss she slowly tore the pages of a book until it snowed paper, black bits of alphabet, white bits of empty margin. Paula's snore traveled down the hall to him. He writhed out of bed and groped for a lamp. With it he lit up a decrepit table covered with ancient fragile model airplanes. Some had rubber-band propellers, some were papered over a skeleton of balsa-wood ribs. A game of Monopoly lay under a samite tissue of dust. His hand fell on two old envelopes, one already browning, and without hesitation he pulled the letters out and read them:

Today was two special holidays in one, Camp Day and Sacco and Vanzetti Day. We had to put on white shirts and white shorts and go to the casino to hear Chaver Rosenbloom talk about Sacco and Vanzetti. They were a couple of Italians who were killed for loving the poor. Chaver Rosenbloom cried, and so did Mickey but I didn't. Mickey keeps forgetting to wipe himself in the toilet but I make him.

Paula and Ben: thanks so much for the little knitted suit and the clown rattle. The box was a bit smashed in but the rattle came safe anyhow. Stevie will look adorable in his new blue suit when he gets big enough for it. He already seems to like the duck on the collar. It will keep him good and warm too. Josh has been working very hard these days preparing for a course in the American Novel and asks me to tell you he'll write as soon as he can. We all send love, and Stevie sends a kiss for Grandma and Pa. *P.S.* Mickey drove down in a pink Mercedes last week. We all had quite a chat and told him he should settle down!

Heroes, martyrdom, a baby. Hatred for these made his eyelids quiver. Ordinariness. Everything a routine. Whatever man touches becomes banal like man. Animals don't contaminate nature. Only man the corrupter, the anti-divinity. All other species live within the pulse of nature. He despised these ceremonies and rattles and turds and kisses. The pointlessness of their babies. Wipe one generation's ass for the sake of wiping another generation's ass: this was his whole definition of civilization. He pushed back the airplanes, cleared a front patch of table with his elbow, found his pen, wrote:

Dear Niece of Vorovsky:

It is very strange to me to feel I become a Smasher, I who was born to being humane and filled with love for our darling Human Race.

But nausea for his shadowy English, which he pursued in dread, passion, bewilderment, feebleness, overcame him. He started again in his own tongue—

Unknown Hannah:

I am a man writing you in a room of the house of another man. He and I are secret enemies, so under his roof it is difficult to write the truth. Yet I swear to you I will speak these words with my heart's whole honesty. I do not remember either your face or your body. Vaguely your angry voice. To me you are an abstraction. I ask whether the ancients had any physical representation of the Future, a goddess Futura, so to speak. Presumably she would have blank eyes, like Justice. It is an incarnation of the Future to whom this letter is addressed. Writing to the Future one does not expect an answer. The Future is an oracle for whose voice one cannot wait in inaction. One must do to be. Although a Nihilist, not by choice but by conviction, I discover in myself an unwillingness to despise survival. Often I have spat on myself for having survived the deathcamps—survived them drinking tea in New York!—but today when I heard carried on your tongue some old syllables of mine I was again wheedled into tolerance of survival. The sound of a dead language on a live girl's tongue! That baby should follow baby is God's trick on us, but surely we too can have a trick on God? If we fabricate with our syllables an immortality passed from the spines of the old to the shoulders of the young, even God cannot spite it. If the prayer-load that spilled upward from the mass graves should somehow survive! If not the thicket of lamentation itself, then the language on which it rode. Hannah, youth itself is nothing unless it keeps its promise to grow old. Grow old in Yiddish, Hannah, and carry fathers and uncles into the future with you. Do this. You, one in ten thousand maybe, who were born with the gift of Yiddish in your mouth, the alphabet of Yiddish in your palm, don't make ash of these! A little while ago there were twelve million people—not including babies—who lived inside this tongue, and now what is left? A language that never had a territory except Jewish mouths, and half the Jewish mouths on earth already stopped up with German worms. The rest jabber Russian, English, Spanish, God knows what. Fifty

years ago my mother lived in Russia and spoke only broken
Russian, but her Yiddish was like silk. In Israel they give the
language of Solomon to machinists. Rejoice—in Solomon's
time what else did the mechanics speak? Yet whoever forgets
Yiddish courts amnesia of history. Mourn—the forgetting has
already happened. A thousand years of our travail forgotten.
Here and there a word left for vaudeville jokes. Yiddish, I
call on you to choose! Yiddish! Choose death or death. Which
is to say death through forgetting or death through translation. Who will redeem you? What act of salvation will restore you? All you can hope for, you tattered, you withered,
is translation in America! Hannah, you have a strong mouth,
made to carry the future—

But he knew he lied, lied, lied. A truthful intention is not
enough. Oratory and declamation. A speech. A lecture. He
felt himself an obscenity. What did the dead of Jews have to
do with his own troubles? His cry was ego and more ego.
His own stew, foul. Whoever mourns the dead mourns himself. He wanted someone to read his poems, no one could
read his poems. Filth and exploitation to throw in history.
As if a dumb man should blame the ears that cannot hear him.
He turned the paper over and wrote in big letters:

EDELSHTEIN GONE,

and went down the corridor with it in pursuit of Paula's snore.
Taken without ridicule a pleasant riverside noise. Bird. More
cow to the sight: the connubial bed, under his gaze, gnarled
and lumped—in it this old male and this old female. He was
surprised on such a cold night they slept with only one blanket,
gauzy cotton. They lay like a pair of kingdoms in summer.
Long ago they had been at war, now they were exhausted
into downy truce. Hair all over Baumzweig. Even his leg-
hairs gone white. Nightstands, a pair of them, on either side
of the bed, heaped with papers, books, magazines, lampshades
sticking up out of all that like figurines on a prow—the bedroom was Baumzweig's second office. Towers of back issues
on the floor. On the dresser a typewriter besieged by Paula's
toilet water bottles and face powder. Fragrance mixed with
urinous hints. Edelshtein went on looking at the sleepers. How
reduced they seemed, each breath a little demand for more,
more, more, a shudder of jowls; how they heaved a knee, a
thumb; the tiny blue veins all over Paula's neck. Her night-

gown was stretched away and he saw that her breasts had dropped sidewise and, though still very fat, hung in pitiful creased bags of mole-dappled skin. Baumzweig wore only his underwear: his thighs were full of picked sores.

He put EDELSHTEIN GONE between their heads. Then he took it away—on the other side was his real message: secret enemies. He folded the sheet inside his coat pocket and squeezed into his shoes. Cowardly. Pity for breathing carrion. All pity is self-pity. Goethe on his deathbed: more light!

In the street he felt liberated. A voyager. Snow was still falling, though more lightly than before, a night-colored blue. A veil of snow revolved in front of him, turning him around. He stumbled into a drift, a magnificent bluish pile slanted upward. Wetness pierced his feet like a surge of cold blood. Beneath the immaculate lifted slope he struck stone—the stair of a stoop. He remembered his old home, the hill of snow behind the study-house, the smoky fire, his father swaying nearly into the black fire and chanting, one big duck, the stupid one, sliding on the ice. His mother's neck too was finely veined and secretly, sweetly, luxuriantly odorous. Deeply and gravely he wished he had worn galoshes—no one reminds a widower. His shoes were infernos of cold, his toes dead blocks. Himself the only life in the street, not even a cat. The veil moved against him, turning, and beat on his pupils. Along the curb cars squatted under humps of snow, blue-backed tortoises. Nothing moved in the road. His own house was far, Vorovsky's nearer, but he could not read the street sign. A building with a canopy. Vorovsky's hat. He made himself very small, small as a mouse, and curled himself up in the fur of it. To be very, very little and live in a hat. A little wild creature in a burrow. Inside warm, a mound of seeds nearby, licking himself for cleanliness, all sorts of weather leaping down. His glasses fell from his face and with an odd tiny crack hit the lid of a garbage can. He took off one glove and felt for them in the snow. When he found them he marveled at how the frames burned. Suppose a funeral on a night like this, how would they open the earth? His glasses were slippery as icicles when he put them on again. A crystal spectrum delighted him, but he could not see the passageway, or if there was a canopy. What he wanted from Vorovsky was Hannah.

There was no elevator. Vorovsky lived on the top floor, very high up. From his windows you could look out and see

people so tiny they became patterns. It was a different building, not this one. He went down three fake-marble steps and
saw a door. It was open: inside was a big black room knobby
with baby carriages and tricycles. He smelled wet metal like
a toothpain: life! Peretz tells how on a bitter night a Jew outside the window envied peasants swigging vodka in a hovel—
friends in their prime and warm before the fire. Carriages and
tricycles, instruments of Diaspora. Baumzweig with his picked
sores was once also a baby. In the Diaspora the birth of a
Jew increases nobody's population, the death of a Jew has no
meaning. Anonymous. To have died among the martyrs—
solidarity at least, a passage into history, one of the marked
ones, *kiddush ha-shem.*—A telephone on the wall. He pulled
off his glasses, all clouded over, and took out a pad with
numbers in it and dialed.

"Ostrover?"

"Who is this?"

"*Yankel* Ostrover, the writer, or Pisher Ostrover the
plumber?"

"What do you want?"

"To leave evidence," Edelshtein howled.

"Never mind! Make an end! Who's there?"

"The Messiah."

"Who is this?—Mendel, it's you?"

"Never."

"Gorochov?"

"That toenail? Please. Trust me."

"Fall into a hole!"

"This is how a man addresses his Redeemer?"

"It's five o'clock in the morning! What do you want? Bum!
Lunatic! Cholera! Black year! Plague! Poisoner! Strangler!"

"You think you'll last longer than your shroud, Ostrover?
Your sentences are an abomination, your style is like a
pump, a pimp has a sweeter tongue—"

"Angel of Death!"

He dialed Vorovsky but there was no answer.

The snow had turned white as the white of an eye. He
wandered toward Hannah's house, though he did not know
where she lived, or what her name was, or whether he had
ever seen her. On the way he rehearsed what he would say to
her. But this was not satisfactory, he could lecture but not
speak into a face. He bled to retrieve her face. He was in
pursuit of her, she was his destination. Why? What does a

man look for, what does he need? What can a man retrieve? Can the future retrieve the past? And if retrieve, how redeem? His shoes streamed. Each step was a pond. The herons in spring, red-legged. Secret eyes they have: the eyes of birds —frightening. Too open. The riddle of openness. His feet poured rivers. Cold, cold.

> Little old man in the cold,
> come hop up on the stove,
> your wife will give you a crust with jam.
> Thank you, muse, for this little psalm.

He belched. His stomach was unwell. Indigestion? A heart attack? He wiggled the fingers of his left hand: though frozen they tingled. Heart. Maybe only ulcer. Cancer, like Mireleh? In a narrow bed he missed his wife. How much longer could he expect to live? An unmarked grave. Who would know he had ever been alive? He had no descendants, his grandchildren were imaginary. *O my unborn grandson* . . . Hackneyed. *Ungrandfathered ghost* . . . Too baroque. Simplicity, purity, truthfulness.

He wrote:

Dear Hannah:

You made no impression on me. When I wrote you before at Baumzweig's I lied. I saw you for a second in a public place, so what? Holding a Yiddish book. A young face on top of a Yiddish book. Nothing else. For me this is worth no somersault. Ostrover's vomit!—that popularizer, vulgarian, panderer to people who have lost the memory of peoplehood. A thousand times a pimp. Your uncle Chaim said about you: "She writes." A pity on his judgment. Writes! Writes! Potatoes in a sack! Another one! What do you write? When will you write? How will you write? Either you'll become an editor of *Good Housekeeping*, or, if serious, join the gang of so-called Jewish novelists. I've sniffed them all, I'm intimate with their smell. Satirists they call themselves. Picking at their crotches. What do they *know*, I mean of *knowledge*? To satirize you have to know something. In a so-called novel by a so-called Jewish novelist ("*activist-existential*"—listen, I understand, I read everything!)—Elkin, Stanley, to keep to only one example—the hero visits Williamsburg to contact a so-called "miracle rabbi." Even the word *rabbi!* No, listen—to me, a descendant of the Vilna Gaon myself, the *guter yid* is a charlatan and his *chasidim* are victims, never mind if willing or not. But that's not the point. You have to KNOW SOMETHING! At least the difference between a *rav* and a *rebbeh!* At least a *pinteleh* here and there! Otherwise where's the joke, where's the satire, where's the mockery? American-born! An ignoramus mocks only himself. *Jewish* novelists! Savages! The allrightnik's children, all they know is to curse the allrightnik! Their Yiddish! One word here, one word there. *Shikseh* on one page, *putz* on the other, and that's the whole vocabulary! And when they give a try at phonetic rendition! Darling God! If they had mothers and fathers, they crawled out of the swamps. Their grandparents were tree-squirrels if that's how they held their mouths. They know ten words for, excuse me, penis, and when it comes to a word for learning they're impotent!

Joy, joy! He felt himself on the right course at last. Daylight was coming, a yellow elephant rocked silently by in the road. A little light burned eternally on its tusk. He let it slide past, he stood up to the knees in the river at home, whirling with joy. He wrote:

TRUTH!

But this great thick word, Truth!, was too harsh, oaken; with his finger in the snow he crossed it out.

I was saying: indifference. I'm indifferent to you and your kind. Why should I think you're another species, something better? Because you knew a shred of a thread of a poem of mine? Ha! I was seduced by my own vanity. I have a foolish tendency to make symbols out of glimpses. My poor wife, peace on her, used to ridicule me for this. Riding in the subway once I saw a beautiful child, a boy about twelve. A Puerto Rican, dusky, yet he had cheeks like pomegranates. I once knew, in Kiev, a child who looked like that. I admit to it. A portrait under the skin of my eyes. The love of a man for a boy. Why not confess it? Is it against the nature of man to rejoice in beauty? "This is to be expected with a childless man"—my wife's verdict. That what I wanted was a son. Take this as a complete explanation: if an ordinary person cannot

The end of the sentence flew like a leaf out of his mind ... it was turning into a quarrel with Mireleh. Who quarrels with the dead? He wrote:

Esteemed Alexei Yosifovitch:

You remain. You remain. An illumination. More than my
own home, nearer than my mother's mouth. Nimbus. Your
father slapped my father. You were never told. Because I
kissed you on the green stairs. The shadow-place on the landing where I once saw the butler scratch his pants. They sent
us away shamed. My father and I, into the mud.

Again a lie. Never near the child. Lying is like a vitamin, it
has to fortify everything. Only through the doorway, looking,
looking. The gleaming face: the face of flame. Or would test
him on verb-forms: *kal, nifal, piel, pual, hifil, hofal, hispael.*
On the afternoons the Latin tutor came, crouched outside the
threshold, Edelshtein heard *ego, mei, mihi, me, me.* May
may. Beautiful foreign nasal chant of riches. Latin! Dirty
from the lips of idolators. An apostate family. Edelshtein and
his father took their coffee and bread, but otherwise lived on
boiled eggs: the elder Kirilov one day brought home with
him the *mashgiach* from the Jewish poorhouse to testify to the
purity of the servants' kitchen, but to Edelshtein's father the
whole house was *treyf*, the *mashgiach* himself a hired impos-
tor. Who would oversee the overseer? Among the Kirilovs
with their lying name money was the best overseer. Money
saw to everything. Though they had their particular talent.
Mechanical. Alexei Y. Kirilov, engineer. Bridges, towers. Con-
sultant to Cairo. Builder of the Aswan Dam, assistant to
Pharaoh for the latest Pyramid. To set down such a fantasy
about such an important Soviet brain . . . poor little Alexei,
Avremeleh, I'll jeopardize your position in life, little corpse
of Babi Yar.

Only focus. Hersh! Scion of the Vilna Gaon! Prince of rationality! Pay attention!

He wrote:

The gait—the prance, the hobble—of Yiddish is not the
same as the gait of English. A big headache for a translator
probably. In Yiddish you use more words than in English.
Nobody believes it but it's true. Another big problem is
form. The moderns take the old forms and fill them up with
mockery, love, drama, satire, etc. Plenty of play. But STILL
THE SAME OLD FORMS, conventions left over from the last
century even. It doesn't matter who denies this, out of

pride: it's true. Pour in symbolism, impressionism, be complex, be subtle, be daring, take risks, break your teeth—whatever you do, it still comes out Yiddish. *Mamaloshen* doesn't produce *Wastelands*. No alienation, no nihilism, no dadaism. With all the suffering no smashing! No INCOHERENCE! Keep the latter in mind, Hannah, if you expect to make progress. Also: please remember that when a goy from Columbus, Ohio, says "Elijah the Prophet" he's not talking about *Eliohu hanovi*. Eliohu is one of us, a *folksmensh*, running around in second-hand clothes. Theirs is God knows what. The same biblical figure, with exactly the same history, once he puts on a name from King James, COMES OUT A DIFFERENT PERSON. Life, history, hope, tragedy, they don't come out even. They talk Bible Lands, with us it's *eretz yisroel*. A misfortune.

Astonished, he struck up against a kiosk. A telephone! On a street corner! He had to drag the door open, pulling a load of snow. Then he squeezed inside. His fingers were sticks. Never mind the pad, he forgot even where the pocket was. In his coat? Jacket? Pants? With one stick he dialed Vorovsky's number: from memory.

"Hello, Chaim?"

"This is Ostrover."

"Ostrover! Why Ostrover? What are you doing there? I want Vorovsky."

"Who's this?"

"Edelshtein."

"I thought so. A persecution, what is this? I could send you to jail for tricks like before—"

"Quick, give me Vorovsky."

"I'll *give* you."

"Vorovsky's not home?"

"How do I know if Vorovsky's home? It's dawn, go ask Vorovsky!"

Edelshtein grew weak: "I called the wrong number."

"Hersheleh, if you want some friendly advice you'll listen to me. I can get you jobs at fancy out-of-town country clubs, Miami Florida included, plenty of speeches your own style, only what they need is rational lecturers not lunatics. If you carry on like tonight you'll lose what you have."

"I don't have anything."

"Accept life, Edelshtein."

"Dead man, I appreciate your guidance."

"Yesterday I heard from Hollywood, they're making a

movie from one of my stories. So now tell me again who's dead."

"The puppet the ventriloquist holds in his lap. A piece of log. It's somebody else's language and the dead doll sits there."

"Wit, you want them to make movies in Yiddish now?"

"In Talmud if you save a single life it's as if you saved the world. And if you save a language? Worlds maybe. Galaxies. The whole universe."

"Hersheleh, the God of the Jews made a mistake when he didn't have a son, it would be a good occupation for you."

"Instead I'll be an extra in your movie. If they shoot the *shtetl* on location in Kansas send me expense money. I'll come and be local color for you. I'll put on my *shtreiml* and walk around, the people should see a real Jew. For ten dollars more I'll even speak *mamaloshen*."

Ostrover said, "It doesn't matter what you speak, envy sounds the same in all languages."

Edelshtein said, "Once there was a ghost who thought he was still alive. You know what happened to him? He got up one morning and began to shave and he cut himself. And there was no blood. No blood at all. And he still didn't believe it, so he looked in the mirror to see. And there was no reflection, no sign of himself. He wasn't there. But he still didn't believe it, so he began to scream, but there was no sound, no sound at all—"

There was no sound from the telephone. He let it dangle and rock.

He looked for the pad. Diligently he consulted himself: pants cuffs have a way of catching necessary objects. The number had fallen out of his body. Off his skin. He needed Vorovsky because he needed Hannah. Worthwhile maybe to telephone Baumzweig for Vorovsky's number, Paula could look it up—Baumzweig's number he knew by heart, no mistake. He had singled out his need. Svengali, Pygmalion, Rasputin, Dr. (jokes aside) Frankenstein. What does it require to make a translator? A secondary occupation. Parasitic. But your own creature. Take this girl Hannah and train her. His alone. American-born but she had the advantage over him, English being no worm on her palate; also she could read his words in the original. Niece of a vanquished mind—still, genes are in reality God, and if Vorovsky had a little talent for translation why not the niece?—Or the other. Russia. The one in the Soviet Union who wrote two stanzas in Yiddish. In Yid-

dish! And only twenty! Born 1948, same year they made up
to be the Doctors' Plot, Stalin already very busy killing Jews,
Markish, Kvitko, Kushnirov, Hofshtein, Mikhoels, Susskin,
Bergelson, Feffer, Gradzenski with the wooden leg. All slaughtered. How did Yiddish survive in the mouth of that girl? Nurtured in secret. Taught by an obsessed grandfather, a crazy
uncle: Marranos. The poem reprinted, as they say, in the
West. (The West! If a Jew says "the West," he sounds like an
imbecile. In a puddle what's West, what's East?) Flowers,
blue sky, she yearns for the end of winter: very nice. A zero,
and received like a prodigy! An aberration! A miracle! Because
composed in the lost tongue. As if some Neapolitan child
suddenly begins to prattle in Latin. Not the same. Little verses
merely. Death confers awe. Russian: its richness, directness.
For "iron" and "weapon" the same word. A *thick* language, a
world-language. He visualized himself translated into Russian,
covertly, by the Marranos' daughter. To be circulated, in type-
script, underground: to be read, read!

Understand me, Hannah—that our treasure-tongue is derived from strangers means nothing. 90 per cent German
roots, 10 per cent Slavic: irrelevant. The Hebrew take for
granted without percentages. We are a people who have
known how to forge the language of need out of the language of necessity. Our reputation among ourselves as a nation of scholars is mostly empty. In actuality we are a mob
of working people, laborers, hewers of wood, believe me.
Leivik, our chief poet, was a house painter. Today all phar-
macists, lawyers, accountants, haberdashers, but tickle the
lawyer and you'll see his grandfather sawed wood for a living. That's how it is with us. Nowadays the Jew is forgetful, everybody with a profession, every Jewish boy a professor—justice seems less urgent. Most don't realize this quiet
time is only another Interim. Always, like in a terrible Wag-
nerian storm, we have our interludes of rest. So now. Once
we were slaves, now we are free men, remember the bread
of affliction. But listen. Whoever cries Justice! is a liberated
slave. Whoever honors Work is a liberated slave. They accuse Yiddish literature of sentimentality in this connection.
Very good, true. True, so be it! A dwarf at a sewing machine
can afford a little loosening of the heart. I return to Leivik.
He could hang wallpaper. I once lived in a room he papered
yellow vines. Rutgers Street that was. A good job, no bubbles,
no peeling. This from a poet of very morbid tendencies. Mani
Leib fixed shoes. Moishe Leib Halpern was a waiter, once in

a while a handyman. I could tell you the names of twenty poets of very pure expression who were operators, pressers, cutters. In addition to fixing shoes Mani Leib was also a laundryman. I beg you not to think I'm preaching Socialism. To my mind politics is dung. What I mean is something else: Work is Work, and Thought is Thought. Politics tries to mix these up, Socialism especially. The language of a hard-pressed people works under the laws of purity, dividing the Commanded from the Profane. I remember one of my old teachers. He used to take attendance every day and he gave his occupation to the taxing council as "attendance-taker"—so that he wouldn't be getting paid for teaching Torah. This with five pupils, all living in his house and fed by his wife! Call it splitting a hair if you want, but it's the hair of a head that distinguished between the necessary and the merely needed. People who believe that Yiddish is, as they like to say, "richly intermixed," and that in Yiddishkeit the presence of the Covenant, of Godliness, inhabits humble things and humble words, are under a delusion or a deception. The slave knows exactly when he belongs to God and when to the oppressor. The liberated slave who is not forgetful and can remember when he himself was an artifact, knows exactly the difference between God and an artifact. A language also knows whom it is serving at each moment. I am feeling very cold right now. Of course you see that when I say liberated I mean self-liberated. Moses not Lincoln, not Franz Josef. Yiddish is the language of auto-emancipation. Theodor Herzl wrote in German but the message spread in *mamaloshen*— my God cold. Naturally the important thing is to stick to what you learned as a slave including language, and not to speak their language, otherwise you will become like them, acquiring their confusion between God and artifact and consequently their taste for making slaves, both of themselves and others.

Slave of rhetoric! This is the trouble when you use God for a Muse. Philosophers, thinkers—all cursed. Poets have it better: most are Greeks and pagans, unbelievers except in natural religion, stones, stars, body. This cube and cell. Ostrover had already sentenced him to jail, little booth in the vale of snow; black instrument beeped from a gallows. The white pad—something white—on the floor. Edelshtein bent for it and struck his jaw. Through the filth of the glass doors morning rose out of the dark. He saw what he held:

"ALL OF US ARE HUMANS TOGETHER
BUT SOME HUMANS SHOULD DROP DEAD."

DO YOU FEEL THIS?

IF SO CALL TR 5-2530 IF YOU WANT TO
KNOW WHETHER YOU WILL SURVIVE IN
CHRIST'S FIVE-DAY INEXPENSIVE
ELECT-PLAN

"AUDITORY PHRENOLOGY"
PRACTICED FREE FREE

(PLEASE NO ATHEISTS OR CRANK CALLS
WE ARE SINCERE SCIENTIFIC SOUL-SOCIOLOGISTS)

ASK FOR ROSE OR LOU
WE LOVE YOU

He was touched and curious, but withdrawn. The cold lit him unfamiliarly: his body a brilliant hollowness, emptied of organs, cleansed of debris, the inner flanks of him perfect lit glass. A clear chalice. Of small change he had only a nickel and a dime. For the dime he could CALL TR 5-2530 and take advice appropriate to his immaculateness, his transparency. Rose or Lou. He had no satire for their love. How manifold and various the human imagination. The simplicity of an ascent lured him, he was alert to the probability of levitation but disregarded it. The disciples of Reb Moshe of Kobryn also disregarded feats in opposition to nature—they had no awe for their master when he hung in air, but when he slept —the miracle of his lung, his breath, his heartbeat! He lurched from the booth into rushing daylight. The depth of snow sucked off one of his shoes. The serpent too prospers without feet, so he cast off his and weaved on. His arms, particularly his hands, particularly those partners of mind his fingers, he was sorry to lose. He knew his eyes, his tongue, his stinging loins. He was again tempted to ascend. The hillock was profound. He outwitted it by creeping through it, he drilled patiently into the snow. He wanted to stand then, but without legs could not. Indolently he permitted himself to rise. He went only high enough to see the snowy sidewalks, the mounds in gutters and against stoops, the beginning of business time. Lifted light. A doorman fled out of a building wearing ear-muffs, pulling a shovel behind him like a little tin cart. Edelshtein drifted no higher than the man's shoulders. He watched the shovel pierce the snow, tunneling down, but there was no bottom, the earth was without foundation.

He came under a black wing. He thought it was the first blindness of Death but it was only a canopy.

The doorman went on digging under the canopy; under the canopy Edelshtein tasted wine and felt himself at a wedding, his own, the canopy covering his steamy gold eyeglasses made blind by Mireleh's veil. Four beings held up the poles: one his wife's cousin the postman, one his own cousin the druggist; two poets. The first poet was a beggar who lived on institutional charity—Baumzweig; the second, Silverman, sold ladies' elastic stockings, the kind for varicose veins. The postman and the druggist were still alive, only one of them retired. The poets were ghosts, Baumzweig picking at himself in bed also a ghost, Silverman long dead, more than twenty years —*lideleh-shreiber* they called him, he wrote for the popular theater: "Song to Steerage": *Steerage, steerage, I remember the crowds, the rags we took with us we treated like shrouds, we tossed them away when we spied out the shore, going re-born through the Golden Door*. . . . Even on Second Avenue 1905 was already stale, but it stopped the show, made fevers, encores, tears, yells. Golden sidewalks. America the bride, under her fancy gown nothing. Poor Silverman, in love with the Statue of Liberty's lifted arm, what did he do in his life besides raise up a post at an empty wedding, no progeny?

The doorman dug out a piece of statuary, an urn with a stone wreath.

Under the canopy Edelshtein recognized it. Sand, butts, a half-naked angel astride the wreath. Once Edelshtein saw a condom in it. Found! Vorovsky's building. There is no God, yet who brought him here if not the King of the Universe? Not so bad off after all, even in a snowstorm he could find his way, an expert, he knew one block from another in this desolation of a world.

He carried his shoe into the elevator like a baby, an orphan, a redemption. He could kiss even a shoe.

In the corridor laughter, toilets flushing; coffee stabbed him.

He rang the bell.

From behind Vorovsky's door, laughter, laughter!

No one came.

He rang again. No one came. He banged. "Chaim, crazy man, open up!" No one came. "A dead man from the cold knocks, you don't come? Hurry up, open, I'm a stick of ice, you want a dead man at your door? Mercy! Pity! Open up!"

No one came.

He listened to the laughter. It had a form; a method, rather: some principle, closer to physics than music, of arching up and sinking back. Inside the shape barks, howls, dogs, wolves, wilderness. After each fright a crevice to fall into. He made an anvil of his shoe and took the doorknob for an iron hammer and thrust. He thrust, thrust. The force of an iceberg.

Close to the knob a panel bulged and cracked. Not his fault. On the other side someone was unused to the lock.

He heard Vorovsky but saw Hannah.

She said: "What?"

"You don't remember me? I'm the one that recited to you tonight my work from several years past, I was passing by in your uncle's neighborhood—"

"He's sick."

"What, a fit?"

"All night. I've been here the whole night. The whole night—"

"Let me in."

"Please go away. I just told you."

"In. What's the matter with you? I'm sick myself, I'm dead from cold! Hey, Chaim! Lunatic, stop it!"

Vorovsky was on his belly on the floor, stifling his mouth with a pillow as if it were a stone, knocking his head down on it, but it was no use, the laughter shook the pillow and came yelping out, not muffled but increased, darkened. He laughed and said "Hannah" and laughed.

Edelshtein took a chair and dragged it near Vorovsky and sat. The room stank, a subway latrine.

"Stop," he said.

Vorovsky laughed.

"All right, merriment, very good, be happy. You're warm, I'm cold. Have mercy, little girl—tea. Hannah. Boil it up hot. Pieces of flesh drop from me." He heard that he was speaking Yiddish, so he began again for her. "I'm sorry. Forgive me. A terrible thing to do. I was lost outside, I was looking, so now I found you, I'm sorry."

"It isn't a good time for a visit, that's all."

"Bring some tea also for your uncle."

"He can't."

"He can maybe, let him try. Someone who laughs like this is ready for a feast—*flanken, tsimmis, rosselfleysh*—" In Yiddish he said, "In the world-to-come people dance at parties like this, all laughter, joy. The day after the Messiah people laugh like this."

Vorovsky laughed and said "Messiah" and sucked the pillow spitting. His face was a flood: tears ran upside down into his eyes, over his forehead, saliva sprang in puddles around his ears. He was spitting, crying, burbling, he gasped, wept, spat. His eyes were bloodshot, the whites showed like slashes, wounds; he still wore his hat. He laughed, he was still laughing. His pants were wet, the fly open, now and then seeping. He dropped the pillow for tea and ventured a sip, with his tongue, like an animal full of hope—vomit rolled up with the third swallow and he laughed between spasms, he was still laughing, stinking, a sewer.

Edelshtein took pleasure in the tea, it touched him to the root, more gripping on his bowel than the coffee that stung the hall. He praised himself with no meanness, no bitterness: prince of rationality! Thawing, he said, "Give him *schnapps*, he can hold *schnapps*, no question."

"He drank and he vomited."

"Chaim, little soul," Edelshtein said, "what started you off? Myself. I was there. I said it, I said graves, I said smoke. I'm the responsible one. Death. Death, I'm the one who said it. Death you laugh at, you're no coward."

"If you want to talk business with my uncle come another time."

"Death is business?"

Now he examined her. Born 1945, in the hour of the death-camps. Not selected. Immune. The whole way she held herself looked immune—by this he meant American. Still, an exhausted child, straggled head, remarkable child to stay through the night with the madman. "Where's your mother?" he said. "Why doesn't she come and watch her brother? Why does it fall on you? You should be free, you have your own life."

"You don't know anything about families."

She was acute: no mother, father, wife, child, what did he know about families? He was cut off, a survivor. "I know your uncle," he said, but without belief: in the first place Vorovsky had an education. "In his right mind your uncle doesn't want you to suffer."

Vorovsky, laughing, said "Suffer."

"He likes to suffer. He wants to suffer. He admires suffering. All you people want to suffer."

Pins and needles: Edelshtein's fingertips were fevering. He stroked the heat of the cup. He could feel. He said, " 'You people'?"

"You Jews."

"Aha. Chaim, you hear? Your niece Hannah—on the other side already, never mind she's acquainted with *mamaloshen*. In one generation, 'you Jews.' You don't like suffering? Maybe you respect it?"

"It's unnecessary."

"It comes from history, history is also unnecessary?"

"History's a waste."

America the empty bride. Edelshtein said, "You're right about business. I came on business. My whole business is waste."

Vorovsky laughed and said "Hersheleh Frog Frog Frog."

"I think you're making him worse," Hannah said. "Tell me what you want and I'll give him the message."

"He's not deaf."

"He doesn't remember afterward—"

"I have no message."

"Then what do you want from him?"

"Nothing. I want from you."

"Frog Frog Frog Frog Frog."

Edelshtein finished his tea and put the cup on the floor and for the first time absorbed Vorovsky's apartment: until now Vorovsky had kept him out. It was one room, sink and stove behind a plastic curtain, bookshelves leaning over not with books but journals piled flat, a sticky table, a sofa-bed, a desk, six kitchen chairs, and along the walls seventy-five cardboard boxes which Edelshtein knew harbored two thousand copies of Vorovsky's dictionary. A pity on Vorovsky, he had a dispute with the publisher, who turned back half the printing to him. Vorovsky had to pay for two thousand German-English mathematical dictionaries, and now he had to sell them himself, but he did not know what to do, how to go about it. It was his fate to swallow what he first excreted. Because of a mishap in business he owned his life, he possessed what he was, a slave, but invisible. A hungry snake has to eat its tail all the way down to the head until it disappears.

Hannah said: "What could I do for you"—flat, not a question.

"Again 'you.' A distinction, a separation. What I'll ask is this: annihilate 'you,' annihilate 'me.' We'll come to an understanding, we'll get together."

She bent for his cup and he saw her boot. He was afraid of a boot. He said mildly, nicely, "Look, your uncle tells me you're one of us. By 'us' he means writer, no?"

"By 'us' you mean Jew."

"And you're not a Jew, *meydeleh?*"

"Not your kind."

"Nowadays there have to be kinds? Good, bad, old, new—"

"Old and new."

"All right! So let it be old and new, fine, a reasonable beginning. Let old work with new. Listen, I need a collaborator. Not exactly a collaborator, it's not even complicated like that. What I need is a translator."

"My uncle the translator is indisposed."

At that moment Edelshtein discovered he hated irony. He yelled, "Not your uncle. You! You!"

Howling, Vorovsky crawled to a tower of cartons and beat on them with his bare heels. There was an alteration in his laughter, something not theatrical but of the theater—he was amused, entertained, clowns paraded between his legs.

"You'll save Yiddish," Edelshtein said, "you'll be like a Messiah to a whole generation, a whole literature, naturally you'll have to work at it, practice, it takes knowledge, it takes a gift, a genius, a born poet—"

Hannah walked in her boots with his dirty teacup. From behind the plastic he heard the faucet. She opened the curtain and came out and said: "You old men."

"Ostrover's pages you kiss!"

"You jealous old men from the ghetto," she said.

"And Ostrover's young, a young prince? Listen! You don't see, you don't follow—translate me, lift me out of the ghetto, it's my life that's hanging on you!"

Her voice was a whip. "Bloodsuckers," she said. "It isn't a translator you're after, it's someone's soul. Too much history's drained your blood, you want someone to take you over, a dybbuk—"

"Dybbuk! Ostrover's language. All right, I need a dybbuk, I'll become a golem, I don't care, it doesn't matter! Breathe in me! Animate me! Without you I'm a clay pot!" Bereaved, he yelled, "Translate me!"

The clowns ran over Vorovsky's charmed belly.

Hannah said: "You think I have to read Ostrover in translation? You think translation has anything to do with what Ostrover is?"

Edelshtein accused her, "Who taught you to read Yiddish? —A girl like that, to know the letters worthy of life and to be ignorant! 'You Jews,' 'you people,' you you you!"

"I learned, my grandfather taught me, I'm not responsible for it, I didn't go looking for it, I was smart, a golden head, same as now. But I have my own life, you said it yourself, I don't have to throw it out. So pay attention, Mr. Vampire: even in Yiddish Ostrover's not in the ghetto. Even in Yiddish he's not like you people."

"He's not in the ghetto? Which ghetto, what ghetto? So where is he? In the sky? In the clouds? With the angels? Where?"

She meditated, she was all intelligence. "In the world," she answered him.

"In the marketplace. A fishwife, a *kochleffel,* everything's his business, you he'll autograph, me he'll get jobs, he listens to everybody."

"Whereas you people listen only to yourselves."

In the room something was absent.

Edelshtein, pushing into his snow-damp shoe, said into the absence, "So? You're not interested?"

"Only in the mainstream. Not in your little puddles."

"Again the ghetto. Your uncle stinks from the ghetto? Graduated, 1924, the University of Berlin, Vorovsky stinks from the ghetto? Myself, four God-given books not one living human being knows, I stink from the ghetto? God, four thousand years since Abraham hanging out with Jews, God also stinks from the ghetto?"

"Rhetoric," Hannah said. "Yiddish literary rhetoric. That's the style."

"Only Ostrover doesn't stink from the ghetto."

"A question of vision."

"Better say visions. He doesn't know real things."

"He knows a reality beyond realism."

"American literary babies! And in your language you don't have a rhetoric?" Edelshtein burst out. "Very good, he's achieved it, Ostrover's the world. A pantheist, a pagan, a goy."

"That's it. You've nailed it. A Freudian, a Jungian, a sensibility. No little love stories. A contemporary. He speaks for everybody."

"Aha. Sounds familiar already. For humanity he speaks? Humanity?"

"Humanity," she said.

"And to speak for Jews isn't to speak for humanity? We're not human? We're not present on the face of the earth? We don't suffer? In Russia they let us live? In Egypt they don't want to murder us?"

"Suffer suffer," she said. "I like devils best. They don't think only about themselves and they don't suffer."

Immediately, looking at Hannah—my God, an old man, he was looking at her little waist, underneath it where the little apple of her womb was hidden away—immediately, all at once, instantaneously, he fell into a chaos, a trance, of truth, of actuality: was it possible? He saw everything in miraculous reversal, blessed—everything plain, distinct, understandable, true. What he understood was this: that the ghetto was the real world, and the outside world only a ghetto. Because in actuality who was shut off? Who then was really buried, removed, inhabited by darkness? To whom, in what little space, did God offer Sinai? Who kept Terach and who followed Abraham? Talmud explains that when the Jews went into Exile, God went into Exile also. Babi Yar is maybe the real world, and Kiev with its German toys, New York with all its terrible intelligence, all fictions, fantasies. Unreality.

An infatuation! He was the same, all his life the same as this poisonous wild girl, he coveted mythologies, specters, animals, voices. Western Civilization his secret guilt, he was ashamed of the small tremor of his self-love, degraded by being ingrown. Alexei with his skin a furnace of desire, his trucks and trains! He longed to be Alexei. Alexei with his German toys and his Latin! Alexei whose destiny was to grow up into the world-at-large, to slip from the ghetto, to break out into engineering for Western Civilization! Alexei, I abandon you! I'm at home only in a prison, history is my prison, the ravine my house, only listen—suppose it turns out that the destiny of the Jews is vast, open, eternal, and that Western Civilization is meant to dwindle, shrivel, shrink into the ghetto of the world—what of history then? Kings, Parliaments, like insects, Presidents like vermin, their religion a row of little dolls, their art a cave smudge, their poetry a lust—Avremeleh, when you fell from the ledge over the ravine into your grave, for the first time you fell into reality.

To Hannah he said: "I didn't ask to be born into Yiddish. It came on me."

He meant he was blessed.

"So keep it," she said, "and don't complain."

With the whole ferocity of his delight in it he hit her mouth.
The madman again struck up his laugh. Only now was it possible to notice that something had stopped it before. A missing
harp. The absence filled with bloody laughter, bits of what
looked like red pimento hung in the vomit on Vorovsky's chin,
the clowns fled, Vorovsky's hat with its pinnacle of fur dangled on his chest—he was spent, he was beginning to fall into
the quake of sleep, he slept, he dozed, roars burst from him,
he hiccuped, woke, laughed, an enormous grief settled in him,
he went on napping and laughing, grief had him in its teeth.

Edelshtein's hand, the cushiony underside of it, blazed from
giving the blow. "You," he said, "you have no ideas, what
are you?" A shred of learning flaked from him, what the sages
said of Job ripped from his tongue like a peeling of the tongue
itself, *he never was, he never existed.* "You were never born,
you were never created!" he yelled. "Let me tell you, a dead
man tells you this, at least I had a life, at least I understood
something!"

"Die," she told him. "Die now, all you old men, what are
you waiting for? Hanging on my neck, him and now you, the
whole bunch of you, parasites, hurry up and die."

His palm burned, it was the first time he had ever slapped
a child. He felt like a father. Her mouth lay back naked on
her face. Out of spite, against instinct, she kept her hands
from the bruise—he could see the shape of her teeth, turned a
little one on the other, imperfect, again vulnerable. From fury
her nose streamed. He had put a bulge in her lip.

"Forget Yiddish!" he screamed at her. "Wipe it out of your
brain! Extirpate it! Go get a memory operation! You have no
right to it, you have no right to an uncle, a grandfather! No
one ever came before you, you were never born! A vacuum!"

"You old atheists," she called after him. "You dead old
socialists. Boring! You bore me to death. You hate magic,
you hate imagination, you talk God and you hate God, you
despise, you bore, you envy, you eat people up with your disgusting old age—cannibals, all you care about is your own
youth, you're finished, give somebody else a turn!"

This held him. He leaned on the door frame. "A turn at
what? I didn't offer you a turn? An opportunity of a lifetime?
To be published now, in youth, in babyhood, early in life?
Translated I'd be famous, this you don't understand. Hannah,
listen," he said, kindly, ingratiatingly, reasoning with her like
a father, "you don't have to like my poems, do I ask you to

like them? I don't ask you to like them, I don't ask you to respect them, I don't ask you to love them. A man my age, do I want a lover or a translator? Am I asking a favor? No. Look," he said, "one thing I forgot to tell you. A business deal. That's all. Business, plain and simple. I'll pay you. You didn't think I wouldn't pay, God forbid?"

Now she covered her mouth. He wondered at his need to weep; he was ashamed.

"Hannah, please, how much? I'll pay, you'll see. Whatever you like. You'll buy anything you want. Dresses, shoes—" *Gottenyu*, what could such a wild beast want? "You'll buy more boots, all kinds of boots, whatever you want, books, everything—" He said relentlessly, "You'll have from me money."

"No," she said, "no."

"Please. What will happen to me? What's wrong? My ideas aren't good enough? Who asks you to believe in my beliefs? I'm an old man, used up, I have nothing to say any more, anything I ever said was all imitation. Walt Whitman I used to like. Also John Donne. Poets, masters. We, what have we got? A Yiddish Keats? Never—" He was ashamed, so he wiped his cheeks with both sleeves. "Business. I'll pay you," he said.

"No."

"Because I laid a hand on you? Forgive me, I apologize. I'm crazier than he is, I should be locked up for it—"

"Not because of that."

"Then why not? *Meydeleh*, why not? What harm would it do you? Help out an old man."

She said desolately, "You don't interest me. I would have to be interested."

"I see. Naturally." He looked at Vorovsky. "Goodbye, Chaim, regards from Aristotle. What distinguishes men from the beasts is the power of ha-ha-ha. So good morning, ladies and gentlemen. Be well. Chaim, live until a hundred and twenty. The main thing is health."

In the street it was full day, and he was warm from the tea. The road glistened, the sidewalks. Paths crisscrossed in unexpected places, sleds clanged, people ran. A drugstore was open and he went in to telephone Baumzweig: he dialed, but on the way he skipped a number, heard an iron noise like a weapon, and had to dial again. "Paula," he practiced, "I'll come back for a while, all right? For breakfast maybe," but instead he changed his mind and decided to CALL TR 5-2530. At the other end of the wire it was either Rose or Lou. Edelshtein told the eunuch's voice, "I believe with you about some should drop dead. Pharaoh, Queen Isabella, Haman, that pogromchik King Louis they call in history Saint, Hitler, Stalin, Nasser—" The voice said, "You're a Jew?" It sounded Southern but somehow not Negro—maybe because schooled, polished: "Accept Jesus as your Saviour and you shall have Jerusalem restored." "We already got it," Edelshtein said. *Meshiachseiten!* "The terrestrial Jerusalem has no significance. Earth is dust. The Kingdom of God is within. Christ released man from Judaic exclusivism." "Who's excluding who?" Edelshtein said. "Christianity is Judaism universalized. Jesus is Moses publicized for ready availability. Our God is the God of Love, your God is the God of Wrath. Look how He abandoned you in Auschwitz." "It wasn't only God who didn't notice." "You people are cowards, you never even tried to defend yourselves. You got a wide streak of yellow, you don't know how to hold a gun." "Tell it to the Egyptians," Edelshtein said. "Everyone you come into contact with turns into your enemy. When you were in Europe every nation despised you. When you moved to take over the Middle East the Arab Nation, spic faces like your own, your very own blood-kin, began to hate you. You are a bone in the throat of all mankind." "Who gnaws at bones? Dogs and rats only." "Even your food habits are abnormal, against the grain of quotidian delight. You refuse to seethe a lamb in the milk of its mother. You will not eat a fertilized egg because it has a spot of blood on it. When you wash your hands you chant. You pray in a debased jargon, not in the beautiful sacramental English of our Holy Bible." Edelshtein said, "That's right, Jesus spoke the King's English." "Even now, after the good Lord knows how many years in America, you talk with a kike accent. You kike, you Yid."

Edelshtein shouted into the telephone, "Amalekite! Titus! Nazi! The whole world is infected by you anti-Semites! On account of you children become corrupted! On account of you I lost everything, my whole life! On account of you I have no translator!"

Homage to Benny Leonard

Meyer Liben

"What wrong with him?" asked Mr. Flaxman, as Davey got up from the table, where he had sat morosely through the meal, and walked off.

Mrs. Flaxman shrugged, as though to say that she could not choose among the numerous possibilities.

When, a moment later, Davey walked back into the dining room to pull out the ball which was securely lodged between the floor and the bottom of the bureau, his father asked him, "What it is, David?"

It was David's turn to shrug his shoulders. "Nothing, Pop."

"A fine nothing," said his father. "One could die looking at you."

"I'm telling you, Pop, it's nothing," and he walked slowly out of the house.

When the door closed quietly behind him, did not slam, Mr. Flaxman said to his wife, "What is it, they don't tell you anything?"

There was an implied criticism here, the burden for the child's nonconfiding was suddenly put on the mother.

"You were probably no different at that stage, that's how the children are."

Mr. Flaxman was momentarily bemused, as he thought of his far-off childhood, the childhood that is twice as far off for the immigrant as for the native-born.

"To tell you the truth," he said, "who remembers?"

Since the problem had not come into full light, he shook it off, the more so when his wife said, "I wonder what's bothering him. You think he's not feeling well? Maybe I'll take his temperature."

Mr. Flaxman shook the thing further away from him, shook it almost into nonbeing.

The sports pages of that morning's newspaper told the story of Davey's grief. It was the defeat of Benny Leonard, one of the three defeats this remarkable champion was ever to suffer in the ring.

Benny was the boy's hero. On the short side himself, putting his reliance on skill, speed, dexterity, what the kids called "form," it was only natural that Davey should identify this way with the peerless lightweight.

Stories he had heard at home of the Old World pogroms and persecutions had created an uncertainty, a fear, which required a defender. This defender was required against no present foe but against some unknown future enemy, even against the monstrous foes of the past—Haman, Antiochus Epiphanes, the thundering Black Hundreds.

It was no accident that at this time (later his heroes were the mighty figures Ruth and Dempsey) he needed the prince-hero, the 135-pounder who could weave, parry, outguess his opponent, jab, feint, dance off, and yet throw the sudden knockout punch, and then come dancing into the middle of the ring, his dark hair unruffled, saying into the microphone: "Hi Mom, he never even touched me."

At this moment Daniel Mendoza would not do, but Benny Leonard would.

He remembered his mother's story. She was taking care of the store in their Russian village. Suddenly the cry "Cossacks!" She quickly locked up the store, ran desperately. How Davey wished he could have been there to defend her. . . .

"Hi Davey."

It was Chick, also out in the street for that glorious hour between supper and sleep.

"What's eatin' you, Davey?"

When Davey mentioned the fight, Chick was surprised. He couldn't understand that much of a reaction.

"So what," said Chick, "you can't win them all."

Chick was one of those kids who had more easily thrown off his ghetto past. He did not seem to carry within him the ancient walled cities, the night-time assaults and terrors; he did not dream of the bearded Jew shot to death in the tunnels under the New York Central Railway up on Park Avenue. He took for granted the prevailing freedom, was not drawn to the ancient midnight, nor was he disturbed by vague and monstrous presentiments, menacing shadows. He was well-adjusted historically.

This rather flippant attitude on Chick's part both angered and relieved Davey, the anger because his friend did not share his woe, the relief because his friend kept him from sinking deeper and deeper into this woefulness.

It was not yet dark, just light enough to see a ball, so they had a catch, throwing the ball back and forth in a leisurely manner—slow balls, curves, floaters, and an occasional fireball down the groove. Allie and Richie joined them, and they got into a quick game of boxball, playing under the lamp post. Then it was too late to play, and they sauntered down the block, toward the candy store.

"Last one down is a rotten egg," said Chick, and the four of them were off in a flash. Allie, a P.S.A.L. runner, won easily, by four or five boxes. Richie, who was kind of heavy, pulled up a game last.

"You're the rotten egg," said Chick, but the satisfaction was not abiding.

Inside the candy store they picked and chose among the sponges, the caramels, the licorices, the creams, in the secure and exciting candy world.

Coming out, at their ease, chewing, or biting, or sucking, or crunching, they paused near a group of the Big Guys who were hanging around in front of the store. They stood close enough to the Big Guys to hear everything that was being said, but far enough away (they hoped) not to disturb them.

Included among these Big Guys was a lad who was not so much a stranger (for he was one of those nomadic types who thought it nothing to wander three or four blocks from his own block) as what you might call a "border figure"; he hung around enough so that he was no stranger, but still he did not belong, because he did not live on the block. There was always an element of suspicion attached to one who did not live on the block. He was called "The Gate," or when he was addressed directly, "Gate." This nickname apparently referred to the figure he once had, wide and formidable. There were some signs of that old figure, out of which he had grown, and yet he kept the nickname (like a tall "Pee Wee" or a gray-haired "Red"). A later school of sociologists may decide that the nickname "Gate" refers to the blocking maneuver, founded on superstition, or suspicion, in a dice game.

Now the conversation of the Big Guys was not of a particularly profound sort. It related to given individuals, mixed praise with the most severe criticism, the foulest maledictions, and was punctuated by expectorations geared for aim or distance. But to Davey and his friends, age conferred, if not dignity, a certain awe, because of that extra measure of experience, the activities just beyond them, so they listened, hoping to get closer to the unknown, the forbidden, and to be initiated painlessly into the mystery of the stage ahead.

But this cynical adoration on the part of the youngsters (for it was not exactly improvement they were looking for) did not predispose *all* of the Big Guys in their favor. Some were pleased, some paid them no mind, but The Gate, who looked around and saw these blemishes on the landscape, said: "Whatta you kids hangin' roun' for?"

At this question the four of them, in a kind of reflex movement, seemed to come closer together, but nobody made a move, for it was clear that the taunter was not serious in his intentions.

The scattered interchange of praise and invective went on; two of the older fellows lit up cigarettes, but The Gate was not one of those two.

"Beat it, you shrimps," he said.

This statement was not yet the one requiring flight (though it was a move in that direction from the previous question) because it was a command, but without a threat attached.

None of the Big Guys showed much interest in The Gate's annoyance, they looked at it as a kind of eccentricity, but with a sure knowledge that there *was* a motive, inexplicable to be sure, but the kind of motive that could induce any one of them, under similar pressures, to behave quite the same way. One of them said, tolerantly, "Aw, leave the kids alone, Gate."

But this friendly admonition only angered him the more. It was as though he was being opposed not only by the silent four, but by these contemporaries of his in whose company he was still somewhat of an outsider, where he still had to prove himself.

"Get goin'," said The Gate, "befaw I roon yiz."

Here was the command, and the threat, but no overt move. The Gate's rhetorical string was played out—his next move was pursuit. Again one of the Big Guys put a cautionary word to him, asking: "What's the diff if they stay here?" implying the acceptance and even enjoyment of the kids' somewhat idle homage.

"Because they're a buncha wise kids, that's what," said The

Gate, and it was just then that Davey tossed up his ball, catching it in his backward-cupped hand.

Here, finally, was a reason, an act of insubordination to justify The Gate's wrath. He had been publicly humiliated.

"Aw right now," he said, and then he made his move. His intentions were obviously to disperse this group, swiftly, by this move in their direction, and then to return to the charmed circle, quietly triumphant.

To his surprise (and deepening chagrin), one of the four detached himself from the group, and advanced toward him, on his toes, in the approved boxing stance. The taunter was being taunted. In the few seconds between Davey's first move and his near approach, The Gate realized in what an absurd predicament he now found himself, forced to do battle with a kid three years younger and maybe thirty pounds lighter. To take on four of the kids was one thing; to find himself isolated with the one was monstrous. A victory could be only hollow and meaningless, a defeat catastrophic. He had no way of coming out at all. He looked longingly at Chick, Allie, and Richie, hoping they would move in to do battle, but they had stopped in their headlong flight, and were watching in fascination as their comrade-in-arms advanced on the enemy.

"Go way, ya runt," said The Gate to Davey, "go back tu da cradle."

In reply, Davey threw a left jab, which grazed The Gate's cheek.

Some of the Big Guys snickered. It was easy for them to turn against this suspect border figure.

The Gate had to protect himself, for to be hit by the kid was in itself an embarrassment, perhaps not so bad as sloughing him, but certainly shameful enough. The Gate's position was deteriorating fast, he could find help neither from his friends nor from his enemies.

Davey, meanwhile, was desperately trying to remember everything he had read about his hero's style. "Keep jabbin' him," he said to himself, "jab him crazy, look for the opening, and if you don't find it move back. Then jab away again."

He followed his own instructions to the letter. The Gate had to adopt a fighting stance in order to avoid the ignominy of being hit. Davey was fighting against an immovable target, for if The Gate were to start moving forward that would constitute an offensive, and The Gate realized that after he was out of this absurd predicament he would have to be able to say: "The kid went crazy, I just kept blocking his punches."

But that turned out not to be the case, for every now and then one of Davey's blows landed, and each jab was a monstrous humiliation for the older boy.

Davey was in a kind of euphoria, imitating the image of himself, and every now and then realizing that it was all real, that he had fled the imaginary world where victory was dearly but surely won and was struggling here in the street, where the issue was always in doubt. Once more he jabbed at The Gate, struck him lightly under the eye, and danced off, but not before The Gate, helpless and infuriated, struck out blindly and hit Davey high up on the cheek.

The Gate advanced threateningly.

"Why doncha grow up?" he asked, but Davey's answer was a long left jab. One of the Big Guys snickered.

This ambiguous bout was brought to an end by a passerby, one of those gents whose sense of justice is outraged by the sight of an obviously unequal struggle (as contrasted to one of those gents whose sense of exactly what is outraged by the sight of an obviously equal struggle).

"Here, break it up, you two."

The Gate turned toward this gentleman with a look of the deepest gratitude. "You are a veritable Nestor," he seemed to be saying, "a depository of the most profound truths buried in the heart of mankind."

Davey was perhaps less pleased with the turn of events, and would have been even more less-pleased had his cheekbone not begun to swell and cause some discomfort.

"That'll loin ya," said The Gate, as Davey walked off with his friends, but this remark was meant for what record?

Davey was considerably cheered, he understood as well as the next one that the Big Guy had pulled his punches, but he was pleased with his own exhibition. Looking back, he saw himself in the classic weave, felt the acclaim of his invisible mentor.

"That was nice goin'," said Richie admiringly, and Davey felt also the approbation of the others. Then they walked each other home, and finally Davey and Chick stood together in the early darkness. They spoke seriously of matters of import, of the latest trade in the American League, of the next club meeting, of the distance of the furthest star.

"So long," said Chick, "see ya."

"So long," said Davey, and he sprinted to the door of his apartment, then opened the door slowly, hoping to avoid at least a direct appearance before his parents.

He reached his room without being seen, and raised a warning finger to his lips at his brother Danny, as he opened and closed the door.

"Who socked you?" asked the younger brother.

"The Gate," said Davey, and he gave a blow-by-blow description.

Danny was proud, envious, and disbelieving.

"You don't have to believe me," said Davey, "just ask anyone tomorrow."

Then he got onto his bed and started on his homework. He wasn't at it long when his sister Joan, who was between the two boys in age, entered noiselessly.

"Did you see my *Little Women*?" she asked.

Davey denied any knowledge of the whereabouts of this work; Danny denied any knowledge of the very meaning of the question.

"It's a book," she said, "and I'm sure you know where it is."

The last part of the sentence was directed to Davey, who had been facing the wall, but now turned round to meet the gaze of his accuser.

She gasped with interest.

"What happened to you?" she asked.

"Oh, it's nothing," he said, "but don't tell Mom and Pop about it."

"If it's nothing," she asked, "why can't I tell them?"

"Instead of being so smart," he said, "why don't you think of something that will help?"

"Beefsteak," said Danny, who was steeped in all sorts of esoteric lore, "that will reduce the swelling."

"That's the same as steak," said Davey to his sister. "See if there's any in the kitchen."

She went and returned with a piece of steak in her hand.

"Great," said Davey, and he applied the meat to his cheek.

There was an instant of silence; then he opened his mouth with every intention of shrieking bloody murder, remembered the danger of disclosure, and bit into the meat, his eyes shut in agony.

"What's the matter?" gasped Joan.

"It burns," he said, "real bad."

They both looked at Danny, whose look of puzzlement suddenly passed into the area of understanding.

"Naturally," he said, "Mom salted the meat already."

"You're a girl," said Davey to Joan, "you should know all about these things."

"Don't bother me," said Joan, as she beat a retreat in the face of her brother's repeated admonitions to say absolutely nothing.

"They'll see it in the morning," said Danny sagaciously.

But Davey was not taking such a long view. He asked Danny to bring in some milk and crackers, and they ate and drank together.

Then it was Danny's bedtime, and Davey, to avoid discovery and because he was tired, got into bed himself. Deep in his soul he exulted, having fought in the manner of his peerless champion, and for his vindication.

In Dreams Begin Responsibilities

Delmore Schwartz

1

I think it is the year 1909. I feel as if I were in a motion picture theatre, the long arm of light crossing the darkness and spinning, my eyes fixed on the screen. This is a silent picture as if an old Biograph one, in which the actors are dressed in ridiculously old-fashioned clothes, and one flash succeeds another with sudden jumps. The actors too seem to jump about and walk too fast. The shots themselves are full of dots and rays, as if it were raining when the picture was photographed. The light is bad.

It is Sunday afternoon, June 12th, 1909, and my father is walking down the quiet streets of Brooklyn on his way to visit my mother. His clothes are newly pressed and his tie is too tight in his high collar. He jingles the coins in his pockets, thinking of the witty things he will say. I feel as if I had by now relaxed entirely in the soft darkness of the theatre; the organist peals out the obvious and approximate emotions on which the audience rocks unknowingly. I am anonymous, and I have forgotten myself. It is always so when one goes to the movies, it is, as they say, a drug.

My father walks from street to street of trees, lawns and houses, once in a while coming to an avenue on which a street-car skates and gnaws, slowly progressing. The conductor, who has a handle-bar mustache helps a young lady wearing a hat like a bowl with feathers on to the car. She lifts her long skirts slightly as she mounts the steps. He leisurely makes change and rings his bell. It is obviously Sunday, for everyone is wearing Sunday clothes, and the street-car's noises emphasize the quiet of the holiday. Is not Brooklyn the City of Churches? The shops are closed and their shades drawn, but for an occasional stationery store or drug-store with great green balls in the window.

My father has chosen to take this long walk because he likes to walk and think. He thinks about himself in the future and so arrives at the place he is to visit in a state of mild exaltation. He pays no attention to the houses he is passing, in which the Sunday dinner is being eaten, nor to the many trees which patrol each street, now coming to their full leafage and the time when they will room the whole street in cool shadow. An occasional carriage passes, the horse's hooves falling like stones in the quiet afternoon, and once in a while an automobile, looking like an enormous upholstered sofa, puffs and passes.

My father thinks of my mother, of how nice it will be to introduce her to his family. But he is not yet sure that he wants to marry her, and once in a while he becomes panicky about the bond already established. He reassures himself by thinking of the big men he admires who are married: William Randolph Hearst, and William Howard Taft, who has just become President of the United States.

My father arrives at my mother's house. He has come too early and so is suddenly embarrassed. My aunt, my mother's sister, answers the loud bell with her napkin in her hand, for the family is still at dinner. As my father enters, my grandfather rises from the table and shakes hands with him. My mother has run upstairs to tidy herself. My grandmother asks my father if he has had dinner, and tells him that Rose will be downstairs soon. My grandfather opens the conversation by remarking on the mild June weather. My father sits uncomfortably near the table, holding his hat in his hand. My grandmother tells my aunt to take my father's hat. My uncle, twelve years old, runs into the house, his hair touseled. He shouts a greeting to my father, who has often given him a nickel, and then runs upstairs. It is evident that the respect in which my father is held in this household is tempered by a good deal of mirth. He is impressive, yet he is very awkward.

2

Finally my mother comes downstairs, all dressed up, and my father being engaged in conversation with my grandfather becomes uneasy, not knowing whether to greet my mother or continue the conversation. He gets up from the chair clumsily and says "hello" gruffly. My grandfather watches, examining their congruence, such as it is, with a critical eye, and meanwhile rubbing his bearded cheek roughly, as he always does when he reflects. He is worried; he is afraid that my father will not make a good husband for his oldest daughter. At this point something happens to the film, just as my father is saying something funny to my mother; I am awakened to myself and my unhappiness just as my interest was rising. The audience begins to clap impatiently. Then the trouble is cared for but the film has been returned to a portion just shown, and once more I see my grandfather rubbing his bearded cheek and pondering my father's character. It is difficult to get back into the picture once more and forget myself, but as my mother giggles at my father's words, the darkness drowns me.

My father and mother depart from the house, my father shaking hands with my mother once more, out of some unknown uneasiness. I stir uneasily also, slouched in the hard chair of the theatre. Where is the older uncle, my mother's older brother? He is studying in his bedroom upstairs, studying for his final examination at the College of the City of New York, having been dead of rapid pneumonia for the last twenty-one years. My mother and father walk down the same quiet streets once more. My mother is holding my father's arm and telling him of the novel which she has been reading; and my father utters judgments of the characters as the plot is made clear to him. This is a habit which he very much enjoys, for he feels the utmost superiority and confidence when he approves and condemns the behavior of other people. At times he feels moved to utter a brief "Ugh,"—whenever the story becomes what he would call sugary. This tribute is paid to his manliness. My mother feels satisfied by the interest which she has awakened; she is showing my father how intelligent she is, and how interesting.

They reach the avenue, and the street-car leisurely arrives. They are going to Coney Island this afternoon, although my mother considers that such pleasures are inferior. She has made up her mind to indulge only in a walk on the boardwalk and a pleasant dinner, avoiding the riotous amusements as being beneath the dignity of so dignified a couple.

My father tells my mother how much money he has made in the past week, exaggerating an amount which need not have been exaggerated. But my father has always felt that actualities somehow fall short. Suddenly I begin to weep. The determined old lady who sits next to me in the theatre is annoyed and looks at me with an angry face, and being intimidated, I stop. I drag out my handkerchief and dry my face, licking the drop which has fallen near my lips. Meanwhile I have missed something, for here are my mother and father alighting at the last stop, Coney Island.

3

They walk toward the boardwalk, and my father commands my mother to inhale the pungent air from the sea. They both breathe in deeply, both of them laughing as they do so. They have in common a great interest in health, although my father is strong and husky, my mother frail. Their minds are full of theories of what is good to eat and not good to eat, and sometimes they engage in heated discussions of the subject, the whole matter ending in my father's announcement, made with a scornful bluster, that you have to die sooner or later anyway. On the boardwalk's flagpole, the American flag is pulsing in an intermittent wind from the sea.

My father and mother go to the rail of the boardwalk and look down on the beach where a good many bathers are casually walking about. A few are in the surf. A peanut whistle pierces the air with its pleasant and active whine, and my father goes to buy peanuts. My mother remains at the rail and stares at the ocean. The ocean seems merry to her; it pointedly sparkles and again and again the pony waves are released. She notices the children digging in the wet sand, and the bathing costumes of the girls who are her own age. My father returns with the peanuts. Overhead the sun's lightning strikes and strikes, but neither of them are at all aware of it. The boardwalk is full of people dressed in their Sunday clothes and idly strolling. The tide does not reach as far as the boardwalk, and the strollers would feel no danger if it did. My mother and father lean on the rail of the boardwalk and absently stare at the ocean. The ocean is becoming rough; the waves come in slowly, tugging strength from far back. The moment before they somersault, the moment when they arch their backs so beautifully, showing green and white veins amid the black, that moment is intolerable. They finally crack, dashing fiercely upon the sand, actually driving, full force downward, against the sand, bouncing upward and forward, and at last petering out into a small stream which races up the beach and then is recalled. My parents gaze absentmindedly at the ocean, scarcely interested in its harshness. The sun overhead does not disturb them. But I stare at the terrible sun which breaks up sight, and the fatal, merciless, passionate ocean, I forget my parents. I stare fascinated and finally, shocked by the indifference of my father and mother, I burst out weeping once more. The old lady next to me pats me on the shoulder and says "There, there, all of this is only a movie, young man, only a movie," but I look up once more at the terrifying sun and the terrifying ocean, and being unable to control my tears, I get up and go to the men's room, stumbling over the feet of the other people seated in my row.

4

When I return, feeling as if I had awakened in the morning sick for lack of sleep, several hours have apparently passed and my parents are riding on the merry-go-round. My father is on a black horse, my mother on a white one, and they seem to be making an eternal circuit for the single purpose of snatching the nickel rings which are attached to the arm of one of the posts. A hand-organ is playing; it is one with the ceaseless circling of the merry-go-round.

For a moment it seems that they will never get off the merry-go-round because it will never stop. I feel like one who looks down on the avenue from the 50th story of a building. But at length they do get off; even the music of the hand-organ has ceased for a moment. My father has acquired ten rings, my mother only two, although it was my mother who really wanted them.

They walk on along the boardwalk as the afternoon descends by imperceptible degrees into the incredible violet of dusk. Everything fades into a relaxed glow, even the ceaseless murmuring from the beach, and the revolutions of the merry-go-round. They look for a place to have dinner. My father suggests the best one on the boardwalk and my mother demurs, in accordance with her principles.

However they do go to the best place, asking for a table near the window, so that they can look out on the boardwalk and the mobile ocean. My father feels omnipotent as he places a quarter in the waiter's hand as he asks for a table. The place is crowded and here too there is music, this time from a kind of string trio. My father orders dinner with a fine confidence.

As the dinner is eaten, my father tells of his plans for the future, and my mother shows with expressive face how interested she is, and how impressed. My father becomes exultant. He is lifted up by the waltz that is being played, and his own future begins to intoxicate him. My father tells my mother that he is going to expand his business, for there is a great deal of money to be made. He wants to settle down. After all, he is twenty-nine, he has lived by himself since he was thirteen, he is making more and more money, and he is envious of his married friends when he visits them in the cozy security of their homes, surrounded, it seems, by the calm domestic pleasures, and by delightful children, and then, as the waltz reaches the moment when all the dancers swing madly, then, then with awful daring, then he asks my mother to marry him, although awkwardly enough and puzzled, even in his excitement, at how he had arrived at the proposal, and she, to make the whole business worse, begins to cry, and my father looks nervously about, not knowing at all what to do now, and my mother says: "It's all I've wanted from the moment I saw you," sobbing, and he finds all of this very difficult, scarcely to his taste, scarcely as he had thought it would be, on his long walks over Brooklyn Bridge in the revery of a fine cigar, and it was then that I stood up in the theatre and shouted: "Don't do it. It's not too late to change your minds, both of you. Nothing good will come of it, only remorse, hatred, scandal, and two children whose characters are monstrous." The whole audience turned to look at me, annoyed, the usher came hurrying down the aisle flashing his searchlight, and the old lady next to me tugged me down into my seat, saying: "Be quiet. You'll be put out, and you paid thirty-five cents to come in." And so I shut my eyes because I could not bear to see what was happening. I sat there quietly.

5

But after awhile I begin to take brief glimpses, and at length I watch again with thirsty interest, like a child who wants to maintain his sulk although offered the bribe of candy. My parents are now having their picture taken in a photographer's booth along the boardwalk. The place is shadowed in the mauve light which is apparently necessary. The camera is set to the side on its tripod and looks like a Martian man. The photographer is instructing my parents in how to pose. My father has his arm over my mother's shoulder, and both of them smile emphatically. The photographer brings my mother a bouquet of flowers to hold in her hand but she holds it at the wrong angle. Then the photographer covers himself with the black cloth which drapes the camera and all that one sees of him is one protruding arm and his hand which clutches the rubber ball which he will squeeze when the picture is finally taken. But he is not satisfied with their appearance. He feels with certainty that somehow there is something wrong in their pose. Again and again he issues from his hidden place with new directions. Each suggestion merely makes matters worse. My father is becoming impatient. They try a seated pose. The photographer explains that he has pride, he is not interested in all of this for the money, he wants to make beautiful pictures. My father says: "Hurry up, will you? We haven't got all night." But the photographer only scurries about apologetically, and issues new directions. The photographer charms me. I approve of him with all my heart, for I know just how he feels, and as he criticizes each revised pose according to some unknown idea of rightness, I become quite hopeful. But then my father says angrily: "Come on, you've had enough time, we're not going to wait any longer." And the photographer, sighing unhappily, goes back under his black covering, holds out his hand, says: "One, two, three, Now!", and the picture is taken, with my father's smile turned to a grimace and my mother's bright and false. It takes a few minutes for the picture to be developed and as my parents sit in the curious light they become quite depressed.

6

They have passed a fortune-teller's booth, and my mother wishes to go in, but my father does not. They begin to argue about it. My mother becomes stubborn, my father once more impatient, and then they begin to quarrel, and what my father would like to do is walk off and leave my mother there, but he knows that that would never do. My mother refuses to budge. She is near to tears, but she feels an uncontrollable desire to hear what the palm-reader will say. My father consents angrily, and they both go into a booth which is in a way like the photographer's, since it is draped in black cloth and its light is shadowed. The place is too warm, and my father keeps saying this is all nonsense, pointing to the crystal ball on the table. The fortune-teller, a fat, short woman, garbed in what is supposed to be Oriental robes, comes into the room from the back and greets them, speaking with an accent. But suddenly my father feels that the whole thing is intolerable; he tugs at my mother's arm, but my mother refuses to budge. And then, in terrible anger, my father lets go of my mother's arm and strides out, leaving my mother stunned. She moves to go after my father, but the fortune-teller holds her arm tightly and begs her not to do so, and I in my seat am shocked more than can ever be said, for I feel as if I were walking a tight-rope a hundred feet over a circus-audience and suddenly the rope is showing signs of breaking, and I get up from my seat and begin to shout once more the first words I can think of to communicate my terrible fear and once more the usher comes hurrying down the aisle flashing his searchlight, and the old lady pleads with me, and the shocked audience has turned to stare at me, and I keep shouting: "What are they doing? Don't they know what they are doing? Why doesn't my mother go after my father? If she does not do that, what will she do? Doesn't my father know what he is doing?"—But the usher has seized my arm and is dragging me away, and as he does so, he says: "What are *you* doing? Don't you know that you can't do whatever you want to do? Why should a young man like you, with your whole life before you, get hysterical like this? Why don't you *think* of what you're doing? You can't act like this even if other people aren't around! You will be sorry if you do not do what you should do, you can't carry on like this, it is not right, you will find that out soon enough, everything you do matters too much," and he said that dragging me through the lobby of the theatre into the cold light, and I woke up into the bleak winter morning of my 21st birthday, the window-sill shining with its lip of snow, and the morning already begun.

America! America!

Delmore Schwartz

When Shenandoah Fish returned from Paris in 1936, he was unable to do very much with himself, he was unable to write with the great fluency and excitement of previous years. Some great change had occurred in the human beings he knew in his native city, whom he had sought out before his stay in Europe. The depression had occurred to these human beings. It had reached the marrow at last; after years, the full sense of the meaning of the depression had modified their hopes and their desires very much. The boys with whom Shenandoah had gone to school no longer lived in the same neighborhood, they no longer saw much of each other, they were somewhat embarrassed when they met, some of them were married now, and many of them were ashamed of what they had made or what had been made of their lives. After visits which concluded in perplexity, Shenandoah ceased to try to renew his old friendships. They no longer existed and they were not going to rise from the grave of the dead years.

Yet Shenandoah was not troubled by his idleness. He would have liked to be in Paris again, and he expected to go back next year. He did not know then that it would be impossible for him to go back. Meanwhile, as his mother said, he was taking it easy, and enjoying an indolence and a relaxation which, though peculiar in him, seemed unavoidable after the prolonged and intense activity of the year before.

He slept late each morning, and then he sat for a long time at the breakfast-table, listening to his mother's talk as she went about her household tasks. It was simple and pleasant to shift attention back and forth between what his mother said and the morning newspaper, for in the morning sunlight, the kitchen's whiteness was pleasant, the newspaper was always interesting in the strength of attention possible in the morning, and Shenandoah found his mother's monologue pleasant too. She spoke always of her own life or of the lives of her friends; of what had been; what might have been; of fate, character and accident; and especially of the mystery of the family life, as she had known it and reflected upon it.

After two months of idleness, Shenandoah began to feel uneasy about these breakfast pleasures. The emotion which often succeeded extended idleness returned again, the emotion of a loss or lapse of identity. "Who am I? what am I?" Shenandoah began once more to say to himself, and although he knew very well that this was only the projection of some other anxiety, although he knew that to work too was merely to deceive himself about this anxiety, nonetheless the intellectual criticism of his own emotions was as ever of no avail whatever.

On the morning when this uneasiness of the whole being overtook Shenandoah seriously, his mother's monologue began to interest him more and more, much more than ever before, although she spoke of human beings who, being of her own generation, did not really interest Shenandoah in themselves. She began to speak of the Baumanns, whom she had known well for thirty years.

The Baumanns, said Mrs. Fish, had given Shenandoah a silver spoon when he was born. Mrs. Fish brought forth the silver and showed Shenandoah his initials engraved in twining letters upon the top of the spoon. Shenandoah took the spoon and toyed with it nervously, looking at the initials as he listened to his mother.

The friendship of the Fish family with the Baumann family had begun in the period just before the turn of the century. Shenandoah's father, who was now dead, had gone into what was then entitled the insurance *game*. The word rang in Shenandoah's mind, and he noted again his mother's fine memory for the speech other people used. Mr. Baumann who was twenty years older than Shenandoah's father, had already established himself in the business of insurance; he had been successful from the start because it was just the kind of business for a man of his temperament.

Shenandoah's mother proceeded to explain in detail how insurance was a genial medium for a man like Mr. Baumann. The important thing in insurance was to win one's way into the homes and into the confidences of other people. Insurance could not be sold as a grocer or a druggist sells his *goods* (here Shenandoah was moved again by his mother's choice of words); you could not wait for the customer to come to you;

nor could you like the book salesman go from house to house, plant your foot in the doorway, and start talking quickly before the housewife shut the door in your face. On the contrary, it was necessary to become friendly with a great many people, who, when they came to know you, and like you, and trust you, take your advice about the value of insurance.

It was necessary to join the lodges, societies, and associations of your own class and people. This had been no hardship to Mr. Baumann who enjoyed groups, gatherings, and meetings of all kinds. He had in his youth belonged to the association of the people who came from the old country, and when he married, he joined his wife's association. Then he joined the masonic lodge, and in addition he participated in the social life of the neighborhood synagogue, although he was in fact an admirer of Ingersoll. Thus he came to know a great many people, and visited them with unfailing devotion and regularity, moved by his love of being with other human beings. A visit was a complicated act for him. It required that he enter the house with much amiability, and tell his host that he had been thinking of him and speaking of him just the other day, mentioning of necessity that he had just *dropped* in for a moment. Only after protestations of a predictable formality, was Mr. Baumann persuaded to sit down for a cup of tea. Once seated, said Mrs. Fish (imposing from time to time her own kind of irony upon the irony which sang in Shenandoah's mind at every phase of her story), once seated it was hours before Mr. Baumann arose from the dining-room table on which a fresh table-cloth had been laid and from which the lace cover and the cut-glass had been withdrawn.

Mr. Baumann drank tea in the Russian style, as he often explained; he drank it from a glass, not from a cup: a cup was utterly out of the question. And while he drank and ate, he discoursed inimitably and authoritatively upon *every topic of the day,* but especially upon his favorite subjects, the private life of the kings and queens of Europe, Zionism, and the new discoveries of science. A silent amazement often mounted in his listeners at the length of time that he was capable of eating, drinking, and talking; until at last, since little was left upon the table, he absentmindedly took up the crumbs and poppyseeds from the tablecloth.

Mrs. Fish had not known Mr. Baumann until he was near middle age. But she had heard that even in his youth, he had looked like a banker. As he grew older and became quite plump, this impression was strengthened, for he took to pince-nez glasses, and handsome vests with white piping. Shenandoah remembered that Mr. Baumann resembled some photographs of the first J. P. Morgan. His friends were delighted with all the aspects of his being, but they took especial satisfaction in his appearance. They were shamed often enough into allowing him to *write* a new insurance policy for them, for it was a time of general prosperity for these people: most of them were rising in the world, after having come to America as grown or half-grown children. Their first insecurity was passed and hardly borne in mind, except in the depths of consciousness; and now they were able to *afford* an insurance policy, just as they were able to look down on newcomers to America, and their own early lives in America, a state of being which was expressed by the word, *greenhorn*. Mr. Baumann's friendship was a token of their progress; they liked him very much, they were flattered by his company, and when he paid them a visit, he conferred upon the household a sense of the great world, even of intellectuality. This pleased the husband often because of what it implied to his wife; it implied that although he, the husband, was too busy a man in the dress business to know much of these worldly matters, yet he was capable of having the friendship and *bringing into the house* this amiable and cultivated man who spoke English with a Russian accent which was extremely refined.

Shenandoah's mother explained then that in the insurance business a good man like Mr. Baumann soon arrives at the point where there is no urgent need to acquire new customers and to write new policies. One can live in comfortable style off the commissions due you as the premiums continue to be paid from year to year. You must maintain your friendship with the policyholders, so that the stress of hard times as it recurs does not make them give up their policies or stop paying the premiums. But this need of reassuring and cajoling policyholders did not for Mr. Baumann interfere with a way of life in which one slept late in the morning and made breakfast the occasion for the most painstaking scrutiny of the morning newspaper. One can go for vacations whenever one pleases, and Mr. Baumann went often with his family, on religious holidays and on national holidays. In fact, Mr. Baumann had frequently written some of his best policies during the general high spirits which are the rule on vacations and at resorts. He was at his best at such times and amid such well-being.

Here Shenandoah recognized in his mother's tone the resentment she had always felt toward those who lived well and permitted nothing to stop their enjoyment of life. It was the resentment of one who had herself never felt the inclination to live well, and regarded it as unjustified, except on the part of the very rich, or during holidays.

Mrs. Fish continued, saying that an insurance man is faced with one unavoidable duty, that of putting in an appearance at the funerals of human beings with whom he has been acquainted, even though he has not known them very well. This is a way of paying tribute to one of the irreducible facts upon which the insurance business is founded. And it provides the starting-point for useful and leading conversation.

"Yes," Mr. Baumann often said, "I was at L——'s funeral today." His tone implied the authoritative character of his presence.

"Yes," he reiterated with emphasis, squeezing the lemon into his tea, "we all have to go, sooner or later!"

Then he dwelt on the interesting incidents at the funeral, the children's lack of understanding, the widow's hysterical weeping, the life-like appearance of the corpse.

"He looked," said Mr. Baumann, "just like he was taking a nap."

And indeed, apart from *doing business,* Mr. Baumann enjoyed funerals for their own sake, for they were comprehensive gatherings of human beings with whom he had everything in common and to whom he was a very interesting and very *well-informed* man, even a man, as he seemed to some and to himself, who was a sage although without rabbinical trappings.

Here, having said this with unconscious disdain, Mrs. Fish finished ironing a tablecloth, folded it carefully, placed it with other ironed linens, took a new piece, and permitted herself no pause in her monologue.

She said that Mrs. Baumann was the one person who was unable to take Mr. Baumann with the seriousness he expected and received in all quarters. She preferred the neighborhood rabbi as a sage. She and her husband shared so many interests that there was a natural and extensive antagonism between them. Whatever gentleman occupied the rabbinical position in the neighborhood synagogue surpassed her husband at his own game, so far as she was concerned: surpassed him in unction, suavity, and fecundity of opinion.

Next to her husband, Mrs. Baumann seemed small and almost tiny. She was nervous and anxious, while he was always assured; and he merely smiled when she attacked him or criticized him before other people, or told him that he was talking too much, or said that he did not know what he was talking about. However, they loved the same things, and some of her resentment of her husband had as its source his freedom to have a full social life while she had to take care of the children. For her children, her friends, and all things Jewish, she had an inexhaustible charity, indulgence, and attentiveness, and consequently she sometimes neglected her household in order to make many visits and tell many stories, stories of patient detail and analysis which had to do with her friends. In the time before the World War, Freud and Bergson were celebrated in Jewish newspapers as Jews who had made a great fame for themselves in the Gentile world. Mrs. Baumann relished their fame to the point of making out a misleading and mistaken version of their doctrines; and in this way, Shenandoah's father, who visited the Baumann household very often before his marriage, learned of the teachings of Freud and passed them on to the salesmen who worked for him in the real estate business.

Only one thing excited Mrs. Baumann more than the success of a musician or an inventor who was Jewish; and that one thing was a new fad, especially fads about food. She often spoke of herself as having a new *fad*, and she often said that everyone should have fads. For the word pleased her, and some of its connotations had never occurred to her. She said often that she wished that she were a vegetarian.

As Shenandoah listened to his mother, he became nervous. He was not sure at any given moment whether the cruelty of the story was in his own mind or in his mother's tongue. And his own thoughts, which had to do with his own life, and seemed to have nothing to do with these human beings, began to trouble him.

What is it, he said to himself, that I do not see in myself, because it is of the present, as they did not see themselves? How can one look at oneself? No one sees himself.

As the Baumann children grew up, they seemed to gain vitality from the intensive social life of the household. For their small apartment near a great park came to be a kind of community center on Sunday nights. All whom Mr. Baumann met on his leisurely rounds were invited to come at any time. Both husband and wife knew very well how glad lonely human beings are to have a house to visit, a true household; and especially the human beings who have gone from the community life of the old country and foundered amid the immense alienation of metropolitan life. And the Baumanns also knew, although they were too wise to express the belief, that it was very important to have something to eat amid the talk, for people do not continue very long without the desire to eat; and in addition, the conversations, the jokes and the comments are improved, heightened, or excited by food and drink, by sandwiches, cake, and coffee; and the food one gets in another's household seems *exceptionally appetizing.*

Shenandoah as he listened tried to go back by imagination or imaginative sympathy to the lives of these people. Certainly in the old country there had been periods when food was scarce, so that one of the most wonderful things about America was the abundance of food. But it was impossible for Shenandoah, who had always been well-fed, to convince himself that he knew what their feelings about food had been. He returned to his mother who had begun genre studies of Sunday nights in the Baumann household.

Each of the Baumann children as they grew up amid these scenes of much sociability acquired social talents which gained them gratifying applause from the visitors, who were expected, in any case, in a profound, unspoken understanding, to make much of the children of any household. Dick, the oldest of the three children, learned to play the piano very cleverly, and he recited limericks and parodies. Sidney, the youngest one, was enchanted by the Sunday nights to the extent that he brought his neighborhood cronies to the house, which was a revelation most children avoided and dreaded because they were ashamed that their parents spoke broken English or a foreign tongue.

Sidney was less gifted than his brother; yet he was liked a good deal because he was small and *cute.* Martha, the girl, suffered from the intense aversions, shames, and frustrations of girlhood; and, as her father remarked, she *took it out* upon the piano, playing romantic music from morning to night. She was very smart and clever; and her remarks were often so biting that she was scolded helplessly, vainly, and tirelessly by her mother. Visitors, however, were charmed and not annoyed, when she was *fresh.* And as she became older, she defended herself by saying that she had learned her wit and irony at the Sunday night school of gossip, when all who were present analyzed the failings of their absent friends. Nonetheless, despite her bitter remarks about the household, she loved its regime very much, though annoyed to see how she depended upon it to nourish the depths of her being.

It was when Dick and Martha were old enough to need jobs that Shenandoah's father and Mr. Baumann went into partnership in the real estate business. Shenandoah's father had been in business *for himself* for some time and he had prospered greatly. It was his need of capital, which however he might have secured elsewhere, and his fondness for the Baumann's household which had made him suggest the partnership. The suggestion was made in a moment of weakness and well-being, when Mr. Fish had just enjoyed a fine dinner at the Baumann's. Whenever Shenandoah's father was pleased and had enjoyed himself very much, he suffered from these generous and unexpected impulses; but this did not prevent him from repairing the evil consequences of his magnanimity with an equally characteristic ruthlessness as soon as it was obvious that it not only had been costly (for then, he might forget about it), but that the cost would continue.

The difficulty soon showed itself, for Mr. Baumann and Dick made it clear that their habits of life were not going to be changed merely because they were now part of a *going concern*. Father and son arrived at work an hour before noon, which permitted them just enough time to look at the mail before departing for an unhurried lunch. They *drew* handsome salaries, and this was what troubled Shenandoah's father most of all. When it was a question of making a sale, Mr. Baumann often allowed his interests of the moment, which were often international in scope, to make him oblivious of *the deal*. He ingratiated himself with the customer very well, but this process ingratiated the customer with Mr. Baumann, and thus the mutual bloom of friendship, made business matters unimportant or a matter for tact and delicacy. Dick followed in his father's footsteps. He took customers to the ball game, which was well enough except that he too forgot the true and ulterior purpose of this spending of the firm's money. In three months, Shenandoah's father appreciated his error to the full; and for a week of half-sleepless nights, he strove to think of a way to free himself of his pleasure-loving partner. In the end, and as often before, he found only a brutal method; he sent Mr. Baumann a letter stating his grievances and dissolving the partnership. For a time, this summary dismissal ended the friendship of the two families. But Mr. Baumann was utterly unable to sustain a grudge, although his wife was unable to forget one, and *pestered* him about his weakness in forgiving those who had injured him.

Dick Baumann seemed to be unable to keep a job and he showed few signs of being able to make his way in the world. But he was popular, he had an *immense* number of friends, he was in request all over because he was always truly and literally the life of every party. At one such party, he met his future wife, an extremely beautiful girl who was also successful and had her own business. She was the only child of a mother deserted by her husband, and never had she been so charmed as by Dick, by Dick's parodies, imitations, out-goingness, and his fine air of well-being and happiness. Although somewhat perplexed by the girl's intense and fond looks, since he had not paid much attention to her, Dick had invited her to the Baumann ménage, where Mrs. Baumann immediately fell in love with her. Dick was pliant and suggestible, Mrs. Baumann was the only strong-willed one in the family, and soon she had arranged matters in such a way that after a certain amount of urging on her part, everyone recognized the inevitability of the marriage.

First, however, Dick had to make a living. His intended had her handsome business, which she *ran* with a cousin. But this did not seem right to Mrs. Baumann; it offended her sense of propriety. She expected that it would end very soon, and she spoke of its ending all the time. She insisted that it must end before the marriage took place, since it was not only intolerable that a wife should make her own living, should go to work each day, but it was wrong that the wife should earn more money than the husband. As it happened, Dick was in no hurry to get married. He wished to please his mother, as he wished to please all. But from morning until night, he enjoyed being *single;* yet he did not conceive of his marriage as bringing about any great change in his habits, or any new goodness.

Shenandoah listened with an interest which increased continuously; and yet his own thoughts intervened many times. He reflected upon his separation from these people, and he felt that in every sense he was removed from them by thousands of miles, or by a generation, or by the Atlantic Ocean. What he cared about, only a few other human beings, separated from each other too, also cared about; and whatever he wrote as an author did not enter into the lives of these people, who should have been his genuine relatives and friends, for he had been surrounded by their lives since the day of his birth, and in an important sense, even before then. But since he was an author of a certain kind, he was a monster to them. They would be pleased to see his name in print and to hear that he was praised at times, but they would never be interested in what he wrote. They might open one book, and turn the pages; but then perplexity and boredom would take hold of them, and they would say, perhaps from politeness and certainly with humility, that this was too *deep* for them, or too *dry*. The lower middle-class of the generation of Shenandoah's parents had engendered perversions of its own nature, children full of contempt for every thing important to their parents. Shenandoah had thought of this gulf and perversion before, and he had shrugged away his unease by assuring himself that this separation had nothing to do with the important thing, which was the work itself. But now as he listened, as he felt uneasy and sought to dismiss his emotion, he began to feel that he was wrong to suppose that the separation, the contempt, and the gulf had nothing to do with his work; perhaps, on the contrary, it was the center; or perhaps it was the starting-point and compelled the innermost motion of the work to be flight, or criticism, or denial, or rejection.

Mrs. Fish had gone to the roof for more wash. She told Shenandoah as she returned that it was time for him to dress (for he had been in dressing-gown and pajamas all the while), and in her imperative tone, he recognized the strain and the resistance which was part of the relationship of mother and son; which had its cause in the true assumption that mother and son would disagree about what was the right thing to do, no matter what the problem might be.

The *engagement* of Dick and Susan was a protracted one; and after two years, the youthful couple had begun to take their intermediate state for granted. Mrs. Baumann in pride told her friends that Susan *practically* lived with them. It was by no means unusual for Susan to be at the Baumann household on every weekday evening, and on such evenings, as Dick read the sport pages with care, his mother interrupted him persistently to demand that he admire Susan's profile as she sat near the window, sewing. Susan was very beautiful indeed; and her business grew more and more prosperous as

Dick went from job to job, unperturbed that a girl waited for him, a fact to which Mrs. Baumann often summoned his attention.

At last, being impatient, Mrs. Baumann arranged that the marriage should occur at the beginning of one of Dick's business ventures, the capital for which had been provided by Mr. Baumann and Susan. It was as if, remarked Shenandoah's mother, Mrs. Baumann was afraid to await the outcome of the new venture. And she had been right, for within eight months the business had to be given up to avoid bankruptcy, and Susan had to return to work as an assistant where before she had been *her own boss,* a humiliation which left Susan without any further illusions about her mother-in-law. The two never again managed to get along very well, although Mrs. Baumann's admiration of her daughter-in-law remained undisturbed. Mrs. Baumann was unable to understand Dick's failure to get rich, for no one failed to be delighted by his charm and his intelligence; and he always seemed to have a great deal of information about each new business. But somehow he was unable to make a success of it, or even to make it *pay.*

After his marriage, Dick frequented his parents' household as often as before marriage, a simple enough matter since he and his bride had taken an apartment near the parents to please Mrs. Baumann. And when Susan had to go back to work, it became convenient for the young married couple to have dinner every night with the whole Baumann family, a procedure Susan resented very much, although she was of a divided heart, since she too often enjoyed the conviviality of the family circle as much as before marriage.

One subject prevailed above others in the Baumann circle, the wonders of America, a subject much loved by all the foreign-born, but discussed in the Baumann household with a scope, intensity, subtlety, and gusto which was matchless, so far as Mrs. Fish knew. One reason for this subject's triumph was Mr. Baumann's interest in science, and one reason was that he was very much pleased with America.

When the first plane flew, when elevators became common, when the new subway was built, some newspaper reader in the Baumann household would raise his head, announce the wonder, and exclaim:

"You see: America!"

When the toilet-bowl flushed like Niagara, when a suburban homeowner killed his wife and children, and when a Jew was made a member of President Theodore Roosevelt's cabinet, the excited exclamation was:

"America! America!"

The expectations of these human beings who had come in their youth to the new world had not been fulfilled in the least. They had above all expected to be rich, and they had come with a very different image of what their new life was to be. But a thing more marvellous than fulfillment had transformed their expectations. They had been amazed to the pitch where they knew that their imaginations were inadequate to conceive the future of this incredible society. They expected and did not doubt that all the wonders would continue and increase; and Mr. Baumann maintained, against rising and rocking laughter, that his grandchildren would return from business by a means of transit which resembled the cash carriers which fly through tubes in department stores. Mrs. Baumann's conception of the future was less mechanical and scientific. She hoped and expected her grandchildren would be millionaires and grandsons, rabbis, or philosophers like Bergson.

Sidney, the youngest child, had arrived at the age when it was expected that he too should earn a living for himself. But the disappointments Dick had caused were nothing to the difficulties Sidney made. Dick had been an indifferent student, but Sidney flatly refused to continue school at all after a certain time, and he displayed unexampled finickiness about the job Mr. Baumann's friends gave him, or helped him to get. He left his job as a shipping clerk because he did not like *the class of people* with whom he had to work, and he refused to take a job during July and August on the ground that he suffered greatly from summer heat, a defense natural to him after the many family discussions of health, food, and exercise. His mother always defended and *humored him*, saying that his health was delicate. But Mr. Baumann was often made furious and at times of an insane anger by his youngest son's indolence. Mrs. Baumann pointed out that Sidney was to be admired, after all, since in being unable to work he showed a sensitivity to *the finer things in life*. But Mr. Baumann knew too much of the world not to be concerned about the fact that both of his sons appeared to be unable to make out well in the world. In anger, he blamed his wife and his wife's family; but on other occasions, he discussed the problem with his friends, once with Shenandoah's father after the two were reconciled.

"I'll tell you what to do," said Mrs. Fish, "but you won't do it."

"Tell me," said Mr. Baumann, although he knew well enough he was not likely to take his friend's advice.

"Ship Sidney out into the world," said Shenandoah's father, "make him stand on his own two feet. As long as he has a place to come home to and someone else to give him money for cigarettes, and plenty of company in the house, he's not going to worry about losing a job."

"But if a boy does not have ambition," Mr. Baumann replied, "is that enough? I always say, it all depends on the individual. His home has nothing to do with it. It is always the character of the person that counts."

"Sure it depends on character," said Mr. Fish, "but a fellow only finds out about his own character when he's all by himself, with no one to help him. Why if I had been your son," said Shenandoah's father, flattered that his advice was asked and wishing to please his friend, "I would have quit work myself and taken it easy and enjoyed the pleasant evenings."

A year after, Sidney was sent to Chicago to be *on his own,* although not before he had been given the addresses of many friends and relatives of the family. In three months, he was back; he had quarreled with his boss about working hours and he had exhausted his funds. He was welcomed into the bosom of the family with unconcealed joy. Although Mr. Baumann grumbled, and Martha addressed habitual ironic remarks to her brother as *a captain of industry,* no one had failed to feel his absence keenly and to be pleased deeply by his return.

"Well: you can try in New York as well as Chicago," said Mr. Baumann, "a smart boy like you is bound to get started sooner or later."

Mrs. Baumann believed that Sidney would fall in love one day, and this would prove the turning point. Either he would meet a rich girl who would be infatuated with *his personality,* or he would meet some poor girl and his desire to marry her would inspire him. In America, everyone or almost everyone was successful. Mrs. Baumann had seen too many fools make out very well to be able to believe otherwise.

And now all he had heard moved Shenandoah to remember all he himself knew of the Baumann family. The chief formal occasions of the Fish family had always been marked by the presence of the Baumanns. Each incident cited by his mother suggested another one to Shenandoah, and he began to interrupt his mother's story and tell her what he himself remembered. She would seize whatever he mentioned and augment it with her own richness of knowledge and experience.

As a girl, Martha had suffered an attack of polio, which left her with a curvature of the spine, which in turn made it unlikely that she would be able to have children. Martha had then decided that this defect and her plainness of appearance, a plainness which, although she did not know this truth, disappeared in her natural vivacity and wit—would prevent her from getting a husband. She would be an old maid, the worst of shames from the point of view of a Jewish mother. The belief that she would never marry heightened Martha's daring wit and *nerve*. She was the one who continued her father's intellectual interests. As he would cite the authors he had read in Russia as a young man, Pushkin, Lermontov, and Tolstoy, so she was much taken with Bernard Shaw and H. G. Wells, and spoke with bitter passion about women's suffrage.

And then, to the amazement of all, a young doctor who had frequented the household, a very shy young man who was already very successful, asked Martha to marry him, pale with fear that she would laugh at him and attack him with her famous sharpness and scorn. When she told him that he would have to go through life without children, he replied with a fine simplicity that he loved her and expected her to make a home for him which would be like her mother's household.

This marriage became the greatest satisfaction of the Baumanns' life, although it did not *compensate* for the shortcomings of the sons in business. Mrs. Baumann tirelessly praised her son-in-law, and marvelled infinitely at his magnanimity in marrying a girl who was unable to have children. She took especial pride in his being a very good doctor, a fact which impressed the women of her acquaintance because they wished most of all for sons or sons-in-law who were doctors. But it was for Mrs. Baumann a triumph chiefly because of her passionate interest in health.

Martha's harshness and sharpness rose to new heights with her marriage, and she became more relentless than ever with her brother, while often Maurice, her husband, found it necessary to protest gently, from a profound gentleness of heart, because she had once again called both brothers *failures*.

Maurice had an admiration for the arts which gave him the conventional independence of conventional business values. He tried to argue with Martha that she was being *very conventional* and accepting conventional views of what *success* was. Martha, inspired by an enjoyment of her own brutality of speech, replied that there was one thing the Baumanns were wonderfully successful at, and that was marriage: they made first-class marriages. She was referring then not only to her own husband's prosperity and generosity, but also to Susan, who had started her own business again, and for years now had supported her husband and herself, and provided Dick with the capital for each new enterprise he attempted, spurred by his mother's anguish at the way things were.

Martha became more impatient with her family year by year, and after a time she did not wish to see them at all. But Maurice gently insisted that she pay her parents a weekly visit, and he sought to soothe the parents' hurt feelings when Martha saw to it that they lived in a suburb distant from the Baumann household.

America! America! The expression began to recur in Shenandoah's mind, like a phrase of music heard too often the day before. He was moved, and in a way shocked, as his mother was too, that Martha the family rebel, the one who had repudiated the family circle many times, should be the one who made out well in life. Shenandoah's mother amazed him by remarking that the two sons were unsuccessful because they were like their father, who had been successful, however, because of what he was. The sons had followed the father and yet for some unclear cause or causes, the way of life which had helped him to prosper prevented them from prospering.

And now Shenandoah remembered his last meeting with Mrs. Baumann, two years before. Late in the afternoon in October, as Shenandoah rewrote a poem, Mrs. Baumann's voice had come through the closed bedroom door. And he had been annoyed because he now had to come from his room, pale and abstracted, his mind elsewhere, to greet his mother's friends. It turned out that Mrs. Baumann had come with a friend, a woman of her own age, and when Shenandoah entered the living room, Mrs. Baumann, as voluble as Mr. Fish, told Shenandoah in a rush the story of her friendship with this woman.

They had come to America on the same boat in the year

1888, and this made them *ship sisters*. And then, although their friendship had continued for some years, one day at a picnic of the old country's society, a sudden storm had disturbed the summer afternoon, everyone had run for cover, and they had not seen each other for the next nineteen years. And Mrs Baumann seemed to feel that the summer thunderstorm had somehow been the reason for their long and unmotivated separation. The two old women drank tea and continued to tell the youthful author about their lives and how they felt about their lives; Shenandoah was suddenly relaxed and empty, now that he had stopped writing; he listened to them and drank tea too. Mrs. Baumann told Shenandoah that in her sixty-five years of life she had known perhaps as many as a thousand human beings fairly well, and when she tried to sleep at night, their faces came back to her so clearly that she believed she could draw their faces, if she were a painter. She was sickened and horrified by this plenitude of memory, although it was wholly clear why she found the past appalling. Yet these faces kept her from falling asleep very often, and consequently she was pleased and relieved to hear the milkman's wagon, which meant that soon the darkness would end and she would get up, make breakfast for her family and return to the world of daylight. Mrs. Baumann felt that perhaps she ought to see a psychoanalyst, like Freud, to find out what was wrong with her.

Her companion offered advice at this point; she said that everyone should have *a hobby*. Her own hobby was knitting and she felt that without her knitting in the morning, she would *go crazy*. This woman's daughter had married a *Gentile*, and she was permitted to visit her only child on monthly occasions when the husband had absented himself. Her one longing, one which she knew would never be satisfied, was to return and visit the old country.

"You would like it there," she said to Shenandoah, speaking of the country of her young girlhood. Shenandoah was flattered.

And as he listened to the two old women, Shenandoah tried to imagine their arrival in the new world and their first impression of the city of New York. But he knew that his imagination failed him, for nothing in his own experience was comparable to the great displacement of body and mind which their coming to America must have been.

Although almost finished with her ironing, Mrs. Fish was far from finished with her story. She was able to illustrate all that she said with fresh or renewed memories. And what she said bloomed in Shenandoah's mind in forms which would have astonished and angered her. Her words descended into the marine world of his mind and were transformed there, even as swimmers and deep-sea divers seen in a film, moving underwater through new pressures and compulsions, and raising heavy arms to free themselves from the dim and dusky green weight of underseas.

Shenandoah's mother now had progressed to the period of great prosperity in America. The worst animosity had come to exist between Mr. Baumann and his son Sidney, for whenever Sidney was criticized by his father for not earning his own living, he replied by citing the success of his father's friends, many of whom were becoming rich. Few of them had the charm or presence of Mr. Baumann, but they were able to give their sons a start in life. Sidney, an avid reader of newspapers like his mother, had acquired a host of examples of immigrants who had made a million dollars. The movie industry was for Sidney a standing example of his father's ineptitude, his failure to make the most of opportunity in the land of promise. It seemed unfair to go outside the family circle of friends, but Sidney was merciless when criticized, and *stopped at nothing*. And Mr. Baumann was left helpless by Sidney's attack, for he felt there was something wrong not only with the comparisons his son made, but the repeated and absolute judgment that his life had not been successful. He himself was satisfied and felt successful. He had always provided for his wife and his children, and kept them in comfort. It was true that he did not work very hard, but then there was no need to work very hard, he made out well enough, since he had an income from the insurance policies he had written for the last thirty years, when the premiums were paid or when the policy was renewed. Yet Sidney used these professions as obvious admissions of weakness. He observed that the sons of other men had a *ten-dollar bill* to spend on a girl on Saturday nights, but he did not. The more unsuccessful he was, the more outrageous became his verbal assault upon his father for not having made a million dollars. He was provoked to these attacks by renewed efforts to get him to work, and by the citation of young men of his age who would soon be wealthy men in their own right, although they came from the households of parents who were really *common*.

During the period of great prosperity the Baumanns and

Shenandoah's mother became intimate friends, since Shenandoah's father had left her. And often Mrs. Baumann and Mrs. Fish discussed the fate of the Baumann children. Mrs. Fish had once given Mrs. Baumann what she still regarded as very good advice, she had told her friend that the salvation of the family would have been the summer hotel business, which they had once considered seriously as an enterprise. No one would have been better suited for that business than the Baumanns, and this was indeed a *high compliment*.

When his mother said such things, Shenandoah suffered for the moment, at any rate, from the illusion that his mother had a far greater understanding of the difficulties of life than he had. It seemed to him at such times that the ignorance he saw in her was a sign of his own arrogant ignorance. Her understanding was less theoretical, less verbal and less abstract than his, and such privations were in fact virtues. She was never deceived about any actual thing by words or ideas, as he often was. And she had just perceived perfectly a profound necessity which he himself knew very well in literature, the necessity that the artist find the adequate subject and the adequate medium for his own powers. No one could deny that the proper medium for the gifted Baumanns was the summer hotel.

What Mrs. Baumann did not understand and sought to explain to herself and Mrs. Fish was the paradox that her sons, who had a good bringing-up unlike many successful young men, had made out so poorly in comparison with most of them. She wished to know whose fault it was, if it were her fault, if she ought to blame herself, as her husband blamed her, for *humoring* and *indulging* the boys. The head start, and the fine home which the boys had, seemed to be a handicap, but this was an impossible thing to think. Mr. Baumann had remembered the advice given him by Mr. Fish, that the boys would be more ambitious if they had no home to come to, and he had distorted this counsel into an explanation which declared that Mrs. Baumann had pampered her sons. Mrs. Baumann returned with this problem many times, eager to be reassured and anxious to be told that on the contrary she was a wonderful mother. Shenandoah's mother was already prepared to blame someone for everything that happened, but she had a general and theoretical interest in the problem which left her free of her natural prepossessions. She observed that one defect of the Baumann sons was their unwillingness to go from door to door for the sake of getting some business. They had not been reared to expect *hard knocks* and rebuffs, and here precisely was where boys of meaner families had the advantage. It was a strange and sad thing, both women agreed, that a certain refinement—nothing like the Four Hundred, *you understand,*—but merely a simple taste for the normal good things of life should be a severe and conclusive handicap. The greatest handicap, said Mrs. Fish, was the fine family circle; this was what had weakened the boys for a world where you had to fight for everything you wanted, and you had to fight all the time just to keep what you had. Mrs. Fish observed again that this was *a cut-rate cut-throat world,* an expression which was her version of the maxim, *dog eat dog.* The best preparation for such a world, as Mrs. Fish's experience had proved many times, was to be born into a family of thirteen children where there was never enough for everyone to eat.

After 1929, when those who had been successful lost so much, Sidney mounted to new summits of scorn. Before 1929, he had been contemptuous of *the system;* now that no one made out well Sidney took the national depression as a personal vindication. Every banker or broker caught in some kind of dishonesty became an instance to Sidney of his own integrity. He suggested that if he had been prepared to do such things, he too might have enjoyed their success.

And now Mr. Baumann was no longer able to support an idle son, for with the hard times people abandoned their insurance or borrowed on it. The father's difficulties and the son's arrogance made their quarrels more and more desperate. As Mr. Baumann dressed to pay a visit one Saturday night, he was unable to find the pair of shoes he wanted. As always, he was concerned about his appearance, and he became very irritated at being unable to find his shoes, and came into his son's bedroom to ask him if he had seen the shoes, and Sidney, outstretched upon his bed, reading and smoking, was annoyed to be interrupted, and replied that his father ought not to be concerned about such a cheap pair of shoes. The shoes were not cheap, in any case, and this typical judgment of his taste by his son, whose standards were derived from his Christmas jobs in fashionable clothing stores, infuriated Mr. Baumann. He hit Sidney with the flat of his hand, and only Mrs. Baumann's screaming entrance prevented a fist-fight. The day after, Sidney had a black eye which he tried to conceal with powder. It was a Sunday and the Baumanns were going to pay a visit. Sidney wished to go with them, being unable to endure solitude at any time, and having nowhere to go that afternoon. But his mother reminded him of his black eye and his father added that he had no clothes, especially no shoes, suitable for the visit they were going to make. When the Baumanns returned at midnight, they found an emergency wagon and the police in front of the apartment house. Sidney had tried to kill himself by turning on the gas in the kitchen, there had been an explosion, and he had not even been injured. Sidney was taken to Bellevue and kept there for a number of months. When visited by his mother, he told her *she should remember* that it was his father who had driven him to insanity. Hearing this, Mr. Baumann retaliated by saying that his son had been unable to be anything but a failure, even at suicide; and he reported to all that at the hospital, Sidney could not be made to take up any of the forms of occupational therapy. It seemed an epitome to Mr. Baumann that even at this extreme his son should refuse to do anything *remotely resembling work.* It was not customary for Mr. Baumann to be as harsh as this with any human being, but nothing would help Mr. Baumann to forget what Sidney had said to him during the early years of the depression, when Mr. Baumann's income had first begun to be sharply curtailed. He said to his father that *the old oil* no longer worked, and when his father said in perplexity and anger, *what oil? what is this oil?,* Sidney had replied, *banana oil!,* laughing with his whole body at his witticism and then explaining to his father that it was foolish to expect to persuade anyone that insurance was anything but *a gyp* by the old methods of striking up a friendship and paying long visits, *spouting* like the neighborhood sage.

Sidney remained under observation, and Dick assisted his wife in her thriving business. He had a child now. Martha and her husband prospered more and more because the practice of medicine was not as bound to general prosperity as business itself. And after an operation and much nervousness, Martha too had a child. Both grandchildren were daughters, which was a disappointment, but which showed, at any rate, that all disappointments were not financial in origin. As Dick often said,

"Money is not everything," to which his sister always replied,

"Money helps," smiling at her own irony.

They were all ashamed of Sidney's *smash-up*, as Dick termed it, but this did not keep them from speaking of it openly with all their friends. Mr. Baumann at seventy was still able to eke out a living for himself and his wife, but he was a disappointed and disillusioned man. He blamed everything on the individual and on his sons' lack of will-power. Mrs. Baumann blamed everything on her husband. She said to Mrs. Fish, however, speaking of Sidney:

"You see: this is what we came to America for forty-five years ago, for this."

Shenandoah was exhausted by his mother's story. He was sick of the mood in which he had listened, the irony and the contempt which had taken hold of each new event. He had listened from such a distance that what he saw was an outline, a caricature, and an abstraction. How different it might seem, if he had been able to see these lives from the inside, looking out.

And now he felt for the first time how closely bound he was to these people. His separation was actual enough, but there existed also an unbreakable unity. As the air was full of the radio's unseen voices, so the life he breathed in was full of these lives and the age in which they had acted and suffered.

Shenandoah went to his room and began to dress for the day. He felt that the contemptuous mood which had governed him as he listened was really self-contempt and ignorance. He thought that his own life invited the same irony. The impression he gained as he looked in the looking-glass was pathetic, for he felt the curious omniscience gained in looking at old photographs where the posing faces and the old-fashioned clothes and the moment itself seem ridiculous, ignorant, and unaware of the period quality which is truly there, and the subsequent revelation of waste and failure.

Mrs. Fish had concluded her story by saying that it was a peculiar but an assured fact that some human beings seemed to be ruined by their best qualities. This shocking statement moved in Shenandoah's mind and became a generalization about the fate of all human beings and his own fate.

"What will become of me?" he said to himself, looking in the looking-glass.

"What will I seem to my children?" he said to himself. "What is it that I do not see now in myself?"

"I do not see myself. I do not know myself. I cannot look at myself truly."

He turned from the looking-glass and said to himself, thinking of his mother's representation of the Baumanns, "No one truly exists in the real world because no one knows all that he is to other human beings, all that they say behind his back, and all the foolishness which the future will bring him."

No Kaddish for Weinstein

Woody Allen

Weinstein lay under the covers, staring at the ceiling in a depressed torpor. Outside, sheets of humid air rose from the pavement in stifling waves. The sound of traffic was deafening at this hour, and in addition to all this his bed was on fire. Look at me, he thought. Fifty years old. Half a century. Next year, I will be fifty-one. Then fifty-two. Using this same reasoning, he could figure out his age as much as five years in the future. So little time left, he thought, and so much to accomplish. For one thing, he wanted to learn to drive a car. Adelman, his friend who used to play dreidel with him on Rush Street, had studied driving at the Sorbonne. He could handle a car beautifully and had already driven many places by himself. Weinstein had made a few attempts to steer his father's Chevy but kept winding up on the sidewalk.

He had been a precocious child. An intellectual. At twelve, he had translated the poems of T. S. Eliot into English, after some vandals had broken into the library and translated them into French. And as if his high I.Q. did not isolate him enough, he suffered untold injustices and persecutions because of his religion, mostly from his parents. True, the old man was a member of the synagogue, and his mother, too, but they could never accept the fact that their son was Jewish. "How did it happen?" his father asked, bewildered. My face looks Semitic, Weinstein thought every morning as he shaved. He had been mistaken several times for Robert Redford, but on each occasion it was by a blind person. Then there was Feinglass, his other boyhood friend: A Phi Beta Kappa. A labor spy, ratting on the workers. Then a convert to Marxism. A Communist agitator. Betrayed by the Party, he went to Hollywood and became the offscreen voice of a famous cartoon mouse. Ironic.

Weinstein had toyed with the Communists, too. To impress a girl at Rutgers, he had moved to Moscow and joined the Red Army. When he called her for a second date, she was pinned to someone else. Still, his rank of sergeant in the Russian infantry would hurt him later when he needed a security clearance in order to get the free appetizer with his dinner at Longchamps. Also, while at school he had organized some laboratory mice and led them in a strike over work conditions. Actually, it was not so much the politics as the poetry of Marxist theory that got him. He was positive that collectivism could work if everyone would learn the lyrics to "Rag Mop." "The withering away of the state" was a phrase that had stayed with him, ever since his uncle's nose had withered away in Saks Fifth Avenue one day. What, he wondered, can be learned about the true essence of social revolution? Only that it should never be attempted after eating Mexican food.

The Depression shattered Weinstein's Uncle Meyer, who kept his fortune under the mattress. When the market crashed, the government called in all mattresses, and Meyer became a pauper overnight. All that was left for him was to jump out the window, but he lacked the nerve and sat on a window sill of the Flatiron Building from 1930 to 1937.

"These kids with their pot and their sex," Uncle Meyer was fond of saying. "Do they know what it is to sit on a window sill for seven years? There you see life! Of course, everybody looks like ants. But each year Tessie—may she rest in peace—made the Seder right out there on the ledge. The family gathered round for Passover. Oy, nephew! What's the world coming to when they have a bomb that can kill more people than one look at Max Rifkin's daughter?"

Weinstein's so-called friends had all knuckled under to the House Un-American Activities Committee. Blotnick was turned in by his own mother. Sharpstein was turned in by his answering service. Weinstein had been called by the committee and admitted he had given money to the Russian War Relief, and then added, "Oh, yes, I bought Stalin a dining-room set." He refused to name names but said if the committee insisted he would give the heights of the people he had met at meetings. In the end he panicked, and instead of taking the Fifth Amendment, took the Third, which enabled him to buy beer in Philadelphia on Sunday.

Weinstein finished shaving and got into the shower. He lathered himself, while steaming water splashed down his bulky back. He thought, Here I am at some fixed point in time and space, taking a shower. I, Isaac Weinstein. One of God's creatures. And then, stepping on the soap, he slid across the floor and rammed his head into the towel rack. It had been a bad week. The previous day, he had got a bad haircut and was still not over the anxiety it caused him. At first the barber had snipped judiciously, but soon Weinstein realized he had gone too far. "Put some back!" he screamed unreasonably.

"I can't," the barber said. "It won't stick."

"Well, then give it to me, Dominic! I want to take it with me!"

"Once it's on the floor of the shop it's mine, Mr. Weinstein."

"Like hell! I want my hair!"

He blustered and raged, and finally felt guilty and left. Goyim, he thought. One way or another, they get you.

Now he emerged from the hotel and walked up Eighth Avenue. Two men were mugging an elderly lady. My God, thought Weinstein, time was when one person could handle that job. Some city. Chaos everyplace. Kant was right: The mind imposes order. It also tells you how much to tip. What a wonderful thing, to be conscious! I wonder what the people in New Jersey do.

He was on his way to see Harriet about the alimony payments. He still loved Harriet, even though while they were married she had systematically attempted to commit adultery with all the *R*'s in the Manhattan telephone directory. He forgave her. But he should have suspected something when his best friend and Harriet took a house in Maine together for three years, without telling him where they were. He didn't *want* to see it—that was it. His sex life with Harriet had stopped early. He slept with her once on the night they first met, once on the evening of the first moon landing, and once to test if his back was all right after a slipped disc. "It's no damn good with you, Harriet," he used to complain. "You're too pure. Every time I have an urge for you I sublimate it by planting a tree in Israel. You remind me of my mother." (Molly Weinstein, may she rest in peace, who slaved for him and made the best stuffed derma in Chicago—a secret recipe until everyone realized she was putting in hashish.)

For lovemaking, Weinstein needed someone quite opposite. Like LuAnne, who made sex an art. The only trouble

was she couldn't count to twenty without taking her shoes
off. He once tried giving her a book on existentialism, but
she ate it. Sexually, Weinstein had always felt inadequate.
For one thing, he felt short. He was five-four in his stocking
feet, although in someone else's stocking feet he could be as
tall as five-six. Dr. Klein, his analyst, got him to see that
jumping in front of a moving train was more hostile than self-
destructive but in either case would ruin the crease in his
pants. Klein was his third analyst. His first was a Jungian, who
suggested they try a Ouija board. Before that, he attended
"group," but when it came time for him to speak he got dizzy
and could only recite the names of all the planets. His problem was women, and he knew it. He was impotent with any
woman who finished college with higher than a B-minus average. He felt most at home with graduates of typing school,
although if the woman did over sixty words a minute he panicked and could not perform.

Weinstein rang the bell to Harriet's apartment, and suddenly she was standing before him. Swelling to maculate giraffe, as usual, thought Weinstein. It was a private joke that
neither of them understood.

"Hello, Harriet," he said.

"Oh, Ike," she said. "You needn't be so damn self-righ-
teous."

She was right. What a tactless thing to have said. He hated
himself for it.

"How are the kids, Harriet?"

"We never had any kids, Ike."

"That's why I thought four hundred dollars a week was a
lot for child support."

She bit her lip, Weinstein bit his lip. Then he bit her lip.
"Harriet," he said, "I . . . I'm broke. Egg futures are down."

"I see. And can't you get help from your *shiksa*?"

"To you, any girl who's not Jewish is a *shiksa*."

"Can we forget it?" Her voice was chocked with recrimina-
tion. Weinstein had a sudden urge to kiss her, or if not her,
somebody.

"Harriet, where did we go wrong?"

"We never faced reality."

"It wasn't my fault. You said it was north."

"Reality *is* north, Ike."

"No, Harriet. Empty dreams are north. Reality is west. False hopes are east, and I think Louisiana is south."

She still had the power to arouse him. He reached out for her, but she moved away and his hand came to rest in some sour cream.

"Is that why you slept with your analyst?" he finally blurted out. His face was knotted with rage. He felt like fainting but couldn't remember the proper way to fall.

"That was therapy," she said coldly. "According to Freud, sex is the royal road to the unconscious."

"Freud said *dreams* are the road to the unconscious."

"Sex, dreams—you're going to nit-pick?"

"Goodbye, Harriet."

It was no use. *Rien à dire, rien à faire*. Weinstein left and walked over to Union Square. Suddenly hot tears burst forth, as if from a broken dam. Hot, salty tears pent up for ages rushed out in an unabashed wave of emotion. The problem was, they were coming out of his ears. Look at this, he thought; I can't even cry properly. He dabbed his ear with Kleenex and went home.

The Facts of Life

Paul Goodman

(revised by the author, 1968)

Childish Ronnie Morris has a wife Martha and a daughter Marcia, aged nine.

Ronnie is middle-aged, ten years older than ourselves, and he has invented a wonderful scheme to milk money from those who make $20,000 a year: he sells them Fine Editions with odd associations, as *The Golden Ass* bound in donkey's hide or *The New Testament* signed by the designer in the blood of a lamb. (He is childish enough to go through with such a profitable idea, instead of dismissing it like the rest of us fools.) He has a two-masted sailboat. In a business way, he knows Picasso and Thomas Benton, and is the expert at the Club in the trade-secrets of the Muses. In the acts of love, he is medium; he went to Dartmouth; but he is only moderately fixated on the period when he was fifth oar, for he had had a period of lust, which has saved him for philosophy and the arts rather than the brokerage.

Martha Morris is an Andalusian type. When she arranges flowers she keeps them under control with wires. She drives at high speeds. Her relations with Ronnie are as usual; she is her little daughter's friend, and every Christmas she and Marcia design a gift-volume for Ronnie's clientèle. She is more political than her husband and her position dramatically to the left of the right wing of the liberal center: a group that finds no representation in Washington but used to have thirty seats in Paris. I could write ads about Martha's teeth as they flash under her nose. The rhythms are delightful of the description of the upper middle class.

Now little Marcia goes to the University Progressive School where many of her schoolmates have fathers in the embassies, but Marcia, too, has been to the Near East in search of that lamb. At school they are taught to express themselves freely, and Marcia is good at colleges.

Marcia has a fight in school today with one of the little gentlemen, her contemporaries. He breaks her photographic plate. The fight is about the nature of chickens' eggs. She stamps on his foot. Being a girl, she still has an advantage in mental age and more words to say; she says a sentence in French. He can't punch her in the nose because it is ungentlemanly. He is inhibited from drawing on his best knowledge because it is dirty; but worse, it is gloomily indistinct, and even on these matters she seems to have more definite information and is about to mention it.

"Shut up!" he argues, "shut up! you're just an old-time Jew."

This perplexing observation, of which she understands neither head nor tail, brings her to a pause; for up to now, at least with Harry—though certainly not with Terry or Larry—she has maintained a queenly advantage. But he has stopped her by drawing on absolutely new information.

In this crisis she does a reckless thing: she dismisses his remark from her mind and launches into a tirade that devastatingly combines contempt and the ability to form complete sentences, till Harry goes away in order not to cry. A reckless, a dangerous thing: because what we thus dismiss enters the regions of anxiety, of loss and unfulfilled desire, and there makes strange friends. It is the prologue to fanatic interests and to falling in love. How new and otherwise real is this observation on its next appearance!

Marcia calls her mother sometimes Momsy and sometimes Martha.

"What did Harry mean," she asks her, "when he called me an old-time shoe?"

"Jew?"

"Yes, he stated I was just an old-time Joo."

Across the woman's face passes, for ever so many reasons, a perceptible tightening. "Oh oh!" feels Marcia along her ears and scalp; and now she is confirmed and doubly confirmed in the suspicions she did not know she had. When she now has to express herself with colored chalks, new and curious objects will swim into the foreground alongside the pool, the clock will become a grandfather's clock, and all be painted Prussian blue, even though Miss Coyle is trying to cajole especially the girls into using warm bright colors, because that is their natural bent.

"Well, he was right, you are a Jewess," says Martha. "It's nothing to be ashamed of."

"Said Joo, not Juice."

"A Jew is a boy; a Jewess is a girl."

"Oh! there are two kinds!"

It's worse and worse. She never thought that Harry was up on anything, but perhaps even his veiled hints conceal something. She feels, it seems inescapable, that boys have a power, surely not obvious in school—and the grownups even take it for granted! She sees it every day, that these same boys when they become men are superior to the women. Yet men's clothes don't *express* anything, and actresses are better than actors. But just this *contradiction* confirms it all the more, for the explanations of contradictions are in the indistinct region —and everything there is mutually involved. Marcia is already working on a system of the mysteries. Especially when Momsy now tries to tell her some reasonable anecdote about Jewesses and Jews, just like a previous astringent account of the chickens and the flowers.

Martha never happens to have told little Marcia that they are all Jews.

"Is Ronnie a Joo?"

"Of course."

"Are Louis and Bernie Joos?"

"Louis is a Jew but Bernie is a Gentile."

"It's a lie, thinks Marcia; they are both the same. They are both effeminate. Why is Martha lying to her?

"What is ser-cum-si-zhum?" asks Marcia, calling the lie.

This inquisition has become intolerable to Martha. "Good night, Marcia," she explains.

"Is Rosina a Juice?" Marcia cries, asking about Ronnie's mistress.

"Marcia! I said good night!"

"Tell me! tell me! is Rosina Juice?"

"No."

"Ah!"

"Why 'Ah!'?"

"Good night, Momsy," says Marcia, kissing her.

Since the habits are formed speediest where there is necessity and yet conscious and deliberate adjustment is embarrassing or tedious, Martha has speedily and long ago learned the few adjustments belonging to Jews of a certain class of money.

The other hotel; not on this list; the right to more chic and modernity, but please no associations with Betsy Ross in tableaux. Of course habits learned by this mechanism are subject to amazing breaches, when submerged desire suddenly asserts itself and the son of Jacob becomes Belmont or Ronnie becomes, as he is, an honorary colonel in the militia. But on the whole, since money is so exchangeable, there are very few special adjustments. They never even came to Marcia's keen perception, especially since none of the Jews whom she is so often with without knowing it, ever mentions them. But there are other meanings, archaically forgotten.

"Since you have to put up with the handicap whether you like it or not," decides Mrs. Ronnie Morris, "why not make an advantage of it, and be proud of it?" She is writing out a check for a subscription to *The Menorah Journal,* the *Harper's* magazine of reformed Jews.

"Never heard such a stupid argument in my life!" says Ronnie. He is very angry, like anyone who has played the game like a gentleman and then finds that the other side goes too far and calls his daughter an old-time Jew. "What's the use of *pretending* you're a Jew, when you're *not* a Jew?" he shouts.

"We are Jews. Don't shout," says Martha.

"I'll go to school and punch that brat's nose."

"Don't."

"Do I pay three hundred dollars a year for him to tell Marcia that she's a Jew?"

"But we are Jews," says Martha, with a new loyalty.

"Since when?" says Ronnie scientifically. "To be a Jew means one of three things: It means first a certain race; but there isn't any Jewish race in anthropology. Look at me, do I look like a Jewish race?"

He looks like a highly brushed and polished moujik.

"No. Secondly: it means a nationality. But even if some Jews think they have a nationality, do I? I went to Jerusalem to pick out a Gentile lamb. Anyway, I can't speak the language. Hebrew isn't the same as Yiddish, you know, even though it looks the same; but I can't speak that either.

"Third: it's a religion. So you see," he concludes, "it's not a matter of not *wanting* to be a Jew or trying to *hide* that you're a Jew, but you *can't* be a Jew if you're *not* a Jew!"

"Don't be a fool," says Martha. "A person's a Jew if his

grandparents were Jews; even one's enough sometimes, depending."

"What sense does that make?"

"Do you think it's by accident," says Martha flatly, "that your mama and papa came to marry Jews and we married Jews?"

She means, thinks Ronnie, when all desire is toward Gentiles, toward retroussé noses and moon-face Hungarians. Does she mean Rosina? She means Bernie.

"I'll ask Louis," says Ronnie; for though he holds sway at the luncheon club, all his ideas come from this poet.

"He's taking Marshy to the Picassos tomorrow."

"Let him tell her, then."

"What! are you going to let your daughter find out the facts from a stranger?"

Having slept on it all night, by morning the little girl has contrived the following working theory:

In the beginning, of course, all babies are alike. Her deep-seated conviction on this point has never been in the least shaken by Momsy's anecdotes about the chickens, for it is plain to observe that all babies are alike. But then comes the moment when the thing is cut off the girls. When this takes place, is not yet clear; but it is planned from the beginning, because you can tell by the names; although sometimes even there is a change of names; with some names you still can't tell; and others are easy to change, like Robert and Roberta or Bernie and Bernice. All of this is an old story.

But now, there are some *chosen* ones, who are supposed to be cut but somehow they get off. Why? They are only *partly* cut—and this is ser-cum-si-zhum, because they use a scissors. These are Joos. For a moment, starting from "Louis," Marcia thinks that she can tell by the names, but then when she thinks of "Ronnie" and of "Terry" and "Larry," two boys in school whom she now knows are Joos (in fact, Terry is and Larry is not), she sees that she can't. The *last* names are connected with marrying and have nothing to do with ser-cum-si-zhum.

Now, she sees in a flash, it is *better* to be a Joo, for then you still have the secret power and the thing, but at the same time you can be cleverer like a girl. This is why Larry and Terry are always able to beat her, they have an unfair advantage; but Harry, the dope, is only a boy and not a Joo.

There are also differences among Joos; for instance, Louis is much smarter than Papa. But this *proves* it, for Louis is more like Martha; that is, they cut the *best* amount off him, but not so much from Papa. Anyway, she hates Louis and loves her poor papa. Suddenly an enormous love for poor Harry suffuses her and she begins to tremble and want to go to school; he has so much secret power.

But more important—still lying in bed, Marcia begins to tremble as she thinks about herself—what is a Juice? and besides all these, there are Gen-tiles. (1. [G—] Scrip. One not a Jew.) Martha and Marcia are Juice and Bernie is a Gen-tile. Oh! what a mean thing to say about poor Bernie, that he is not even a Juice, but even worse than a girl; he is not even clever. It is nice of Louis to be so kind to him. So it seems that things go in the following order: Boys, Joos, Juices, Girls, Gen-tiles. Except that it is smartest to be a Joo. But what is it? What is it that they did to Marcia to be a Juice? As she lets her fingers move between her thighs, she breaks into a cold sweat. With a violent dismissal, she leaps from bed.

While she is eating breakfast, an awful emptiness for her boy Harry spreads within her, and she bursts into tears.

Louis, who is intelligent, often cannot resist being cruel and supercilious to Ronnie, so that Ronnie feels like punching him in the nose—but then suddenly, at a poignant touch, even suggested by his own monologue, he relapses into natural melancholia. "To me of course," says he, "your Jewish problem doesn't exist. My paternal parent twelfth removed was Joseph Karo, the author of the *Shulchan Aruch,* or *Table* of the observances; he had established the lineage back to Joseph son of Eli, so that according to the Gentile gospels, we go back to David the son of Jesse and further; but you're a Russian Jew. On my mother's side, I am related to the convert Leo the Hebrew; but that blood throughout is tainted by conversions, my three cousins, Georges de Duchesse, Georges Catala, and Georges Catala-de Duchesse were all converts of Maritain. My cousin Georges Catala-de Duchesse is the Abbot of St. Germain-des-Prés, an *idol*-worshiper, as I told him last summer. It ought to be clear by now, I said, that only Maimonides conceived the relation of God and Man in a way helpful to the Modern Age. This is my faith. "If every Jew would read the *Mishnah Torah,* he would become a perfect snob," says Louis Parigi with pride; "he would set tradition against tradition and not take the insults lying down or by appealing merely to good sense! In our poetry both the Parigis and the de Duchesses look for inspiration to the Prophets. My cousin Georges de Duchesse, on the very eve of his baptism, wrote his rime royal *Habakuk; 'Habakuk,'* as Voltaire said, 'était capable de tout!' But in writing my *Anacreontics* I have drawn on the dipsomaniac rhythms of your Chassidim. By the way, my cousin Georges Catala was married to an eighth removed descendant of the Vilna Gaon, her suicide was the cause of his conversion, which goes to show what comes of marrying with the Ashkenazim. (Are you also related to the Vilna Gaon, like all the other Lithuanians?) On the National issue, I am, like Judah ha-Levi, an allegorical Zionist; but the pathetic desire of a temporal habitation —this destroys, as I see it, just our distinction from the *Goyim*"—(he pronounces *Go-yeem* as if he had stepped from a fastness in Aragon where never a foreign Jew had once set foot);—"but God said—but *God* said," says Louis, raising a forefinger, "Make *Succoth,* Booths." At this quotation, suddenly, he sinks into the deepest gloom. "But," he finishes airily, "except the purity of our Jewish morals, what defense do I have against adultery and sodomy?"

It is especially this breezy ending that makes Ronnie punch him in the nose—almost. It's hard to put up with somebody else's thing.

In the afternoon, in front of the impassive checkerboard of *The Three Musicians,* the little girl again bursts into tears. Louis, who has with some skill been pointing out to her only such features of the difficult paintings as she is adequate to, an underfed and melancholy face, a marvelous mother bathed in rose, the fact that in 1920 the colors are no longer blended, and enveloping it all in fanciful anecdotes—he looks at her in stupefaction.

"It's not fair! It's not fair!" she sobs.

They are alone in the room.

"What's not fair dear?" says Louis.

"It's not fair 'cause it's a myst'ry, and I won't *ever* be able to understand it."

"Why you've been understanding it very well, Marcia. What you said about the colors I didn't see myself, because you're a painter and I'm not."

"You're *lying* to me—'cause it's a secret myst'ry, and I won't ever be able to understand it 'cause I'm only a girl, even if I'm a Juice."

? ?

"I understand about the colors and the poor boy, but I can't understand it *all,* 'cause they cut my thing off when I was little and Picass' is a man— An' I have nothing left but to be a nurse or a ballerina."

He takes her hand, for the tears are rolling down her cheeks.

"—I won't ever be able to make 'em with a myst'ry if I live to be a million years old."

She hides her face in her other arm, and she cries with the pent-up anxiety of her third to her ninth years.

The guard hastily goes into the other gallery.

On the walls, the impassive objects stare from side to side.

The tears glisten in Louis's eyes. "This Holy Spirit," he says—he thinks he says—"is given to us and not made by us. It's not my fault if I cannot any more."

"Ah," she says (he thinks), "maybe if it weren't for the Bernies and the Jackies, the prophetic voice of the Lord of Hosts would not prove so disheartened at the third and fourth verse."

"What a despicable argument!" he cries (he thinks), "if I'm finally tired of that boy, why don't I think so right off and not need these thin arguments to bolster up my courage? Stop staring, you," says he to the unblinking middle Musician, "or I'll punch you in the nose."

"Look, Marshy," he says reasonably to the little girl whose hand he is holding tight, "you can't expect to make pictures right off! You have to develop your power. Just as when you learn to play the piano, you have to begin with finger exercises."

"Oh!" she cries and pulls her hand away. "How could he tell so quick?" she thinks in terror; "Momsy couldn't tell."

"See, this one is easy to understand," he says, pointing to those Three Musicians. "You see, this is an oboe."

What's a Obo?"

"An oboe is a kind of wooden instrument with stops. This part is what the oboe looks like from underneath, which you

can't ordinarily see. This is a guitar; he broke it into two
pieces in order to make the pattern here with this red business.—"

"Can you, Louis?" she seizes his hand, "I mean, can you?
Can you develop your power by finger exercises?"

? ?

"Can you? Can you?"

"Certainly. Every day you'll be able to paint a little better."

"Hurrah!"

Two women come in, tittering at a pyramidal creature that
is like one of the works of the Six Days.

But the silence is twangling with the music of the guitars,
with the guitars of Catalonia, with the cubist harmony by
which the acrobats drift away.

On the school field, the fourth-year boys, in maroon sweat-
suits, are playing the in-tra-mur-al ball game, while Mr. Donlin is umpiring and keeping order. From time to time some
of the little boys have their minds on the game. When his
side is at bat, Harry is sitting on the lowest bench of the
stands and Marcia bounces pebbles on him from above. Outside the iron fence, Timmy and Page McCroskey, who go to
Holy Name Academy, are staring at the clean and distinguished boys within. Mr. Donlin looks a perfect fool, full of
manly baby-talk such as, "Gooood try!" or "C'mon *Terry*,
let's see what you can do!" Sometimes he loses his temper.
One of the boys takes off his clothes and to the amazement
of the Irish boys discloses his delicate limbs in another
maroon uniform of shorts and a shirt with a big U. Amid a
chorus of complaints, Mr. Donlin has to assert his authority
to keep the children from exposing themselves to the cold air.

"Mr. Donlin, Mr. Donlin," mimic the two outside the bars,
"kin I take off my drawers?"

A local merchant-prince, a great contributor to the University, has the exclusive franchise for the manufacture and
sale of these many uniforms. Timmy and Page and their
friends call the U-school the Jew-school. They are envious of
the boundless wealth inside the bars and of the fact that the
girls and boys go to school together. "Why doncha let the
girls play with youse?" shouts little Timmy. Page, who is a
year younger and much bolder, cries, "Mr. Donlin, kin I take
off my drawers and show the girls my prick?"

On the large field, which is used for the high-school games, the baseball, thrown by weak arms and tapped by little bats, makes little hops and arcs. Terry, distracted by the remark from the fence, drops a little pop-fly and the runners stream across the plate. Mr. Donlin advances to the fence, shouting without profanity, go away or he'll punch them in the nose. From a little distance, they shout in chorus "Jew School, Jew School!" and some of the little scholars, who at other times announce proudly that they go to the University P'rgressive School (as if they went to college), now turn pink. "Play ball!" shouts Mr. Donlin in a manly voice.

Now all the little feelings are afire.

Marcia and Harry, however, have heard nothing. They have now progressed from the first stage of touching-yet-not-touching by throwing things at each other, to the next stage of punching and pulling shoelaces.

To the Irish boys, so systematically kept in order by their father and by the priest and Brothers to whom even their mother defers, there is no way of doubting that non-Catholics enjoy a full sexual freedom. They *know*, in fact, that the Reformation began with fornication; and even more enviable are the Jews, as is proved by the anti-Semitism, otherwise incomprehensible, that forms so large a part of the instruction by the Brothers. And along with this yearning, they observe this wealth and beauty and privilege through the bars. So is consolidated that deep sentiment of inferiority which will tomorrow need firearms to soothe.

To the little rich boys, on the other hand, it is obvious that freedom lies outside the bars among those wild boys whose dirty language makes them tremble with terror and stirs unconquerable lust in each one when he is alone; who can stay out late and wear hats decorated with paper clips and beg for pennies from strangers. So even before the first clash, the rich boys feel physically and morally powerless and would like to be the slaves of the poor ones, and it will require all the machinery of the state to treat them with an iron hand.

But why should I make the case any simpler than is necessary? For Timmy also hates little Page, just as he hates the Brothers in school; and among the U-boys there are the families going up and families falling down, and the case, for instance, of tubby Billy, whose parents are slipping and climbing at the same time, and who will tomorrow be satisfied and avenged by burning for a hustler if his name happens to be

Woodrow, until with a sinking heart he one day learns that Woodrow isn't a family name, but a war name, after President Wilson.

Fascinated, Timmy is watching Marcia wrestling with Harry and pulling his hair, while he is trying to concentrate on his teammate at bat: "Make it be a good one! Make it be a good one!" he cries; and then he chases Marcia up the stands. Pressed between the bars still he is white, Timmy follows them with his stare, above him, through the stands. But she jumps down and runs across the field toward the building, and then they both disappear. Poor Timmy stares at the gray door which has just closed.—So in each heart are fixed the types of love, after the girls who seem to be easy, who have the reputation of being available, who are easy and available in idea though never in fact. The Jewish girls to the Irish boys like Timmy, and the Irish girls to the Jewish boys like Ronnie, and the sailors to Louis. But for the most part, it is just one's own kind that is really available (and really desirable, and deeply forbidden!), and that we live with in the end, as Ronnie with Martha, and Louis with Bernie; these are no doubt also types of love, but too few to give us any pleasure.

"Knock knock!" cries Page McCroskey.

"Play ball!" shouts Mr. Donlin.

"Knock knock, Mr. Donlin, knock knock!" he screams.

"Don't pay any attention, play ball," says Mr. Donlin.

"Who's there?" answered Larry.

"Cohen!"

"Don't pay any attention!" cries Mr. Donlin.

"Cohen who?" answers a voice.

"Who said it?" shouts Mr. Donlin authoritatively.

"Cohen fuck yourself!" cry Page and Timmy together.

One of the boys throws a stone at them.

"You cocksuckers!" says Timmy, casting his eyes about for some resource.

"Shut up, McCroskey," says Terry, "or I'll tell somethin' on you, but I don't want to make you shamed."

"Do you believe that pile o' shit that O'Hara said?" says Timmy wildly.

"Naw, I *saw* it!" says Terry.

"What did O'Hara say?" says Page.

A foul ball jumps out over the fence.

"H'yaann! H'yaann!" sing Page and Timmy and run down the block with the ball, grasping off their hats.

"Where's Harry Riesling? He's supposed to be coaching on first," says the beaten Mr. Donlin.

But Marcia and Harry are in one of the empty rooms where they have never been before (it is part of the high school), and she is telling him all about Picass'. He explains to her that he likes Terry and Larry swell, but he hates his big brother; but he promises just not to notice him any more. "He probably hates your papa as much as you hate *him*," Marcia observes judiciously, "so that's something you know on *him*." This insight, this knowledge, casts such an angel light on Harry's usually puzzled countenance that Marcia turns and stares at him. He explains to her that he likes geography and history, but Miss Jensen doesn't make it interesting the way Mr. Bee used to, and that's why he's not smart. When Marcia tells him that she was in Egypt and the Near-East (as opposed to the Far-East), he is struck with admiration. But different now is his admiration and his pleasure and pride in her ability to form complete sentences, as if she were a teacher whom he can kiss and lick and not even have to stand up and recite, from the animosity he felt yesterday when she was so goddamned smart. She draws on the blackboard the dolphins playing on the *Ile de France*'s prow.

"There are geniuses in every race," says Ronnie passionately, with all the energy of his desire for Rosina; "but both per capita and absolutely there are more of them among the Jews."

"I thought you said there was no Jewish race?"

"There's not, but the facts, and you can't get around it. Einstein, Ehrlich, Freud."

"Yes, the Jews are always going in for syphilis or psychoanalysis or the fourth dimension," says Martha.

"Picasso—"

"Ha, the same thing!"

"Proust—"

"There you have it!" says Martha triumphantly. "I'm not saying the Jews are not geniuses, but they're *queer*, they're just queer, that's all."

"What about Dali? He's not a Jew."

"Will you please tell me what you're trying to prove by

that? I thought you were trying to prove that all the Jews, including yourself, were geniuses."

"No, but you said that Proust and Picasso were Jews."

"*I* said it? *I* said it?"

"I didn't say you said it especially; they *are* Jews, *half-Jews*."

"Oh, don't be a fool."

Ronnie says nothing.

"And let me tell you another thing," says Martha, "you Jews are not doing yourselves any favor by putting yourselves forward so much. If Felix Frankfurter is so smart as he's supposed to be, he knows that especially just now there's no place for another Jew on the Supreme Court bench. Every Jew that gets on the Supreme Court makes it just so much harder for us and Marcia. Where do you think I'm going to be able to send her to college?"

"That's a fine way of looking at it!" cries Ronnie. "It's true enough," he thinks; but Martha has always been ahead of him on national and international affairs.

"You're a Jew, so all right!" says Mrs. Ronnie Morris née de Havilland. "It's nothing to be ashamed of. But why bring it up in public? Who asks you?"

"Who?" says Ronnie, bewildered.

"But trust a Jew to put himself forward as if he were something peculiar! If it weren't for the Jews there wouldn't be any anti-Semitism."

"Who?" asks Ronnie.

The Magic Barrel

Bernard Malamud

Not long ago there lived in uptown New York, in a small almost meager room, though crowded with books, Leo Finkle, a rabbinical student in the Yeshivah University. Finkle, after six years of study, was to be ordained in June and had been advised by an acquaintance that he might find it easier to win himself a congregation if he were married. Since he had no present prospects of marriage, after two tormented days of turning it over in his mind, he called in Pinye Salzman, a marriage broker whose two-line advertisement he had read in the *Forward*.

The matchmaker appeared one night out of the dark fourth-floor hallway of the graystone rooming house where Finkle lived, grasping a black, strapped portfolio that had been worn thin with use. Salzman, who had been long in the business, was of slight but dignified build, wearing an old hat, and an overcoat too short and tight for him. He smelled frankly of fish, which he loved to eat, and although he was missing a few teeth, his presence was not displeasing, because of an amiable manner curiously contrasted with mournful eyes. His voice, his lips, his wisp of beard, his bony fingers were animated, but give him a moment of repose and his mild blue eyes revealed a depth of sadness, a characteristic that put Leo a little at ease although the situation, for him, was inherently tense.

He at once informed Salzman why he had asked him to come, explaining that his home was in Cleveland, and that but for his parents, who had married comparatively late in life, he was alone in the world. He had for six years devoted himself almost entirely to his studies, as a result of which, understandably, he had found himself without time for a social life and the company of young women. Therefore he thought it the better part of trial and error—of embarrassing fumbling—to call in an experienced person to advise him on these matters. He remarked in passing that the function of the marriage broker was ancient and honorable, highly approved in the Jewish community, because it made practical the necessary without hindering joy. Moreover, his own parents had been brought together by a matchmaker. They had made, if not a financially profitable marriage—since neither had possessed any worldly goods to speak of—at least a successful one in the sense of their everlasting devotion to each other. Salzman listened in embarrassed surprise, sensing a sort of apology. Later, however, he experienced a glow of pride in his work, an emotion that had left him years ago, and he heartily approved of Finkle.

The two went to their business. Leo had led Salzman to the only clear place in the room, a table near a window that overlooked the lamp-lit city. He seated himself at the matchmaker's side but facing him, attempting by an act of will to suppress the unpleasant tickle in his throat. Salzman eagerly unstrapped his portfolio and removed a loose rubber band from a thin packet of much-handled cards. As he flipped through them, a gesture and sound that physically hurt Leo, the student pretended not to see and gazed steadfastly out the window. Although it was still February, winter was on its last legs, signs of which he had for the first time in years begun to notice. He now observed the round white moon, moving high in the sky through a cloud menagerie, and watched with half-open mouth as it penetrated a huge hen, and dropped out of her like an egg laying itself. Salzman, though pretending through eyeglasses he had just slipped on, to be engaged in scanning the writing on the cards, stole occasional glances at the young man's distinguished face, noting with pleasure the long, severe scholar's nose, brown eyes heavy with learning, sensitive yet ascetic lips, and a certain, almost hollow quality of the dark cheeks. He gazed around at shelves of books and let out a soft, contented sigh.

When Leo's eyes fell upon the cards, he counted six spread out in Salzman's hand.

"So few?" he asked in disappointment.

"You wouldn't believe me how much cards I got in my office," Salzman replied. "The drawers are already filled to the top, so I keep them now in a barrel, but is every girl good for a new rabbi?"

Leo blushed at this, regretting all he had revealed of himself in a curriculum vitae he had sent to Salzman. He had thought it best to acquaint him with his strict standards and specifications, but in having done so, felt he had told the marriage broker more than was absolutely necessary.

He hesitantly inquired, "Do you keep photographs of your clients on file?"

"First comes family, amount of dowry, also what kind promises," Salzman replied, unbuttoning his tight coat and settling himself in the chair. "After comes pictures, rabbi."

"Call me Mr. Finkle. I'm not yet a rabbi."

Salzman said he would, but instead called him doctor, which he changed to rabbi when Leo was not listening too attentively.

Salzman adjusted his horn-rimmed spectacles, gently cleared his throat and read in an eager voice the contents of the top card:

"Sophie P. Twenty four years. Widow one year. No children. Educated high school and two years college. Father promises eight thousand dollars. Has wonderful wholesale business. Also real estate. On the mother's side comes teachers, also one actor. Well known on Second Avenue."

Leo gazed up in surprise. "Did you say a widow?"

"A widow don't mean spoiled, rabbi. She lived with her husband maybe four months. He was a sick boy she made a mistake to marry him."

"Marrying a widow has never entered my mind."

"This is because you have no experience. A widow, especially if she is young and healthy like this girl, is a wonderful person to marry. She will be thankful to you the rest of her life. Believe me, if I was looking now for a bride, I would marry a widow."

Leo reflected, then shook his head.

Salzman hunched his shoulders in an almost imperceptible gesture of disappointment. He placed the card down on the wooden table and began to read another:

"Lily H. High school teacher. Regular. Not a substitute. Has savings and new Dodge car. Lived in Paris one year. Father is successful dentist thirty-five years. Interested in professional man. Well Americanized family. Wonderful opportunity."

"I knew her personally," said Salzman. "I wish you could see this girl. She is a doll. Also very intelligent. All day you could talk to her about books and theyater and what not. She also knows current events."

"I don't believe you mentioned her age?"

"Her age?" Salzman said, raising his brows. "Her age is thirty-two years."

Leo said after a while, "I'm afraid that seems a little too old."

Salzman let out a laugh. "So how old are you, rabbi?"

"Twenty-seven."

"So what is the difference, tell me, between twenty-seven and thirty-two? My own wife is seven years older than me. So what did I suffer?—Nothing. If Rothschild's a daughter wants to marry you, would you say on account her age, no?"

"Yes," Leo said dryly.

Salzman shook off the no in the yes. "Five years don't mean a thing. I give you my word that when you will live with her for one week you will forget her age. What does it mean five years—that she lived more and knows more than somebody who is younger? On this girl, God bless her, years are not wasted. Each one that it comes makes better the bargain."

"What subject does she teach in high school?"

"Languages. If you heard the way she speaks French, you will think it is music. I am in the business twenty-five years, and I recommend her with my whole heart. Believe me, I know what I'm talking, rabbi."

"What's on the next card?" Leo said abruptly.

Salzman reluctantly turned up the third card:

"Ruth K. Nineteen years. Honor student. Father offers thirteen thousand cash to the right bridegroom. He is a medical doctor. Stomach specialist with marvelous practice. Brother in law owns own garment business. Particular people."

Salzman looked as if he had read his trump card.

"Did you say nineteen?" Leo asked with interest.

"On the dot."

"Is she attractive?" He blushed. "Pretty?"

Salzman kissed his finger tips. "A little doll. On this I give you my word. Let me call the father tonight and you will see what means pretty."

But Leo was troubled. "You're sure she's that young?"

"This I am positive. The father will show you the birth certificate."

"Are you positive there isn't something wrong with her?" Leo insisted.

"Who says there is wrong?"

"I don't understand why an American girl her age should go to a marriage broker."

A smile spread over Salzman's face.

"So for the same reason you went, she comes."

Leo flushed. "I am pressed for time."

Salzman, realizing he had been tactless, quickly explained. "The father came, not her. He wants she should have the best, so he looks around himself. When we will locate the right boy he will introduce him and encourage. This makes a better marriage than if a young girl without experience takes for herself. I don't have to tell you this."

"But don't you think this young girl believes in love?" Leo spoke uneasily.

Salzman was about to guffaw but caught himself and said soberly, "Love comes with the right person, not before."

Leo parted dry lips but did not speak. Noticing that Salzman had snatched a glance at the next card, he cleverly asked, "How is her health?"

"Perfect," Salzman said, breathing with difficulty. "Of course, she is a little lame on her right foot from an auto accident that it happened to her when she was twelve years, but nobody notices on account she is so brilliant and also beautiful."

Leo got up heavily and went to the window. He felt curiously bitter and upbraided himself for having called in the marriage broker. Finally, he shook his head.

"Why not?" Salzman persisted, the pitch of his voice rising.

"Because I detest stomach specialists."

"So what do you care what is his business? After you marry her do you need him? Who says he must come every Friday night in your house?"

Ashamed of the way the talk was going, Leo dismissed Salzman, who went home with heavy, melancholy eyes.

Though he had felt only relief at the marriage broker's departure, Leo was in low spirits the next day. He explained it as arising from Salzman's failure to produce a suitable bride for him. He did not care for his type of clientele. But when Leo found himself hesitating whether to seek out another matchmaker, one more polished than Pinye, he wondered if it could be—his protestations to the contrary, and although he honored his father and mother—that he did not, in essence, care for the matchmaking institution? This thought he quickly put out of mind yet found himself still upset. All day he ran around in the woods—missed an important appointment, forgot to give out his laundry, walked out of a Broadway cafeteria without paying and had to run back with the ticket in his hand; had even not recognized his landlady in the street when she passed with a friend and courteously called out, "A good evening to you, Doctor Finkle." By nightfall, however, he had regained sufficient calm to sink his nose into a book and there found peace from his thoughts.

Almost at once there came a knock on the door. Before Leo could say enter, Salzman, commercial cupid, was standing in the room. His face was gray and meager, his expression hungry, and he looked as if he would expire on his feet. Yet the marriage broker managed, by some trick of the muscles, to display a broad smile.

"So good evening. I am invited?"

Leo nodded, disturbed to see him again, yet unwilling to ask the man to leave.

Beaming still, Salzman laid his portfolio on the table. "Rabbi, I got for you tonight good news."

"I've asked you not to call me rabbi. I'm still a student."

"Your worries are finished. I have for you a first-class bride."

"Leave me in peace concerning this subject." Leo pretended lack of interest.

"The world will dance at your wedding."

"Please, Mr. Salzman, no more."

"But first must come back my strength," Salzman said weakly. He fumbled with portfolio straps and took out of the leather case an oily paper bag, from which he extracted a hard, seeded roll and a small, smoked white fish. With a quick motion of his hand he striped the fish out of its skin and began ravenously to chew. "All day in a rush," he muttered.

Leo watched him eat.

"A sliced tomato you have maybe?" Salzman hesitantly inquired.

"No."

The marriage broker shut his eyes and ate. When he had finished he carefully cleaned up the crumbs and rolled up the remains of the fish, in the paper bag. His spectacled eyes roamed the room until he discovered, amid some piles of books, a one-burner gas stove. Lifting his hat he humbly asked, "A glass tea you got, rabbi?"

Conscience-stricken, Leo rose and brewed the tea. He served it with a chunk of lemon and two cubes of lump sugar, delighting Salzman.

After he had drunk his tea, Salzman's strength and good spirits were restored.

"So tell me, rabbi," he said amiably, "you considered some more the three clients I mentioned yesterday?"

"There was no need to consider."

"Why not?"

"None of them suits me."

"What then suits you?"

Leo let it pass because he could give only a confused answer.

Without waiting for a reply, Salzman asked, "You remember this girl I talked to you—the high school teacher?"

"Age thirty-two?"

But, surprisingly, Salzman's face lit in a smile. "Age twenty-nine."

Leo shot him a look. "Reduced from thirty-two?"

"A mistake," Salzman avowed. "I talked today with the dentist. He took me to his safety deposit box and showed me the birth certificate. She was twenty-nine years last August. They made her a party in the mountains where she went for her vacation. When her father spoke to me the first time I forgot to write the age and I told you thirty-two, but now I remember this was a different client, a widow."

"The same one you told me about? I thought she was twenty-four?"

"A different. Am I responsible that the world is filled with widows?"

"No, but I'm not interested in them, nor for that matter, in school teachers."

Salzman pulled his clasped hands to his breast. Looking at the ceiling he devoutly exclaimed, "Yiddishe kinder, what can I say to somebody that he is not interested in high school teachers? So what then you are interested?"

Leo flushed but controlled himself.

"In what else will you be interested," Salzman went on, "if you not interested in this fine girl that she speaks four languages and has personally in the bank ten thousand dollars? Also her father guarantees further twelve thousand. Also she has a new car, wonderful clothes, talks on all subjects, and she will give you a first-class home and children. How near do we come in our life to paradise?"

"If she's so wonderful, why wasn't she married ten years ago?"

"Why?" said Salzman with a heavy laugh. "—Why? Because she is *partikiler*. This is why. She wants the *best*."

Leo was silent, amused at how he had entangled himself. But Salzman had aroused his interest in Lily H., and he began seriously to consider calling on her. When the marriage broker observed how intently Leo's mind was at work on the facts he had supplied, he felt certain they would soon come to an agreement.

Late Saturday afternoon, conscious of Salzman, Leo Finkle walked with Lily Hirschorn along Riverside Drive. He walked briskly and erectly, wearing with distinction the black fedora he had that morning taken with trepidation out of the dusty hat box on his closet shelf, and the heavy black Saturday coat he had thoroughly whisked clean. Leo also owned a walking stick, a present from a distant relative, but quickly put temptation aside and did not use it. Lily, petite and not unpretty, had on something signifying the approach of spring. She was au courant, animatedly, with all sorts of subjects, and he weighed her words and found her surprisingly sound—score another for Salzman, whom he uneasily sensed to be somewhere around, hiding perhaps high in a tree along the street, flashing the lady signals with a pocket mirror; or perhaps a cloven-hoofed Pan, piping nuptial ditties as he danced his invisible way before them, strewing wild buds on the walk and purple grapes in their path, symbolizing fruit of a union, though there was of course still none.

Lily startled Leo by remarking, "I was thinking of Mr. Salzman, a curious figure, wouldn't you say?"

Not certain what to answer, he nodded.

She bravely went on, blushing, "I for one am grateful for his introducing us. Aren't you?"

He courteously replied, "I am."

"I mean," she said with a little laugh—and it was all in good taste, or at least gave the effect of being not in bad—"do you mind that we came together so?"

He was not displeased with her honesty, recognizing that she meant to set the relationship aright, and understanding that it took a certain amount of experience in life, and courage, to want to do it quite that way. One had to have some sort of past to make that kind of beginning.

He said that he did not mind. Salzman's function was traditional and honorable—valuable for what it might achieve, which, he pointed out, was frequently nothing.

Lily agreed with a sigh. They walked on for a while and she said after a long silence, again with a nervous laugh, "Would you mind if I asked you something a little bit personal? Frankly, I find the subject fascinating." Although Leo shrugged, she went on half embarrassedly, "How was it that you came to your calling? I mean was it a sudden passionate inspiration?"

Leo, after a time, slowly replied, "I was always interested in the Law."

"You saw revealed in it the presence of the Highest?"

He nodded and changed the subject. "I understand that you spent a little time in Paris, Miss Hirschorn?"

"Oh, did Mr. Salzman tell you, Rabbi Finkle?" Leo winced but she went on, "It was ages ago and almost forgotten. I remember I had to return for my sister's wedding."

And Lily would not be put off. "When," she asked in a trembly voice, "did you become enamored of God?"

He stared at her. Then it came to him that she was talking not about Leo Finkle, but of a total stranger, some mystical figure, perhaps even passionate prophet that Salzman had dreamed up for her—no relation to the living or dead. Leo trembled with rage and weakness. The trickster had obviously sold her a bill of goods, just as he had him, who'd expected to become acquainted with a young lady of twenty-nine, only to behold, the moment he laid eyes upon her strained and anxious face, a woman past thirty-five and aging rapidly. Only his self control had kept him this long in her presence.

"I am not," he said gravely, "a talented religious person," and in seeking words to go on, found himself possessed by shame and fear. "I think," he said in a strained manner, "that I came to God not because I loved Him, but because I did not."

This confession he spoke harshly because its unexpectedness shook him.

Lily wilted. Leo saw a profusion of loaves of bread go flying like ducks high over his head, not unlike the winged loaves by which he had counted himself to sleep last night. Mercifully, then, it snowed, which he would not put past Salzman's machinations.

He was infuriated with the marriage broker and swore he would throw him out of the room the minute he reappeared. But Salzman did not come that night, and when Leo's anger had subsided, an unaccountable despair grew in its place. At first he thought this was caused by his disappointment in Lily, but before long it became evident that he had involved himself with Salzman without a true knowledge of his own intent. He gradually realized—with an emptiness that seized him with six hands—that he had called in the broker to find him a bride because he was incapable of doing it himself. This terrifying insight he had derived as a result of his meeting and conversation with Lily Hirschorn. Her probing questions had somehow irritated him into revealing—to himself more than her—the true nature of his relationship to God, and from that it had come upon him, with shocking force, that apart from his parents, he had never loved anyone. Or perhaps it went the other way, that he did not love God so well as he might, because he had not loved man. It seemed to Leo that his whole life stood starkly revealed and he saw himself for the first time as he truly was—unloved and loveless. This bitter but somehow not fully unexpected revelation brought him to a point of panic, controlled only by extraordinary effort. He covered his face with his hands and cried.

The week that followed was the worst of his life. He did not eat and lost weight. His beard darkened and grew ragged. He stopped attending seminars and almost never opened a book. He seriously considered leaving the Yeshivah, although he was deeply troubled at the thought of the loss of all his years of study—saw them like pages torn from a book, strewn over the city—and at the devastating effect of this decision upon his parents. But he had lived without knowledge of himself, and never in the Five Books and all the Commentaries—mea culpa—had the truth been revealed to him. He did not know where to turn, and in all this desolating loneliness there was no *to whom*, although he often thought of Lily but not once could bring himself to go downstairs and make the call. He became touchy and irritable, especially with his landlady, who asked him all manner of personal questions; on the other hand, sensing his own disagreeableness, he waylaid her on the stairs and apologized abjectly, until mortified, she ran from him. Out of this, however, he drew the consolation that he was a Jew and that a Jew suffered. But gradually, as the long and terrible week drew to a close, he regained his composure and some idea of purpose in life: to go on as planned. Although he was imperfect, the ideal was not. As for his quest of a bride, the thought of continuing afflicted him with anxiety and heartburn, yet perhaps with this new knowledge of himself he would be more successful than in the past. Perhaps love would now come to him and a bride to that love. And for this sanctified seeking who needed a Salzman?

The marriage broker, a skeleton with haunted eyes, returned that very night. He looked, withal, the picture of frustrated expectancy—as if he had steadfastly waited the week at Miss Lily Hirschorn's side for a telephone call that never came.

Casually coughing, Salzman came immediately to the point: "So how did you like her?"

Leo's anger rose and he could not refrain from chiding the matchmaker: "Why did you lie to me, Salzman?"

Salzman's pale face went dead white, the world had snowed on him.

"Did you not state that she was twenty-nine?" Leo insisted.

"I give you my word—"

"She was thirty-five, if a day. *At least* thirty-five."

"Of this don't be too sure. Her father told me—"

"Never mind. The worst of it was that you lied to her."

"How did I lie to her, tell me?"

"You told her things about me that weren't true. You made me out to be more, consequently less than I am. She had in mind a totally different person, a sort of semi-mystical Wonder Rabbi."

"All I said, you was a religious man."

"I can imagine."

Salzman sighed. "This is my weakness that I have," he confessed. "My wife says to me I shouldn't be a salesman, but when I have two fine people that they would be wonderful to be married, I am so happy that I talk too much." He smiled wanly. "This is why Salzman is a poor man."

Leo's anger left him. "Well, Salzman, I'm afraid that's all."

The marriage broker fastened hungry eyes on him.

"You don't want any more a bride?"

"I do," said Leo, "but I have decided to seek her in a different way. I am no longer interested in an arranged marriage. To be frank, I now admit the necessity of premarital love. That is, I want to be in love with the one I marry."

"Love?" said Salzman, astounded. After a moment he remarked, "For us, our love is our life, not for the ladies. In the ghetto they—"

"I know, I know," said Leo. "I've thought of it often. Love,

I have said to myself, should be a by-product of living and worship rather than its own end. Yet for myself I find it necessary to establish the level of my need and fulfill it."

Salzman shrugged but answered, "Listen, rabbi, if you want love, this I can find for you also. I have such beautiful clients that you will love them the minute your eyes will see them."

Leo smiled unhappily. "I'm afraid you don't understand."

But Salzman hastily unstrapped his portfolio and withdrew a manila packet from it.

"Pictures," he said, quickly laying the envelope on the table.

Leo called after him to take the pictures away, but as if on the wings of the wind, Salzman had disappeared.

March came. Leo had returned to his regular routine. Although he felt not quite himself yet—lacked energy—he was making plans for a more active social life. Of course it would cost something, but he was an expert in cutting corners; and when there were no corners left he would make circles rounder. All the while Salzman's pictures had lain on the table, gathering dust. Occasionally as Leo sat studying, or enjoying a cup of tea, his eyes fell on the manila envelope, but he never opened it.

The days went by and no social life to speak of developed with a member of the opposite sex—it was difficult, given the circumstances of his situation. One morning Leo toiled up the stairs to his room and stared out the window at the city. Although the day was bright his view of it was dark. For some time he watched the people in the street below hurrying along and then turned with a heavy heart to his little room. On the table was the packet. With a sudden relentless gesture he tore it open. For a half-hour he stood by the table in a state of excitement, examining the photographs of the ladies Salzman had included. Finally, with a deep sigh he put them down. There were six, of varying degrees of attractiveness, but look at them long enough and they all became Lily Hirschorn: all past their prime, all starved behind bright smiles, not a true personality in the lot. Life, despite their frantic yoohooings, had passed them by; they were pictures in a brief case that stank of fish. After a while, however, as Leo attempted to return the photographs into the envelope, he found in it another, a snapshot of the type taken by a machine for a quarter. He gazed at it a moment and let out a cry.

Her face deeply moved him. Why, he could at first not say.

It gave him the impression of youth—spring flowers, yet age —a sense of having been used to the bone, wasted; this came from the eyes, which were hauntingly familiar, yet absolutely strange. He had a vivid impression that he had met her before, but try as he might he could not place her although he could almost recall her name, as if he had read it in her own handwriting. No, this couldn't be; he would have remembered her. It was not, he affirmed, that she had an extraordinary beauty —no, though her face was attractive enough; it was that *something* about her moved him. Feature for feature, even some of the ladies of the photographs could do better; but she leaped forth to his heart—had *lived,* or wanted to—more than just wanted, perhaps regretted how she had lived—had somehow deeply suffered: it could be seen in the depths of those reluctant eyes, and from the way the light enclosed and shone from her, and within her, opening realms of possibility: this was her own. Her he desired. His head ached and eyes narrowed with the intensity of his gazing, then as if an obscure fog had blown up in the mind, he experienced fear of her and was aware that he had received an impression, somehow, of evil. He shuddered, saying softly, it is thus with us all. Leo brewed some tea in a small pot and sat sipping it without sugar, to calm himself. But before he had finished drinking, again with excitement he examined the face and found it good: good for Leo Finkle. Only such a one could understand him and help him seek whatever he was seeking. She might, perhaps, love him. How she had happened to be among the discards in Salzman's barrel he could never guess, but he knew he must urgently go find her.

Leo rushed downstairs, grabbed up the Bronx telephone book, and searched for Salzman's home address. He was not listed, nor was his office. Neither was he in the Manhattan book. But Leo remembered having written down the address on a slip of paper after he had read Salzman's advertisement in the "personals" column of the *Forward.* He ran up to his room and tore through his papers, without luck. It was exasperating. Just when he needed the matchmaker he was nowhere to be found. Fortunately Leo remembered to look in his wallet. There on a card he found his name written and a Bronx address. No phone number was listed, the reason— Leo now recalled—he had originally communicated with Salzman by letter. He got on his coat, put a hat on over his skull cap and hurried to the subway station. All the way to the far end of the Bronx he sat on the edge of his seat. He was more than once tempted to take out the picture and see if the girl's face was as he remembered it, but he refrained, allowing the snapshot to remain in his inside coat pocket, content to have her so close. When the train pulled into the station he was waiting at the door and bolted out. He quickly located the street Salzman had advertised.

The building he sought was less than a block from the subway, but it was not an office building, nor even a loft, nor a store in which one could rent office space. It was a very old tenement house. Leo found Salzman's name in pencil on a soiled tag under the bell and climbed three dark flights to his apartment. When he knocked, the door was opened by a thin, asthmatic, gray-haired woman, in felt slippers.

"Yes?" she said, expecting nothing. She listened without listening. He could have sworn he had seen her, too, before but knew it was an illusion.

"Salzman—does he live here? Pinye Salzman," he said, "the matchmaker?"

She stared at him a long minute. "Of course."

He felt embarrassed. "Is he in?"

"No." Her mouth, though left open, offered nothing more.

"The matter is urgent. Can you tell me where his office is?"

"In the air." She pointed upward.

"You mean he has no office?" Leo asked.

"In his socks."

He peered into the apartment. It was sunless and dingy, one large room divided by a half-open curtain, beyond which he could see a sagging metal bed. The near side of a room was crowded with rickety chairs, old bureaus, a three-legged table, racks of cooking utensils, and all the apparatus of a kitchen. But there was no sign of Salzman or his magic barrel, probably also a figment of the imagination. An odor of frying fish made Leo weak to the knees.

"Where is he?" he insisted. "I've got to see your husband."

At length she answered, "So who knows where he is? Every time he thinks a new thought he runs to a different place. Go home, he will find you."

"Tell him Leo Finkle."

She gave no sign she had heard.

He walked downstairs, depressed.

But Salzman, breathless, stood waiting at his door.

Leo was astounded and overjoyed. "How did you get here before me?"

"I rushed."

"Come inside."

They entered. Leo fixed tea, and a sardine sandwich for Salzman. As they were drinking he reached behind him for the packet of pictures and handed them to the marriage broker.

Salzman put down his glass and said expectantly, "You found somebody you like?"

"Not among these."

The marriage broker turned away.

"Here is the one I want." Leo held forth the snapshot.

Salzman slipped on his glasses and took the picture into his trembling hand. He turned ghastly and let out a groan.

"What's the matter?" cried Leo.

"Excuse me. Was an accident this picture. She isn't for you."

Salzman frantically shoved the manila packet into his portfolio. He thrust the snapshot into his pocket and fled down the stairs.

Leo, after momentary paralysis, gave chase and cornered the marriage broker in the vestibule. The landlady made hysterical outcries but neither of them listened.

"Give me back the picture, Salzman."

"No." The pain in his eyes was terrible.

"Tell me who she is then."

"This I can't tell you. Excuse me."

He made to depart, but Leo, forgetting himself, seized the matchmaker by his tight coat and shook him frenziedly.

"Please," sighed Salzman. *"Please."*

Leo ashamedly let him go. "Tell me who she is," he begged. "It's very important for me to know."

"She is not for you. She is a wild one—wild, without shame. This is not a bride for a rabbi."

"What do you mean wild?"

"Like an animal. Like a dog. For her to be poor was a sin. This is why to me she is dead now."

"In God's name, what do you mean?"

"Her I can't introduce to you," Salzman cried.

"Why are you so excited?"

"Why, he asks," Salzman said, bursting into tears. "This is my baby, my Stella, she should burn in hell."

Leo hurried up to bed and hid under the covers. Under the covers he thought his life through. Although he soon fell asleep he could not sleep her out of his mind. He woke, beating his breast. Though he prayed to be rid of her, his prayers went unanswered. Through days of torment he endlessly struggled not to love her; fearing success, he escaped it. He then concluded to convert her to goodness, himself to God. The idea alternately nauseated and exalted him.

He perhaps did not know that he had come to a final decision until he encountered Salzman in a Broadway cafeteria. He was sitting alone at a rear table, sucking the bony remains of a fish. The marriage broker appeared haggard, and transparent to the point of vanishing.

Salzman looked up at first without recognizing him. Leo had grown a pointed beard and his eyes were weighted with wisdom.

"Salzman," he said, "love has at last come to my heart."

"Who can love from a picture?" mocked the marriage broker.

"It is not impossible."

"If you can love her, then you can love anybody. Let me show you some new clients that they just sent me their photographs. One is a little doll."

"Just her I want," Leo murmured.

"Don't be a fool, doctor. Don't bother with her."

"Put me in touch with her, Salzman," Leo said humbly. "Perhaps I can be of service."

Salzman had stopped eating and Leo understood with emotion that it was now arranged.

Leaving the cafeteria, he was, however, afflicted by a tormenting suspicion that Salzman had planned it all to happen this way.

Leo was informed by letter that she would meet him on a certain corner, and she was there one spring night, waiting under a street lamp. He appeared, carrying a small bouquet of violets and rosebuds. Stella stood by the lamp post, smoking. She wore white with red shoes, which fitted his expectations, although in a troubled moment he had imagined the dress red, and only the shoes white. She waited uneasily and shyly. From afar he saw that her eyes—clearly her father's—were filled with desperate innocence. He pictured, in her, his own redemption. Violins and lit candles revolved in the sky. Leo ran forward with flowers outthrust.

Around the corner, Salzman, leaning against a wall, chanted prayers for the dead.

Twilight in Southern California

Daniel Fuchs

The novelty business was shot to pieces; the whole bottom had dropped out of the market. Mr. Honti, who manufactured the gadgets and gewgaws, was going through terrible financial troubles, dunned and driven on all sides, everything crashing down on his head, and Morley felt this was no time to run out on him. Morley Finch was a young physician who had opened a practice in Los Angeles just two or three years ago. He and his wife had been taken up by the Hontis, had gone up there to the swimming pool in Coldwater Canyon almost every Saturday, and Morley didn't see how they could stop going there now. The trouble was Barbara, his wife. She hated those visits. She said Mr. Honti was unbalanced.

"I'm willing to do anything you want," Barbara said, cool and trim and beautiful. She was wearing a beige linen jumper, a white organdie blouse, and white pumps and gloves, and she was ready to leave—except, of course, she plainly didn't want to.

They were in the office, and the frantic six-lane traffic outside on Wilshire Boulevard was ripping along as it everlastingly did. "That's very nice of you," Morley said. He stepped on the scales, weighed himself, stepped off. Every Saturday, after office hours, Barbara came to pick him up, and every Saturday there was this little struggle, this tortured ticktacktoe. Mr. Honti wasn't unbalanced and Barbara knew it. She just couldn't stand him or the rest of them up there. She couldn't stand the noise, the kissing of hands, the way they constantly talked about people making boom-tarra-ra, the way they openly pinched the women. Whenever she went there, the first thing she did was find a place and sit down.

"If I don't want to go, you get mad," Barbara said. "If I say let's go, you say I'm insincere. I don't know what to do."

"Maybe I could think up some excuse." Morley said. "Maybe I could tell them I was called away to the hospital." After

all, he was a doctor. But his voice trailed off and he gave
it up. He really wanted to go there—because he liked them,
or understood them, with all their peculiar ways, or because
he felt guilty toward them, or whatever it was. And besides
there was no use trying to lie to them. They were so quick, so
intelligent. They always knew what was going on in your
mind. Mr. Honti hadn't been able to pay his monthly doctor's
bill—there had been some trouble at the bank with a check—
and if Morley and Barbara failed to appear this afternoon,
Honti would think it was because of the bad check, and then
he'd get all hurt and humiliated and miserable.

"He gives me a bad check and *I'm* the one that has to feel
bad about it," Morley said. "I don't even know why I want
to go there."

"Anything you want to do," Barbara said, despondent.

The swimming pool was in a hollow, fringed with poplar
trees, just below the house. Mr. Honti was still in town, down
in Beverly Hills somewhere, doing business or trying to do
business. Morley and Barbara hadn't arrived, and the only
one sitting with Mrs. Honti at the pool was a man named
Edmond Oleam. Lily Honti was a great coffee drinker. She
had an electric percolator out there with her on the lawn,
but Oleam wouldn't accept a cup. He had no heart for coffee. He was also in the novelty business, also in distressed
financial circumstances, but, in addition, his wife had left him
and he had a stiff neck. All these things were more or less
connected—the business slump, his wife's leaving him, the stiff
neck. When the business started to go slack, his wife moved
out. In retaliation, Oleam went on a diet and took a course
of bar-bell exercises. That was why he had the stiff neck, from
the bar bells. Lily Honti finished her coffee and promptly filled
the cup again. "Sad for the children," she said in passing,
meaning these separations. There was a child involved, a boy
now at a military academy near San Diego.

"Sad for the grownups, too," Oleam said.

He looked at the poplar trees, distracted. The leaves kept
dropping into the pool, and in any case poplars weren't suitable for the dry southern California climate. They needed
lots of water, became brittle, and were liable to break and
go falling down on top of you at any time. If you wanted to
pull them out, it would cost you hundreds of dollars. Every-

thing was unsatisfactory, Oleam thought, looking at the trees. Everything turned out badly. And the thought of his wife, only a mile or two away over the hills, living with a Mr. Larry Scorbell in another canyon—Benedict Canyon. Scorbell was not in the novelty business.

"She fell in love," Oleam said gently, wryly. "The fact that he owns three millinery factories had nothing to do with it."

"What should she do—hate him because he is rich?" Lily said. "What is she—a bobby-soxer? Why shouldn't she love him if he has money? Can anybody show me a better reason?"

"You have no ideals," Oleam said.

"This is perfect for you," Lily went on. "You are fat, you are lazy. Maybe this will wake you up."

"Stop," he said.

"Why are you crying—that you have lost her? You know what your life was. You got up late, you lay in bed, you did nothing. When you went to the office, you called her on the phone every minute—did anything come in the mail, was there a telegram, did somebody call up? Anything for an excuse."

"It wasn't for an excuse," Oleam said. "I was anxious. I was hoping for something good to happen."

"Baloney, you were spying on her."

"I was not!" Oleam said. "Nobody understands! You don't know what it is when a business goes sour, when you wait and pray for something to develop."

"Be still," Lily said. Morley and Barbara were approaching, walking down the path from the house. "Now, behave yourself. Watch how you talk—you will frighten her. She is a child. She comes from New Hampshire. How are you, my sweethearts?" Lily said, turning to them, her eyes shining with mischief. "Come—sit down, sit down."

All at once, there was a cloud; everything darkened, there was a strange, muted whoosh of wind, and then they heard an ominous, creeping, tearing patter. Oleam gave a start of fear and jumped up. He thought it was one of the poplars breaking, but it was just a quick rain coming on. "Bring in the cushions!" Lily said, screaming with delight, enjoying the upset. Morley grabbed up an armful, and Oleam wrestled with the big chaise pads. The pads were cumbersome, he couldn't manage them, and suddenly he twisted his stiff neck and felt a stab of pain. "Oh, help me, Dr. Finch," he started to say, calling to Morley. But Oleam didn't say "Dr. Finch."

Oleam said "Gladys," which was his wife's name. And now, standing in the shelter of the porch, he realized what he had said, and it was as though he had been punctured. The heart all went out of him and he gave way. He thought of that soft, suntanned, warm little body all cuddled up in bed, no longer his, no longer his, now in Benedict Canyon with Larry Scorbell, making boom-tarra-ra there at least two times a day, and he sobbed aloud in deep, hopeless anguish.

The sun came flooding back through the poplar trees. The rain was over. "Behold!" Lily said. They put the cushions back and grouped themselves around the pool. It was the kind of rain people find hard to believe when you tell them about it; they were just around the bend or just across the road, they say, and it didn't rain there at all.

At least if there was only a funicular up Coldwater Canyon, Alexander Honti said to himself as he trudged bitterly up the road to his home. They had eaten up the car, Lily and he. The loan company had taken it away, and now the sun beat on his head as though he were back in the desert wilderness, in the time of the Pharaohs again. He had been able to accomplish nothing in town. In days of crisis, the money men became inaccessible, the go-betweens became arrogant and contemptuous, and the secretaries everywhere turned into fierce, haughty virgins. I should commit suicide and get through with it once for all, Honti said to himself—only, what was the use, who would cry? He had no patience; otherwise he would have done it long ago. In a last, desperate effort, he had put all his eggs in one basket. He had signed Tony Brewer, an inventor-designer, laying out eight hundred dollars hard cash in advance. In the novelty business, if you had an ace designer, you could make a beginning, you could do something; the banks at least would *talk* to you. But, no fate had had to intervene. Brewer had promptly come down with a paralytic stroke; the loudmouths in the trade had diligently passed the good word around; and in no time Honti had been marked lousy again, from Culver City to Burbank, the eight hundred dollars going down the drain along with everything else.

Honti now walked over the rise of ground to the pool. He saw the people assembled there and greeted them lustily, holding up his palm like an Indian on a calendar saluting the morning sun. "My star is risen!" he said, overheated and all wound up, the blood racing in his brain. "Mrs. Maveen has predicted that exactly at three-thirty sharp good news will arrive, my fortunes will change for the better, and everything henceforth will be rosy and serene!" Mrs. Maveen was a professional palm reader who lived in a stucco bungalow on Sunset Boulevard. Honti pretended he was joking, out of reckless despair, out of bravado, but actually he was superstitious and seriously hoped the prophecy would come true. What else was there for him, anyway? "See?" he said, pointing to a line on his palm. "There is the good luck, according to Mrs. Maveen, in the stucco bungalow. This is where it says I must positively get the good news at three-thirty sharp." He paused. He stood gazing at Barbara, forgetting his troubles for the moment. He was always glad to see her. Morley was wearing a pair of swimming trunks, but she hadn't changed, and she looked lovely in that outfit, pure and clean and untouched, with those white pumps and gloves. Honti became softly playful. He beamed at her, treating her like a little child. "Snow-white teeth," he said. "Such deep-blue eyes. So blond. Your face is like a fire. I could warm my hands." He suddenly remembered the check that had bounced. The great big smile ebbed away. He winced. He had promised to straighten everything out at the bank and call Morley right back. He had, of course, done neither. He couldn't face the Doctor now and turned instead on Oleam. "Why did you have to be noble and give Gladys the car?" Honti referred to the settlement Oleam had made at the time of the separation. He could have borrowed Oleam's machine, spared himself the climb up the whole mountain.

"Well, I was in love," Oleam said.

"You have no backbone!" Honti said. "You are a pickpocket. You are less than a pickpocket. You are an oboe!" Honti was putting on his show, as usual, but the truth was he himself didn't know how much of it was kidding. He took off his glasses and placed them on a table. He sat down on the grass, slipped out of his trousers and went on undressing, preparing himself for a dip in the pool. Maybe that would cool him off. Maybe a swim would lower his blood pressure and settle him down. He looked up at the sky and scratched his nose.

"Hobo," Lily said, bland and airy over her coffee cup. "Speak correct English. 'You are an hobo.'"

"Bassoon!" Honti roared, getting to his feet. "Do not correct me! I know where I speak. You are a bassoon and he is an oboe. Watch but your own English!"

"Mr. Alexander Honti is in fine fettle," Oleam said, shy and wistful in his manner. "When he is onstage, all are forbidden to breathe. He must monopolize the center of attraction."

"Edmond is right," Lily said. "If business is bad for you, why must you take it out on him? He has heartaches, too."

"Feed the dog!" Honti bellowed. They had a dog, Fidelio— an ungainly creature, large and ill-proportioned, with an unfortunate, sensitive personality. They sometimes forgot about the dog for days at a stretch, and during their frequent arguments Honti generally brought the subject up, putting the whole blame on Lily.

"Why do you insist on stirring me up?" he went on, shouting at her and at Oleam both. "Is it a plot? Do you wish me to die of high blood pressure?" He turned to Barbara and Morley. "He is spineless!" Honti said, speaking not about the dog but about Oleam. "In Paris, on the Champs-Elysées, a man kicked him in the behind and he started running away without even looking back to see who had done it to him."

"A slander!" Oleam said, disgusted. "How he exaggerates and misrepresents everything. I did *not* run without looking back."

"Believe me!" Honti said, reaching down and holding Barbara by the shoulders as she sat there in a cane chair. "I know him. He is the kind of a man who goes into the public phone booths and sticks his fingers into the slot—you know, for the coins. He bets on racing horses and has dealings with bookies. He looks at television—" Honti checked himself. He took his hands off Barbara and stepped back. "Do not be alarmed. We are normal people. It is just our way." He tried to make amends. He beamed broadly again and became skittish. He bulged his eyes out. He mugged. "It is harmless! Actually, I am very fond of Mr. Oleam. In spite of appearances, I am really very much like him in disposition. I do not seem like him because when I am with *him,* I do not have to be like *me,* which is a *godsend.* Prepare yourself for a shock." He was now barefoot, wearing just his undershorts and one of those flowery tropical shirts. He took off the tropical shirt and stood revealed. There were thick masses of hair on his chest, on his shoulders, all over his arms. "Is it not horrible?" he said with a gleam in his eye. What was so painful was he loved this child, he dearly wanted her esteem, while all the time she disapproved and found him offensive. "Am I not ugly? Like a huge bear in the forest. Would you believe it, once I was a babe in arms and my parents called me Skellbillie? It was my pet name." He turned about and threw himself into the pool. He parted the water with a tremendous smash, disappeared for a moment, then reappeared. He was already turned around, facing them. He stretched his arm out and pointed sternly. "Do not talk about me."

What a deplorable mess I am, Honti said to himself as he flopped about in the water. How ugly it was to be in need, to be obliged always to find some way of disguising your despair. He had only meant to be amusing. He thought now of Morley and the look on his face while he, Honti, was going through his antics. Morley had grinned, had stopped grinning, had glanced constantly at his sweet young wife, nervous and uneasy. Honti remembered the tight, stiff smile on *her* face, the way she had flinched when he put his hands on her shoulders. Why did he always have to act like such a fool in front of her? How could he ever expect her to have any respect for her? He made himself a freak; he raved; he jumped up and down; he was a punchinello, a gargoyle. And what, Honti asked himself as he thrashed through the water—and what would happen Monday morning, the shop opening again and him with no funds for the payroll?

He vowed to reform. From now on, in the child's presence he would always be controlled, dignified. He would conduct himself like any well-adjusted gentleman. He would make agreeable small conversation. "And how is Morley's practice progressing?" he would remark to her. "Very well, I hope? Goodness, what a becoming frock you have on."

Then he heard it. He was in the water and they were all sitting up there, high and dry, but he heard it and they didn't; somebody was ringing the doorbell. Honti looked up at the house. A messenger had arrived. It was the prophecy, Mrs. Maveen's prediction. It had to be! It was a cable, a telegram come to save him, a bonanza!

"Here, boy!" Honti started clambering out of the pool. "Here! Down here we are!"

The others on the lawn looked up, startled. They saw the messenger and were instantly excited, too. After all, it was somewhere around three-thirty, the time that Mrs. Maveen had stipulated. "Oh, swiftly!" Lily called out to the messenger. "Swiftly, swiftly, young man!" Oleam took up the cry, and so did Morley.

"See, you must have faith!" Honti exulted, hopping. "You must believe—Here, boy!" The messenger came stumbling down the path, all upset and unnerved by the tumult, but when he reached them and they saw the box in his hands, they immediately fell silent. The jubilee was finished.

It wasn't a bonanza. It was a cake—a homemade chocolate layer cake. Mrs. Carneal, the mother-in-law of the inventor-designer, of Tony Brewer, had sent it. Mrs. Carneal, a fine, pious elderly lady, had deeply appreciated Honti's generosity when he hadn't asked for his eight hundred dollars back. Honti couldn't have got it back anyway—the money was already spent—but Mrs. Carneal didn't know that, and she told everybody what a grand, upstanding soul Mr. Honti was. "Thinking of you," the card in the box said. Honti sent the messenger away. For a while, nobody spoke.

" 'Thinking of you!' " Lily said, going back to her percolator and plopping down on the cushions again. "Everything is ducky."

"You pay for your sins," Honti said, standing there, holding the box. He was exhausted, winded.

"His star is risen!" Lily said, trilling. "We shall have good fortune, seven years of milk and honey!"

"Feed the dog!" Honti roared at her, his eyes shut tight.

"He is not here," she said. "He is wandering. He is looking for you since early morning, since you went to business."

The dog was remarkably sympathetic, psychic. Whenever Honti was in the dumps, Fidelio seemed to know it and went looking for him, to be near his master, to share his distress, to comfort him. The two had missed connections all day.

Honti put the cake down on a table and rubbed his face with both his hands. "Then drink yourself to death," he said to his wife. "In Berlin, in Prague, in Paris, they chased me like an animal in the fields, and now, finally, in sunny California I am condemned to end my days a bankrupt living with a witch. I am the dog. Fidelio is I. No wonder he is neurotic." Honti was running everything together, feeling sorry for the dog, chastising himself. "He is neglected. It is my fault. I must take care of him. The S.P.C.A. should lock me up. Morley," he said suddenly, thinking of the bad check, almost seeking out the punishment, the mortification. "Morley, I did not call you back about the bank, because, as I knew you would know,

I had nothing to say—*Do not be alarmed!*" he burst out at Barbara, turning on her now in his misery. She sat rigid in the cane chair, big-eyed. "I told you—it is just our way! It means nothing. We are emotional, we overstate everything. . . . Oh, look at her! She sits there dying by inches. Somebody would think— Oh, goodbye." He plunged into the pool again, putting an end to it. And what would be, he asked himself as he sank into the greenish, opalescent depths—what would be when they finished eating up the house, with the swimming pool and the grounds and the garden? It was like a tune you couldn't get out of your head.

The poplar leaves fluttered listlessly in the slight breeze, showing now their shiny side, now their pale, velvety underside. A hummingbird skidded into, and then out of, a hibiscus blossom the size of a grapefruit. Over it all, the golden sunshine poured down, ever benign, ever patient. "My neck," Oleam said, far away among his private troubles. "It pains."

Lily gazed vacantly at her husband, swimming in the pool. She had her own troubles, and her mind was far away, too. "When the news came that Brewer was stricken, that all was lost, I was on the balcony in the hall," she said, "looking down on Alexander while he stood downstairs by the telephone. Right away, I knew it was a catastrophe; his poor little bald spot turned white."

"Lily," Oleam said, grieving. "Lily, I would like to ask you for an advice. Should I telephone Gladys for an appointment? Should I go over there and have a meeting with them?"

Morley squirmed with discomfort. For the fortieth time, he glanced at Barbara and reproached himself. Why did he have to bring her here? She didn't like these people. She didn't understand how it really was with them. She took everything at its face value and thought they were cynical, corrupt, and materialistic. Barbara often went along with Morley on his calls, waiting alone outside in the car, and when his patients forgot to pay their bills, as they generally did, she was always bitter about it. She said they were deliberately taking advantage of him. She didn't understand how broke they were, how hardpressed and bedevilled. She didn't understand they were constitutionally bedevilled. She understood nothing. Honti was still chopping and flailing around in the water, and Morley knew he ought to take Barbara home now, quickly, while everything was still quiet, before the explosions started going off again, but he stood rooted to the spot. He couldn't make a move. There was always the difficulty of getting away gracefully. If he and Barbara left too abruptly, it would seem pointed, a reflection on the Hontis, and their feelings would be hurt. So again Morley was torn; again he felt guilty.

"Lily, you do not answer me," Oleam wailed. "Should I go there and discuss the situation—you know, calmly, amicably? Would it be advisable?"

"Why must you interfere and pester?" Lily said, her voice dreamy and lazy. "Leave her alone. It will be good for her, an experience, and you will benefit, too."

"Now," Morley said to himself. "Now."

But just then Oleam rose to his feet and said, "I think I will get a drink of water. Maybe it will make me feel better." He started walking toward the house, his pace altering oddly as he went. The closer he got to the house, the more he seemed to hurry. At the end, he was almost running.

"Barbara," Morley finally said, "I guess we ought to be getting started. I—" He stopped. Honti had climbed out of the pool and was heading directly for Barbara. He grabbed at her hand. She wouldn't let him have it. She shrank back and fidgeted. She didn't know what he was after, and she was, poor thing, frightened by him as he swarmed all over her. He was so big and hairy, the water sluicing off him, and without his glasses he squinted horribly. "Let me," he said. "Oh, just— please!" She gave a shriek and bolted. "Barbara!" Morley called in dismay, but there was no stopping her. Knocking the chair over, she fled for her life, toward the garden in the back.

Honti stared after her. "Has everyone taken leave of their senses?" he asked indignantly. It appeared that he had only wanted to look at her wristwatch. Swimming in the water, thinking of Mrs. Maveen, he had suddenly decided to see how close it actually was to three-thirty. "Not that I expect anything from Mrs. Maveen or from anybody else!" Honti said, still dripping water. "I am doomed! Everything goes against me. I have exhausted the whole list of misfortunes. The only thing now is to start all over again from the beginning."

Morley kept swallowing, in pain. It was all so awkward, so garish, and so completely unnecessary. There had been nothing for Barbara to be afraid of. Without his glasses, Honti could barely see; that was why he had had to come up so

close, swarming all over her and bringing his nose right up to
her hand. "I'll go after her," Morley mumbled. "It's all right.
Please just ignore it." He started slowly toward the garden.

Barbara was standing near some oleander bushes. "What
did you think he was going to do to you, anyway?" Morley
said to her sharply.

"I didn't know what to expect," she blurted out. "How do
I know *what* they do? They're depraved! They're degener-
ate—"

"He only wanted to see the time," Morley said. He told her
how it had happened—Honti in the water thinking of Mrs.
Maveen, wondering if it was three-thirty, pinning his hopes
on palmists and their nutty predictions. "Why did you have
to do an awful thing like that?" Morley said. "What's the
matter with you? You sat like a mummy. Every time you
smiled, you acted as though it was killing you."

"I'm sorry," Barbara said, turning away from him. "I mis-
understood. I'll go back and apologize to him." But suddenly
she was crying, pressing her face against the pink oleander
blossoms, and all the sharpness went out of Morley. In the
stillness now, he felt lost and his heart ached—because his
wife looked so lovely, because it was true, after all, that Honti
was ugly and repellent, and because the sunlight over everything was so clear and brilliant.

Suddenly, he became aware of a commotion going on behind him in the distance. Oleam, at the house, seemed to be
shouting furiously, calling something to the Hontis. Now the
Hontis themselves went racing up the path, Lily following
after her husband, screaming out wildly at him as they ran.
Morley was puzzled, even alarmed, but he couldn't leave
Barbara crying alone in the garden.

"All right, finish," he said, and told her something was
happening at the house, that he wanted to go up there.

"Soon," she said, blubbering. "Just give me a minute—I'll
be with you right away."

This is what happened at the pool. Honti was still carrying
on, still cursing his luck, when Lily took it into her head to
look at her wristwatch. She had one on, too. "If you wanted
to know the time," she said, "then why didn't you ask in a
civilized way? You are an idiot. You have no taste, and scare
innocent people." Somewhere far off, an automobile horn got

stuck and started blowing. "It is half past three," Lily said.

Right on the dot, almost before the words were out of her mouth, they heard Oleam shouting "Good news! Good news!" from the terrace, and Honti started to tremble.

"Brewer is on the telephone!" Oleam shouted down to them. "He wants to talk to you!"

"But he is paralyzed!" Lily said. "Don't raise your hopes—you'll only be disappointed!"

"Lubitchka, my dearest," Honti said. There were tears in his eyes, and his voice was husky. He knew she meant well, that she was only trying to save him from himself, from his senseless elations, but he deeply believed in oracles, in signs. It was a lunatic world, and who knew the answers to the riddles or why things happened as they did? Maybe Mrs. Maveen really had an inside line. "Lubitchka, my birdling," Honti said, "is it not strange? Is it not mysterious? Like magic—we didn't even hear the telephone ringing."

"Edmond was standing right by it. He picked it up," Lily said. She tried to explain about Oleam's pestering Gladys and Scorbell for an appointment, but Honti didn't listen. He put on his glasses and started up the path to the house. "Alexander, my watch doesn't even keep good time!" Lily shouted after him. "It was not half past three!"

"A miracle!" he insisted, running and gasping for breath, his eyes still brimming.

He was right and Lily wrong. Brewer was out of the hospital, still partly paralyzed on his left side but ready for work. He had four small children, the two youngest mere infants, and he told Honti to go right ahead—to raise capital, to schedule meetings with the money men. He, Brewer, would be there, willing and able. Honti put the phone back on the rest and prepared to go into action immediately, Saturday afternoon or no Saturday afternoon.

"You will have a downfall!" Lily cried. "You know you—How you will suffer!"

He turned away from her. Morley and Barbara came into the hall, staring and wondering, but Honti had no time for them, either, and let them wonder. He had to think. In the novelty business, there were levels and levels of importance. Standing at the very top was a certain Mr. Marcellus. This man controlled a good deal of the available investment capital. If he nodded, you functioned. Mr. Marcellus was austere and forbidding by temperament, a czar, his time was holy, and he could be approached only through go-betweens. Honti went to work on the phone and dug them up, one after another. They brushed him off without ceremony. Their time was holy, too. In the crisis, everyone had become snooty, and nowadays you needed a go-between to talk to a go-between. Honti wiped the sweat off his bald spot. The phone in his hand was hot. He thought of Mr. Zeitz—not a go-between, a relative. Zeitz had entrée on his wife's sister's side; the sister was married to a Marcellus somewhere. Honti got busy on the phone again.

"My dear Zeitz," he began, speaking gingerly, because dealing with relations was ticklish and you had to follow a rigid etiquette. "Can you do me a great big private favor? I would like to pay you for it, and, of course, there definitely would be a sizable consideration involved, only it all becomes so complicated. This is something just between you and I. . . ." Honti went on deftly, sketching out the situation, but Zeitz, who came from no village himself, smoothly double-talked right back. Zeitz said he fully appreciated the potential, but prestigewise it was imperative for him to protect his integrity. This meant, in plain English, that Zeitz wasn't going to wear out his welcome with Marcellus by bringing him trash. Honti and Zeitz understood each other perfectly and finished their conversation.

"Well?" Lily said as Honti hung up. "Nothing doing?"

" 'Thinking of you'!" Honti said savagely. " 'Don't call us, we'll call you!' You have to eat your heart out before they let you finalize a dollar—"

He broke off. Oleam was back. He had slipped away during the excitement, and had gone out to the garage. He had rummaged around there and had found an old neck brace. He had put it on, for his stiff neck, for the sake of the impression, and now, in the middle of everything, he was parading around like a peacock that had lost its wits. "I have my appointment with Gladys and Mr. Scorbell," Oleam said, in bliss, almost humming. "I am invited for cocktails, very stylish. We will discuss matters. We will see what will eventuate."

"Rejoice!" Honti roared. "Our fortunes are made! We shall hold a fiesta!" He broke off. His eyes went deep, and again he turned tenderly to Lily—his wife, his lifelong friend, his business partner. "Lubitchka, my angel," he said, "why shouldn't I deal with Mr. Marcellus direct? Who says I can't call him up myself? After all, I am somebody, too. I have position. Why not?"

He made his mind up on the instant, grimly set his jaw, and strode back to the phone. Everyone crept up silently and stood near him as he dialled the number. He got through to Marcellus's residence. Honti could hear the phone there ringing. Somebody picked it up—the butler. Honti squared his shoulders, drew his breath in. Now he rolled the words out, weighty and important. "This is Mr. Alexander Honti, of Paris, calling. I wish to speak in person with Mr. Anton Marcellus— *Don't hang gup!*" It was useless. Honti heard the click. He slammed his own phone down on the rest. "May a fire devour them, Mr. Marcellus and the butler together! May floods engulf them! May cancers and ulcers fester in their bellies! May their tongues grow swollen and hang out from their mouths like beards—" He stopped, transfixed. He had the answer. He knew exactly where he could get financing. Everything became dead quiet. In the hush, Oleam suddenly shivered, because Honti was staring at him so strangely.

"The milliner," Honti said. "Scorbell." That would be his salvation. Why hadn't he thought of it before? Scorbell was rich, owned factories. Honti would take over Oleam's appointment. Honti would go there for the cocktails.

"No!" Oleam said. Honti silenced him with a bellow. He was ecstatic, carried away. The hall couldn't hold him, and he swirled into the living room. He had grovelled, he had fasted and prayed, he had turned himself inside out, and now, at last, came victory. Honti trumpeted with joy.

"He is flying, flying!" Lily said. "He will bust!"

He sent her back to the phone, to call up Gladys and pave the way, so that he would come invited. There was a flurry of movement, Lily going to the hall and Morley saying it was time to leave. Laughing and happy, the young Doctor started out for the dressing rooms at the pool, to change back into his clothes. Barbara lingered. Honti could tell she was remorseful. She knew now how unjust, how cruel, she had been to him and no doubt wanted to apologize formally, but he was far too happy to be bothered with trifles.

He saw it all. He couldn't stop talking. He would get his backing, he would recoup, he would be a power in the industry again. Everyone would smile. He would be popular, universally admired. His visions soared. He would give an enormous party. He would throw a tent over the garden, hire live musicians, rent dishes from the rental people, and make all the guests sign the guestbook, so that he would have tangible evidence when the income-tax officials came to question the deductions. Honti even had the menu all worked out—veal, peaches and plums, wild rice, shrimp in aspic, salad. . . . But then some devil got hold of him. Honti couldn't leave well enough alone, and everything came jarring to a halt.

He meant no harm. He did it only out of rapture, out of sheer, bouncing gladness. He pinched Barbara. In an amazing burst of anger, she flared up and cracked him. She cracked him with surprising force, too, in one blow destroying three hundred and fifty dollars' worth of bridgework on his lower jaw.

"Oh, you are disgusting!" she said bitterly, and turned on her heel and walked out of the house, to wait for her husband outside at the car.

Honti was dazed. The first thought that occurred to him was how ludicrous he would look, talking to Scorbell in the millions and no teeth in his mouth. But then Honti forgot about the teeth and a general depression set in. The plans, the happy hopes, the visions all fell away from him. To take their place came a terrible, pitiless clarity. It was the letdown Lily had been predicting. The cycle was completed. He sat down on a chair, sick and dreary.

He had meant to borrow Morley's car for the trip over to Benedict Canyon. Now Honti had no machine, he had no teeth, and he could also see that he wasn't going to get his financing so fast. Scorbell was no dumbbell. A man didn't own three factories by throwing his money around indiscriminately. Honti sat in the gloom of the living room and didn't stir. Black thoughts crowded in his head. He had been feeling so good. Everything had been so wonderful. Why, he asked himself over and over again—why did he have to go and pinch her? He was a pariah. He wasn't fit for human company.

"It is demeaning," Oleam said mournfully, not referring to the pinch—he hadn't even noticed the incident. He was still protesting because Honti was taking away his appointment. Oleam thought it wasn't becoming to bring business matters into a delicate situation like this. It would put the whole affair in a different light. "It is not right," Oleam said sorrowfully, still in the neck brace. "It is cheap. It is vulgar. Scorbell will think we are all adventurers and finaglers."

Morley was driving along Mulholland Drive, on top of the hills, heading for Laurel Canyon, which would take them down to the Crescent Heights section, where they lived. Barbara sat next to him, tight-lipped and flushed. He had never seen her in such a mood and was half afraid to talk to her. She refused to tell him anything. She was just too furious to explain. He racked his brains. It was so tantalizing. He had thought everything was fine and settled. When he left the living room, they were dancing with glee. What in the world could have gone wrong?

"After the way you made me feel!" Barbara said. "After I reproached myself and was even going to go to him and apologize!"

"But what happened?" Morley begged. "If you would only tell me—what did he *do*?"

He stopped short. The car was coasting and came to a stop. The motor had failed. Morley put the brakes on and fiddled with the starter. Then he remembered that the gas line had a slow leak in it. They were out of gas. The car had a number of things the matter with it and needed an overhaul job, but Morley had been putting it off, because he was always so short. There was nothing to do now but start walking to a gas station. Suddenly, Barbara burst into tears.

"All the hours I sat in the car by myself, listening to the dopey radio," she said. She was thinking of the unpaid bills, of the times she had waited alone outside while Morley made his calls.

He frowned. He felt helpless and confused, and didn't know what to say to her. He left her weeping and got out of the car. Sadly, he began the long hike down to the foot of Laurel Canyon, where the nearest gas station was.

Honti was also on Mulholland Drive, but farther to the west, toward Benedict Canyon. He was walking to Scorbell's place—to try there, to keep the appointment. The air was clean. The view extended for miles on either side. The earth lay still and impassive, touched with the solitude of great spaces. Honti felt shrunken in spirit. He was weary. He thought of the few decades that were given to a man, three or four, or five at the most. How swiftly they had gone for him, in what a frenzy. There had hardly been time to stop for anything.

When he was a boy, he used to soak lima beans in water overnight and then plant them in flowerpots. All day long, he would carry the flowerpot from window sill to window sill, to give his plant the benefit of the shifting sun. Honti remembered that home—the warmth there and the peace. He remembered walking with his father along the river in Frankfurt, on a wintry day, holding his father's hand, passing some great cathedral; after all the years, Honti could still see in his mind the clouds etched against the sky that day, like frost on a windowpane. Honti thought of some bricklayers he had seen in Paris, when he and Lily had tried there, when they had thought maybe, maybe in Paris . . . The bricklayers, high up on the scaffolding, had been caught in a sudden shower and covered themselves with their empty plaster troughs, huddling like turtles. These, and perhaps a half-dozen others, were the images, the memories, that Honti at the age of fifty had collected to treasure. He loved that moment with the bricklayers, and the light in Paris, and the rivers of France, the Hudson River Valley in this country, and the incredible California sunshine; the tragedy was that they did not love him back. Everywhere he was rejected, everywhere a trespasser. "Forgive me!" Honti suddenly said, pleading quietly but with all his heart and soul. "Forgive me! Forgive me!" Yes, it was his fault. He had trespassed, he had transgressed; he had committed abominations, stretched the truth and kited checks. He must have committed all the sins, for you weren't punished for nothing in this world, and God knew all Honti's lifetime had been a punishment.

He humbly pleaded for forgiveness high on the mountaintop. To his left were the harbors, the beaches, the glinting Pacific Ocean. To the right lay the floor of the San Fernando Valley and, beyond that, the sullen ranges of the San Gabriels.

Avoiding all distractions, ignoring the rabbits and squirrels, ignoring the other dogs as they came out to meet him, ready to fight or frolic, Fidelio was heading back to the house by a series of paths and short cuts. He was hungry. He had been searching all day long. He had been to the barbershop, the restaurants and drugstores, the Turkish bath. He had looked for Honti at the houses of all his friends. Hoping that his master was home, that all was well, he came loping through the thickets and arrived at the clearing. He paused, breathing hard, disappointed. The swimming pool looked abandoned. The lawn was strewn with empty chairs. Fidelio went up to and sniffed an old beach shoe on the tiled edge of the pool, a squiggly wet towel, a torn bathing cap without the strap, the chocolate layer cake. Then he slipped into the bushes and began loping again, resuming his search.

The Heart of the Artichoke

Herbert Gold

1

My father, his horny hands black with sulphur, lit a cigar
with a brief, modest, but spectacular one-handed gesture, his
thumbnail crr-racking across the blue-headed kitchen match;
when he described his first job in America, selling water to
the men building the skyscrapers, teetering across the girders
for fifteen cents a pail, green flecks fumed and sailed in his
yellowish Tartar eyes; he peeled an artichoke with both hands
simultaneously, the leaves flying toward his mouth, crossing
at the napkin politely tucked at the master juggler's collar,
until with a groan that was the trumpet of all satisfaction he
attained the heart; he—but he was a man of capabilities, such
feats apart.

As my mother said of him before they married, "He's
well-off. Lots of personality." Older than the other women of
her family, she used the word *well-off* in a primitive sense, to
signify a general relationship with the world, not subtracting
from the term all but its usual financial refrain: "Well-off
very, he's a Buick. . . ." But she took the word from Aunt
Sarah and Aunt Ethel; it's important that the vocabulary derives from economic security, to be extended outward only by
an exceptional act of vitality. We, my brothers and I, could
never eat enough for her. "Don't aggravate me. Eat. Eat,"
she would say.

"We already ate," I pointed out.

"But look at your father!"

He was eating. He ate with silent respect for food, a great
deal, and not out of gluttony but with appreciation for his own
labor in it. He knew the cost. In each spoonful of soup carried with music to his mouth I heard the winds whistling
through the branches of the knaedloch trees; I saw the farmers' trucks, laden with chopped liver, musing in his crocodile

eyes. "Eat," he pronounced at intervals, assuaging his love for us, "eat, eat."

We ate with a hunger in our bellies or in a filial loyalty while his was in his heart. Wearing a sheepskin coat which came as a gift from Mother and Pitkin's with the no-overhead, a silvery-pronged crate-hammer arming his back pocket, he climbed into the cab of his truck before dawn on market days, his wife's lips still parted against their single pillow while he checked off a list measured in gross over a breakfast of liver-and-onions with the other fruitmen in Solly's Market Tearoom. Perhaps at the earlier moment of supper, while we heedlessly digested, carloads of artichokes were coming in at the Food Terminal for the Thursday morning auction. He would get the best for Jack's Food & Vegetable: *The Best is the Best Buy*.

"Always," my mother piously breathed after him. She was proud of his slogan. "He made it up himself one day I remember it, he was by the cooler sorting asparagus. Lots of personality, loads," she informed Aunt Ethel and Aunt Sarah. "Eat," she said to me. "The nice ovenbaked potato."

I once asked the address of the poor hungry man in China who would be glad to finish my potato. "I'll send it to him with Mr. Kennedy the mailman," I suggested.

"I need your backtalk like I need my own brother Morton's agar-agar oil for his constipation, Henry Ford should take him. A whole tablespoon," she said. "I need it." Repenting of my sarcasm, I never believed in the poor hungry man, although I had recently become convinced of China at least in Geography.

My father had the knowledge of things—how to hoist an orange crate in a movement like a dance, how to tell an honest farmer from one who will hide his bad Pascal or Iceberg under bravado and a show of good ones, whom to trust in the fleet meetings of money at a fruit auction; this is already a great deal. Only once was he famously tricked, and by Uncle Morton, a man who installed automatic sprinkling pipes in his lawn ("For show! for the neighbors!" my mother communicated, outraged) but spent his Sundays tightening the faucets and complaining that his daughters filled the bathtub too full. (How clean can you get?)

Well, this brother-in-law, exalted by cupidity in one federally sponsored moment, suggested a partnership in the property in order to eliminate my father's competition at an auction: Should brothers, or almost-brothers, bid each other up like cats and dogs? No, the answer.

Afterwards, the deal secured, my father approached, tendering a hand-rolled cigar fraternally-in-law and saying, "Nu Mort, now about the partnership I think well we should let Henry there in the Republic Building, not that Hank from 105th Street, Henry a reliable man Hazelton Hotels uses him, draw up the papers—"

"Partners! hah!" Villainous Uncle Morton, performing for some secret inner croak of applause, permitted himself laughter at such innocence. "I'm partners me only with my wife" —and they haven't spoken since, nor have his daughters and I, cousins all.

But this was real estate, not food, which was the true sphere of my father's power; besides, such an error brings scope and savor to a legend of paternal infallibility. He could say, or let my mother say, while above the broad cheekbones his eyes glittered like two long plump lima beans on sidewalk display in the sun: "The only time Jake got it but good, it was that time with the Woodward property, his own brother-in-law my brother, they run a house in the Heights and two cars—they need it?—a Buick sure and a Chevie for Yetta and the kids, may his breath turn sour in his old age—"

And his daughters' too. Amen.

As my mother talked, my father measured us from under a vast biblical forehead which had sojourned in Kamenetz-Podolsk; it was a forehead that barely escaped the scars of reprisal for a tradesman's life given to a man who needed labor in the open air. He wrestled out this frozen compression, these knotty ravages, at the cost of an over-quickening in the work of the store, wielding cases with a plunging violence and mounting trucks like a burly fruitstore tomcat. Over-happiness too is a threat, Zarathustra said. The yellow flecks of his long narrow eyes fumed in contemplation. His sons were strange animals, born in America.

Question-shaped, my belly in advance of my thoughts, I had unnoticed by all but myself become skinny, pimply, shrewd, and poetic. I trained myself to wake at dawn, not for work like my father or to drink formula like my youngest brother, but because of the possibility that Pattie Donahue might feel my presence and stir in response to it; I believed in telepathy, tuning in on no messages because no one sent me any. I searched her face during Miss Baxter's Reading and The Library How To Use It for a sign of complicity (received no answer); I never spoke to her, for reasons of shyness and reasons of magic. She had aquarium eyes, profoundly green, profoundly empty, and a mouth like a two-cent Bull's Eye candy, and pale transparent fingers busy as fins. She powdered her nose in public, no longer picking it; she touched her ears to make sure of their presence on the beach of her head; patiently she plucked the angora from her mittens off the front of her cardigan, with this gesture of pale-boned fingers exploring herself and me. Together only abstractly, we were linked by both imagining atrocious ways to wish her well.

I let her swim again in my memory. She considered the future by judging it with the deliberate active forgetfulness of a fish floating asleep under ice: power through patience. Pattie Donahue wanted more than love, more than strength; she wanted mastery in denial, divinity in refusal of her own blood. Up the ladder to godhood or down to fishliness? That was her one risk in life. Seaweed is good for you! Lots of iodine! She had a repertory of head-tuckings, wiggles, peeps, curtseys, suckings, winks, herself charmed by herself; she was crippled for eternity, condemned to increase by parthenogenesis. She could not laugh with her body because her body could never move to another's, sway as it might under the seas of her ambition. Bemused, pious, she granted herself an adoring hand, fingers straddling to squeeze her sweater at the root of milk and psychology. Recall that princess who could undress before a slave because she did not regard him as a human being? We are all sometimes slaves.

Slavishly I kneeled for her chamois penwiper where it fell behind her desk in Music and Singing.

"Oh thank you," she said.

"Never mind, never mind"—me melting like March ice in a spring pool of timidity and chagrin.

"Oh don't stop me, Daniel Berman. Thank you indeed. My mother says I need practice how to be gracious. Please let me do thank you. Oh thank you, Daniel Berman. . . ."

This too is a sort of excess!—and I let her take me under the green grasp of her greedy eyes. The fishy princess pouted, ducked, abstractly reached; I worshipped this body shivering and glistening under bracelets like scale. I saw her as age. Age during that time signifies secret power, secret passion, and the death which follows age is known only as the death which follows love. Girls, born queens, are always older than boys, ten-thousand-eyed drones, living for love, empty-headed, precariously housebroken. "Oh thank you really," said Princess Pattie Donahue, her royal sardine, queen of the hive.

She was gracious on me.

One day, the talk of the Horace Greeley Junior High playground, a pride for events beyond me took her; she wore a shiny black brassiere which hung in lank splendor beneath the faintly distended yarn of her sweater and the morning's accretion of pink angora. She plucked, she pinched; in my poems I never found a rhyme for Donahue. Desire for a girl with nipples like tapioca spots! She went out, it was alleged, with high school seniors.

It was at this era of sudden sweat and pubic rancor that the issue of working in the store afternoons or at least Saturdays became prominent. "To help out," my father said.

"To learn the value of a dollar," my mother said.

"To know what's what in life," my father said.

"To learn the value of a dollar," my mother said.

"To find out it's like something to be a man," my father said.

"To learn the value of a dollar," my mother said.

"To see how people—"

"To learn the value—"

"To help—"

"To learn—"

There always remained another word to propose on the subject. "I have homework to do?" I asked, making this a question because the whole world knew I did no homework.

"Your cousin Bernie works in his father's store," my mother said. "He's learning the value."

"Your cousin Irwin works in his father's store," my father said. "Very mature kit, grown-up. Knows what's what."

No fonder of my cousins, I began to work in the store. At first there were compensations besides learning the value and knowing what's what; for example, I quickly suspected the potentialities of stacking Jello. Its six delicious box colors made possible the development of a penchant toward baroque in counter displays. I gave over to fantasy in exercises of pure structure; I brought art to Dried Desserts (end of the first aisle), evolving from a gothic striving and simplicity to a rococo exuberance, raspberry mounting lemon in commercial embrace. The Jello man beamed and said I had talent. He promised me an autographed photograph of Jack Benny from his sample case, the signature printed as good as original, the *same identical thing*. I stood off, narrow-eyed, architectural, three loose boxes in each hand. While orange buttresses flew and lime vaulted over naves of cherry, my father grew impatient. "Is that all you got on your mind, the playboy?" It was not all, but he was right: there is a limit to what one can do with Jello. And what finally happened to my dream of a celestial engineering? Bananas were sliced into it.

I knew that my friends were playing touch football in the street or perhaps, if it were late afternoon, amorously lobbing rocks onto Pattie Donahue's front porch. Pity the man with an unemployed throwing-arm! Aproned and earth-bound despite my Buster Brown aviator shoes, I stood in exile among the creak of shopping baskets and a cash-register clank, such matters unmusical where a rumor of roller skates on a girl's sidewalk pledges passion eternal and a well-placed rock portends an invitation to Rosalie Fallon's second annual traditional Hallowe'en party; these are suburban verities which held even in the prehistory before Mayor Cassidy's first reign, when I began my studies of how to pee in an enamelled pot. A marksman now, I turned sullen despite my skill, sour as a strawberry plucked too early; my father knew their need to ripen wild in the sun, unfingered by ambitious farmwives. I was a bad crop, green through, lazy for spite.

"Stop slouching," my mother said. "Stand up like a mench. Bernie *likes* the store. He stays and works even when Uncle Abe says go home, here's a quarter."

I learned contempt for my cousins, the submissive ones, who worked so that they could spend dimes like grown-ups instead of nickels in the Chippewa Lake slot machines. No amount of labor could harden their gluey hands. Irwin had flat feet, a moustache at fourteen because his mother did not tell him to shave, the habit of standing too close when he talked, and, as luck would have it, a talent for projecting his bad breath with such accuracy that any customer's sales resistance must have died in the first whiff. Later he learned to brush his tongue, shave his armpits, sprinkle himself with Johnson's Baby Powder, and rinse his mouth with spearmint mouthwash. Anything for a client. He gave up his soul, a pulpy one at that, which resided in the crevices of his teeth.

Bernie, Narcissus Gaynesbargh the Go-getter, developed an artist's pure love for illness, hospitals, and operations. He saved up enough—"All by his lonesome," bragged Aunt

Sarah—for an operation which joined his ears more cunningly to his head. "Clark Gable can let himself go, he's a big man already, but not my Bernie," his mother proudly recounted. "Today he looks a million—stand frontways, Bernie! And how tall is your Daniel?"

Bernie had enough left over in his account to have his piles removed during the after-Christmas slow spell. *Carpe Diem:* he obeyed our junior high motto, constantly improving himself, a medically-made man, an expert on vitamin pills, eye exercises, and local anesthesia. He was also judicially-made; let us not omit the subtle alterations in the orthography of his name. Imagine the legal nightmare in which a Ginsberg-into-Gaynesbargh signifies more rebirth than immolation! The suicide was a complete success. Neither his ears nor his ancestors stuck out, although the stitching showed.

"*They* will marry nice rich girls from New York City, you'll see," my mother threatened me. Later both took Marital Engineering courses, one at Miami University and the other at Cornell, and it paid, because Bernie married a nice rich shoe business from Hartford and Irwin married a wholesale Divan & Studio Couch, a steady thing.

"But," as my mother said, "you can't measure happiness in dollars and cents. There are things more important especially with taxes these days. A sweet little wife, a nice little family. . . ."

"Have a piece Sanders." Aunt Sarah consoled her with the Continental assortment. "I got it by Sanders Chocolates when I went downtown to look for my new Person Lamb yesterday. Purse-and-lamb, I mean. Who knows maybe I'll settle for a Shirt Beaver, the season's almost over."

Not even Aunt Sarah can distract my mother when philosophy comes over her. "You could marry in a low element, maybe he wouldn't really be rich only pretending, living high, that kind of a click—"

"My Irwin hm hm, you should know he sent me a this year's pillow direct from the factory to me," Aunt Sarah might remark. "He don't have to put birds in his vest, my Irwin."

"Don't tell me, I know," Mother groaned. "Some people are real type bigshots, some people have to make look big to themselves with escalator heels and Scotch shoelaces, who ever heard?"

"My Irwin—"

"What, you crazy? He's a nice steady boy your Irwin, clean-cut, a neat dresser. I'm mentioning it so happens one of those fast clicks, oh, oh."

"Ho," breathed Aunt Sarah.

They communed in silence over the family shame. They clopped the bitter memory from their outraged palates. They drew the lesson from what befell poor Cousin Bessie, who returned from a vacation—he had a nice job with the government, too—with pierced ears and coral earrings, a pair of chartreuse silk slacks, and a new man to replace the one who broke his head. "My new husband," she announced, indicating a plump individual with oily sunburned pouches under his eyes, Novelty-style shoelaces, and a sky-blue Kalifornia Kravate with a silver-lightning pin, the tie tucked into a Hickock Kowboy-type belt: "Roland, he's in the wholesale business in Los Angeles."

"Wholesale what?" Mother had asked, suspicious already.

"Just wholesale," Cousin Bessie said equably. Roland smiled to show the gap in his teeth bridged by invisible platinum. His little woman spoke for him: "He has the biggest outlet in Los Angeles."

"Ellay," he corrected her.

Later, after Uncle Moish from Indian River Drive discovered that this Roland was a bad-type thief off the legit, not a dealer in factory-to-you eliminate-the-middleman low-costs, they helped Bessie out again. She promised to be more careful next season. She was pushing thirty-five, although the family loyally counted only the last twenty-seven of them; she had combed the summer time mountains and the winter time seaside since she buried Lester. Mother took three deep breaths and announced, addressing her in the ceremonial third person while Bessie wept wholesale tears: "Next time she should vacate a week ten days in Atlantic City on the Atlantic, the sun, the salt water taffy, she should meet a nice steady New York type fella, she still got her health why not? Knock on wood. Just he shouldn't have the biggest outlet in Ellay."

Still my cousins were generally nice, steady, and successful even at that early time. I was recalcitrant, a failure in affairs.

"The whole world knows. Aunt Ethel and Aunt Sarah know, it should happen to me I try to be a good mama to you. The whole city knows."

Aunt Sarah encouraged my mother in her own way.

" '*Mama*,' my Bernie tell me,"—and her eyes moistened over such devotion—" 'Mama,' he says, 'you look like sugar in the urine again. What did I tell you about those two-dollar Sanders assortments?' . . . . So thoughtful," she concluded, folding her arms across a high stalwart bone of her *garment*, leaning back, and waiting for my mother to tell something good about me. I couldn't even read an oral thermometer. After a while she sighed for pity, yawned for contentment, and added soothingly, "Your Danny working nice in the store these days maybe? Just tell him about my Bernie, he'll learn, you got to encourage."

"I look in the looking glass I ask myself why, I got no answer. A son of mine, why? A thirteen-years-old lump," she encouraged.

It wasn't laziness. That's a maternal answer. I would have worked in other ways, and did; if I could have remained at some comprehensible task, delivering orders perhaps, building shelves, loading the truck, or manipulating the stock in the basement, I might have attained a fulfillment equal in its way to Cousin Bernie's avarice for operations. The constant pouring of commands from a triumphant father shivered and shattered my sense for work: he wanted me by his side, proud of an eldest son, any eldest son. For good reasons of his own —he had been poor, he wanted me to see what he had done for himself and for us all—he urged me to learn the pleasure of a direct delicious manipulation of money, its worn old touch of cloth, its warmth of hands and pockets, its smell of sex and work, its color of economy or death in our world, signed in those days by Andrew W. Mellon. "Here! it says right here. Read it yourself. That's the Secretary of the Treasury of the United States of America, U. S. A., his own autograph."

"Oh, for God's sake. Jake, you can notice such things?" —my mother discovering new depths, she a modest economist, my father not.

"Notice notice," he admitted virtuously. Money was poetry, a symbol of life and power on one side, economy and death for him with the White House on the other, but only a symbol —how could I understand such metaphysics, ungraduate-schooled in that epoch of despair with girls and ambitions of purity? My agile Tartar-eyed father made the distinction by enjoying both the earning and the spending, finding his truth higgledy-piggledy in an exploit of strapping a load-and-a-healthy-half on his 1928 White Motors truck or in giving

himself to a snack of artichoke with Kraft's dressing, the heart
his end but the money-colored leaves loved for what they were.

He wanted me to clerk, to *wait on trade,* then, to be an
aproned catalyst toward the final term. How could I take
money from Mrs. Donahue, whose daughter no one but Tom
Moss knew I loved, while Pattie herself teased her mouth with
an end of lipstick without glancing at me in my feminizing
wraparound? My languishing yip should have betrayed me:
"That'll be just three sixty-five, please," recited as I had been
taught. It did not; no one saw me. The money joined money
in the new Serv-a-slip cash register. *O love me, Pattie! look!*
—and I feared that she would. I gave the cash to Hannah, the
cashier, my father's deputy while he bargained with the
Wheaties jobber for bonus Eversharps and an electric fan-
flame wood-glow fireplace.

"Okay, Little Jack, you're picking up now. I'll tell your pa.
Just keep the hands out of the pockets when you're making
a sale. Say thank you to the customer." Hannah had a tongue
cracked and ridged, mounds at the meaty sides and fissures
among the yellowish scale, betrothed to dyspepsia. These
wounds came of a continual talking confused with a continual
eating. No one knew a remedy. She suffered unsilently, chewing Baseball Gum. "I said take hands out of pockets that's a
boy. I said say thank you to the nice customer."

"Thank you, Mrs. Donahue," I mumbled miserably.

I carried Mrs. Donahue's order to her Hudson. Pattie
moved ahead, her rump twitching like a snapdragon delicately
pinched. I fled as she fumbled with her purse for a tip. The
next Monday, inspecting my approach from her station at the
side entrance to Horace Greeley Junior High, without taking
her eyes off mine she bent significantly to whisper into her
friend Rosalie Fallon's ear. To stifle their laughter the two of
them made paws of their silly adored hands at their mouths.
This gesture insured politeness and (reward for a suburban
virtue) the secret renewal of laughter when the grocery boy
had passed. Sober and unblinking, Pattie nonchalantly rubbed
her edible kneecap.

"Don't call me Little Jack," I told Hannah once more without hope. "Call me my name."

"Okay. . . . Little Jack," she said, humorously chewing.

Sometimes I carried a book to work, wearing it piously
between my shirt and my chest, and then hid with it and a
cigarette in the basement among the cases of Libby's Whole

Sliced Pineapple and Hinz-zuzz Pork and Beans with Tomato Sauce. The whitewashed walls sweated; the storeroom smelled of dampness, rat poison, cardboard packing cases, and a broken bottle of soy sauce. Here I was happy, the complicated atmosphere making me dizzy as I perched corrupt with one of Andy's Wing butts on a peak of pineapple under the dusty 40-watt bulb. Sometimes I put down the Poe (I had memorized *Ulalume* without being able to pronounce it) and moodily considered my childhood, before Pattie Donahue and before my parents had decided I was a man, when I had sometimes visited this range of cans and bottles to leap like a goat among it in my innocence. I practiced a tragic sigh, inhaling soy.

Always my father roared down the stairway to discover me. "YOU THINK YOU CAN KID ME, HAH? The A & P can't even kid me, I got a list of your tricks—"

I stood up with no answer, understanding that he would forever find me, silent in my wished chagrin. I could not explain to him the disgrace of working in a store in a neighborhood where boys had important unexplainable things to do, secret clubs and fatal loafing, while their fathers managed offices for Standard Machines or handled law cases for insurance companies downtown. I wanted him to commute instead of work, like the others; I could not tell either of us the reason for my stubborn reluctance to follow him to the market, racy and challenging though it was. I felt a justice in his despair with me. A coward, I hid each time.

"Your mother says today you'll be good, I say I'll find you sneaking off with a book."

I studied his boots on the cement and deeply assented. He had looked in the backroom to see if I were filling orders, giving me the benefit of a doubt and profligate hope which is still my debt.

"Nu, what do you say for yourself? I'm going crazy upstairs, it's a big one-cent-sale, the Saturday help's no good these days. . . . Hah?"

I said nothing.

"Why not tell me another lie, you'll be good like you promised I should be happy?"

I stared, Poe sweaty in my hands.

"So why don't you at least say you had to go to the toilet, the mensroom?"—a treble note of exasperation hidden in his bass, wanting an excuse for me, loving his oldest.

I refused this. I was over-moral for a moment, going on thirteen, as he was over-happy; I despised anything but extreme commitments, surrender to his world or defiance of it.

"What's the matter, you constipated? You got stomach trouble?"—pretending that I had given us this excuse, unable to bear our misery together.

He watched the tears silently fill my eyes.

He relented; he appealed to me, trying to preserve his anger by shouting; he betrayed his helplessness by heavily sitting down beside me on the canned pineapple. "What's the matter, you hungry, you want your mother should make you a tomato and balonny sandwich with Kraft's Miracle Whip dressing?"

"I want to go upstairs and help out," I whispered at last.

Reconciled, unable to preserve animus, he bumped against me up the narrow steps. Instead of letting me sink into the crowd of customers reaching with their lists and their clippings of advertisements at the counters, he ordered me to go to lunch with him, knowing that I liked this. To have the Business Men's special with Dad in a restaurant was one of the compensations; choosing food is the act of a god—only gods and business men don't have mothers to tell them what to eat, filling their plates with it. It was a pure joy although a bad restaurant; we had to go there because Guy Mallin owed my father two hundred dollars, which he never paid and we couldn't eat through by the time he left his wife and ran off to Montreal with Stella, the waitress, and a week's receipts. (When this happened Dad tried, although he knew little about the restaurant business, to help out poor Mrs. Mallin, who had no children but only a thyroid condition to give her an interest in life.) Both of us would have preferred an egg roll and hamburger steak at Louie's, the Chinaman across the street, and our unity on this—winking across the table as fast-talking Guy Mallin approached—cleared the hatred of civilizations between father and son. I should insist on this: the storm confined itself to its direct object, my laziness, rising like an east wind to its peak on the busy day, Saturday or before holidays, then falling away. "You learn with meet people," he only said. "You learn with know their ways."

After we finished our lunch I hid in the basement of the store to read Edgar Allan Poe.

2

As the months went by, the ruses deepened and the anger
swam like some exiled bull carp in the deepest pools of the
natures of my mother, my father, and me. Pattie Donahue
had definitively given up roller skating in the street, and not
only on bricked Pittsburg Road but also on the mellifluous
asphalt of Chesterton Avenue. We were freshmen in junior
high, seventh graders learning dignity from a Social Dancing
teacher added to the curriculum by the Board of Education
which decided that Grace and Poise (formerly Comportment)
were as essential as geography and algebra to the Young Men
& Women of Tomorrow, be they bond salesmen like their
fathers or *homemakers* like their mothers. The Real Estate
Taxpayers League issued a protest against educational frills;
pioneering virtues that made our country great, assessment already excessive, it argued. Artichokes, bulky and hard to handle, were coming into season again.

Shamefully I pretended to be sleeping Saturday mornings
when my father had gotten up at three or earlier. Mother was
more violent, my father more deeply hurt—the denial, after
all, was of him. She nagged constantly; yet on Saturdays when
I stayed motionless slugabed, her pride in sleep—"It's very
healthy"—protected me there. Later, my father telephoning to
ask if I had arisen yet, he fell silent before her report, pressing the receiver to his ear amid the mob of shoppers importu-
nate about fork-tongued Hannah's dais, and he darkly said
nothing while Mother repeated infuriated with me but stubborn in her allegiance to health: "Let the kid sleep just one
more morning, kids need sleep. It's good for them."

Having vacuumed, she herself got ready to go to the store
for *relief*. Out of some relic of pride I could not bring myself to feign until she would safely leave me among my angry
bedclothes in the occult reproach of a house. "I'm up," I
fatally admitted. I reached for a paltry revenge in wearing
yesterday's socks. She edified me in a steady torrent on the
streetcar to the store:

"No good! big lump! lazy good-for-nothing! You're thirteen
already and look at you!"

"Twelve," I corrected her.

" 'Please Daddy I want to work in the store like a big man,'
Bernie always says. Aunt Sarah says. Such a go-getter! But

what do you say?—look ma the dog wet the rug I'm twelve years old. Aunt Sarah says I should stop aggravating myself. Please give a look my waricose weins from standing up." She had forgotten that the effect of threatening to telephone Aunt Sarah when I was *bad* had been dissipated years ago with the advent of Unlimited Calls. Sometimes I had even offered to dial the number for her.

"A big lump like you he should give me a rest, take the load off your feet Ma like Bernie, not trouble trouble all the time."

"Why is it you always say I'm thirteen when it's something you want me to do and know I'm twelve?" I asked, a savant without rimless glasses: "And when I want to do something I can't because I'm not old enough, I'm only eleven? My birthday is July twentieth at six o'clock in the morning."

"I remember," she said morosely. "And a fine night I had with you in Mount Sinai all night too, they almost had to use force-its. Dr. Shapiro said my bones were so delicate close together. . . . Thirteen, going on now. Even Uncle Morton knows about you, I'm so ashamed in the family why I told Aunt Ethel I'll never hold my head high again, at least Morton he got daughters they keep themselves clean at least not so much aggravation, all right so worry a tiny bit they should marry nice, but not heartache a no-good like you day in day out—"

Outside the streetcar the first autumn leaves were burning in piles on the street, sending up an odor redolent of freedom in the open air. My friends flamboyantly loitered on the Saturday streets, chalk in their mouths, their hearts unfettered. Pattie Donahue was perhaps walking alone in Rocky River Park, just waiting for me telepathically to find her.

The store opened about us with the intense plushy smell of old vegetables. Hannah was comforting old Mrs. Simmons, a childless widow whose husband had been manager of the Guarantee Trust, Rocky River branch; she generally admitted herself among us with the distant face of someone who disliked the smell of the inside of her own nose, but now she claimed to have seen a spider in a hand of bananas. "It probably wasn't a deadly poisonous banana spider," Hannah said. "Did it have a lot of legs? Furry ones from Costo Rico?"

"A South American banana spider! oh!" Mrs. Simmons, realizing that it was a foreign element, rolled her eyes in search of a pleasant place to faint.

"Probably not deadly poisonous, though. Probably just

a sleepy little old banana spider from the deadly jungles of Hatey." Mrs. Simmons fainted. That is, considering her dignity and the aristocratic unpaid bills in the drawer with Hannah's sandwiches, she *swooned.* "Anyway no one else saw it, the thousand-legger bug, the horrible deadly spider," Hannah mused on, rubbing Mrs. Simmons' wrists without taking off her Ovaltine Birthstone & Goodluck Ring.

"Ouch, you're scratching," said Mrs. Simmons.

My father, harried but always expecting the best, greeted me with an order. Stack the oranges, wait on Mrs. Simmons, put on your apron, what's the matter with you? . . . Could I confess the chief reason for my tardiness, a hope that telepathic pressure concentrated among my bedclothes might compel Mrs. Donahue to buy her Ohio State hothouse tomatoes and Swansdown ready-mix no-sift cake flour before my surrender to penance in a wraparound? *Develop Your Will Increase Your Power. Sample Booklet Fool Your Friends. 25c Coin or Stamps.* No, I could not. My father's will developed, he spoke a language in which existed no vocabulary to explain that, among the people with whom he chose to bring me up, it was more important to run end in a pick-up touch football game, spinning craftily about the young trees planted by the Our Street Beautiful committee, than to fill orders in sour old orange crates on Saturday afternoons. We all paid, in our various ways, a price for those trees and for the privilege of overhead doors on our garages and colonial-style magazine racks for our Saturday Evening Posts. He did not draw the consequences of his ambition for me; if he judged our neighborhood to be better than that of his childhood, then our neighborhood would judge his world. In a develop-your-will (Fool Your Friends) like my father's, the only lack was the will to find my will-less longing. He worked! Mother worked! Like dogs!—They were right, but they could not see through to my rightness, forgetting a child's hunger to belong. Ulalume might have been for the ages, but Rosalie Fallon and Pattie tongued their malicious pencils and wrote my fate in their Slam Books. He knew he was a foreigner, my father did; I had to discover it in pain, shame before my parents, and self-judging. "I earned my own living when I was thirteen, and proud of it," he had said.

"Your father earned his own living when he was twelve," Mother remarked contentedly in explanation, "and he is proud of it. *Proud* of it."

"Thirteen he said," I said.

"Proud he said," she said.

He studied me in sorrow and silence, figuring with his short black-nailed thick-knuckled hands reaching for the silvery crating hammer in his back pocket. I was just a kid. I even looked like him. Hannah said so. Even Guy Mallin said I was a chip off the. Hey kid? You want a Business Men's plate with chocolate ice cream instead of the green peas with butter sauce? It should be easy to figure. . . . "Gravy on that there ice cream haw-haw yessir, hey kid? Gravy!" Guy Mallin roared. "A real chip if I ever saw one, Jake. I'm telling you listen to me now. Your eyes. Your chin. His mother's, a sweet little woman you got there, nose. Yessir. Your hair. Off the old block there, Jake. Good material, hey? It won't be long before it's *Jake & Son*, what-do-you-say? I'm telling you now Jake you heard what I said."

"Maybe things are different these days," he told me. "You ain't the way I was."

My father had the gift of listening to the artichokes at the top of a load in such a way—they informed him in a language which only he and the artichokes spoke—that he always knew when their brothers at the bottom were defective, defeated, edged with rust or shriveled from a stingy soil. Silent in their hampers, they communicated by the violence of love, all knowing their role on this occasion as opportunities, each thick-leafed one, for a sociable debating between farmer and merchant, green, crisp, candid, and nutritive after a pleasant journeying into the hands of women. They accepted the gift of himself which my father made, their shoots curly for him, their unbaked hearts shy in a bra of ticklish felt. Buy us! sell us!—they asked nothing more. Artichokes understood my father, and his sympathy for vegetables arose to meet theirs for him. Devotion—he gave this freely. He accepted, too, being stuck with thorns.

Unfortunately I, even in those days, was not an artichoke —perhaps not so rewarding, my heart not luscious with a dab of miracle-whip, stunted in fact, even hornier, full of bad character and a brooding plant rust. "Lots of personality," my mother had said, feebly defending me when as a child I had refused to shell lima beans for the store with the rest of the family on Friday nights. "Everyone says he takes after your side, Jake. Ethel says, Sarah says."

"Since I was thirteen! I got scars on my back, the bucket

cut me, the greenhorn I didn't get a pad cloth. Look at Irwin, look at Bernie born the same week like you in Mount Sinai, you was the first so I got your mother a semi-private. A healthy kid like you, he sleeps all morning Saturday."

"Since he was twelve years old a greenhorn," Mother mournfully intoned. "Who ever heard of it?"

Pattie Donahue plucked at her sweater and pouted with kiss-proof lipstick (maybe) over teeth lucky to serve her. Lewis Snyder, the sheik, told stories about Rosalie Fallon and Pattie. Tom Moss told me. "The liar," we agreed, ferociously believing him.

Such matters flowed in time; the store remained outside time, its claim ripening through the spines but as incredible to me as a heartless artichoke to my father. The store gulped me down. I evaded, I squirmed, I stubbornly bent, receded, and persisted like heartburn, taking all shapes but in fact knowing only itself, which has no shape and a mysterious matter.

"You don't want, what kind of a reason is that?" my mother demanded, fertile as Hera in argument. "No reason, that's what kind."

I couldn't explain to myself or to them, much less to Aunt Sarah or to Aunt Ethel, to Hannah, Guy Mallin, or Cousin Bernie the Smarty. Let him marry a nice rich girl from New York Queens in the clothing business, I don't care, I sacrilegiously insisted. My single purpose was love for Pattie Donahue, whose father carried a portfolio to work in his airless pink little hands; she would love only the elaborate loungers, the conspicuous consumers—a little Veblenite she was! You Americans all long for the useless, the hymen no proper end; it feathers no beds, it fleshes no bellies—this Mother and Dad might have pointed out if they had argued their philosophy. I sensed, too, that my father's agility and strength and love, moving among the objects all his in the store, were a threat to me, the more dangerous because—one of his few fatal thoughts outside the moment—he was beginning to see Jack's Fruit & Vegetable in terms of immortality for both of us. He asked only a sign of recognition for this gift to me.

I refused his gift daily now. Even the Jello counter fell into ruins. My ultimate denial lay outside morality, essential to character. My father was over-happy, over-moral. I crouched like a troll under a mushroom in the cellar, a troll who read *Ulalume* and murmured, "Pattie Donahue!" with dilated eyes in the shadow of a shipment from Procter & Gamble. Poor Dad!

We can measure his desolation. He left his struggle and joyous head-on combat with farmers, jobbers, salesmen, Saturday help, policemen, wilting lettuce and pears which remained green until they rotted, competitors, the chain stores, the landlord, debtors, creditors, the delivery truck, the account books, the government, insects, rodents, spoilage, wastage, heat, cold, the margin of profit, draw items, push merchandise, merchandise which he could not get, premiums, samplers, one-cent giveaways, Christmas trees on January second and Easter candy in May, children who skated through a display of jars of olives (the olives lined up one by one in bottles shaped like a straw, optically illusive, expensive all the same), Mr. Jenkins who insisted on Aunt Mary's pancake mix and would not be content with Aunt Jemimah's or any other Aunt's because he wanted to honor in this way his poor dead old Aunt Mary his mother's sister, Mrs. Rawlings the klepto whose chauffeur dropped her off at the store every morning to slip a bottle of vanilla extract into her pink muff (her daughter paid, but we had to keep score), the charity ladies and the lottery girls, the kids selling advertisements in their parochial school bulletins, the beggars who claimed to have had a store just like his in Phoenix, Arizona, until they hit a run of bad luck back in '29 (he was unanimously elected to a directory circulated by a syndicate of beggars, Phoenix & Miami Beach Chapter), the faithful customers who tried to convert him to their religions, Mrs. Colonel Greenough who came with tears to tell him that her husband forbade her to shop at Jack's Fruit & Vegetable any longer because the colonel himself had given him three months to read a book on technocracy and he had not yet complied (she bought a farewell bouquet of cauliflower before she left), the high school teacher who wanted to pay an overdue bill in the privacy of her chamber, the judges asking support both moral and ah financial in the coming primaries, the tax collectors, the bill collectors, the garbage collectors, the health inspectors, the housing inspectors, the zoning inspectors, electricians, refrigerator repair men, insurance which only covered fires begun by safety matches when his fire had resulted from a cigar butt, illness among his clerks, jealousies, rivalries, romances, extended lunch hours, female troubles which (a gentleman) he could not publicly doubt, inventories, lentil soup in cans labelled liver pate, children, who descended like locusts to remove all the tops from the Ralston boxes to send away as a mark of esteem for Tom Mix, the electric cash register playing Chopin in a short circuit, Hannah who had B. O., Andy who left his hair among the macaroons, Myrna who showed too much of her bosom in order to encourage Mr. Tramme to take an extra cantaloupe, and other problems which I'll not mention because I want to avoid making a list.

My father abandoned his direct response to these issues in order to *use psychology* on me. He appealed in subtle ways. He tried to *get me interested*. His Tartar eyes were made to squint for laughter and appetite, not cunning. My heart contracts with sadness for him now, sadness and regret. He came to me on the porch one Sunday afternoon, his great arms slack at his sides, saying, "Say!" in the way of a good fellow, and asked me to write a paragraph for his weekly advertisement in the neighborhood throwaway. I responded, too, working hard at a composition modelled on The Raven, sharpening three pencils into oblivion before I finished. Proudly I announced to Tom Moss the prospect of publication in the West Side Advertiser.

The work never appeared. Trochees had no place next to bargains in Crisco. The Crisco people paid half and supplied the engraving; the Spry people, not caught napping at the shortening, offered to pay sixty per cent and sent my mother a portable sunlamp for her sinuses. I wasn't even impregnated with Vitamin D or viosterol from Wisconsin, living by Poe and Pattie. Psychology failed; my father came as an alien to such maneuvres. Nevermore!

One day I sneaked out of the store at 4:30, made my own dinner of Laub's rye, Blue Moon pimento cheese with those taste-delightful little chopped-up pieces of real pimento, Krunchy peanut butter (kan't remember the brand), and Thursday's spoiled milk; then I went to an Edward G. Robinson with Tom Moss. The three of us stood off the coppers for a reel and a half, and when they finally got Edward G. the camera noticed a paper boat which sailed down the gutter in the symbolic rain. "Just like The Strange Case of Monsieur Whatsizname," I pedantically reminded Tom. We fought back our tears, magnificent to THE END, ate a dime's worth of evergreen mints, and went divvies on a Spicy Detective to read under the Jantzen's Swimsuit for That Lee-*uscious* Look billboard on the way home. I told him about Pattie and he told me about Rosalie Fallon. Our patient listening to each other was more than politesse; we learned through it although the histories remained classically similar, unmodified in months except for the time Rosalie kicked Tom in the shins when he complimented her by rubbing one of the last March snowballs in her face. He rolled up his pantleg to show me the wound once more. I accused him of preserving it with salt. He denied this. He accused me of envy. I lowered my eyes. Tom was a lady-killer, he was; I'll never understand how he did it.

"Well, goodnight Tom. Good luck with Rosalie."

"Well, goodnight Dan. I'll ask Lewis Snyder about Pattie. He took Virginia Thompson out on a date and maybe she knows something. He'll tell me if I ask him because I know something on him."

Goodnight. . . . Goodnight. . . . In that midworld of childish seriousness and the first adult frivolity of passion Tom and I needed the sense of banding together, our sufferings held in common while our sense of them remained untouchable, pariahs of glandular enthusiasm in a structure built of economy. He gave me the Spicy to hide in the garage. I had often dreamed of moving through an atmosphere of glue, invisibly held from my family's home in an empty night. Empty?—full of unknown excess. Now I whistled, leaving Tom Moss an hour before midnight, forgetting that I had last seen my parents seven hours earlier when my father had said, "Wait on trade!" and I had crept out the back door where Andy was boxing strawberries and beet greens were blackening in the sun.

The door to our house was locked. The windows were dark. There was no key under the mat. The crickets suddenly deafened me, like in the movies. I thought I knew, then, how Edward G. felt when the boys went over to the South Side mob, but found a basement window open, crawled through the coal chute, and significantly murmured Pattie's name out of the side of my mouth. Ulalume Donahue, Killer Berman's moll. . . . I'd have flipped a quarter with disdain except that it was too dark and I had no quarter. *Dad!* I thought. I worried about the gas stove upstairs. Maybe they were all dead and so I should bang on the door until they let me in to sleep in my own bed. What if there were rats in the basement? Big ones like in the Paris sewers with Gene Valgene? The washing machine opened its mouth at me in the darkness. *Mother!* I thought. If the water pipes broke and I got drowned they'd be sorry. They'd be sorry someday when I spit blood into my monogrammed handkerchief from sleeping all alone in a damp basement. They would be sorry. I was sorry. *Mother and Dad!* I thought.

Without taking off my shoes I slept on the extra kitchen table in the basement, amid dirty laundry (my pillow) and old hatreds (my dreams).

3

Even this passed. The next Saturday I was as faithful as Irwin, as true as Bernie with his eyes like spoiled oysters. I tasted during one evening the delights of approval, staying up with Mother and Dad while we discussed the day's business, counted the receipts, and discussed the pros and cons of tangle displays against neat pyramids of cans or fruit. I spoke for tangle displays, Mother for order; Dad listened to us both, sipping his tea with little Ahs through his lump of sugar, and reserved decision. He tried to lasso my head as he used to in a ring of cigar smoke. "It's too big," he complained. "Just like mine, a size seven seven-eights. So look what needs a hat! You want a Stetson?"

We had a long late supper, and before going to bed he slipped me three dollar bills in a secret conspiratorial gesture while Mother stacked the dishes.

"I saw! I saw!" she cried out, her eyes peeping bright in the mirror over the sink. We all giggled together.

Dad slapped her rump, yawned, and said, "Nothing like a good day's work, hey?" in his imitation of Guy Mallin.

"Jake, you crazy?" At peace with each other, we parted. "And don't forget whose birthday is next month," my mother said: "Yours. You'll be thirteen, kiddel."

She had it right this time. It was a real truce; I knew its joys. But had anything been altered? As aphoristic Aunt Ethel might say, "A leopard coat can't change its spots."

A few days afterward I received a letter. The envelope carried my name on the outside, together with the smart-alecky title *Master,* all printed in green ink. I studied it, marvelling, my first mail since the revolutionary discovery of INCREASE YOUR WILL POWER FOOL YOUR FRIENDS, and for that I had sent away a coupon and a quarter. I sniffed it. I licked the ink

and made a smear of what our art teacher called *graded area.*
I tasted my name in green, finding it more subtle than black
but just as lucid. At last I decided to open the letter.

It was an invitation from Mr. B. Franklyn Wilkerson to
go on a Nature Walk a week from Saturday. Mr. Wilkerson,
who taught General Science to the seventh grade, had worked
out a plan to augment his income during the summer vacation
by conveying flower names and leaf shapes to suburban scholars. Small, swarthy, with three daughters and thin black hair
artfully spaced and glued into place to cover his scalp, Mr.
Wilkerson recited Science (general) with his neck petrified
for fear a sudden breeze or emotion might betray his baldness. Zealous, he devoted himself to general science textbooks,
turning the pages slowly to avoid drafts. A real scientist would
have perforated the pages. He was but a general scientist,
however, combining, as he thought, the virtues of the practical
and the theoretical in Elevating the Young, an intellectual sort
whose pink resentful mouth and clenched neck gave him the
expression of someone who had swallowed a banana sideways.

The first walk, a free trial, would take place on a Saturday,
and the Saturday before the Fourth, the third-busiest day of
the year in the store. I decided not to go.

Tom Moss was going. Lewis Snyder, who had dates alone
with girls, was going. I learned that several of them, including
Rosalie Fallon and Pattie Donahue, would be botanically present. I decided to go.

We met, everyone carrying lunch but me, at eleven-thirty.
Mother didn't know about it; I had run away from the
store, taking my cap from under the cash register and, for
some last scruple, telling Hannah to tell my father that I had
gone. "Where?"—but I disappeared without answering, subtle
as a hungry tomcat unable to hide its rut, sneaking around
corners with its yellow eyes scheming. Lewis Snyder had a
scout canteen filled with near-beer left over after repeal. I
suspected him of planning to offer Pattie some.

Pedantic, amorous, shifty-eyed general scientists, we followed Mr. Wilkerson into the Rocky River reservation. He
wore a checkered golf cap, its band black with Sta-Neet, and
showed how he had taught his wife to wrap his lunch—cello-
phane insulated the devilled eggs each from each. "Practical.
Sanitary, germ-free. Vitamins spoil in the open air," he advised us.

Tom Moss, my friend the sceptic, whispered to me that he

thought it was supposed to be *good* for you to be out in the fresh-air, and then went to step on Rosalie Fallon's heels.

We penetrated the woods, already hungry. "Now right here on your left children we find an interesting phenomenon page one hundred and forty-eight in Brenner's figure sixteen that orange growth over there with the black spots now that's a wild spermaphore," Mr. Wilkerson remarked. "Ess. Pee. Ee. Arrh—"

"Looks like a toadstool to me," I said.

"Spermaphore. Silver spoons unreliable poor quality silver these days no workmanship. Damp places. Twenty-four on a picnic without a general scientist. Could have told them. Whole party dead in eight to ten hours. Horrible. Too bad. Ess, pee, ee—"

A voice occurred behind me, whispering, "Hello, Daniel Berman." It was Pattie. "Toadstools are very poisonous,"— she leaned sociably. "Do you like are you fond of mushrooms?"

I soared into paradise at her feet. "My mother cooks spermaphores with meat loaf," I said, "and stuffed peppers."

"Oh!"—a gasp of scandal. "She does not. You'll all be dead. . . . Does she?"

"Yes," I lied, death-defying—what could be a better beginning between lovers? All lies come true in a world of such supple twelve-year-old facts. It was cool here across the city from the store. Birds soon to be falsely named cocked their heads in the trees and lectured us. Someplace customers swarmed amid the imperatives of telephones and the distance between my father and me widened past even the nine-month doubt separating an instant of giving from the birth of a son. Fatherhood, a metaphysical idea, was being taken from Dad as Mrs. Rawlings slipped her daily bottle of vanilla extract into her bosom, no one to distract her, and as Mr. Wilkerson bravely broke the perfidious spermaphore with a five-foot stick, no academician he, a man of general action in science. Rosalie Fallon gave her pressed-lip assent and moral outrage against hypocritical silver spoons while my thoughts fled back from the store to recall prepared speeches of passion for Miss Donahue, known by Killer Berman and Edward G. as Ulalume or The Lost Lenore.

"Oh-h-h," she was saying.

"Look the bug," I replied.

She pretended to be scared, not. I knew. Death and complicity—love is not a biological gesture in suburban children, O Mr. Wilkerson! I had forgotten my speeches and Ulalume.

Despite this meeting I again felt deserted, lunchless at lunchtime. Tom Moss pretended not to notice: excuse him his hunger. "Where's yours?" Pattie asked, her mouth full.

"Don't have any. My mother didn't. Not hungry anyway."

Girls always have enough to give. Suburban girls (economical) always have enough to invest. Sweetly she murmured, "You can have one of my bacon and tomato-motto sandwiches and a bite of cottage cheese with the canopy, please do." Smiling, licking her lipstick, her eyes calculating under the modest fluttering venereal lids, she whispered intimately: "And a cookie—the one with the candied cherry in the middle, please do, really."

"Oh!" I protested.

Take take, my mother would have said.

"Really, I don't mind, please do," said dainty Miss Patricia Donahue.

I did.

Later, when we bid farewell to sporting, big-toothed, intellectual (generally scientific) Mr. Wilkerson, and thanked him for a lovely nice afternoon, and promised to ask our parents to fork over five smackeroos for a Program of Nature Walks, Pattie Donahue allowed it to be known that I was walking her home. Under the circumstances even Lewis Snyder had to count it a date with a girl alone; the evidence whelmed, overwhelmed. I obeyed the protocol. We had a coke and then an ice cream stick. That Snyder must have been eating his heart out, at least aggravated. All right then—I soliloquied with Tom Moss *qua* Conscience & Scorekeeper—half-credit then for a daytime date.

"Did you get a free one?" I asked.

She read her ice cream stick. "No," she said.

"Neither did I. Don't believe in luck anyway"—and I expounded my philosophy of will power concentrate your way to fame and/or fortune. I tried to recite *Ulalume* but forgot it.

My mother's arches were hurting in her Enna Jetticks, but she avoided my father so that he would not order her home. Andy was making off to the vegetable cooler with a bagful of macaroons. Basketwood splintered under orders; customers fidgeted untended; my father wiped his forehead with a paper towel from the pine forests of Maine, leaving crumbs of lint, and mourned me.

"I never knew you were so smart," said Pattie Donahue.

We had fallen silent, sitting on the front steps of her house in the shadow of a bush where her mother could not see us. Up the street someone was hosing his car, an incontinent sound, in preparation for a Fourth of July trip. The afternoon was over. Pattie Donahue, an economical creature, an Indian giver, took back her gift in a way which expressed her genius. Business acumen. Operating costs and turnover. Appraising me with her turtle-round eyes, shrewd to calculate the value of an investment, she first created a bear market by sighing Ohh, rustling her dress, and accidentally touching my arm with her transparent turquoise-veined hands. Cologned and dusted with powder, she breathed on me.

"Yes!" I spilled out, naked in summer smells. "Do you like me, Pattie? I like you."

"Sure I like you"—disappointment and a pout that it had been so easy. Even economy becomes sport with such a housekeeper. "Sure I like you but you're too fat."

"Fat?" I repeated stupidly.

Her laughter tinkled in the July calm by the watered bush. "Fat I mean skinny. I mean you're just a *grocery* boy, you. You just grub around a certain store I could name all the Saturdays *I* ever heard about, except I suppose today—"

She was a sly old creature, that Pattie Donahue. The lips: *grocery boy*. The frozen iris: the same. Her laughter caroled forth, free, enterprising, resolute, the investment paying off in a Saturday afternoon dividend of power. Not all men are men, her laughter told her. This is a profit forever, my face told her.

"Oh but—oh but—oh but—" I said.

She put her little hand to her mouth and delicately closed it. Tee-hee. She looked at me, unblinking. My father, knowing he was a foreigner, could have accepted this in the perspective of history. I had to discover a fact without a past; it leapt out at me like some fierce fish from the glittering shale of Pattie Donahue's economical eyes.

I stood up. "Thank you for the sandwich and the cookie," I said. (The cookie with a preserved cherry on it.)

"Oh me no," she said.

"I was hungry."

"Oh you're welcome really," she said. "Thank you for the coke. Thank you for the ice cream."

"Goodbye, Pattie."

"It was nice, Daniel Berman," she said, "truly very nice."

4

I prowled, growing up fast that afternoon. I climbed a fat hump of a mailbox for packages and, my hands hanging in front, or my elbows on my knees and my fists in my cheeks, I watched the traffic on Parkside Boulevard. I did not choose the sentimental places, the tree by the lake, the woods where the river on which we skated in winter spread out like a sheet. I began to understand how the lost Lenore really got mislaid, without a dark conversational bird, without a tomb, without even a long metrical sigh. A heavy July sky lowered and thick-ened above me. I perched on the box like an animal in a dream.

But I was no animal in no dream. I was wide-awake, me, itchy, straddling a mailbox. Once someone mailed a book between my legs. I did not stop to wonder whether it were some quaint and curious volume, this being already forgotten lore. I studied the houses squatting like fat-necked bullfrogs along the boulevard, puzzled over the nay-saying mouths and step of the emerging strollers, celebrated and grieved for the crystallizing structure of my judgment (my *complexes*), no longer contained by sad and pretty words—grieved but did not cry.

Long after dark I finally went home. My parents were in the kitchen, talking in low voices, the relieved hawing of Sat-urday nights absent today. Entering at the street, I went di-rectly to my room and lay down on the bed. I made none of the dramatic flourishes of locking the door or pushing the footstool in front of it.

"Daniel!"

Doltish, I wondered if this were what it felt like to be an adult. It was true that for weeks I had been awakening mornings with my bite clamped, my jaw aching, and my tongue plunged against my teeth. Was that the seeding for Pattie Donahue's educational crop? her economy predicted by my extravagance in sleep?

"Daniel!"—Mother's voice. I went. Mother stood by the kitchen table. Dad sat without looking at me, his head low-ered, his hands about a bowl of soup. "You should come when I called you," she said.

"I did come."

"When I called you I said. Not whenever you please." She

looked at my father and waited for him to speak. He did not. We all waited for him, the challenged one, amid the summer smell of flypaper in the kitchen and the buzzing of the wily flies.

Resentfully I broke the stillness: "I went on a naturewalk."

"What?—what?"

"I learned what's a toadstool and the names of birds. A naturewalk. Mr. Wilkerson general science from junior high, he—"

"And what about Mr. and Mrs. Slave-their-head-off, I suppose your parents by the store?" my mother asked. The sarcasm gave me hope; it was, after all, only dialectic again. How soon hope returns! We dwell in it even after the exile to which Pattie Donahue's laughter and nibbling teeth send us.

Turning to my father, whose head bent over the table in a way I only remembered afterward—his brother had died and Mother said he was crying because he was sad and I didn't believe her because daddies don't cry—I appealed to him with a manly challenge: "Almost everyone I know went on the naturewalk."

He did not yet look up.

"It's educational. Mr. Wilkerson says. Tom Moss was there. Almost everyone in our grade Seven-B Seven-A was there—"

"Lookit my waricose from standing up all day working like a horse eating my heart out," Mother said. "You should take a load off my feet, not I should carry you like a baby you're going on fourteen."

"Thirteen," I said.

"Going on anyway," she insisted, "*going* on. That's what it means. Big lummox. Look at my waricose go on look lookit."

She could not know—my cruelty at twelve years, soon thirteen!—that my only concern was for surgery on the distended veins, as other women had, instead of wearing the lumpy corset that bulged about her calves under webbed brown stockings. My garment, she called it. Like taxes, Jake says. Teeth too, O! Sarah had the same trouble after Bernie and she took calcium. You ask me I think better injections in the arm, injections.

Dad listened watchfully over the soup in the evening heat. He hunched and studied vegetables in the bowl.

See how I admit the two of them to paper. Put my refusal of their world, which was their deepest gift to me, beside a son's longed-for and imagined love for his parents. Let me call myself a liar, but don't you be quick to do it. "Want to playboy around all your life dreaming smoke in the head?" my father used to ask me, and yet he loved me despite the law that we cannot love someone who refuses our gifts. I did not see the power and light of his world, in which the four causes were felt in action with my mother, vegetables, and the Saturday specials; I had looked for light and power in Pattie and Poe while all the Aristotelian potencies and more lay waiting for me with the combustible garbage swept into the backyard at closing time each evening. The backroom, emptied and cleaned, was filled and emptied of carrot tops, beet greens, and the furry blue glow of spoiled oranges. I stalled; my father waited. I looked; my father watched.

A week earlier I had overheard Mother murmuring into the telephone. "So how's your Bernie? My Daniel shouldn't be better, he got a all-A report card and with a B plus in gymnistics, he gained two pounds by the scale but he's full of complexes, still a heart-ache in the store. . . . Yah. . . . I read in the paper it's complexes, Jake says he'll grow out. . . ."

But only the complexes kept growing out. It's because I really like my parents that it costs me so much to speak kindly of them. I remember how my father offered me his entire world and I threw it in his face like a rotten orange because he left out one little lump of an Atlantis, my *own* world.

"Listen to your father he's talking," my mother said. He had not yet spoken, but she knew him well and knew he now would. "You take his fifteen cents for a movie, don't you? Listen to your father."

Still sitting in his washed-out shirt crusted with salt under the armpits, in his old blue serge work pants, once dress-up with the sharpy stripe down the legs, more generous than fathers have a right to be, he tried to help me expiate my sin in a ritual of reprimand. No ceremony could heal him this time, but he waited. This time before the beginning: "At your age I was a man," he said.

He was right.

He swayed over the soup, food breathing back into his body the prayers he had forgotten in leaving his own father. His swaying shoulders heavily sloped and remembered. His father had forbidden him to go to godless America, better to die than to be unfaithful. This too he had forgotten, his father struck down by a Cossack's rifle, but the chant in his voice and the dance of his shoulders remembered.

"Look at you"—he could not. "Are you a man?"

No. Right again.

"A playboy. A nature-walker. A eater of ice cream."

All true. I still like ice cream, especially with Hershey's chocolate syrup. He taught me quality in food, my father. I waited for him to force me to make myself what we both agreed I should be; no ceremony could compel it though only ceremony could confirm it. Still I had to choose. Untheological, without brand names, we improvised ritual.

"A lollypop!" my mother shrilled, thinking she was on her husband's side. Here she was wrong. I was not a lollypop.

"Let me tell it, Rose," my father said softly, as if this were an incident on their trip to South Haven. "It's my turn to tell it, Rose."

"I don't care"—me turning in my pointed shoes perforated for ventilation and sweet beauty's sake under the eyes of Pattie. I mourned her now, blaming my birth. "I don't care about you." I lowered my gaze to my father's stubby foreign feet in steel-backed boots. "None of the kids have to do it. I don't care about you and your store."

He needed an instant for this. I gave it to him overflowing. "And—your—store."

His hand floated up like a speck fuming on the eyes; his fist crashed down on the enamelled table like the plunging claw of a crate-hammer. "Oh! Oh!"—Mother. Soup splashed out on his pants and ran weeping with little red carrot eyes.

His gaze was prophetic in mine. "*Some kits help out in the store,*" he said.

"We were practically supposed to go," I said, neither retreating nor regretting, gaining time and learning patience. "Mr. Wilkerson is a teacher."

"*Some kits remember their father and mother.*"

Everyone knows where it hurts when you begin to cry—that place at the back of the throat. Pins jabbed under my eyelids. My palate ached. The tears hurt most in that instant before they break out. . . . And then I imagined cologned Pattie's cool laughter at my father's pronunciation of the *d* in *kits* ("—remember their father and mother"), and then drunk with the idea of the murder of someone I loved, my belly awash at the thought, I screamed him to his feet:

"I won't, I *won't* work in your store. I don't want it. It's not my life. I hate it. I hate it!"

He stood huge over me, smelling of leafy vegetables and

sweat, smelling of his strength and his terror because he would have to beat me. This is the reek of power, what the men at the Food Terminal understood when Ollie the Agent tried to shake down him first of the West Side men. . . . The opponents were uneven. He had wise muscles, protected by years of work and good eating, the skills of use, the satisfactions of his time of life. He had three sons, only one of those baby brothers of mine lying awake to listen. His swaying body knew it loved me as his father had loved him, the woman carrying her child on a belly or breast, the man taking his son only at the eye or the fist. There must have been a great satisfaction in his fear and love at that moment.

My sole weapon was exactly my dissatisfaction. My father's arms swam with veins among the curled oily hairs on his light bluish freckled flesh. No bow-straight shoulders like Atlas the World's Most Perfect Develop It! No Culver Academy athlete calling for Pattie Donahue in his uniform at Christmastime! It was a body which had worked well and been used with pleasure, a happy body, soup on the pants, making its own purpose and content with this.

Mine, as I have said: discontented. I looked for a use for it. I said:

"And you and your grocery boys and everyone! *I hate you!*"

Mother was crying and stacking the dishes in the sink when his open hand—generous! open!—struck my shoulder. I flew back and then up at him, slipping past his collar rough as a dog's tongue. Mother screamed. I climbed him, flailing; he was planted on the floor and he rocked under my weight for a moment, both of us silently straining toward each other and apart, our sweat pouring together while Mother screamed on and on—the malignant smell of hate and fear becoming the myrrh of two men fighting, the sweet cunning of love and death. I clung to his great neck to strangle it. His beard scratched my arms. He hugged my ribs, forcing them up—cracking!—pushing my hair out, lengthening my bones, driving my voice deep. Savagely he told me his life, wringing my childhood from me. I took this after his long day and had nothing to give in return but my unfleshed arms roped about his neck. We embraced like this.

The broken blood fled for a window into my mouth. I felt myself fainting.

Abruptly I lunged down, perhaps permitted to beg free.

His weighty old-country strength: my agile sporting slyness: as he glanced for pity at my mother I threw myself like a pole against his knees in a playground stunt performed without thinking. The trick uprooted his legs; he crashed; his forehead above the unsurprised Tartar eyes hit my mother's foot when he fell.

He sat up and started to his feet as she held him. I could not breathe, my chest frozen. I turned from his sprawling. I let him hear me choke and then ran to my room. Yes, I had wanted to win, but now, fatalistic, in an instant guessing ahead, I made the highest demand on a father: that he know he had beaten me too, only because he had let it happen.

"What's happening to us all?"—those first tears of old age. "What's happening to us?" Dad was crying in the bathroom with the door shut and the water running in the sink so that no one would hear an old man with an ingrate son. He had locked Mother out, who was dry-eyed now, figuring.

If I am bereaved of my sons, the first Jacob said, *then am I bereaved.* To fight back was all I needed; he had given too much. Economy in Pattie! my father a spendthrift!—such knowledge comes late to me now.

The Old System

Saul Bellow

It was a thoughtful day for Dr. Braun. Winter. Saturday.
The short end of December. He was alone in his apartment
and woke late, lying in bed until noon, in the room kept very
dark, working with a thought—a feeling: Now you see it, now
you don't. Now a content, now a vacancy. Now an important
individual, a force, a necessary existence; suddenly nothing.
A frame without a picture, a mirror with missing glass. The
feeling of necessary existence might be the aggressive, in-
stinctive vitality we share with a dog or an ape. The difference
being in the power of the mind or spirit to declare *I am*. Plus
the inevitable inference *I am not*. Dr. Braun was no more
pleased with being than with its opposite. For him an age of
equilibrium seemed to be coming in. How nice! Anyway, he
had no project for putting the world in rational order, and
for no special reason he got up. Washed his wrinkled but not
elderly face with freezing tap water, which changed the night-
time white to a more agreeable color. He brushed his teeth.
Standing upright, scrubbing the teeth as if he were looking
after an idol. He then ran the big old-fashioned tub to sponge
himself, backing into the thick stream of the Roman faucet,
soaping beneath with the same cake of soap he would apply
later to his beard. Under the swell of his belly, the tip of his
parts, somewhere between his heels. His heels needed scrubbing. He dried himself with yesterday's shirt, an economy.
It was going to the laundry anyway. Yes, with the self-respect-
ing expression human beings inherit from ancestors for whom
bathing was a solemnity. A sadness.

But every civilized man today cultivated an unhealthy self-
detachment. Had learned from art the art of amusing self-
observation and objectivity. Which, since there had to be
something amusing to watch, required art in one's conduct.
Existence for the sake of such practices did not seem worth
while. Mankind was in a confusing, uncomfortable, disagree-

able stage in the evolution of its consciousness. Dr. Braun
(Samuel) did not like it. It made him sad to feel that the
thought, art, belief of great traditions should be so misem-
ployed. Elevation? Beauty? Torn into shreds, into ribbons for
girls' costumes, or trailed like the tail of a kite at Happenings.
Plato and the Buddha raided by looters. The tombs of
Pharaohs broken into by desert rabble. And so on, thought
Dr. Braun as he passed into his neat kitchen. He was well
pleased by the blue-and-white Dutch dishes, cups hanging,
saucers standing in slots.

He opened a fresh can of coffee, much enjoyed the fragrance from the punctured can. Only an instant, but not to
be missed. Next he sliced bread for the toaster, got out the
butter, chewed an orange; and he was admiring long icicles on
the huge red, circular roof tank of the laundry across the alley,
the clear sky, when he discovered that a sentiment was
approaching. It was said of him, occasionally, that he did not
love anyone. This was not true. He did not love anyone
steadily. But unsteadily he loved, he guessed, at an average
rate.

The sentiment, as he drank his coffee, was for two cousins
in upstate New York, the Mohawk Valley. They were dead.
Isaac Braun and his sister Tina. Tina was first to go. Two
years later, Isaac died. Braun now discovered that he and
Cousin Isaac had loved each other. For whatever use or
meaning this fact might have within the peculiar system of
light, movement, contact, and perishing in which he tried to
find stability. Toward Tina, Dr. Braun's feelings were less
clear. More passionate once, but at present more detached.

Isaac's wife, after he died, had told Braun, "He was proud
of you. He said, 'Sammy has been written up in *Time,* in all
the papers, for his research. But he never says a word about
his scientific reputation!' "

"I see. Well, computers do the work, actually."

"But you have to know what to put into these computers."

This was more or less the case. But Braun had not continued
the conversation. He did not care much for being *first* in his
field. People were boastful in America. Matthew Arnold, a
not entirely appetizing figure himself, had correctly observed
this in the U.S. Dr. Braun thought this native American
boastfulness had aggravated a certain weakness in Jewish immigrants. But a proportionate reaction of self-effacement was
not praiseworthy. Dr. Braun did not want to be interested in

this question at all. However, his cousin Isaac's opinions had some value for him.

In Schenectady there were two more Brauns of the same family, living. Did Dr. Braun, drinking his coffee this afternoon, love them, too? They did not elicit such feelings. Then did he love Isaac more because Isaac was dead? There one might have something.

But in childhood, Isaac had shown him great kindness. The others, not very much.

Now Braun remembered certain things. A sycamore tree beside the Mohawk River. Then the river couldn't have been so foul. Its color, anyhow, was green, and it was powerful and dark, an easy, level force—crimped, green, blackish, glassy. A huge tree like a complicated event, with much splitting and thick chalky extensions. It must have dominated an acre, brown and white. And well away from the leaves, on a dead branch, sat a gray-and-blue fish hawk. Isaac and his little cousin Braun passed in the wagon—the old coarse-tailed horse walking, the steady head, in blinders, working onward. Braun, seven years old, wore a gray shirt with large bone buttons and had a short summer haircut. Isaac was dressed in work clothes, for in those days the Brauns were in the secondhand business—furniture, carpets, stoves, beds. His senior by fifteen years, Isaac had a mature business face. Born to be a man, in the direct Old Testament sense, as that bird on the sycamore was born to fish in water. Isaac, when he had come to America, was still a child. Nevertheless his old-country Jewish dignity was very firm and strong. He had the outlook of ancient generations on the New World. Tents and kine and wives and maidservants and manservants. Isaac was handsome, Braun thought—dark face, black eyes, vigorous hair, and a long scar on the cheek. Because, he told his scientific cousin, his mother had given him milk from a tubercular cow in the old country. While his father was serving in the Russo-Japanese War. Far away. In the Yiddish metaphor, on the lid of hell. As though hell were a caldron, a covered pot. How those old-time Jews despised the goy wars, their vainglory and obstinate *Dummheit*. Conscription, mustering, marching, shooting, leaving the corpses everywhere. Buried, unburied. Army against army. Gog and Magog. The czar, that weak, whiskered arbitrary and woman-ridden man, decreed that Uncle Braun would be swept away to Sakhalin. So by irrational decree, as in *The Arabian Nights,* Uncle

Braun, with his greatcoat and short humiliated legs, little beard, and great eyes, left wife and child to eat maggoty pork. And when the War was lost Uncle Braun escaped through Manchuria. Came to Vancouver on a Swedish ship. Labored on the railroad. He did not look so strong, as Braun remembered him in Schenectady. His chest was deep and his arms long, but the legs like felt, too yielding, as if the escape from Sakhalin and trudging in Manchuria had been too much. However, in the Mohawk Valley, monarch of used stoves and fumigated mattresses—dear Uncle Braun! He had a small, pointed beard, like George V, like Nick of Russia. Like Lenin, for that matter. But large, patient eyes in his wizened face, filling all of the space reserved for eyes.

A vision of mankind Braun was having as he sat over his coffee Saturday afternoon. Beginning with those Jews of 1920.

Braun as a young child was protected by the especial affection of his cousin Isaac, who stroked his head and took him on the wagon, later the truck, into the countryside. When Braun's mother had gone into labor with him, it was Issac whom Aunt Rose sent running for the doctor. He found the doctor in the saloon. Faltering, drunken Jones, who practiced among Jewish immigrants before those immigrants had educated their own doctors. He had Isaac crank the Model T. And they drove. Arriving, Jones tied Mother Braun's hands to the bedposts, a custom of the times.

Having worked as a science student in laboratories and kennels, Dr. Braun had himself delivered cats and dogs. Man, he knew, entered life like these other creatures, in a transparent bag or caul. Lying in a bag filled with transparent fluid, a purplish water. A color to mystify the most rational philosopher. What is this creature that struggles for birth in its membrane and clear fluid? Any puppy in its sac, in the blind terror of its emergence, any mouse breaking into the external world from this shining, innocent-seeming blue-tinged transparency!

Dr. Braun was born in a small wooden house. They washed him and covered him with mosquito netting. He lay at the foot of his mother's bed. Tough Cousin Isaac dearly loved Braun's mother. He had great pity for her. In intervals of his dealing, of being a Jewish businessman, there fell these moving reflections of those who were dear to him.

Aunt Rose was Dr. Braun's godmother, held him at his circumcision. Bearded, nearsighted old Krieger, fingers stained with chicken slaughter, cut away the foreskin.

Aunt Rose, Braun felt, was the original dura mater—the primal hard mother. She was not a big woman. She had a large bust, wide hips, and old-fashioned thighs of those corrupted shapes that belong to history. Which hampered her walk. Together with poor feet, broken by the excessive female weight she carried. In old boots approaching the knee. Her face was red, her hair powerful, black. She had a straight sharp nose. To cut mercy like a cotton thread. In the light of her eyes Braun recognized the joy she took in her hardness. Hardness of reckoning, hardness of tactics, hardness of dealing and of speech. She was building a kingdom with the labor of Uncle Braun and the strength of her obedient sons. They had their shop, they had real estate. They had a hideous synagogue of such red brick as seemed to grow in upstate New York by the will of the demon spirit charged with the ugliness of America in that epoch, which saw to it that a particular comic ugliness should influence the soul of man. In Schenectady, in Troy, in Gloversville, Mechanicville, as far west as Buffalo. There was a sour paper mustiness in this synagogue. Uncle Braun not only had money, he also had some learning and he was respected. But it was a quarrelsome congregation. Every question was disputed. There was rivalry, there were rages; slaps were given, families stopped speaking. Pariahs, thought Braun, with the dignity of princes among themselves.

Silent, with silent eyes crossing and recrossing the red water tank bound by twisted cables, from which ragged ice hung down and white vapor rose, Dr. Braun extracted a moment four decades gone in which Cousin Isaac had said, with one of those archaic looks he had, that the Brauns were descended from the tribe of Naphtali.

"How do we know?"

"People—families—*know*."

Braun was reluctant, even at the age of ten, to believe such things. But Isaac, with the authority of a senior, almost an uncle, said, "You'd better not forget it."

As a rule, he was gay with young Braun. Laughing against the tension of the scar that forced his mouth to one side. His eyes black, soft, and flaming. Off his breath, a bitter fragrance that translated itself to Braun as masculine earnestness and gloom. All the sons in the family had the same sort of laugh. They sat on the open porch. Sundays, laughing, while Uncle Braun read aloud the Yiddish matrimonial advertisements. "Attractive widow, 35, dark-favored, owning her own dry-goods business in Hudson, excellent cook, Orthodox, well-bred, refined. Plays the piano. Two intelligent, well-behaved children, eight and six."

All but Tina, the obese sister, took part in this satirical Sunday pleasure. Behind the screen door, she stood in the kitchen. Below, the yard, where crude flowers grew—zinnias, plantain lilies, trumpet vine on the chicken shed.

Now the country cottage appeared to Braun, in the Adirondacks. A stream. So beautiful! Trees, full of great strength. Wild strawberries, but you must be careful about the poison ivy. In the drainage ditches, polliwogs. Braun slept in the attic with Cousin Mutt. Mutt danced in his undershirt in the morning, naked beneath, and sang an obscene song:

> "I stuck my nose up a nanny goat's ass
> And the smell was enough to blind me."

He was leaping on bare feet, and his thing bounded from thigh to thigh. Going into saloons to collect empty bottles, he had learned this. A ditty from the stokehold. Origin, Liverpool or Tyneside. Art of the laboring class in the machine age.

An old mill. A pasture with clover flowers. Braun, seven years old, tried to make a clover wreath, pinching out a hole in the stems for other stems to pass through. He meant the wreath for fat Tina. To put it on her thick savory head, her smoky black harsh hair. Then in the pasture, little Braun overturned a rotten stump with his foot. Hornets pursued and bit him. He screamed. He had painful crimson lumps all over his body. Aunt Rose put him to bed and Tina came huge into the attic to console him. An angry fat face, black eyes, and the dilated nose breathing at him. Little Braun, stung and burning. She lifted her dress and petticoat to cool him with her body. The belly and thighs swelled before him. Braun felt too small and frail for this ecstasy. By the bedside was a chair, and she sat. Under the dizzy heat of the shingled roof, she rested her legs upon him, spread them wider, wider. He saw the barbarous and coaly hair. He saw the red within. She parted the folds with her fingers. Parting, her dark nostrils opened, the eyes looked white in her head. She motioned that he should press his child's genital against her fat-flattened thighs. Which, with agonies of incapacity and pleasure, he did. All was silent. Summer silence. Her sexual odor. The flies and gnats stimulated by delicious heat or the fragrance. He heard a mass of flies tear themselves from the windowpane. A sound of detached adhesive. Tina did not kiss, did not embrace. Her face was menacing. She was defying. She was drawing him—taking him somewhere with her. But she promised nothing, told him nothing.

When he recovered from his bites, playing once more in the yard, Braun saw Issac with his fiancée, Clara Sternberg, walking among the trees, embracing very sweetly. Braun tried to go with them, but Cousin Isaac sent him away. When he still followed, Cousin Isaac turned him roughly toward the cottage. Little Braun then tried to kill his cousin. He wanted with all his heart to club Isaac with a piece of wood. He was still stuck by the incomparable happiness, the luxury of that pure murderousness. Rushing toward Isaac, who took him by the back of the neck, twisted his head, held him under the pump. He then decreed that little Braun must go home, to Albany. He was far too wild. Must be taught a lesson. Cousin Tina said in private, "Good for *you*, Sam. I hate him, too." She took Braun with her dimpled, inept hand and walked down the road with him in the Adirondack dust. Her gingham-fitted bulk. Her shoulders curved, banked, like the earth of the hill-cut road. And her feet turned outward by the terrifying weight and deformity of her legs.

Later she dieted. Became for a while thinner, more civilized. Everyone was more civilized. Little Braun became a docile, bookish child. Did very well at school.

All clear? Quite clear to the adult Braun, considering his fate no more than the fate of others. Before his tranquil look, the facts arranged themselves—rose, took a new arrangement. Remained awhile in the settled state and then changed again. We were getting somewhere.

Uncle Braun died angry with Aunt Rose. He turned his face to the wall with his last breath to rebuke her hardness. All the men, his sons, burst out weeping. The tears of the women were different. Later, too, their passion took other forms. They bargained for more property. And Aunt Rose defied Uncle Braun's will. She collected rents in the slums of Albany and Schenectady from properties he had left to his sons. She dressed herself in the old fashion, calling on nigger tenants or the Jewish rabble of tailors and cobblers. To her the old Jewish words for these trades—*Schneider, Schuster*—were terms of contempt. Rents belonging mainly to Isaac she banked in her own name. Riding ancient streetcars in the factory slums. She did not need to buy widow's clothes. She had always worn suits, they had always been black. Her hat was three-cornered, like the town crier's. She let the black braid hang behind, as though she were in her own kitchen. She had trouble with bladder and arteries, but ailments did not keep her at home and she had no use for doctoring and drugs. She blamed Uncle Braun's death on Bromo-Seltzer, which, she said, had enlarged his heart.

Isaac did not marry Clara Sternberg. Though he was a manufacturer, her father turned out on inquiry to have started as a cutter and have married a housemaid. Aunt Rose would not tolerate such a connection. She took long trips to make genealogical investigations. And she vetoed all the young women, her judgments severe without limit. "A false dog." "Candied poison." "An open ditch. A sewer. A born whore!"

The woman Isaac eventually married was pleasant, mild, round, respectable, the daughter of a Jewish farmer.

Aunt Rose said, "Ignorant. A common man."

"He's honest, a hard worker on the land," said Isaac. "He recites the Psalms even when he's driving. He keeps them under his wagon seat."

"I don't believe it. A son of Ham like that. A cattle dealer. He stinks of manure." And she said to the bride in Yiddish, "Be so good as to wash thy father before bringing him to the synagogue. Get a bucket and scalding water, and 20 Mule Team Borax and ammonia, and a horse brush. The filth is ingrained. Be sure to scrub his hands."

The rigid madness of the Orthodox. Their haughty, spinning, crazy spirit.

Tina did not bring her young man from New York to be examined by Aunt Rose. Anyway, he was neither young, nor handsome, nor rich. Aunt Rose said he was a minor hoodlum, a slugger. She had gone to Coney Island to inspect his family —a father who sold pretzels and chestnuts from a cart, a mother who cooked for banquets. And the groom himself— so thick, so bald, so grim, she said, his hands so common and his back and chest like fur, a fell. He was a beast, she told young Sammy Braun. Braun was a student then at Rensselaer Polytechnic and came to see his aunt in her old kitchen—the great black-and-nickel stove, the round table on its oak pedestal, the dark-blue-and-white check of the oilcloth, a still life of peaches and cherries salvaged from the secondhand shop. And Aunt Rose, more feminine with her corset off and a gaudy wrapper over her thick Victorian undervests, camisoles, bloomers. Her silk stockings were gartered below the knee and the wide upper portions, fashioned for thighs, drooped down flimsy, nearly to her slippers.

Tina was then handsome, if not pretty. In high school she took off eighty pounds. Then she went to New York City without getting her diploma. What did *she* care for such things! said Rose. And how did she get to Coney Island by herself? Because she was perverse. Her instinct was for freaks. And there she met this beast. This hired killer, this second Lepke of Murder, Inc. Upstate, the old woman read the melodramas of the Yiddish press, which she embroidered with her own ideas of wickedness.

But when Tina brought her husband to Schenectady, installing him in her father's secondhand shop, he turned out to be a big innocent man. If he had ever had guile, he lost it with his hair. His baldness was total, like a purge. He had a sentimental, dependent look. Tina protected him. Here Dr. Braun had sexual thoughts, about himself as a child and about her childish bridegroom. And scowling, smoldering Tina, her angry tenderness in the Adirondacks, and how she was beneath, how hard she breathed in the attic, and the violent strength and obstinacy of her crinkled, sooty hair.

Nobody could sway Tina. That, thought Braun, was probably the secret of it. She had consulted her own will, kept her own counsel for so long, that she could accept no outer guidance. Anyone who listened to others seemed to her weak.

When Aunt Rose lay dead, Tina took from her hand the ring Isaac had given her many years ago. Braun did not remember the entire history of that ring, only that Isaac had loaned money to an immigrant who disappeared, leaving this jewel, which was assumed to be worthless but turned out to be valuable. Braun could not recall whether it was ruby or emerald; nor the setting. But it was the one feminine adornment Aunt Rose wore. And it was supposed to go to Isaac's wife, Sylvia, who wanted it badly. Tina took it from the corpse and put it on her own finger.

"Tina, give that ring to me. Give it here," said Isaac.

"No. It was hers. Now it's mine."

"It was not Mama's. You know that. Give it back."

She outfaced him over the body of Aunt Rose. She knew he would not quarrel at the deathbed. Sylvia was enraged. She did what she could. That is, she whispered, "Make her!" But it was no use. He knew he could not recover it. Besides, there

were too many other property disputes. His rents in Aunt
Rose's savings bank.

But only Isaac became a millionaire. The others simply
hoarded, old immigrant style. He never sat waiting for his
legacy. By the time Aunt Rose died, Isaac was already worth a
great deal of money. He had put up an ugly apartment
building in Albany. To him, an achievement. He was out with
his men at dawn. Having prayed aloud while his wife, in
curlers, pretty but puffy with sleepiness, sleepy but obedient,
was in the kitchen fixing breakfast. Isaac's Orthodoxy only
increased with his wealth. He soon became an old-fashioned
Jewish paterfamilias. With his family he spoke a Yiddish
unusually thick in old Slavic and Hebrew expressions. Instead
of "important people, leading citizens," he said *"Anshe ha-ir,"*
Men of the City. He, too, kept the Psalms near. As active,
worldly Jews for centuries had done. One copy lay in the glove
compartment of his Cadillac. To which his great gloomy sister
referred with a twist of the face—she had become obese again,
wider and taller, since those Adirondack days. She said, "He
reads the Tehillim aloud in his air-conditioned Caddy when
there's a long freight train at the crossing. That crook! He'd
pick God's pocket!"

One could not help thinking what fertility of metaphor there
was in all of these Brauns. Dr. Braun himself was no exception. And what the exception might be, despite twenty-five
years of specialization in the chemistry of heredity, he couldn't
say. How a protein molecule might carry such propensities of
ingenuity, and creative malice and negative power. Originating
in an invisible ferment. Capable of printing a talent or a vice
upon a billion hearts. No wonder Isaac Braun cried out to his
God when he sat seated in his great black car and the freights
rumbled in the polluted shimmering of this once-beautiful
valley.

> Answer me when I call, O God of my
> righteousness.

"But what do you think?" said Tina. "Does he remember
his brothers when there is a deal going? Does his give his only
a sister a chance to come in?"

Not that there was any great need. Cousin Mutt, after he
was wounded at Iwo Jima, returned to the appliance business.
Cousin Aaron was a C.P.A. Tina's husband, bald Fenster,

branched into housewares in his secondhand shop. Tina was back of that, of course. No one was poor. What irritated Tina was that Isaac would not carry the family into real estate, where the tax advantages were greatest. The big depreciation allowances, which she understood as legally sanctioned graft. She had her money in savings accounts at a disgraceful two and a half percent, taxed at the full rate. She did not trust the stock market.

Isaac had tried, in fact, to include the Brauns when he built the shopping center at Robbstown. At a risky moment, they abandoned him. A desperate moment, when the law had to be broken. At a family meeting, each of the Brauns had agreed to put up $25,000, the entire amount to be given under the table to Ilkington. Old Ilkington headed the board of directors of the Robbstown Country Club. Surrounded by factories, the club was moving farther into the country. Isaac had learned this from the old caddie master when he gave him a lift, one morning of fog. Mutt Braun had caddied at Robbstown in the early twenties, had carried Ilkington's clubs. Isaac knew Ilkington, too, and had a private talk with him. The old goy, now seventy, retiring to the British West Indies, had said to Isaac, "Off the record. One hundred thousand. And I don't want to bother about Internal Revenue." He was a long, austere man with a marbled face. Cornell 1910 or so. Cold but plain. And, in Isaac's opinion, fair. Developed as a shopping center, properly planned, the Robbstown golf course was worth half a million apiece to the Brauns. The city in the postwar boom was spreading fast. Isaac had a friend on the zoning board who would clear everything for five grand. As for the contracting, he offered to do it all on his own. Tina insisted that a separate corporation be formed by the Brauns to make sure the building profits were shared equally. To this Isaac agreed. As head of the family, he took the burden upon himself. He would have to organize it all. Only Aaron the C.P.A. could help him, setting up the books. The meeting, in Aaron's office, lasted from noon to three P.M. All the difficult problems were examined. Four players, specialists in the harsh music of money, studying a score. In the end, they agreed to perform.

But when the time came, ten A.M. on a Friday, Aaron balked. He would not do it. And Tina and Mutt also reneged. Isaac told Dr. Braun the story. As arranged, he came to Aaron's office carrying the $25,000 for Ilkington in an old briefcase. Aaron, now forty, smooth, shrewd, and dark, had the habit of writing tiny neat numbers on his memo pad as he spoke to you. Dark fingers quickly consulting the latest tax publications. He dropped his voice very low to the secretary on the intercom. He wore white-on-white shirts and silk-brocade ties, signed "Countess Mara." Of them all, he looked most like Uncle Braun. But without the beard, without the kingly pariah derby, without the gold thread in his brown eye. In many externals, thought scientific Braun, Aaron and Uncle Braun were drawn from the same genetic pool. Chemically, he was the younger brother of his father. The differences within were due possibly to heredity. Or perhaps to the influence of business America.

"Well?" said Isaac, standing in the carpeted office. The grandiose desk was superbly clean.

"How do you know Ilkington can be trusted?"

"I think he can."

"*You* think. He could take the money and say he never heard of you in all his life."

"Yes, he might. But we talked that over. We have to gamble."

Probably on his instructions, Aaron's secretary buzzed him. He bent over the instrument and out of the corner of his mouth he spoke to her very deliberately and low.

"Well, Aaron," said Isaac. "You want me to guarantee your investment? Well? Speak up."

Aaron had long ago subdued his thin tones and spoke in the gruff style of a man always sure of himself. But the sharp breaks, mastered twenty-five years ago, were still there. He stood up with both fists on the glass of his desk, trying to control his voice.

He said through clenched teeth, "I haven't slept!"

"Where is the money?"

"I don't have that kind of cash."

"No?"

"You know damn well. I'm a certified accountant. I'm in no position . . ."

"And what about Tina—Mutt?"

"I don't know anything about them."

"Talked them out of it, didn't you? I have to meet Ilkington at noon. Sharp. Why didn't you tell me sooner?"

Aaron said nothing.

Isaac dialed Tina's number and let the phone ring. Certain

that she was there, gigantically listening to the steely, beady drilling of the telephone. He let it ring, he said, about five minutes. He made no effort to call Mutt. Mutt would do as Tina did.

"I have an hour to raise this dough."

"In my bracket," Aaron said, "the twenty-five would cost me more than fifty."

"You could have told me this yesterday. Knowing what it means to me."

"You'll turn over a hundred thousand to a man you don't know? Without a receipt? Blind? Don't do it."

But Isaac had decided. In our generation, Dr. Braun thought, a sort of playboy capitalist has emerged. He gaily takes a flier in rebuilt office machinery for Brazil, motels in East Africa, high-fidelity components in Thailand. A hundred thousand means little. He jets down with a chick to see the scene. The governor of a province is waiting in his Thunderbird to take the guests on jungle expressways built by graft and peons to a surf-and-champagne weekend where the executive, youthful at fifty, closes the deal. But Cousin Isaac had put his stake together penny by penny, old style, starting with rags and bottles as a boy; then fire-salvaged goods; then used cars; then learning the building trades. Earth moving, foundations, concrete, sewage, wiring, roofing, heating systems. He got his money the hard way. And now he went to the bank and borrowed $75,000, at full interest. Without security, he gave it to Ilkington in Ilkington's parlor. Furnished in old goy taste and disseminating an old goy odor of tiresome, silly, respectable things. Of which Ilkington was clearly so proud. The applewood, the cherry, the wing tables and cabinets, the upholstery with a flavor of dry paste, the pork-pale colors of gentility. Ilkington did not touch Isaac's briefcase. He did not intend, evidently, to count the bills, nor even to look. He offered Isaac a martini. Isaac, not a drinker, drank the clear gin. At noon. Like something distilled in outer space. Having no color. He sat there sturdily, but felt lost—lost to his people, his family, lost to God, lost in the void of America. Ilkington drank a shaker of cocktails, gentlemanly, stony, like a high slab of something generically human, but with few human traits familiar to Isaac. At the door he did not say he would keep his word. He simply shook hands with Isaac, saw him to the car. Isaac drove home and sat in the den of his bungalow. Two whole days.

Then on Monday, Ilkington phoned to say that the Robbstown directors had decided to accept his offer for the property. A pause. Then Ilkington added that no written instrument could replace trust and decency betweén gentlemen.

Isaac took possession of the country club and filled it with a shopping center. All such places are ugly. Dr. Braun could not say why this one struck him as especially brutal in its ugliness. Perhaps because he remembered the Robbstown Club. Restricted, of course. But Jews could look at it from the road. And the elms had been lovely—a century or older. The light, delicate. And the Coolidge-era sedans turning in, with small curtains at the rear window, and holders for artificial flowers. Hudsons, Auburns, Bearcats. Only machinery. Nothing to feel nostalgic about.

Still, Braun was startled to see what Isaac had done. Perhaps in an unconscious assertion of triumph—in the vividness of victory. The green acres reserved, it was true, for mild idleness, for hitting a little ball with a stick, were now paralyzed by parking for five hundred cars. Supermarket, pizza joint, chop suey, laundromat, Robert Hall clothes, a dime store.

And this was only the beginning. Isaac became a millionaire. He filled the Mohawk Valley with housing developments. And he began to speak of "my people," meaning those who lived in the buildings he had raised. He was stingy with land, he built too densely, it was true, but he built with benevolence. At six in the morning, he was out with his crews. He lived very simply. Walked humbly with his God, as the rabbi said. A Madison Avenue rabbi, by this time. The little synagogue was wiped out. It was as dead as the Dutch painters who would have appreciated its dimness and its shaggy old peddlers. Now there was a *temple* like a World's Fair pavilion. Isaac was president, having beaten out the father of a famous hoodlum, once executioner for the Mob in the Northeast. The worldly rabbi with his trained voice and tailored suits, like a Christian minister except for the play of Jewish cleverness in his face, hinted to the old-fashioned part of the congregation that he had to pour it on for the sake of the young people. America. Extraordinary times. If you wanted the young women to bless Sabbath candles, you had to start their rabbi at $20,000, and add a house and a Jaguar.

Cousin Isaac, meantime, grew more old-fashioned. His car

was ten years old. But he was a strong sort of man. Self-assured, a dark head scarcely thinning at the top. Upstate women said he gave out the positive male energy they were beginning to miss in men. He had it. It was in the manner with which he picked up a fork at the table, the way he poured from a bottle. Of course, the world had done for him exactly what he had demanded. That meant he had made the right demand and in the right place. It meant his reading of life was metaphysically true. Or that the Old Testament, the Talmud, and Polish Ashkenazi Orthodoxy were irresistible.

But that wouldn't altogether do, thought Dr. Braun. There was more there than piety. He recalled his cousin's white teeth and scar-twisted smile when he was joking. "I fought on many fronts," Cousin Isaac said, meaning women's bellies. He often had a sound American way of putting things. Had known the back stairs in Schenectady that led to the sheets, the gripping arms and spreading thighs of workingwomen. The Model T was parked below. Earlier, the horse waited in harness. He got great pleasure from masculine reminiscences. Recalling Dvorah the greenhorn, on her knees, hiding her head in pillows while her buttocks soared, a burst of kinky hair from the walls of whiteness, and her feeble voice crying, "*Nein.*" But she did not mean it.

Cousin Mutt had no such anecdotes. Shot in the head at Iwo Jima, he came back from a year in the hospital to sell Zenith, Motorola, and Westinghouse appliances. He married a respectable girl and went on quietly amid a bewildering expansion and transformation of his birthplace. A computer center taking over the bush-league park where a scout had him spotted before the war as material for the majors. On most important matters, Mutt went to Tina. She told him what to do. And Isaac looked out for him, whenever possible buying appliances through Mutt for his housing developments. But Mutt took his problems to Tina. For instance, his wife and her sister played the horses. Every chance they got, they drove to Saratoga, to the trotting races. Probably no great harm in this. The two sisters with gay lipstick and charming dresses. And laughing continually with their pretty jutting teeth. And putting down the top of the convertible.

Tina took a mild view of this. Why shouldn't they go to the track? Her fierceness was concentrated, all of it, on Braun the millionaire.

"That whoremaster!" she said.

"Oh, no. Not in years and years," said Mutt.

"Come, Mutt. I know whom he's been balling. I keep an eye on the Orthodox. Believe me, I do. And now the governor has put him on a commission. Which is it?"

"Pollution."

"Water pollution, that's right. Rockefeller's buddy."

"Well, you shouldn't, Tina. He's our brother."

"He feels for *you*."

"Yes, he does."

"A multimillionaire—lets you go on drudging in a little business? He's heartless. A heartless man."

"It's not true."

"What? He never had a tear in his eye unless the wind was blowing," said Tina.

Hyperbole was Tina's greatest weakness. They were all like that. The mother had bred it in them.

Otherwise, she was simply a gloomy, obese woman, sternly combed, the hair tugged back from her forehead, tight, so that the hairline was a fighting barrier. She had a totalitarian air. And not only toward others. Toward herself, also. Absorbed in the dictatorship of her huge person. In a white dress, and with the ring on her finger she had seized from her dead mother. By a *putsch* in the bedroom.

In her generation—Dr. Braun had given up his afternoon to the hopeless pleasure of thinking affectionately about his dead—in her generation, Tina was also old-fashioned for all her modern slang. People of her sort, and not only the women, cultivated charm. But Tina willed consistently to appeal for nothing, to have no charm. Absolutely none. She never tried to please. Her aim must have been majesty. Based on what? She had no great thoughts. She built on her own nature. On a primordial idea, hugely blown up. Somewhat as her flesh in its dress of white silk, as last seen by Cousin Braun some years ago, was blown up. Some sub-suboffice of the personality, behind a little door of the brain where the restless spirit never left its work, had ordered this tremendous female form, all of it, to become manifest, with dark hair on the forearms, conspicuous nostrils in the white face, and black eyes staring. The eyes had an affronted expression; sometimes a look of sulphur; a clever look—they had all the looks, even the look of kindness that came from Uncle Braun. The old man's sweetness. Those who try to interpret humankind through its eyes are in for much strangeness—perplexity.

The quarrel between Tina and Isaac lasted for years. She accused him of shaking off the family when the main chance came. He had refused to cut them in. He said that they had all deserted him at the zero hour. Eventually the brothers made it up. Not Tina. She wanted nothing to do with Isaac. In the first phase of enmity she saw to it that he should know exactly what she thought of him. Brothers, aunts, and old friends reported what she was saying about him. He was a crook. Mama had lent him money; he would not repay; that was why she had collected those rents. Also, Isaac had been a silent partner of Zaikas, the Greek, the racketeer from Troy. She said that Zaikas had covered for Isaac, who was implicated in the state-hospital scandal. Zaikas took the fall, but Isaac had to put $50,000 in Zaikas's box at the bank. The Stuyvesant Bank, that was. Tina said she even knew the box number. Isaac said little to these slanders, and after a time they stopped.

And it was when they stopped that Isaac actually began to feel the anger of his sister. He felt it as head of the family, the oldest living Braun. After he had not seen his sister for two or three years, he began to remind himself of Uncle Braun's affection for Tina. The only daughter. The youngest. Our baby sister. Thoughts of the old days touched his heart. Having gotten what he wanted, Tina said to Mutt, he could redo the past in sentimental colors. Isaac would remember that in 1920 Aunt Rose wanted fresh milk, and the Brauns kept a cow in the pasture by the river. What a beautiful place. And how delicious it was to crank the Model T and drive at dusk to milk the cow beside the green water. Driving, they sang songs. Tina, then ten years old, must have weighed two hundred pounds, but the shape of her mouth was very sweet, womanly—perhaps the pressure of the fat, hastening her maturity. Somehow she was more feminine in childhood than later. It was true that at nine or ten she sat on a kitten in the rocker, unaware, and smothered it. Aunt Rose found it dead when her daughter stood up. "You huge thing," she said to her daughter, "you animal." But even this Isaac recollected with amused sadness. And since he belonged to no societies, never played cards, never spent an evening drinking, never went to Florida, never went to Europe, never went to see the State of Israel, Isaac had plenty of time for reminiscences. Respectable elms about his house sighed with him for the past. The squirrels were orthodox. They dug and saved. Mrs. Isaac Braun wore no cosmetics. Except a touch of lipstick when going out in public. No mink coats. A comfortable Hudson seal, yes. With a large fur button on the belly. To keep her, as he liked her, warm. Fair, pale, round, with a steady innocent look, and hair worn short and symmetrical. Light brown, with kinks of gold. One gray eye, perhaps, expressed or came near. expressing slyness. It must have been purely involuntary. At least there was not the slightest sign of conscious criticism or opposition. Isaac was master. Cooking, baking, laundry, all housekeeping, had to meet his standard. If he didn't like the smell of the cleaning woman, she was sent away. It was an ample plain old-fashioned respectable domestic life on an East European model completely destroyed in 1939 by Hitler and Stalin. Those two saw to the eradication of the old conditions, made sure that certain modern concepts became social realities. Maybe the slightest troubling ambiguity in one of Cousin Sylvia's eyes was the effect of a suppressed historical comment. As a woman, Dr. Braun considered, she had more than a glimmering of this modern transformation. Her husband was a multimillionaire. Where was the life this might have bought? The houses, servants, clothes, and cars? On the farm she had operated machines. As his wife, she was obliged to forget how to drive. She was a docile, darling woman, and she was in the kitchen baking spongecake and chopping liver, as Isaac's mother had done. Or should have done. Without the flaming face, the stern meeting brows, the rigorous nose, and the club of powerful braid lying on her spine. Without Aunt Rose's curses.

In America, the abuses of the Old World were righted. It was appointed to be the land of historical redress. However, Dr. Braun reflected, new uproars filled the soul. Material details were of the greatest importance. But still the largest strokes were made by the spirit. Had to be! People who said this were right.

Cousin Isaac's thoughts: a web of computations, of frontages, elevations, drainage, mortgages, turn-around money. And since, in addition, he had been a strong, raunchy young man, and this had never entirely left him (it remained only as witty comment), his piety really did appear to be put on. Superadded. The Psalm-saying at building sites. *When I consider the heavens, the work of Thy fingers . . . what is Man that Thou art mindful of him?* But he evidently meant it all.

He took off whole afternoons before high holidays. While his fair-faced wife, flushed with baking, noted with the slightly Biblical air he expected of her that he was bathing, changing upstairs. He had visited the graves of his parents. Announcing, "I've been to the cemetery."

"Oh," she said with sympathy, the one beautiful eye full of candor. The other fluttering with a minute quantity of slyness.

The parents, stifled in the clay. Two crates, side by side. Grass of burning green sweeping over them, and Isaac repeating a prayer to the God of Mercy. And in Hebrew with a Baltic accent at which modern Israelis scoffed. September trees, yellow after an icy night or two, now that the sky was blue and warm, gave light instead of shadow. Isaac was concerned about his parents. Down there, how were they? The wet, the cold, above all the worms worried him. In frost, his heart shrank for Aunt Rose and Uncle Braun, though as a builder he knew they were beneath the frost line. But a human power, his love, affected his practical judgment. It flew off. Perhaps as a builder and housing expert (on two of the governor's commissions, not one) he especially felt his dead to be unsheltered. But Tina—they were her dead, too—felt he was still exploiting Papa and Mama and that he would have exploited her, too, if she had let him.

For several years, at the same season, there was a scene between them. The pious thing before the Day of Atonement was to visit the dead and to forgive the living—forgive and ask forgiveness. Accordingly, Isaac went annually to the old home. Parked his Cadillac. Rang the bell, his heart beating hard. He waited at the foot of the long, enclosed staircase. The small brick building, already old in 1915 when Uncle Braun had bought it, passed to Tina, who tried to make it modern. Her ideas came out of *House Beautiful*. The paper with which she covered the slanted walls of the staircase was unsuitable. It did not matter. Tina, above, opened the door, saw the masculine figure and scarred face of her brother and said, "What do you want?"

"Tina! For God's sake, I've come to make peace."

"What peace! You swindled us out of a fortune."

"The others don't agree. Now, Tina, we are brother and sister. Remember Father and Mother. Remember . . ."

She cried down at him, "You son of a bitch, I *do* remember! Now get the hell out of here."

Banging the door, she dialed her brother Aaron, lighting

one of her long cigarettes. "He's been here again," she said.
"What shit! He's not going to practice his goddamn religion
on me."

She said she hated his Orthodox cringe. She could take
him straight. In a deal. Or a swindle. But she couldn't bear
his sentiment.

As for herself, she might smell like a woman, but she
acted like a man. And in her dress, while swooning music
came from the radio, she smoked her cigarette after he was
gone, thundering inside with great flashes of feeling. For
which, otherwise, there was no occasion. She might curse
him, thought Dr. Braun, but she owed him much. Aunt
Rose, who had been such a harsh poet of money, had left
her daughter needs—such needs! Quiet middle-age domestic
decency (husband, daughter, furnishings) did nothing for
needs like hers.

So when Isaac Braun told his wife that he had visited
the family graves, she knew that he had gone again to see
Tina. The thing had been repeated. Isaac, with a voice and
gesture that belonged to history and had no place or parallel
in upstate industrial New York, appealed to his sister in the
eyes of God, and in the name of souls departed, to end her
anger. But she cried from the top of the stairs, "Never! You
son of a bitch, never!" and he went away.

He went home for consolation, and walked to the synagogue later with an injured heart. A leader of the congregation, weighted with grief. Striking breast with fist in old-
fashioned penitence. The new way was the way of understate-
ment. Anglo-Saxon restraint. The rabbi, with his Madison
Avenue public-relations airs, did not go for these European
Judaic, operatic fist-clenchings. Tears. He made the cantor
tone it down. But Isaac Braun, covered by his father's
prayer shawl with its black stripes and shedding fringes,
ground his teeth and wept near the ark.

These annual visits to Tina continued until she became
sick. When she went into the hospital, Isaac phoned Dr.
Braun and asked him to find out how things really stood.

"But I'm not a medical doctor."

"You're a scientist. You'll understand it better."

Anyone might have understood. She was dying of cancer
of the liver. Cobalt radiation was tried. Chemotherapy. Both
made her very sick. Dr. Braun told Isaac, "There is no hope."

"I know."

"Have you seen her?"

"No. I hear from Mutt."

Isaac sent word through Mutt that he wanted to come to her bedside.

Tina refused to see him.

And Mutt, with his dark sloping face, unhandsome but gentle, dog-eyed, softly urged her, "You should, Tina."

But Tina said, "No. Why should I? A Jewish deathbed scene, that's what he wants. No."

"Come, Tina."

"No," she said, even firmer. Then she added, "I hate him." As though explaining that Mutt should not expect her to give up the support of this feeling. And a little later she added, in a lower voice, as though speaking generally, "I can't help him."

But Isaac phoned Mutt daily, saying, "I have to see my sister."

"I can't get her to do it."

"You've got to explain it to her. She doesn't know what's right."

Isaac even telephoned Fenster, though, as everyone was aware, he had a low opinion of Fenster's intelligence. And Fenster answered, "She says you did us all dirt."

"I? She got scared and backed out. I had to go it alone."

"You shook us off."

Quite simple-mindedly, with the directness of the Biblical fool (this was how Isaac saw him, and Fenster knew it), he said, "You wanted it all for yourself, Isaac."

That they should let him, ungrudgingly, enjoy his great wealth, Isaac told Dr. Braun, was too much to expect. Of human beings. And he was very rich. He did not say how much money he had. This was a mystery in the family. The old people said, "He himself doesn't know."

Isaac confessed to Dr. Braun, "I never understood her." He was much moved, even then, a year later.

Cousin Tina had discovered that one need not be bound by the old rules. That, Isaac's painful longing to see his sister's face being denied, everything was put into a different sphere of advanced understanding, painful but truer than the old. From her bed she appeared to be directing this research.

"You ought to let him come," said Mutt.

"Because I'm dying?"

Mutt, plain and dark, stared at her, his black eyes momentarily vacant as he chose an answer. "People recover," he said.

But she said, with peculiar indifference to the fact, "Not this time." She had already become gaunt in the face and high in the belly. Her ankles were swelling. She had seen this in others and understood the signs.

"He calls every day," said Mutt.

She had had her nails done. A dark-red, almost maroon color. One of those odd twists of need or desire. The ring she had taken from her mother was now loose on the finger. And, reclining on the raised bed, as if she had found a moment of ease, she folded her arms and said, pressing the lace of the bed jacket with her finger tips, "Then give Isaac my message, Mutt. I'll see him, yes, but it'll cost him money."

"Money?"

"If he pays me twenty thousand dollars."

"Tina, that's not right."

"Why not! For my daughter. She'll need it."

"No, she doesn't need that kind of dough." He knew what Aunt Rose had left. "There's plenty and you know it."

"If he's got to come, that's the price of admission," she said. "Only a fraction of what he did us out of."

Mutt said simply, "He never did me out of anything." Curiously, the shrewdness of the Brauns was in his face, but he never practiced it. This was not because he had been wounded in the Pacific. He had always been like that. He sent Tina's message to Isaac on a piece of business stationery, BRAUN APPLIANCES, 42 CLINTON. Like a contract bid. No word of commitment, not even a signature.

For 20 grand cash Tina says yes otherwise no.

In Dr. Braun's opinion, his Cousin Tina had seized upon the force of death to create *a situation of opera*. Which at the same time was a situation of parody. As he stated it to himself, there was a feedback of mockery. Death the horrid bridegroom, waiting with a consummation life had never offered. Life, accordingly, she devalued, filling up the clear light remaining (which should be reserved for beauty, miracle, nobility) with obese monstrosity, rancor, failure, self-torture.

Isaac, on the day he received Tina's terms, was scheduled to go out on the river with the governor's commission on pollution. A boat was sent by the Fish and Game Department

to take the five members out on the Hudson. They would go
south as far as Germantown. Where the river, with mountains
on the west, seems a mile wide. And back again to Albany.
Isaac would have cancelled this inspection, he had so much
thinking to do, was so full of things. "Overthronged" was the
odd term Braun chose for it, which seemed to render Isaac's
state best. But Isaac could not get out of this official excursion.
His wife made him take his Panama hat and wear a light suit.
He bent over the side of the boat, hands clasped tight on the
dark-red, brass-joined rail. He breathed through his teeth. At
the back of his legs, in his neck, his pulses beating; and in the
head an arterial swell through which he was aware, one-
sidedly, of the air streaming, and gorgeous water. Two young
professors from Rensselaer lectured on the geology and
wildlife of the upper Hudson and on the industrial and
community problems of the region. The towns were dumping
raw sewage into the Mohawk and the Hudson. You could
watch the flow from giant pipes. Cloacae, said the professor
with his red beard and ruined teeth. Much dark metal in his
mouth, pewter ridges instead of bone. And a pipe with which
he pointed to the turds yellowing the river. The cities, spilling
their filth. How dispose of it? Methods were discussed—treatment plants. Atomic power. And finally he presented an
ingenious engineering project for sending all waste into the
interior of the earth, far under the crust, thousands of feet into
deeper strata. But even if pollution were stopped today, it
would take fifty years to restore the river. The fish had
persisted but at last abandoned their old spawning grounds.
Only a savage scavenger eel dominated the water. The river
great and blue in spite of the dung pools and the twisting of
the eels.

One member of the governor's commission had a face
remotely familiar, long and high, the mouth like a latch,
cheeks hollow, the bone warped in the nose, and hair fading.
Gentle. A thin person. His thoughts on Tina, Issac had missed
his name. But looking at the printed pages prepared by the
staff, he saw that it was Ilkington Junior. This quiet, likable
man examining him with such meaning from the white
bulkhead, long trousers curling in the breeze as he held the
metal rail behind him.

Evidently he knew about the $100,000.

"I think I was acquainted with your father," Isaac said, his
voice very low.

"You were, indeed," said Ilkington. He was frail for his height; his skin was pulled tight, glistening on the temples, and a reddish blood lichen spread on his cheekbones. Capillaries. "The old man is well."

"Well. I'm glad."

"Yes. He's well. Very feeble. He had a bad time, you know."

"I never heard."

"Oh, yes, he invested in hotel construction in Nassau and lost his money."

"All of it?" said Isaac.

"All his legitimate money."

"I'm very sorry."

"Lucky he had a little something to fall back on."

"He did?"

"He certainly did."

"Yes, I see. That *was* lucky."

"It'll last him."

Isaac was glad to know and appreciated the kindness of Ilkington's son in telling him. Also the man knew what the Robbstown Country Club had been worth to him, but did not grudge him, behaved with courtesy. For which Isaac, filled with thankfulness, would have liked to show gratitude. But what you showed, among these people, you showed with silence. Of which, it seemed to Isaac, he was now beginning to appreciate the wisdom. The native, different wisdom of gentiles, who had much to say but refrained. What was this Ilkington Junior? He looked into the pages again and found a paragraph of biography. Insurance executive. Various government commissions. Probably Isaac could have discussed Tina with such a man. Yes, in heaven. On earth they would never discuss a thing. Silent impressions would have to do. Incommunicable diversities, kindly but silent contact. The more they had in their heads, the less people seemed to know how to tell it.

"When you write to your father, remember me to him."

Communities along the river, said the professor, would not pay for any sort of sewage-treatment plants. The Federal Government would have to arrange it. Only fair, Isaac considered, since Internal Revenue took away to Washington billions in taxes and left small change for the locals. So they pumped the excrements into the waterways. Isaac, building along the Mohawk, had always taken this for granted. Build-

ing squalid settlements of which he was so proud. . . . Had
been proud.

He stepped onto the dock when the boat tied up. The State
Game Commissioner had taken an eel from the water to show
the inspection party. It was writhing toward the river in swift,
powerful loops, tearing its skin on the planks, its crest of fin
standing. *Treph!* And slimy black, the perishing mouth open.

The breeze had dropped and the wide water stank. Isaac
drove home, turning on the air conditioner of his Cadillac. His
wife said, "What was it like?"

He had no answer to give.

"What are you doing about Tina?"

Again, he said nothing.

But knowing Issac, seeing how agitated he was, she predicted that he would go down to New York City for advice.
She told this later to Dr. Braun, and he saw no reason to
doubt it. Clever wives can foretell. A fortunate husband will
be forgiven his predictability.

Isaac had a rabbi in Williamsburg. He was Orthodox
enough for that. And he did not fly. He took a compartment
on the Twentieth Century when it left Albany just before
daybreak. With just enough light through the dripping gray to
see the river. But not the west shore. A tanker covered by
smoke and cloud divided the bituminous water. Presently the
mountains emerged.

They wanted to take the old crack train out of service. The
carpets were filthy, the toilets stank. Slovenly waiters in the
dining car. Isaac took toast and coffee, rejecting the odors of
ham and bacon by expelling breath. Eating with his hat on.
Racially distinct, as Dr. Braun well knew. A blood group
characteristically eastern Mediterranean. The very finger-
prints belonging to a distinctive family of patterns. The nose,
the eyes long and full, the skin dark, slashed near the mouth
by a Russian doctor in the old days. And looking out as they
rushed past Rhinecliff, Isaac saw, with the familiarity of
hundreds of journeys, the grand water, the thick trees—illumi-
nated space. In the compartment, in captive leisure, shut up
with the foul upholstery, the rattling door. The old arsenal,
Bannerman's Island, the playful castle, yellow-green willows
around it, and the water sparkling, as green as he remembered
it in 1910—one of the forty million foreigners coming to
America. The steel rails, as they were then, the twisting

currents and the mountain round at the top, the wall of rock curving steeply into the expanding river.

From Grand Central, carrying a briefcase with all he needed in it, Isaac took the subway to his appointment. He waited in the anteroom, where the rabbi's bearded followers went in and out in long coats. Dressed in business clothes, Isaac, however, seemed no less archaic than the rest. A bare floor. Wooden seats, white stippled walls. But the windows were smeared, as though the outside did not matter. Of these people, many were survivors of the German holocaust. The rabbi himself had been through it as a boy. After the war, he had lived in Holland and Belgium and studied sciences in France. At Montpellier. Biochemistry. But he had been called—summoned—to these spiritual duties in New York; Isaac was not certain how this had happened. And now he wore the full beard. In his office, sitting at a little table with a green blotting pad, and a pen and note paper. The conversation was in the *jargón*—in Yiddish.

"Rabbi, my name is Issac Braun."

"From Albany. Yes, I remember."

"I am the eldest of four—my sister, the youngest, the *muzínka,* is dying."

"Are you sure of this?"

"Of cancer of the liver, and with a lot of pain."

"Then she is. Yes, she is dying." From the very white, full face, the rabbi's beard grew straight and thick in rich bristles. He was a strong, youthful man, his stout body buttoned tightly, straining in the shiny black cloth.

"A certain thing happened soon after the war. An opportunity to buy a valuable piece of land for building. I invited my brothers and my sister to invest with me, Rabbi. But on the day . . ."

The rabbi listened, his white face lifted toward a corner of the ceiling, but fully attentive, his hands pressed to the ribs, above the waist.

"I understand. You tried to reach them that day. And you felt abandoned."

"They deserted me, Rabbi, yes."

"But that was also your good luck. They turned their faces from you, and this made you rich. You didn't have to share."

Isaac admitted this but added, "If it hadn't been one deal, it would have been another."

"You were destined to be rich?"

"I was sure to be. And there were so many opportunities."

"Your sister, poor thing, is very harsh. She is wrong. She has no ground for complaint against you."

"I am glad to hear that," said Isaac. "Glad," however, was only a word, for he was suffering.

"She is not a poor woman, your sister?"

"No, she inherited property. And her husband does pretty well. Though I suppose the long sickness costs."

"Yes, a wasting disease. But the living can only will to live. I am speaking of Jews. They wanted to annihilate us. To give our consent would have been to turn from God. But about your problem: Have you thought of your brother Aaron? He advised the others not to take the risk."

"I know."

"It was to his interest that she should be angry with you, and not with them."

"I realize that."

"He is guilty. He is sinning against you. Your other brother is a good man."

"Mutt? Yes, I know. He is decent. He barely survived the war. He was shot in the head."

"But is he still himself?"

"Yes, I believe so."

"Sometimes it takes something like that. A bullet through the head." The rabbi paused and turned his round face, the black quill beard bent on the folds of shiny cloth. And then, as Isaac told him how he went to Tina before the high holidays, he looked impatient, moving his head forward, but his eyes turning sideward. "Yes. Yes." He was certain that Isaac had done the right things. "Yes. You have the money. She grudged you. Unreasonable. But that's how it seems to her. You are a man. She is only a woman. You are a rich man."

"But, Rabbi," said Isaac, "now she is on her deathbed, and I have asked to see her."

"Yes? Well?"

"She wants money for it."

"Ah? Does she? Money?"

"Twenty thousand dollars. So that I can be let into the room."

The burly rabbi was motionless, white fingers on the armrests of the wooden chair. "She knows she is dying, I suppose?" he said.

"Yes."

"Yes. Our Jews love deathbed jokes. I know many. Well. America has not changed everything, has it? People assume that God has a sense of humor. Such jokes made by the dying in anguish show a strong and brave soul, but skeptical. What sort of woman is your sister?"

"Stout. Large."

"I see. A fat woman. A chunk of flesh with two eyes, as they used to say. Staring at the lucky ones. Like an animal in a cage, perhaps. Separated. By sensual greed and despair. A fat child like that—people sometimes behave as though they were alone when such a child is present. So those little monster souls have a strange fate. They see people as people are when no one is looking. A gloomy vision of mankind."

Isaac respected the rabbi. Revered him, thought Dr. Braun. But perhaps he was not old-fashioned enough for him, notwithstanding the hat and beard and gabardine. He had the old tones, the manner, the burly poise, the universal calm judgment of the Jewish moral genius. Enough to satisfy anyone. But there was also something foreign about him. That is, contemporary. Now and then there was a sign of the science student, the biochemist from the south of France, from Montpellier. He would probably have spoken English with a French accent, whereas Cousin Isaac spoke like anyone else from upstate. In Yiddish they had the same dialect—White Russian. The Minsk region. The Pripet Marshes, thought Dr. Braun. And then returned to the fish hawk on the brown and chalky sycamore beside the Mohawk. Yes. Perhaps. Among these recent birds, finches, thrushes, there was Cousin Isaac with more scale than feather in his wings. A more antique type. The ruddy brown eye, the tough muscles of the jaw working under the skin. Even the scar was precious to Dr. Braun. He knew the man. Or rather, he had the longing of having known. For these people were dead. A useless love.

"You can afford the money?" the rabbi asked. And when Isaac hesitated, he said, "I don't ask you for the figure of your fortune. It is not my concern. But could you give her the twenty thousand?"

And Isaac, looking greatly tired, said, "If I had to."

"It wouldn't make a great difference in your fortune?"

"No."

"In that case, why shouldn't you pay?"

"You think I should?"

"It's not for me to tell you to give away so much money.

But you gave—you gambled—you trusted the man, the goy."

"Ilkington? That was a business risk. But Tina? So you believe I should pay?"

"Give in. I would say, judging the sister by the brother, there is no other way."

Then Isaac thanked him for his time and his opinion. He went out into the broad daylight of the street, which smelled of muck. The tedious mortar of tenements, settled out of line, the buildings sway-backed, with grime on grime, as if built of castoff shoes, not brick. The contractor observing. The ferment of sugar and roasting coffee was strong, but the summer air moved quickly in the damp under the huge machine-trampled bridge. Looking about for the subway entrance, Isaac saw instead a yellow cab with a yellow light on the crest. He first told the driver, "Grand Central," but changed his mind at the first corner and said, "Take me to the West Side Air Terminal." There was no fast train to Albany before late afternoon. He could not wait on Forty-second Street. Not today. He must have known all along that he would have to pay the money. He had come to get strength by consulting the rabbi. Old laws and wisdom on his side. But Tina from the deathbed had made too strong a move. If he refused to come across, no one could blame him. But he would feel greatly damaged. How would he live with himself? Because he made these sums easily now. Buying and selling a few city lots. Had the price been $50,000, Tina would have been saying that he would never see her again. But $20,000— the figure was a shrewd choice. And Orthodoxy had no remedy. It was entirely up to him.

Having decided to capitulate, he felt a kind of deadly recklessness. He had never been in the air before. But perhaps it was high time to fly. Everyone had lived enough. And anyway, as the cab crept through the summer lunch-time crowds on Twenty-third Street, there seemed plenty of human-kind already.

On the airport bus, he opened his father's copy of the Psalms. The black Hebrew letters only gaped at him like open mouths with tongues hanging down, pointing upward, flaming but dumb. He tried—forcing. It did no good. The tunnel, the swamps, the auto skeletons, machine entrails, dumps, gulls, sketchy Newark trembling in fiery summer, held his attention minutely. As though he were not Isaac Braun but a man who took pictures. Then in the plane running with concentrated fury to take off—the power to pull away from the magnetic earth; and more: When he saw the ground tilt backward, the machine rising from the runway, he said to himself in clear internal words, *"Shema Yisroel,"* Hear, O Israel, God alone is God! On the right, New York leaned gigantically seaward, and the plane with a jolt of retracted wheels turned toward the river. The Hudson green within green, and rough with tide and wind. Isaac released the breath he had been holding, but sat belted tight. Above the marvelous bridges, over clouds, sailing in atmosphere, you know better than ever that you are no angel.

The flight was short. From Albany airport, Isaac phoned his bank. He told Spinwall, with whom he did business there, that he needed $20,000 in cash. "No problem," said Spinwall. "We have it."

Isaac explained to Dr. Braun, "I have passbooks for my savings accounts in my safe-deposit box."

Probably in individual accounts of $10,000, protected by federal deposit insurance. He must have had bundles of these.

He went through the round entrance of the vault, the mammoth delicate door, circular, like the approaching moon seen by space navigators. A taxi waited as he drew the money and took him, the dollars in his briefcase, to the hospital. Then at the hospital, the hopeless flesh and melancholy festering and drug odors, the splashy flowers and wrinkled garments. In the large cage elevator that could take in whole beds, pulmotors, and laboratory machines, his eyes were fixed on the silent, beautiful Negro woman dreaming at the control as they moved slowly from lobby to mezzanine, from mezzanine to first. The two were alone, and since there was no going faster, he found himself observing her strong, handsome legs, her bust, the gold wire and glitter of her glasses, and the sensual bulge in her throat, just under the chin. In spite of himself, struck by these as he slowly rose to his sister's deathbed.

At the elevator, as the gate opened, was his brother Mutt. "Issac!"

"How is she?"

"Very bad."

"Well, I'm here. With the money."

Confused, Mutt did not know how to face him. He seemed frightened. Tina's power over Mutt had always been great.

Though he was three or four years her senior. Isaac somewhat understood what moved him and said, "That's all right, Mutt, if I have to pay. I'm ready. On her terms."

"She may not even know."

"Take it. Say I'm here. I want to see my sister, Mutt."

Unable to look at Issac, Mutt received the briefcase and went in to Tina. Isaac moved away from her door without glancing through the slot. Because he could not stand still, he moved down the corridor, hands clasped behind his back. Past the rank of empty wheelchairs. Repelled by these things which were made for weakness. He hated such objects, hated the stink of hospitals. He was sixty years old. He knew the route he, too, must go, and soon. But only knew, did not yet feel it. Death still was at a distance. As for handing over the money, about which Mutt was ashamed, taking part unwillingly in something unjust, grotesque—yes, it was farfetched, like things women imagined they wanted in pregnancy, hungry for peaches, or beer, or eating plaster from the walls. But as for himself, as soon as he handed over the money, he felt no more concern for it. It was nothing. He was glad to be rid of it. He could hardly understand this about himself. Once the money was given, the torment stopped. Nothing at all. The thing was done to punish, to characterize him, to convict him of something, to put him in a category. But the effect was just the opposite. What category? Where was it? If she thought it made him suffer, it did not. If she thought she understood his soul better than anyone—his poor dying sister; no, she did not.

And Dr. Braun, feeling with them this work of wit and despair, this last attempt to exchange significance, rose, stood, looking at the shafts of ice, the tatters of vapor in winter blue.

Then Tina's private nurse opened the door and beckoned to Isaac. He hurried in and stopped with a suffocated look. Her upper body was wasted and yellow. Her belly was huge with the growth, and her legs, her ankles were swollen. Her distorted feet had freed themselves from the cover. The soles like clay. The skin was tight on her skull. The hair was white. An intravenous tube was taped to her arm, and other tubes from her body into excretory jars beneath the bed. Mutt had laid the briefcase before her. It had not been unstrapped. Fleshless, hair coarse, and the meaning of her black eyes impossible to understand, she was looking at Isaac.

"Tina!"

"I wondered," she said.

"It's all there."

But she swept the briefcase from her and in a choked voice said, "No. Take it." He went to kiss her. Her free arm was lifted and tried to embrace him. She was too feeble, too drugged. He felt the bones of his obese sister. Death. The end. The grave. They were weeping. And Mutt, turning away at the foot of the bed, his mouth twisted open and the tears running from his eyes. Tina's tears were much thicker and slower.

The ring she had taken from Aunt Rose was tied to Tina's wasted finger with dental floss. She held out her hand to the nurse. It was all prearranged. The nurse cut the thread. Tina said to Isaac. "Not the money. I don't want it. You take Mama's ring."

And Dr. Braun, bitterly moved, tried to grasp what emotions were. What good were they! What were they for! And no one wanted them now. Perhaps the cold eye was better. On life, on death. But, again, the cold of the eye would be proportional to the degree of heat within. But once humankind had grasped its own idea, that it was human and human through such passions, it began to exploit, to play, to disturb for the sake of exciting disturbance, to make an uproar, a crude circus of feelings. So the Brauns wept for Tina's death. Isaac held his mother's ring in his hand. Dr. Braun, too, had tears in his eyes. Oh, these Jews—these Jews! Their feelings, their hearts! Dr. Braun often wanted nothing more than to stop all this. For what came of it? One after another you gave over your dying. One by one they went. You went. Childhood, family, friendship, love were stifled in the grave. And these tears! When you wept them from the heart, you felt you justified something, understood something. But what did you understand? Again, *nothing!* It was only an imitation of understanding. A promise that mankind might —*might,* mind you—eventually, through its gift which might —*might* again!—be a divine gift, comprehend why it lived. Why life, why death.

And again, why these particular forms—these Isaacs and these Tinas? When Dr. Braun closed his eyes, he saw, red on black, something like molecular processes—the only true heraldry of being. As later, in the close black darkness when the short day ended, he went to the dark kitchen window to have a look at stars. These things cast outward by a great begetting spasm billions of years ago.

Criers and Kibitzers, Kibitzers and Criers

Stanley Elkin

Greenspahn cursed the steering wheel shoved like the hard edge of someone's hand against his stomach. Goddamn lousy cars, he thought. Forty-five hundred dollars and there's not room to breathe. He thought sourly of the smiling salesman who had sold it to him, calling him Jake all the time he had been in the showroom: Lousy *podler*. He slid across the seat, moving carefully as though he carried something fragile, and eased his big body out of the car. Seeing the parking meter, he experienced a dark rage. They don't let you live, he thought. *I'll put your nickels in the meter for you, Mr. Greenspahn,* he mimicked the Irish cop. Two dollars a week for the lousy grubber. Plus the nickels that were supposed to go into the meter. And they talked about the Jews. He saw the cop across the street writing out a ticket. He went around his car, carefully pulling at the handle of each door, and he started toward his store.

"Hey there, Mr. Greenspahn," the cop called.

He turned to look at him. "Yeah?"

"Good morning."

"Yeah. Yeah. Good morning."

The grubber came toward him from across the street. Uniforms, Greenspahn thought, only a fool wears a uniform.

"Fine day, Mr. Greenspahn," the cop said.

Greenspahn nodded grudgingly.

"I was sorry to hear about your trouble, Mr. Greenspahn. Did you get my card?"

"Yeah, I got it. Thanks." He remembered something with flowers on it and rays going up to a pink Heaven. A picture of a cross yet.

"I wanted to come out to the chapel but the brother-in-law was up from Cleveland. I couldn't make it."

"Yeah," Greenspahn said. "Maybe next time."

The cop looked stupidly at him, and Greenspahn reached into his pocket.

"No. No. Don't worry about that, Mr. Greenspahn. I'll take care of it for now. Please, Mr. Greenspahn, forget it this time. It's okay."

Greenspahn felt like giving him the money anyway. Don't mourn for me, *podler*, he thought. Keep your two dollars' worth of grief.

The cop turned to go. "Well, Mr. Greenspahn, there's nothing anybody can say at times like this, but you know how I feel. You got to go on living, don't you know."

"Sure," Greenspahn said. "That's right, Officer." The cop crossed the street and finished writing the ticket. Greenspahn looked after him angrily, watching the gun swinging in the holster at his hip, the sun flashing brightly on the shiny handcuffs. *Podler*, he thought, afraid for his lousy nickels. There'll be an extra parking space sooner than he thinks.

He walked toward his store. He could have parked by his own place but out of habit he left his car in front of a rival grocer's. It was an old and senseless spite. Tomorrow he would change. What difference did it make, one less parking space? Why should he walk?

He felt bloated, heavy. The bowels, he thought. I got to move them soon or I'll bust. He looked at the street vacantly, feeling none of the old excitement. What did he come back for, he wondered suddenly, sadly. He missed Harold. Oh my God. Poor Harold, he thought. I'll never see him again. I'll never see my son again. He was choking, a big pale man beating his fist against his chest in grief. He pulled a handkerchief from his pocket and blew his nose. That was the way it was, he thought. He would go along flat and empty and dull, and all of a sudden he would dissolve in a heavy, choking grief. The street was no place for him. His wife was crazy, he thought, swiftly angry. "Be busy. Be busy," she said. What was he, a kid, that because he was making up somebody's lousy order everything would fly out of his mind? The bottom dropped out of his life and he was supposed to go along as though nothing had happened. His wife and the cop, they had the same psychology. Like in the movies after the horse kicks your head in you're supposed to get up and ride him so he can throw you off and finish the job. If he could get a buyer he would sell, and that was the truth.

Mechanically he looked into the windows he passed. The displays seemed foolish to him now, petty. He resented the wooden wedding cakes, the hollow watches. The manikins were grotesque, giant dolls. Toys, he thought bitterly. Toys. That he used to enjoy the displays himself, had even taken a peculiar pleasure in the complicated tiers of cans, in the amazing pyramids of apples and oranges in his own window, seemed incredible to him. He remembered he had liked to look at the little living rooms in the window of the furniture store, the wax models sitting on the couches offering each other tea. He used to look at the expensive furniture and think, *Merchandise.* The word had sounded rich to him, and mysterious. He used to think of camels on a desert, their bellies slung with heavy ropes. On their backs they carried *merchandise.* What did it mean, any of it? Nothing. It meant nothing.

He was conscious of someone watching him.

"Hello, Jake."

It was Margolis from the television shop.

"Hello, Margolis. How are you?"

"Business is terrible. You picked a hell of a time to come back."

A man's son dies and Margolis says business is terrible. Margolis, he thought, jerk, son of a bitch.

"You can't close up a minute. You don't know when somebody might come in. I didn't take coffee since you left," Margolis said.

"You had it rough, Margolis. You should have said something, I would have sent some over."

Margolis smiled helplessly, remembering the death of Greenspahn's son.

"It's okay, Margolis." He felt his anger tug at him again. It was something he would have to watch, a new thing with him but already familiar, easily released, like something on springs.

"Jake," Margolis whined.

"Not now, Margolis," he said angrily. He had to get away from him. He was like a little kid, Greenspahn thought. His face was puffy, swollen, like a kid about to cry. He looked so meek. He should be holding a hat in his hand. He couldn't stand to look at him. He was afraid Margolis was going to make a speech. He didn't want to hear it. What did he need a speech? His son was in the ground. Under all that earth. Under all that dirt. In a metal box. Airtight, the funeral director told him. Oh my God, *airtight. Vacuum-sealed.* Like a can of coffee. His son was in the ground and on the street the models in the windows had on next season's dresses. He would hit Margolis in his face if he said one word.

Margolis looked at him and nodded sadly, turning his palms out as if to say, "I know. I know." Margolis continued to look at him and Greenspahn thought, He's taking into account, that's what he's doing. He's taking into account the fact that my son has died. He's figuring it in and making apologies for me, making an allowance, like he was doing an estimate in his head what to charge a customer.

"I got to go, Margolis."

"Sure, me too," Margolis said, relieved. "I'll see you, Jake. The man from R.C.A. is around back with a shipment. What do I need it?"

Greenspahn walked to the end of the block and crossed the street. He looked down the side street and saw the *shul* where that evening he would say prayers for his son.

He came to his store, seeing it with distaste. He looked at the signs, like the balloons in comic strips where they put the words, stuck inside against the glass, the letters big and red like it was the end of the world, the big whitewash numbers on the glass thickly. A billboard, he thought.

He stepped up to the glass door and looked in. Frank, his produce man, stood by the fruit and vegetable bins taking the tissue paper off the oranges. His butcher, Arnold, was at the register talking to Shirley, the cashier. Arnold saw him through the glass and waved extravagantly. Shirley came to the door and opened it. "Good morning there, Mr. Greenspahn," she said.

"Hey, Jake, how are you?" Frank said.

"How's it going, Jake?" Arnold said.

"Was Siggie in yet? Did you tell him about the cheese?"

"He ain't been in this morning, Jake," Frank said.

"How about the meat? Did you place the order?"

"Sure, Jake," Arnold said. "I called the guy Thursday."

"Where are the receipts?" he asked Shirley.

"I'll get them for you, Mr. Greenspahn. You already seen them for the first two weeks you were gone. I'll get last week's."

She handed him a slip of paper. It was four hundred and seventy dollars off the last week's low figure. They must have had a picnic, Greenspahn thought. No more though. He looked at them, and they watched him with interest. "So," he said. "So."

"Nice to have you back, Mr. Greenspahn," Shirley told him, smiling.

"Yeah," he said, "yeah."

"We got a shipment yesterday, Jake, but the *schvartze* showed up drunk. We couldn't get it all put up," Frank said.

Greenspahn nodded. "The figures are low," he said.

"It's business. Business has been terrible. I figure it's the strike," Frank said.

"In West Virginia the miners are out and you figure that's why my business is bad in this neighborhood?"

"There are repercussions," Frank said. "All industries are affected."

"Yeah," Greenspahn said, "yeah. The pretzel industry. The canned chicken noodle soup industry."

"Well, business has been lousy, Jake," Arnold said testily.

"I guess maybe it's so bad, now might be a good time to sell. What do you think?" Greenspahn said.

"Are you really thinking of selling, Jake?" Frank asked.

"You want to buy my place, Frank?"

"You know I don't have that kind of money, Jake," Frank said uneasily.

"Yeah," Greenspahn said, "yeah."

Frank looked at him, and Greenspahn waited for him to say something else, but in a moment he turned and went back to the oranges. Some thief, Greenspahn thought. Big shot. I insulted him.

"I got to change," he said to Shirley. "Call me if Siggie comes in."

He went into the toilet off the small room at the rear of the store. He reached for the clothes he kept there on a hook on the back of the door and saw, hanging over his own clothes, a woman's undergarments. A brassiere hung by one cup over his trousers. What is it here, a locker room? Does she take baths in the sink? he thought. Fastidiously he tried to remove his own clothes without touching the other garments, but he was clumsy, and the underwear, together with his trousers, tumbled in a heap to the floor. They looked, lying there, strangely obscene to him, as though two people, desperately in a hurry, had dropped them quickly and were somewhere near him even now, perhaps behind the very door, making love. He picked up his trousers and changed his clothes. Taking a hanger from a pipe under the sink, he hung the clothes he had worn to work and put the hanger on the hook. He stooped to pick up Shirley's underwear. Placing it on the hook, his hand rested for a moment on the brassiere. He was immediately ashamed. He was terribly tired. He put his head through the loop of his apron and tied the apron behind the back of the old blue sweater he wore even in summer. He turned the sink's single tap and rubbed his eyes with water. Bums, he thought. Bums. You put up mirrors to watch the customers so they shouldn't get away with a stick of gum, and in the meanwhile Frank and Arnold walk off with the whole store. He sat down to try to move his bowels and the apron hung down from his chest like a barber's sheet. He spread it across his knees. I must look like I'm getting a haircut, he thought irrelevantly. He looked suspiciously at Shirley's underwear. My movie star. He wondered if it was true what Arnold told him, that she used to be a 26-girl. Something was going on between her and that Arnold. Two bums, he thought. He knew they drank together after work. That was one thing, bad enough, but were they screwing around in the back of the store? Arnold had a family. You couldn't trust a young butcher. It was too much for him. Why didn't he just sell and get the hell out? Did he have to look for grief? Was he making a fortune that he had to put up with it? It was crazy. All right, he thought, a man in business, there were things a man in business put up with. But this? It was crazy. Everywhere he was beset by thieves and cheats. They kept pushing him, pushing him. What did it mean? Why did they do it? All right, he thought, when Harold was alive was it any different? No, of course not, he knew plenty then too. But it didn't make as much difference. Death is an education, he thought. Now there wasn't any reason to put up with it. What did he need it? On the street, in the store, he saw everything. Everything. It was as if everybody else were made out of glass. Why all of a sudden was he like that?

Why? he thought. Jerk, because they're hurting *you*, that's why.

He stood up and looked absently into the toilet. "Maybe I need a laxative," he said aloud. Troubled, he left the toilet.

In the back room, his "office," he stood by the door to the toilet and looked around. Stacked against one wall he saw four or five cases of soups and canned vegetables. Against the meat locker he had pushed a small table, his desk. He went to it to pick up a pencil. Underneath the telephone was a pad of note paper. Something about it caught his eye and he picked up the pad. On the top sheet was writing, his son's. He used to come down on Saturdays sometimes when they were busy; evidently this was an order he had taken down over the phone. He looked at the familiar writing and thought his heart would break. Harold, Harold, he thought. My God, Harold, you're dead. He touched the sprawling, hastily written letters, the carelessly spelled words, and thought absently, He must have been busy. I can hardly read it. He looked at it more closely. "He was in a hurry," he said, starting to sob. "My God, *he* was in a hurry." He tore the sheet from the pad, and folding it, put it into his pocket. In a minute he was able to walk back out into the store.

In the front Shirley was talking to Siggie, the cheese man. Seeing him up there leaning casually on the counter, Greenspahn felt a quick anger. He walked up the aisle toward him.

Siggie saw him coming. "*Shalom*, Jake," he called.

"I want to talk to you."

"Is it important, Jake, because I'm in some terrific hurry. I still got deliveries."

"What did you leave me?"

"The same, Jake. The same. A couple pounds blue. Some Swiss. Delicious," he said, smacking his lips.

"I been getting complaints, Siggie."

"From the Americans, right? Your average American don't know from cheese. It don't mean nothing." He turned to go.

"Siggie, where you running?"

"Jake, I'll be back tomorrow. You can talk to me about it."

"Now."

He turned reluctantly. "What's the matter?"

"You're leaving old stuff. Who's your wholesaler?"

"Jake, Jake," he said. "We already been over this. I pick up the returns, don't I?"

"That's not the point."

"Have you ever lost a penny on account of me?"

"Siggie, who's your wholesaler? Where do you get the stuff?"

"I'm cheaper than the dairy, right? Ain't I cheaper than the dairy? Come on, Jake. What do you want?"

"Siggie, don't be a jerk. Who are you talking to? Don't be a jerk. You leave me cheap, crummy cheese, the dairies are ready to throw it away. I get everybody else's returns. It's old when I get it. Do you think a customer wants a cheese it goes off like a bomb two days after she gets it home? And what about the customers who don't return it? Thy think I'm gypping them and they don't come back. I don't want the *schlak* stuff. Give me fresh or I'll take from somebody else."

"I couldn't give you fresh for the same price, Jake. You know that."

"The same price."

"Jake," he said, amazed.

"The same price. Come on, Siggie, don't screw around with me."

"Talk to me tomorrow. We'll work something out." He turned to go.

"Siggie," Greenspahn called after him. "Siggie." He was already out of the store. Greenspahn clenched his fists. "The bum," he said.

"He's always in a hurry, that guy," Shirley said.

"Yeah, yeah," Greenspahn said. He started to cross to the cheese locker to see what Siggie had left him.

"Say, Mr. Greenspahn," Shirley said, "I don't think I have enough change."

"Where's the *schvartze?* Send him to the bank."

"He ain't come in yet. Shall I run over?"

Greenspahn poked his fingers in the cash drawer. "You got till he comes," he said.

"Well," she said, "if you think so."

"What do we do, a big business in change? I don't see customers stumbling over each other in the aisles."

"I told you, Jake," Arnold said, coming up behind him. "It's business. Business is lousy. People ain't eating."

"Here," Greenspahn said, "give me ten dollars. I'll go myself." He turned to Arnold. "I seen some stock in the back. Put it up, Arnold."

"I should put up the stock?" Arnold said.

"You told me yourself, business is lousy. Are you here to keep off the streets or something? What is it?"

"What do you pay the *schvartze* for?"

"He ain't here," Greenspahn said. "When he comes in I'll have him cut up some meat, you'll be even."

He took the money and went out into the street. It was lousy, he thought. You had to be able to trust them or you could go crazy. Every retailer had the same problem; he winked his eye and figured, All right, so I'll allow a certain percentage for shrinkage. You made it up on the register. But in his place it was ridiculous. They were professionals. Like the Mafia or something. What did it pay to aggravate himself, his wife would say. Now he was back he could watch them. *Watch* them. He couldn't stand even to be in the place. They thought they were getting away with something, the *podlers*.

He went into the bank. He saw the ferns. The marble tables where the depositors made out their slips. The calendars, carefully changed each day. The guard, a gun on his hip and a white carnation in his uniform. The big safe, thicker than a wall, shiny and open, in the back behind the sturdy iron gate. The tellers behind their cages, small and quiet, as though they went about barefooted. The bank officers, gray-haired and well dressed, comfortable at their big desks, solidly official behind their engraved name-plates. That was something, he thought. A bank. A bank was something. And no shrinkage.

He gave his ten-dollar bill to a teller to be changed.

"Hello there, Mr. Greenspahn. How are you this morning? We haven't seen you lately," the teller said.

"I haven't been in my place for three weeks," Greenspahn said.

"Say," the teller said, "that's quite a vacation."

"My son passed away."

"I didn't know," the teller said. "I'm very sorry, sir."

He took the rolls the teller handed him and stuffed them into his pocket. "Thank you," he said.

The street was quiet. It looks like a Sunday, he thought. There would be no one in the store. He saw his reflection in a window he passed and realized he had forgotten to take his apron off. It occurred to him that the apron somehow gave him the appearance of being very busy. An apron did that, he thought. Not a business suit so much. Unless there was a briefcase. A briefcase and an apron, they made you look busy. A uniform wouldn't. Soldiers didn't look busy, policemen didn't. A fireman did, but he had to have that big hat on. Schmo, he thought, a man your age walking in the street in an apron. He wondered if the vice-presidents at the bank had noticed his apron. He felt the heaviness again.

He was restless, nervous, disappointed in things.

He passed the big plate window of "The Cookery," the restaurant where he ate his lunch, and the cashier waved at him, gesturing that he should come in. He shook his head. For a moment when he saw her hand go up he thought he might go in. The men would be there, the other business people, drinking cups of coffee, cigarettes smearing the saucers, their sweet rolls cut into small, precise sections. Even without going inside he knew what it would be like. The criers and the kibitzers. The criers, earnest, complaining with a peculiar vigor about their businesses, their gas mileage, their health; their despair articulate, dependably lamenting their lives, vaguely mourning conditions, their sorrow something they could expect no one to understand. The kibitzers, deaf to grief, winking confidentially at the others, their voices high-pitched in kidding or lowered in conspiracy to tell of triumphs, of men they knew downtown, of tickets fixed, or languishing goods moved suddenly and unexpectedly, of the windfall that was life; their fingers sticky, smeared with the sugar from their rolls.

What did he need them, he thought. Big shots. What did they know about anything? Did they lose sons?

He went back to his place and gave Shirley the silver.

"Is the *schvartze* in yet?" he asked.

"No, Mr. Greenspahn."

I'll dock him, he thought. I'll dock him.

He looked around and saw that there were several people in the store. It wasn't busy, but there was more activity than he had expected. Young housewives from the university. Good shoppers, he thought. Good customers. They knew what they could spend and that was it. There was no monkey business about prices. He wished his older customers would take lessons from them. The ones who came in wearing their fur coats and who thought because they knew him from his old place that entitled them to special privileges. In a supermarket. Privileges. Did A&P give discounts? The National? What did they want from him?

He walked around straightening the shelves. Well, he thought, at least it wasn't totally dead. If they came in like this all day he might make a few pennies. A few pennies, he thought. A few dollars. What difference does it make?

A salesman was talking to him when he saw her. The man was trying to tell him something about a new product, some detergent, ten cents off on the box, something, but Greenspahn couldn't take his eyes off her.

"Can I put you down for a few trial cases, Mr. Greenspahn? In Detroit when the stores put it on the shelves . . ."

"No," Greenspahn interrupted him. "Not now. It don't sell. I don't want it."

"But, Mr. Greenspahn, I'm trying to tell you. This is something new. It hasn't been on the market more than three weeks."

"Later, later," Greenspahn said. "Talk to Frank, don't bother me."

He left the salesman and followed the woman up the aisle, stopping when she stopped, turning to the shelves, pretending to adjust them. One egg, he thought. She touches one egg, I'll throw her out.

It was Mrs. Frimkin, the doctor's wife. An old customer and a chisler. An expert. For a long time she hadn't been in because of a fight they'd had over a thirty-five-cent delivery charge. He had to watch her. She had a million tricks. Sometimes she would sneak over to the eggs and push her finger through two or three of them. Then she would smear a little egg on the front of her dress and come over to him complaining that he'd ruined her dress, that she'd picked up the eggs "in good faith," thinking they were whole. "In good faith," she'd say. He'd have to give her the whole box and charge her for a half dozen just to shut her up. An expert.

He went up to her. He was somewhat relieved to see that she wore a good dress. She risked the egg trick only in a housecoat.

"Jake," she said, smiling at him.

He nodded.

"I heard about Harold," she said sadly. "The doctor told me. I almost had a heart attack when I heard." She touched his arm. "Listen," she said. "We don't know. We just don't know. Mrs. Baron, my neighbor from when we lived on Drexel, didn't she fall down dead in the street? Her daughter was getting married in a month. How's your wife?"

Greenspahn shrugged. "Something I can do for you, Mrs. Frimkin?"

"What am I, a stranger? I don't need help. Fix, fix your shelves. I can take what I need."

"Yeah," he said, "yeah. Take." She had another trick. She came into a place, his place, the A&P, it didn't make any difference, and she priced everything. She even took notes. He knew she didn't buy a thing until she was absolutely convinced she couldn't get it a penny cheaper some place else.

"I only want a few items. Don't worry about me," she said.

"Yeah," Greenspahn said. He could wring her neck, the lousy *podler*.

"How's the fruit?" she asked.

"You mean confidentially?"

"What else?"

"I'll tell you the truth," Greenspahn said. "It's so good I don't like to see it get out of the store."

"Maybe I'll buy a banana."

"You couldn't go wrong," Greenspahn said.

"You got a nice place, Jake. I always said it."

"So buy something," he said.

"We'll see," she said mysteriously. "We'll see."

They were standing by the canned vegetables and she reached out her hand to lift a can of peas from the shelf. With her palm she made a big thing of wiping the dust from the top of the can and then stared at the price stamped there. "Twenty-seven?" she asked, surprised.

"Yeah," Greenspahn said. "It's too much?"

"Well," she said.

"I'll be damned," he said. "I been in the business twenty-two years and I never did know what to charge for a tin of peas."

She looked at him suspiciously, and with a tight smile gently replaced the peas. Greenspahn glared at her, and then, seeing Frank walk by, caught at his sleeve, pretending he had business with him. He walked up the aisle holding Frank's elbow, conscious that Mrs. Frimkin was looking after them.

"The lousy *podler*," he whispered.

"Take it easy, Jake," Frank said. "She could be a good customer again. So what if she chisels a little? I was happy to see her come in."

"Yeah," Greenspahn said, "happy." He left Frank and went toward the meat counter. "Any phone orders?" he asked Arnold.

"A few, Jake. I can put them up."

"Never mind," Greenspahn said. "Give me." He took the slips Arnold handed him. "While it's quiet I'll do them."

He read over the orders quickly and in the back of the store selected four cardboard boxes with great care. He picked the stock from the shelves and fit it neatly into the boxes, taking a kind of pleasure in the diminution of the stacks. Each time he put something into a box he had the feeling that there was that much less to sell. At the thick butcher's block behind the meat counter, bloodstains so deep in the wood they seemed almost a part of its grain, he trimmed fat from a thick roast. Arnold, beside him, leaned heavily against the paper roll. Greenspahn was conscious that Arnold watched him.

"Bernstein's order?" Arnold asked.

"Yeah," Greenspahn said.

"She's giving a party. She told me. Her husband's birthday."

"Happy birthday."

"Yeah," Arnold said. "Say, Jake, maybe I'll go eat."

Greenspahn trimmed the last piece of fat from the roast before he looked up at him. "So go eat," he said.

"I think so," Arnold said. "It's slow today. You know?" Greenspahn nodded.

"Well, I'll grab some lunch. Maybe it'll pick up in the afternoon."

He took a box and began filling another order. He went to the canned goods in high, narrow, canted towers. That much less to sell, he thought bitterly. It was endless. You could never liquidate. There were no big deals in the grocery business. He thought hopelessly of the hundreds of items in his store, of all the different brands, the different sizes. He was terribly aware of each shopper, conscious of what each put into the shopping cart. It was awful, he thought. He wasn't selling diamonds. He wasn't selling pianos. He sold bread, milk, eggs. You had to have volume or you were dead. He was losing money. On his electric, his refrigeration, the signs in his window, his payroll, his specials, his stock. It was the chain stores. They had the parking. They advertised. They gave stamps. Two percent right out of the profits— it made no difference to them. They had the tie-ins. Fantastic. Their own farms, their own dairies, their own bakeries, their own canneries. Everything. The bastards. He was committing suicide to fight them.

In a little while Shirley came up to him. "Is it all right if I get my lunch now, Mr. Greenspahn?"

Why did they ask him? Was he a tyrant? "Yeah, yeah. Go eat. I'll watch the register."

She went out, and Greenspahn, looking after her, thought, Something's going on. First one, then the other. They meet each other. What do they do, hold hands? He fit a carton of eggs carefully into a box. What difference does it make? A slut and a bum.

He stood at the checkout counter, and pressing the orange key, watched the *No Sale* flag shoot up into the window of the register. He counted the money sadly.

Frank was at the bins trimming lettuce. "Jake, you want to go eat I'll watch things," he said.

"Not yet," Greenspahn said.

An old woman came into the store and Greenspahn recognized her. She had been in twice before that morning and both times had bought two tins of the coffee Greenspahn was running on a special. She hadn't bought anything else. Already he had lost twelve cents on her. He watched her carefully and saw with a quick rage that she went again to the coffee. She picked up another two tins and came toward the checkout counter. She wore a bright red wig which next to her very white, ancient skin gave her the appearance of a clown. She put the coffee down on the counter and looked up at Greenspahn timidly. He made no effort to ring up the sale. She stood for a moment and then pushed the coffee toward him.

"Sixty-nine cents a pound," she said. "Two pounds is a dollar thirty-eight. Six cents tax is a dollar forty-four."

"Lady," Greenspahn said, "don't you ever eat? Is that all you do is drink coffee?" He stared at her.

Her lips began to tremble and her body shook. "A dollar forty-four," she said. "I have it right here."

"This is your sixth can, lady. I lose money on it. Do you know that?"

The woman continued to tremble. It was as though she were very cold.

"What do you do, lady? Sell this stuff door-to-door? Am I your wholesaler?"

Her body continued to shake, and she looked out at him from behind faded eyes as though she were unaware of the terrible movements of her body, as though they had, ultimately, nothing to do with her, that really she existed, hiding, crouched, somewhere behind the eyes. He had the impression that, frictionless, her old bald head bobbed beneath the wig. "All right," he said finally, "a dollar forty-four. I hope you have more luck with the item than I had." He took the money from her and watched her as she accepted her package wordlessly and walked out of the store. He shook his head. It was all a pile of crap, he thought. He had a vision of the woman on back porches, standing silently at back doors open on their chains, sadly extending the coffee.

He wanted to get out. Frank could watch the store. If he stole, he stole.

"Frank," he said, "it ain't busy. Watch things. I'll eat."

"Go on, Jake. Go ahead. I'm not hungry, I got a cramp. Go ahead."

"Yeah."

He walked toward the restaurant. On his way he had to pass a National; seeing the crowded parking lot, he felt his stomach tighten. He paused at the window and pressed his face against the glass and looked in at the full aisles. Through the thick glass he saw women moving silently through the store. He stepped back and read the advertisements on the window. My fruit is cheaper, he thought. My meat's the same, practically the same.

He moved on. Passing the familiar shops, he crossed the street and went into "The Cookery." Pushing open the heavy glass door, he heard the babble of the lunchers, the sound rushing to his ears like the noise of a suddenly unmuted trumpet. Criers and kibitzers, he thought. Kibitzers and criers.

The cashier smiled at him. "We haven't seen you, Mr. G. Somebody told me you were on a diet," she said.

Her too, he thought. A kibitzer that makes change.

He went toward the back. "Hey, Jake, how are you?" a man in a booth called. "Sit by us."

He nodded at the men who greeted him, and pulling a chair from another table, placed it in the aisle facing the booth. He sat down and leaned forward, pulling the chair's rear legs into the air so that the waitress could get by. Sitting there in the aisle, he felt peculiarly like a visitor, like one there only temporarily, as though he had rushed up to the table merely to say hello or to tell a joke. He knew what it was. It was the way kibitzers sat. The others, cramped in the booth but despite this giving the appearance of lounging there, their lunches begun or already half eaten, somehow gave him the impression that they had been there all day.

"You missed it, Jake," one of the men said. "We almost got Traub here to reach for a check last Friday. Am I lying, Margolis?"

"He almost did, Jake. He really almost did."

"At the last minute he jumped up and down on his own arm and broke it."

The men at the table laughed, and Greenspahn looked at Traub sitting little and helpless between two big men. Traub looked down shame-faced into his Coca-Cola.

"It's okay, Traub," the first man said. "We know. You got all those daughters getting married and having big weddings at the same time. It's terrible. Traub's only got one son. And do you think he'd have the decency to get married so Traub could one time go to a wedding and just enjoy himself? No, *he's* not *old* enough. But he's old enough to turn around and get himself bar mitzvah'd, right, Traub? The lousy kid."

Greenspahn looked at the men in the booth and at many-daughtered Traub, who seemed as if he were about to cry. Kibitzers and criers, he thought. Everywhere it was the same. At every table. The two kinds of people like two different sexes that had sought each other out. Sure, Greenspahn thought, would a crier listen to another man's complaints? Could a kibitzer kid a kidder? But it didn't mean anything, he thought. Not the jokes, not the grief. It didn't mean anything. They were like birds making noises in a tree. But try to catch them in a deal. They'd murder you. Every day they came to eat their lunch and make their noises. Like cowboys on television hanging up their gun belts to go to a dance.

But even so, he thought, they were the way they pretended to be. Nothing made any difference to them. Did they lose sons? Not even the money they earned made any difference to them finally.

"So I was telling you," Margolis said, "the guy from the Chamber of Commerce came around again today."

"He came to me too," Paul Gold said.

"Did you give?" Margolis asked.

"No, of course not."

"Did he hit you yet, Jake? Throw him out. He wants contributions for decorations. Listen, those guys are on the take from the paper-flower people. It's fantastic what they get for organizing the big stores downtown. My cousin on State Street told me about it. I told him, I said, 'Who needs the Chamber of Commerce? Who needs Easter baskets and colored eggs hanging from the lamppost?' "

"Not when the ring trick still works, right, Margolis?" Joe Fisher said.

Margolis looked at his lapel and shrugged lightly. It was the most modest gesture Greenspahn had ever seen him make. The men laughed. The ring trick was Margolis' invention. "A business promotion," he had told Greenspahn. "Better than Green Stamps." He had seen him work it. Margolis would stand at the front of his store and signal to some guy who stopped for a minute to look at the TV sets in his window. He would rap on the glass with his ring to catch his attention. He would smile and say something to him, anything. It didn't make any difference; the guy in the street couldn't hear him. As Greenspahn watched, Margolis had turned to him and winked slyly as if to say, "Watch this. Watch how I get this guy." Then he had looked back at the customer outside, and still smiling broadly had said, "Hello, schmuck. Come on in, I'll sell you something. That's right, jerk, press your greasy nose against the glass to see who's talking to you. Shade your eyes. That-a-jerk. Come on in, I'll sell you something." Always the guy outside would come into the store to find out what Margolis had been saying to him. "Hello there, sir," Margolis would say, grinning. "I was trying to tell you that the model you were looking at out there is worthless. Way overpriced. If the boss knew I was talking to you like this I'd be canned, but what the hell? We're all working people. Come on back here and look at a real set."

Margolis was right. Who needed the Chamber of Commerce? Not the kibitzers and criers. Not even the Gold boys. Criers. Greenspahn saw the other one at another table. Twins, but they didn't even look like brothers. Not even they needed the paper flowers hanging from the lamppost. Paul Gold shouting to his brother in the back, "Mr. Gold, please show this gentleman something stylish." And they'd go into the act, putting on a thick Yiddish accent for some white-haired old man with a lodge button in his lapel, giving him the business. Greenspahn could almost hear the old man telling the others at the Knights of Columbus Hall, "I picked this suit up from a couple of Yids on Fifty-third, real greenhorns. But you've got to hand it to them. Those people really know material."

Business was a kind of game with them, Greenspahn thought. Not even the money made any difference.

"Did I tell you about these two kids who came in to look at rings?" Joe Fisher said. "Sure," he went on, "two kids. Dressed up. The boy's a regular *mensch*. I figure they've been downtown at Peacock's and Field's. I think I recognized the girl from the neighborhood. I say to her boy friend—a nice kid, a college kid, you know, he looks like he ain't been bar mitzvah'd yet—'I got a ring here I won't show you the price. Will you give me your check for three hundred dollars right now? No appraisal? No bringing it to Papa on approval? No nothing?'

" 'I'd have to see the ring,' he tells me.

"Get this. I put my finger over the tag on a ring *I* paid eleven hundred for. *A big ring.* You got to wear smoked glasses just to look at it. Paul, I mean it, this is some ring. I'll give you a price for your wife's anniversary. No kidding, this is some ring. Think seriously about it. We could make it up into a beautiful cocktail ring. Anyway, this kid stares like a big dummy. I think he's turned to stone. He's scared. He figures something's wrong a big ring like that for only three hundred bucks. His girl friend is getting edgy, she thinks the kid's going to make a mistake, and she starts shaking her head. Finally he says to me, listen to this, he says, 'I wasn't looking for anything that large, Anyway, it's not a blue stone.' Can you imagine? Don't tell me about shoppers. I get prizes."

"What would you have done if he said he wanted the ring?" Traub asked.

"What are you, crazy? He was strictly from wholesale. It was like he had a sign on his suit. Don't you think I can tell a guy who's trying to get a price idea from a real customer?"

"Say, Jake," Margolis said, "ain't that your cashier over there with your butcher?"

Greenspahn looked around. It was Shirley and Arnold. He hadn't seen them when he came in. They were sitting across the table from each other—evidently they had not seen him either—and Shirley was leaning forward, her chin on her palms. Sitting there, she looked like a young girl. It annoyed him. It was ridiculous. He knew they met each other. What did he care? It wasn't his business. But to let themselves be seen. He thought of Shirley's brassiere hanging in his toilet. It was reckless. They were reckless people. All of them, Arnold and Shirley and the men in the restaurant. Reckless people.

"They're pretty thick with each other, ain't they?" Margolis said.

"How should I know?" Greenspahn said.

"What do you run over there at that place of yours, a lonely hearts club?"

"It's not my business. They do their work."

"Some work," Paul Gold said.

"I'd like a job like that," Joe Fisher said.

"Ain't he married?" Paul Gold said.

"I'm not a policeman," Greenspahn said.

"Jake's jealous because he's not getting any," Joe Fisher said.

"Loudmouth," Greenspahn said, "I'm a man in mourning." The others at the table were silent. "Joe was kidding," Traub, the crier, said.

"Sure, Jake," Joe Fisher said.

"Okay," Greenspahn said. "Okay."

For the rest of the lunch he was conscious of Shirley and Arnold. He hoped they would not see him, or if they did that they would make no sign to him. He stopped listening to the stories the men told. He chewed on his hamburger wordlessly. He heard someone mention George Stein, and he looked up for a moment. Stein had a grocery in a neighborhood that was changing. He had said that he wanted to get out. He was looking for a setup like Greenspahn's. He could speak to him. Sure, he thought. Why not? What did he need the aggravation? What did he need it? He owned the building the store was in. He could live on the rents. Even Joe Fisher was a tenant of his. He could speak to Stein, he thought, feeling he had made up his mind about something. He waited until Arnold and Shirley had finished their lunch and then went back to his store.

In the afternoon Greenspahn thought he might be able to move his bowels. He went into the toilet off the small room at the back of the store. He sat, looking up at the high ceiling. In the smoky darkness above his head he could just make out the small, square tin-ceiling plates. They seemed pitted, soiled, like patches of war-ruined armor. Agh, he thought, the place is a pigpen. The sink bowl was stained dark, the enamel chipped, long fissures radiating like lines on the map of some wasted country. The single faucet dripped steadily. Greenspahn thought sadly of his water bill. On the knob of the faucet he saw again a faded blue S. S. he thought, what the hell does S stand for? H hot, C cold. What the hell kind of faucet is S? Old clothes hung on a hook on the back of the door. A man's blue wash pants hung inside out, the zipper split like a peeled banana, the crowded concourse of seams at the crotch like carelessly sewn patches.

He heard Arnold in the store, his voice raised exaggeratedly. He strained to listen.

"*Forty-five,*" he heard Arnold say.

"*Forty-five, Pop.*" He was talking to the old man. Deaf, he came in each afternoon for a piece of liver for his supper.

"I can't give you two ounces. I told you. I can't break the set." He heard a woman laugh. Shirley? Was Shirley back there with him? What the hell, he thought. It was one thing for them to screw around with each other at lunch, but they didn't have to bring it into the store. *"Take eight ounces. Invite someone over for dinner. Take eight ounces. You'll have for four days. You won't have to come back."* He was a wise guy, that Arnold. What did he want to do, drive the old man crazy? What could you do? The old man liked a small slice of liver. He thought it kept him alive.

He heard footsteps coming toward the back room and voices raised in argument.

"I'm sorry," a woman said, "I don't know how it got there. Honest. Look, I'll pay. I'll pay you for it."

"You bet, lady," Frank's voice said.

"What do you want me to do?" the woman pleaded.

"I'm calling the cops," Frank said.

"For a lousy can of salmon?"

"It's the principle. You're a crook. You're a lousy thief, you know that? I'm calling the cops. We'll see what jail does for you."

"Please," the woman said. "Mister, please. This whole thing is crazy. I never did anything like this before. I haven't got any excuse, but please, can't you give me a chance?" The woman was crying.

"No chances," Frank said. "I'm calling the cops. You ought to be ashamed, lady. A woman dressed like you are. What are you, sick or something? I'm calling the cops." He heard Frank lift the receiver.

"Please," the woman sobbed. "My husband will kill me. I have a little kid, for Christ's sake."

Frank replaced the phone.

"Ten bucks," he said quietly.

"What's that?"

"Ten bucks and you don't come in here no more."

"I haven't got it," she said.

"All right, lady. The hell with you. I'm calling the cops."

"You bastard," she said.

"Watch your mouth," he said. "Ten bucks."

"I'll write you a check."

"Cash," Frank said.

"Okay, okay," she said. "Here."

"Now get out of here, lady." Greenspahn heard the

woman's footsteps going away. Frank would be fumbling now with his apron, trying to get the big wallet out of his front pocket. Greenspahn flushed the toilet and waited.

"Jake?" Frank asked, frightened.

"Who was she?"

"Jake, I never saw her before, honest. Just a tramp. She gave me ten bucks. She was just a tramp, Jake."

"I told you before. I don't want trouble," Greenspahn said angrily. He came out of the toilet. "What is this, a game with you?"

"Look, I caught her with the salmon. Would you want me to call the cops for a can of salmon? She's got a kid."

"Yeah, you got a big heart, Frank."

"I would have let you handle it if I'd seen you. I looked for you, Jake."

"You shook her down. I told you before about that."

"Jake, it's ten bucks for the store. I get so damned mad when somebody like that tries to get away with something."

"*Podler*," Greenspahn shouted. "You're through here."

"Jake," Frank said. "She was a tramp." He held the can of salmon in his hand and offered it to Greenspahn as though it were evidence.

Greenspahn pushed his hand aside. "Get out of my store. I don't need you. Get out. I don't want a crook in here."

"Who are you calling names, Jake?"

Greenspahn felt his rage, immense, final. It was on him at once, like an animal that had leaped upon him in the dark. His body shook with it. Frightened, he warned himself uselessly that he must be calm. A *podler* like that, he thought. He wanted to hit him in the face.

"Please, Frank. Get out of here," Greenspahn said.

"Sure," Frank screamed. "Sure, sure," he shouted. Greenspahn, startled, looked at him. He seemed angrier then even himself. Greenspahn thought of the customers. They would hear him. What kind of a place, he thought. What kind of a place? "Sure," Frank yelled, "fire me, go ahead. A regular holy man. A saint! What are you, God? He smells everybody's rottenness but his own. Only when your own son—may he rest—when your own son slips five bucks out of the cash drawer, that you don't see."

Greenspahn could have killed him. "Who says that?"

Frank caught his breath.

"Who says that?" Greenspahn repeated.

"Nothing, Jake. It was nothing. He was going on a date probably. That's all. It didn't mean nothing."

"Who calls him a thief?"

"Nobody. I'm sorry."

"My dead son? You call my dead son a thief?"

"Nobody called anybody a thief. I didn't know what I was saying."

"In the ground. Twenty-three years old and in the ground. Not even a wife, not even a business. Nothing. He had nothing. He wouldn't take. Harold wouldn't take. Don't call him what you are. He should be alive today. You should be dead. You should be in the ground where he is. *Podler. Mumser*," he shouted. "*I saw the lousy receipts, liar*," he screamed.

In a minute Arnold was there and was putting his arm around him. "Calm down, Jake. Come on now, take it easy. What happened back here?" he asked Frank.

Frank shrugged.

"Get him away," Greenspahn pleaded. Arnold signaled Frank to get out and led Greenspahn to the chair near the table he used as a desk.

"You all right now, Jake? You okay now?"

Greenspahn was sobbing heavily. In a few moments he looked up. "All right," he said. "The customers. Arnold, please. The customers."

"Okay, Jake. Just stay back here and wait till you feel better."

Greenspahn nodded. When Arnold left him he sat for a few minutes and then went back into the toilet to wash his face. He turned the tap and watched the dirty basin fill with water. It's not even cold, he thought sadly. He plunged his hands into the sink and scooped up warm water, which he rubbed into his eyes. He took a handkerchief from his back pocket and unfolded it and patted his face carefully. He was conscious of laughter outside the door. It seemed old, brittle. For a moment he thought of the woman with the coffee. Then he remembered. The porter, he thought. He called his name. He heard footsteps coming up to the door.

"That's right, Mr. Greenspahn," the voice said, still laughing.

Greenspahn opened the door. His porter stood before him in torn clothes. His eyes, red, wet, looked as though they were bleeding. "You sure told that Frank," he said.

"You're late," Greenspahn said. "What do you mean coming in so late?"

"I been to Harold's grave," he said.

"What's that?"

"I been to Mr. Harold's grave," he repeated. "I didn't get to the funeral. I been to his grave cause of my dream."

"Put the stock away," Greenspahn said. "Some more came in this afternoon."

"I will," he said. "I surely will." He was an old man. He had no teeth and his gums lay smooth and very pink in his mouth. He was thin. His clothes hung on him, the sleeves of the jacket rounded, puffed from absent flesh. Through the rents in shirt and trousers Greenspahn could see the grayish skin, hairless, creased, the texture like the pit of a peach. Yet he had a strength Greenspahn could only wonder at, and could still lift more stock than Arnold or Frank or even Greenspahn himself.

"You'd better start now," Greenspahn said uncomfortably.

"I tell you about my dream, Mr. Greenspahn?"

"No dreams. Don't tell me your dreams."

"It was about Mr. Harold. Yes, sir, about him. Your boy that's dead, Mr. Greenspahn."

"I don't want to hear. See if Arnold needs anything up front."

"I dreamed it twice. That means it's true. You don't count on a dream less you dream it twice."

"Get away with your crazy stories. I don't pay you to dream."

"That time on Halsted I dreamed the fire. I dreamed that twice."

"Yeah," Greenspahn said, "the fire. Yeah."

"I dreamed that dream twice. Them police wanted to question me. Same names, Mr. Greenspahn, me and your boy we got the same names."

"Yeah. I named him after you."

"I tell you that dream, Mr. Greenspahn? It was a mistake. Frank was supposed to die. Just like you said. Just like I heard you say it just now. And he will. Mr. Harold told me in the dream. Frank he's going to sicken and die his own self." The porter looked at Greenspahn, the red eyes filling with blood. "If you want it," he said. "That's what I dreamed, and I dreamed about the fire on Halsted the same way. Twice."

"You're crazy. Get away from me."

"That's a true dream. It happened just that very way."

"Get away. Get away," Greenspahn shouted.

"My name's Harold, too."

"You're crazy. Crazy."

The porter went off. He was laughing. What kind of a madhouse? Were they all doing it on purpose? Everything to aggravate him? For a moment he had the impression that this was what it was. A big joke, and everybody was in on it but himself. He was being *kibitzed* to death. Everything. The cop. The receipts. His cheese man. Arnold and Shirley. The men in the restaurant. Frank and the woman. The *schvartze*. Everything. He wouldn't let it happen. What was he, crazy or something? He reached into his pocket for his handkerchief, but pulled out a piece of paper. It was the order Harold had taken down over the phone and left on the pad. Absently he unfolded it and read it again. Something occurred to him. As soon as he had the idea he knew it was true. The order had never been delivered. His son had forgotten about it. It couldn't be anything else. Otherwise would it still have been on the message pad? Sure, he thought, what else could it be? Even his son. What did he care? What the hell did he care about the business? Greenspahn was ashamed. It was a terrible thought to have about a dead boy. Oh God, he thought. Let him rest. He was a boy, he thought. Twenty-three years old and he was only a boy. No wife. No business. Nothing. Was the five dollars so important? In helpless disgust he could see Harold's sly wink to Frank as he slipped the money out of the register. Five dollars, Harold, *five dollars,* he thought, as though he were admonishing him. "Why didn't you come to me, Harold?" he sobbed. "Why didn't you come to your father?"

He blew his nose. It's crazy, he thought. Nothing pleases me. Frank called him God. Some God, he thought. I sit weeping in the back of my store. The hell with it. The hell with everything. Clear the shelves, that's what he had to do. Sell the groceries. Get rid of the meats. Watch the money pile up. Sell, sell, he thought. That would be something. Sell everything. He thought of the items listed on the order his son had taken down. Were they delivered? He felt restless. He hoped they were delivered. If they wern't they would have to be sold again. He was very weary. He went to the front of the store.

It was almost closing time. Another half hour. He couldn't stay to close up. He had to be in *shul* before sundown. He had to get to the *minion*. They would have to close up for him. For a year. If he couldn't sell the store, for a year he wouldn't be in his own store at sundown. He would have to trust them to close up for him. Trust who? he thought. My Romeo, Arnold? Shirley? The crazy *schvartze?* Only Frank could do it. How could he have fired him? He looked for him in the store. He was talking to Shirley at the register. He would go up and talk to him. What difference did it make? He would have had to fire all of them. Eventually he would have to fire everybody who ever came to work for him. He would have to throw out his tenants, even the old ones, and finally whoever rented the store from him. He would have to keep on firing and throwing out as long as anybody was left. What difference would one more make?

"Frank," he said. "I want you to forget what we talked about before."

Frank looked at him suspiciously. "It's all right," Greenspahn reassured him. He led him by the elbow away from Shirley. "Listen," he said, "we were both excited before. I didn't mean it what I said."

Frank continued to look at him. "Sure, Jake," he said finally. "No hard feelings." He extended his hand.

Greenspahn took it reluctantly. "Yeah," he said.

"Frank," he said, "do me a favor and close up the place for me. I got to get to the *shul* for the *minion.*"

"I got you, Jake."

Greenspahn went to the back to change his clothes. He washed his face and hands and combed his hair. Carefully he removed his working clothes and put on the suit jacket, shirt and tie he had worn in the morning. He walked back into the store.

He was about to leave when he saw that Mrs. Frimkin had come into the store again. That's all right, he told himself, she can be a good customer. He needed some of the old customers now. They could drive you crazy, but when they bought, they bought. He watched as she took a cart from the front and pushed it through the aisles. She put things in the cart as though she were in a hurry. She barely glanced at the prices. That was the way to shop, he thought. It was a pleasure to watch her. She reached into the frozen-food locker and took out about a half-dozen packages. From the towers of canned goods on his shelves she seemed to take down only the largest cans. In minutes her shopping car was overflowing. That's some order, Greenspahn thought. Then he watched as she went to the stacks of bread at the bread counter. She picked up a packaged white bread, and first looking around to see if anyone was watching her, bent down quickly over the loaf, cradling it to her chest as though it were a football. As she stood, Greenspahn saw her brush crumbs from her dress, then put the torn package into her cart with the rest of her purchases.

She came up to the counter where Greenspahn stood and unloaded the cart, pushing the groceries toward Shirley to be checked out. The last item she put on the counter was the wounded bread. Shirley punched the keys quickly. As she reached for the bread, Mrs. Frimkin put out her hand to stop her. "Look," she said, "what are you going to charge me for the bread? It's damaged. Can I have it for ten cents?"

Shirley turned to look at Greenspahn.

"Out," he said. "Get out, you *podler*. I don't want you coming in here any more. You're a thief," he shouted. "A thief."

Frank came rushing up. "Jake, what is it? What is it?"

"Her. That one. A crook. She tore the bread. I seen her."

The woman looked at him defiantly. "I don't have to take that," she said. "I can make plenty of trouble for you. You're crazy. I'm not going to be insulted by somebody like you."

"Get out of here," Greenspahn shouted, "before I have you locked up."

The woman backed away from him, and when he stepped forward she turned and fled.

"Jake," Frank said, putting his hand on Greenspahn's shoulder. "That was a big order. So she tried to get away with a few pennies. What does it mean? You want me to find her and apologize?"

"Look," Greenspahn said, "she comes in again I want to know about it. I don't care what I'm doing. I want to know about it. She's going to pay me for that bread."

"Jake," Frank said.

"No," he said. "I mean it."

"Jake, it's ten cents."

"*My* ten cents. No more," he said. "I'm going to *shul*."

He waved Frank away and went into the street. Already the sun was going down. He felt urgency. He had to get there before the sun went down.

That night Greenspahn had the dream for the first time.

He was in the synagogue waiting to say prayers for his son. Around him were the old men, the *minion*, their faces brittle and pale. He recognized them from his youth. They had been old even then. One man stood by the window and watched the sun. At a signal from him the others would begin. There was always some place in the world where the prayers were being said, he thought, some place where the sun had just come up or just gone down, and he supposed there was always a *minion* to watch it and to mark its progress, the prayers following God's bright bird, going up in sunlight or in darkness, always, everywhere. He knew the men never left the *shul*. It was the way they kept from dying. They didn't even eat, but there was about the room the foul lemony smell of urine. Sure, Greenspahn thought in the dream, stay in the *shul*. That's right. Give the *podlers* a wide berth. All they have to worry about is God. Some worry, Greenspahn thought. The man at the window gave the signal and they all started to mourn for Greenspahn's son, their ancient voices betraying the queer melody of the prayers. The rabbi looked at Greenspahn and Greenspahn, imitating the old men, began to rock back and forth on his heels. He tried to sway faster than they did. I'm younger, he thought. When he was swaying so quickly that he thought he would be sick were he to go any faster, the rabbi smiled at him approvingly. The man at the window shouted that the sun was approaching the danger point in the sky and that Greenspahn had better begin as soon as he was ready.

He looked at the strange thick letters in the prayer book. "Go ahead," the rabbi said, "think of Harold and tell God."

He tried then to think of his son, but he could recall him only as he was when he was a baby standing in his crib. It was unreal, like a photograph. The others knew what he was thinking and frowned. "Go ahead," the rabbi said.

Then he saw him as a boy on a bicycle, as once he had seen him at dusk as he looked out from his apartment, riding the gray sidewalks, slapping his buttocks as though he were on a horse. The others were not satisfied.

He tried to imagine him older but nothing came of it. The rabbi said, "Please, Greenspahn, the sun is almost down. You're wasting time. Faster. Faster."

All right, Greenspahn thought. All right. Only let me think. The others stopped their chanting.

Desperately he thought of the store. He thought of the woman with the coffee, incredibly old, older than the old men who prayed with him, her wig fatuously red, the head beneath it shaking crazily as though even the weight and painted fire of the thick, bright hair were not enough to warm it.

The rabbi grinned.

He thought of the *schvartze*, imagining him on an old cot, on a damp and sheetless mattress, twisting in a fearful dream. He saw him bent under the huge side of red, raw meat he carried to Arnold.

The others were still grinning, but the rabbi was beginning to look a little bored. He thought of Arnold, seeming to watch him through the *schvartze's* own red, mad eyes, as Arnold chopped at the fresh flesh with his butcher's axe.

He saw the men in the restaurant. The criers, ignorant of hope, the *kibitzers*, ignorant of despair. Each with his pitiful piece broken from the whole of life, confidently extending only half of what there was to give.

He saw the cheats with their ten dollars and their stolen nickels and their luncheon lusts and their torn breads.

All right, Greenspahn thought. He saw Shirley naked but for her brassiere. It was evening and the store was closed. She lay with Arnold on the butcher's block.

"The boy," the rabbi said impatiently, "*the boy*."

He concentrated for a long moment while all of them stood by silently. Gradually, with difficulty, he began to make something out. It was Harold's face in the coffin, his expression at the very moment of death itself, before the undertakers had had time to tamper with it. He saw it clearly. It was soft, puffy with grief; a sneer curled the lips. It was Harold, twenty-three years old, wifeless, jobless, sacrificing nothing even in the act of death, leaving the world with his life not started.

The rabbi smiled at Greenspahn and turned away as though he now had other business.

"No," Greenspahn called, "wait. Wait."

The rabbi turned and with the others looked at him.

He saw it now. They all saw it. The helpless face, the sly wink, the embarrassed, slow smug smile of guilt that must, volitionless as the palpitation of a nerve, have crossed Harold's face when he had turned, his hand in the register, to see Frank watching him.

Under the Marquee

Wallace Markfield

Let it be winter, 1935, with snow in the air and the clouds dark as Egypt. Far from his mother's house now he walks in the perfect peace of Saturday, when there is nothing that is not for his pleasure.

No demerits redden his Delaney card.

None seek his blood in the school yard, or play "sallugee" with his hat.

At Chinese handball he is not good, but good enough.

His lima bean plant overflows the pot.

The substitute teacher took his part against Lionel Jacobs; saying, you are stocky, and stocky is not like chubby.

Only he, of all the first row boys, is not a listener in music.

He eats delicatessen tonight.

His Cousin Yuss will bring him the *Journal* jokes.

On Monday he traces his Benjamin Franklin drawing on good paper, fills the ink wells, works on his raffia mat.

Prince of the present, king of the future, he strips the silver foil from a Hershey Kiss, holds it without biting or sucking between his front teeth, then surrenders it to the wash of spittle. Far off, but not so far off that he cannot see the pennants sailing out in every direction from the giant chains, is the marquee. It is as natural to him as a tree. By squinting, by tilting his glasses against his brows, he makes out the "M" of Majestic, which is quite unlike any other "M" and moves him powerfully.

Baruch attuh he silently prays, let there be no line.

Adonai and *Elohanu,* if there is a line let it reach only to the appetizing store; and if it must reach so far, let it not go beyond the first window, beyond the nuts and dried fruits.

If, *Adonai Echad,* you have made the line long, say even to the bakery, and I must wait and wait, let no harm come to me from the cashier, let her not judge my size or question my age, let her fingers swiftly punch out a half-price ticket.

Before he knows for sure he must cover an avenue block, and during his long progress, he makes himself into another creature, one that is altogether what it should be. He sniffs in, but does not swallow; he passes a hedge but strips none of its few leaves; he goes by the crazy shoemaker's window without knocking on the glass, without yelling "Yar-yar-yar!" or making jerkfiend faces; he lays not even a finger upon guarded deposit bottles and cigar boxes that hold newsstand change; he neither seeks nor avoids pavement cracks; he does not rock his hands like Cagney's or pit them, one against the other, in deadly dogfights; he takes no clean flesh wound in arm or shoulder; he draws no bow string, flips no grenades, ties down no gun belt, parries no blade; he holds back the two-fingered whistle for Rin-Tin-Tin, the Tarzan yell, the whinny of the wild black stallion smelling men or fire.

But even so there is a line, and he feels his weight increase. The full tumult brings over the manager, a red, nervous, sharp-nosed man, barely taller than the tallest on the line. Anger billows from him, clings to him, almost like an emanation. With a long wooden pointer he chivvys the line, and he snaps his fingers at each child as if he would snap him off the earth. Scuffling, scuffing, all pellmell behind him, and he singlefiles them and marches them with synchronized steps back and back to form a new line. By the time they reach the bakery there is a rebellious shudder; by the appetizing store there are some who jeer and bray and back-talk. From one set of lips a "Dopey mutt!" seeps out. The manager crimps brows and rakes the wiseguy with his gaze, humbling and gentling him in the way that Ken Maynard will humble and gentle a wild mustang. Then, with the shade of a smile, he asks, "Hey, 'glues.' You know anything about 'glues'?" "Because when you open that mouth next time you'll 'glues' your teeth."

All grin the manager's grin.

Now the line is slackening.

Now gaps appear.

Now some awaken to the truth of things: far up front the line moves.

Now he is nearer by five cement boxes to the cashier's cage.

Now he is bumped rudely from behind, and when he wheels, fisty, full of turbulence in his belly, Rubin Metz is leering at him like a Katzenjammer Kid. He bumps back, taking care to give as much, but only as much as he has gotten. And he says, harshly wooing, "Hey, hey Rubin! Where, do you know where you're going to sit?"

Rubin offers the information eagerly: "On my ass."

He outwaits Rubin's excessive laughter, then shuts his eyes for a long moment. "You want to make up to save seats?"

"I made up already." Many expressions cross Rubin's face, but malice presides. "I'm saving for Solly and Labey and Morty and Ozzey."

Though he wishes Rubin dead at his feet, he says only, "Ozzey?", and makes a small smashing sound.

While they advance by two cement squares, and two more, Rubin tells how Ozzey stands with him and his. How he can punch a ball across two-and-a-half sewers. How what is his Ozzey gives and lends out, even 15-cent Spauldings, color pictures from the *Book of Knowledge, Boy's Life* and the *National Geographic,* aviator goggles, the Doc Savage signet ring. How Ozzey names the make and year of each and every car. How Ozzey has a secret grip for ticket toss, a killing slice in box ball. How Ozzey lights matches in Home Room. How when it was his turn to mark papers for Miss Probst he gave only 75s. How when hit by Rabbi Meltzer, Ozzey hits back.

For answer he distends his cheeks and stretches his lower lips out stupidly.

"Ozzey can beat you up," says Rubin, in a dry official tone.

"Ozzey can beat me up. Yeah. Ofcourseofcourseofcourse!"

"Any day in the week."

"Any day in the week."

"He beat up Stanley Bloom—"

"He beat up Stanley Bloom."

"—and Stanley Bloom beats you up."

"Stanley Bloom beats you up. Ofcourseofcourseofcourse!"

Then Rubin, in slow motion and using many faces, pantomimes his fight with Stanley Bloom. There is Stanley chalking his brief case. There is his slow, soft, girlish slap at Stanley's neck. There is the taking off of his glasses. There is Stanley dancing away, and there is Stanley lunging in like a fencer to chalk his briefcase again, and also his hair. There is the smile he holds and holds on his face. There is his apish charge, and there is Stanley's ballet grace. There is the feeble flapping of his open hands, and there is the bang-bang-bang of Stanley's boney dukes. There is his awe and pity at the sight of his own blood. There is the return of his glasses, the lowering of his face as he puts them on, the turning inward of his feet. There is the nice way Stanley offers his hand, and there is the sissy way he takes it. There is Stanley basking in the gaze of all, and there is his own thick, dumb-ox stance and his eyes locking to the horizon.

"I'll learn you to box," Rubin says.

"*Learn* me!"

He turns his back on Rubin. Who tells him, "Puh . . . puh . . . puh . . . puh-puh-puh-puh . . . that's how you chin." Who tugs at his muffler, bawling, "Pull the chain!" and "Flush the bowl!" Who tweaks a hair on his neck. Who treads on the heels of his shoes. Who blows great wet kissing noises in his ear.

All coiled up and vibrating, he puts his face only an inch from Rubin's face. "You think you're such a wise guy, but you're not such a wise guy. You're a,"—His voice thins out—

Laughter seeps up and down the line.

"I'm what dogs make in a street. What, what do dogs make in a street?"

Two or three chant reasonable suggestions, which he pretends to mull over, then finally turns aside.

"They make . . . in the street, it's in the street . . . itkinbe round . . . itkinbe not round . . . itkinbe long, long and thin . . . itkinbe short and fat . . . in a street, they make it in a street, longandthinshortandfat . . . A HOLE!"

He fetches shrill whoops from the line, and from Rubin a look of special caution. "A hole," he crows, seeking to revive the laughter. But there is only the urgent pressure of the line stirring, then moving him so swiftly that for an instant he is out of step. Three stores and one-and-a-half cement boxes from the front, he inhales, or thinks he inhales, many tonic odors: the cashier lady, who comes to him as a blend of Dugan's white bread, porkey franks and heavily fried eggs; the gum, phlegm, rust, pits and peel of the water fountain; the gamey plush and leather of the seats; the cotton wool, like dirty dog fur, where the seats are ruined; the musty damp air creeping through the fire doors. . . .

Fat and Skinny had a race,
All around the steeplechase,
Fat fell down and broke his face,
That's how Skinny won the race.

. . . Rubin is singing very, very slowly, huffing and puffing to show Fat's hard effort, Fat's shame and defeat.

"Lousy . . ." he launches against the choking in his throat. Then Rubin hammers his shoulders.

Then the front of Rubin's knees are suddenly fitted to the backs of his knees.

Then Rubin deftly dips, and he dips with Rubin.

Then, knees still sagging, he turns.

Then he lifts hands against Rubin.

Then Rubin lifts hands against him.

Then his arm flies out in a spasm of rage and alarm.

Then, to his immense surprise, Rubin is going "Woo!" and "Stinkercockeye!"

For with the broken button on his sleeve or the brass-buckled end of his glove he has burst the greenish cold sore alongside Rubin's lip.

He hears, "Pus!"

Also, "Stitches!"

And, "Lockjaw!"

"Hit me," he begs, while the line boils over. "Rubey?" He slaps himself. "Hard on the face even."

But Rubin only sniffles softly and flaps his hands.

"I'll take off my glasses. Hey, come on, I'm taking it off, on the face, anywhere, do it—"

"—burns, woo! Woowooitburns!"

Now the manager draws near, walking as though his feet were on fire. His sour gaze sweeps over them, his pointer parts them.

"Ho-kay, you . . . you . . . youyouyouyouyou!" The pointer takes in half the line. "Out, out, step out for the black-list."

None move; all whimper.

"Blacklist means no movies. Not in here, not in the whole circuit. Not in the *Aperion* and not in the *Garfield*. Not in the *Boulevard*, not in the *Claridge*, not in the *Festival*, not in the *Wynmore*, not in the *Emerald*, not in the *Fine Arts*. Unless . . . unleh-hess . . . one chance. . . ."

The pointer whacks the sidewalk once.

"Who started? Who—who is the troublemaking individual and rotten person that doesn't, that shouldn't deserve Kartoon Kavalcade privileges plus selected short subjects? Let me hear from his own mouth while he has teeth in it."

". . . a bloodpoison," Rubin is saying.

". . . pushing, pestering," he is saying.

"I got time," the manager chimes in. "I, I got all . . . the time . . . in . . . the . . . world. *I* know what happens in the chapter. *I* saw the Betty Boop. *I* saw the Charlie Chase. *I* saw *The Silver Bullet,* and how they kill Tom Tyler's father, and how Tom Tyler practices with his father's gun and makes a special silver bullet for the bad guy—"

Whereupon Rubin, eyes shining with unshed tears, shows the tiny squibbles of blood on his face and on his handkerchief, tells what befell him at the hands of sissy, an unfair hitter, a crybaby sneak, a dirty mouth.

"You called him that? What he said is what you said?"

"That's unfair. That's very highly unfair because . . . because. . . ."

"I only teased," Rubin maintains.

"You *teased!*"

"He can't take a tease."

"I can't take a tease? Waha, I can't take a tease, nahmuch, I—'

"—you know about Dublin?" the manager comes in sweetly. "Dublin, Ireland?"

"—like this he was pushing."

"Because where Ireland my hand is where you'll be Dublin over. Because I'm not concerned who gives a tease and I'm not interested who takes a tease. Because what I'm interested in—*what* I'm concerned for is to run a nice theater. With nice kids coming and enjoying. Nice kids. That's all. That's asking too much? Is . . . that . . . asking too much?"

He waits for the chirping of "No's."

"So what—what is a nice kid? A nice kid doesn't have to be a hundred per cent perfect. He's wild? *Let* him be wild. Let him be a *regular* guy. Let him run and jump and carry on and hit a little. But—I goes *one* but. I want him honest. He has to be honest, and if he's honest he'll go very far with me."

The pointer swishes up, out, out toward infinity.

"So—so-ho, what he said you said is what. . . ."

". . . I said . . . *sortof*Isaid."

"You're honest, you're going far with me. You know how far you're going? You're going," the manager lowers his voice confidentially—"You're going-g-g"—the manager's hand hooks under his armpit, squeezes and yanks—"around the corner, away the hell from my theater, that's where you're going with me."

And the manager pulls.

And he pulls back.

And bellies and behinds cram instantly together.

And his place in the line is usurped, absorbed, as though it never was.

And shivering, squinting, feeling strangely drowsy, he yields himself to the manager.

And in close-lock-step they pass the cashier's cage.

And they pass under the marquee.

And he sees many boys and girls who are familiar to him; he sees Myron Boroff, Vinnie Fastine, Bert Lubell, Lila Werfel, Hershel Kramer and the Edelson twins, Zeena and Miriam.

And they come to the corner.

And they round the corner.

And they draw abreast of the wall where it says NOW PLAYING, then to where it says COMING NEXT WEEK, then to where it says only COMING SOON.

And the manager's stride slackens and he pauses, turning his head so that their glances graze.

"You love your mother and dad?"

A sob blurs his reply.

"You'd want—you'd like me to call them up on the telephone and tell them they have a son, that they've been raising a boy who uses smut words?"

Taking great care with his voice he says, "Nah."

"How are you in your school, what kind of marks?"

"All right," he gets out. "I *think* all right."

"You *thi-ink* all right?"

". . . a good average."

"Spell average," the manager flashes in.

"Average, A,V,E . . . A,V,E,R,A,G,E, average."

"Piece, like in I want a piece of cake."

"That piece is an I,E word."

"What about capitol, when you're talking about a city?"

"*O, L.*"

"*O*, L. O. You're sure, then, you say *O* absolutely?" The manager examines his eyes, his face, his whole being.

"We just"—He chokes down something hot and raw—"justjustjust only had them!"

"One 'just,'" warns the manager. "Just one 'just' to me!"

He tries an agreeable smile, saying, "I meant it was a homonym and *we just* had them. Like 'capitol' when it's a city and 'capital' when it's money, like B,E,A,R and B,A—"

"—you know that, you're so-ho smart in vocabulary then why, why do you have to use smut words?"

Dull-eyed, droopy-lidded, he hangs his head forward. And suffers a rap from the pointer, a mussing of his hair.

"Ho-kay," the manager says. "I am going . . . to take . . . a . . . chance on you."

He pretends not to divine the manager's meaning.

"*Should* I take a chance on you? Should I have *con*fidence?"

Slowly, solemnly and distinctly, as though reciting the Pledge of Allegiance, he counsels the manager to take the chance, to have confidence.

"I want to hear your name and address. I want also what school, what class and what teacher."

He gladly throws in his Home Room number and Assembly seat.

And the manager's arm comes around him, turns him, rests and remains strongly on his shoulder.

And he takes care not to resist this arm, not to shy, not to flick a muscle nor show on his face the smallest desire to free himself.

And he matches his steps to the manager's steps.

And where it says COMING NEXT WEEK the manager tells him that from all this he will learn something.

And when they round the corner the manager tells him that what he will learn will be common sense.

And under the marquee the manager tells him that what he will learn is that common sense cannot be learned.

And when he is last on a new line, yet only three from the front, the manager tells him that common sense is not common.

"Once—wuh-hunce you can have that straight in your mind—"

He hears the chime and fluttery whir of the ticket machine.

"You'll never forget it through your life—"

The orange and black of his own ticket springs out.

"—make it a habit, a habit and a practice to use it—"

He straddles the threshold of the lobby, blinks against its pure golden light.

"That's C-O-M-M-O-N S-E-N-S-E," the manager's voice rumbles after.

Next is the voice of an usher crying, "Get the number for LUCKY NUMBER any number could be a LUCKY NUMBER what are you holding up the line come on. . . ."

Next is the voice of the doorman, laden with guile, delighting in itself.

"Say you whatyearwereyouborn? You, big fellow, you!"

"Eleven." He speaks as though through a yawn. "I'll be eleven."

He begins a humble, scoffing, wheedling, "Ah, ah, come on. . . ." He strives desperately to engage the doorman's fingers with his ticket.

"You're not twelve?"

"Not even eleven. You know when—"

"—you're twelve, twelve-and-a-half; go buy a full price."

". . . first *be* eleven."

"Move, scrammo, let people pass!"

"How do you know how old I am? Hah, how do you know, hah? *You* know, you!"—A blare of Movietone music sends his blood storming—"HeywillyaCOMEon!"

"Bye-bye, get going, so long."

"I'm justjustjust asking you how do you know how old I am. Just answer my question, come on, it's a fair question. . . ."

"That's a half price, that is *some* half price." The doorman raises his voice for the benefit of other ears. "What you call"—His arms curve out, describe a heavy front, a heavier behind—"a husky."

"Not your business," he lets out in a slow breath. "Nobody asked you an opinion; who asked you, so what are—"

"Tell him, 'Bite your tongue.' " A quieting hand is laid upon him, "Tell him, 'You can't afford to talk, Mister, you're not such a skinny rail.' " His head is drawn into the clotted yellow depths of a sheepskin coat. "Tell him, 'Mister, not everybody can be a perfect beauty like you.' " He squirms, gets a one-eyed glimpse of a round, soft-nosed, heavy-lipped May Robeson face. "Tell him, 'I'm with my Aunty, I happen to be with my Aunty.' " His head is knuckled like a ball, kneaded like a potato pancake, then pressed into sheepskin. "Tell him, 'My Aunty is putting her full price on top of my half price; my Aunty is taking me in with her; my Aunty who with God's help is getting now on her feet from an operation where three of the biggest professors had her on the table two hours and thirty-four minutes by the clock and for who any excitement is the worst poison. . . .'"

They go together into the semi-darkness, into the insane noise, the applause and the one giggly tremulous *boooooh* that sets itself against the voice of President Roosevelt. Near the candy counter he lags, starts to swing away, but she takes fresh hold of him, saying, "You need it? You need it badly."

He hoarsely answers, "Black Crows. Black Crows is a licorice."

"Sonny, Sonny, do without it."

"Black Crows is justjustjust licorice, Black Crows is no chocolate."

She changes her grip, clamping him against her side like a pocketbook, steering him toward the aisle that is farthest from the candy counter, saying that she means well, that the harm she wishes him should fall upon her and hers, that now is the time to watch himself, that when he gets older he will see and realize the importance of appearance, that he would be better off and a hundred times healthier with a piece of fruit.

And as they turn into the full darkness of the aisle, she gives him a choice of apples or oranges.

"MacIntosh or Delicious, navel or with seeds?"

She turns, humps her back, makes a few modest motions inside her coat and brings forth, little by little, a paper bag. She snaps off rubber bands, pinches them over a wrist, hisses a few short fitful notes between her teeth. She waits till the bag crinkles, crackles open, and when the crinkle and crackle are loudest and sharpest and prickling his flesh she plunges in more swiftly and boldly with frantic, thrashing, cumbersome motions, shakes out one, two, three lumpy envelopes.

"I even got here a persimmon, but I wouldn't advise you a persimmon on account of it got too much——"

"——us enjoy!"

"——worse than a child!"

"——wet on me!"

"——donwannaseedonseeweewannasee!"

While she deals with each of the voices, while she is blinded by the usher's flash, he veers off and runs on tip-toe, unbuttoning, peeling off, loosening, folding and refolding. Back and forth and up and down the rows he passes, peeping through one lens, then another, muttering a muted "Zitaken?", getting back only a righteous "Zitaken, zitaken!" There is nothing in the middle, and there is nothing in the back, and what he sees on the sides would put him under the glow of the Fire Exit signs.

Once he forgets to stoop as he crosses the pit, and his shadow bulks on the screen like King Kong.

"——race the clock to halt the ravages of Old Man River."

Once he thinks there is a seat where there is no seat, and he is roughly handled before he blunders out of the row.

"——for our dedicated men of science."

Once, in the middle of the middle, there is a seat and he loses it because a man will not uncross his legs to let him by.

"——an ermine trim to guard against cool ocean breezes."

Once he accidentally-on-purpose sits where there is a coat, where the seat is positively taken, and the outcry brings an usher.

"Monkeys is . . . de cwaziest pipple!"

To himself he murmurs a "Ma."

He stretches and sustains the syllable into "Maahahahaha-hahahah."

An old terror rears up in his mind.

That harm has come to her.

That they are seeking him.

That they are asking Eugene Zimmer and Henney Orloff if they know where he went, by what streets and at what time.

That his father has gone to the *Emerald,* his Cousin Yuss to the *Wynmore,* his Aunt Pearlie to the *Claridge.*

That they hear news of his mother's death.

And walking backwards up the aisle he stumbles against an usher, who chides him with, "I'll get you another pair of glasses, foureyes, hey foureyes, you can't see . . . ?"

And he follows the usher back down the aisle till they are one, two, three, four rows from the front.

And quietly, stealthily, he enters his row, making himself as small as possible and lifting his feet.

And he sits without knocking the seat in front of him, and when the elbow he plants on an arm rest is shoved away he offers no contest.

And he tunnels under his coat, and turns right, left, and half-round, and sees that he is not in the presence of his enemies.

And then, then for the first time, he lifts his eyes to the light of the screen.

Defender of the Faith

Philip Roth

In May of 1945, only a few weeks after the fighting had ended in Europe, I was rotated back to the States, where I spent the remainder of the war with a training company at Camp Crowder, Missouri. We had been racing across Germany so swiftly during the late winter and spring that when I boarded the plane that drizzly morning in Berlin, I couldn't believe our destination lay to the west. My mind might inform me otherwise, but there was an inertia of the spirit that told me we were flying to a new front where we would disembark and continue our push eastward—eastward until we'd circled the globe, marching through villages along whose twisting, cobbled streets crowds of the enemy would watch us take possession of what up till then they'd considered their own. I had changed enough in two years not to mind the trembling of the old people, the crying of the very young, the uncertain fear in the eyes of the once-arrogant. After two years I had been fortunate enough to develop an infantryman's heart which, like his feet, at first aches and swells, but finally grows horny enough for him to travel the weirdest paths without feeling a thing.

Captain Paul Barrett was to be my C. O. at Camp Crowder. The day I reported for duty he came out of his office to shake my hand. He was short, gruff, and fiery, and indoors or out he wore his polished helmet liner down on his little eyes. In Europe he had received a battlefield commission and a serious chest wound, and had been returned to the States only a few months before. He spoke easily to me, but was, I thought, unnecessarily abusive towards the troops. At the evening formation, he introduced me.

"Gentlemen," he called. "Sergeant Thurston, as you know, is no longer with this Company. Your new First Sergeant is Sergeant Nathan Marx here. He is a veteran of the European theater and consequently will take no shit."

I sat up late in the orderly room that evening, trying half-heartedly to solve the riddle of duty rosters, personnel forms, and morning reports. The CQ slept with his mouth open on a mattress on the floor. A trainee stood reading the next day's duty roster, which was posted on the bulletin board directly inside the screen door. It was a warm evening and I could hear the men's radios playing dance music over in the barracks.

The trainee, who I knew had been staring at me whenever I looked groggily into the forms, finally took a step in my direction.

"Hey, Sarge—we having a G.I. party tomorrow night?" A G.I. party is a barracks-cleaning.

"You usually have them on Friday nights?"

"Yes," and then he added mysteriously, "that's the whole thing."

"Then you'll have a G.I. party."

He turned away and I heard him mumbling. His shoulders were moving and I wondered if he was crying.

"What's your name, soldier?" I asked.

He turned, not crying at all. Instead his green-speckled eyes, long and narrow, flashed like fish in the sun. He walked over to me and sat on the edge of my desk.

He reached out a hand. "Sheldon," he said.

"Stand on your own two feet, Sheldon."

Climbing off the desk, he said, "Sheldon Grossbart." He smiled wider at the intimacy into which he'd led me.

"You against cleaning the barracks Friday night, Grossbart? Maybe we shouldn't have G.I. parties—maybe we should get a maid." My tone startled me: I felt like a Charlie McCarthy, with every top sergeant I had ever known as my Edgar Bergen.

"No, Sergeant." He grew serious, but with a seriousness that seemed only to be the stifling of a smile. "It's just G.I. parties on Friday night, of all nights . . ."

He slipped up to the corner of the desk again—not quite sitting, but not quite standing either. He looked at me with those speckled eyes flashing and then made a gesture with his hand. It was very slight, no more than a rotation back and forth of the wrist, and yet it managed to exclude from our affairs everything else in the orderly room, to make the two of us the center of the world. It seemed, in fact, to exclude everything about the two of us except our hearts. "Sergeant Thurston was one thing," he whispered, an eye flashing to the sleeping CQ "but we thought with you here, things might be a little different."

"We?"

"The Jewish personnel."

"Why?" I said, harshly.

He hesitated a moment, and then, uncontrollably, his hand went up to his mouth. "I mean . . ." he said.

"What's on your mind?" Whether I was still angry at the "Sheldon" business or something else, I hadn't a chance to tell—but clearly I was angry.

". . . we thought you . . . Marx, you know, like Karl Marx. The Marx brothers. Those guys are all . . . M-A-R-X, isn't that how you spell it, Sergeant?"

"M-A-R-X."

"Fishbein said—" He stopped. "What I mean to say, Sergeant—" His face and neck were red, and his mouth moved but no words came out. In a moment, he raised himself to attention, gazing down at me. It was as though he had suddenly decided he could expect no more sympathy from me than from Thurston, the reason being that I was of Thurston's faith and not his. The young man had managed to confuse himself as to what my faith really was, but I felt no desire to straighten him out. Very simply, I didn't like him.

When I did nothing but return his gaze, he spoke, in an altered tone. "You see, Sergeant," he explained to me, "Friday nights, Jews are supposed to go to services."

"Did Sergeant Thurston tell you you couldn't go to them when there was a G.I. party?"

"No."

"Did he say you had to stay and scrub the floors?"

"No, Sergeant."

"Did the Captain say you had to stay and scrub the floors?"

"That isn't it, Sergeant. It's the other guys in the barracks." He leaned toward me. "They think we're goofing off. But we're not. That's when Jews go to services, Friday night. We have to."

"Then go."

"But the other guys make accusations. They have no right."

"That's not the Army's problem, Grossbart. It's a personal problem you'll have to work out yourself."

"But it's un*fair*."

I got up to leave. "There's nothing I can do about it," I said.

Grossbart stiffened in front of me. "But this is a matter of *religion,* sir."

"Sergeant."

"I mean 'Sergeant,'" he said, almost snarling.

"Look, go see the chaplain. The I.G. You want to see Captain Barrett, I'll arrange an appointment."

"No, no. I don't want to make trouble, Sergeant. That's the first thing they throw up to you. I just want my rights!"

"Damn it, Grossbart, stop whining. You have your rights. You can stay and scrub floors or you can go to *shul—*"

The smile swam in again. Spittle gleamed at the corners of his mouth. "You mean church, Sergeant."

"I mean *shul,* Grossbart!" I walked past him and outside. Near me I heard the scrunching of a guard's boots on gravel. In the lighted windows of the barracks the young men in T-shirts and fatigue pants were sitting on their bunks, polishing their rifles. Suddenly there was a light rustling behind me. I turned and saw Grossbart's dark frame fleeing back to the barracks, racing to tell his Jewish friends that they were right —that like Karl and Harpo, I was one of them.

The next morning, while chatting with the Captain, I recounted the incident of the previous evening, as if to unburden myself of it. Somehow in the telling it seemed to the Captain that I was not so much explaining Grossbart's position as defending it.

"Marx, I'd fight side by side with a nigger if the fellow proved to me he was a man. I pride myself," the Captain said looking out the window, "that I've got an open mind. Consequently, Sergeant, nobody gets special treatment here, for the good *or* the bad. All a man's got to do is prove himself. A man fires well on the range, I give him a weekend pass. He scores high in PT, he gets a weekend pass. He *earns* it." He turned from the window and pointed a finger at me. "You're a Jewish fellow, am I right, Marx?"

"Yes, sir."

"And I admire you. I admire you because of the ribbons on your chest, not because you had a hem stitched on your dick before you were old enough to even know you had one. I judge a man by what he shows me on the field of battle,

Sergeant. It's what he's got *here*," he said, and then, though I expected he would point to his heart, he jerked a thumb towards the buttons straining to hold his blouse across his belly. "Guts," he said.

"Okay, sir. I only wanted to pass on to you how the men felt."

"Mr. Marx, you're going to be old before your time if you worry about how the men feel. Leave that stuff to the Chaplain—pussy, the clap, church picnics with the little girls from Joplin, that's all his business, not yours. Let's us train these fellas to shoot straight. If the Jewish personnel feels the other men are accusing them of goldbricking . . . well, I just don't know. Seems awful funny how suddenly the Lord is calling so loud in Private Grossman's ear he's just got to run to church."

"Synagogue," I said.

"Synagogue is right, Sergeant. I'll write that down for handy reference. Thank you for stopping by."

That evening, a few minutes before the company gathered outside the orderly room for the chow formation, I called the CQ, Corporal Robert LaHill, in to see me. LaHill was a dark burly fellow whose hair curled out of his clothes wherever it could. He carried a glaze in his eyes that made one think of caves and dinosaurs. "LaHill," I said, "when you take the formation, remind the men that they're free to attend church services *whenever* they are held, provided they report to the orderly room before they leave the area."

LaHill didn't flicker; he scratched his wrist, but gave no indication that he'd heard or understood.

"LaHill," I said, "*church*. You remember? Church, priest, Mass, confession . . ."

He curled one lip into a ghastly smile; I took it for a signal that for a second he had flickered back up into the human race.

"Jewish personnel who want to attend services this evening are to fall out in front of the orderly room at 1900." And then I added, "By order of Captain Barrett."

A little while later, as a twilight softer than any I had seen that year dropped over Camp Crowder, I heard LaHill's thick, inflectionless voice outside my window: "Give me your ears, troopers. Toppie says for me to tell you that at 1900 hours all Jewish personnel is to fall out in front here if they wants to attend the Jewish Mass."

At seven o'clock, I looked out of the orderly-room window and saw three soldiers in starched khakis standing alone on the dusty quadrangle. They looked at their watches and fidgeted while they whispered back and forth. It was getting darker, and alone on the deserted field they looked tiny. When I walked to the door I heard the noises of the G.I. party coming from the surrounding barracks—bunks being pushed to the wall, faucets pounding water into buckets, brooms whisking at the wooden floors. In the windows big puffs of cloth moved round and round, cleaning the dirt away for Saturday's inspection. I walked outside and the moment my foot hit the ground I thought I heard Grossbart, who was now in the center, call to the other two, "Ten-*hut*!" Or maybe when they all three jumped to attention, I imagined I heard the command.

At my approach, Grossbart stepped forward. "Thank you, sir," he said.

"Sergeant, Grossbart," I reminded him. "You call officers 'Sir.' I'm not an officer. You've been in the Army three weeks—you know that."

He turned his palms out at his sides to indicate that, in truth, he and I lived beyond convention. "Thank you, anyway," he said.

"Yes," the tall boy behind him said. "Thanks a lot."

And the third whispered, "Thank you," but his mouth barely fluttered so that he did not alter by more than a lip's movement, the posture of attention.

"For what?" I said.

Grossbart snorted, happily. "For the announcement before. The Corporal's announcement. It helped. It made it . . ."

"Fancier." It was the tall boy finishing Grossbart's sentence.

Grossbart smiled. "He means formal, sir. Public," he said to me. "Now it won't seem as though we're just taking off, goldbricking, because the work has begun."

"It was by order of Captain Barrett," I said.

"Ahh, but you pull a little weight . . ." Grossbart said. "So we thank you." Then he turned to his companions. "Sergeant Marx, I want you to meet Larry Fishbein."

The tall boy stepped forward and extended his hand. I shook it. "You from New York?" he asked.

"Yes."

"Me too." He had a cadaverous face that collapsed inward from his cheekbone to his jaw, and when he smiled—as he did at the news of our communal attachment—revealed a mouthful of bad teeth. He blinked his eyes a good deal, as though he were fighting back tears. "What borough?" he asked.

I turned to Grossbart. "It's five after seven. What time are services?"

"*Shul,*" he smiled, "is in ten minutes. I want you to meet Mickey Halpern. This is Nathan Marx, our Sergeant."

The third boy hopped forward. "Private Michael Halpern." He saluted.

"Salute officers, Halpern." The boy dropped his hand, and in his nervousness checked to see if his shirt pockets were buttoned on the way down.

"Shall I march them over, sir?" Grossbart asked, "or are you coming along?"

From behind Grossbart, Fishbein piped up. "Afterwards they're having refreshments. A Ladies' Auxiliary from St. Louis, the rabbi told us last week."

"The chaplain," whispered Halpern.

"You're welcome to come along," Grossbart said.

To avoid his plea, I looked away, and saw, in the windows of the barracks, a cloud of faces staring out at the four of us.

"Look, hurry out of here, Grossbart."

"Okay, then," he said. He turned to the others. "Double time, *march!*" and they started off, but ten feet away Grossbart spun about, and running backwards he called to me, "Good *shabus,* sir." And then the three were swallowed into the Missouri dusk.

Even after they'd disappeared over the parade grounds, whose green was now a deep twilight blue, I could hear Grossbart singing the double-time cadence, and as it grew dimmer and dimmer it suddenly touched some deep memory—as did the slant of light—and I was remembering the shrill sounds of a Bronx playground, where years ago, beside the Grand Concourse, I had played on long spring evenings such as this. Those thin fading sounds . . . It was a pleasant memory for a young man so far from peace and home, and it brought so very many recollections with it that I began to grow exceedingly tender about myself. In fact, I indulged my-

self to a reverie so strong that I felt within as though a hand
had opened and was reaching down inside. It had to reach so
very far to touch me. It had to reach past those days in the
forests of Belgium and the dying I'd refused to weep over;
past the nights in those German farmhouses whose books
we'd burned to warm us, and which I couldn't bother to
mourn; past those endless stretches when I'd shut off all softness I might feel for my fellows, and managed even to deny
myself the posture of a conqueror—the swagger that I, as a
Jew, might well have worn as my boots whacked against the
rubble of Münster, Braunschweig, and finally Berlin.

But now one night noise, one rumor of home and time
past, and memory plunged down through all I had anesthetized
and came to what I suddenly remembered to be myself. So it
was not altogether curious that in search of more of me I
found myself following Grossbart's tracks to Chapel No. 3
where the Jewish services were being held.

I took a seat in the last row, which was empty. Two rows
in front sat Grossbart, Fishbein, and Halpern, each holding
a little white dixie cup. Fishbein was pouring the contents of
his cup into Grossbart's, and Grossbart looked mirthful as the
liquid drew a purple arc between his hand and Fishbein's. In
the glary yellow light, I saw the chaplain on the pulpit chanting the first line of the responsive reading. Grossbart's prayerbook remained closed on his lap; he swished the cup around.
Only Halpern responded in prayer. The fingers of his right
hand were spread wide across the cover of the book, and his
cap was pulled down low onto his brow so that it was round
like a *yarmulke* rather than long and pointed. From time to
time, Grossbart wet his lips at the cup's edge; Fishbein, his
long yellow face, a dying light bulb, looked from here to
there, leaning forward at the neck to catch sight of the faces
down the row, in front—then behind. He saw me and his eyelids beat a tattoo. His elbow slid into Grossbart's side, his
neck inclined towards his friend, and then, when the congregation responded, Grossbart's voice was among them. Fishbein looked into his book now too; his lips, however, didn't
move.

Finally it was time to drink the wine. The chaplain smiled
down at them as Grossbart swigged in one long gulp, Halpern sipped, meditating, and Fishbein faked devotion with an
empty cup.

At last the chaplain spoke: "As I look down amongst the
congregation—" he grinned at the word, "this night, I see

many new faces, and I want to welcome you to Friday night services here at Camp Crowder. I am major Leo Ben Ezra, your chaplain . . ." Though an American, the chaplain spoke English very deliberately, syllabically almost, as though to communicate, above all, to the lip-readers in the audience. "I have only a few words to say before we adjourn to the refreshment room where the kind ladies of the Temple Sinai, St. Louis, Missouri, have a nice setting for you."

Applause and whistling broke out. After a momentary grin, the chaplain raised his palms to the congregation, his eyes flicking upward a moment, as if to remind the troops where they were and Who Else might be in attendance. In the sudden silence that followed, I thought I heard Grossbart's cackle —"Let the goyim clean the floors!" Were those the words? I wasn't sure, but Fishbein, grinning, nudged Halpern. Halpern looked dumbly at him, then went back to his prayerbook, which had been occupying him all through the rabbi's talk. One hand tugged at the black kinky hair that stuck out under his cap. His lips moved.

The rabbi continued. "It is about the food that I want to speak to you for a moment. I know, I know, I know," he intoned, wearily, "how in the mouths of most of you the *trafe* food tastes like ashes. I know how you gag, some of you, and how your parents suffer to think of their children eating foods unclean and offensive to the palate. What can I tell you? I can only say close your eyes and swallow as best you can. Eat what you must to live and throw away the rest. I wish I could help more. For those of you who find this impossible, may I ask that you try and try, but then come to see me in private where, if your revulsion is such, we will have to seek aid from those higher up."

A round of chatter rose and subsided; then everyone sang "Ain Kelohanoh"; after all those years I discovered I still knew the words.

Suddenly, the service over, Grossbart was upon me. "Higher up? He means the General?"

"Hey, Shelly," Fishbein interrupted, "he means God." He smacked his face and looked at Halpern. "How high can you go!"

"Shhh!" Grossbart said. "What do you think, Sergeant?"

"I don't know. You better ask the chaplain."

"I'm going to. I'm making an appointment to see him in private. So is Mickey."

Halpern shook his head. "No, no, Sheldon . . ."

"You have rights, Mickey. They can't push us around."

"It's okay. It bothers my mother, not me . . ."

Grossbart looked at me. "Yesterday he threw up. From the hash. It was all ham and God knows what else."

"I have a cold—that was why," Halpern said. He pushed his *yamalkah* back into a cap.

"What about you, Fishbein?" I asked. "You kosher too?"

He flushed, which made the yellow more gray than pink. "A little. But I'll let it ride. I have a very strong stomach. And I don't eat a lot anyway . . ." I continued to look at him, and he held up his wrist to re-enforce what he'd just said. His watch was tightened to the last hole and he pointed that out to me. "So I don't mind."

"But services are important to you?" I asked him.

He looked at Grossbart. "Sure, sir."

"Sergeant."

"Not so much at home," said Grossbart, coming between us, "but away from home it gives one a sense of his Jewishness."

"We have to stick together," Fishbein said.

I started to walk towards the door; Halpern stepped back to make way for me.

"That's what happened in Germany," Grossbart was saying, loud enough for me to hear. "They didn't stick together. They let themselves get pushed around."

I turned. "Look, Grossbart, this is the Army, not summer camp."

He smiled. "So?" Halpern tried to sneak off, but Grossbart held his arm. "So?" he said again.

"Grossbart," I asked, "how old are you?"

"Nineteen."

"And you?" I said to Fishbein.

"The same. The same month even."

"And what about him?" I pointed to Halpern, who'd finally made it safely to the door.

"Eighteen," Grossbart whispered. "But he's like he can't tie his shoes or brush his teeth himself. I feel sorry for him."

"I feel sorry for all of us, Grossbart, but just act like a man. Just don't overdo it."

"Overdo what, sir?"

"The sir business. Don't overdo that," I said, and I left him standing there. I passed by Halpern but he did not look up. Then I was outside, black surrounded me—but behind I heard Grossbart call, "Hey, Mickey, *liebschen,* come on back. Refreshments!"

Liebschen! My grandmother's word for me!

One morning, a week later, while I was working at my desk, Captain Barrett shouted for me to come into his office. When I entered, he had his helmet liner squashed down so that I couldn't even see his eyes. He was on the phone, and when he spoke to me, he cupped one hand over the mouthpiece.

"Who the fuck is Grossbart?"

"Third platoon, Captain," I said. "A trainee."

"What's all this stink about food? His mother called a goddam congressman about the food . . ." He uncovered the mouthpiece and slid his helmet up so I could see the curl of his bottom eyelash. "Yes, sir," he said into the phone. "Yes, sir. I'm still here, sir. I'm asking Marx here right now . . ."

He covered the mouthpiece again and looked back to me. "Lightfoot Harry's on the phone," he said, between his teeth. "This congressman calls General Lyman who calls Colonel Sousa who calls the Major who calls me. They're just dying to stick this thing on me. What's a matter," he shook the phone at me, "I don't feed the troops? What the hell is this?"

"Sir, Grossbart is strange . . ." Barrett greeted that with a mockingly indulgent smile. I altered my approach. "Captain, he's a very orthodox Jew and so he's only allowed to eat certain foods."

"He throws up, the congressman said. Every time he eats something his mother says he throws up!"

"He's accustomed to observing the dietary laws, Captain."

"So why's his old lady have to call the White House!"

"Jewish parents, sir, they're apt to be more protective than you expect. I mean Jews have a very close family life. A boy goes away from home, sometimes the mother is liable to get very upset. Probably the boy *mentioned* something in a letter and his mother misinterpreted."

"I'd like to punch him one right in the mouth. There's a goddam war on and he wants a silver platter!"

"I don't think the boy's to blame, sir. I'm sure we can straighten it out by just asking him. Jewish parents worry—"

"*All* parents worry, for Christ sake. But they don't get on their high horse and start pulling strings—"

I interrupted, my voice higher, tighter than before. "The home life, Captain, is so very important . . . but you're right, it may sometimes get out of hand. It's a very wonderful thing, Captain, but because it's so close, this kind of thing—"

He didn't listen any longer to my attempt to present both myself and Lightfoot Harry with an explanation for the letter. He turnel back to the phone. "Sir?" he said. "Sir, Marx here tells me Jews have a tendency to be pushy. He says he thinks he can settle it right here in the Company . . . Yes, sir . . . I *will* call back, sir, soon as I can . . ." He hung up. "Where are the men, Sergeant?"

"On the range."

With a whack on the top, he crushed his helmet over his eyes, and charged out of his chair. "We're going for a ride."

The Captain drove and I sat beside him. It was a hot spring day and under my newly starched fatigues it felt as though my armpits were melting down onto my sides and chest. The roads were dry and by the time we reached the firing range, my teeth felt gritty with dust though my mouth had been shut the whole trip. The Captain slammed the brakes on and told me to get the hell out and find Grossbart.

I found him on his belly, firing wildly at the 500 feet target. Waiting their turns behind him were Halpern and Fishbein. Fishbein, wearing a pair of rimless G.I. glasses I hadn't seen on him before, gave the appearance of an old peddler who would gladly have sold you the rifle and cartridges that were slung all over him. I stood back by the ammo boxes, waiting for Grossbart to finish spraying the distant targets. Fishbein straggled back to stand near me.

"Hello, Sergeant Marx."

"How are you?" I mumbled.

"Fine, thank you. Sheldon's really a good shot."

"I didn't notice."

"I'm not so good, but I think I'm getting the hang of it now . . . Sergeant, I don't mean to, you know, ask what I shouldn't . . ." The boy stopped. He was trying to speak intimately but the noise of the shooting necessitated that he shout at me.

"What is it?" I asked. Down the range I saw Captain Barrett standing up in the jeep, scanning the line for me and Grossbart.

"My parents keep asking and asking where we're going. Everybody says the Pacific. I don't care, but my parents . . . If I could relieve their minds I think I could concentrate more on my shooting."

"I don't know where, Fishbein. Try to concentrate anyway."

"Sheldon says you might be able to find out—"

"I don't know a thing, Fishbein. You just take it easy, and don't let Sheldon—"

"*I'm* taking it easy, Sergeant. It's at home—"

Grossbart had just finished on the line and was dusting his fatigues with one hand. I left Fishbein's sentence in the middle.

"Grossbart, the Captain wants to see you."

He came toward us. His eyes blazed and twinkled. "Hi!"

"Don't point that goddam rifle!"

"I wouldn't shoot you, Sarge." He gave me a smile wide as as a pumpkin as he turned the barrel aside.

"Damn you, Grossbart—this is no joke! Follow me."

I walked ahead of him and had the awful suspicion that behind me Grossbart was *marching*, his rifle on his shoulder, as though he were a one-man detachment.

At the jeep he gave the Captain a rifle salute. "Private Sheldon Grossbart, sir."

"At ease, Grossman." The captain slid over to the empty front seat, and crooking a finger, invited Grossbart closer.

"Bart, sir. Sheldon Gross*bart*. It's a common error." Grossbart nodded to me—*I* understand, he indicated. I looked away, just as the mess truck pulled up to the range, disgorging a half dozen K.P.'s with rolled-up sleeves. The mess sergeant screamed at them while they set up the chow line equipment.

"Grossbart, your mama wrote some congressman that we don't feed you right. Do you know that?" the Captain said.

"It was my father, sir. He wrote to Representative Franconi that my religion forbids me to eat certain foods."

"What religion is that, Grossbart?"

"Jewish."

"Jewish, *sir*," I said to Grossbart.

"Excuse me, sir. 'Jewish, sir.' "

"What have you been living on?" the Captain asked. "You've been in the Army a month already. You don't look to me like you're falling to pieces."

"I eat because I have to, sir. But Sergeant Marx will testify to the fact that I don't eat one mouthful more than I need to in order to survive."

"Marx," Barrett asked, "is that so?"

"I've never seen Grossbart eat, sir," I said.

"But you heard the rabbi," Grossbart said. "He told us what to do, and I listened."

The Captain looked at me. "Well, Marx?"

"I still don't know what he eats and doesn't eat, sir."

Grossbart raised his rifle, as though to offer it to me. "But, Sergeant—"

"Look, Grossbart, just answer the Captain's questions!" I said sharply.

Barrett smiled at me and I resented it. "All right, Grossbart," he said, "what is it you want? The little piece of paper? You want out?"

"No, sir. Only to be allowed to live as a Jew. And for the others, too."

"What others?"

"Fishbein, sir, and Halpern."

"They don't like the way we serve either?"

"Halpern throws up, sir. I've seen it."

"I thought *you* throw up."

"Just once, sir. I didn't know the sausage was sausage."

"We'll give menus, Grossbart. We'll show training films about the food, so you can identify when we're trying to poison you."

Grossbart did not answer. Out before me, the men had been organized into two long chow lines. At the tail end of one I spotted Fishbein—or rather, his glasses spotted me. They winked sunlight back at me like a friend. Halpern stood next to him, patting inside his collar with a khaki handkerchief. They moved with the line as it began to edge up towards the food. The mess sergeant was still screaming at the K.P.'s, who stood ready to ladle out the food, bewildered. For a moment I was actually terrorized by the thought that somehow the mess sergeant was going to get involved in Grossbart's problem.

"Come over here, Marx," the Captain said to me. "Marx, you're a Jewish fella, am I right?"

I played straight man. "Yes, sir."

"How long you been in the Army? Tell this boy."

"Three years and two months."

"A year in combat, Grossbart. Twelve goddam months in combat all through Europe. I admire this man," the Captain said, snapping a wrist against my chest. "But do you hear him peeping about the food? Do you? I want an answer, Grossbart. Yes or no."

"No, sir."

"And why not? He's a Jewish fella."

"Some things are more important to some Jews than other things to other Jews."

Barrett blew up. "Look, Grossbart, Marx here is a good man, a goddam *hero*. When you were sitting on your sweet ass in school, Sergeant Marx was killing Germans. Who does more for the Jews, you by throwing up over a lousy piece of sausage, a piece of firstcut meat—or Marx by killing those Nazi bastards? If I were a Jew, Grossbart, I'd kiss this man's feet. He's a goddam hero, you know that? And *he* eats what we give him. Why do you have to cause trouble is what I want to know! What is it you're buckin' for, a discharge?"

"No, sir."

"I'm talking to a *wall!* Sergeant, get him out of my way." Barrett pounced over to the driver's seat. "I'm going to see the chaplain!" The engine roared, the jeep spun around, and then, raising a whirl of dust, the Captain was headed back to camp.

For a moment, Grossbart and I stood side by side, watching the jeep. Then he looked at me and said, "I don't want to start trouble. That's the first thing they toss up to us."

When he spoke I saw that his teeth were white and straight, and the sight of them suddenly made me understand that Grossbart actually did have parents: that once upon a time someone had taken little Sheldon to the dentist. He was someone's son. Despite all the talk about his parents, it was hard to believe in Grossbart as a child, an heir—as related by blood to anyone, mother, father, or, above all, to me. This realization led me to another.

"What does your father do, Grossbart?" I asked, as we started to walk back towards the chow line.

"He's a tailor."

"An American?"

"Now, yes. A son in the Army," he said, jokingly.

"And your mother?" I asked.

He winked. "A *ballabusta*—she practically sleeps with a dustcloth in her hand."

"She's also an immigrant?"

"All she talks is Yiddish, still."

"And your father too?"

"A little English. 'Clean,' 'Press,' 'Take the pants in . . .' That's the extent of it. But they're good to me . . ."

"Then, Grossbart—" I reached out and stopped him. He

turned towards me and when our eyes met his seemed to jump back, shiver in their sockets. He looked afraid. "Grossbart, then you were the one who wrote that letter, weren't you?"

It took only a second or two for his eyes to flash happy again. "Yes." He walked on, and I kept pace. "It's what my father *would* have written if he had known how. It was his name, though. *He* signed it. He even mailed it. I sent it home. For the New York postmark."

I was astonished, and he saw it. With complete seriousness, he thrust his right arm in front of me. "Blood is blood, Sergeant," he said, pinching the blue vein in his wrist.

"What the hell *are* you trying to do, Grossbart? I've seen you eat. Do you know that? I told the Captain I don't know what you eat, but I've seen you eat like a hound at chow."

"We work hard, Sergeant. We're in training. For a furnace to work, you've got to feed it coal."

"If you wrote the letter, Grossbart, then why did you say you threw up all the time?"

"I was really talking about Mickey there. But he would never write, Sergeant, though I pleaded with him. He'll waste away to nothing if I don't help. Sergeant, I used my name, my father's name, but it's Mickey and Fishbein too I'm watching out for."

"You're a regular Messiah, aren't you?"

We were at the chow line now.

"That's a good one, Sergeant." He smiled. "But who knows? Who can tell? Maybe you're the Messiah . . . a little bit. What Mickey says is the Messiah is a collective idea. He went to Yeshivah, Mickey, for a while. He says *together* we're the Messiah. Me a little bit, you a little bit . . . You should hear that kid talk, Sergeant, when he gets going."

"Me a little bit, you a little bit. You'd like to believe that, wouldn't you, Grossbart? That makes everything so clean for you."

"It doesn't seem too bad a thing to believe, Sergeant. It only means we should all give a little, is all . . ."

I walked off to eat my rations with the other noncoms.

Two days later a letter addressed to Captain Barrett passed over my desk. It had come through the chain of command—from the office of Congressman Franconi, where it had been received, to General Lyman, to Colonel Sousa, to Major

Lamont, to Captain Barrett. I read it over twice while the Captain was at the officers' mess. It was dated May 14th, the day Barrett had spoken with Grossbart on the rifle range.

Dear Congressman:

First let me thank you for your interest in behalf of my son, Private Sheldon Grossbart. Fortunately, I was able to speak with Sheldon on the phone the other night, and I think I've been able to solve our problem. He is, as I mentioned in my last letter, a very religious boy, and it was only with the greatest difficulty that I could persuade him that the religious things to do—what God Himself would want Sheldon to do—would be to suffer the pangs of religious remorse for the good of his country and all mankind. It took some doing, Congressman, but finally he saw the light. In fact, what he said (and I wrote down the words on a scratch pad so as never to forget), what he said was, "I guess you're right, Dad. So many millions of my fellow Jews gave up their lives to the enemy, the least I can do is live for a while minus a bit of my heritage so as to help end this struggle and regain for all the children of God dignity and humanity." That, Congressman, would make any father proud.

By the way, Sheldon wanted me to know—and to pass on to you—the name of a soldier who helped him reach this decision: SERGEANT NATHAN MARX. Sergeant Marx is a combat veteran who is Sheldon's First Sergeant. This man has helped Sheldon over some of the first hurdles he's had to face in the Army, and is in part responsible for Sheldon's changing his mind about the dietary laws. I know Sheldon would appreciate any recognition Marx could receive.

Thank you and good luck. I look forward to seeing your name on the next election ballot.

Respectfully,

SAMUEL E. GROSSBART

Attached to the Grossbart communiqué was a communiqué addressed to General Marshall Lyman, the post commander, and signed by Representative Charles E. Franconi of the House of Representatives. The communiqué informed General Lyman that Sergeant Nathan Marx was a credit to the U.S. Army and the Jewish people.

What was Grossbart's motive in recanting? Did he feel he'd gone too far? Was the letter a strategic retreat—a crafty attempt to strengthen what he considered our alliance? Or had he actually changed his mind, via an imaginary dialogue between Grossbart *père* and *fils?* I was puzzled, but only for a few days—that is, only until I realized that whatever his reasons, he had actually decided to disappear from my life: he was going to allow himself to become just another trainee. I saw him at inspection but he never winked; at chow formations but he never flashed me a sign; on Sundays, with the other trainees, he would sit around watching the noncoms' softball team, for whom I pitched, but not once did he speak an unnecessary or unusual word to me. Fishbein and Halpern retreated from sight too, at Grossbart's command I was sure. Apparently he'd seen that wisdom lay in turning back before he plunged us over into the ugliness of privilege undeserved. Our separation allowed me to forgive him our past encounters, and, finally, to admire him for his good sense.

Meanwhile, free of Grossbart, I grew used to my job and my administrative tasks. I stepped on a scale one day and discovered I had truly become a noncombatant: I had gained seven pounds. I found patience to get past the first three pages of a book. I thought about the future more and more, and wrote letters to girls I'd known before the war—I even got a few answers. I sent away to Columbia for a Law School catalogue. I continued to follow the war in the Pacific, but it was not my war and I read of bombings and battles like a civilian. I thought I could see the end in sight and sometimes at night I dreamed that I was walking on streets of Manhattan—Broadway, Third Avenue, and 116th Street, where I had lived those three years I'd attended Columbia College. I curled myself around these dreams and I began to be happy.

And then one Saturday when everyone was away and I was alone in the orderly room reading a month-old copy of *The Sporting News,* Grossbart reappeared.

"You a baseball fan, Sergeant?"

I looked up. "How are you?"

"Fine," Grossbart said. "They're making a soldier out of me."

"How are Fishbein and Halpern?"

"Coming along," he said. "We've got no training this afternoon. They're at the movies."

"How come you're not with them?"

"I wanted to come over and say hello."

He smiled—a shy, regular-guy smile, as though he and I well knew that our friendship drew its sustenance from unexpected visits, remembered birthdays, and borrowed lawnmowers. At first it offended me, and then the feeling was swallowed by the general uneasiness I felt at the thought that everyone on the post was locked away in a dark movie theater and I was here alone with Grossbart. I folded my paper.

"Sergeant," he said, "I'd like to ask a favor. It is a favor and I'm making no bones about it."

He stopped, allowing me to refuse him a hearing—which, of course, forced me into a courtesy I did not intend. "Go ahead."

"Well, actually it's two favors."

I said nothing.

"The first one's about these rumors. Everybody says we're going to the Pacific."

"As I told your friend Fishbein, I don't know. You'll just have to wait to find out. Like everybody else."

"You think there's a chance of any of us going East?"

"Germany," I said, "maybe."

"I meant New York."

"I don't think so, Grossbart. Offhand."

"Thanks for the information, Sergeant," he said.

"It's not information, Grossbart. Just what I surmise."

"It certainly would be good to be near home. My parents . . . you know." He took a step towards the door and then turned back. "Oh the other thing. May I ask the other?"

"What is it?"

"The other thing is—I've got relatives in St. Louis and they say they'll give me a whole Passover dinner if I can get down there. God, Sergeant, that'd mean an awful lot to me."

I stood up. "No passes during basic, Grossbart."

"But we're off from now till Monday morning, Sergeant. I could leave the post and no one would ever know."

"I'd know. You'd know."

"But that's all. Just the two of us. Last night I called my aunt and you should have heard her. 'Come, come,' she said. 'I got gefilte fish, *chrain*, the works!' Just a day, Sergeant, I'd take the blame if anything happened."

"The captain isn't here to sign a pass."

"You could sign."

"Look, Grossbart—"

"Sergeant, for two months practically I've been eating *trafe* till I want to die."

"I thought you'd made up your mind to live with it. To be minus a little bit of heritage."

He pointed a finger at me. "You!" he said. "That wasn't for you to read!"

"I read it. So what."

"That letter was addressed to a congressman."

"Grossbart, don't feed me any crap. You *wanted* me to read it."

"Why are you persecuting me, Sergeant?"

"Are you kidding!"

"I've run into this before," he said, "but never from my own!"

"Get out of here, Grossbart! Get the hell out of my sight!"

He did not move. "Ashamed, that's what you are. So you take it out on the rest of us. They say Hitler himself was half a Jew. Seeing this, I wouldn't doubt it!"

"What are you trying to do with me, Grossbart? What are you after? You want me to give you special privileges, to change the food, to find out about your orders, to give you weekend passes."

"You even talk like a goy!" Grossbart shook his fist. "Is this a weekend pass I'm asking for? Is a Seder sacred or not?"

Seder! It suddenly occurred to me that Passover had been celebrated weeks before. I confronted Grossbart with the fact.

"That's right," he said. "Who says no? A month ago, and *I* was in the field eating hash! And now all I ask is a simple favor—a Jewish boy I thought would understand. My aunt's willing to go out of her way—to make a Seder a month later—" He turned to go, mumbling.

"Come back here!" I called. He stopped and looked at me. "Grossbart, why can't you be like the rest? Why do you have to stick out like a sore thumb? Why do you beg for special treatment?"

"Because I'm a Jew, Sergeant. I *am* different. Better, maybe not. But different."

"This is a war, Grossbart. For the time being *be* the same."

"I refuse."

"What?"

"I refuse. I can't stop being me, that's all there is to it." Tears came to his eyes. "It's a hard thing to be a Jew. But

now I see what Mickey says—it's a harder thing to stay one."
He raised a hand sadly toward me. "Look at you."

"Stop crying!"

"Stop this, stop that, stop the other thing! You stop, Sergeant. Stop closing your heart to your own!" And wiping his face with his sleeve, he ran out of the door. "The least we can do for one another . . . the least . . ."

An hour later I saw Grossbart headed across the field. He wore a pair of starched khakis and carried only a little leather ditty bag. I went to the door and from the outside felt the heat of the day. It was quiet—not a soul in sight except over by the mess hall four K.P.'s sitting round a pan, sloped forward from the waists, gabbing and peeling potatoes in the sun.

"Grossbart!" I called.

He looked toward me and continued walking.

"Grossbart, get over here!"

He turned and stepped into his long shadow. Finally he stood before me.

"Where are you going?" I said.

"St. Louis. I don't care."

"You'll get caught without a pass."

"So I'll get caught without a pass."

"You'll go to the stockade."

"I'm in the stockade." He made an about-face and headed off.

I let him go only a step: "Come back here," I said, and he followed me into the office, where I typed out a pass and signed the Captain's name and my own initials after it.

He took the pass from me and then, a moment later, he reached out and grabbed my hand. "Sergeant, you don't know how much this means to me."

"Okay. Don't get in any trouble."

"I wish I could show you how much this means to me."

"Don't do me any favors. Don't write any more congressmen for citations."

Amazingly, he smiled. "You're right. I won't. But let me do something."

"Bring me a piece of that gefilte fish. Just get out of here."

"I will! With a slice of carrot and a little horseradish. I won't forget."

"All right. Just show your pass at the gate. And don't tell *anybody*."

"I won't. It's a month late, but a good Yom Tov to you."

"Good Yom Tov, Grossbart," I said.

"You're a good Jew, Sergeant. You like to think you have a hard heart, but underneath you're a fine decent man. I mean that."

Those last three words touched me more than any words from Grossbart's mouth had the right to. "All right, Grossbart. Now call me 'sir' and get the hell out of here."

He ran out the door and was gone. I felt very pleased with myself—it was a great relief to stop fighting Grossbart. And it had cost me nothing. Barrett would never find out, and if he did, I could manage to invent some excuse. For a while I sat at my desk, comfortable in my decision. Then the screen door flew back and Grossbart burst in again. "Sergeant!" he said. Behind him I saw Fishbein and Halpern, both in starched khakis, both carrying ditty bags exactly like Grossbart's.

"Sergeant, I caught Mickey and Larry coming out of the movies. I almost missed them."

"Grossbart, did I say tell no one?"

"But my aunt said I could bring friends. That I should, in fact."

"I'm the Sergeant, Grossbart—not your aunt!"

Grossbart looked at me in disbelief; he pulled Halpern up by his sleeve. "Mickey, tell the Sergeant what this would mean to you."

"Grossbart, for God's sake, spare us—"

"Tell him what you told me, Mickey. How much it would mean."

Halpern looked at me and, shrugging his shoulders, made his admission. "A lot."

Fishbein stepped forward without prompting. "This would mean a great deal to me and my parents, Sergeant Marx."

"No!" I shouted.

Grossbart was shaking his head. "Sergeant, I could see you denying me, but how you can deny Mickey, a Yeshivah boy, that's beyond me."

"I'm not denying Mickey anything. You just pushed a little too hard, Grossbart. *You* denied him."

"I'll give him my pass, then," Grossbart said. "I'll give him my aunt's address and a little note. At least let him go."

In a second he had crammed the pass into Halpern's pants' pocket. Halpern looked at me, Fishbein too. Grossbart was at the door, pushing it open. "Mickey, bring me a piece of gefilte fish at least." And then he was outside again.

The three of us looked at one another and then I said, "Halpern, hand that pass over."

He took it from his pocket and gave it to me. Fishbein had now moved to the doorway, where he lingered. He stood there with his mouth slightly open and then pointed to himself. "And me?" he asked.

His utter ridiculousness exhausted me. I slumped down in my seat and felt pulses knocking at the back of my eyes. "Fishbein," I said, "you understand I'm not trying to deny you anything, don't you? If it was my Army I'd serve gefilte fish in the mess hall. I'd sell kugel in the PX, honest to God."

Halpern smiled.

"You understand, don't you, Halpern?"

"Yes, Sergeant."

"And you, Fishbein? I don't want enemies. I'm just like you—I want to serve my time and go home. I miss the same things you miss."

"Then, Sergeant," Fishbein interrupted, "why don't you come too?"

"Where?"

"To St. Louis. To Shelley's aunt. We'll have a regular Seder. Play hide-the-matzah." He gave a broad, black-toothed smile.

I saw Grossbart in the doorway again, on the other side of the screen.

"Pssst!" He waved a piece of paper. "Mickey, here's the address. Tell her I couldn't get away."

Halpern did not move. He looked at me and I saw the shrug moving up his arms into his shoulders again. I took the cover off my typewriter and made out passes for him and Fishbein. "Go," I said, "the three of you."

I thought Halpern was going to kiss my hand.

That afternoon, in a bar in Joplin, I drank beer and listened with half an ear to the Cardinal game. I tried to look squarely at what I'd become involved in, and began to wonder if perhaps the struggle with Grossbart wasn't as much my fault as his. What was I that I had to *muster* generous feelings? Who was I to have been feeling so grudging, so tight-hearted?

After all, I wasn't being asked to move the world. Had I a right, then, or a reason, to clamp down on Grossbart, when that meant clamping down on Halpern, too? And Fishbein, that ugly agreeable soul, wouldn't he suffer in the bargain also? Out of the many recollections that had tumbled over me these past few days, I heard from some childhood moment my grandmother's voice: "What are you making a *tsimas?*" It was what she would ask my mother when, say, I had cut myself with a knife and her daughter was busy bawling me out. I would need a hug and a kiss and my mother would moralize! But my grandmother knew—mercy overrides justice. I should have known it, too. Who was Nathan Marx to be such a pennypincher with kindness? Surely, I thought, the Messiah himself—if he should ever come—won't niggle over nickels and dimes. God willing, he'll hug and kiss.

The next day, while we were playing softball over on the Parade Grounds, I decided to ask Bob Wright, who was noncom in charge over at Classification and Assignment, where he thought our trainees would be sent when their cycle ended in two weeks. I asked casually, between innings, and he said, "They're pushing them all into the Pacific. Shulman cut the orders on your boys the other day."

The news shocked me, as though I were father to Halpern, Fishbein, and Grossbart.

That night I was just sliding into sleep when someone tapped on the door. "What is it?"

"Sheldon."

He opened the door and came in. For a moment I felt his presence without being able to see him. "How was it?" I asked, as though to the darkness.

He popped into sight before me. "Great, Sergeant." I felt my springs sag; Grossbart was sitting on the edge of the bed. I sat up.

"How about you?" he asked. "Have a nice weekend?"

"Yes."

He took a deep paternal breath. "The others went to sleep . . ." We sat silently for a while, as a homey feeling invaded my ugly little cubicle: the door was locked, the cat out, the children safely in bed.

"Sergeant, can I tell you something? Personal?"

I did not answer and he seemed to know why. "Not

about me. About Mickey. Sergeant, I never felt for any-body like I feel for him. Last night I heard Mickey in the bed next to me. He was crying so, it could have broken your heart. Real sobs."

"I'm sorry to hear that."

"I had to talk to him to stop him. He held my hand, Sergeant—he wouldn't let it go. He was almost hysterical. He kept saying if he only knew where we were going. Even if he knew it *was* the Pacific, that would be better than nothing. Just to know."

Long ago, someone had taught Grossbart the sad law that only lies can get the truth. Not that I couldn't believe in Halpern's crying—his eyes *always* seemed red-rimmed. But, fact or not, it became a lie when Grossbart uttered it. He was entirely strategic. But then—it came with the force of indictment—so was I! There are strategies of aggression, but there are strategies of retreat, as well. And so, recogniz-ing that I, myself, had not been without craft and guile, I told him what I knew. "It is the Pacific."

He let out a small gasp, which was not a lie. "I'll tell him. I wish it was otherwise."

"So do I."

He jumped on my words. "You mean you think you could do something? A change maybe?"

"No, I couldn't do a thing."

"Don't you know anybody over at C & A?"

"Grossbart, there's nothing I can do. If your orders are for the Pacific then it's the Pacific."

"But Mickey."

"Mickey, you, me—everybody, Grossbart. There's noth-ing to be done. Maybe the war'll end before you go. Pray for a miracle."

"But—"

"Good night, Grossbart." I settled back, and was relieved to feel the springs upbend again as Grossbart rose to leave. I could see him clearly now; his jaw had dropped and he looked like a dazed prizefighter. I noticed for the first time a little paper bag in his hand.

"Grossbart"—I smiled—"my gift?"

"Oh, yes, Sergeant. Here, from all of us." He handed me the bag. "It's egg roll."

"Egg roll?" I accepted the bag and felt a damp grease spot on the bottom. I opened it, sure that Grossbart was joking.

"We thought you'd probably like it. You know, Chinese egg roll. We thought you'd probably have a taste for—"

"Your aunt served egg roll?"

"She wasn't home."

"Grossbart, she invited you. You told me she invited you and your friends."

"I know. I just reread the letter. *Next* week."

I got out of bed and walked to the window. It was black as far off as I could see. "Grossbart," I said. But I was not calling him.

"What?"

"What are you, Grossbart? Honest to God, what are you?"

I think it was the first time I'd asked him a question for which he didn't have an immediate answer.

"How can you do this to people?" I asked.

"Sergeant, the day away did us all a world of good. Fishbein, you should see him, he *loves* Chinese food."

"But the Seder," I said.

"We took second best, Sergeant."

Rage came charging at me. I didn't sidestep—I grabbed it, pulled it in, hugged it to my chest.

"Grossbart, you're a liar! You're a schemer and a crook! You've got no respect for anything! Nothing at all! Not for me, for the truth, not even for poor Halpern! You use us all—"

"Sergeant, Sergeant, I feel for Mickey, honest to God, I do. I *love* Mickey. I try—"

"You try! You feel!" I lurched towards him and grabbed his shirt front. I shook him furiously. "Grossbart, get out. Get out and stay the hell away from me! Because if I see you, I'll make your life miserable. *You understand that?*"

"Yes."

I let him free, and when he walked from the room I wanted to spit on the floor where he had stood. I couldn't stop the fury from rising in my heart. It engulfed me, owned me, till it seemed I could only rid myself of it with tears or an act of violence. I snatched from the bed the bag Grossbart had given me and with all my strength threw it out the window. And the next morning, as the men policed the area around the barracks, I heard a great cry go up from one of the trainees who'd been anticipating only this morning handful of cigarette butts and candy wrappers. "Egg roll!" he shouted. "Holy Christ, Chinese goddam egg roll!"

A week later when I read the orders that had come down from C & A I couldn't believe my eyes. Every single trainee was to be shipped to Camp Stoneham, California, and from there to the Pacific. Every trainee but one: Private Sheldon Grossbart was to be sent to Fort Monmouth, New Jersey. I read the mimeographed sheet several times. Dee, Farrell, Fishbein, Fuselli, Fylypowycz, Glinicki, Gromke, Gucwa, Halpern, Hardy, Helebrandt . . . right down to Anton Zygadlo, all were to be headed West before the month was out. All except Grossbart. He had pulled a string and I wasn't it.

I lifted the phone and called C & A.

The voice on the other end said smartly, "Corporal Shulman, sir."

"Let me speak to Sergeant Wright."

"Who is this calling, sir?"

"Sergeant Marx."

And to my surprise, the voice said, *"Oh."* Then: "Just a minute, Sergeant."

Shulman's *oh* stayed with me while I waited for Wright to come to the phone. Why *oh*? Who was Shulman? And then, so simply, I knew I'd discovered the string Grossbart had pulled. In fact, I could hear Grossbart the day he'd discovered Shulman, in the PX, or the bowling alley, or maybe even at services. "Glad to meet you. Where you from? Bronx? Me too. Do you know so-and-so? And so-and-so? Me too! You work at C & A? Really? Hey, how's chances of getting East? Could you do something? Change something? Swindle, cheat, lie? We gotta help each other, you know . . . if the Jews in Germany . . ."

At the other end Bob Wright answered. "How are you, Nate? How's the pitching arm?"

"Good. Bob, I wonder if you could do me a favor." I heard clearly my own words and they so reminded me of Grossbart that I dropped more easily than I could have imagined into what I had planned. "This may sound crazy, Bob, but I got a kid here on orders to Monmouth who wants them changed. He had a brother killed in Europe and he's hot to go to the Pacific. Say he'd feel like a coward if he wound up stateside. I don't know, Bob, can anything be done? Put somebody else in the Monmouth slot?"

"Who?" he asked cagily.

"Anybody. First guy on the alphabet. I don't care. The kid just asked if something could be done."

"What's his name?"

"Grossbart, Sheldon."

Wright didn't answer.

"Yeah," I said, "he's a Jewish kid, so he thought I could help him out. You know."

"I guess I can do something," he finally said. "The Major hasn't been around here for weeks—TDY to the golf course. I'll try, Nate, that's all I can say."

"I'd appreciate it, Bob. See you Sunday," and I hung up, perspiring.

And the following day the corrected orders appeared: Fishbein, Fuselli, Fylypowycz, Glinicki, Grossbart, Gucwa, Halpern, Hardy . . . Lucky Private Harley Alton was to go to Fort Monmouth, New Jersey, where for some reason or other, they wanted an enlisted man with infantry training.

After chow that night I stopped back at the orderly room to straighten out the guard duty roster. Grossbart was waiting for me. He spoke first.

"You son of a bitch!"

I sat down at my desk and while he glared down at me I began to make the necessary alterations in the duty roster.

"What do you have against me?" he cried. "Against my family? Would it kill you for me to be near my father, God knows how many months he has left to him."

"Why?"

"His heart," Grossbart said. "He hasn't had enough troubles in a lifetime, you've got to add to them. I curse the day I ever met you, Marx! Shulman told me what happened over there. There's no limit to your anti-Semitism, is there! The damage you've done here isn't enough. You have to make a special phone call! You really want me dead!"

I made the last few notations in the duty roster and got up to leave. "Good night, Grossbart."

"You owe me an explanation!" He stood in my path.

"Sheldon, you're the one who owes explanations."

He scowled. "To *you*?"

"To me, I think so, yes. Mostly to Fishbein and Halpern."

"That's right, twist things around. I owe nobody nothing, I've done all I could do for them. Now I think I've got the right to watch out for myself."

"For each other we have to learn to watch out, Sheldon. You told me yourself."

"You call this watching out for me, what you did?"

"No. For all of us."

I pushed him aside and started for the door. I heard his furious breathing behind me, and it sounded like steam rushing from the engine of his terrible strength.

"You'll be all right," I said from the door. And, I thought, so would Fishbein and Halpern be all right, even in the Pacific, if only Grossbart could continue to see in the obsequiousness of the one, the soft spirituality of the other, some profit for himself.

I stood outside the orderly room, and I heard Grossbart weeping behind me. Over in the barracks, in the lighted windows, I could see the boys in their T-shirts sitting on their bunks talking about their orders, as they'd been doing for the past two days. With a kind of quiet nervousness, they polished shoes, shined belt buckles, squared away underwear, trying as best they could to accept their fate. Behind me, Grossbart swallowed hard, accepting his. And then, resisting with all my will an impulse to turn and seek pardon for my vindictiveness, I accepted my own.

Back to Bread

Michael Seide

That week it was my turn to have lunch at one o'clock. The boss wanted to have someone in the factory all the time in case a customer called up or a package came in. But when one eats alone, an hour for lunch is much too much. I would dive into that cheap excuse for a cafeteria across Madison Avenue (when I ate with the bunch we went to Childs basement on Fifth Avenue) and scramble out again in fifteen minutes flat. I would then stroll a bit down the block and stop and look doubtfully north and south, chewing a soggy toothpick and wondering what to do with myself until two o'clock. Usually I would end up by returning to my building where I would sit down on the stairs in the back of the lobby and laze there on a cool marble step while other slaves scurried in and out the elevator, chasing business.

Thursday afternoon, I had just plumped down on the second step and was putting a match to a Camel, when Jimmy, the elevator boy, came strutting over for me to feel his muscle. The scrapper was but six months out of County Sligo, Ireland, and already he wanted to be a cop. He flexed his uniformed arm and puffed into my face, bragging and insisting; but I held him off, glancing away in annoyance. All at once I blushed so hard that Jimmy straightened and dropped his club of an arm in surprise. I was staring beyond him, my face a cartoon of frank delight and incredulity. He turned swiftly to see who had come into the lobby and saw *her* (arm in arm with Glickman) enter the elevator.

"Why, do you know the lady?" he asked, puzzled by my nutty look.

"What lady?" I said.

"Oh, now, man!" he laughed.

"Come on, Tarzan," I said, "get to work."

"But first feel," he begged hurriedly. "Go on, man, take a feel of it!"

I felt his muscle.

"Where is it?" I said.

"What?" he bellowed. "Where is it, you say?"

He moved away, shaking his fist at my grin.

But you little nitwit (I swore softly at myself), why the blush?

Yet recognition had been swift and sure (she was dead, who was it had told me, and I had lazily accepted the rumor—or had the fool mixed her up with someone else?) and the sudden heelclicking fact of her (Madeline!) had given me an exquisite kick in the heart. A glimpse of her had peeled fifteen years off my toughening hide and I had become once again a bashful and fascinated child, that same mousy seven-year-old who had once nibbled at the edges of the peculiar charm and mystery that had been young Mrs. Madeline Singer: a woman who had never been completely explained.

So I tried to analyze that blush. It felt fine to have something exciting to think about. I lit a second cigarette from the glowing butt of the first and reached out eagerly to feel the muscle of that time fifteen years ago.

It was early summer then in East New York, Brooklyn. And my mother said to me, It is getting warm and you must go get a short haircut. You are a big boy now and can go without me. Here, she said, is twenty-five cents (don't lose it or I'll cripple you!) and just tell the man to take it all off in the back and leave me a little nicely in the front. And I looked so stupid she began to shake me and I dropped the quarter and she yelled and I ducked and picked it up and ran out of the house. The barber was a sad and attractive man. Whenever there was no one to shave or clip, he would console himself by blowing into his clarinet. You could hear it wail and tootle many times a day, liquefying the sunshine. He lifted me onto a board placed across the arms of the chair and asked me kindly, How do you want it, Sonny? And I said, Short, flattered to be asked. Cut it very short. So he clipped me to the bone. And when I came home and my mother saw my baldy she screamed and smacked me once on the top of my skull, then grabbed it to her bosom and felt of it gingerly and then, holding me off, began to grin, then laughed until she cried. Aw, gee.

Come here, my darling dope, my mother said and dried her eyes, I'll give you a piece of bread and butter. And please, she said, angrily slicing and spreading, please get out of my sight before I give you everything I have on my heart. I stumped downstairs, munching bread spiced with tears. I was ashamed to show myself freely so I paused before the new bakery next door. As I worried the greasy bread and yearned for the powdered crullers I saw in the window, a little sissy came popping out of the store and began to inspect me frankly. I dared him with my eyes to say something about my baldy. I felt I could lick with him one hand easy because he was dressed too clean and looked too nice to know his right fist from his left.

"Kibba kibba koo?" he inquired pertly.

I merely stared.

"Kibba?" he croaked, coming closer. "Kumb?"

I began to back away.

"My name's Albert," he said suddenly in nice English. "What's yours?"

I told him, avoiding the hand he extended to touch my head.

"What happened?" he asked with a friendly smile.

But I pointed to his mouth and asked him to say it again. He gibbled and gabbled. It was fascinating to watch his Adam's apple do tricks. But what did those funny words mean? He shrugged. They were not meant to mean. It was all a trick. It was a secret language meant to mystify.

"I'll show you how to do it," he said, "if you let me rub your head."

That was it: my head of no hair. You let someone rub it as if it were Aladdin's lamp and lovely things begin to happen to you. You receive your first lesson in a magical form of communication. Then you enter with Albert his grandmother's enchanting bakery. Mrs. Weber is tiny behind the counter, a simple soul gawking at you with a seed roll in her hand. You follow Albert shyly. You see a bearded man at a table with a marble top. He is hunched greedily over a glass of tea, snug in his vest, a tilted *yahmelkeh* on his head. He watches you approach with alert and sarcastic eyes. He chuckles and nabs you, pawing over your baldy with a hot hand, roaring with delight. Mr. Weber likes you. Everybody likes you. You funny kid, you.

"Wait for me," Albert whispered as we entered the back kitchen. "I have to eat now. It won't take long."

I whispered back I would wait. But why must we whisper? Because at a window barred against the petty thieves of the neighborhood sat a very handsome lady—sat strangely still, a noiseless newspaper in her lap. Albert seemed afraid to approach her.

"Madeline," he ventured softly.

She turned upon him in inquisition her enormous eyes.

"Yes?"

"I'm hungry, Madeline."

"So?"

"Gramma's busy in the store."

"Then you must wait."

"But I'm so hungry."

She turned away.

"You must wait," she said.

She said he must wait and it was final. It was terrible the way she said he must wait. She really meant it. Terrible seemed the finality of her stiff position at the barred window. She meant to sit so (she was dressed with simple elegance: a cameo pinning the neck of her white frilled shirtwaist; a voluminous navy blue skirt flowing from her tiny waist) until every cake rotted and newsprint decomposed and flies buzzed no more.

Mrs. Weber quietly entered the kitchen. Mr. Weber shuffled after in floppy bedroom slippers. Seeing them, Albert went to sit down at a round table spread with a rose-patterned oilcloth. They were going to have lunch. Without Madeline? I backed up to a steamer trunk which lay on its side against the wall and climbed it noiselessly.

"Oooouhhh!" Mr. Weber groaned voluptuously as he stretched higher and higher. He staggered away on trembling legs, then dropped his arms and suddenly whacked himself fiercely on the chest. Albert giggled. Mr. Weber winked at me out of a horrible funnyface, then deftly plucked Albert out of his chair and began to grapple with him in a rough and noisy show of affection. Mrs. Weber hurried over, wildly flapping her spoon towards Madeline at the window. Mr. Weber repulsed her with a tyrant's glare.

"Hah?" he grunted breathlessly.

Mrs. Weber tried to make him understand.

"Shah-shah-shah!" he jeered, brusquely shooing her away.

Then without warning, with startling agility, he skipped over to Madeline.

"Come, Maddy!" he said tartly, clutching her arm. "You'll wear out the best chair. Up, I say!"

She clicked her tongue in irritation at this pesky gnat of a man.

"Well?" he shook her. "Well, well?"

She calmly freed her arm. He tucked in his chin and stared fixedly at her cold disobedient face. Suddenly he crouched before her. His bearded jaw drooped inanely. He began to sway as though drunk, wobbling a loose idiotic head in droll mimicry.

"Ach, I'm dying!" he moaned and tottered. "Friends . . . God . . . Mamma darling, save me! Can't you see I'm *dying?*"

"Please, Papa," she said, "you bother me."

He straightened testily.

"Please, daughter," he cried in genuine distress, "you *worry* me!"

"Leave me alone, Papa."

"No, I can't stand it!" He slapped his forehead. "To think that good-for-nothing should make you act this way. Sweet God in heaven! *He* should change you overnight into a dummy!" He paced up and down with murder in his heart, his feet slapping viciously on the linoleum. "But why, Maddy?" he said, coming to a sudden halt before her. "Why did he hit you?"

She sighed with the impossibility of explaining.

"Tell me, darling, why?"

"How excited you are, Papa!" she said, smiling for the first time. "Why are you so excited?"

"What!" he cried, flabbergasted. "I shouldn't be excited about it?"

"Now, Papa," she said gently, folding up the newspaper. "You go and sit down. Please. There's absolutely nothing to worry about, I tell you."

"Sit down?" He glanced behind him in bewilderment. "What for? What kind of monkey business is this? You think your Papa is an old fool?"

"My Papa is a very smart man," she smiled. "But I'm sorry to say he's a very excitable man too."

"Tut-tut-tut!" he cried. "An excitable man! His daughter leaves her husband (God knows why!) and he should sit down and say nothing. Very nice! An excitable man!"

"But a *smart* man."

"Sure, sure!"

"See?" she said. "Just look at you. Now isn't it foolish to talk? What's there to tell? I've been miserable all these years and I've told no one."

"But your own Papa!"

"Certainly not!" she laughed vivaciously. "He would have become terribly excited!"

"She's laughing!" he cried, astonished. "Sweet God! What am I to think of this queer daughter of mine?"

"Only the best," she said. "Laugh with her, Papa."

He shook his head disconsolately.

"Ah, Papa, Papa!" she mocked, reaching out to touch his arm. "Where did you ever get such a funny face?"

He caught hold of her hand, suddenly smiling.

"So, Maddy?" he said.

"What, Papa?"

"It's all over, eh?"

"It's all over."

"No more Sol?"

"No more Sol."

"Why, darling?" His smile deepened ingratiatingly. "Why?"

"Aren't you hungry, Papa?"

"Just because the man slapped you?"

"Huh?" she said, craning her neck towards the stove. "What's there good to eat?"

He laughed outright. "All right." He patted her hand. "I believe you. When you say it's finished, it's finished. Only tell me this, please. What are you going to do now?"

"I'll be a nurse again, Papa."

"A nurse," he considered, rapidly blinking his eyes. "Fine, a nurse. I approve."

"Thank you," she smiled. "That's very kind of you."

"Sure," he said, "you can begin right now. Nurse me. I'm a very sick man."

"Oh, yes, very sick!"

He snapped his head down and kissed her loudly on the cheek.

"Feh!" she cried.

She ducked as he came at her again.

"What a bear!" she laughed. "Now I'm sure he's hungry!"

"Hungry?" he started, coming wholly to himself. "Hungry? Oh, my god, what time is it?" He hustled away to the sink and began to soap his hands. "Ruth," said he to his wife, violently rinsing and splashing, "please set the table at once!" And Mrs. Weber did as she was told.

And me? A friendly fly buzzed round my head. Otherwise the kid with the baldy was utterly forgotten. And I liked it that way.

A bell jangled. All looked up.

"Someone's in the store," said Albert, putting his nose back into a glass of milk. Mrs. Weber left the table. I saw Madeline (she had been rolling breadcrumbs, pensively kneading the soft clay of a sad past) frown and nudge her father: who's that little boy? My heart began a thump-thump.

"You still here?" Mr. Weber gawked at me. And when I lowered my head and did not answer, he ordered, "Come over here!" I slipped down and went over.

"Here," he said, reaching across the table and spearing a fat hunk of sponge cake. "Eat it!"

I stepped back, shaking my head.

"Take it!" he roared.

I took it.

"Albert's new friend," he chuckled. "Look at him, Maddy! Just look at that boy, will you?"

She smiled at me gently.

"He blushes," she said.

I sure did.

"What's your name?" she asked.

She smelled like sponge cake.

"What?" she said, her eyes sparkling.

I said it again.

"Oh!" she laughed. "Nice boy!"

"All right!" Mr. Weber suddenly clapped his hands. "Out, Albert! Out with the both of you! Out, out!"

So we were chased out by this benevolent tyrant, this excitable man. But I was back the next day, and the day after that, and almost every day of that memorable summer, to receive frequent gifts of cake with which my giddy and fragrant sense of Madeline was always mixed up.

I did not see her often. She came and went at mysterious hours. But when she was there glorifying the back kitchen, she liked to see me perched on that trunk. I felt that. And yet I do not remember her ever speaking to me again, except once.

It was weeks later when she was once again at the table with her father.

"But, darling," Mr. Weber was saying, "why don't you wait, please?"

"No, Papa, no."

Mr. Weber tugged hard at his beard.

"See Sol again, Maddy," he urged plaintively. "For my sake. Talk to the man. What can you lose?"

"Papa," she said, "I'm going to be free!"

"Every day the poor man comes and looks for you."

"Free, Papa!"

Mr. Weber sighed and smiled helplessly.

"Will it be so nice to be free?" he said.

"Oh, Papa!"

"And then?" he said. "Would you again?"

"Again?"

"Would you marry again?"

"Ah, you would like that?"

"Sure, Maddy."

"All right." Her eyes gleamed mischievously and she pointed at me. "I'll wait for him!"

Mr. Weber roared.

"Oh, you shouldn't laugh, Papa." She suddenly frowned. She turned to me and beckoned. When I got to the table, she took my hand and caressed it.

"This is a fine boy!" she said.

"He likes cake very much," Mr. Weber grinned.

"He is quiet and good," she said.

Her hand cupped my hot cheek and she drew me tenderly to her.

"You would wait for me, wouldn't you?"

I wanted to say I would.

"Say, you would," she implored. "Say, yes."

I tried to say it.

"Say it!"

"Yes," I said, and she hugged me tight.

Oh, and I meant it.

One night at supper, my father said to my mother, Sarah, why don't you take the boy for a haircut? You can wipe up the floor with the mop he's got. Why do you wait until he is so overgrown? And I butt in and said, I don't want a haircut, Pa. You don't want? said my father. Why don't you want? Because, I said. My father smiled at me. Sometimes you are very stupid, he said. Do you know that sometimes you are very stupid? I don't care, Pa, I said. I just don't want a haircut. Sarah, he appealed to my mother, please do me a favor. See that he gets a haircut tomorrow. I won't go, I said. You'll see, Pa, I just won't go. Tomorrow, Sarah, said my father. School will be next week, and I want he should look presentable. Aw, I said, the hell with school! My father flushed and bit his lips. My mother sighed. Better

leave him alone, she said. His Mr. Weber died today.
Weber, Weber? said my father nervously. Who is this Mr.
Weber? The man from the bakery next door, said my
mother. My father blinked at the ceiling. Bakery? he said.
Weber? Ach, said my mother, the poor man! He went to
take a bath and there he died in the water! My father
swallowed and put down his spoon. He said something under
his breath and began to nod his head. Then he shook himself
free of what he was thinking. His mild gray eyes surveyed
me kindly. Why is it, he said, you never finish your bread?
You used to like bread. Do you want more butter? He thickly buttered my untouched slice. Eat it, he said, it's good
for you. I nibbled the bread of peace. The taste of cake
slowly whitened in my mouth.

Yep, I sat there on the stairs in the lobby and philosophized,
I sure kissed the lock that morning when I went to call for
Albert. That is the way it goes: death (a powerful riddle in
itself) leaves too many things unexplained. Kibba kibba
koo, it says, and thinks it has said a lot.

I stretched out my leg and dug into my pants pocket for
a cigarette. My mouth felt very ripe for a smoke. But the
crumpled pack was empty.

I was debating with myself whether I had enough time to
run out and get another pack, when I saw Glickman step out
of the elevator. He was laughing backwardly at Jimmy.

"Hey, Glickman!" I called.

Glickman came prancing over in a boxer's vicious pose.

"Come on, kiddo!" he urged. "Let me smack you one!
Just one!"

It was disgusting. Everybody wanted to fight.

"Let's have one of your fancy cigarettes," I said, parrying.

Glickman smoked Murads. He clawed in his coat pocket,
extravagantly anxious to please. "A cigarette anytime!" He
was a silk underwear contractor with a factory in Brooklyn
of thirty machines. He could not mention his age (which was
fifty) without spitting. You had to admire such sincere self-
disgust. He was a shrunken five feet five. He tried to be
one of the boys. The band of his straw hat was gaily colored.
"Where's your lovely boss?" he asked, lighting up a Murad
for himself.

"Who knows?" I said. "Who cares? This is my lunch
hour."

"How about it, kiddo? Think there's any work for me
today?"

"Glickman, the ladykiller," I grinned. "Who is she?"

"Who is who?"

"That lady, Glickman," I said. "I saw you."

I liked to kid him.

His eyes lit up. "Oh, her," he said. "My cousin."

"Yeah?" I said, getting excited.

He put one foot on the step I was sitting on, and leaned over me. A bit of blood brightened his rutted skin.

"Kiddo," he said, and paused. Then rapidly, "I've slept more times with that woman than you got hair on your chest!"

"Oh, get out!" I yelled, jerking back as if I had been stabbed.

He gaped at me.

"What's a matter

"Oh, nothing, nothing!" I said, standing up.

"What did I say?" he asked anxiously.

I took a last deliberate drag on the Murad, then squashed it underfoot.

"Listen, Glickman," I said. "I hope you're lying about this. I know you're a big shot. You don't have to lie to prove it, you know."

"Say," he said resentfully, "what's a matter with you? You know I don't lie."

"That's what I used to think," I said. "Only this time I happen to know the lady!"

"What?" he said. "What're you talking about?"

"That's right," I said. "When I was a kid."

"Yeah?" he said. "What's her name?"

"Singer," I said. "Madeline Singer."

He threw down his cigarette and spat after it.

"I talk too damn much," he said.

I had to laugh.

"Take it easy," I sneered.

"Listen, kiddo," he said plaintively. "Don't mind what I said. I was only kidding."

"Oh, yeah?"

"Sure," he said. "I was only shooting my mouth off. Forget it, willya?"

"Aa, Glickman," I said, "why don't you stop lying?"

He licked his trembling lips.

"Now, kiddo," he said, "don't talk like that."

"Well, you're lying, aren't you?"

His face was screwed up as if he had a bellyache.

"Well," I insisted, "aren't you?"

"Christ, kiddo!" he blurted out. "Why bother me? Everybody knows her!"

"What's that?"

"Sure!" he cried in defensive anger. "All Brooklyn's had her!"

That was about all I could take.

"I got to go now," I mumbled, stepping down. "I'm late." He grabbed my arm.

"Say, kiddo?"

"Yeah?"

His grip worked appealingly.

"See if there's any work for me, willya?"

I could not look long into his pathetic eyes.

"All right, Glickman," I said, turning away, "come up later. I'll see the boss. Come up later."

The Man Who Studied Yoga

Norman Mailer

1

I would introduce myself if it were not useless. The name
I had last night will not be the same as the name I have tonight. For the moment, then, let me say that I am thinking of
Sam Slovoda. Obligingly, I study him. Sam Slovoda who is
neither ordinary nor extraordinary, who is not young nor yet
old, nor tall nor short. He is sleeping, and it is fit to describe
him now, for like most humans he prefers sleeping to not
sleeping. He is a mild pleasant-looking man who has just
turned forty. If the crown of his head reveals a little bald
spot, he has nourished in compensation the vanity of a mustache. He has generally when he is awake an agreeable manner, at least with strangers; he appears friendly, tolerant, and
genial. The fact is that like most of us, he is full of envy, full
of spite, a gossip, a man who is pleased to find others are as
unhappy as he, and yet—this is the worst to be said—he is a
decent man. He is better than most. He would prefer to see
a more equitable world, he scorns prejudice and privilege, he
tries to hurt no one, he wishes to be liked. I will go even
further. He has one serious virtue—he is not fond of himself,
he wishes he were better. He would like to free himself of
envy, of the annoying necessity to talk about his friends, he
would like to love people more; specifically, he would like
to love his wife more, and to love his two daughters without
the tormenting if nonetheless irremediable vexation that they
closet his life in the dusty web of domestic responsibilities and
drudging for money.

How often he tells himself with contempt that he has the
cruelty of a kind weak man.

May I state that I do not dislike Sam Slovoda; it is just that
I am disappointed in him. He has tried too many things and
never with a whole heart. He has wanted to be a serious

novelist and now merely indulges the ambition; he wished to be of consequence in the world, and has ended, temporarily perhaps, as an overworked writer of continuity for comic magazines; when he was young he tried to be a bohemian and instead acquired a wife and family. Of his appetite for a variety of new experience I may say that it is matched only by his fear of new people and novel situations.

I will give an instance. Yesterday, Sam was walking along the street and a bum approached him for money. Sam did not see the man until too late; lost in some inconsequential thought, he looked up only in time to see a huge wretch of a fellow with a red twisted face and an outstretched hand. Sam is like so many; each time a derelict asks for a dime, he feels a coward if he pays the money, and is ashamed of himself if he doesn't. This once, Sam happened to think, "I will not be bullied," and hurried past. But the bum was not to be lost so easily. "Have a heart, Jack," he called after in a whiskey voice, "I need a drink bad." Sam stopped, Sam began to laugh. "Just so it isn't for coffee, here's a quarter," he said, and he laughed, and the bum laughed. "You're a man's man," the bum said. Sam went away pleased with himself, thinking about such things as the community which existed between all people. It was cheap of Sam. He should know better. He should know he was merely relieved the situation had turned out so well. Although he thinks he is sorry for bums, Sam really hates them. Who knows what violence they can offer?

At this time, there is a powerful interest in Sam's life, but many would ridicule it. He is in the process of being psychoanalyzed. Myself, I do not jeer. It has created the most unusual situation between Sam and me. I could go into details but they are perhaps premature. It would be better to watch Sam awaken.

His wife, Eleanor, has been up for an hour, and she has shut the window and neglected to turn off the radiator. The room is stifling. Sam groans in the stupor which is neither sleep nor refreshment, opens one eye, yawns, groans again, and lies twisted, strangled and trussed in pajamas which are too large for him. How painful it is for him to rise. Last night there was a party, and this morning, Sunday morning, he is awakening with a hangover. Invariably, he is depressed in the morning, and it is no different today. He finds himself in the flat and familiar dispirit of nearly all days.

It is snowing outside. Sam finally lurches to the window,

and opens it for air. With the oxygen of a winter morning
clearing his brain, he looks down six stories into the giant
quadrangle of the Queens housing development in which he
lives, staring morosely at the inch of slush which covers the
monotonous artificial park that separates his apartment building
from an identical structure not two hundred feet away. The
walks are black where the snow has melted, and in the children's playground, all but deserted, one swing oscillates back
and forth, pushed by an irritable little boy who plays by himself among the empty benches, swaddled in galoshes, muffler,
and overcoat. The snow falls sluggishly, a wet snow which
probably will turn to rain. The little boy in the playground
gives one last disgusted shove to the swing and trudges away
gloomily, his overshoes leaving a small animal track behind
him. Back of Sam, in the four-room apartment he knows like
a blind man, there is only the sound of Eleanor making breakfast.

Well, thinks Sam, depression in the morning is a stage of
his analysis, Dr. Sergius has said.

This is the way Sam often phrases his thoughts. It is not
altogether his fault. Most of the people he knows think that
way and talk that way, and Sam is not the strongest of men.
His language is doomed to the fashion of the moment. I
have heard him remark mildly, almost apologetically, about
his daughters: "My relation with them still suffers because I
haven't worked through all my feminine identifications." The
saddest thing is that the sentence has meaning to Sam even if
it will not have meaning to you. A great many ruminations,
discoveries, and memories contribute their connotation to
Sam. It has the significance of a cherished line of poetry to
him.

Although Eleanor is not being analyzed, she talks in a similar way. I have heard her remark in company, "Oh, you know
Sam, he not only thinks I'm his mother, he blames me for
being born." Like most women, Eleanor can be depended
upon to employ the idiom of her husband.

What amuses me is that Sam is critical of the way others
speak. At the party last night he was talking to a Hollywood
writer, a young man with a great deal of energy and enthusiasm. The young man spoke something like this: "You see,
boychick, I can spike any script with yaks, but the thing I
can't do is heartbreak. My wife says she's gonna give me heartbreak. The trouble is I've had a real solid-type life. I mean I've

had my ups and downs like all of humanity, but there's never been a shriek in my life. I don't know how to write shrieks."

On the trip home, Sam had said to Eleanor, "It was disgraceful. A writer should have some respect for language."

Eleanor answered with a burlesque of Sam's indignation. "Listen, I'm a real artist-type. Culture is for comic-strip writers."

Generally, I find Eleanor attractive. In the ten years they have been married she has grown plump, and her dark hair which once was long is now cropped in a mannish cut of the prevailing mode. But, this is quibbling. She still possesses her best quality, a healthy exuberance which glows in her dark eyes and beams in her smile. She has beautiful teeth. She seems aware of her body and pleased with it. Sam tells himself he would do well to realize how much he needs her. Since he has been in analysis he has come to discover that he remains with Eleanor for more essential reasons than mere responsibility. Even if there were no children, he would probably cleave to her.

Unhappily, it is more complicated than that. She is always —to use their phrase—competing with him. At those times I do not like Eleanor, I am irritated by her lack of honesty. She is too sharp-tongued, and she does not often give Sam what he needs most, a steady flow of uncritical encouragement to counteract the harshness with which he views himself. Like so many who are articulate on the subject, Eleanor will tell you that she resents being a woman. As Sam is disappointed in life, so is Eleanor. She feels Sam has cheated her from a proper development of her potentialities and talent, even as Sam feels cheated. I call her dishonest because she is not so ready as Sam to put the blame on herself.

Sam, of course, can say all this himself. It is just that he experiences it in a somewhat different way. Like most men who have been married for ten years, he finds that his wife is not quite real to him. Last night at the party, there were perhaps half a dozen people whom he met for the first time, and he talked animatedly with them, sensing their reactions, feeling their responses, aware of the life in them, as they were aware of the life in him. Eleanor, however, exists in his nerves. She is a rather vague embodiment, he thinks of her as "she" most of the time, someone to conceal things from. Invariably, he feels uneasy with her. It is too bad. No matter how inevitable,

I am always sorry when love melts into that pomade of affection, resentment, boredom and occasional compassion which is the best we may expect of a man and woman who have lived together a long time. So often, it is worse, so often no more than hatred.

They are eating breakfast now, and Eleanor is chatting about the party. She is pretending to be jealous about a young girl in a strapless evening gown, and indeed, she does not have to pretend altogether. Sam, with liquor inside him, had been leaning over the girl; obviously he had coveted her. Yet, this morning, when Eleanor begins to talk about her, Sam tries to be puzzled.

"Which girl was it now?" he asks a second time.

"Oh, you know, the hysteric," Eleanor sys, "the one who was parading her bazooms in your face." Eleanor has ways of impressing certain notions upon Sam. "She's Charlie's new girl."

"I didn't know that," Sam mutters. "He didn't seem to be near her all evening."

Eleanor spreads marmalade over her toast and takes a bite with evident enjoyment. "Apparently, they're all involved. Charles was funny about it. He said he's come to the conclusion that the great affairs of history are between hysterical women and detached men."

"Charles hates women," Sam says smugly. "If you notice, almost everything he says about them is a discharge of aggression." Sam has the best of reasons for not liking Charles. It takes more than ordinary character for a middle-aged husband to approve of a friend who moves easily from woman to woman.

"At least Charles discharges his aggression," Eleanor remarks.

"He's almost a classic example of the Don Juan complex. You notice how masochistic his women are?"

"I know a man or two who's just as masochistic."

Sam sips his coffee. "What made you say the girl was an hysteric?"

Eleanor shrugs. "She's an actress. And I could see she was a tease."

"You can't jump to conclusions," Sam lectures. "I had the impression she was a compulsive. Don't forget you've got to distinguish between the outer defenses, and the more deeply rooted conflicts."

I must confess that this conversation bores me. As a sample it is representative of the way Sam and Eleanor talk to each other. In Sam's defense I can say nothing; he has always been too partial to jargon.

I am often struck by how eager we are to reveal all sorts of supposedly ugly secrets about ourselves. We can explain the hatred we feel for our parents, we are rather pleased with the perversions to which we are prone. We seem determinedly proud to be superior to ourselves. No motive is too terrible for our inspection. Let someone hint, however, that we have bad table manners and we fly into a rage. Sam will agree to anything you may say about him, provided it is sufficiently serious —he will be the first to agree he has fantasies of murdering his wife. But tell him that he is afraid of waiters, or imply to Eleanor that she is a nag, and they will be quite annoyed.

Sam has noticed this himself. There are times when he can hear the jargon in his voice, and it offends him. Yet, he seems powerless to change his habits.

An example: He is sitting in an armchair now, brooding upon his breakfast, while Eleanor does the dishes. The two daughters are not home; they have gone to visit their grandmother for the weekend. Sam had encouraged the visit. He had looked forward to the liberty Eleanor and he would enjoy. For the past few weeks the children had seemed to make the most impossible demands upon his attention. Yet now they are gone and he misses them, he even misses their noise. Sam, however, cannot accept the notion that many people are dissatisfied with the present, and either dream of the past or anticipate the future. Sam must call this ambivalence over possessions. Once he even felt obliged to ask his analyst, Dr. Sergius, if ambivalence over possessions did not characterize him almost perfectly, and Sergius, whom I always picture with the flat precision of a coin's head—bald skull and horn-rimmed glasses—answered in his German accent, "But, my dear Mr. Slovoda, as I have told you, it would make me happiest if you did not include in your reading these psycho-analytical text-works."

At such rebukes, Sam can only wince. It is so right, he tells himself, he is exactly the sort of ambitious fool who uses big words when small ones would do.

2

While Sam sits in the armchair, gray winter light is entering the windows, snow falls outside. He sits alone in a modern seat, staring at the gray, green, and beige decor of their living room. Eleanor was a painter before they were married, and she has arranged this room. It is very pleasant, but like many husbands, Sam resents it, resents the reproductions of modern painters upon the wall, the slender coffee table, a free-form poised like a spider on wire legs, its feet set onto a straw rug. In the corner, most odious of all, is the playmate of his children, a hippopotamus of a television-radio-and-phonograph cabinet with a blind monstrous snout of the video tube.

Eleanor had set the Sunday paper near his hand. Soon, Sam intends to go to work. For a year, he has been giving a day once or twice a month to a bit of thought and a little writing on a novel he hopes to begin some time. Last night he told himself he would work today. But he has little enthusiasm now. He is tired, he is too depressed. Writing for the comic strips seems to exhaust his imagination.

Sam reads the paper as if he were peeling an enormous banana. Flap after flap of newsprint is stripped away and cast upon the straw rug until only the magazine section is left. Sam glances through it with restless irritability. A biography of a political figure runs its flatulent prose into the giant cross-word puzzle at the back. An account of a picturesque corner of the city becomes lost in statistics and exhortations on juvenile delinquency, finally to emerge with photographs about the new style of living which desert architecture provides. Sam looks at a wall of windows in rotogravure with a yucca tree framing the pool.

There is an article about a workingman. His wife and his family are described, his apartment, his salary and his budget. Sam reads a description of what the worker has every evening for dinner, and how he spends each night of the week. The essay makes its point; the typical American workingman must watch his pennies, but he is nonetheless secure and serene. He would not exchange his life for another.

Sam is indignant. A year ago he had written a similar article in an attempt to earn some extra money. Subtly, or so he thought, he had suggested that the average workingman was raddled with insecurity. Naturally, the article had been re-jected.

Sam throws the magazine section away. Moments of such anger torment him frequently. Despite himself, Sam is en-raged at editorial dishonesty, at the smooth strifeless world which such articles present. How angry he is—how angry and how helpless. "It is the actions of men and not their sentiments which make history," he thinks to himself, and smiles wryly. In his living room he would go out to tilt the windmills of a vast, powerful, and hypocritical society; in his week of work he labors in an editorial cubicle to create space-ships, violent death, women with golden tresses and wanton breasts, men who act with their fists and speak with patriotic slogans.

I know what Sam feels. As he sits in the armchair, the Sun-day papers are strewn around him, carrying their war news, the murders, their parleys, their entertainments, mummery of a real world which no one can grasp. It is terribly frustrat-ing. One does not know where to begin.

Today, Sam considers himself half a fool for having been a radical. There is no longer much consolation in the thought that the majority of men who succeed in a corrupt and ac-quisitive society are themselves obligatorily corrupt, and one's failure is therefore the price of one's idealism. Sam can-not recapture the pleasurable bitterness which resides in the notion that one has suffered for one's principles. Sergius is too hard on him for that.

They have done a lot of work on the subject. Sergius feels that Sam's concern with world affairs has always been spu-rious. For example, they have uncovered in analysis that Sam wrote his article about the worker in such a way as to make certain it would be refused. Sam, after all, hates editors; to have such a piece accepted would mean he is no better than they, that he is mediocrity. So long as he fails he is not obliged to measure himself. Sam, therefore, is being unrealistic. He rejects the world with his intellect, and this enables him not to face the more direct realities of his present life.

Sam will argue with Sergius but it is very difficult. He will say, "Perhaps you sneer at the radicals because it is more comfortable to ignore such ideas. Once you became interested it might introduce certain unpleasant changes in your life."

"Why," says Sergius, "do you feel it so necessary to assume that I am a bourgeois interested only in my comfort?"

"How can I discuss these things," says Sam, "if you insist

that my opinions are the expression of neurotic needs, and your opinions are merely dispassionate medical advice?"

"You are so anxious to defeat me in an argument," Sergius will reply. "Would you admit it is painful to relinquish the sense of importance which intellectual discussion provides you?"

I believe Sergius has his effect. Sam often has thoughts these days which would have been repellent to him years ago. For instance, at the moment, Sam is thinking it might be better to live the life of a worker, a simple life, to be completely absorbed with such necessities as food and money. Then one could believe that to be happy it was necessary only to have more money, more goods, less worries. It would be nice, Sam thinks wistfully, to believe that the source of one's unhappiness comes not from oneself, but from the fault of the boss, or the world, or bad luck.

Sam has these casual daydreams frequently. He likes to think about other lives he might have led, and he envies the most astonishing variety of occupations. It is easy enough to see why he should wish for the life of an executive with the power and sense of command it may offer, but virtually from the same impulse Sam will wish himself a bohemian living in an unheated loft, his life a catch-as-catch-can from day to day. Once, after reading an article, Sam even wished himself a priest. For about ten minutes it seemed beautiful to him to surrender his life to God. Such fancies are common, I know. It is just that I, far better than Sam, know how serious he really is, how fanciful, how elaborate, his imagination can be.

The phone is ringing. Sam can hear Eleanor shouting at him to answer. He picks up the receiver with a start. It is Marvin Rossman, who is an old friend, and Marvin has an unusual request. They talk for several minutes, and Sam squirms a little in his seat. As he is about to hang up, he laughs. "Why, no, Marvin, it gives me a sense of adventure," he says.

Eleanor has come into the room toward the end of this conversation. "What is it all about?" she asks.

Sam is obviously a bit agitated. Whenever he attempts to be most casual, Eleanor can well suspect him. "It seems," he says slowly, "that Marvin has acquired a pornographic movie."

"From whom?" Eleanor asks.

"He said something about an old boy friend of Louise's."

Eleanor laughs. "I can't imagine Louise having an old boy friend with a dirty movie."

"Well, people are full of surprises," Sam says mildly.

"Look, here," says Eleanor suddenly. "Why did he call us?"

"It was about our projector."

"They want to use it?" Eleanor asks.

"That's right." Sam hesitates. "I invited them over."

"Did it ever occur to you I might want to spend my Sunday some other way?" Eleanor asks crossly.

"We're not doing anything," Sam mumbles. Like most men, he feels obliged to act quite nonchalant about pornography. "I'll tell you, I am sort of curious about the film. I've never seen one, you know."

"Try anything once, is that it?"

"Something of the sort." Sam is trying to conceal his excitement. The truth is that in common with most of us, he is fascinated by pornography. It is a minor preoccupation, but more from lack of opportunity than anything else. Once or twice, Sam has bought the sets of nude photographs which are sold in marginal bookstores, and with guilty excitement has hidden them in the apartment.

"Oh, this is silly," Eleanor says. "You were going to work today."

"I'm just not in the mood."

"I'll have to feed them," Eleanor complains. "Do we have enough liquor?"

"We can get beer." Sam pauses. "Alan Sperber and his wife are coming too."

"Sam, you're a child."

"Look, Eleanor," says Sam, controlling his voice, "if it's too much trouble, I can take the projector over there."

"I ought to make you do that."

"Am I such an idiot that I must consult you before I invite friends to the house?"

Eleanor has the intuition that Sam, if he allowed himself, could well drown in pornography. She is quite annoyed at him, but she would never dream of allowing Sam to take the projector over to Marvin Rossman's where he could view the movie without her—that seems indefinably dangerous. Besides she would like to see it, too. The mother in Eleanor is certain it cannot hurt her.

"All right, Sam," she says, "but you are a child."

More exactly, an adolescent, Sam decides. Ever since Marvin phoned, Sam has felt the nervous glee of an adolescent locking himself in the bathroom. "Anal fixation," Sam thinks automatically.

While Eleanor goes down to buy beer and cold cuts in a delicatessen, Sam gets out the projector and begins to clean it. He is far from methodical in this. He knows the machine is all right, he has shown movies of Eleanor and his daughters only a few weeks ago, but from the moment Eleanor left the apartment, Sam has been consumed by an anxiety that the projection bulb is burned out. Once he has examined it, he begins to fret about the motor. He wonders if it needs oiling, he wonders if it needs oiling, he blunders through a drawer of household tools looking for an oil can. It is ridiculous. Sam knows that what he is trying to keep out of his mind are the reactions Sergius will have. Sergius will want to "work through" all of Sam's reasons for seeing the movie. Well, Sam tells himself, he knows in advance what will be discovered: detachment, not wanting to accept Eleanor as a sexual partner, evasion of responsibility, etc. etc. The devil with Sergius. Sam has never seen a dirty movie, and he certainly wants to.

He feels obliged to laugh at himself. He could not be more nervous, he knows, if he were about to make love to a woman he had never touched before. It is really disgraceful.

When Eleanor comes back, Sam hovers about her. He is uncomfortable with her silence. "I suppose they'll be here soon," Sam says.

"Probably."

Sam does not know if he is angry at Eleanor or apprehensive that she is angry at him. Much to his surprise he catches her by the waist and hears himself saying, "You know, maybe tonight when they're gone . . . I mean, we do have the apartment to ourselves." Eleanor moves neither toward him nor away from him. "Darling, it's not because of the movie," Sam goes on, "I swear. Don't you think maybe we could . . ."

"Maybe," says Eleanor.

3

The company has arrived, and it may be well to say a word or two about them. Marvin Rossman who has brought the film is a dentist, although it might be more accurate to describe him as a frustrated doctor. Rossman is full of statistics and items of odd information about the malpractice of physicians, and he will tell these things in his habitually gloomy voice, a voice so slow, so sad, that it almost conceals the humor of his remarks. Or, perhaps, that is what creates his humor. In his spare time, he is a sculptor, and if Eleanor may be trusted, he is not without talent. I often picture him working in the studio loft he has rented, his tall bony frame the image of dejection. He will pat a piece of clay to the armature, he will rub it sadly with his thumb, he will shrug, he does not believe that anything of merit could come from him. When he talked to Sam over the phone, he was pessimistic about the film they were to see. "It can't be any good," he said in his melancholy voice. "I know it'll be a disappointment." Like Sam, he has a mustache, but Rossman's will droop at the corners.

Alan Sperber who has come with Rossman is the subject of some curiosity for the Slovodas. He is not precisely womanish; in fact, he is a large plump man, but his voice is too soft, his manners too precise. He is genial, yet he is finicky; waspish, yet bland; he is fond of telling long, rather affected stories, he is always prepared with a new one, but to general conversation he contributes little. As a lawyer, he seems mis-cast. One cannot imagine him inspiring a client to confidence. He is the sort of heavy florid man who seems boyish at forty, and the bow ties and gray flannel suits he wears do not make him appear more mature.

Roslyn Sperber, his wife, used to be a school teacher, and she is a quiet nervous woman who talks a great deal when she is drunk. She is normally quite pleasant, and has only one habit which is annoying to any degree. It is a little flaw, but social life is not unlike marriage in that habit determines far more than vice or virtue. This mannerism which has become so offensive to the friends of the Sperbers is Roslyn's social pretension. Perhaps I should say intellectual pretension. She entertains people as if she were conducting a salon, and in her birdlike voice is forever forcing her guests to accept still another intellectual canapé. "You must hear Sam's view of the world market," she will say, or "Has Louise told you her statistics on divorce?" It is quite pathetic, for she is so eager to please. I have seen her eyes fill with tears at a sharp word from Alan.

Marvin Rossman's wife, Louise, is a touch grim and definite in her opinions. She is a social welfare worker, and will declare herself with force whenever conversation impinges on those matters where she is expert. She is quite opposed to psychoanalysis, and will say without quarter, "It's all very well for people in the upper-middle area—" She is referring to the upper middle class— "but it takes more than a couch to solve the problems of . . ." and she will list narcotics, juvenile delinquency, psychosis, relief distribution, slum housing, and other descriptions of our period. She recites these categories with an odd anticipation. One would guess she was ordering a meal.

Sam is fond of Marvin but he cannot abide Louise. "You'd think she discovered poverty," he will complain to Eleanor.

The Slovodas do feel superior to the Rossmans and the Sperbers. If pressed, they could not offer the most convincing explanation why. I suppose what it comes down to is that Sam and Eleanor do not think of themselves as really belonging to a class, and they feel that the Sperbers and Rossmans are petit bourgeois. I find it hard to explain their attitude. Their company feels as much discomfort and will apologize as often as the Slovodas for the money they have, and the money they hope to earn. They are all of them equally concerned with progressive education and the methods of raising children to be well-adjusted—indeed, they are discussing that now—consider themselves relatively free of sexual taboo, or put more properly, Sam and Eleanor are no less possessive than the others. The Slovodas' culture is not more profound; I should be hard-put to say that Sam is more widely read, more seriously informed, than Marvin or Alan, or for that matter, Louise. Probably, it comes to this: Sam, in his heart, thinks himself a rebel, and there are few rebels who do not claim an original mind. Eleanor has been a bohemian and considers herself more sophisticated than her friends who merely went to college and got married. Louise Rossman could express it more soundly. "Artists, writers, and people of the creative layer have in their occupational ideology the belief that they are classless."

One thing I might remark about the company. They are all being the most unconscionable hypocrites. They have rushed across half the city of New York to see a pornographic film, and they are not at all interested in each other at the moment. The women are giggling like tickled children at remarks which cannot possibly be so funny. Yet, they are all determined to talk for a respectable period of time. No less, it must be serious talk. Roslyn has said once, "I feel so funny at the thought of seeing such a movie," and the others have passed her statement by.

At the moment, Sam is talking about value. I might note that Sam loves conversation and thrives when he can expound an idea. "What are our values today?" he asks. "It's really fantastic when you stop to think of it. Take any bright, talented kid who's getting out of college now."

"My kid brother, for example," Marvin interposes morosely. He passes his bony hand over his sad mustache, and somehow the remark has become amusing, much as if Marvin had said, "Oh, yes, you have reminded me of the trials, the worries, and the cares which my fabulous younger brother heaps upon me."

"All right, take him," Sam says. "What does he want to be?"

"He doesn't want to be anything," says Marvin.

"That's my point," Sam says excitedly. "Rather than work at certain occupations, the best of these kids would rather do nothing at all."

"Alan has a cousin," Roslyn says, "who swears he'll wash dishes before he becomes a businessman."

"I wish that were true," Eleanor interrupts. "It seems to me everybody is conforming more and more these days."

They argue about this. Sam and Eleanor claim the country is suffering from hysteria; Alan Sperber disagrees and says it's merely a reflection of the headlines; Louise says no adequate criteria exist to measure hysteria; Marvin says he doesn't know anything at all.

"More solid liberal gains are being made in this period," says Alan, "than you would believe. Consider the Negro . . ."

"Is the Negro any less maladjusted?" Eleanor shouts with passion.

Sam maneuvers the conversation back to his thesis. The values of the young today, and by the young I mean the cream of the kids, the ones with ideas, are a reaction of indifference to the culture crisis. It really is despair. All they know is what they don't want to do."

"That is easier," Alan says genially.

"It's not altogether unhealthy," Sam says. "It's a corrective for smugness and the false value of the past, but it has created new false value." He thinks it worth emphasizing. "False value seems always to beget further false value."

"Define your terms," says Louise, the scientist.

"No, look," Sam says, "there's no revolt, there's no acceptance. Kids today don't want to get married, and . . ."

Eleanor interrupts. "Why should a girl rush to get married? She loses all chance for developing herself."

Sam shrugs. They are all talking at once. "Kids don't want

to get married," he repeats, "and they don't want not to get married. They merely drift."

"It's a problem we'll all have to face with our own kids in ten years," Alan says, "although I think you make too much of it, Sam."

"My daughter," Marvin states. "She's embarrassed I'm a dentist. Even more embarrassed than I am." They laugh.

Sam tells a story about his youngest, Carol Ann. It seems he had a fight with her, and she went to her room. Sam followed, he called through the door.

"No answer," Sam says. "I called her again, 'Carol Ann.' I was a little worried you understand, because she seemed so upset, so I said to her, 'Carol Ann, you know I love you.' What do you think she answered?"

"What?" asks Roslyn.

"She said, 'Daddie, why are you so anxious?' "

They all laugh again. There are murmurs about what a clever thing it was to say. In the silence which follows, Roslyn leans forward and says quickly in her high voice, "You must get Alan to tell you his wonderful story about the man who studied yogi."

"Yoga," Alan corrects, "It's too long to tell."

The company prevails on him.

"Well," says Alan, in his genial courtroom voice, "it concerns a friend of mine named Cassius O'Shaughnessy."

"You don't mean Jerry O'Shaughnessy, do you?" asks Sam.

Alan does not know Jerry O'Shaughnessy. "No, no, this is Cassius O'Shaughnessy," he said. "He's really quite an extraordinary fellow." Alan sits plumply in his chair, fingering his bow-tie. They are all used to his stories, which are told in a formal style and exhibit the attempt to recapture a certain note of urbanity, wit, and elan which Alan has probably copied from someone else. Sam and Eleanor respect his ability to tell these stories, but they resent the fact that he talks *at* them.

"You'd think we were a jury of his inferiors," Eleanor has said. "I hate being talked down to." What she resents is Alan's quiet implication that his antecedents, his social position, in total his life outside the room is superior to the life within. Eleanor now takes the promise from Alan's story by remarking, "Yes, and let's see the movie when Alan has finished."

"Sssh," Roslyn says.

"Cassius was at college a good while before me," says Alan,

"but I knew him while I was an undergraduate. He would drop in and visit from time to time. An absolutely extraordinary fellow. The most amazing career. You see, he's done about everything."

"I love the way Alan tells it," Roslyn pipes nervously.

"Cassius was in France with Dos Passos and Cummings, he was even arrested with e.e. After the war, he was one of the founders of the dadaist school, and for awhile I understand he was Fitzgerald's guide to the gold of the Côte d'Azur. He knew everybody, he did everything. Do you realize that before the twenties had ended, Cassius had managed his father's business and then entered a monastery? It is said he influenced T. S. Eliot."

"Today, we'd call Cassius a psychopath," Marvin observes.

"Cassius called himself a great dilettante," Alan answers, "although perhaps the nineteenth-century Russian conception of the great sinner would be more appropriate. What do you say if I tell you this was only the beginning of his career?"

"What's the point?" Louise asks.

"Not yet," says Alan, holding up a hand. His manner seems to say that if his audience cannot appreciate the story, he does not feel obliged to continue. "Cassius studied Marx in the monastery. He broke his vows, quit the Church, and became a Communist. All through the thirties he was a figure in the party, going to Moscow, involved in all the Party struggles. He left only during the Moscow trials."

Alan's manner while he relates such stories is somewhat effeminate. He talks with little caresses of his hand, he mentions names and places with a lingering ease as if to suggest that his audience and he are aware, above all, of nuance. The story as Alan tells it is drawn over-long. Suffice it, that the man about whom he is talking, Cassius O'Shaughnessy, becomes a Trotskyist, becomes an anarchist, is a pacifist during the Second World War, and suffers it from a prison cell.

"I may say," Alan goes on, "that I worked for his defense, and was successful in getting him acquitted. Imagine my dolor when I learned that he had turned his back on his anarchist friends and was living with gangsters."

"This is weird," Eleanor says.

"Weird, it is," Alan agrees. "Cassius got into some scrape, and disappeared. What could you do with him? I learned only recently that he had gone to India and was studying yoga. In fact, I learned it from Cassius himself. I asked him of his experiences at Brahna-puth-thar, and he told me the following story."

Now, Alan's voice alters, he assumes the part of Cassius, and speaks in a tone weary of experience, wise and sad in its knowledge. " 'I was sitting on my haunches contemplating my navel,' Cassius said to me, 'when of a sudden I discovered my navel under a different aspect. It seemed to me that if I were to give a counter-clockwise twist, my navel would unscrew.' "

Alan looks up, he surveys his audience, which is now rapt and uneasy, not certain as yet whether a joke is to come. Alan's thumb and forefinger pluck at the middle of his ample belly, his feet are crossed upon the carpet in symbolic suggestion of Cassius upon his haunches.

" 'Taking a deep breath, I turned, and the abysses of Vishtarni loomed beneath. My navel had begun to unscrew. I knew I was about to accept the reward of three years of contemplation. So,' said Cassius, 'I turned again, and my navel unscrewed a little more. I turned and I turned,' " Alan's fingers now revolving upon his belly, " 'and after a period I knew that with one more turn my navel would unscrew itself forever. At the edge of revelation I took one sweet breath, and turned my navel free.' "

Alan looks up at his audience.

" 'Damn,' said Cassius, 'if my ass didn't fall off.' "

4

The story has left the audience in an exasperated mood. It has been a most untypical story for Alan to tell, a little out of place, not offensive exactly, but irritating and inconsequential. Sam is the only one to laugh with more than bewildered courtesy, and his mirth seems excessive to everyone but Alan, and of course, Roslyn, who feels as if she has been the producer. I suppose what it reduces to is a lack of taste. Perhaps that is why Alan is not the lawyer one would expect. He does not have that appreciation—as necessary in his trade as for an actor—of what is desired at any moment, of that which will encourage, as opposed to that which does not encourage, a stimulating but smooth progression of logic and sentiment. Only a fool would tell so long a story when everyone is awaiting the movie.

Now, they are preparing. The men shift armchairs to cor-

respond with the couch, the projector is set up, the screen is
unfolded. Sam attempts to talk while he is threading the film,
but no one listens. They seem to realize suddenly that a fright-
ful demand has been placed upon them. One does not study
pornography in a living room with a beer glass in one's hand,
and friends at the elbow. It is the most unsatisfactory of com-
promises; one can draw neither the benefit of solitary contemplation nor of social exchange. There is, at bottom, the
same exasperated fright which one experiences in turning the
shower tap and receiving cold water when the flesh has been
prepared for heat. Perhaps that is why they are laughing so
much now that the movie is begun.

A title, *The Evil Act*, twitches on the screen, shot with
scars, holes, and the dust-lines of age. A man and woman are
sitting on a couch, they are having coffee. They chat. What
they say is conveyed by printed words upon an ornately flowered card, interjected between glimpses of their casual ges-
tures, a cup to the mouth, a smile, a cigarette being lit. The
man's name, it seems, is Frankie Idell; he is talking to his wife
Magnolia. Frankie is dark, he is sinister, he confides in Magnolia, his dark counterpart, with a grimace of his brows, black
from make-up pencil.

FRANKIE: She will be here soon.
MAGNOLIA: This time the little vixen will not escape.
FRANKIE: No, my dear, this time we are prepared.
He looks at his watch.
FRANKIE: Listen, she knocks!
    There is a shot of a tall blond woman knocking on the
door. She is probably over thirty, but by her short dress and
ribboned hat, it is suggested that she is a girl of fifteen.
FRANKIE: Come in, Eleanor.

As may be expected, the audience laughs hysterically at
this. It is so wonderful a coincidence. "How I remember
Frankie," says Eleanor Slovoda, and Roslyn Sperber is the
only one not amused. In the midst of the other's laughter, she
says in a worried tone, obviously adrift upon her own concerns, "Do you think we'll have to stop the film in the middle
to let the bulb cool off?" The others hoot, they giggle, they
are weak from the combination of their own remarks and the
action of the plot.

Frankie and Magnolia have sat down on either side of the heroine, Eleanor. A moment passes. Suddenly, stiffly, they attack. Magnolia from her side kisses Eleanor, and Frankie commits an indecent caress.

ELEANOR: How dare you? Stop!
MAGNOLIA: Scream my little one. It will do you no good. The walls are soundproofed.
FRANKIE: We've fixed a way to make you come across.
ELEANOR: This is hideous. I am hitherto undefiled. Do not touch me!

The captions fade away. A new title takes their place. It says, "But There Is No Escape From the Determined Pair." On the fade-in, we discover Eleanor in the most distressing situation. Her hands are tied to loops running from the ceiling, and she can only writhe in helpless perturbation before the deliberate and progressive advances of Frankie and Magnolia. Slowly they humiliate her, with relish they probe her.

The audiences laugh no longer. A hush has come upon them. Eyes unblinking they devour the images upon Sam Slovoda's screen.

Eleanor is without clothing. As the last piece is pulled away, Frankie and Magnolia circle about her in a grotesque of pantomime, a leering of lips, limbs in a distortion of desire. Eleanor faints. Adroitly, Magnolia cuts her bonds. We see Frankie carrying her inert body.

Now, Eleanor is trussed to a bed, and the husband and wife are tormenting her with feathers. Bodies curl upon the bed in postures so complicated, in combinations so advanced, that the audience leans forward, Sperbers, Rossmans, and Slovodas, as if tempted to embrace the moving images. The hands trace abstract circles upon the screen, passes and recoveries upon a white background so illumined that hollows and swells, limb to belly and mouth to undescribables, tip of a nipple, orb of a navel swim in giant magnification, flow and slide in a lurching yawing fall, blotting out the camera eye.

A little murmur, all unconscious, passes from their lips. The audience sways, each now finally lost in himself, communing hungrily with shadows, violated or violating, fantasy triumphant.

At picture's end, Eleanor the virgin whore is released from the bed. She kisses Frankie, she kisses Magnolia. "You dears," she says. "Let's do it again." The projector lamp burns empty light, the machine keeps turning, the tag of film goes slap-tap, slap-tap, slap-tap, slap-tap, slap-tap, slap-tap.

"Sam, turn it off," says Eleanor.

But when the room lights are on, they cannot look at one another. "Can we see it again?" someone mutters. So, again, Eleanor knocks on the door, is tied, defiled, ravished, and made rapturous. They watch it soberly now, the room hot with the heat of their bodies, the darkness a balm for orgiastic vision. To the Deer Park, Sam is thinking, to the Deer Park of Louis XV, were brought the most beautiful maidens of France, and there they stayed, dressed in fabulous silks, perfumed and wigged, the mole drawn upon their cheek, ladies of pleasure awaiting the pleasure of the king. So Louis had stripped an empire, bankrupt a treasury, prepared a deluge, while in his garden on summer evenings the maidens performed their pageants, eighteenth-century tableau of the evil act, beauteous instruments of one man's desire, lewd translation of a king's power. That century men sought wealth so they might use its fruits; this epoch men lusted for power in order to amass more power, a compounding of power into pyramids of abstraction whose yield are cannon and wire enclosure, pillars of statistics to the men who are the kings of this century and do no more in power's leisure time than go to church, claim to love their wives, and eat vegetables.

It is possible, Sam wonders, that each of them here, two Rossmans, two Sperbers, two Slovodas, will cast off their clothes when the movie is done, and perform the orgy which tickles at the heart of their desire. They will not, he knows, they will make jokes when the projector is put away, they will gorge the plate of delicatessen Eleanor provides, and swallow more beer, he among them. He will be the first to make jokes.

Sam is right. The movie has made him extraordinarily alive to the limits of them all. While they sit with red faces, eyes bugged, glutting sandwiches of ham, salami, and tongue, he begins the teasing.

"Roslyn," he calls out, "is the bulb cooled off yet?"

She cannot answer him. She chokes on beer, her face glazes, she is helpless with self-protecting laughter.

"Why are you so anxious, daddie?" Eleanor says quickly.

They begin to discuss the film. As intelligent people they must dominate it. Someone wonders about the actors in the piece, and discussion begins afresh. "I fail to see," says Louise, "why they should be hard to classify. Pornography is a job to the criminal and prostitute element."

"No, you won't find an ordinary prostitute doing this," Sam insists. "It requires a particular kind of personality."

"They have to be exhibitionists," says Eleanor.

"It's all economic," Louise maintains.

"I wonder what those girls felt," Roslyn asks, "I feel sorry for them."

"I'd like to be the camera man," says Alan.

"I'd like to be Frankie," says Marvin sadly.

There is a limit to how long such a conversation may continue. The jokes lapse into silence. They are all busy eating. When they begin to talk again, it is of other things. Each dollop of food sops the agitation which the movie has spilled. They gossip about the party the night before, they discuss which single men are interested in which women, who got drunk, who got sick, who said the wrong thing, who went home with someone else's date. When this is exhausted, one of them mentions a play the others have not seen. Soon they are talking about books, a concert, a one-man show by an artist who is a friend. Dependably, conversation will voyage its orbit. While the men talk of politics, the women are discussing fashions, progressive schools, and recipes they have attempted. Sam is uncomfortable with the division; he knows Eleanor will resent it, he knows she will complain later of the insularity of men and the basic contempt they feel for women's intelligence.

"But you collaborated," Sam will argue. "No one forced you to be with the women."

"Was I to leave them alone?" Eleanor will answer.

"Well, why do the women always have to go off by themselves?"

"Because the men aren't interested in what we have to say."

Sam sighs. He has been talking with interest, but really he is bored. These are nice pleasant people, he thinks, but they are ordinary people, exactly the sort he has spent so many years with, making little jokes, little gossip, living little everyday events, a close circle where everyone mothers the others by his presence. The womb of middle-class life, Sam decides heavily. He is in a bad mood indeed. Everything is laden with dissatisfaction.

Alan has joined the women. He delights in preparing odd dishes when friends visit the Sperbers, and he is describing to Eleanor how he makes blueberry pancakes. Marvin draws closer to Sam.

"I wanted to tell you," he says, "Alan's story reminded me. I saw Jerry O'Shaughnessy the other day."

"Where was he?"

Marvin is hesitant. "It was a shock, Sam. He's on the Bowery. I guess he's become a wino."

"He always drank a lot," says Sam.

"Yeah." Marvin cracks his bony knuckles. "What a stinking time this is, Sam."

"It's probably like the years after 1905 in Russia," Sam says.

"No revolutionary party will come out of this."

"No," Sam says, "nothing will come."

He is thinking of Jerry O'Shaughnessy. What did he look like? what did he say? Sam asks Marvin, and clucks his tongue at the dispiriting answer. It is a shock to him. He draws closer to Marvin, he feels a bond. They have, after all, been through some years together. In the thirties they have been in the Communist Party, they have quit together, they are both weary of politics today, still radicals out of habit, but without enthusiasm and without a cause. "Jerry was a hero to me," Sam says.

"To all of us," says Marvin.

The fabulous Jerry O'Shaughnessy, thinks Sam. In the old days, in the Party, they had made a legend of him. All of them with their middle-class origins and their desire to know a worker-hero.

I may say that I was never so fond of Jerry O'Shaughnessy as was Sam. I thought him a showman and too pleased with himself. Sam, however, with his timidity, his desire to travel, to have adventure and know many woman, was obliged to adore O'Shaughnessy. At least he was enraptured with his career.

Poor Jerry who ends as a bum. He has been everything else. He has been a trapper in Alaska, a chauffeur for gangsters, an officer in the Foreign Legion, a labor organizer. His nose was broken, there were scars on his chin. When he talked about his years at sea or his experiences in Spain, the stenographers and garment workers, the radio writers and unemployed actors would listen to his speeches as if he were the prophet of new romance, and their blood would be charged with the magic of revolutionary vision. A man with tremendous charm. In those days it had been easy to confuse his love for himself with his love for all underprivileged work-ingmen.

"I thought he was still in the Party," Sam says.

"No," says Marvin, "I remember they kicked him out a couple of years ago. He was supposed to have piddled some funds, that's what they say."

"I wish he'd taken the treasury," Sam remarks bitterly. "The Party used him for years."

Marvin shrugs. "They used each other." His mustache droops. "Let me tell you about Sonderson. You know he's still in the Party. The most progressive dentist in New York." They laugh.

While Marvin tells the story, Sam is thinking of other things. Since he has quit Party work, he has studied a great deal. He can tell you about prison camps and the secret police, political murders, the Moscow trials, the exploitation of Soviet labor, the privileges of the bureaucracy; it is all painful to him. He is straddled between the loss of a country he has never seen, and his repudiation of the country in which he lives. "Doesn't the Party seem a horror now?" he bursts out.

Marvin nods. They are trying to comprehend the distance between Party members they have known, people by turns pathetic, likable, or annoying—people not unlike them-selves—and in contrast the immensity of historic logic which deploys along statistics of the dead.

"It's all schizoid," Sam says. "Modern life is schizoid."

Marvin agrees. They have agreed on this many times, bored with the petulance of their small voices, yet needing the comfort of such complaints. Marvin asks Sam if he has given up his novel, and Sam says, "Temporarily." He cannot find a form, he explains. He does not want to write a realistic novel, because reality is no longer realistic. "I don't know what it is," says Sam. "'To tell you the truth I think I'm kidding myself. I'll never finish this book. I just like to en-tertain the idea I'll do something good some day." They sit there in friendly depression. Conversation has cooled. Alan and the women are no longer talking.

"Marvin," asks Louise, "what time is it?"

They are ready to go. Sam must say directly what he had hoped to approach by suggestion. "I was wondering," he whispers to Rossman, "would you mind if I held onto the film for a day or two?"

Marvin looks at him. "Oh, why of course, Sam," he says in his morose voice. "I know how it is." He pats Sam on the shoulder as if, symbolically, to convey the exchange of ownership. They are fellow conspirators.

"If you ever want to borrow the projector," Sam suggests.

"Nah," says Marvin, "I don't know that it would make much difference."

5

It has been, when all is said, a most annoying day. As Sam and Eleanor tidy the apartment, emptying ash trays and washing the few dishes, they are fond neither of themselves nor each other. "What a waste today has been," Eleanor remarks, and Sam can only agree. He has done no writing, he has not been outdoors, and still it is late in the evening, and he has talked too much, eaten too much, is nervous from the movie they have seen. He knows that he will watch it again with Eleanor before they go to sleep; she has given her assent to that. But as is so often the case with Sam these days, he cannot await their embrace with any sure anticipation. Eleanor may be in the mood or Eleanor may not; there is no way he can control the issue. It is depressing; Sam knows that he circles about Eleanor at such times with the guilty maneuvers of a sad hound. Resent her as he must, be furious with himself as he will, there is not very much he can do about it. Often, after they have made love, they will lie beside each other in silence, each offended, each certain the other is to blame. At such times, memory tickles them with a cruel feather. Not always has it been like this. When they were first married, and indeed for the six months they lived together before marriage, everything was quite different. Their affair was very exciting to them; each told the other with some hyperbole but no real mistruth that no one in the past had ever been comparable as lover.

I suppose I am a romantic. I always feel that this is the best time in people's lives. There is, after all, so little we accomplish, and that short period when we are beloved and triumph as lovers is sweet with power. Rarely are we concerned then with our lack of importance; we are too important. In Sam's case, disillusion means even more. Like so many young men, he entertained the secret conceit that he was an extraordinary lover. One cannot really believe this without supporting at the same time the equally secret conviction that one is fundamentally inept. It is—no matter what Sergius would say—a more dramatic and therefore more attractive view of oneself than the sober notion which Sam now accepts with grudging wisdom, that the man as lover is dependent upon the bounty of the woman. As I say, he accepts the notion, it is one of the lineaments of maturity, but there is a part of him which, no matter how harried by analysis, cannot relinquish the antagonism he feels that Eleanor has respected his private talent so poorly, and has not allowed him to confer its benefits upon more women. I mock Sam, but he would mock himself on this. It hardly matters; mockery cannot accomplish everything, and Sam seethes with that most private and tender pain: even worse than being unattractive to the world is to be unattractive to one's mate; or, what is the same and describes Sam's case more accurately, never to know in advance when he shall be undesirable to Eleanor.

I make perhaps too much of the subject, but that is only because it is so important to Sam. Relations between Eleanor and him are not really that bad—I know other couples who have much less or nothing at all. But comparisons are poor comfort to Sam; his standards are so high. So are Eleanor's. I am convinced the most unfortunate people are those who would make an art of love. It sours other effort. Of all artists, they are certainly the most wretched.

Shall I furnish a model? Sam and Eleanor are on the couch, and the projector adjusted to its slowest speed, is retracing the elaborate pantomime of the three principals. If one could allow these shadows a life . . . but indeed such life has been given them. Sam and Eleanor are no more than an itch, a smart, a threshold of satisfaction; the important share of themselves has steeped itself in Frankie, Magnolia, and Eleanor-of-the-film. Indeed the variations are beyond telling. It is the most outrageous orgy performed by five ghosts.

Self-critical Sam! He makes love in front of a movie, and one cannot say that it is unsatisfactory any more than one can say it is pleasant. It is dirty, downright porno dirty, it is a lewd slop-brush slapped through the middle of domestic exasperations and breakfast eggs. It is so dirty that one half of Sam—he is quite divisible into fractions—can be exercised at all. The part that is his brain worries along like a cuckolded burgher. He is taking the pulse of his anxiety. Will he last long enough to satisfy Eleanor. Will the children come back tonight? He cannot help it. In the midst of the circus, he is suddenly convinced the children will walk through the door. "Why are you so anxious, daddie?"

So it goes. Sam the lover is conscious of exertion. One moment he is Frankie Idell, destroyer of virgins—take that! you whore!—at the next, body moving, hands caressing, he is no more than some lines from a psychoanalytical text. He is thinking about the sensitivity of his scrotum. He has read that this is a portent of femininity in a male. How strong is his latent homosexuality, worries Sam, thrusting stiffly, warm sweat running cold. Does he identify with Eleanor-of-the-film?

Technically, the climax is satisfactory. They lie together in the dark, the film ended, the projector humming its lonely revolutions in the quiet room. Sam gets up to turn it off; he comes back and kisses Eleanor upon the mouth. Apparently, she has enjoyed herself more than he; she is tender and fondles the tip of his nose.

"You know, Sam," she says from her space beside him, "I think I saw this picture before."

"When?"

"Oh, you know when. That time."

Sam thinks dully that women are always most loving when they can reminisce about infidelity.

"That time!" he repeats.

"I think so."

Racing forward from memory like the approaching star which begins as a point on the mind and swells to explode the eyeball with its odious image, Sam remembers, and is weak in the dark. It is ten years, eleven perhaps, before they were married, yet after they were lovers. Eleanor had told him, but she has always been vague about details. There had been two men it seemed, and another girl, and all had been drunk. They had seen movie after movie. With reluctant fascination, Sam can conceive the rest. How it had pained him, how excited him. It is years now since he has remembered, but he remembers. In the darkness he wonders at the unreasonableness of jealous pain. That night was impossible to imagine any longer—therefore it is more real; Eleanor his plump wife who presses a pigeon's shape against her housecoat, forgotten heroine of black orgies. It has been meaningless, Eleanor claimed; it was Sam she loved, and the other had been no more than a fancy of which she wished to rid herself. Would it be the same today, thinks Sam, or had Eleanor been loved by Frankie, by Frankie of the other movies, by Frankie of the two men she never saw again on that night so long ago.

The pleasure he gets from this pain, Sam thinks furiously.

It is not altogether perverse. If Eleanor causes him pain, it means after all that she is alive for him. I have often observed that the reality of a person depends upon their ability to hurt us; Eleanor as the vague accusing embodiment of the wife is different, altogether different, from Eleanor who lies warmly in Sam's bed, an attractive Eleanor who may wound his flesh. Thus, brother to the pleasure of pain, is the sweeter pleasure which follows pain. Sam, tired, lies in Eleanor's arms, and they talk with the cozy trade words of old professionals, agreeing that they will not make love again before a movie, that it was exciting, but also not without detachment, that all in all it has been good but not quite right, that she had loved this action he had done, and was uncertain about another. It is their old familiar critique, a sign that they are intimate and well-disposed. They do not talk about the act when it has failed to fire; then they go silently to sleep. But, now, Eleanor's enjoyment having mollified Sam's sense of no enjoyment, they talk with the apologetics and encomiums of familiar mates. Eleanor falls asleep and Sam falls almost asleep, curling next to her warm body, his hand over her round belly with the satisfaction of a sculptor. He is drowsy, and he thinks drowsily that these few moments of creature-pleasure, this brief compassion he can feel for the body that trusts itself to sleep beside him, his comfort in its warmth, is perhaps all the meaning he may ask for his life. That out of disappointment, frustration, and the passage of dreary years come these few moments when he is close to her, and their years together possess a connotation more rewarding than the sum of all which has gone into them.

But then he thinks of the novel he wants to write, and he is wide-awake again. Like the sleeping pill which fails to work and leaves one warped in an exaggeration of the ills which sought the drug, Sam passes through the promise of sex-emptied sleep, and is left with nervous loins, swollen jealousy of an act ten years dead, and sweating irritable resentment of the woman's body which hinders his limbs. He has wasted the day, he tells himself, he has wasted the day as he has wasted so many days of his life, and tomorrow in the office he will be no more than his ten-fingers typing plot and words for Bramba the Venusian and Lee-Lee Deeds, Hollywood Star, while that huge work with which he has cheated himself, holding it before him as a covenant of his worth, that enormous novel which would lift him at a bound from the impasse in which he stifles, whose dozens of characters would develop a vision of life in bountiful complexity, lies foundered, rotting on a beach of purposeless effort. Notes here, pages there, it sprawls through a formless wreck of incidental ideas and half-episodes, utterly without shape. He has not even a hero for it.

One could not have a hero today, Sam thinks, a man of action and contemplation, capable of sin, large enough for good, a man immense. There is only a modern hero damned by no more than the ugliness of wishes whose satisfaction he will never know. One needs a man who could walk the stage, someone who—no matter who, not himself. Someone, Sam thinks, who reasonably could not exist.

The novelist, thinks Sam, perspiring beneath blankets, must live in paranoia and seek to be one with the world; he must be terrified of experience and hungry for it; he must think himself nothing and believe he is superior to all. The feminine in his nature cries for proof he is a man; he dreams of power and is without capacity to gain it; he loves himself above all and therefore despises all that he is.

He is, thinks Sam, he is part of the perfect prescription, and yet he is not a novelist. He lacks energy and belief. It is left for him to write an article some day about the temperament of the ideal novelist.

In the darkness, memories rise, yeast-swells of apprehension. Out of bohemian days so long ago, comes the friend of Eleanor, a girl who had been sick and was committed to an institution. They visited her, Sam and Eleanor, they took the suburban train and sat on the lawn of the asylum grounds while patients circled about intoning a private litany, or shuddering in boob-blundering fright from an insect that crossed their skin. The friend had been silent. She had smiled, she had answered their questions with the fewest words, and had returned again to her study of sunlight and blue sky. As they were about to leave, the girl had taken Sam aside. "They violate me," she said in a whisper. "Every night when the doors are locked, they come to my room and they make the movie. I am the heroine and am subjected to all variety of sexual viciousness. Tell them to leave me alone so I may enter the convent." And while she talked, in a horror of her body, one arm scrubbed the other. Poor tortured friend. They had seen her again, and she babbled, her face had coarsened into an idiot leer.

Sam sweats. There is so little he knows, and so much to know. Youth of the depression with its economic terms, what can he know of madness or religion? They are both so alien to him. He is the mongrel, Sam thinks, brought up without religion from a mother half-Protestant and half-Catholic, and a father half-Catholic and half-Jew. He is the quarter-Jew, and yet he is a Jew, or so he feels himself, knowing nothing of Gospel, tabernacle, or Mass, the Jew through accident, through state of mind. What, whatever did he know of penance? self-sacrifice? mortification of the flesh? the love of his fellow man? Am I concerned with my relation to God? ponders Sam, and smiles sourly in the darkness. No, that has never concerned him, he thinks, not for better not for worse. "They are making the movie," says the girl into the ear of memory, "and so I cannot enter the convent."

How hideous was the mental hospital. A concentration camp, decides Sam. Perhaps it would be the world some day, or was that only his projection of feelings of hopelessness? "Do not try to solve the problems of the world," he hears from Sergius, and pounds a lumpy pillow.

However could he organize his novel? What form to give it? It is so complex. Too loose, thinks Sam, too scattered. Will he ever fall asleep? Wearily, limbs tense, his stomach too keen, he plays again the game of putting himself to sleep. "I do not feel my toes," Sam says to himself, "my toes are dead, my calves are asleep, my calves are sleeping . . ."

In the middle from wakefulness to slumber, in the torpor which floats beneath blankets, I give an idea to Sam. "Destroy time, and chaos may be ordered," I say to him.

"Destroy time, and chaos may be ordered," he repeats after me, and in desperation to seek his coma, mutters back,

"I do not feel my nose, my nose is numb, my eyes are heavy, my eyes are heavy."

So Sam enters the universe of sleep, a man who seeks to live in such a way as to avoid pain, and succeeds merely in avoiding pleasure. What a dreary compromise is life!

Sour or Suntanned,
It Makes No Difference

Johanna Kaplan

What could make sense? The Israeli playwright had such long legs it was hard to believe he was Jewish.

"Little girl," he said, coming up to Miriam with his very short pants and his heavy brown sandals that looked like they were made out of a whole rocky gang's Garrison belts, "little girl, which languages you are speaking?"

But Miriam had not been speaking to anyone: she was walking around the canteen with a milk container going gummy in her hand, and waiting by herself for all the days of camp to be over. There, in the rain, the entire room was sour from milk and muffled from rubber boots and raincoats. The sourness clung to her tongue and whined in her sinuses; locked away from rain and from mud was the whole camp. Soon, some other day, it would get sunny and Snack would be outside on long wooden picnic benches. If you made a mistake and sat down on these benches, splinters crept into your thighs, and if you sat down on the grass instead, insects roamed your whole body. For milk containers and Oreos, this was summer.

"Listen to me, please, little girl. Why you are walking away? I am asking only a simple question. Which languages you are speaking?"

"Right this minute?" Miriam said. "I wasn't speaking anything, can't you even tell?" How he could be smart enough to fix tractors or fool Arabs, let alone write plays, Miriam did not see, not that she said it.

"No, no," said the Israeli playwright. "Bring me please your counselor."

"She's right over there with the garbage," Miriam said, but because she was not at all sure of how words came out of his mouth or went into his head, walked over with him to Fran, who was going around with the basket.

"Amnon!" Fran screamed with her thin sparrow's voice,

and immediately dropped the basket and the empty milk containers like people on TV shows who walk backward into sewers. Miriam had never seen her look so lively: Fran's flat paper face was like the front of a brand-new apartment house, and even though she was nineteen years old, did not wear lipstick. Instead, she got up very early in the morning, before any of the girls in the bunk, just to make sure that she would have enough time to stand in front of the mirror and put on all her black eye makeup. It was how Miriam woke up every morning: Fran standing at the mirror, patting and painting her eyes as if they were an Arts-and-Crafts project. Right after that, Gil Burstein, a Senior boy, went to the loudspeaker to play his bugle, and from that time on there was no way at all to stop anything that came after. Every single morning Miriam woke up in the cold light of a strange bed.

From behind all the black lines, Fran's eyes looked as if she was already set to start flirting, but even so her arm would not let go of Miriam's shoulder. It was just another thing that Miriam did not like. Simply going from one activity to another, the whole bunk walked with their arms linked around each other's waist; at flag-lowering, you joined hands and swayed in a semicircle; in swimming you had to jump for someone else's dripping hand the second the whistle blew; and at any time at all there were counselors standing with their arms around kids for no particular reason. They were all people you hardly knew and would probably never see again; there was no reason to spend a whole summer hugging them.

"Miriam," Fran said, smiling at her as if she were a new baby in somebody's carriage, "do you speak Yiddish?"

"What do you mean?" Miriam said. "Every second? I can, if I have to."

"It's all I ask you," Amnon said and, for the first time, smiled too; from way above his long legs, his face crinkled and seemed smaller, as if he wrote most of his plays right under a bulb that was going bad.

Fran said, "I don't see it. She's very quiet—her voice is much too soft."

It's not making a difference. In America you have microphones falling from the ceiling even in a children's camp you're using only for summer."

"On that huge stage? Are you kidding? She'd fade into

the woodwork. Nobody would even see her. I told you— she's very quiet."

"She is *not* quiet," Amnon said. "Not quiet, only unhappy. It's how I am choosing her. I see her face: unhappy and unhappy."

It was the last thing Miriam wanted anyone to think of. "Everything's perfect," she said, and with all the tightness inside her, quickly gave Fran a smile that tired out the corners of her mouth.

"Probably she wouldn't forget lines. But if she doesn't remember to scream when she gets up there, you're finished."

"I don't believe in screaming," Miriam said, but not so that anyone could hear her. Beneath the ceiling, there were Ping-Pong balls popping through the air like mistaken snow-flakes, and behind her, some girls from her bunk were playing jacks. In the close, headachy damp, Miriam looked at Fran and hated her; in the whole canteen, that was all that there was.

It was getting to Amnon, too; the whole sour room seemed trapped in his face.

"Frances Wishinsky," he said as he watched Fran walk away with the basket. "In England are *boys* named Francis. In England, Wishinsky would already be Williams. England is a worse country, it's true. I have suffered there for eleven months."

Miriam said, "I read that it rains a lot in England," and wondered if the rainy day and gray, stuffy room were what was reminding him.

"Weathers are not so much important to me," Amnon said. "Other things I don't accustom myself so well. For me, terrible weathers I find not so bad as terrible people. For example, I think you're not liking so much your counselor Fran."

But Amnon was a stranger. "She docks us from movies a lot," Miriam said, "but with what they've got here, it doesn't even matter. The last time we went, all they had was Martians. An entire movie about a bunch of miniature green guys running around in space ships."

"You're not liking science fictions? Which kind of films you like to see?"

"All different ones. I just don't see why they can't find enough movies to make up with real people's colors and sizes in them."

"Ah," said long, stretched-out Amnon. "Look here, Miriam, you have been ever in a theater?"

"A children's theater," said Miriam. "They took us once from school." The children's theater, in the auditorium of a big high school in Manhattan, was in a terrible neighborhood: in a building right across the way, a left-alone little girl was standing up completely naked, her whole dark body pressed right against the window in the cold. "She's only a little baby," Miriam had said, but there were people who giggled all the way through the play and couldn't wait to get outside again just to see if she would still be there.

"Children's theater," Amnon said, nodding. "This play we do is also children's theater. Only because it's in Yiddish, the children here will not understand. But what can I do? I am not choosing it, it's not my play, it's not my language."

It was not Miriam's language either, so she said nothing and watched Amnon stare around the room, more and more dissatisfied.

"It is not my medium. I am playwright, not director. What can I do? Many people are coming to see this play who are not interesting themselves in theater and they are not interesting themselves in the children. They are only obsessing themselves with Yiddish. For *this* they will come."

"For what?" said Miriam. "What are they all coming for?" There was a program every Friday night—nobody special came and nobody ever made a fuss about it.

"It will be performance for Parents Day," Amnon said. "In two weeks is coming Parents Day. You know about it, yes?"

But more than yes: Miriam was sure that any parents, seeing what camp was like, would be only too glad to take their children out of it. How much more than yes? It was the one day she was certain of and waited for.

Even before she got there, Miriam had a feeling that camp might not turn out to be her favorite place.

"It's terrific," was what her cousin Dina told her. But it was the same thing that Dina said about going on Ferris-wheel and roller-coaster rides in an amusement park. Coming home from school, her arms full of all her heavy high-school books, she would tell Miriam, "Wait till you start doing things like that! Everybody screams and it's terrific."

"I get dizzy on the merry-go-round," Miriam said, and

was very suspicious. Only a few years before, Dina used to lie around on her bed, setting her stringy strawberry-blond hair and reading love comics. With her extra baby-sitting money, she would buy different-size lipstick brushes, close the door in the bathroom, and completely mess up all her perfectly good but strange-colored brand-new lipsticks. Naturally, Dina's mother did not approve, but all she said was, "All the girls are like that. They all do it, and Miriam will be like that, too." But because she was not like Dina, who and what she would be like was in Miriam's mind very often; it was the reason she looked so closely at people's faces on the street.

"If you'd only smile once in a while," Miriam's aunt said, "you'd look like a different person." But her aunt was a liar, a person who spent her life thinking there was not much children could understand. Just to prove it once, when Miriam was in kindergarten, she gave her aunt a special lie test on purpose: on the day that Israel got started as a country, everyone had the radio on all day and many people put out little flags in their windows.

"Why do they have Jewish flags out?" Miriam asked, very pleased with herself because she had thought up the trick and knew the answer.

"What Jewish flags?" Her aunt's arms were all full of bundles and her fat, soggy face looked very annoyed. "Where? In the window? They're left over from Shabbas."

So Miriam saw she was right, but even when she got older said nothing, because she knew that for the times her mother was sick, she would still have to stick around her aunt's house, listen to some lies, and watch Dina fool around with her friends or do her homework. Whenever her aunt bought fruit, she would say, "It's sweet as sugar," even if it was unripened grapefruit; and when she made lamb chops, she said, "Don't leave over the fat, it's delicious," even though it wasn't.

Sometimes, when Dina and her mother had fights, or when her uncle was yelling on the phone about Socialism, it would seem to Miriam very funny, so to stop them from noticing her giggles, and also to drown out the screaming, she would go into the living room and play the piano. She played from her head songs she had learned in Assembly or Hebrew School, or, even better, melodies that came into her mind like ideas: not real, official songs that people knew, but ones she made up on the spot and could change and fix up if she wanted. It was separate from things that she knew about and completely different from people; often when she played the piano, it seemed to Miriam like reading Chinese in a dream.

"I don't see what's so great about playing without piano books," Dina said. "You can't even read music. Just wait till you start taking lessons from Mrs. Landau and have to start practicing from *books*, then we'll see what a big shot you are."

"I'm not ever going to take from Mrs. Landau," Miriam said. "My mother says she's a very limited person who shouldn't be teaching anybody anything."

"Your mother tells you too much," said her aunt, but in what way this was true she had no idea. "Stalin" was what Miriam's mother called her uncle, and what she said about him was that he simply had nothing in his head and had no way of telling what was true from what wasn't. For this reason, all of his talk about Socialism was just noise-making, and all he was, she said, was a big talker who would believe anyone who was a bigger faker.

The other thing Miriam's mother most often told about was her own life when she was a child, but when she got to that, she talked only half to Miriam and half to someone who wasn't there at all.

"Who could have believed that any place could be as big as Warsaw?" is what she would say. "Streets and more streets, I couldn't understand it. I was the first girl from my town ever to be sent there to school, and I was so smart that when I got there I was the youngest in my class. But all my smartness did me no good—I looked at all the stores and the people, the streetcars and the houses, and all I did was cry constantly." This, Miriam never had any trouble believing; it was a habit her mother never got out of. Whenever the boiler broke down for a day, her mother cried all the time that she washed in cold water, and if the butcher ever sent the wrong kind of chicken, or one with too many pinfeathers on it, she cried for hours after and then started all over again when they were ready to sit down and eat it.

Still, with all the things that she did tell, when it came to camp Miriam's mother said very little.

"You'll meet children from all over. When Dina went, there was a girl from Winnipeg, Canada."

"Was her father a Mountie?"

"How could he be a Mountie?" her mother said. "Ask Dina, I think he was a dentist."

"Then I don't see the point."

"It isn't a question of point, Miriam. In camp you'll have grass and trees and get away. Here all you'd have is the hot city."

But it was the hot, empty city that Miriam loved. The flat, gritty sidewalks, freed of people, widened in the glassy, brilliant glare and in the distance fell away like jungle snow. Hard, strange bits of stone came bubbling up through the pavements: glazed, heated traces of another city that once drummed and droned beneath. In front of all the buildings, just where landlords had planted them, low, wiry shrubs pushed themselves out like rubber plants, and the buildings, rougher and rocklike in the ocher heat, seemed turned into brick that was brick before houses, brick that cooked up from the earth itself. From the sky, the city's summer smell sank into Miriam's skin, and walking along with the slow air, she felt her thin, naggy body skim away to the bricks and the pavement that steamed, in belonging, to the sun. What she would do with a bunch of trees, Miriam did not know.

Only dodge ball, it turned out, could have been invented by human beings: if somebody kept throwing balls at you, it was only natural to try to get away from them, and if you would just be allowed to go far enough, there wouldn't be a problem in the first place. This was what Miriam decided on for all games, so in basketball and volleyball she let other people push and scream for the ball as if there were a sale, and in badminton she watched them jump and yell, "Look at the birdie," like photographers with black clothes in an old-time movie.

Folk dancing was no improvement. "Right over left, left, step, right behind, left, step," Naamah the Yemenite folk dancer sang out instead of words in her dark Yemenite voice, while all her heavy silver jewelry sounded behind her, a rhythm as clear and alone as somebody cracking gum in an empty subway. In a way, Naamah was the most Israeli-looking person Miriam had ever seen; with her tiny, tight, dark features and black, curly hair, she flew around the room like a strange but very beautiful insect, the kind of insect a crazy scientist would let loose in a room and sit up watching till he no longer knew whether it was beautiful or ugly, human or a bug. Sometimes Naamah would pull Miriam out of the circle and sing the special right-over-left song straight into her ear as if *Miriam* were the one who couldn't speak English.

"The grapevine step," she screamed over the music. "It's necessary for all Oriental dance. Not just Israeli. Also the Greeks have it, and it's found modified with the Druse." But it seemed to Miriam like doing arithmetic with your feet, and finally Naamah let her go back into the circle, saying, "Westerners cannot do our dances. They do not have the body."

"I don't know what *she* acts so fancy about," Miriam said in a half-whisper to no one. "Everybody knows that when the Yemenites first came to Israel, they never even saw a toilet before, and when the Israelis gave them brand-new bathrooms, what they did was go over the floor. "

"Shush, Miriam," said Phyllis Axelrod, a tanned, chunky girl in Miriam's bunk. "Don't answer back. If you feel bad, just cry into your pillow. I do it every night and it works."

"What does your pillow have to do with it? That sounds like putting teeth under your pillow so that fairies will give you money."

"You get dimes that way, Miriam. Don't you even want the dimes?"

"If I want a dime, I ask my mother for it. I don't hide teeth and expect fairies, that's not something I believe in."

"My mother wouldn't just hand out dimes like that," Phyllis said, and Miriam immediately felt sorry. She liked Phyllis, though she often seemed not too brilliant; sometimes they were buddies in swimming, and once they snuck out of the water together because Phyllis heard a radio playing inside the little cabaña that was only for counselors. It was the reason that Phyllis cried into her pillow at night: she missed listening to the radio and knowing what was on the Hit Parade, and this gave Miriam the idea that when Phyllis got to be a teenager she might spend all her time hanging around cars in the street, holding up a radio and looking for boys. Sometimes Phyllis also cried because she missed her oldest brother, Ronny, who had just come back from Korea and immediately got married.

"You're not glad about being a sister-in-law?" Miriam asked her.

"It's not that great," Phyllis said. "I just wish I had my regular brother back again, no Army and no wedding." Still, she had a beautiful red-and-gold silk scarf that Ronny had brought back for her from Asia; once she wore it as a shawl when everyone, already in white tops and shorts, had gone out on the road to pick wild flowers for the Friday-evening table. On that road, outside camp just behind the bunks, most of the flowers were tiger lilies, and when Phyllis bent over to pick one, she looked, with her straight black hair and broad brown face, like an Asian girl herself.

It was the closest Miriam got to "children from all over": except for a girl from Teaneck, New Jersey, everyone in her bunk was from New York, mostly from Brooklyn or Queens, both places Miriam had not been to. Still, from what they said, the only difference she could see was that they called Manhattan "going into the city" while people from the Bronx called it "going downtown." Besides Miriam, that meant only Bryna Sue Seligman, who, because she came from Riverdale, would not admit it. Everything that belonged to Bryna, her recorder included, had specially printed stickers, made up by her father who was in the printing business, that said in giant yellow letters BRYNA SUE SELIGMAN, and her favorite book in the world was the Classic Comic of *Green Mansions*. On the very first day they were in camp she asked Miriam, "Don't you wish you were Rima? Isn't *Green Mansions* the most beautiful thing you ever heard of?"

"It's OK," Miriam said; she could not see constantly going barefoot in a hot jungle and having to depend on birds when you had any trouble. But Bryna liked the whole idea so much that just in order to be like Rima, she kept her long red hair loose and hanging down her back, walked around without shoes when she wasn't supposed to, and blew into her recorder, which she couldn't really play, when she lay in bed after Lights Out. Whenever there was any free time, Bryna the bird-girl spent almost all of it either brushing her hair or dusting herself with bath powder, all in her private mirror with the yellow label, moving it constantly from side to side so that there was no part of her she would miss.

"I don't know what I'm doing here," she would say as she stared at herself and brushed all her red hair. "I'm going to be a bareback rider and my mother promised me a camp with horses."

"Jewish camps don't come with horses," Miriam said. "You should have figured that out for yourself. Besides, I thought you said you were going to be a poetess."

"Oh, I am one already," Bryna said. "Any time I feel like it, my father prints up all my poems."

"In yellow?" said Miriam.

"In any color I want. Once I wrote a poem about a rainbow and my father made every line in a different color."

This sounded like a bubble-gum wrapper and no poem, but watching Bryna trace around her suntan marks in the mirror, Miriam decided not to say it.

"I could be going horseback riding in Riverdale right now. Where I live, it's practically the country."

"Where you live is the Bronx," Miriam said. "On your letters you put Bronx, New York, and you even write in a zone number."

"It just so happens that lots of people put Riverdale-on-Hudson, and any time I wanted to, I could."

"You *could*," Miriam said, "but it would probably end up in a museum in Albany."

Because their beds were next to each other, Miriam and Bryna shared a cubby; with all Bryna's yellow labels shining through the shelves like flashbulb suns and the smell of her bath powder always hanging in the air, there was no place that Miriam felt was really hers. Her bathrobe and bathing suits hung like blind midgets in the way; they even got the Bryna bath-powder smell. It made them seem as if they were someone else's clothes and, like something else in camp, had nothing to do with Miriam and her life.

"I could be in a special dramatics camp on a fat scholarship," Bryna said. "The only reason I told them no was that they didn't have any horseback riding, but at least *there* they would have had me starring in a million plays."

"I'm in a play here," said Miriam. It was turning out to be what she had instead of a cubby, and completely faking calmness, she waited for Bryna to faint.

Who could have believed that anyplace could be as big as Warsaw? Probably not anyone in the play: who they were, all of them, were Jews, Nazis, and Polish partisans in the Warsaw ghetto—but where all the streets, more streets, and streetcars could be, the stage gave no idea and Amnon didn't ever say. On the stage was a tiny, crowded Warsaw filled with people who had phlegmy, sad Polish names—Dudek and Vladek, Dunya and Renya—just like in Miriam's mother's stories, and though they were always fighting and singing, there was no way for them to turn out not to be dead. Even the Yiddish song that Miriam had to sing at the end was about a girl who gets taught by her boyfriend how to shoot a gun, and who, one night in the freezing cold, goes out in her beret and shoots up a truckload of Nazis. When the girl is finished, she falls asleep, and the snow coming down makes a garland in her hair. Probably it also freezes her to death, though all it said at the end of the song was: "Exhausted from this small victory, For our new, free generation."

How could a girl who ran out all alone shooting soldiers let herself end up snowed under? And what was the point of people's running through sewers with guns if all they turned into was corpses? It was very hard to explain to Bryna, whose big question was, "Are you starring?"

"Nobody is," Miriam said. "It's not that kind of a play. Half of the time I fake being dead so that nobody finds out and they leave me."

"You mean you don't even *say* anything?"

"I do," Miriam said, "but what I say doesn't do any good. I'm a little girl in braids and I sneak out of the ghetto with my big brother."

Bryna said, "That's your big part? What do you tell him?"

"Nothing. While he's out getting guns, I hide and I hear some Nazi soldiers being so drunk that they start screaming out their plans. And that's when I immediately run back to the ghetto and warn everyone."

"Oh," Bryna said. "So the whole thing is that you copy Paul Revere."

"The only kind of Paul Revere it could be is a Jewish kind. Everyone dies and there are no horses."

Bryna said, "Some play! When we did *The Princess and the Pea,* I was the star, and then when we did *Pocahontas, Red-Skin Lady of Jamestown,* I was the heroine. In *this* moron play, I bet that there isn't even one person with a halfway decent part."

"My part's good," Miriam said. "I'm practically the only one who doesn't turn out to be killed."

"That's because you're a girl."

"No, it's not," Miriam said. "I don't even *know* why, that's just the way the play is."

"Listen, Miriam, I've been in a million plays. Little girls never get killed in any of them."

"Well, in this one they do. In this one the only people who don't wind up dead are me and Gil Burstein."

"*You're* in a play with Gil Burstein? You? Just let me come to rehearsals with you and I'll let you use my expensive bath powder any time you want."

"You can't get out of playing badminton just like that," Miriam told her. "That's only for people in the play."

But play or not, camp was still camp. At night, cold air flew in through the dark from Canada and mixed on the screens with mosquitoes; 6-12 and whispers filled up the air in the bunk and stayed there like ugly wallpaper. How could anyone sleep? Miriam played with the dark like a blind person in a foreign country: in the chilly, quiet strangeness, her bed was as black as a packed-up trunk, and her body, separate in all its sunburned parts, was suddenly as unfamiliar as someone else's toothpaste.

In the daytime, too, camp was still camp: a place dreamed up to be full of things that Miriam could not get out of. Whenever Amnon saw her face, he said, "What's the matter, Miriam?" It was how he kept starting out rehearsals.

"Look here, Mir*iam*," he would say, pronouncing her name the Hebrew way, with the accent on the last syllable. "Look here, Mir*iam*, say me what's wrong."

"Nothing," she said. "Everything's great."

"Why you are saying me 'Nothing' when I see you are crying—have been crying?"

"I wasn't, I'm not, and anyway it's not something I do."

"All girls are sometimes crying."

"Well, not me," Miriam said. "I don't believe in it." For a reason: it sometimes seemed to Miriam that if a person from a foreign country—or even a miniature green man from Mars—ever landed, by accident, in her building and by mistake walked up the six flights of stairs, all he would hear was screaming and crying: mothers screaming and children crying, fathers screaming and mothers crying, televisions screaming and vacuum cleaners crying; he could very easily get the idea that in this place there was no language, and that with all the noises there were no lives.

But crying was the last thing that Miriam thought of once she got to rehearsals. Still in camp, but not really in camp at all, it felt like a very long fire drill in school when you stayed on the street long enough to be not just a child on a line, but almost an ordinary person—someone who could walk in the street where they wanted, into stores, around corners, and maybe, if they felt like it, even disappear into buses.

As soon as Miriam put on her costume and combed her hair into braids, there was nothing on her body that felt like camp, and away from the day outside, nothing to even remind her. On the stage, Jews, Nazis, and Polish partisans were wandering through the streets of shrunken Warsaw, and in a corner, where in the real Warsaw there might have been a gas streetlight, a trolley-car stop, or even her mother's Gymnasium, Miriam and Gil Burstein played dead.

"What's the best can-opener?" Gil whispered.

"I don't know," Miriam said.

"Ex-Lax," said Gil, and laughed into his Ripley's *Believe It or Not.*

"Rest!" Amnon called out. In the middle of the stage, a Polish partisan had just kicked a Jew by mistake and suddenly the girl was crying. Nazi soldiers and Jewish resistance fighters started stampeding across the stage and charging, and Amnon, looking at no one, said, "Always they are playing Indians and Lone Rangers. It's for me completely not possible.

"Rest!" he yelled again; what he meant was "Break." Once, in one of his terrible-English times, Amnon said, "Ninety-Twoth Street Y," and Miriam, thinking suddenly of a giant tooth-building with elevators full of a thousand dentists, could not stop herself from laughing. Other times she thought of asking Amnon why she and Gil were the only ones who managed to end up not dead, but usually during breaks Amnon sat with his long legs stretched out across a whole row of chairs and just talked. He hardly even noticed who was concentrating on Cokes and who was paying attention.

"In Israel now it's not the right climate for art. You understand me?"

"It's much too hot there for people to sit around drawing pictures," Miriam said, and wished that the Arts-and-Crafts counselor could understand this too.

"No," Amnon said. "For me it means in my own country even people are not interesting themselves in my work. Here it's not my language, it's not my country, there is no place for an Israeli writer, there is nothing to do."

Gil Burstein said, "He could always take and autograph

butcher-store windows or foods for Passover. I'm getting sick of this. Who wants a Coke?"

"Me," Miriam said, but knew the truth was that she didn't mind at all. From lying stretched out on the wooden stage for so long, her mind felt empty and the whole rest of her seemed dizzy in a sweet, half-sleepy way. Soon, in this dark auditorium, only the stage would be full of light and the plain wooden floor would hold up for an hour all the mistakes of a place that once had existed. A girl with braids and a too-long dress would run out into the mixed-up streets, and sitting in the audience with many other people, Miriam's mother would know what this place once was like way before and could tell how it actually looked. The girl with braids would sing the last song, and all Miriam's days of camp would finally be over.

Parents Day did not start out with Gil waking people up with his bugle; instead, from the loudspeaker in the office came records of Israeli songs—background music for the whole day, as if it were a movie. The melodies ran out quick and flying, and framed by the music, the whole camp—children, counselors, little white boats, even trees and grass—seemed to be flying away, too, as if after all these weeks they were finally going someplace. Not exactly in the movie herself, Miriam went to the clothesline in the back, checking to make sure no bathing suit of hers was still left on it.

"Miriam, you better come in the front," Phyllis said. There's a whole bunch of people here and they're looking for you."

Right outside the bunk, some girls in a circle were doing the dances that belonged with the melodies, and. squinting there in the sun, practically trapped inside the dance, were Miriam's aunt and uncle, and with them a couple she had never seen before. The man, very short and with gray, curly hair, was dressed just like her uncle: Bermuda shorts, brown cut-out sandals with high socks, and a kind of summer hat that always looked to Miriam like a Jewish baseball cap. His wife, who was taller, had thick, dark braids all across her head, and though her skirt was very long in the sun, there was such a round, calm look in her clothes and on her face that Miriam was sure she had never had to be anybody's mother.

Miriam's aunt said, "There's my niece. Here she is. Miriam, this is Mrs. Imberman and that's Mr. Imberman, they came up with the car."

Miriam's aunt looked exactly the same: every part of her heavy face drooped like the bargain bundles she always carried, and stuck to her cheeks like decals were high pink splotches the color of eyelids—extra supplies of tears she kept up to make sure she was always ready.

"What are *you* doing here?" said Miriam. "You're not my mother. Who asked you to come?"

"Mr. and Mrs. Imberman came here to see a play," her aunt said, "and we're staying right next to them in the same little hotel, and it's not far, and they came with the car, so here we are."

"I didn't say what are *they* doing here. I said what are *you* doing here? And where's my mother?"

"Your mother couldn't come. She was going to write a letter and tell you, but I told her not to because I *know* you, Miriam, that if you knew about it you'd make a fuss, and now I see how right I was."

Turning around, Miriam stared at all the trees and grass that she had there: if they were so wonderful, the least they could do was pay attention to the music and do an Israeli dance.

"For you, your mother is your mother, but for me, she's still my little sister and there are plenty of things still that I have to tell her."

The trees, with all their millions of leaves, did not do even half a grapevine, and Miriam's uncle said, "Imberman, feel how hot it is already here and it's still early. Can you imagine what it's like a day like today in the city?"

"Hot," Mr. Imberman said. They stood there, the two of them, with their Jewish baseball caps, and Miriam thought how her uncle looked when it got too hot in his apartment: he would walk back and forth in his shorts and undershirt, fan himself with a newspaper, and say in Yiddish, "It's hot today in the city. Oh my God, it's hot!" If her uncle and midget Mr. Imberman got together, they could both walk back and forth in a little undershirt parade, fan themselves with two newspapers and, in between saying how hot it was, could have little fights about which countries were faking it with Socialism.

Miriam said, "If my mother were here, she would take me home."

"Why should she take you home? It's good for you to be outside and it's good for you to get used to it."

"Why should I get used to it if I don't like it?"

"Look how nice it is here, Miriam," her uncle said in Yiddish. "Look what you have here—a beautiful blue lake, a sky with sun and clouds that's also blue, big strong trees you can see from a mountain—with birds in them, wide, empty green fields with only grass and flowers. Look how nice."

"The lake is polluted," Miriam said. And it seemed to her that he was describing someplace else entirely—maybe a place in Poland he remembered from when he was young, maybe even a picture on a calendar, but definitely not camp on Parents Day. All the empty green fields were filling up with cars, the grass and flowers were getting covered over with blankets and beach chairs, and pretty soon the birds from the mountain would be able to come down and eat all the leftover food that people brought with them. Except that there was no sand, the whole camp could have been Orchard Beach.

"Let me tell you something," her uncle said. "First I'll tell you a little story about your cousin Dina, and then I'll give you some advice."

"I don't want any advice from you," Miriam said. "You can't even figure out which countries are faking it with Socialism, and if you're supposed to care about it so much, why don't you just write a letter to a person in the country and ask them? All they have to tell you is if they're selfish or if they share around the things they've got."

"Straight from her mother," said Miriam's aunt. "With absolutely no sense that she's talking in front of a child."

"And don't think I can't understand it either. My mother calls *him* Stalin."

Mrs. Imberman said, "Sweetheart, are you in the play?" She bent her head in the sun, and for a second her earrings, turquoise and silver, suddenly turned iridescent.

"Yes," Miriam said and looked up at her: somewhere a man with a sombrero and a mustache had gotten off his donkey and sat down in the heat to fold pieces of silver so that Mrs. Imberman could turn her head in the sun and ask questions of strange children.

"Ah hah," Mrs. Imberman said, "an *aktricekeh*. That's why she's so temperamental."

"I am *not* an actress," Miriam said. "I never was one before and I don't·plan on being one again, and what I'm definitely not going to be is an explorer, so I don't see why I have to get used to so much being outside."

"Listen, Miriam," her uncle said. "Let me tell you what happened with Dina in case she was embarrassed to tell you herself. It happened that Dina didn't feel like giving in her chocolates to the counselor, so she put them under her bed and only took out the box to eat them when it was dark in the bunk at night and she was sitting up in the bed and setting her hair. She figured out that if anyone heard any noises she could tell them it was from the bobby pins and curlers."

"Such a woman's story," Mr. Imberman said in very Polish Yiddish. "I didn't know, Citrin, that you knew such women's stories."

Miriam's aunt said, "You know my Dina. She could set her hair anyplace."

"Anyway, what happened, Miriam, is that once somebody put on a light and saw her, and that's how she made some enemies, and that's why she didn't always love it here."

"I don't set my hair," Miriam said. "It's the one thing I'm lucky about—it's naturally curly, and now I have to get it put in braids for the play, so good-by."

"So quick?" her aunt said. "Good-by, Miriam, look how nice and suntanned she is. Nobody would even know she has a sour face."

Just behind the curtain, Miriam waited bunched up with everyone in their costumes on the hot, quiet stage. Sunk into the scenery, not even Gil Burstein was laughing, and all the Jews, Nazis, and Polish partisans were finally without Cokes in their hands. Amnon, still walking around in his same very short pants, gave Miriam a giant Israeli smile that she had not seen before and could not feel a part of. He said, "Now I don't worry for the play and I don't worry for the audience."

But why anyone would worry for the audience, Miriam could not see. All through the play she kept looking out at them—a little girl in braids and a too-long dress who would end up not dead—and could not tell the face of anyone.

Who they were she did not know and did not want to think about: people, probably, who cried and screamed in their houses, fanned themselves with newspapers, and took along hard-boiled eggs if they went in a car for a half-hour.

The stage did not stop being hot, and lying stretched out on it with Gil Burstein, it seemed to Miriam that they were playing dead right underneath a gas streetlight from a stuffy summer night in the real Warsaw. Way above their heads hung a fat yellow bulb that was surrounded by a thousand insects. In all different shapes and sizes, they kept flying from the empty blue darkness backstage toward this one single glare, till the bulb, ugly and unshaded in the first place, seemed to be growing a beard as sweaty and uneven as a grandfather's. Back and forth, over and around, the different insects crowded and buzzed, all with each other, so that, watching them, Miriam started to wonder whether these were Socialist bugs who believed in sharing with each other what they had, or else bugs who were secretly wishing to keep the whole bulb for themselves and, by politely flying close together, just faking it.

In the woods, just outside the finished-off Warsaw ghetto, the night was bitter cold. Miriam stood up to sing the song of the girl with the velvet face who went out in the blizzard to shoot up the enemy, and knew that no matter how big the stage was, when she sang and played the piano there was nothing about her that was quiet at all. " 'Exhausted from this small victory, For our new, free generation,' " Miriam finally sang, and the curtain fell over her head like the garland of snow on the girl who could end up snowed under.

Left all by herself behind the curtain, Miriam heard crying coming from people in the audience: they were the parents of no one in the play, but were crying now because like somebody's stupid, stupid parakeet, they had learned how to do one thing and one thing only. If anyone yelled out "Budgie!" right now, the entire audience would immediately get up and start flying. Amnon would fly out, too, and Bryna, always a bird-girl, ran up now to Miriam on the stage and right then and there began chirping.

"Guess what?" she said. "Now there are *two* people in my family with red hair. My mother got her hair dyed and I didn't even know it was her till she came over and kissed me."

"Oh," Miriam said, and because she could see that Bryna

had big things on her mind—counting redheads—listened from somewhere for the sound of Amnon's voice letting out his one Israeli-parakeet line: Say-me-what's-wrong-Mir*iam*, Mir*iam*-say-me-the-matter. Standing there on the stage, a little girl in braids and a too-long dress who would end up not dead, Miriam promised herself that never again in her life would anyone look at her face and see in it what Amnon did, but just like the girl who could fake being dead, she would keep all her aliveness a secret.

Waiting for Santy

A CHRISTMAS PLAYLET
(*With a Bow to Mr. Clifford Odets*)

S. J. Perelman

Scene: The sweatshop of S. Claus, a manufacturer of children's toys, on North Pole Street. Time: The night before Christmas.

At rise, seven gnomes, Rankin, Panken, Rivkin, Riskin, Ruskin, Briskin, and Praskin, are discovered working furiously to fill orders piling up at stage right. The whir of lathes, the hum of motors, and the hiss of drying lacquer are so deafening that at times the dialogue cannot be heard, which is very vexing if you vex easily. (Note: The parts of Rankin, Panken, Rivkin, Riskin, Ruskin, Briskin, and Praskin are interchangable, and may be secured directly from your dealer or the factory.)

RISKIN (*filing a Meccano girder, bitterly*)—A parasite, a leech, a bloodsucker—altogether a five-star nogoodnick! Starvation wages we get so he can ride around in a red team with reindeers!

RUSKIN (*jeering*)—Hey, Karl Marx, whyn'tcha hire a hall?

RISKIN (*sneering*)—Scab! Stool pigeon! Company spy! (*They tangle and rain blows on each other. While waiting for these to dry, each returns to his respective task.*)

BRISKIN (*sadly, to Panken*)—All day long I'm painting "Snow Queen" on these Flexible Flyers and my little Irving lays in a cold tenement with the gout.

PANKEN—You said before it was the mumps.

BRISKIN (*with a fatalistic shrug*)—The mumps—the gout—go argue with City Hall.

PANKEN (*kindly, passing him a bowl*)—Here, take a piece fruit.

BRISKIN (*chewing*)—It ain't bad, for wax fruit.

PANKEN (*with pride*)—I painted it myself.

BRISKIN (*rejecting the fruit*)—Ptoo! Slave psychology!

RIVKIN (*suddenly, half to himself, half to the Party*)—
I got a belly full of stars, baby. You make me feel like I
swallowed a Roman candle.

PRASKIN (*curiously*)—What's wrong with the kid?

RISKIN—What's wrong with all of us? The system! Two
years he and Claus's daughter's been making googoo eyes
behind the old man's back.

PRASKIN—So what?

RISKIN (*scornfully*)—So what? Economic determinism!
What do you think the kid's name is—J. Pierpont Rivkin?
He ain't even got for a bottle Dr. Brown's Celery Tonic.
I tell you, it's like gall in my mouth two young people
shouldn't have a room where they could make great music.

RANKIN (*warningly*)—Shhh! Here she comes now! (*Stella
Claus enters, carrying a portable phonograph. She and Rivkin
embrace, place a record on the turntable, and begin a very
slow waltz, unmindful that the phonograph is playing "Cohen
on the Telephone."*)

STELLA (*dreamily*)—Love me, sugar?

RIVKIN—I can't sleep, I can't eat, that's how I love you.
You're a double malted with two scoops of whipped cream;
you're the moon rising over Mosholu Parkway; you're a two
weeks' vacation at Camp Nitgedaiget! I'd pull down the
Chrysler Building to make a bobbie pin for your hair!

STELLA—I've got a stomach full of anguish. Oh, Rivvy,
what'll we do?

PANKEN (*sympathetically*)—Here, try a piece fruit.

RIVKIN (*fiercely*)—Wax fruit—that's been my whole life!
Imitations! Substitutes! Well, I'm through! Stella, tonight I'm
telling your old man. He can't play mumblety-peg with two
human beings! (*The tinkle of sleigh bells is heard offstage,
followed by a voice shouting, "Whoa, Dasher! Whoa,
Dancer!" A moment later S. Claus enters in a gust of mock
snow. He is a pompous bourgeois of sixty-five who affects a
white beard and a false air of benevolence. But tonight the
ruddy color is missing from his cheeks, his step falters, and he
moves heavily. The gnomes hastily replace the marzipan they
have been filching*).

STELLA (*anxiously*)—Papa! What did the specialist say
to you?

CLAUS (*brokenly*)—The biggest professor in the country

. . . the best cardiac man that money could buy. . . . I tell you I was like a wild man.

STELLA—Pull yourself together, Sam!

CLAUS—It's no use. Adhesions, diabetes, sleeping sickness, decalcomania—oh, my God! I got to cut out climbing in chimneys, he says—me, Sanford Claus, the biggest toy concern in the world!

STELLA (*soothingly*)—After all, it's only one man's opinion.

CLAUS—No, no, he cooked my goose. I'm like a broken uke after a Yosian picnic. Rivkin!

RIVKIN—Yes, Sam.

CLAUS—My boy, I had my eye on your for a long time. You and Stella thought you were too foxy for an old man, didn't you? Well, let bygones be bygones. Stella, do you love this gnome?

STELLA (*simply*)—He's the whole stage show at the Music Hall, Papa; he's Toscanini conducting Beethoven's Fifth; he's—

CLAUS (*curtly*)—Enough already. Take him. From now on he's a partner in the firm. (*As all exclaim, Claus holds up his hand for silence.*) And tonight he can take my route and make the deliveries. It's the least I could do for my own flesh and blood. (*As the happy couple kiss, Claus wipes away a suspicious moisture and turns to the other gnomes.*) Boys, do you know what day tomorrow is?

GNOMES (*crowding around expectantly*)—Christmas!

CLAUS—Correct. When you look in your envelopes tonight, you'll find a little present from me—a forty-percent pay cut. And the first one who opens his trap—gets this. (*As he holds up a tear-gas bomb and beams at them, the gnomes utter cries of joy, join hands, and dance around him shouting exultantly. All except Riskin and Briskin, that is, who exchange a quick glance and go underground.*)

CURTAIN

The Loudest Voice

Grace Paley

There is a certain place where dumb-waiters boom, doors slam, dishes crash; every window is a mother's mouth bidding the street shut up, go skate somewhere else, come home. My voice is the loudest.

There, my own mother is still as full of breathing as me and the grocer stands up to speak to her. "Mrs. Abramowitz," he says, "people should not be afraid of their children."

"Ah, Mr. Bialik," my mother replies, "if you say to her or her father 'Ssh,' they say, 'In the grave it will be quiet.' "

"From Coney Island to the cemetery," says my papa. "It's the same subway; it's the same fare."

I am right next to the pickle barrel. My pinky is making tiny whirlpools in the brine. I stop a moment to announce: "Campbell's Tomato Soup. Campbell's Vegetable Beef Soup. Campbell's S-c-otch Broth . . ."

"Be quiet," the grocer says, "the labels are coming off."

"Please, Shirley, be a little quiet," my mother begs me.

In that place the whole street groans: Be quiet! Be quiet! but steals from the happy chorus of my inside self not a tittle or a jot.

There, too, but just around the corner, is a red brick building that has been old for many years. Every morning the children stand before it in double lines which must be straight. They are not insulted. They are waiting anyway.

I am usually among them. I am, in fact, the first, since I begin with "A."

One cold morning the monitor tapped me on the shoulder. "Go to Room 409, Shirley Abramowitz," he said. I did as I was told. I went in a hurry up a down staircase to Room 409, which contained sixth-graders. I had to wait at the desk without wiggling until Mr. Hilton, their teacher, had time to speak.

After five minutes he said, "Shirley?"

"What?" I whispered.

He said, "My! My! Shirley Abramowitz! They told me you had a particularly loud, clear voice and read with lots of expression. Could that be true?"

"Oh, yes," I whispered.

"In that case, don't be silly; I might very well be your teacher someday. Speak up, speak up."

"Yes," I shouted.

"More like it," he said. "Now, Shirley, can you put a ribbon in your hair or a bobby pin? It's too messy."

"Yes!" I bawled.

"Now, now, calm down." He turned to the class. "Children, not a sound. Open at page 39. Read till 52. When you finish, start again." He looked me over once more. "Now, Shirley, you know, I suppose, that Christmas is coming. We are preparing a beautiful play. Most of the parts have been given out. But I still need a child with a strong voice, lots of stamina. Do you know what stamina is? You do? Smart kid. You know, I heard you read 'The Lord is my shepherd' in Assembly yesterday. I was very impressed. Wonderful delivery. Mrs. Jordan, your teacher, speaks highly of you. Now listen to me, Shirley Abramowitz, if you want to take the part and be in the play, repeat after me, 'I swear to work harder than I ever did before.' "

I looked to heaven and said at once, "Oh, I swear." I kissed my pinky and looked at God.

"That is an actor's life, my dear," he explained. "Like a soldier's, never tardy or disobedient to his general, the director. Everything," he said, "absolutely everything will depend on you."

That afternoon, all over the building, children scraped and scrubbed the turkeys and the sheaves of corn off the schoolroom windows. Goodbye Thanksgiving. The next morning a monitor brought red paper and green paper from the office. We made new shapes and hung them on the walls and glued them to the doors.

The teachers became happier and happier. Their heads were ringing like the bells of childhood. My best friend Evie was prone to evil, but she did not get a single demerit for whispering. We learned "Holy Night" without an error. "How wonderful!" said Miss Glacé, the student teacher. "To think that some of you don't even speak the language!" We learned "Deck the Halls" and "Hark! The Herald Angels". . . . They weren't ashamed and we weren't embarrassed.

Oh, but when my mother heard about it all, she said to my father: "Misha, you don't know what's going on there. Cramer is the head of the Tickets Committee."

"Who?" asked my father. "Cramer? Oh yes, an active woman."

"Active? Active has to have a reason. Listen," she said sadly, "I'm surprised to see my neighbors making tra-la-la for Christmas."

My father couldn't think of what to say to that. Then he decided: "You're in America! Clara, you wanted to come here. In Palestine the Arabs would be eating you alive. Europe you had pogroms. Argentina is full of Indians. Here you got Christmas. . . . Some joke, ha?"

"Very funny, Misha. What is becoming of you? If we came to a new country a long time ago to run away from tyrants, and instead we fall into a creeping pogrom, that our children learn a lot of lies, so what's the joke? Ach, Misha, your idealism is going away."

"So is your sense of humor."

"That I never had, but idealism you had a lot of."

"I'm the same Misha Abramovitch, I didn't change an iota. Ask anyone."

"Only ask me," says my mama, may she rest in peace. "I got the answer."

Meanwhile the neighbors had to think of what to say too. Marty's father said: "You know, he has a very important part, my boy."

"Mine also," said Mr. Sauerfeld.

"Not my boy!" said Mrs. Klieg. "I said to him no. The answer is no. When I say no! I mean no!"

The rabbi's wife said, "Its disgusting!" But no one listened to her. Under the narrow sky of God's great wisdom she wore a strawberry-blond wig.

Every day was noisy and full of experience. I was Right-hand Man. Mr. Hilton said: "How could I get along without you, Shirley?"

He said: "Your mother and father ought to get down on their knees every night and thank God for giving them a child like you."

He also said: "You're absolutely a pleasure to work with, my dear, dear child."

Sometimes he said: "For God's sakes, what did I do with the script? Shirley! Shirley! Find it."

Then I answered quietly: "Here it is, Mr. Hilton."

Once in a while, when he was very tired, he would cry out: "Shirley, I'm just tired of screaming at those kids. Will you tell Ira Pushkov not to come in till Lester points to that star the second time?"

Then I roared: "Ira Pushkov, what's the matter with you? Dope! Mr. Hilton told you five times already, don't come in till Lester points to that star the second time."

"Ach, Clara," my father asked, "what does she do there till six o'clock she can't even put the plates on the table?"

"Christmas," said my mother coldly.

"Ho! Ho!" my father said. "Christmas. What's the harm? After all, history teaches everyone. We learn from reading this is a holiday from pagan times also, candles, lights, even Chanukah. So we learn it's not altogether Christian. So if they think it's a private holiday, they're only ignorant, not patriotic. What belongs to history, belongs to all men. You want to go back to the Middle Ages? Is it better to shave your head with a secondhand razor? Does it hurt Shirley to learn to speak up? It does not. So maybe someday she won't live between the kitchen and the shop. She's not a fool."

I thank you, Papa, for your kindness. It is true about me to this day. I am foolish but I am not a fool.

That night my father kissed me and said with great interest in my career, "Shirley, tomorrow's your big day. Congrats."

"Save it," my mother said. Then she shut all the windows in order to prevent tonsillitis.

In the morning it snowed. On the street corner a tree had been decorated for us by a kind city administration. In order to miss its chilly shadow our neighbors walked three blocks east to buy a loaf of bread. The butcher pulled down black window shades to keep the colored lights from shining on his chickens. Oh, not me. On the way to school, with both my hands I tossed it a kiss of tolerance. Poor thing, it was a stranger in Egypt.

I walked straight into the auditorium past the staring children. "Go ahead, Shirley!" said the monitors. Four boys, big for their age, had already started work as propmen and stagehands.

Mr. Hilton was very nervous. He was not even happy. Whatever he started to say ended in a sideward look of sadness. He sat slumped in the middle of the first row and asked me to help Miss Glacé. I did this, although she thought my voice too resonant and said, "Show-off!"

Parents began to arrive long before we were ready. They wanted to make a good impression. From among the yards of drapes I peeked out at the audience. I saw my embarrassed mother.

Ira, Lester, and Meyer were pasted to their beards by Miss Glacé. She almost forgot to thread the star on its wire, but I reminded her. I coughed a few times to clear my throat. Miss Glacé looked around and saw that everyone was in costume and on line waiting to play his part. She whispered, "All right . . ." Then:

Jackie Sauerfeld, the prettiest boy in first grade, parted the curtains with his skinny elbow and in a high voice sang out:

> "Parents dear
> We are here
> To make a Christmas play in time.
> It we give
> In narrative
> And illustrate with pantomime."

He disappeared.

My voice burst immediately from the wings to the great shock of Ira, Lester, and Meyer, who were waiting for it but were surprised all the same.

"I remember, I remember, the house where I was born . . ."

Miss Glacé yanked the curtain open and there it was, the house—an old hayloft, where Celia Kornbluh lay in the straw with Cindy Lou, her favorite doll. Ira, Lester, and Meyer moved slowly from the wings toward her, sometimes pointing to a moving star and sometimes ahead to Cindy Lou.

It was a long story and it was a sad story. I carefully pronounced all the words about my lonesome childhood, while little Eddie Braunstein wandered upstage and down with his shepherd's stick, looking for sheep. I brought up lonesomeness again, and not being understood at all except by some women everybody hated. Eddie was too small for that and Marty Groff took his place, wearing his father's prayer shawl. I announced twelve friends, and half the boys in the fourth grade gathered round Marty, who stood on an orange crate while my voice harangued. Sorrowful and loud, I declaimed about love and God and Man, but because of the terrible deceit of Abie Stock we came suddenly to a famous moment. Marty, whose remembering tongue I was, waited at the foot of the cross. He stared desperately at the audience. I groaned, "My God, my God, why hast thou forsaken me?" The soldiers who were sheiks grabbed poor Marty to pin him up to die, but he wrenched free, turned again to the audience, and spread his arms aloft to show despair and the end. I murmured at the top of my voice, "The rest is silence, but as everyone in this room, in this city—in this world—now knows, I shall have life eternal."

That night Mrs. Kornbluh visited our kitchen for a glass of tea."

"How's the virgin?" asked my father with a look of concern.

"For a man with a daughter, you got a fresh mouth, Abramovitch."

"Here," said my father kindly, "have some lemon, it'll sweeten your disposition."

They debated a little in Yiddish, then fell in a puddle of Russian and Polish. What I understood next was my father, who said, "Still and all, it was certainly a beautiful affair, you have to admit, introducing us to the beliefs of a different culture."

"Well, yes," said Mrs. Kornbluh. "The only thing . . . you know Charlie Turner—that cute boy in Celia's class—a couple others? They got very small parts or no part at all. In very bad taste, it seemed to me. After all, it's their religion."

"Ach," explained my mother, "what could Mr. Hilton do? They got very small voices; after all, why should they holler? The English language they know from the beginning by heart. They're blond like angels. You think it's so important they should get in the play? Christmas . . . the whole piece of goods . . . they own it."

I listened and listened until I couldn't listen any more. Too sleepy, I climbed out of bed and kneeled. I made a little church of my hands and said, "Hear, O Israel . . ." Then I called out in Yiddish, "Please, good night, good night. Ssh." My father said, "Ssh yourself," and slammed the kitchen door.

I was happy. I fell asleep at once. I had prayed for everybody: my talking family, cousins far away, passersby, and all the lonesome Christians. I expected to be heard. My voice was certainly the loudest.

More Outstanding Anthologies from MENTOR Books

☐ **WOMEN AND FICTION: Short Stories by and about Women** edited by Susan Cahill. A unique collection of twenty-six short stories about women—their lives as mysterious and individual as the human personality itself—as perceived by the finest modern women writers, including Katherine Mansfield, Colette, Kate Chopin, Grace Paley, Doris Lessing, Joyce Carol Oates and other great women writers. (#ME1445—$2.25)

☐ **COLONIAL AMERICAN LITERATURE: From Wilderness to Independence** selected and edited, with an Introduction, Commentary and Notes by Robert Douglas Mead. From Indian myths to the Declaration of Independence, a brilliant anthology of pioneer writings describes the creation of our nation. (#MJ1463—$1.95)

☐ **LITERATURE OF THE AMERICAN NATION: From Independence to the Gilded Age**, selected and edited, with an Introduction, Commentary and Notes by Robert Douglas Mead. A brilliant anthology that includes such immortal voices as Edgar Allan Poe, Nathaniel Hawthorne, Herman Melville, Mark Twain and Henry James. (#MJ1470—$1.95)

☐ **THE MENTOR BOOK OF MAJOR AMERICAN POETS** edited by Oscar Williams and Edwin Honig. Selections from the work of Taylor, Emerson, Longfellow, Poe, Whitman, Dickinson, Robinson, S. Crane, Frost, Lindsay, Stevens, Williams, Pound, Moore, Ransom, Millay, MacLeish, Cummings, H. Crane and Auden. Introduction, Notes, Index. (#MJ1381—$1.95)

Other Anthologies in MENTOR and SIGNET CLASSIC
Editions

☐ **BLACK VOICES: AN ANTHOLOGY OF AFRO-AMERICAN LITERATURE edited by Abraham Chapman.** Fiction, autobiography, poetry, and literary criticism by American Negroes, selected from the work of well-known authors as well as younger writers whose work is being published here for the first time. Contributors include Ralph Ellison, Richard Wright, James Weldon Johnson, James Baldwin, Gwendolyn Brooks, and Langston Hughes. (#ME1611—$2.25)

☐ **FOUR CLASSIC AMERICAN NOVELS edited by Willard Thorp.** The complete texts of The Scarlet Letter, Huckleberry Finn, The Red Badge of Courage and Billy Budd anthologized for the first time in a low-priced paperback edition. (#CJ992—$1.95)

☐ **THE MENTOR BOOK OF SHORT PLAYS edited by Richard H. Goldstone and Abraham H. Lass.** A treasury of drama by some of the finest playwrights of the century that includes Anton Chekhov, Thornton Wilder, Tennessee Williams, Gore Vidal, Terence Ratigan and Paddy Chayefsky. (#ME1504—$1.75)

☐ **THE RED BADGE OF COURAGE and Selected Stories by Stephen Crane.** Foreword by R. W. Stallman. The masterpiece of Civil War fiction plus these great short stories: The Open Boat, The Blue Hotel, The Upturned Face and The Bride Comes to Yellow Sky.
(#CQ971—95¢)